FREESTYLE

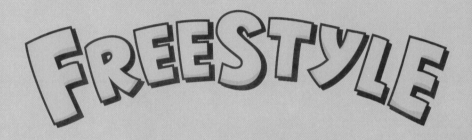

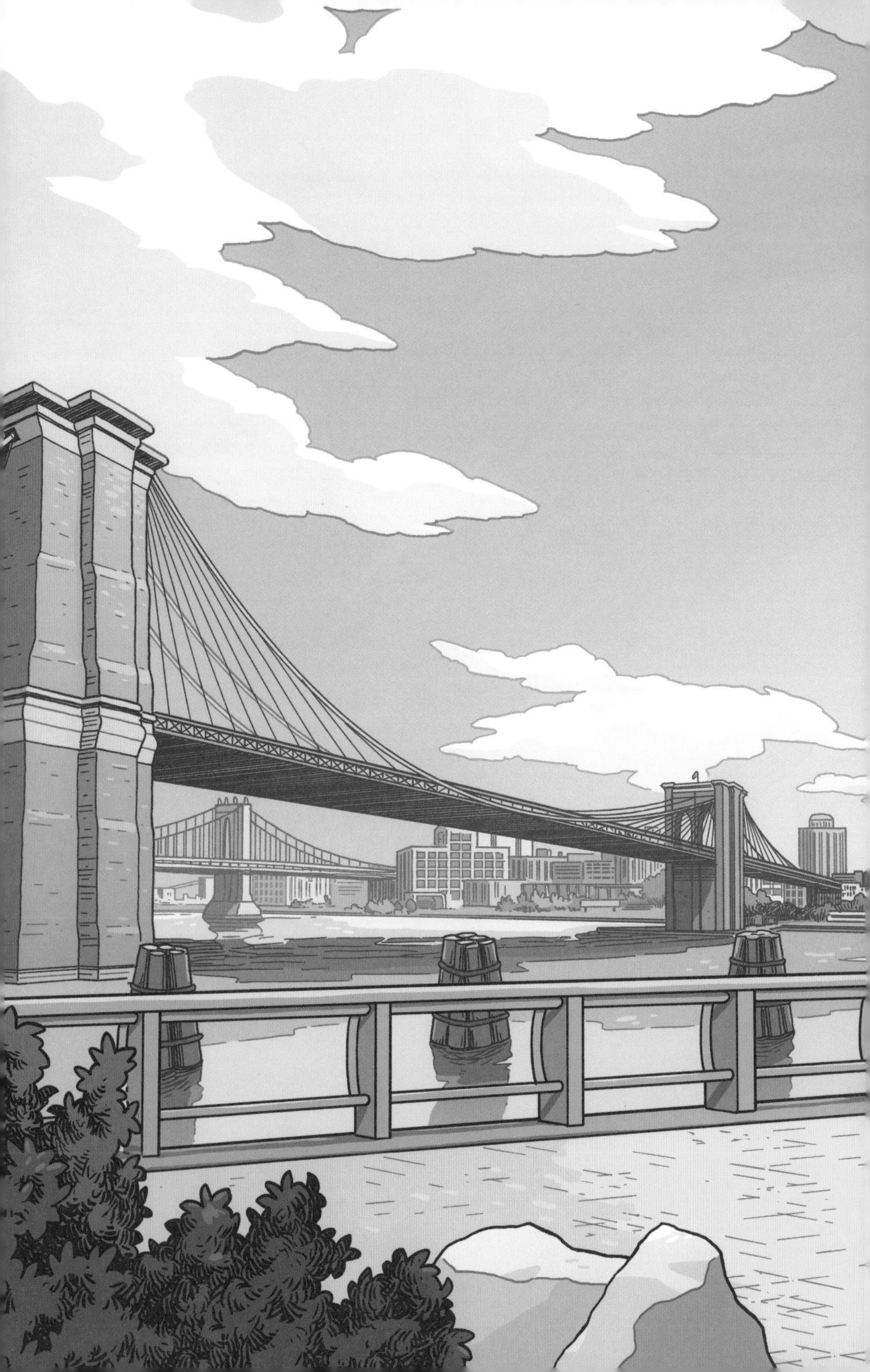

FREESTYLE

GALE GALLIGAN

WITH COLOR BY K CZAP

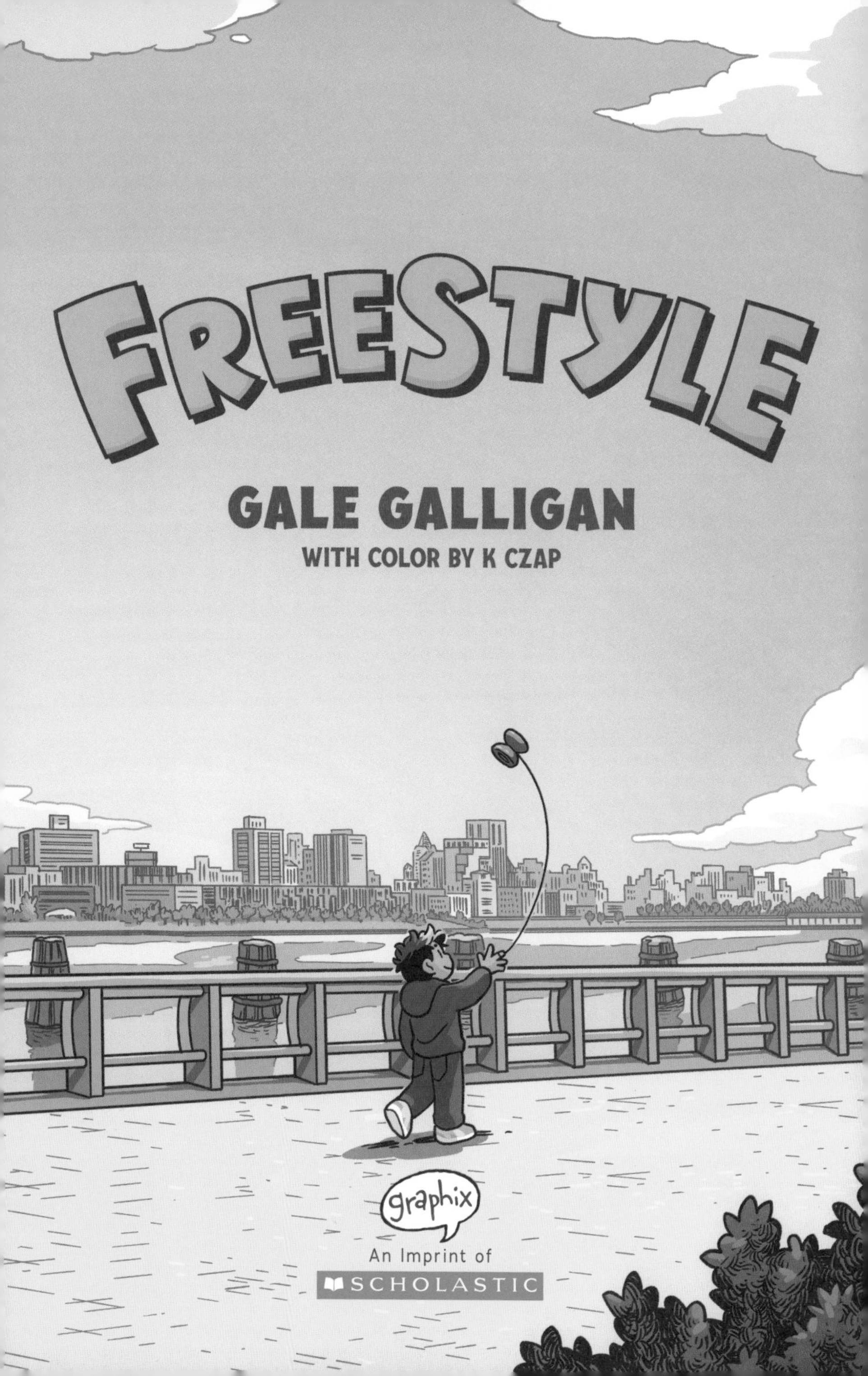

graphix

An Imprint of

SCHOLASTIC

Library of Congress Control Number: 2021948450

ISBN 978-1-338-04581-9 (hardcover)
ISBN 978-1-338-04580-2 (paperback)

10 9 8 7 6 5 4 3 2 1 22 23 24 25 26

Printed in China 62
First edition, October 2022

Edited by Cassandra Pelham Fulton
Book design by Shivana Sookdeo and Carina Taylor
Creative Director: Phil Falco
Publisher: David Saylor

For Robin

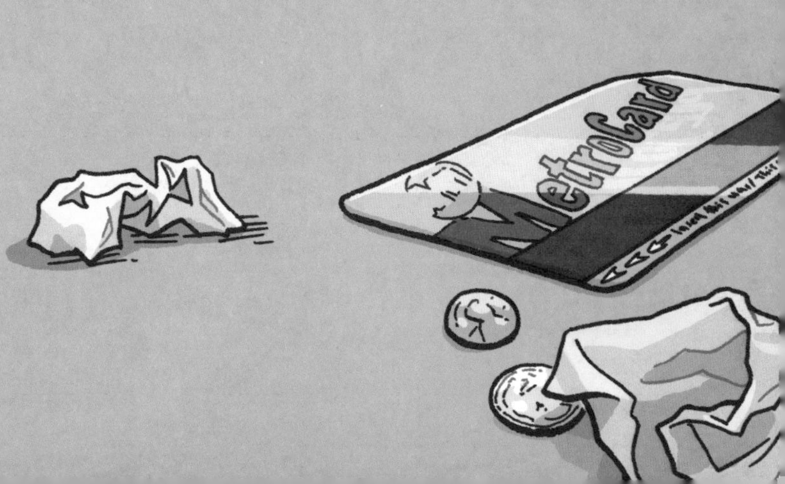
MetroCard

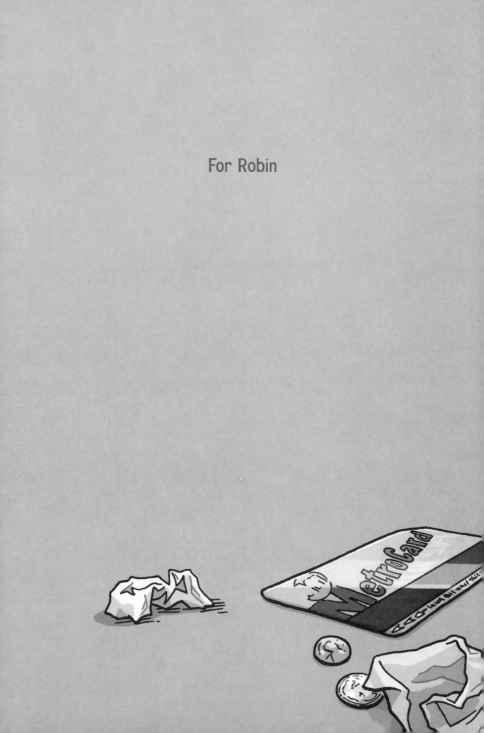

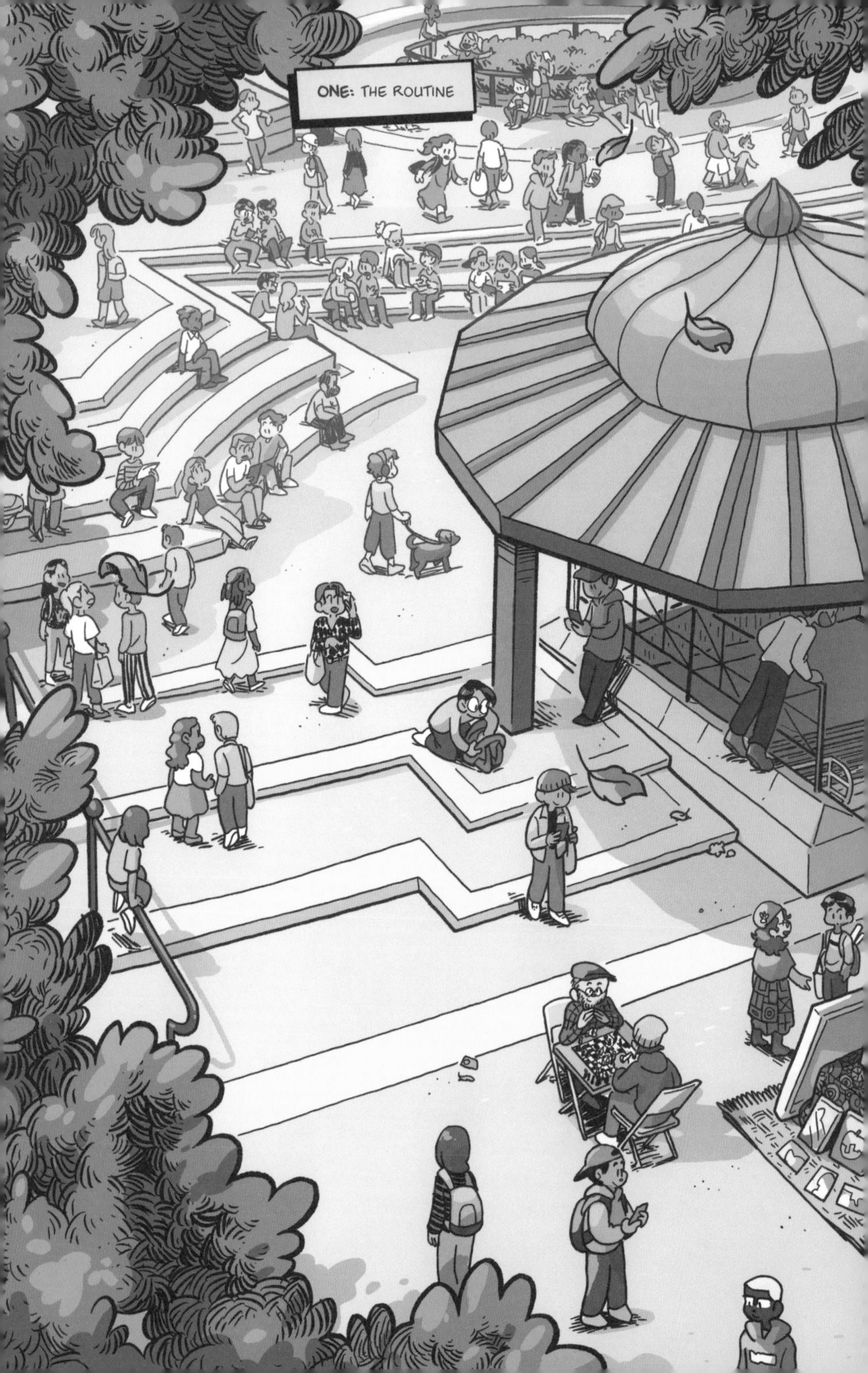
ONE: THE ROUTINE

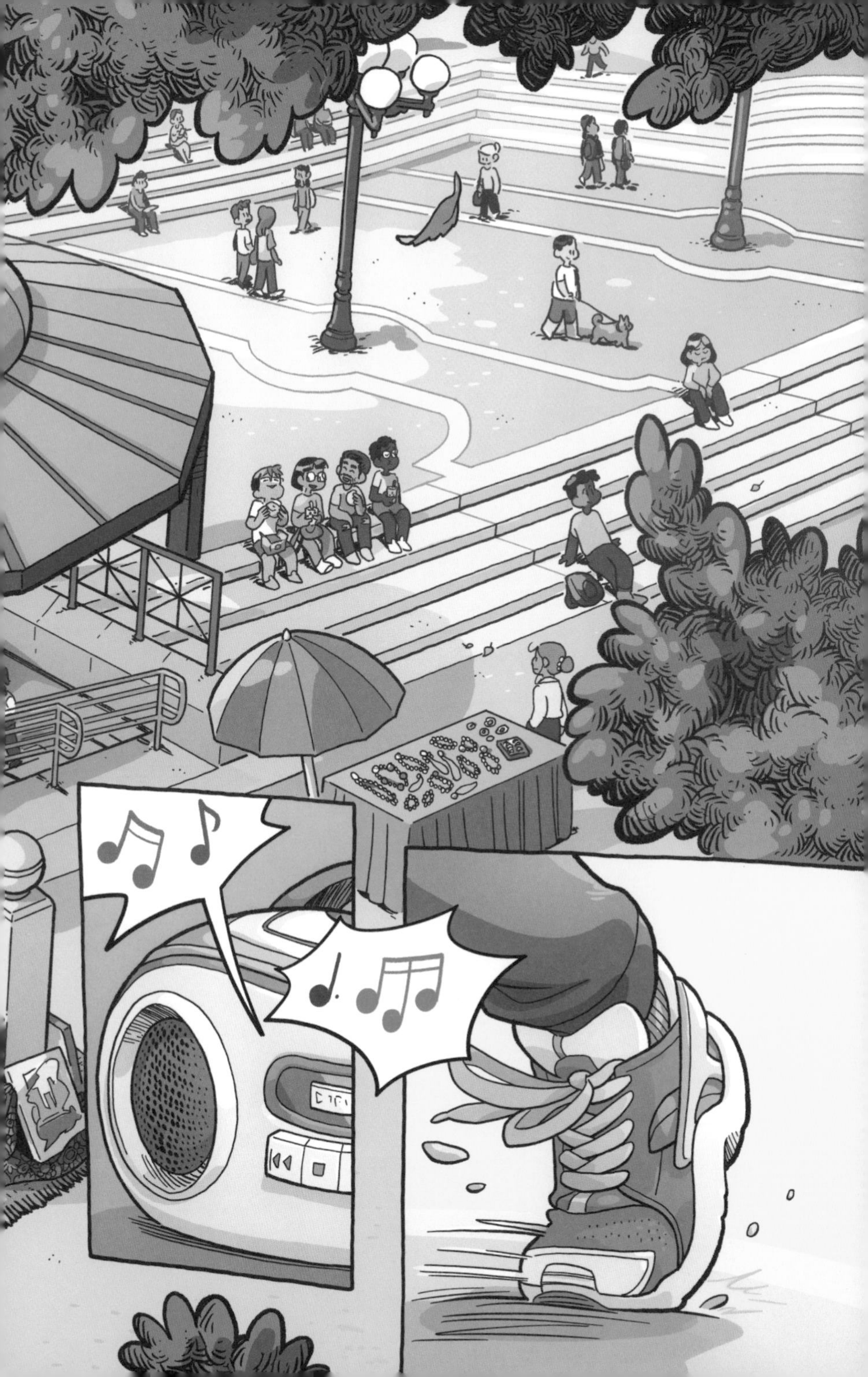

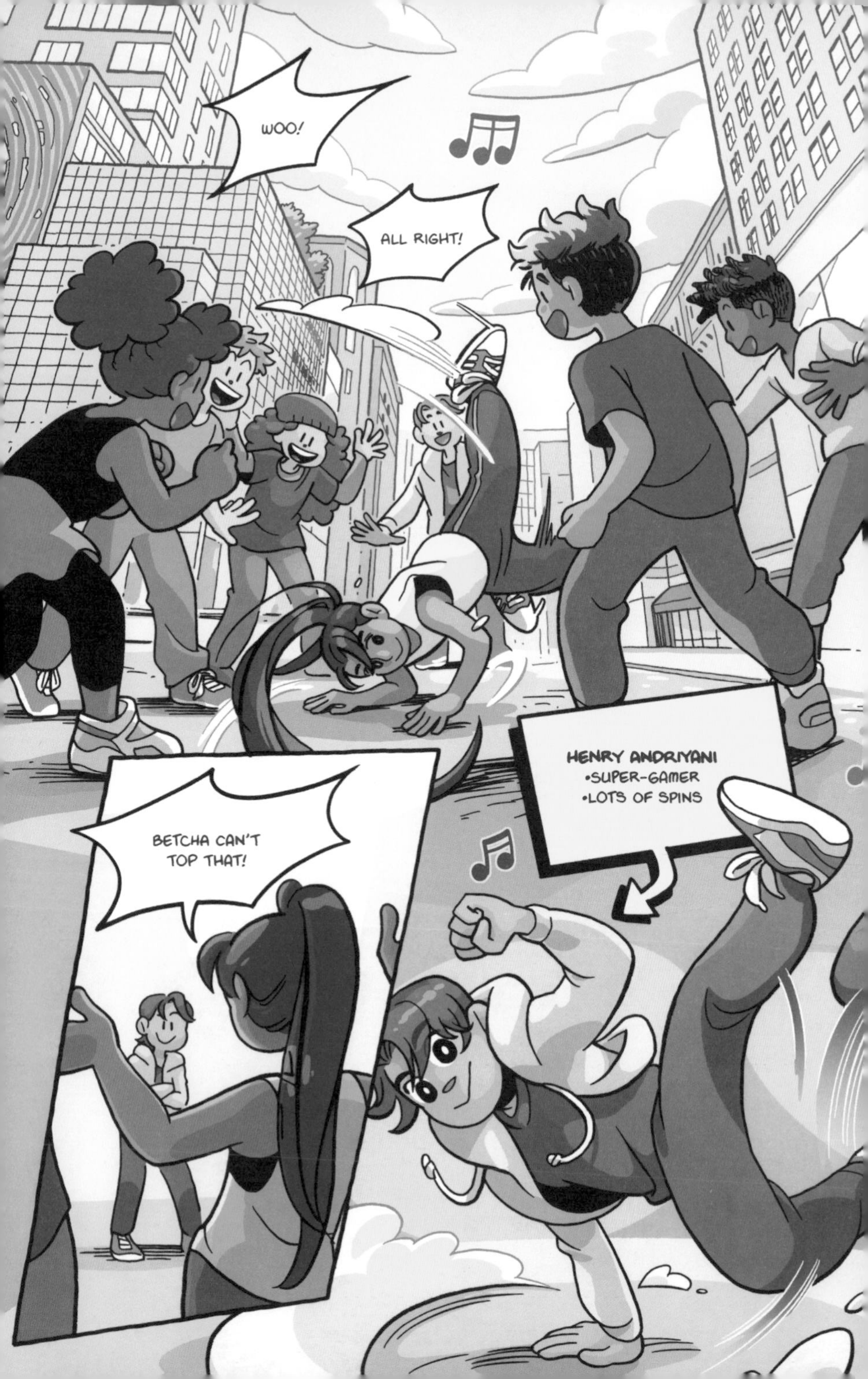
WOO!
ALL RIGHT!
HENRY ANDRIYANI
•SUPER-GAMER
•LOTS OF SPINS
BETCHA CAN'T TOP THAT!

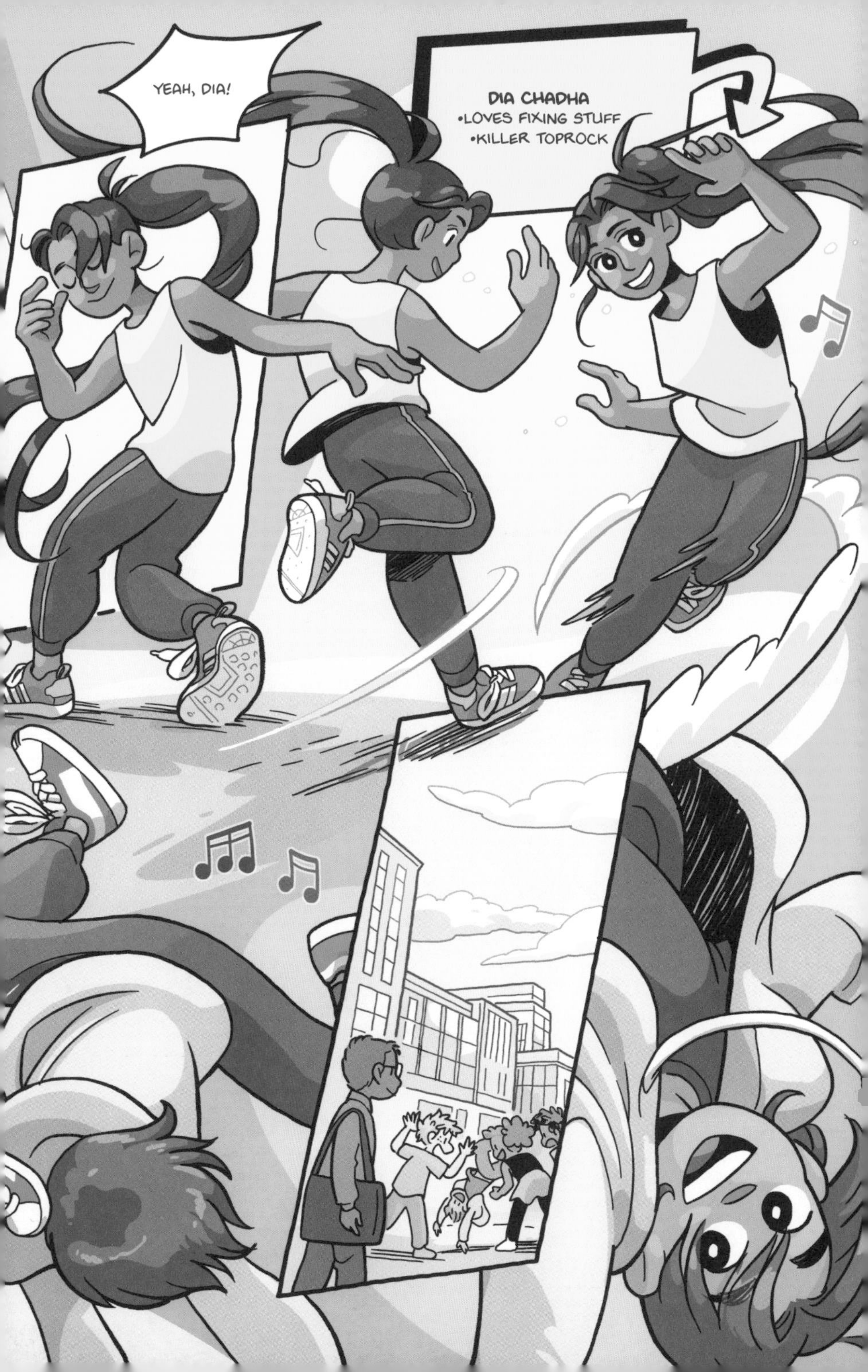
YEAH, DIA!
DIA CHADHA
•LOVES FIXING STUFF
•KILLER TOPROCK

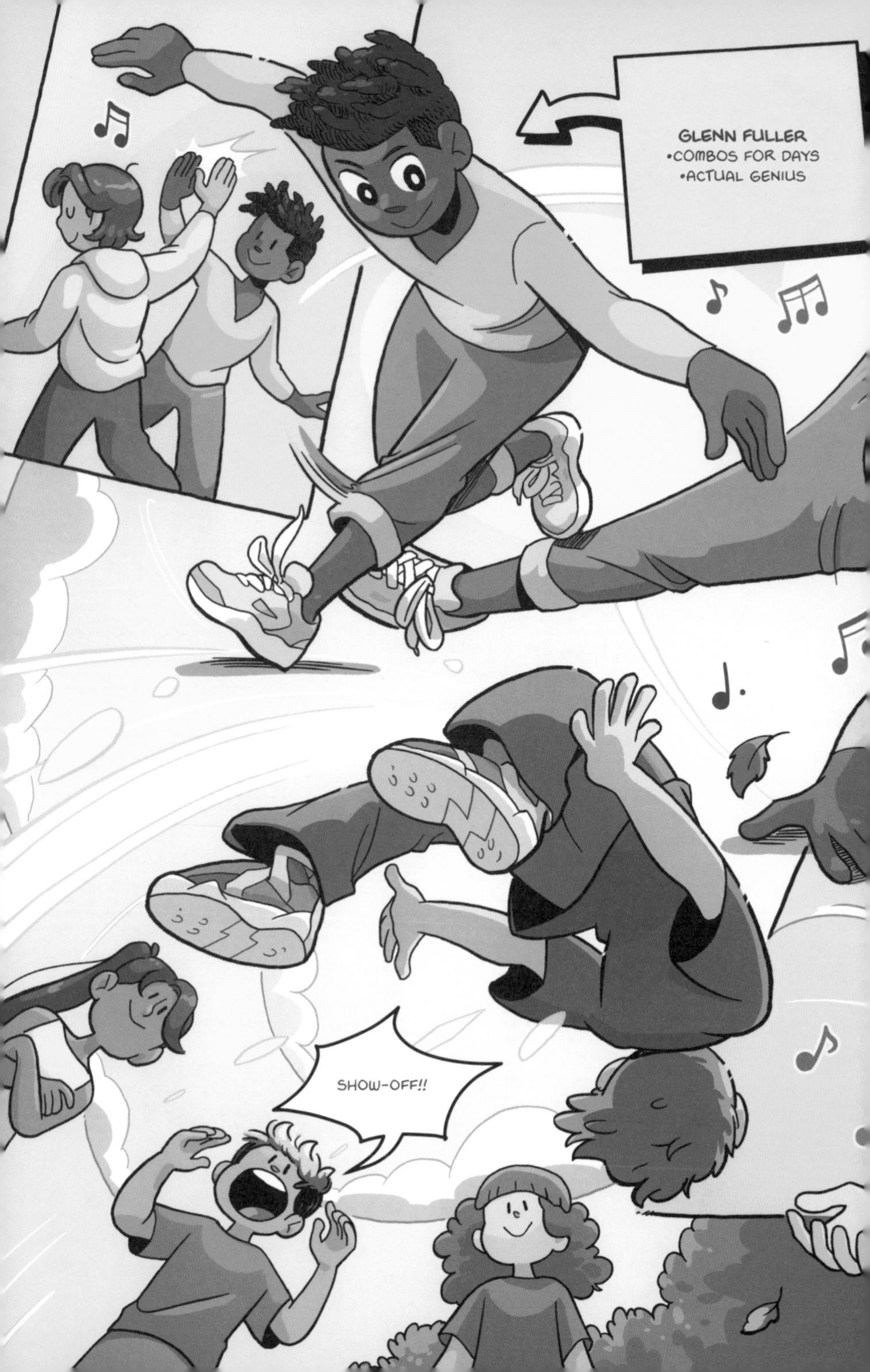
GLENN FULLER
•COMBOS FOR DAYS
•ACTUAL GENIUS
SHOW-OFF!!

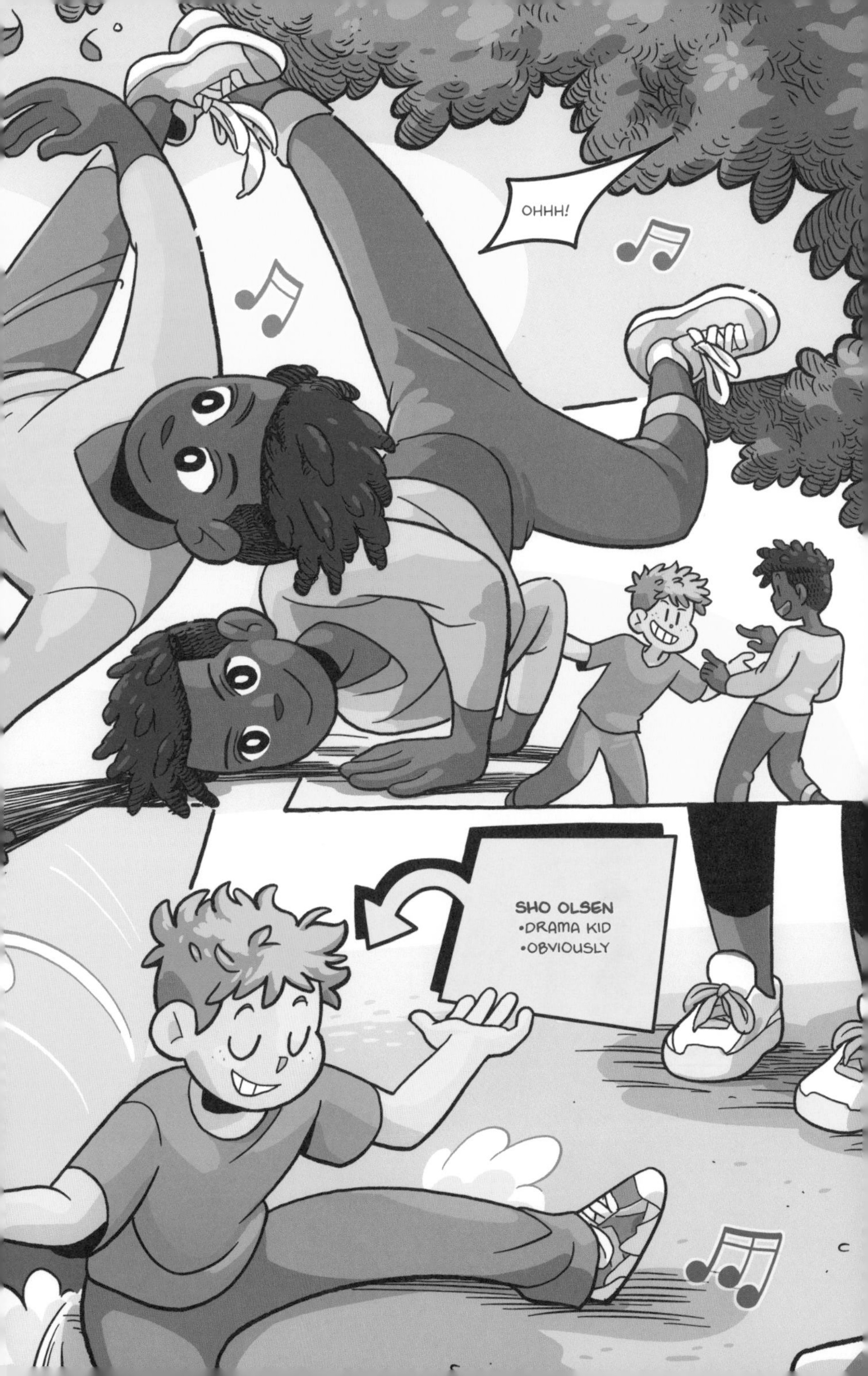
OHHH!
SHO OLSEN
•DRAMA KID
•OBVIOUSLY

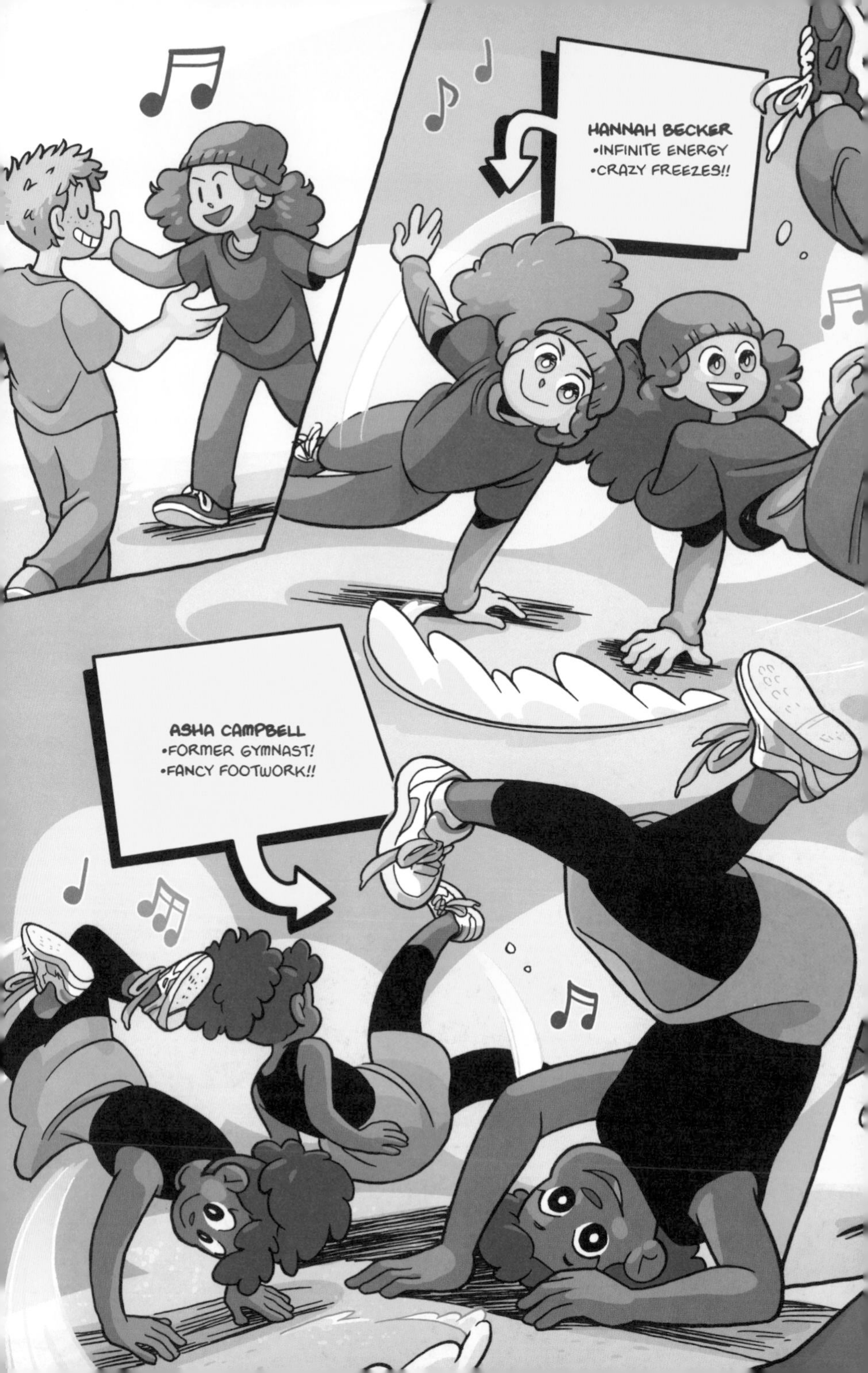
HANNAH BECKER
•INFINITE ENERGY
•CRAZY FREEZES!!
ASHA CAMPBELL
•FORMER GYMNAST!
•FANCY FOOTWORK!!

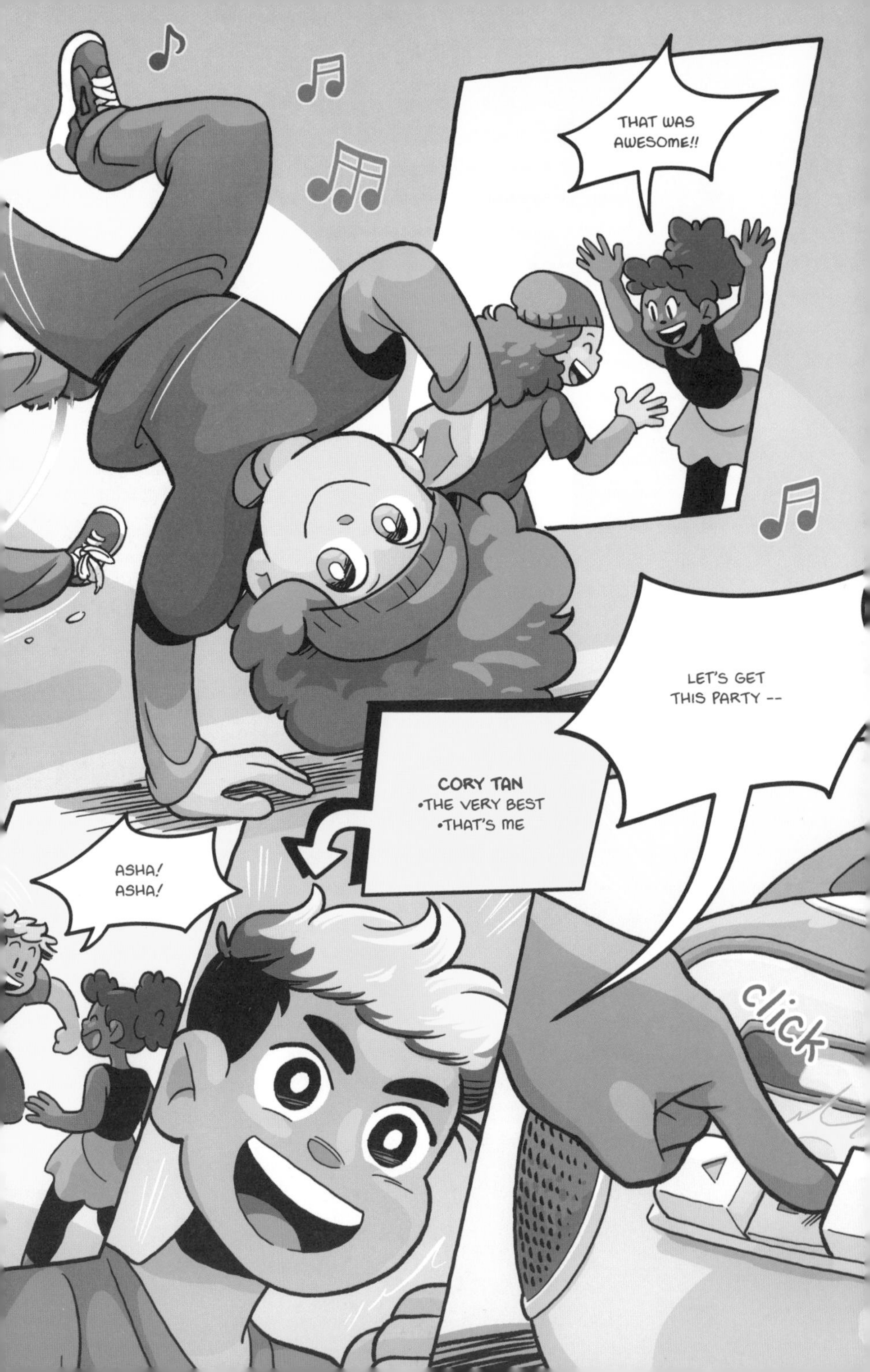

THAT WAS AWESOME!!
CORY TAN
•THE VERY BEST
•THAT'S ME
LET'S GET THIS PARTY --
ASHA! ASHA!
click

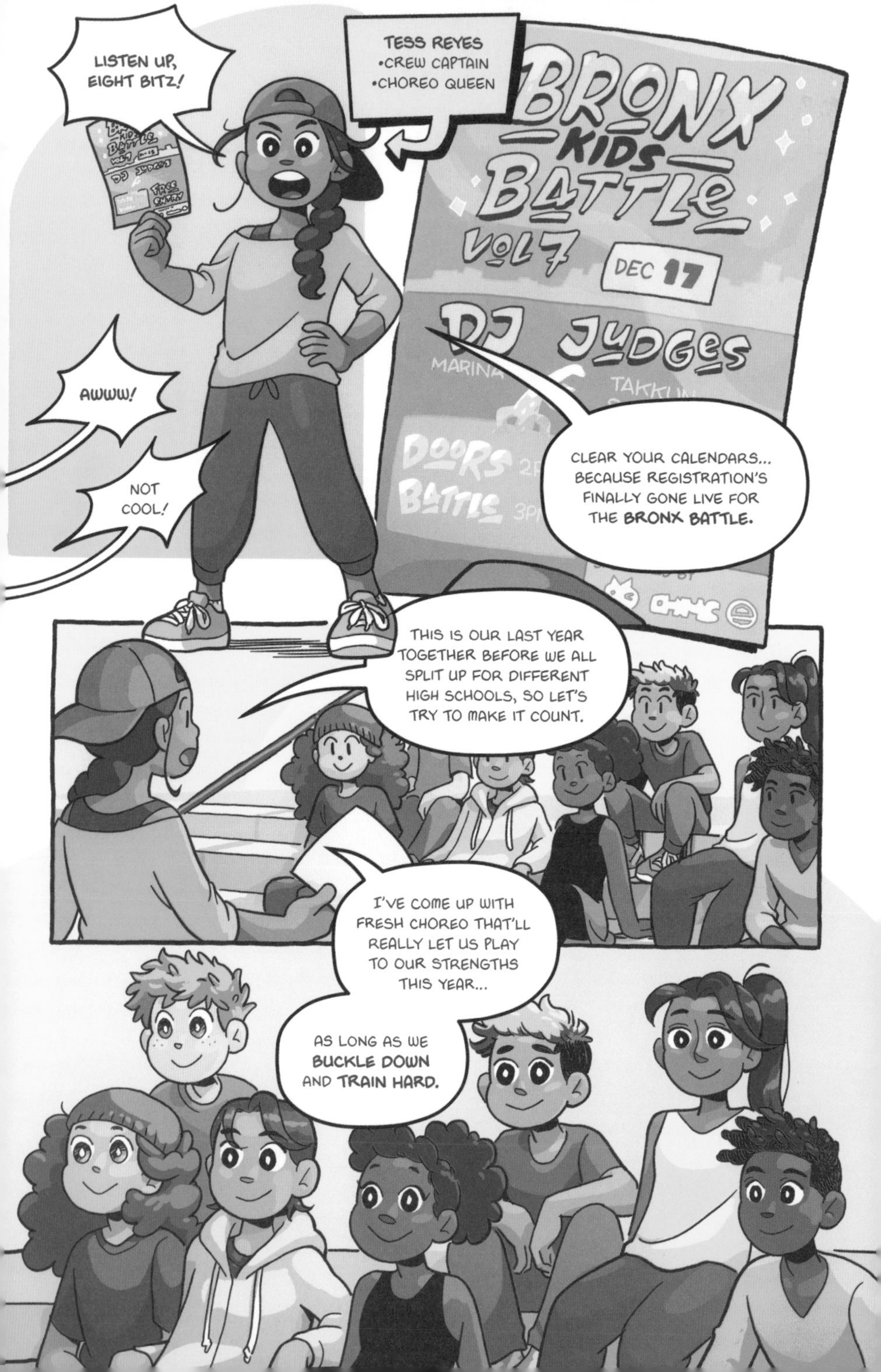
LISTEN UP, EIGHT BITZ!
TESS REYES
•CREW CAPTAIN
•CHOREO QUEEN
BRONX KIDS BATTLE VOL 7
DEC 17
DJ
JUDGES
MARINA
TAKKUN
DOORS
BATTLE
AWWW!
NOT COOL!
CLEAR YOUR CALENDARS... BECAUSE REGISTRATION'S FINALLY GONE LIVE FOR THE **BRONX BATTLE.**
THIS IS OUR LAST YEAR TOGETHER BEFORE WE ALL SPLIT UP FOR DIFFERENT HIGH SCHOOLS, SO LET'S TRY TO MAKE IT COUNT.
I'VE COME UP WITH FRESH CHOREO THAT'LL REALLY LET US PLAY TO OUR STRENGTHS THIS YEAR...
AS LONG AS WE **BUCKLE DOWN** AND **TRAIN HARD.**

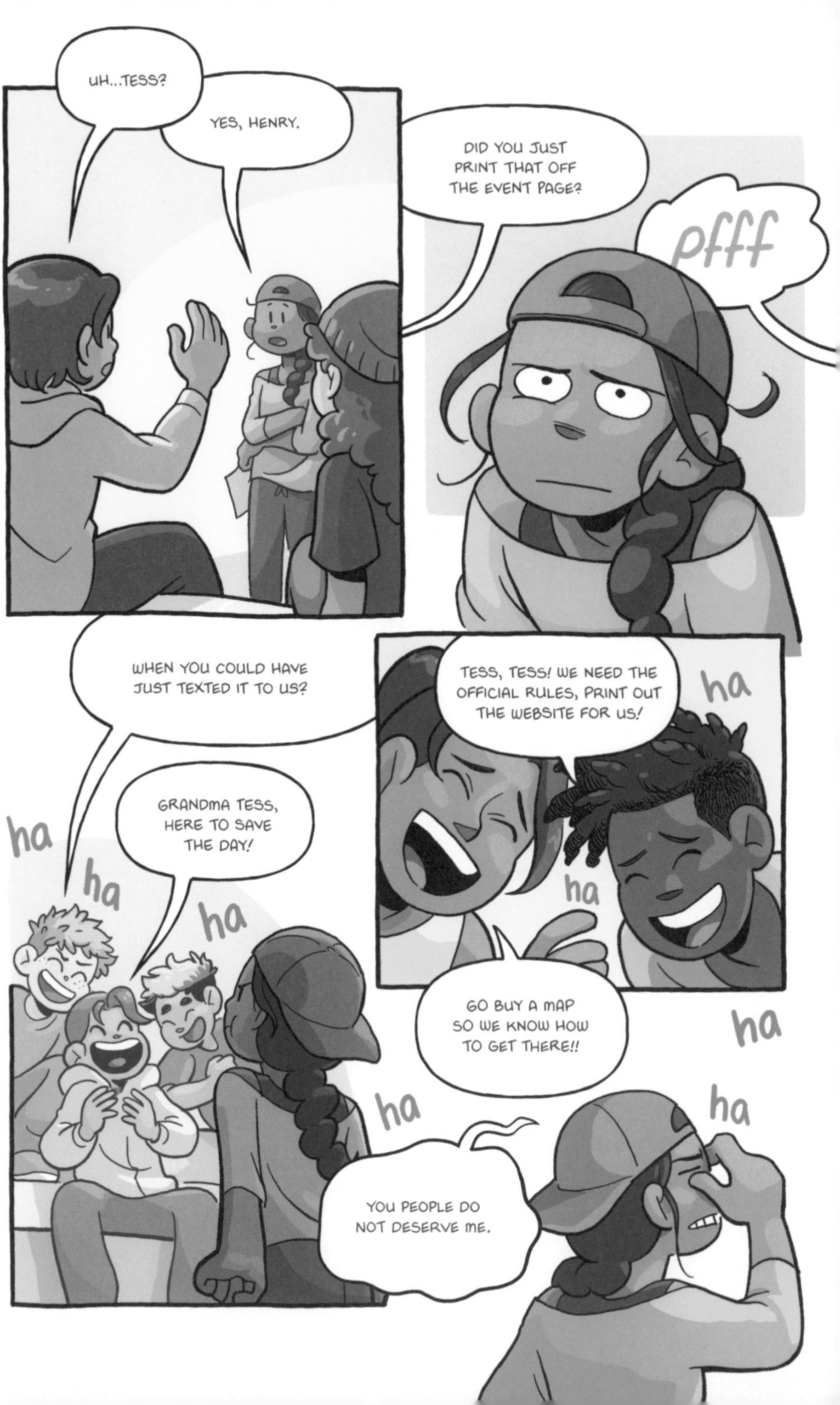
UH...TESS?
YES, HENRY.
DID YOU JUST PRINT THAT OFF THE EVENT PAGE?
pfff
WHEN YOU COULD HAVE JUST TEXTED IT TO US?
GRANDMA TESS, HERE TO SAVE THE DAY!
ha
ha
ha
TESS, TESS! WE NEED THE OFFICIAL RULES, PRINT OUT THE WEBSITE FOR US!
ha
ha
GO BUY A MAP SO WE KNOW HOW TO GET THERE!!
ha
ha
ha
YOU PEOPLE DO NOT DESERVE ME.

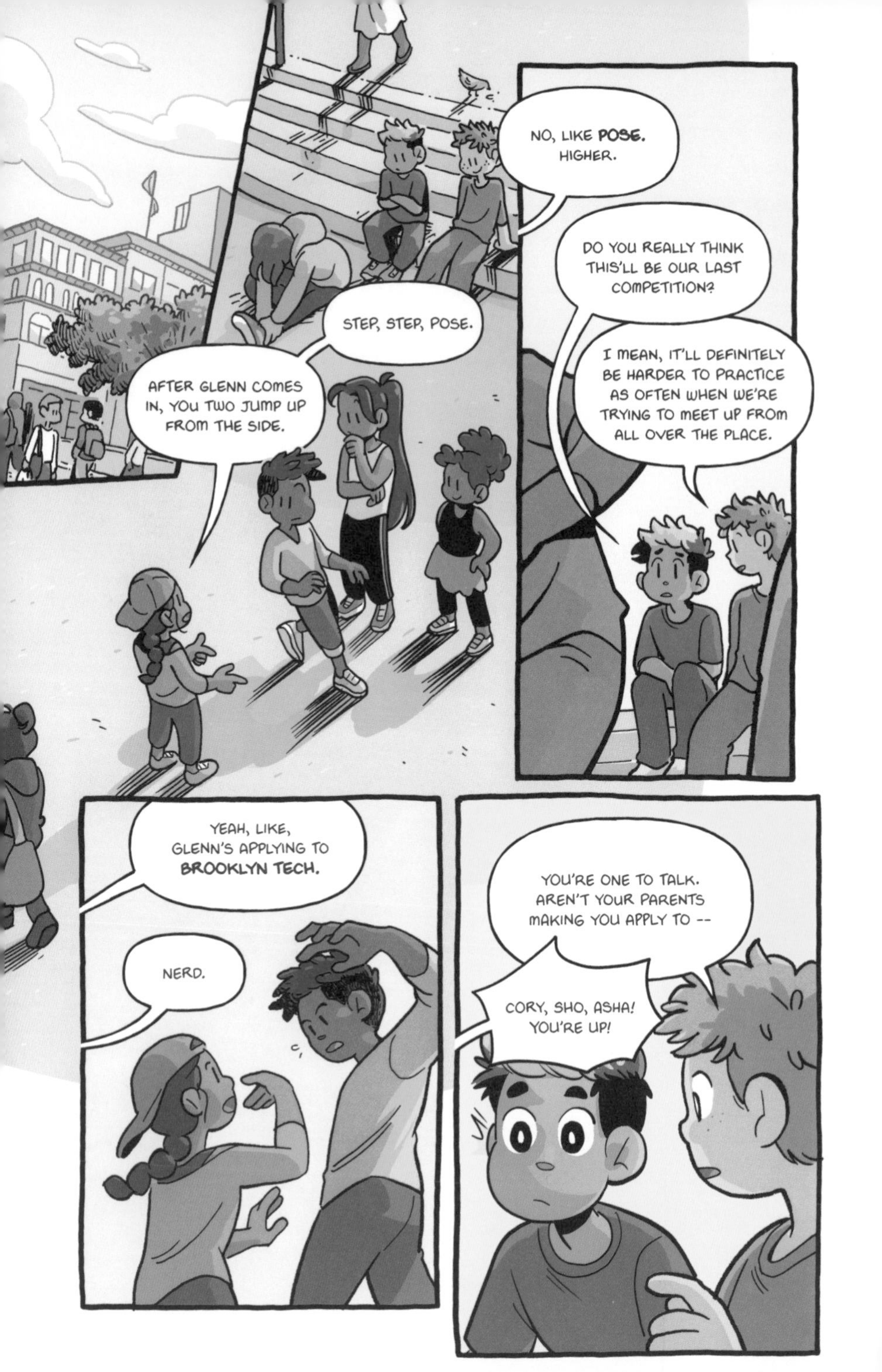
AFTER GLENN COMES IN, YOU TWO JUMP UP FROM THE SIDE.
STEP, STEP, POSE.
NO, LIKE **POSE.** HIGHER.
DO YOU REALLY THINK THIS'LL BE OUR LAST COMPETITION?
I MEAN, IT'LL DEFINITELY BE HARDER TO PRACTICE AS OFTEN WHEN WE'RE TRYING TO MEET UP FROM ALL OVER THE PLACE.
YEAH, LIKE, GLENN'S APPLYING TO **BROOKLYN TECH.**
NERD.
YOU'RE ONE TO TALK. AREN'T YOUR PARENTS MAKING YOU APPLY TO --
CORY, SHO, ASHA! YOU'RE UP!

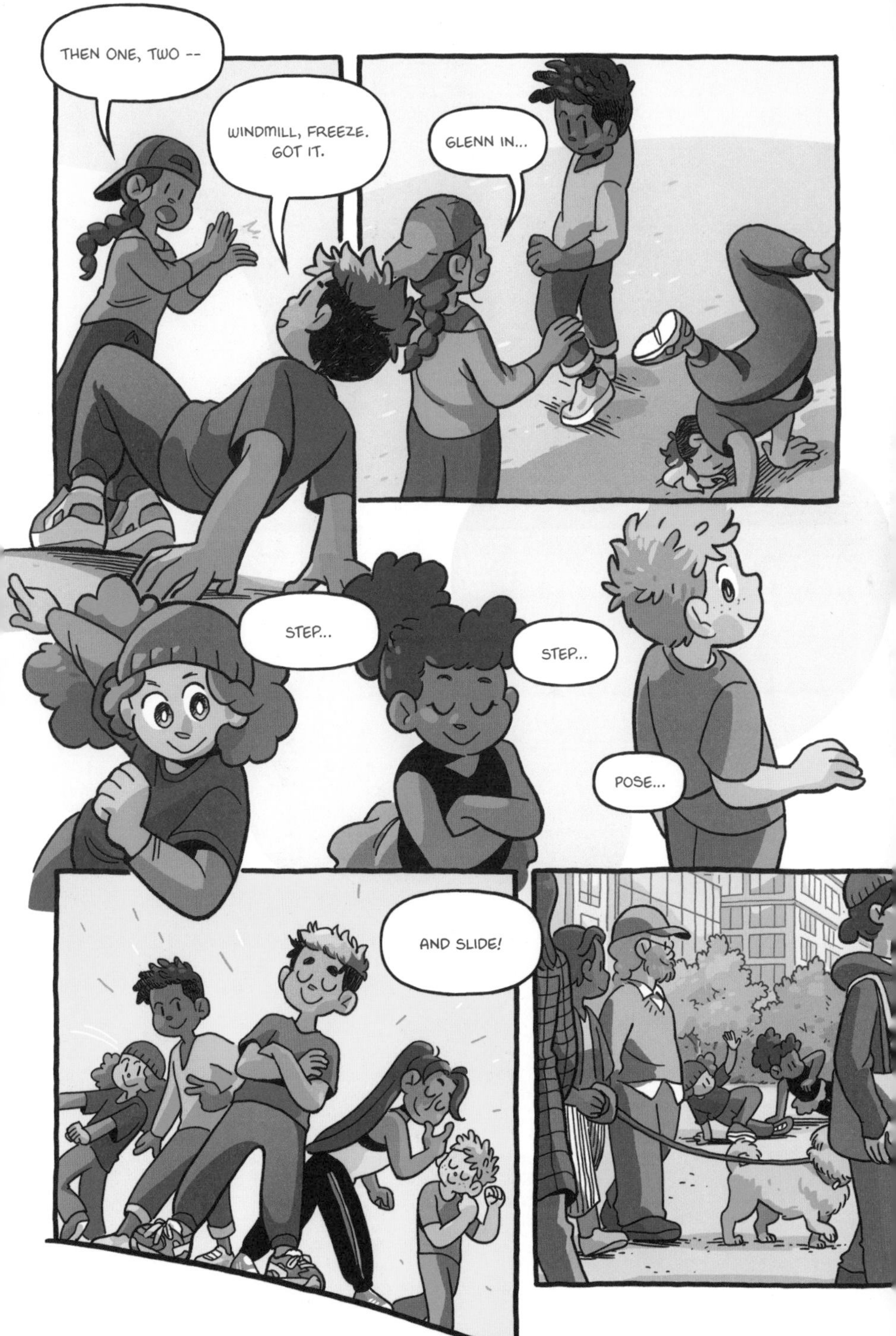
THEN ONE, TWO --
WINDMILL, FREEZE. GOT IT.
GLENN IN...
STEP...
STEP...
POSE...
AND SLIDE!

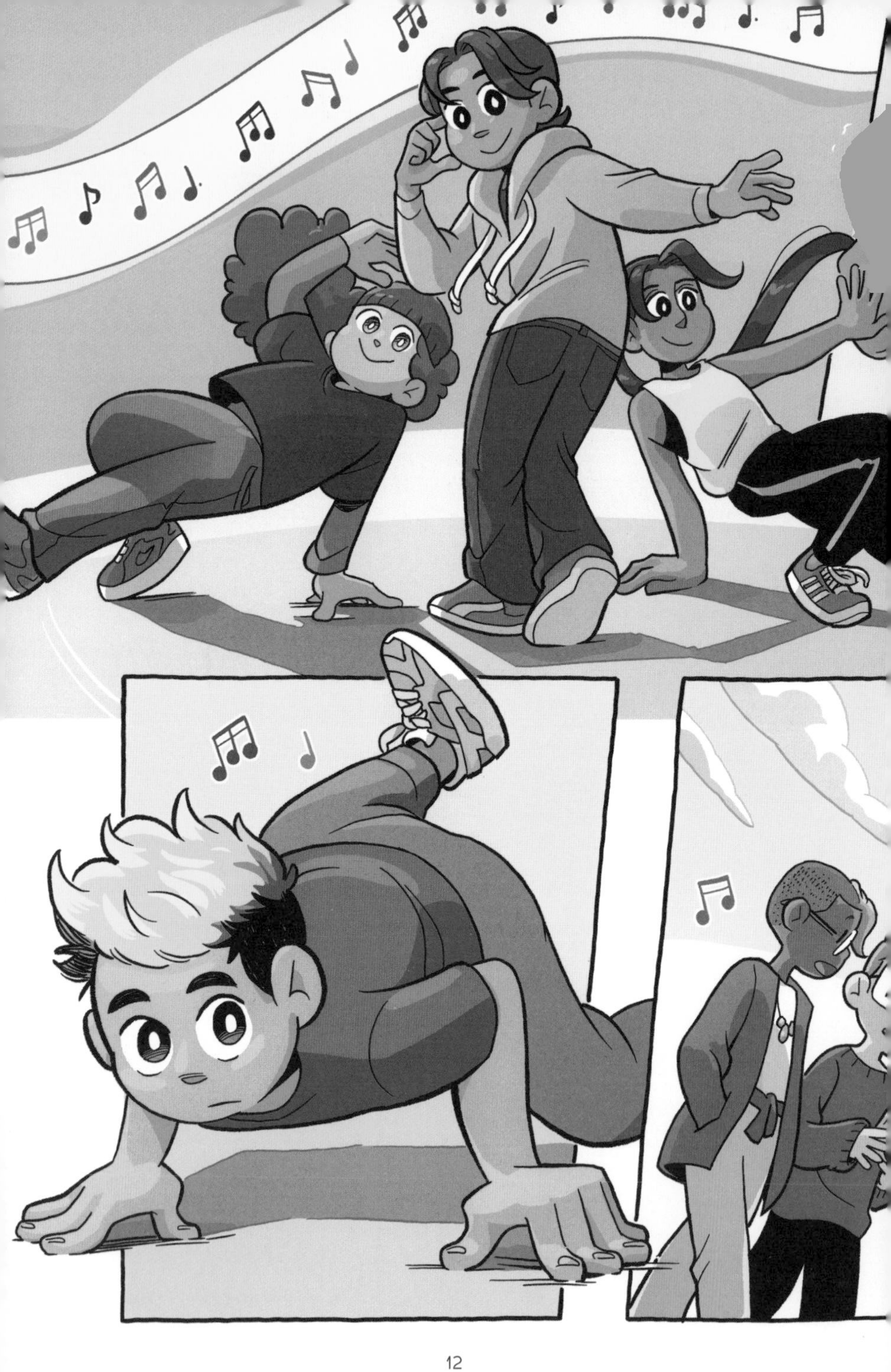

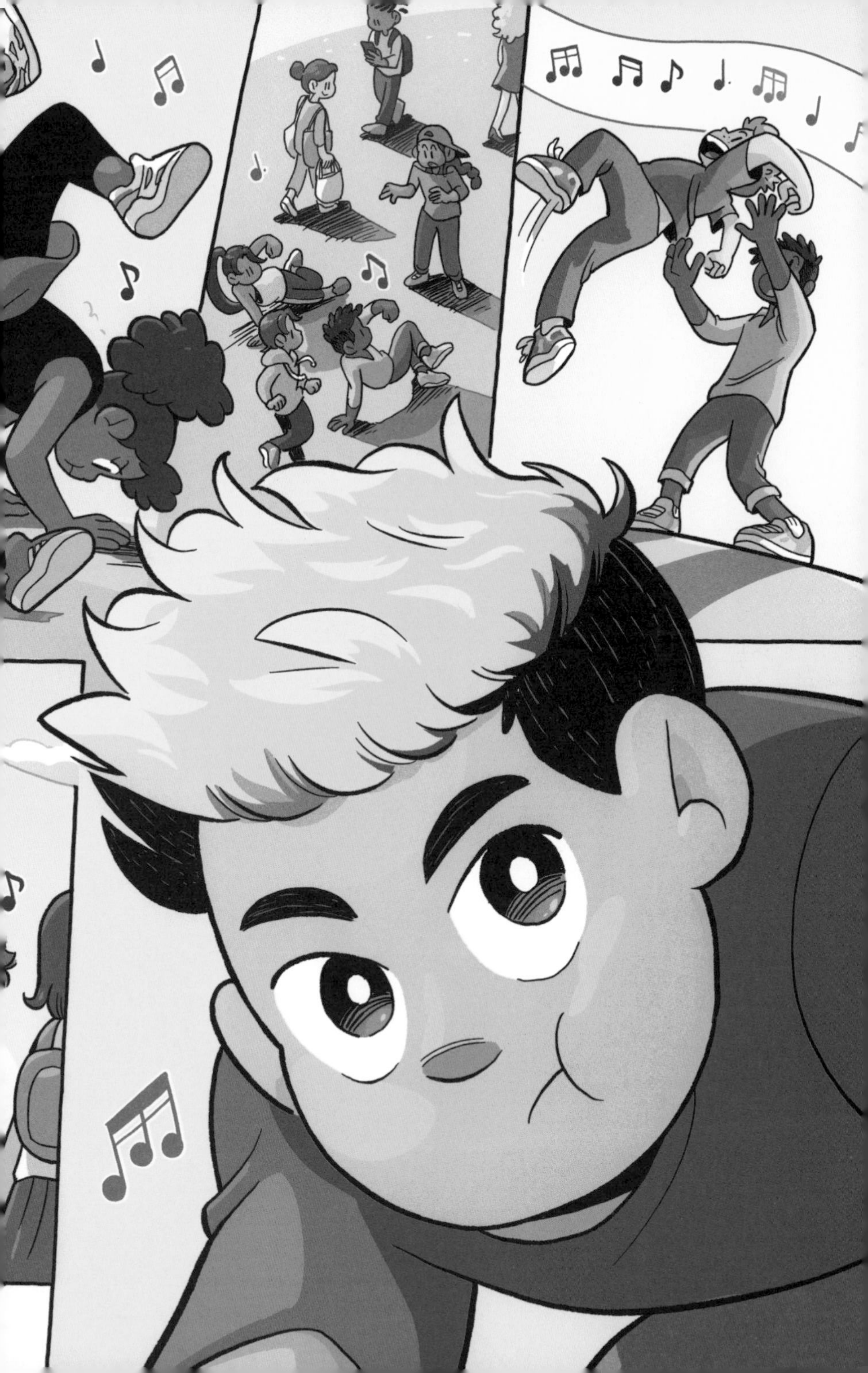

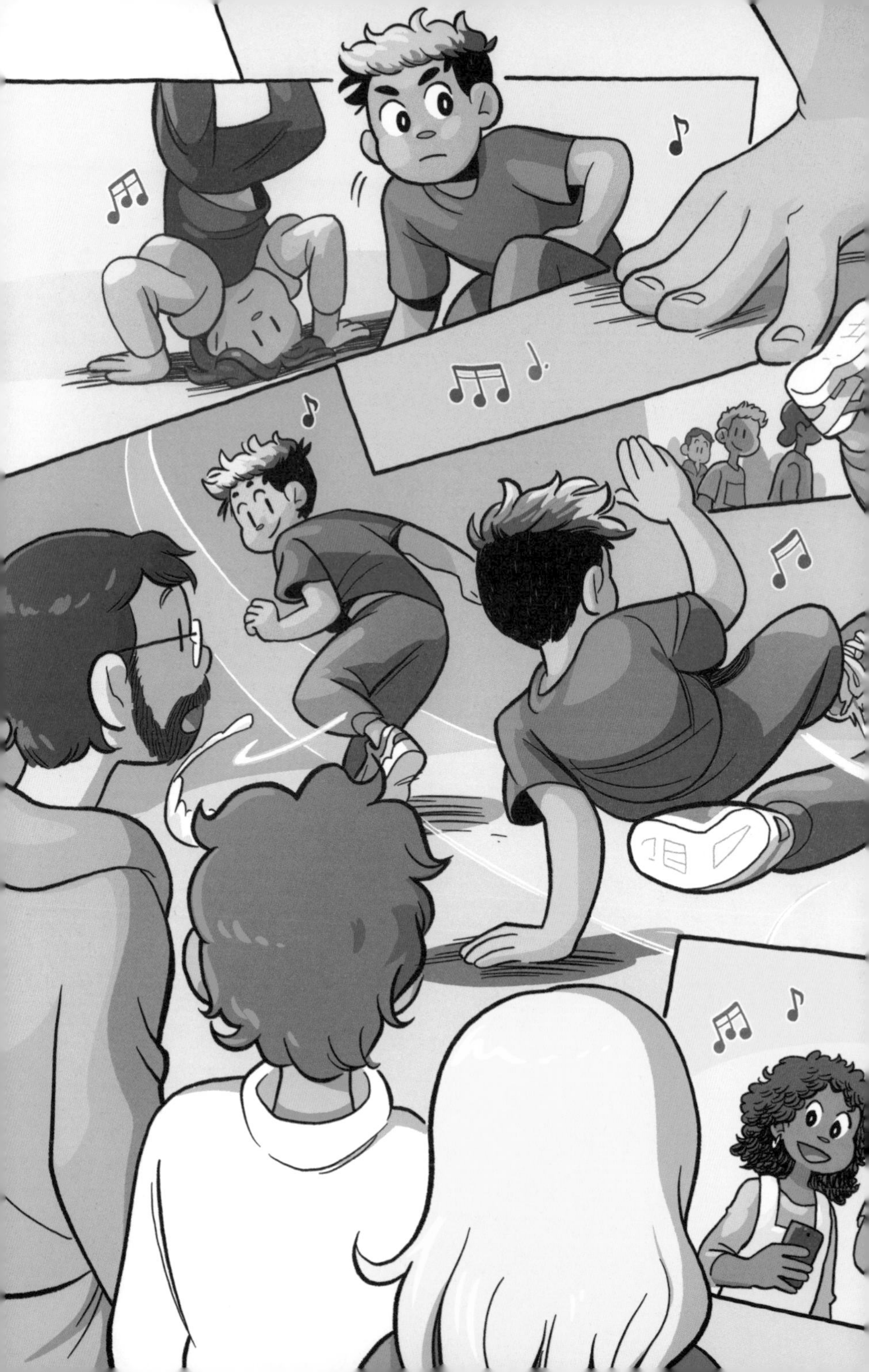

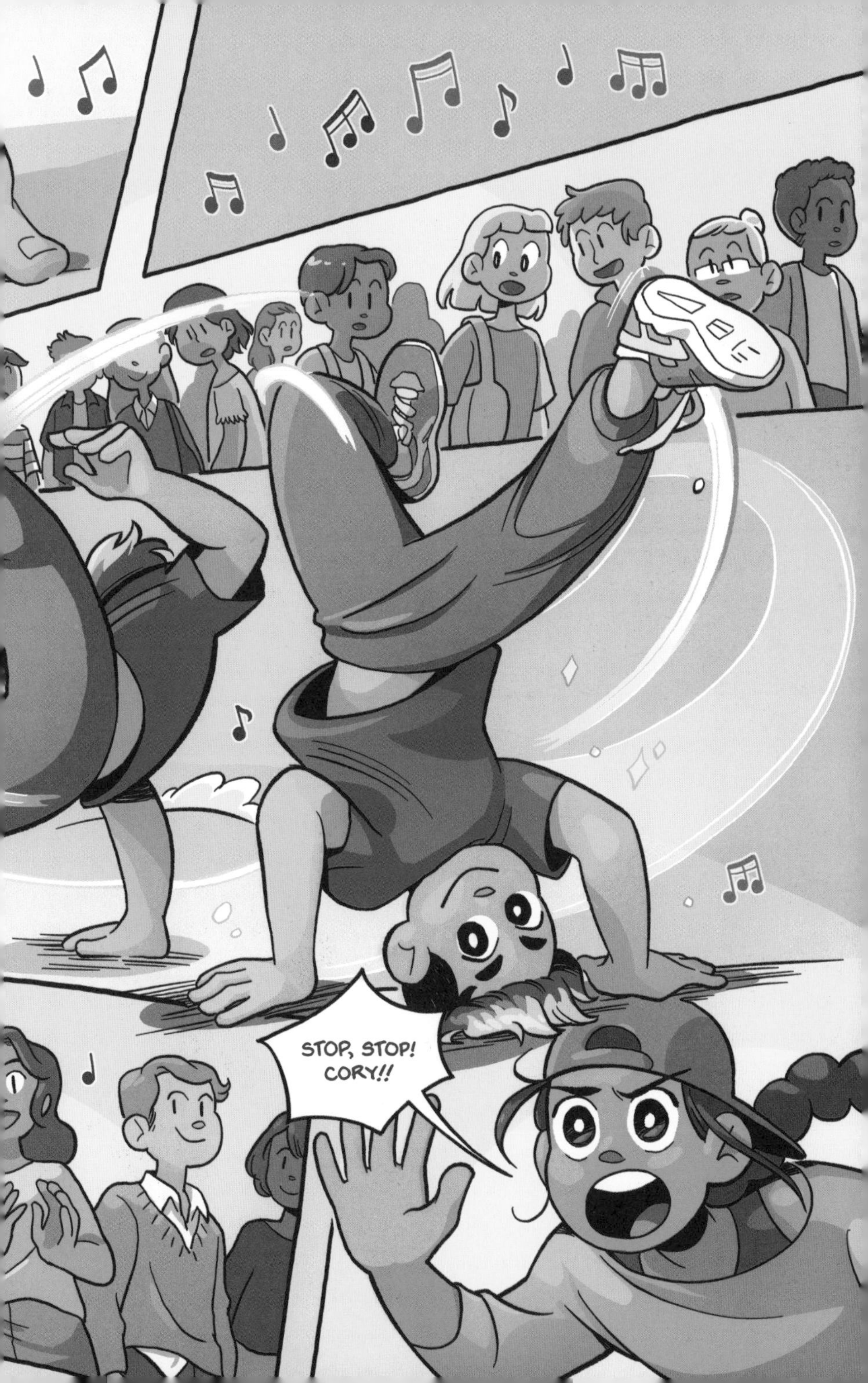
STOP, STOP!
CORY!!

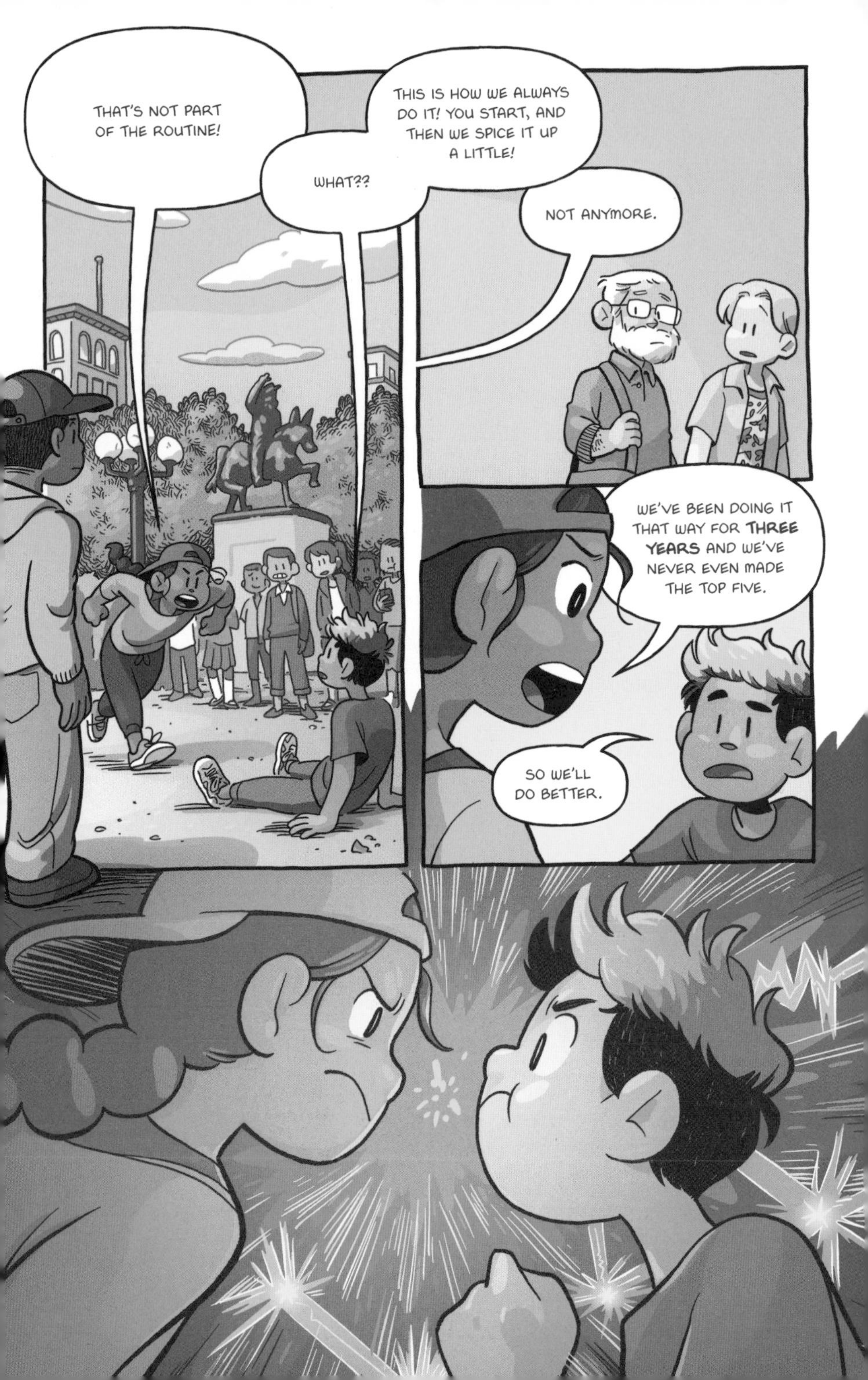
THAT'S NOT PART OF THE ROUTINE!
WHAT??
THIS IS HOW WE ALWAYS DO IT! YOU START, AND THEN WE SPICE IT UP A LITTLE!
NOT ANYMORE.
WE'VE BEEN DOING IT THAT WAY FOR **THREE YEARS** AND WE'VE NEVER EVEN MADE THE TOP FIVE.
SO WE'LL DO BETTER.

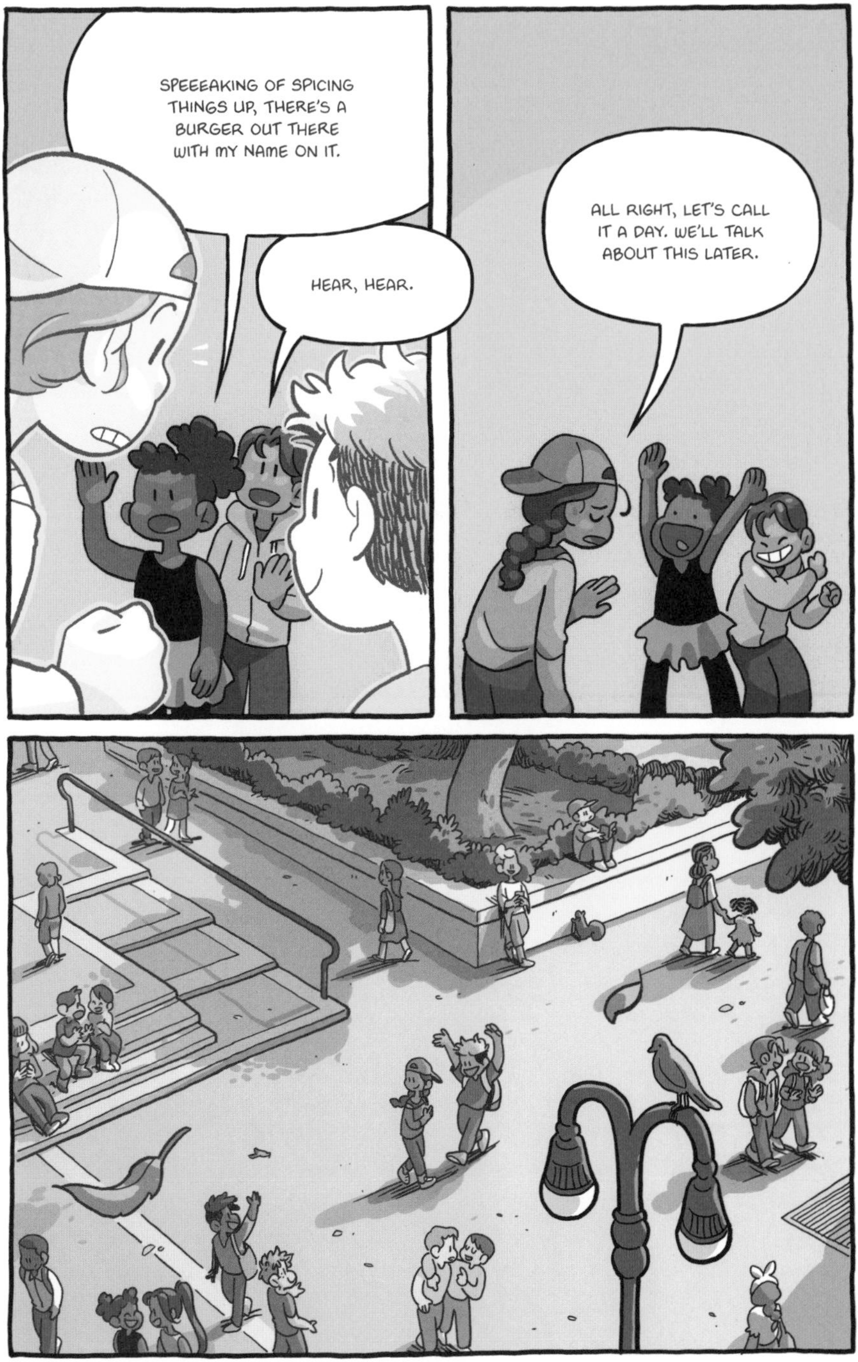
SPEEEAKING OF SPICING THINGS UP, THERE'S A BURGER OUT THERE WITH MY NAME ON IT.
HEAR, HEAR.
ALL RIGHT, LET'S CALL IT A DAY. WE'LL TALK ABOUT THIS LATER.

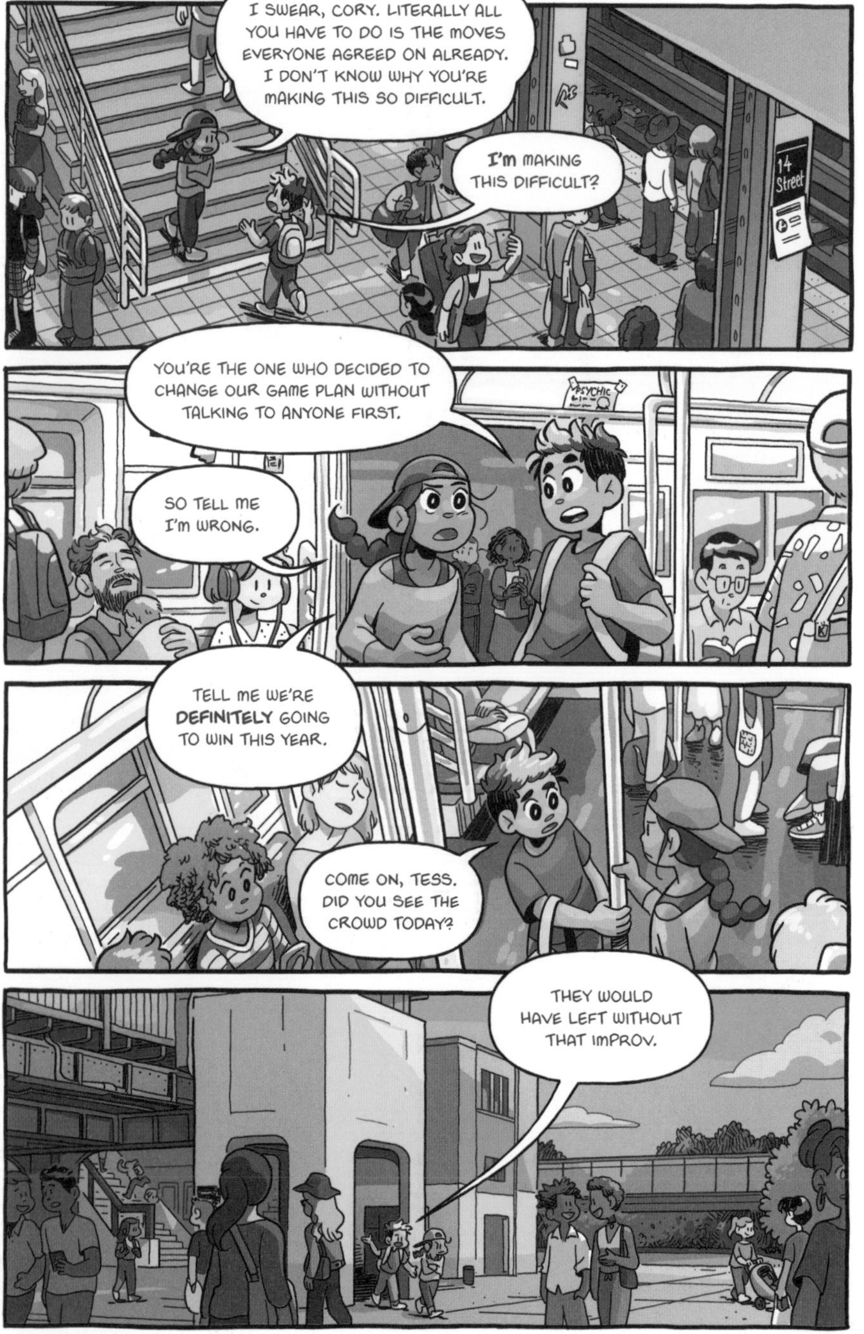
I SWEAR, CORY. LITERALLY ALL YOU HAVE TO DO IS THE MOVES EVERYONE AGREED ON ALREADY. I DON'T KNOW WHY YOU'RE MAKING THIS SO DIFFICULT.
I'M MAKING THIS DIFFICULT?
14 Street
YOU'RE THE ONE WHO DECIDED TO CHANGE OUR GAME PLAN WITHOUT TALKING TO ANYONE FIRST.
SO TELL ME I'M WRONG.
PSYCHIC
TELL ME WE'RE **DEFINITELY** GOING TO WIN THIS YEAR.
COME ON, TESS. DID YOU SEE THE CROWD TODAY?
THEY WOULD HAVE LEFT WITHOUT THAT IMPROV.

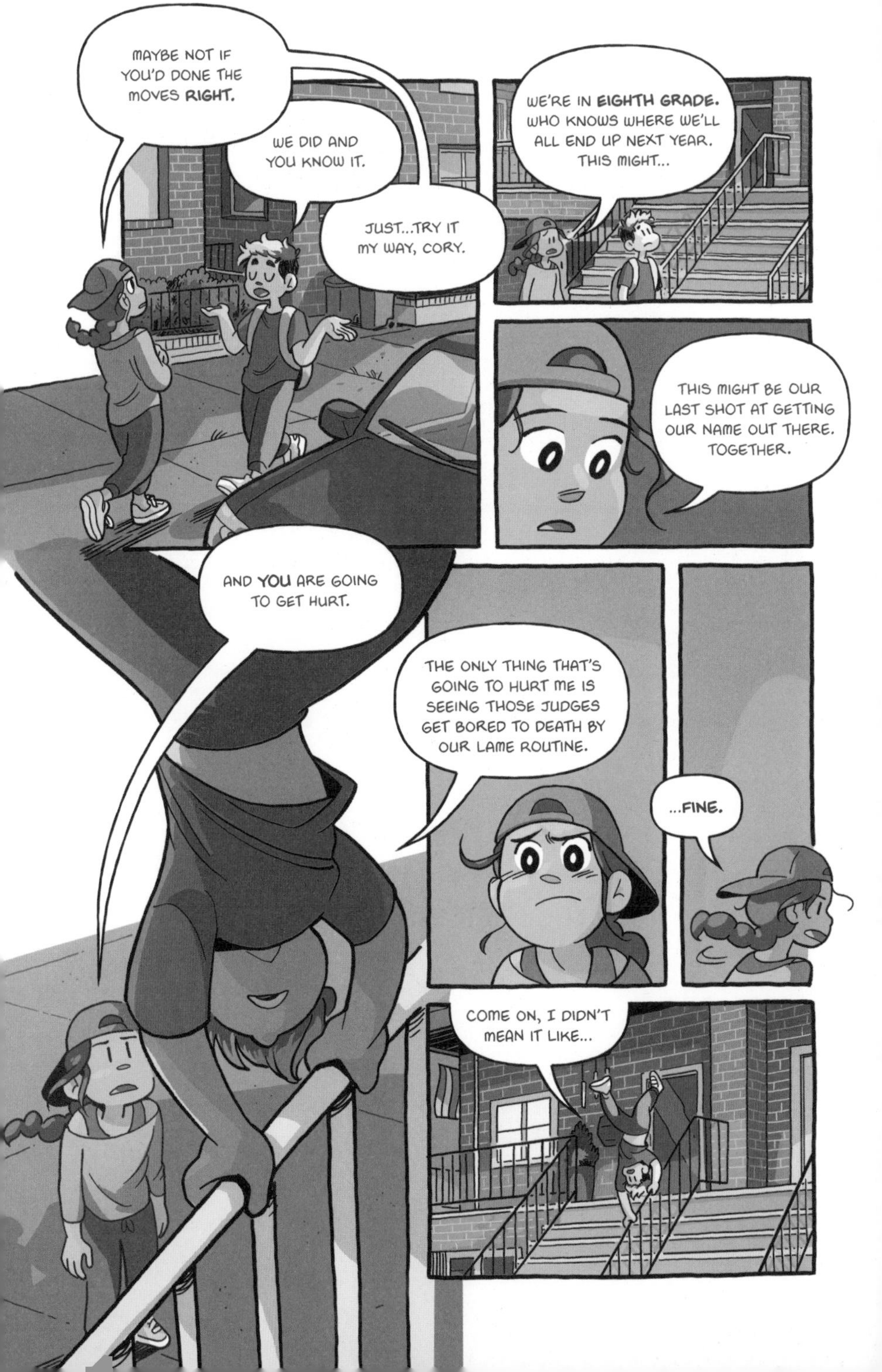
MAYBE NOT IF YOU'D DONE THE MOVES **RIGHT.**
WE DID AND YOU KNOW IT.
JUST...TRY IT MY WAY, CORY.
WE'RE IN **EIGHTH GRADE.** WHO KNOWS WHERE WE'LL ALL END UP NEXT YEAR. THIS MIGHT...
THIS MIGHT BE OUR LAST SHOT AT GETTING OUR NAME OUT THERE. TOGETHER.
AND **YOU** ARE GOING TO GET HURT.
THE ONLY THING THAT'S GOING TO HURT ME IS SEEING THOSE JUDGES GET BORED TO DEATH BY OUR LAME ROUTINE.
...**FINE.**
COME ON, I DIDN'T MEAN IT LIKE...

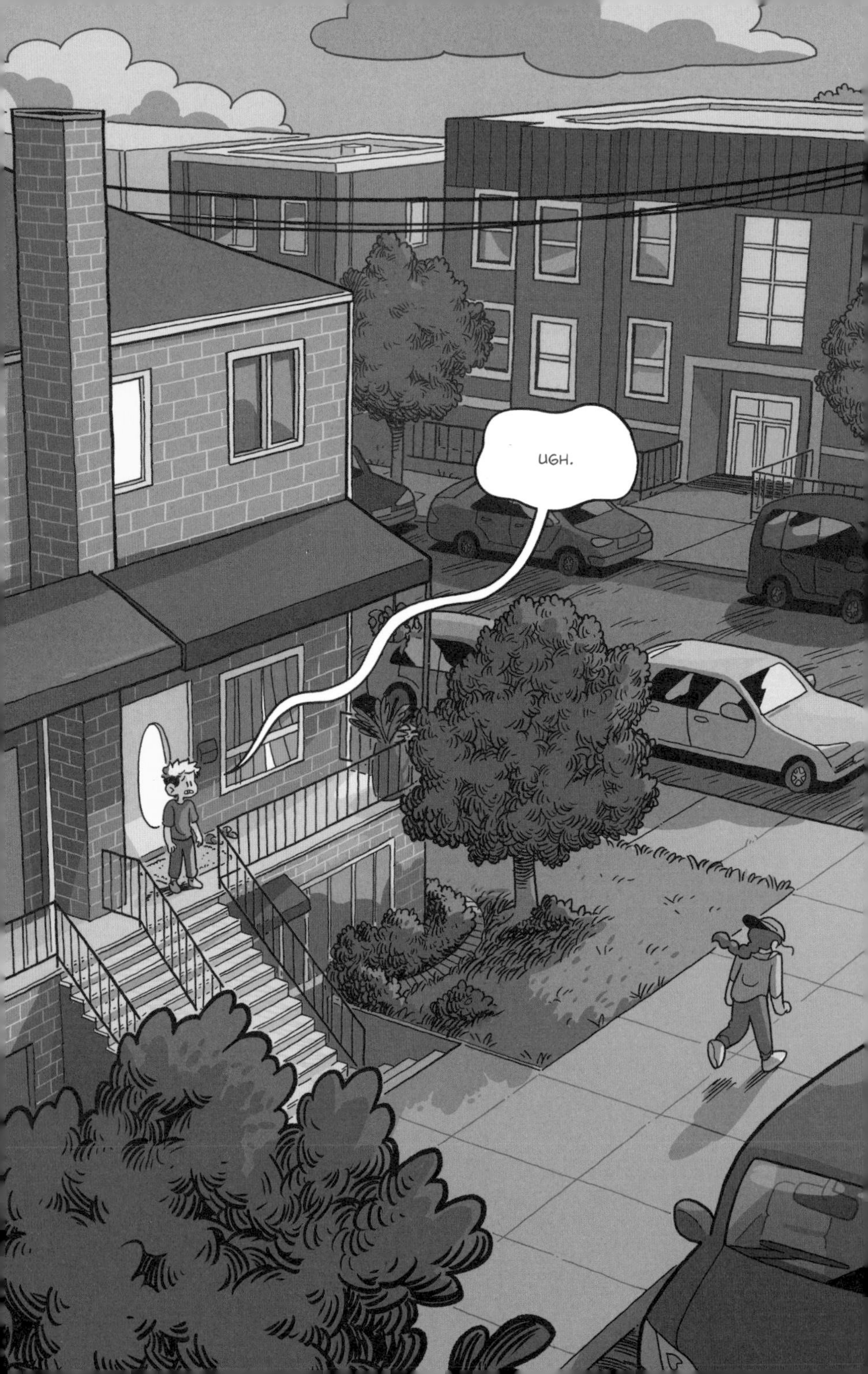
UGH.

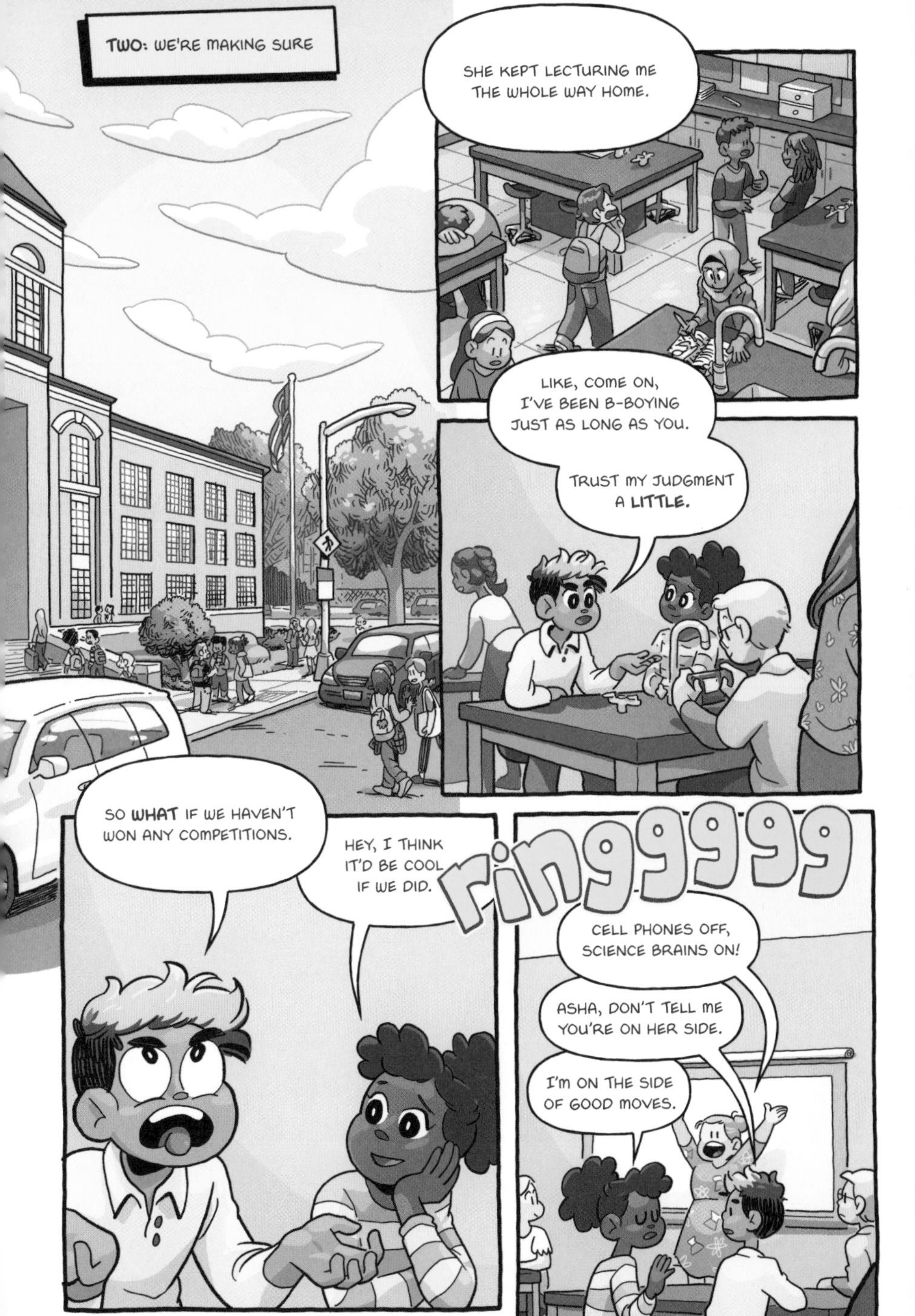
TWO: WE'RE MAKING SURE
SHE KEPT LECTURING ME THE WHOLE WAY HOME.
LIKE, COME ON, I'VE BEEN B-BOYING JUST AS LONG AS YOU.
TRUST MY JUDGMENT A **LITTLE.**
SO **WHAT** IF WE HAVEN'T WON ANY COMPETITIONS.
HEY, I THINK IT'D BE COOL IF WE DID.
ringgggg
CELL PHONES OFF, SCIENCE BRAINS ON!
ASHA, DON'T TELL ME YOU'RE ON HER SIDE.
I'M ON THE SIDE OF GOOD MOVES.

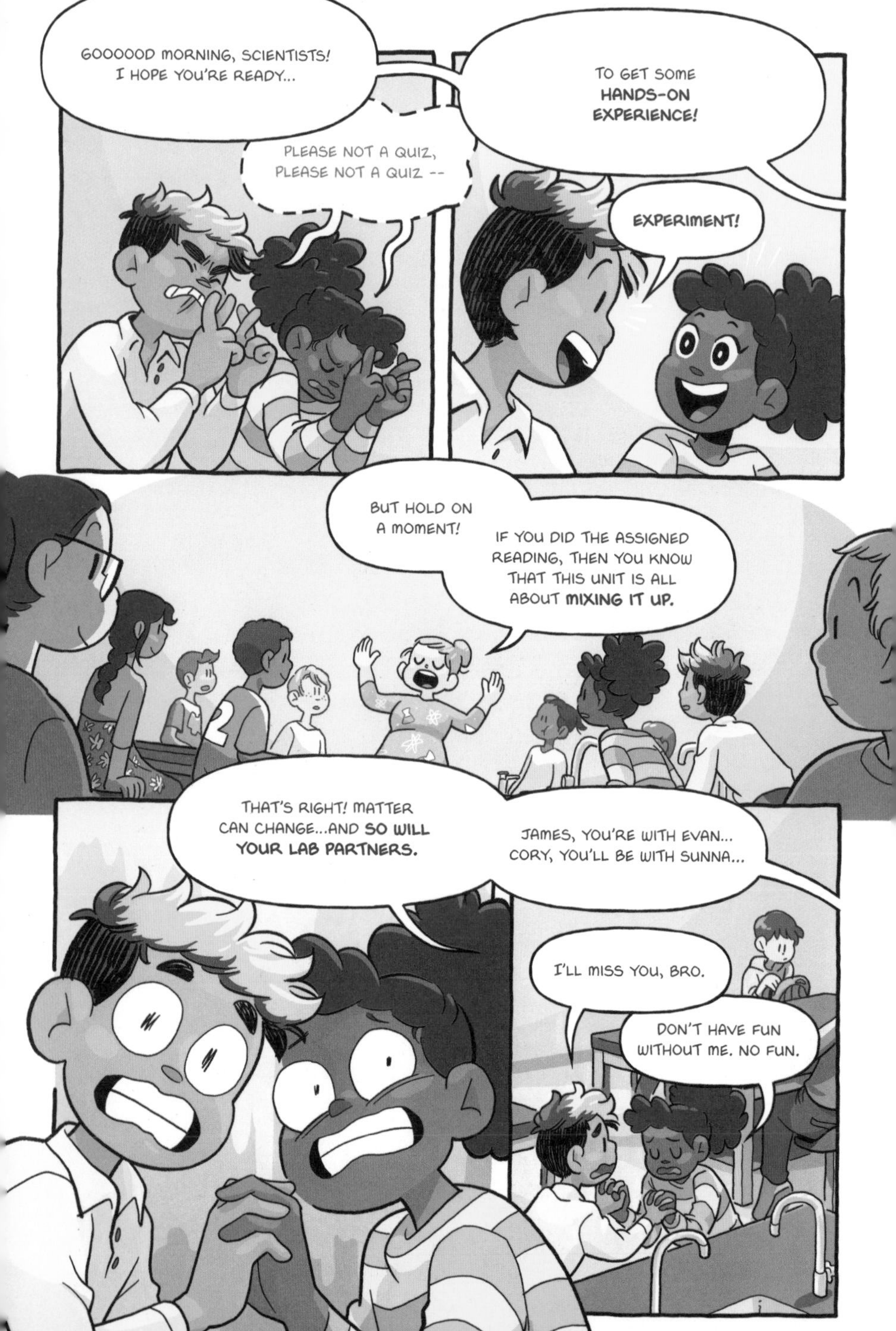
GOOOOOD MORNING, SCIENTISTS! I HOPE YOU'RE READY...
PLEASE NOT A QUIZ, PLEASE NOT A QUIZ --
TO GET SOME HANDS-ON EXPERIENCE!
EXPERIMENT!
BUT HOLD ON A MOMENT!
IF YOU DID THE ASSIGNED READING, THEN YOU KNOW THAT THIS UNIT IS ALL ABOUT MIXING IT UP.
THAT'S RIGHT! MATTER CAN CHANGE...AND SO WILL YOUR LAB PARTNERS.
JAMES, YOU'RE WITH EVAN... CORY, YOU'LL BE WITH SUNNA...
I'LL MISS YOU, BRO.
DON'T HAVE FUN WITHOUT ME. NO FUN.

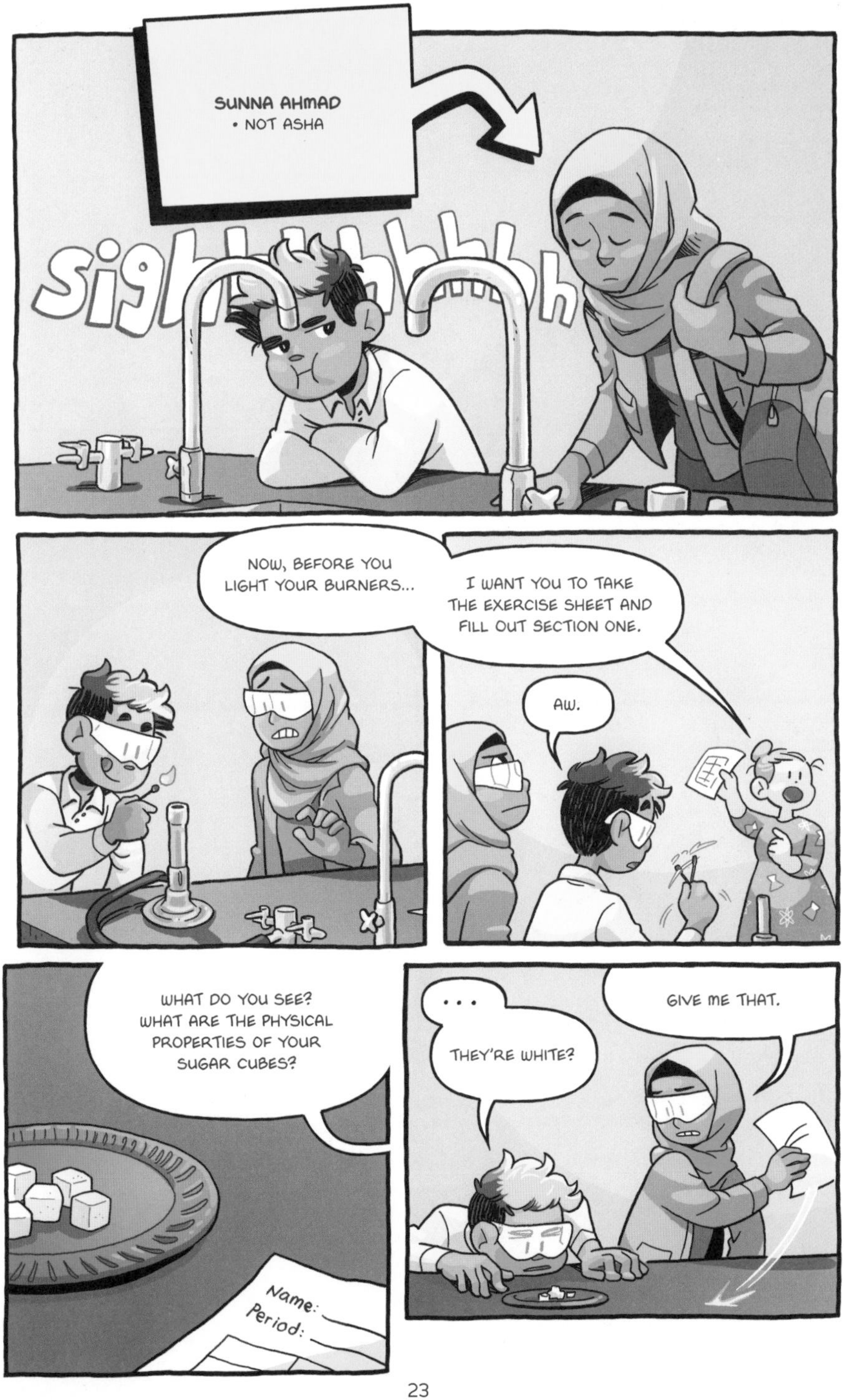

SUNNA AHMAD
• NOT ASHA
sighhhhhhhh
NOW, BEFORE YOU LIGHT YOUR BURNERS...
I WANT YOU TO TAKE THE EXERCISE SHEET AND FILL OUT SECTION ONE.
AW.
WHAT DO YOU SEE? WHAT ARE THE PHYSICAL PROPERTIES OF YOUR SUGAR CUBES?
Name:
Period:
. . .
THEY'RE WHITE?
GIVE ME THAT.

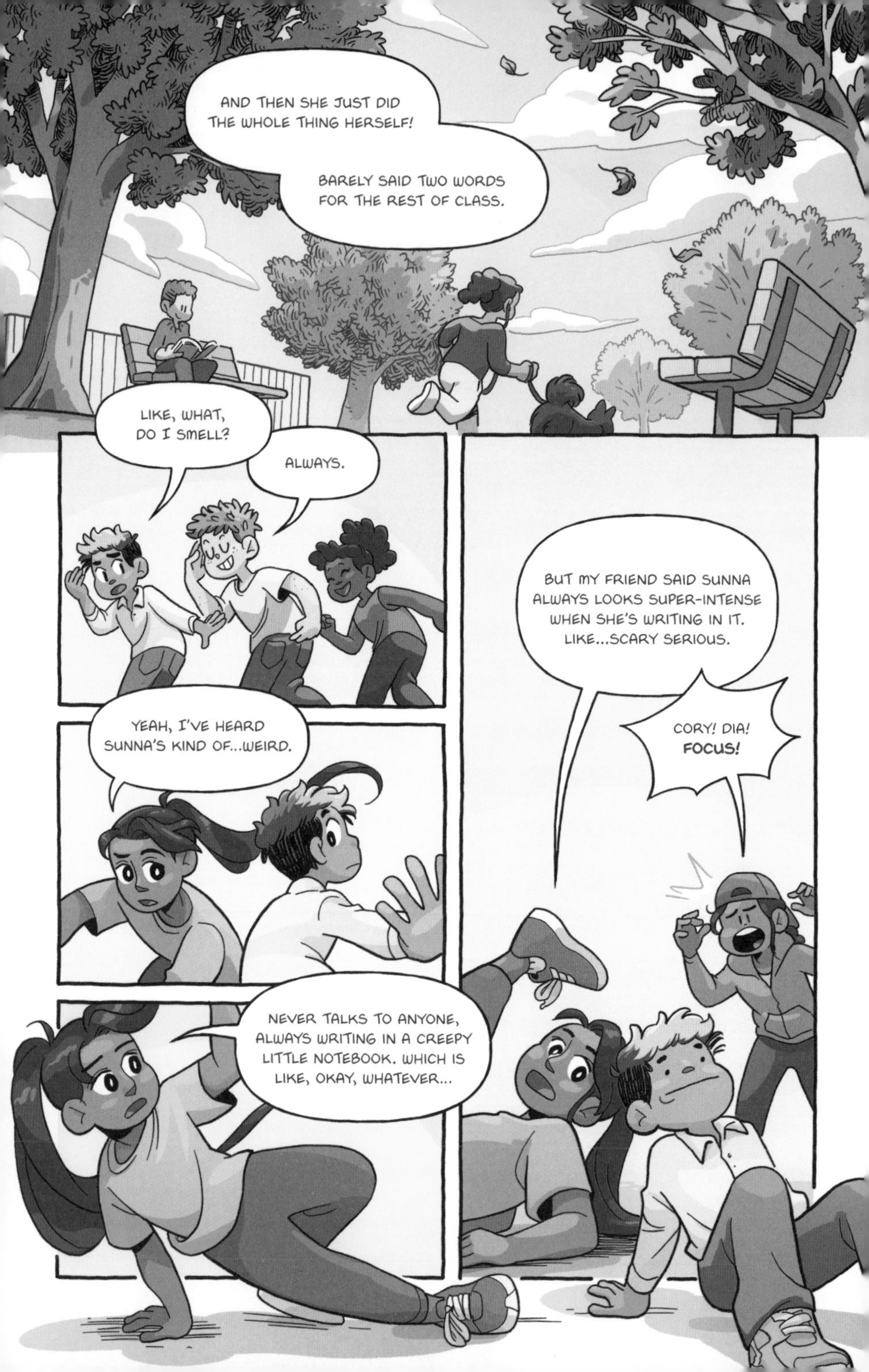
AND THEN SHE JUST DID THE WHOLE THING HERSELF!
BARELY SAID TWO WORDS FOR THE REST OF CLASS.
LIKE, WHAT, DO I SMELL?
ALWAYS.
YEAH, I'VE HEARD SUNNA'S KIND OF...WEIRD.
NEVER TALKS TO ANYONE, ALWAYS WRITING IN A CREEPY LITTLE NOTEBOOK. WHICH IS LIKE, OKAY, WHATEVER...
BUT MY FRIEND SAID SUNNA ALWAYS LOOKS SUPER-INTENSE WHEN SHE'S WRITING IN IT. LIKE...SCARY SERIOUS.
CORY! DIA! **FOCUS!**

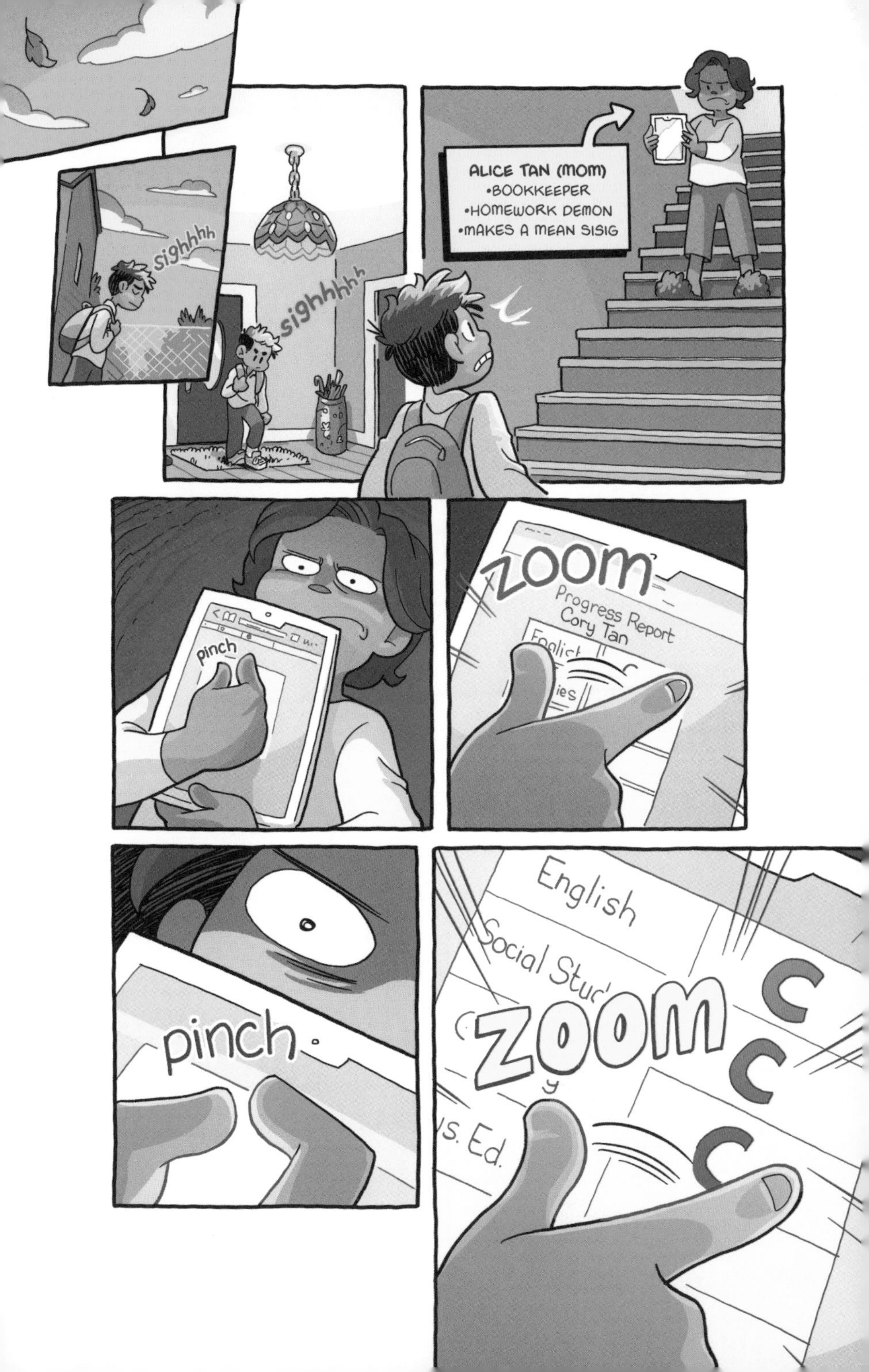

sighhhh
sighhhhh
ALICE TAN (MOM)
•BOOKKEEPER
•HOMEWORK DEMON
•MAKES A MEAN SISIG
pinch
zoom
Progress Report
Cory Tan
pinch
English
Social Stud
ZOOM
C
C
C
s. Ed.

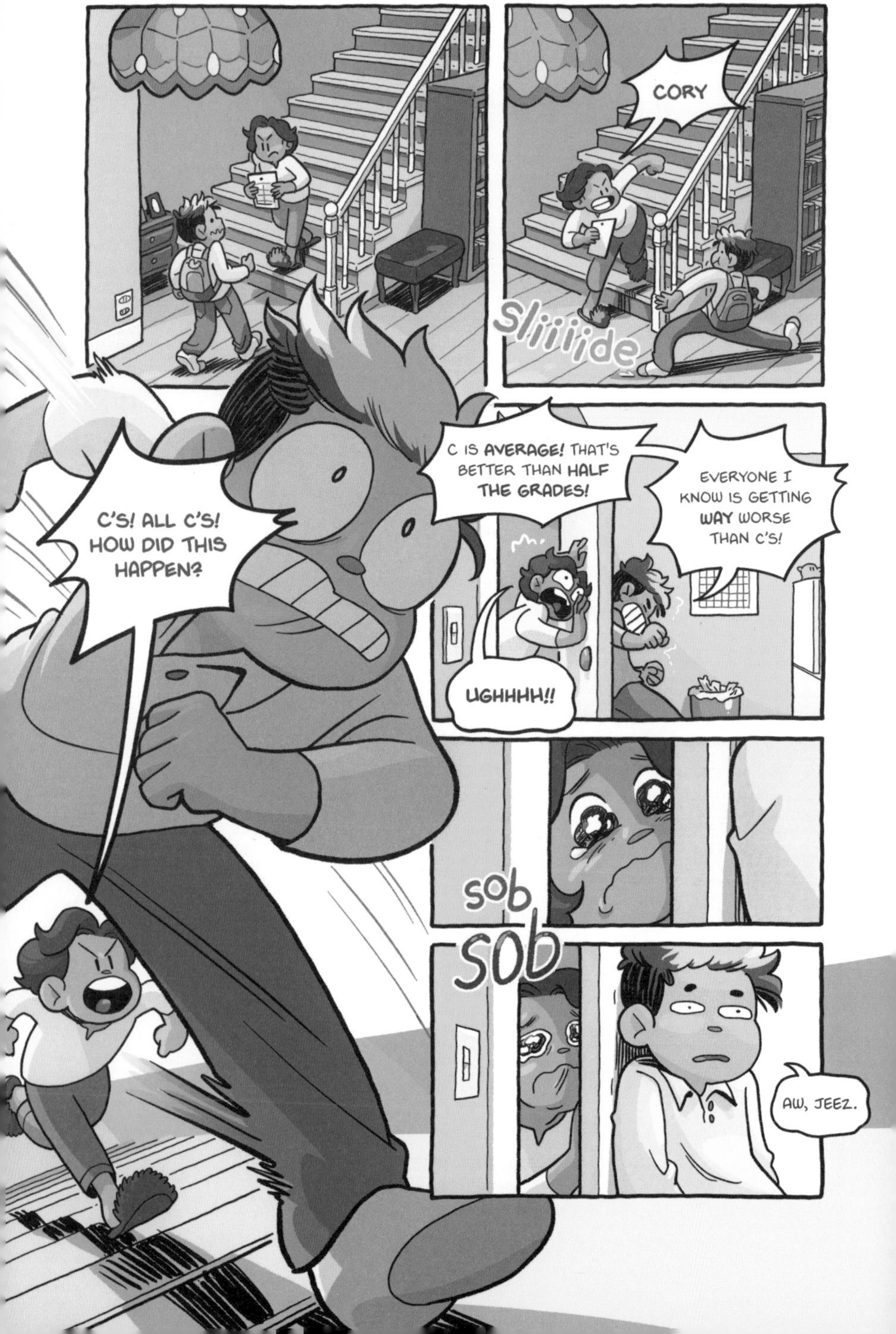
CORY
Sliiiide
C'S! ALL C'S! HOW DID THIS HAPPEN?
C IS AVERAGE! THAT'S BETTER THAN HALF THE GRADES!
EVERYONE I KNOW IS GETTING WAY WORSE THAN C'S!
UGHHHH!!
sob
sob
AW, JEEZ.

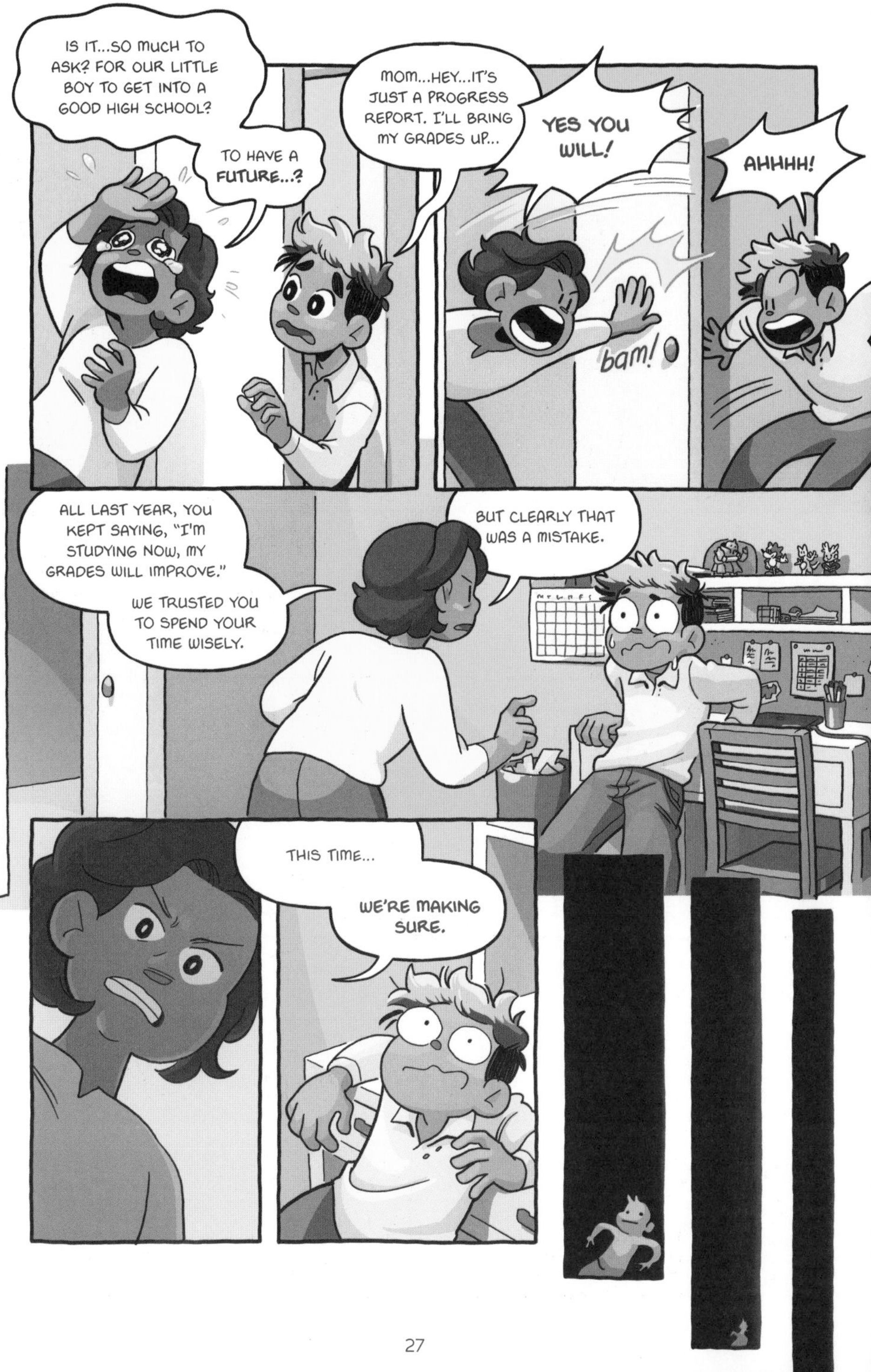

IS IT...SO MUCH TO ASK? FOR OUR LITTLE BOY TO GET INTO A GOOD HIGH SCHOOL?
TO HAVE A FUTURE...?
MOM...HEY...IT'S JUST A PROGRESS REPORT. I'LL BRING MY GRADES UP...
YES YOU WILL!
bam!
AHHHH!
ALL LAST YEAR, YOU KEPT SAYING, "I'M STUDYING NOW, MY GRADES WILL IMPROVE."
WE TRUSTED YOU TO SPEND YOUR TIME WISELY.
BUT CLEARLY THAT WAS A MISTAKE.
THIS TIME...
WE'RE MAKING SURE.

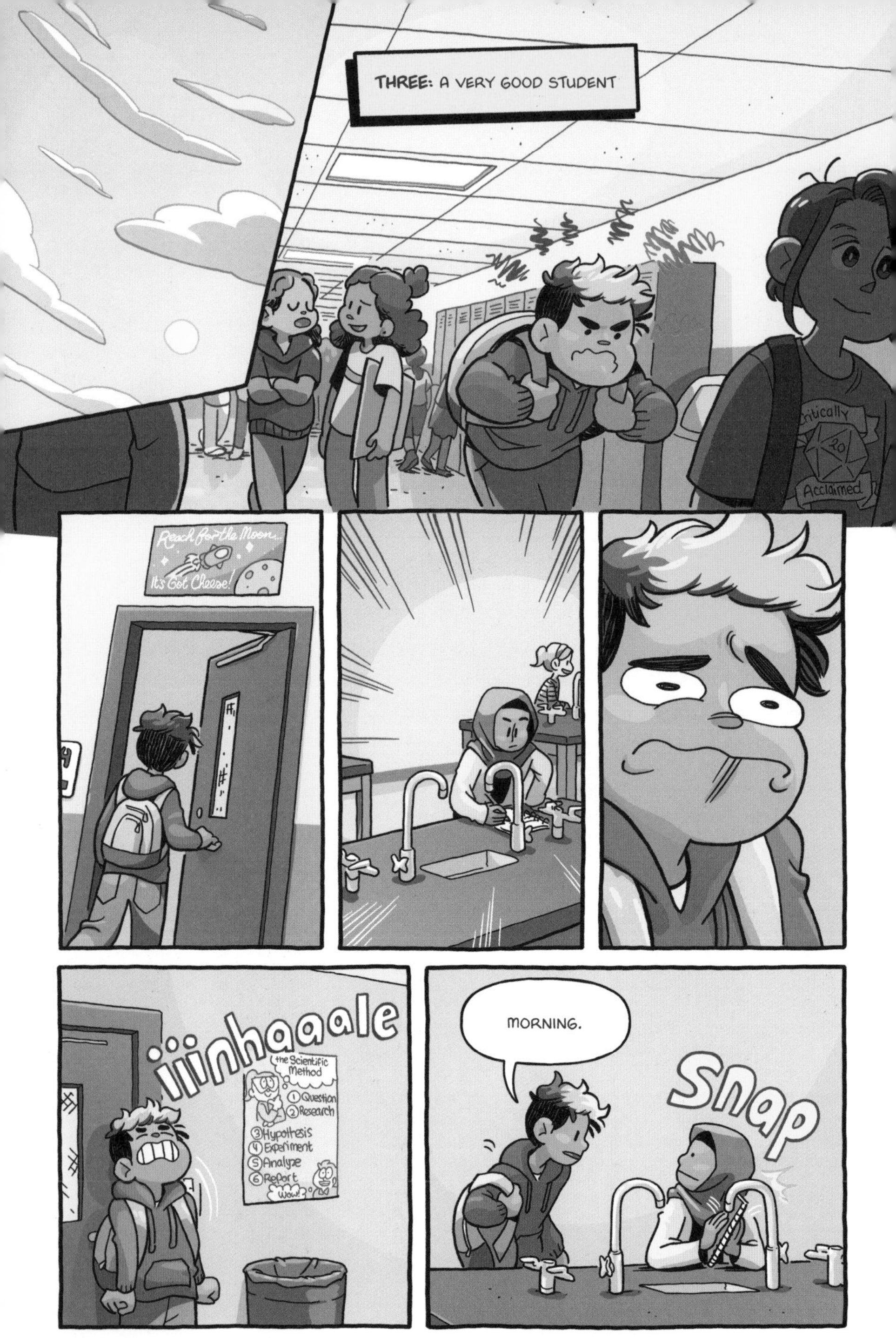
THREE: A VERY GOOD STUDENT
Critically 20 Acclaimed
Reach for the Moon... It's Got Cheese!
iiiinhaaaale
the Scientific Method
① Question
② Research
③ Hypothesis
④ Experiment
⑤ Analyze
⑥ Report
Wow!
MORNING.
SNAP

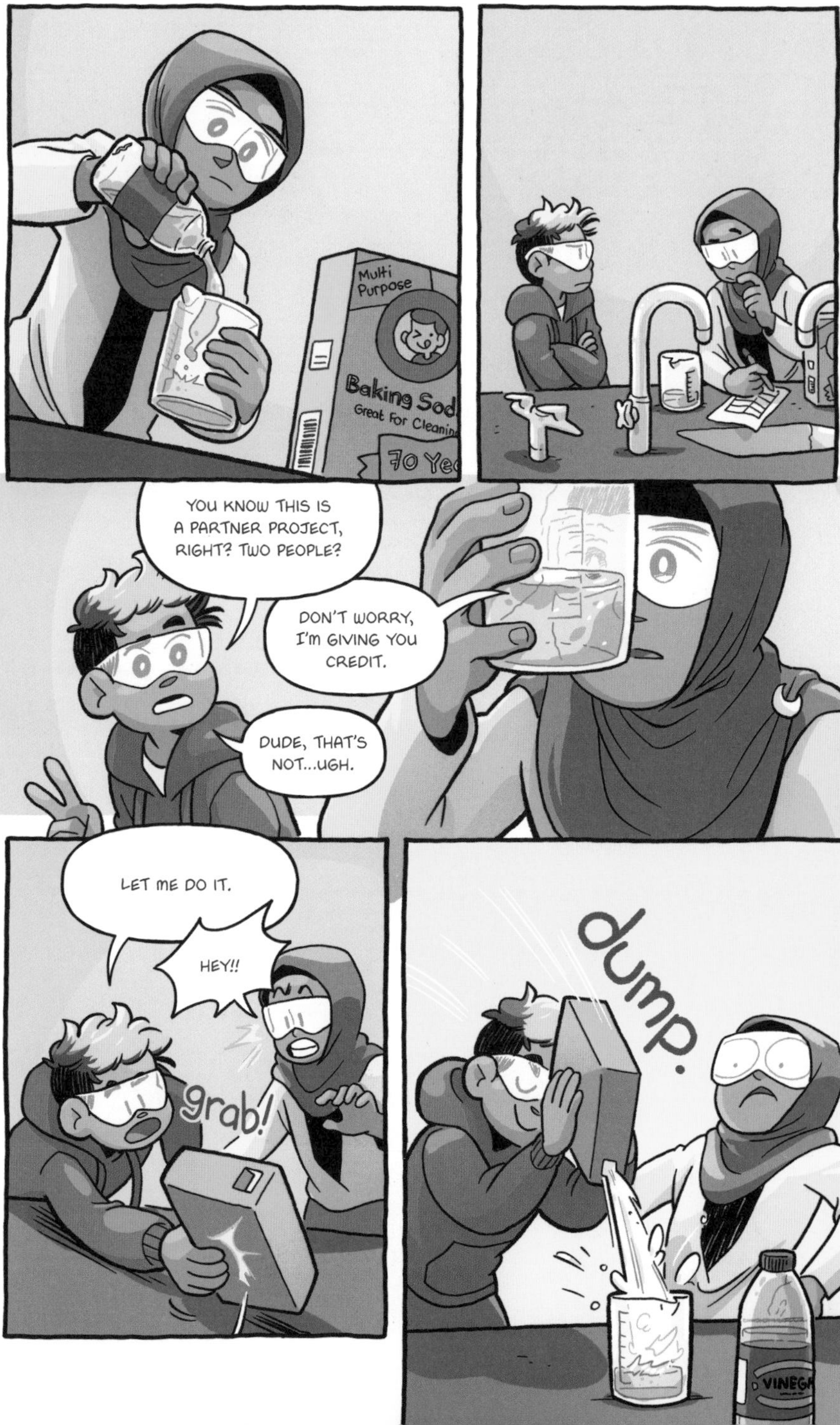
Multi Purpose
Baking Sod
Great For Cleanin
70 Yea
YOU KNOW THIS IS A PARTNER PROJECT, RIGHT? TWO PEOPLE?
DON'T WORRY, I'M GIVING YOU CREDIT.
DUDE, THAT'S NOT...UGH.
LET ME DO IT.
HEY!!
grab!
dump.
VINEG

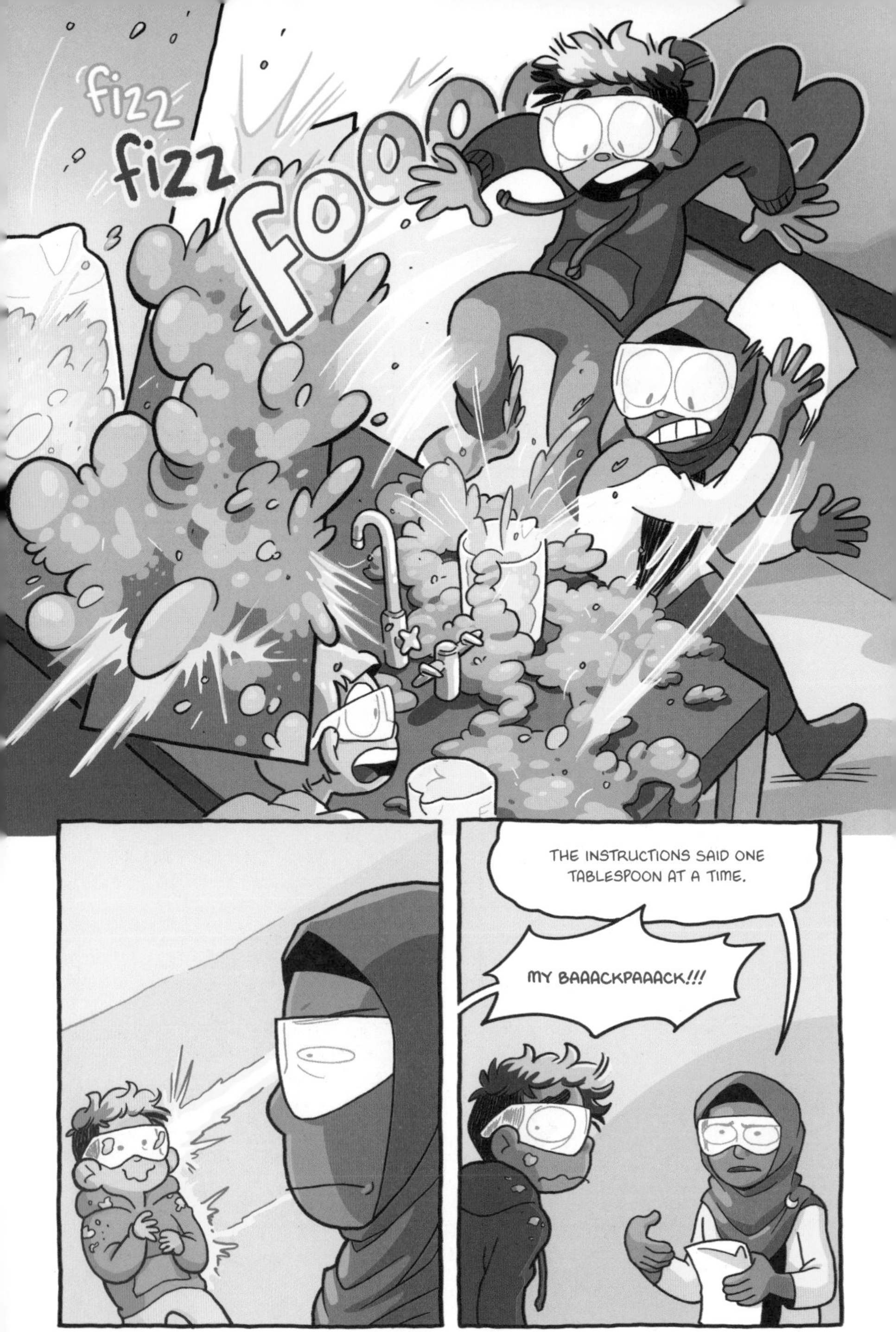
fizz
fizz
FOOOOOM
THE INSTRUCTIONS SAID ONE TABLESPOON AT A TIME.
MY BAAACKPAAACK!!!

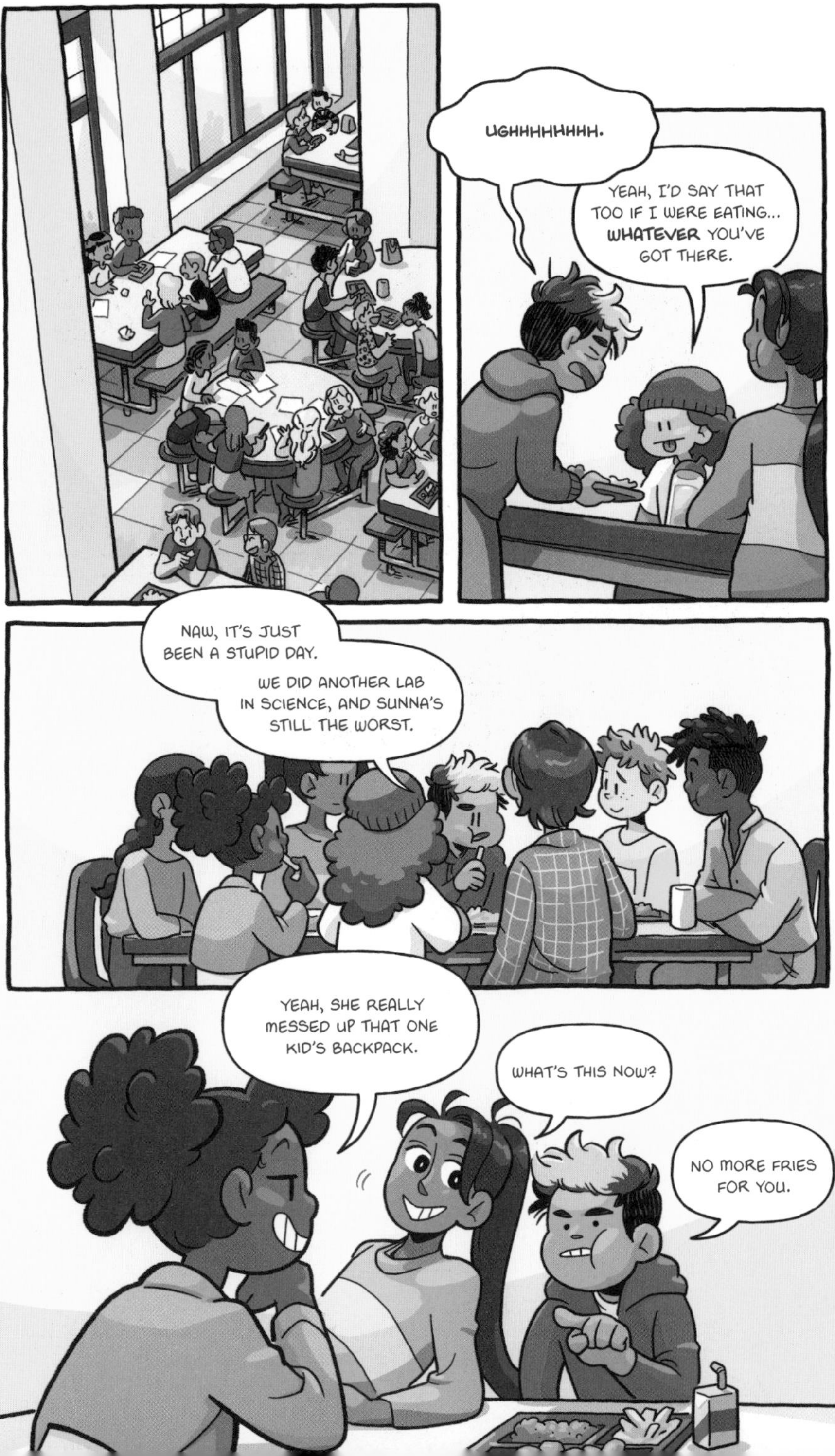
UGHHHHHHHH.
YEAH, I'D SAY THAT TOO IF I WERE EATING... **WHATEVER** YOU'VE GOT THERE.
NAW, IT'S JUST BEEN A STUPID DAY.
WE DID ANOTHER LAB IN SCIENCE, AND SUNNA'S STILL THE WORST.
YEAH, SHE REALLY MESSED UP THAT ONE KID'S BACKPACK.
WHAT'S THIS NOW?
NO MORE FRIES FOR YOU.

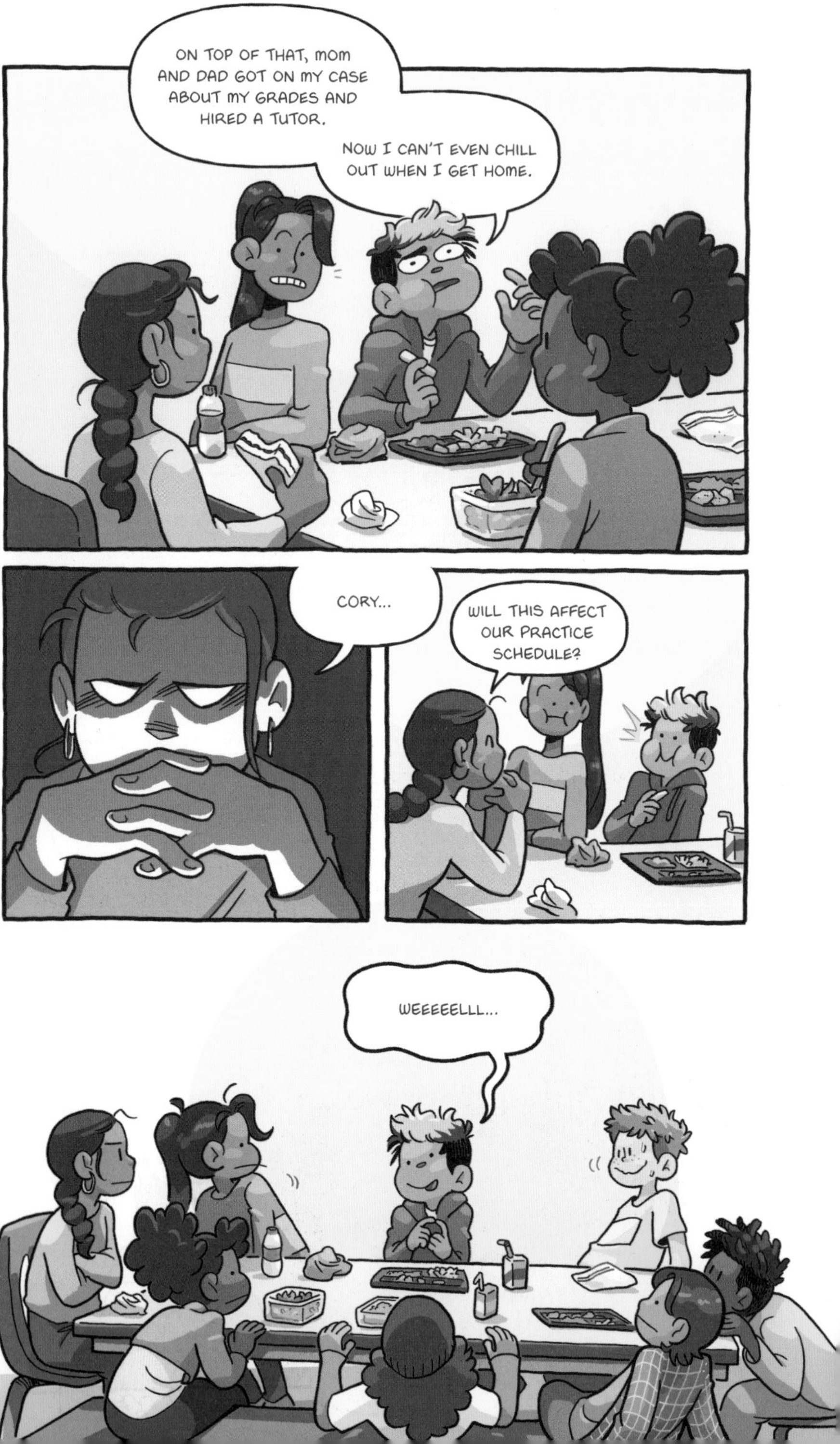
ON TOP OF THAT, MOM AND DAD GOT ON MY CASE ABOUT MY GRADES AND HIRED A TUTOR.
NOW I CAN'T EVEN CHILL OUT WHEN I GET HOME.
CORY...
WILL THIS AFFECT OUR PRACTICE SCHEDULE?
WEEEEELLL...

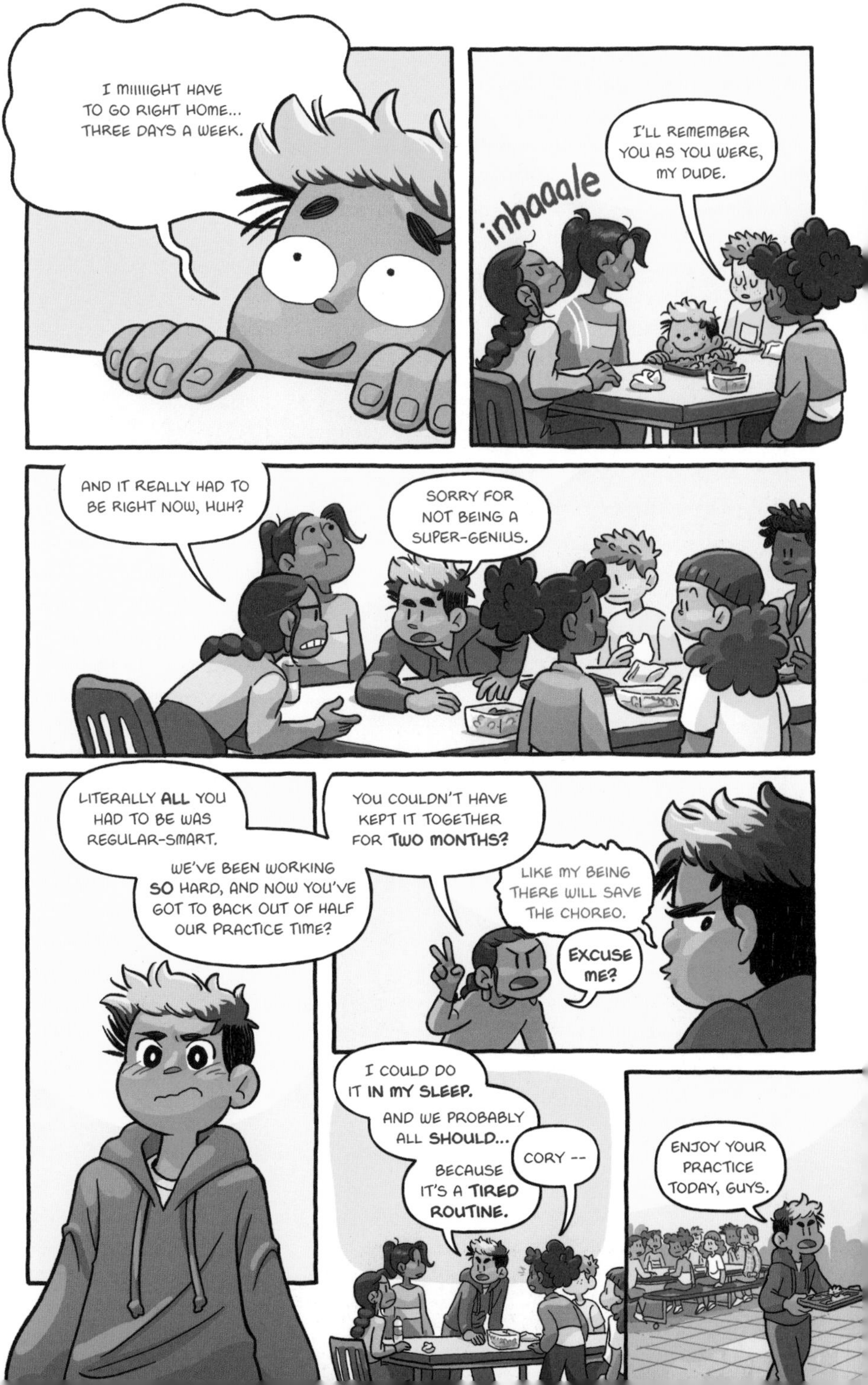
I MIIIIIGHT HAVE TO GO RIGHT HOME... THREE DAYS A WEEK.
inhaaale
I'LL REMEMBER YOU AS YOU WERE, MY DUDE.
AND IT REALLY HAD TO BE RIGHT NOW, HUH?
SORRY FOR NOT BEING A SUPER-GENIUS.
LITERALLY ALL YOU HAD TO BE WAS REGULAR-SMART.
YOU COULDN'T HAVE KEPT IT TOGETHER FOR TWO MONTHS?
WE'VE BEEN WORKING SO HARD, AND NOW YOU'VE GOT TO BACK OUT OF HALF OUR PRACTICE TIME?
LIKE MY BEING THERE WILL SAVE THE CHOREO.
EXCUSE ME?
I COULD DO IT IN MY SLEEP.
AND WE PROBABLY ALL SHOULD...
BECAUSE IT'S A TIRED ROUTINE.
CORY --
ENJOY YOUR PRACTICE TODAY, GUYS.

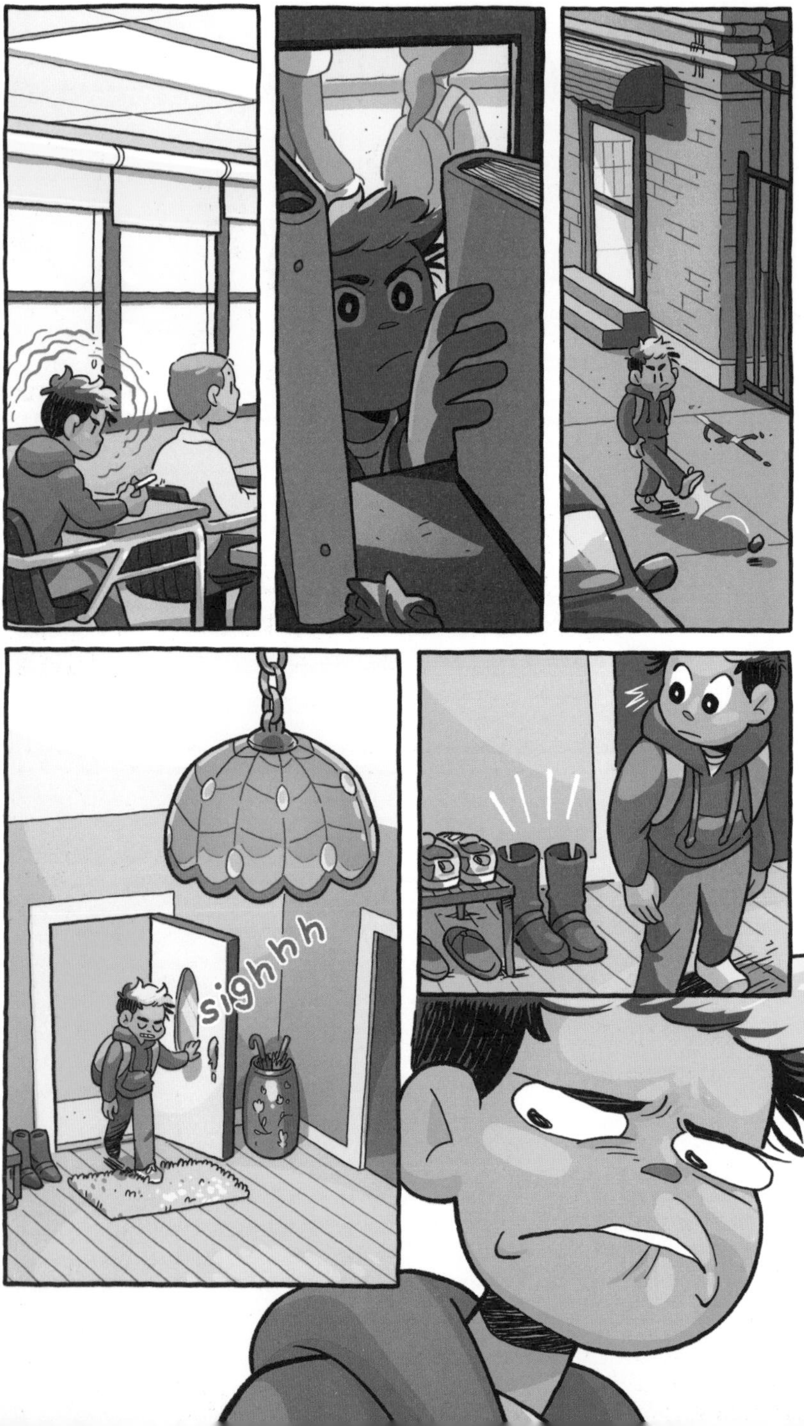
sighhh

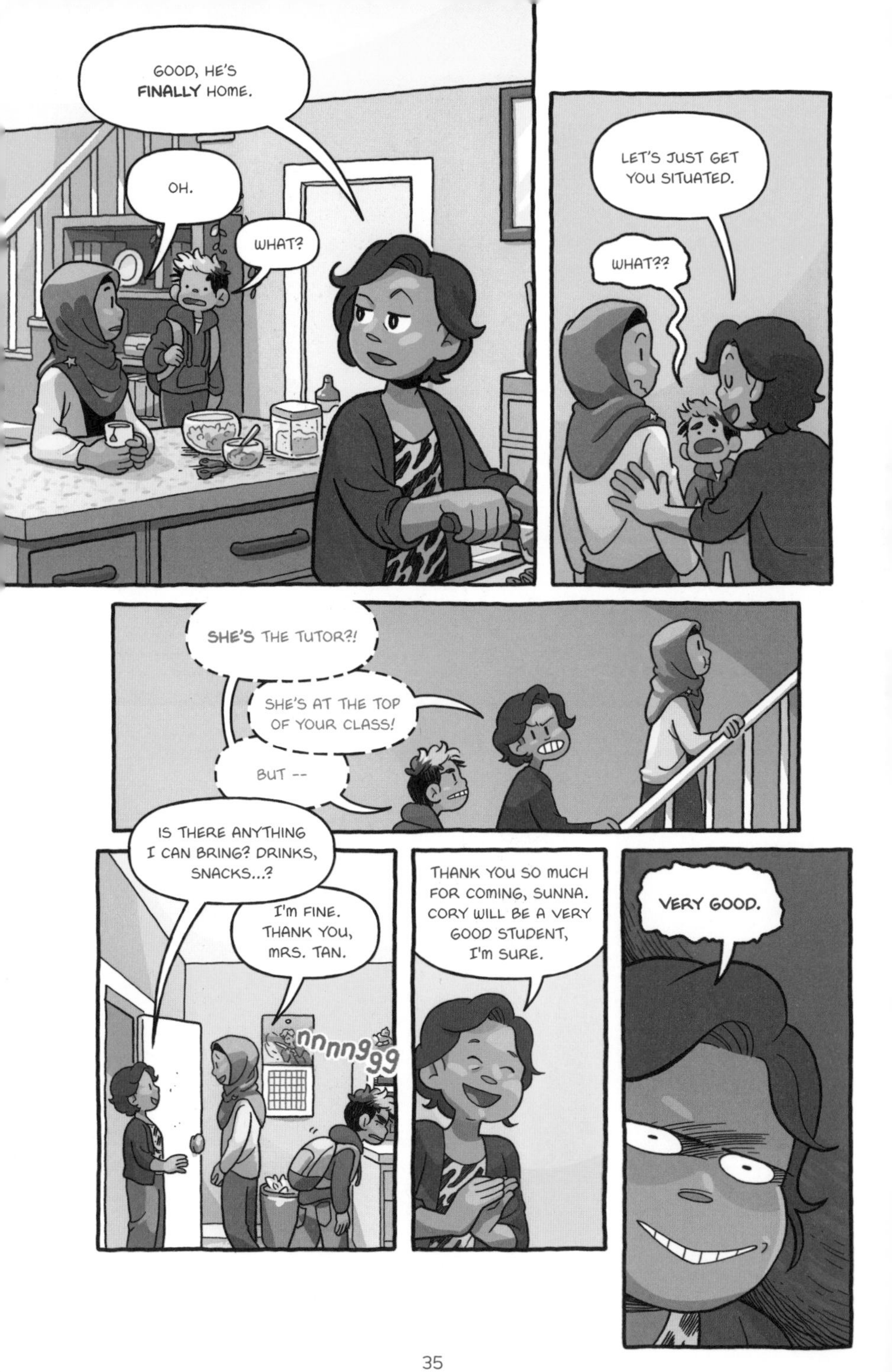
GOOD, HE'S **FINALLY** HOME.
OH.
WHAT?
LET'S JUST GET YOU SITUATED.
WHAT??
SHE'S THE TUTOR?!
SHE'S AT THE TOP OF YOUR CLASS!
BUT --
IS THERE ANYTHING I CAN BRING? DRINKS, SNACKS...?
I'm FINE. THANK YOU, mRS. TAN.
nnnnggg
THANK YOU SO mUCH FOR COMING, SUNNA. CORY WILL BE A VERY GOOD STUDENT, I'm SURE.
VERY GOOD.

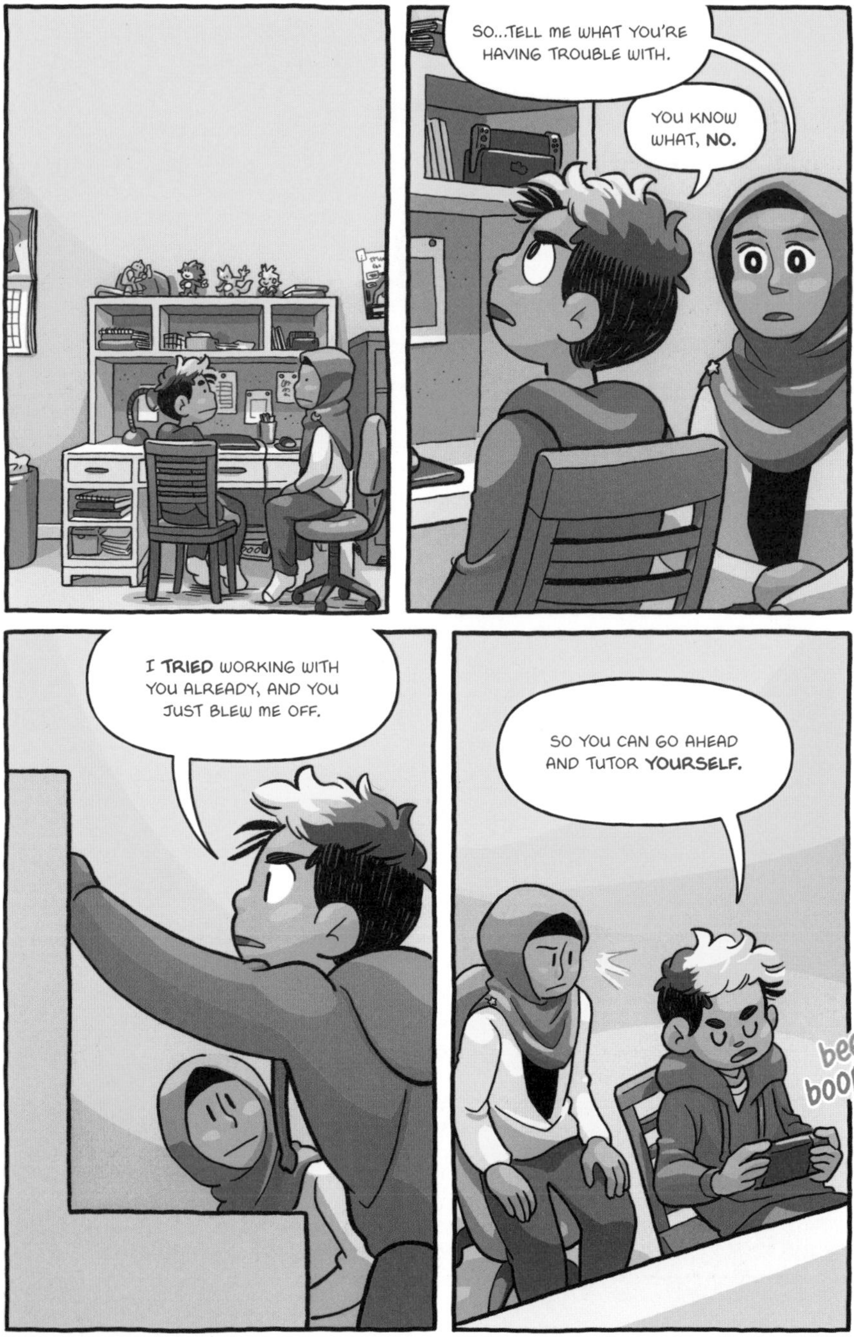
SO...TELL ME WHAT YOU'RE HAVING TROUBLE WITH.
YOU KNOW WHAT, **NO.**
I **TRIED** WORKING WITH YOU ALREADY, AND YOU JUST BLEW ME OFF.
SO YOU CAN GO AHEAD AND TUTOR **YOURSELF.**
beep boop

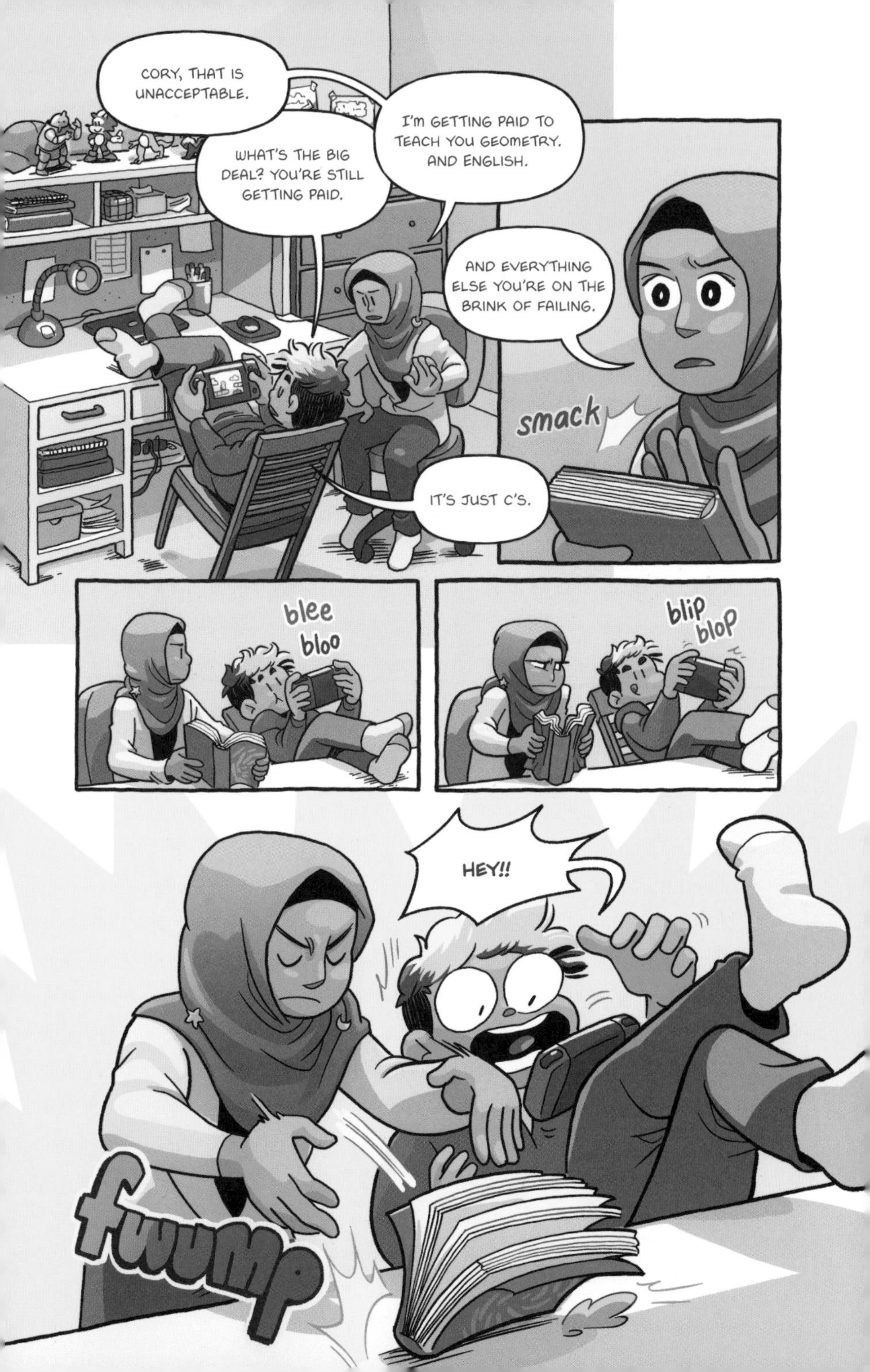

CORY, THAT IS UNACCEPTABLE.
WHAT'S THE BIG DEAL? YOU'RE STILL GETTING PAID.
I'M GETTING PAID TO TEACH YOU GEOMETRY. AND ENGLISH.
AND EVERYTHING ELSE YOU'RE ON THE BRINK OF FAILING.
smack
IT'S JUST C'S.
blee bloo
blip blop
HEY!!
fwump

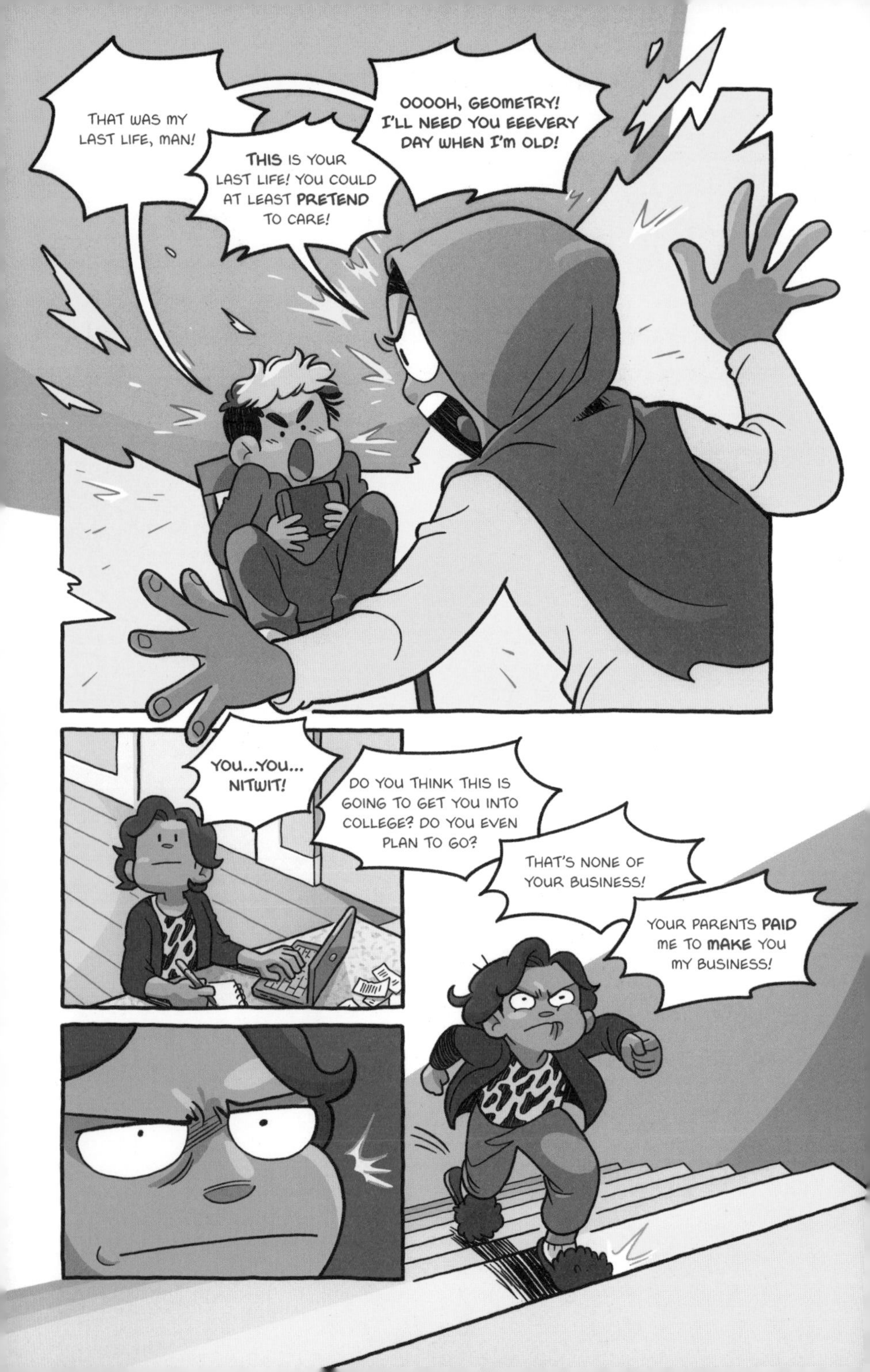
THAT WAS MY LAST LIFE, MAN!
OOOOH, GEOMETRY! I'LL NEED YOU EEEVERY DAY WHEN I'M OLD!
THIS IS YOUR LAST LIFE! YOU COULD AT LEAST PRETEND TO CARE!
YOU...YOU... NITWIT!
DO YOU THINK THIS IS GOING TO GET YOU INTO COLLEGE? DO YOU EVEN PLAN TO GO?
THAT'S NONE OF YOUR BUSINESS!
YOUR PARENTS PAID ME TO MAKE YOU MY BUSINESS!

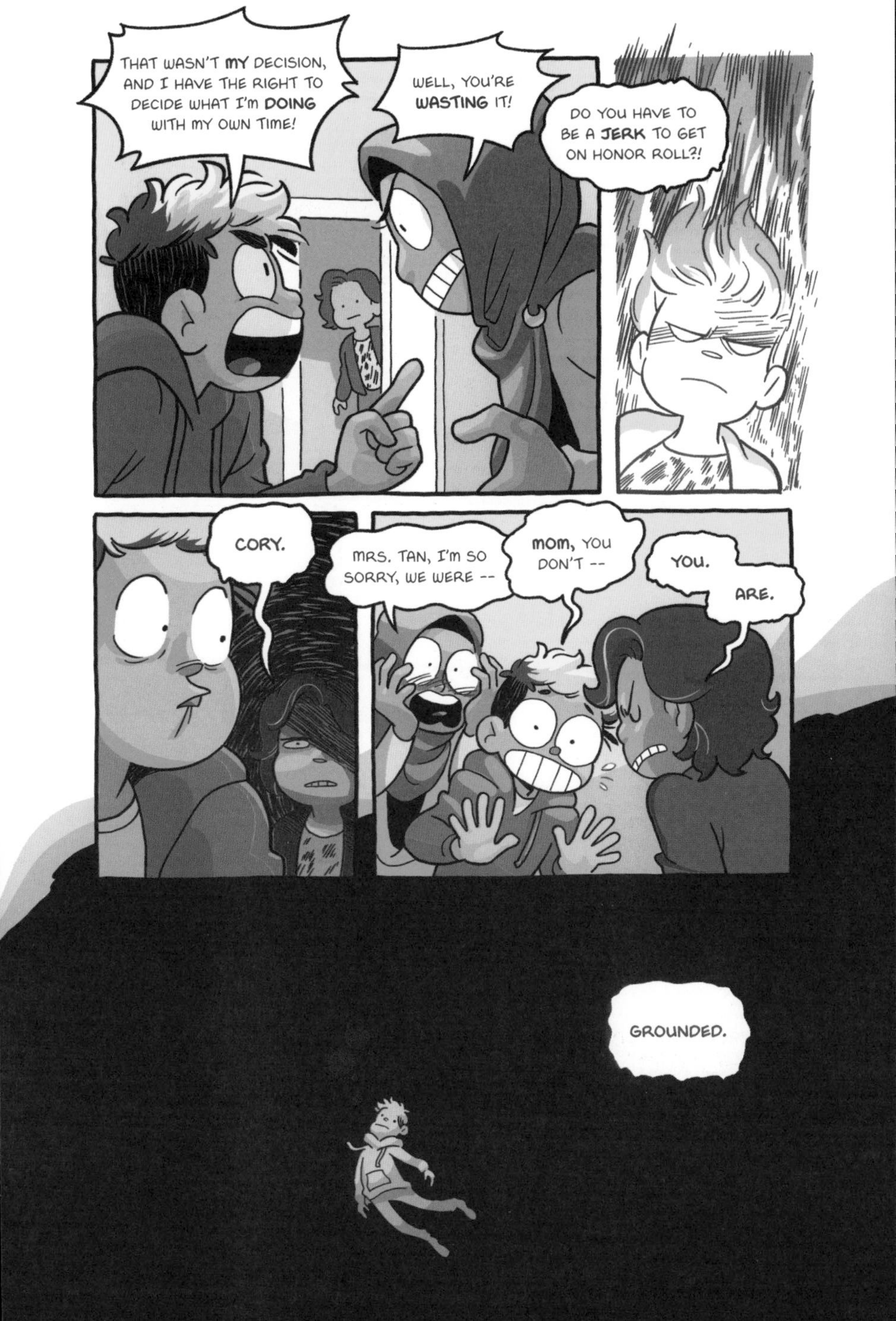

THAT WASN'T MY DECISION, AND I HAVE THE RIGHT TO DECIDE WHAT I'M DOING WITH MY OWN TIME!
WELL, YOU'RE WASTING IT!
DO YOU HAVE TO BE A JERK TO GET ON HONOR ROLL?!
CORY.
MRS. TAN, I'M SO SORRY, WE WERE --
MOM, YOU DON'T --
YOU.
ARE.
GROUNDED.

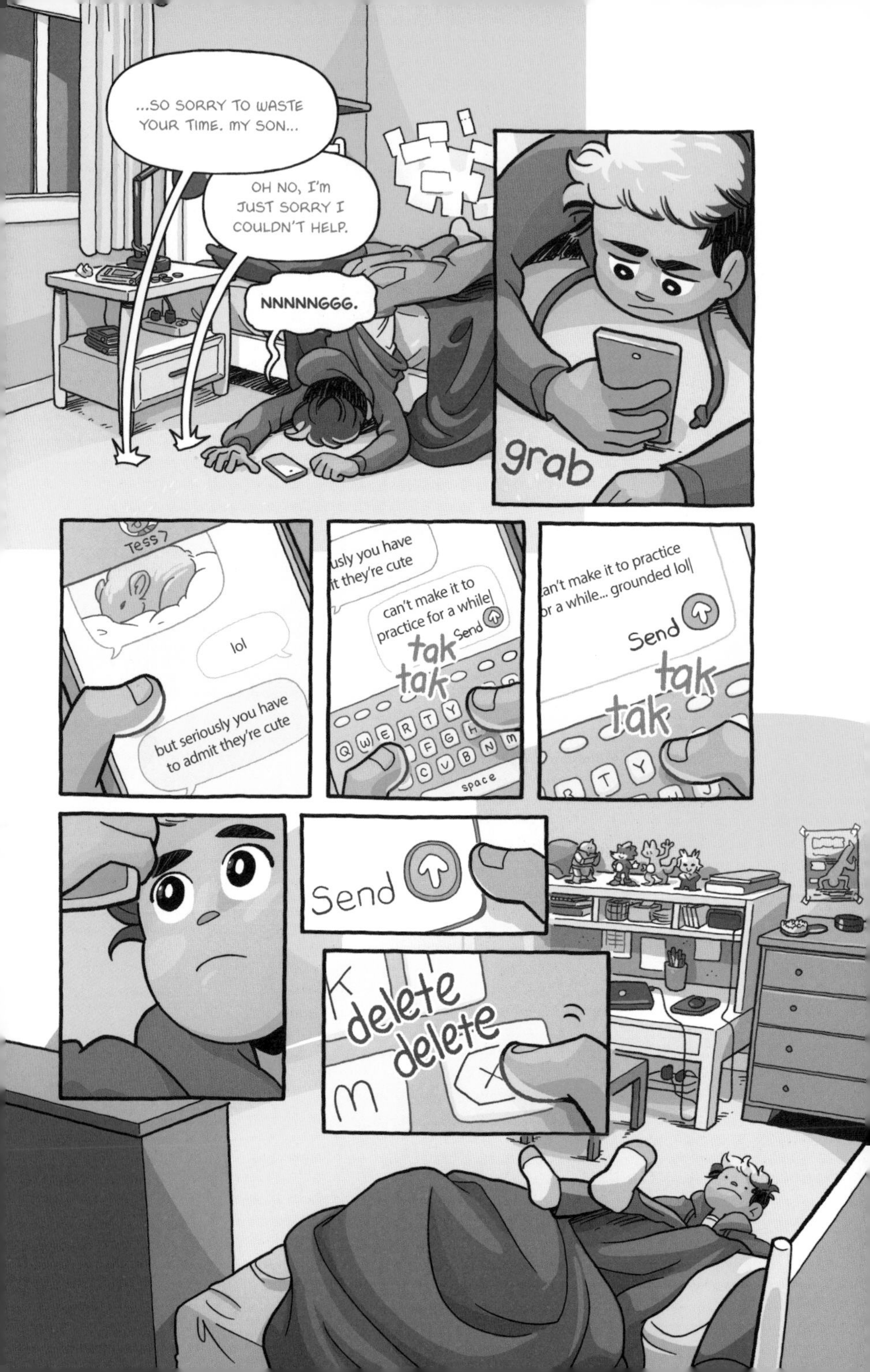
...SO SORRY TO WASTE YOUR TIME. MY SON...
OH NO, I'M JUST SORRY I COULDN'T HELP.
NNNNNGGG.
grab
Tess7
lol
but seriously you have to admit they're cute
usly you have
it they're cute
can't make it to practice for a while
Send
tak
tak
space
can't make it to practice
or a while... grounded lol
Send
tak
tak
Send
delete
delete

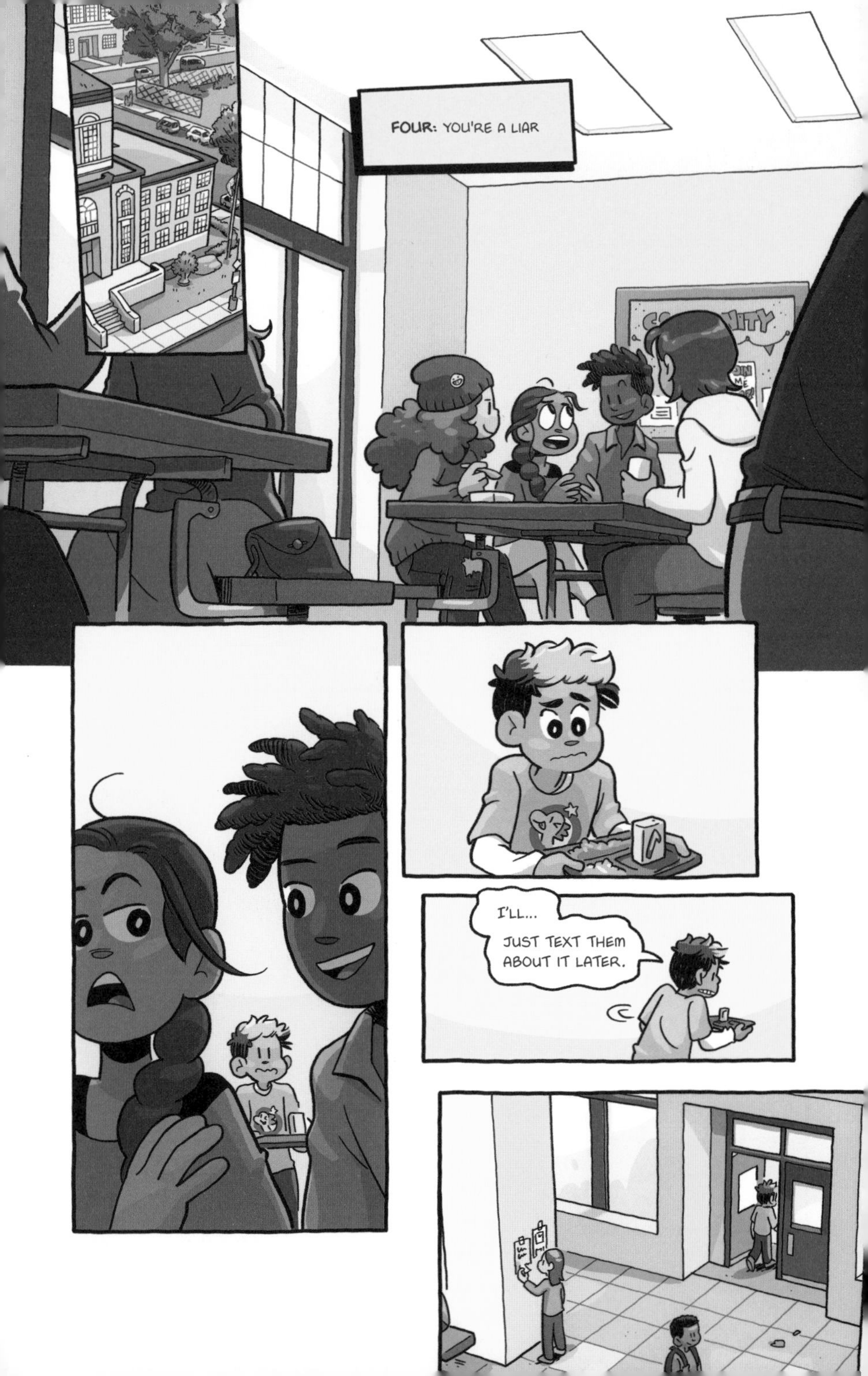
FOUR: YOU'RE A LIAR
I'LL...
JUST TEXT THEM ABOUT IT LATER.

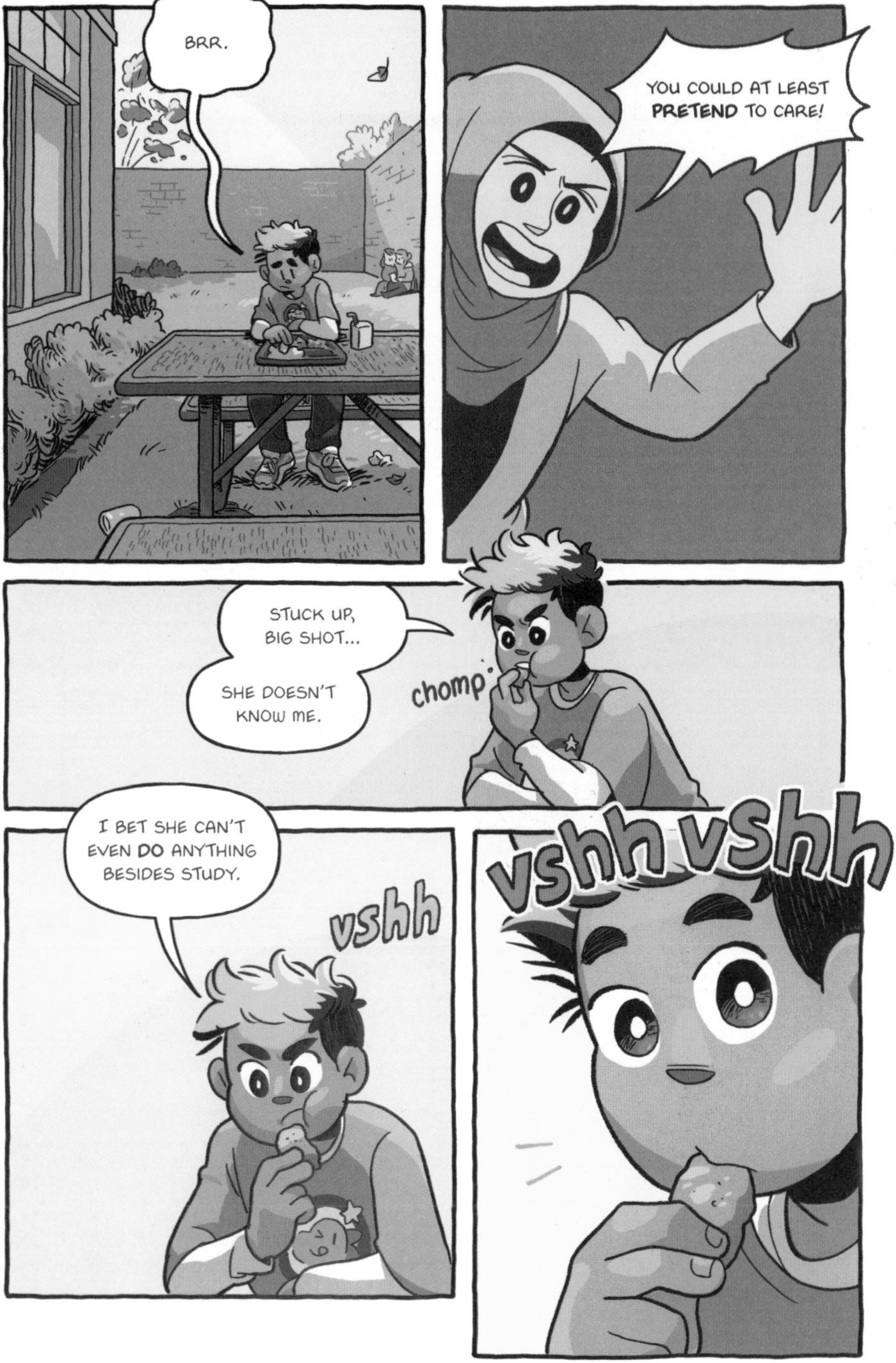
BRR.
YOU COULD AT LEAST **PRETEND** TO CARE!
STUCK UP, BIG SHOT...
SHE DOESN'T KNOW ME.
chomp
I BET SHE CAN'T EVEN **DO** ANYTHING BESIDES STUDY.
vshh
vshh vshh

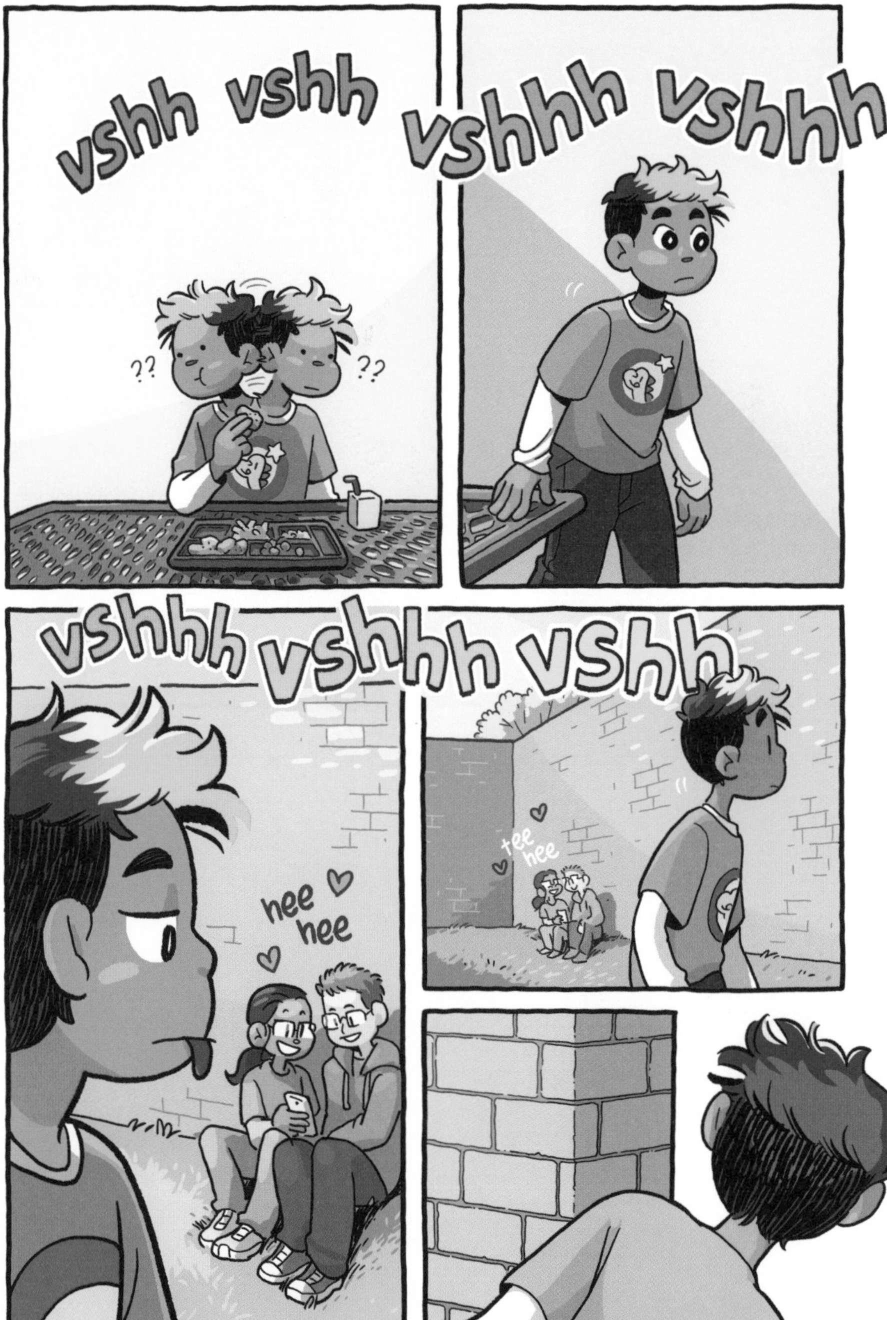
vshh vshh
??
??
vshhh vshhh
vshhh vshhh vshh
hee hee
tee hee

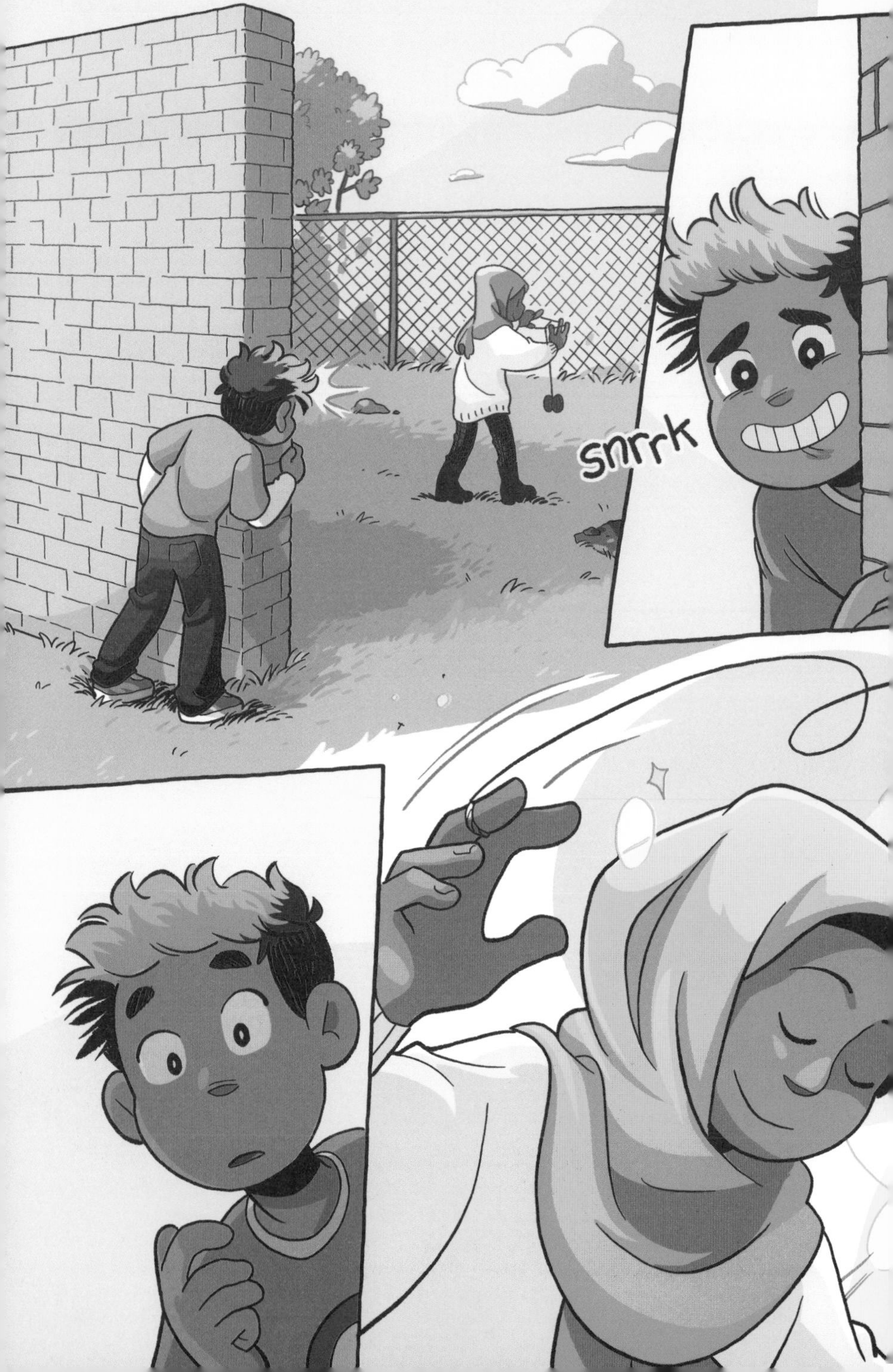
snrrk

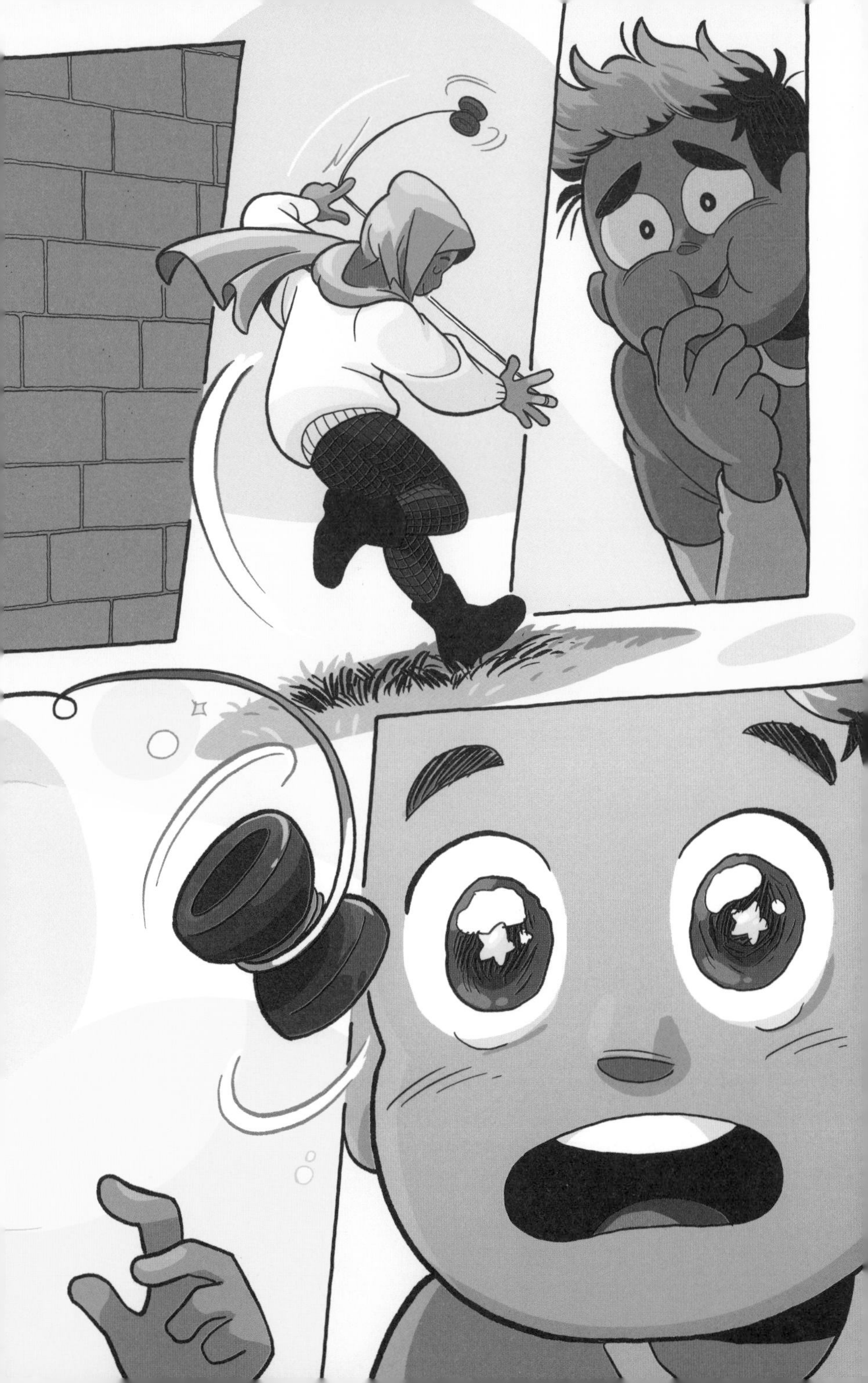

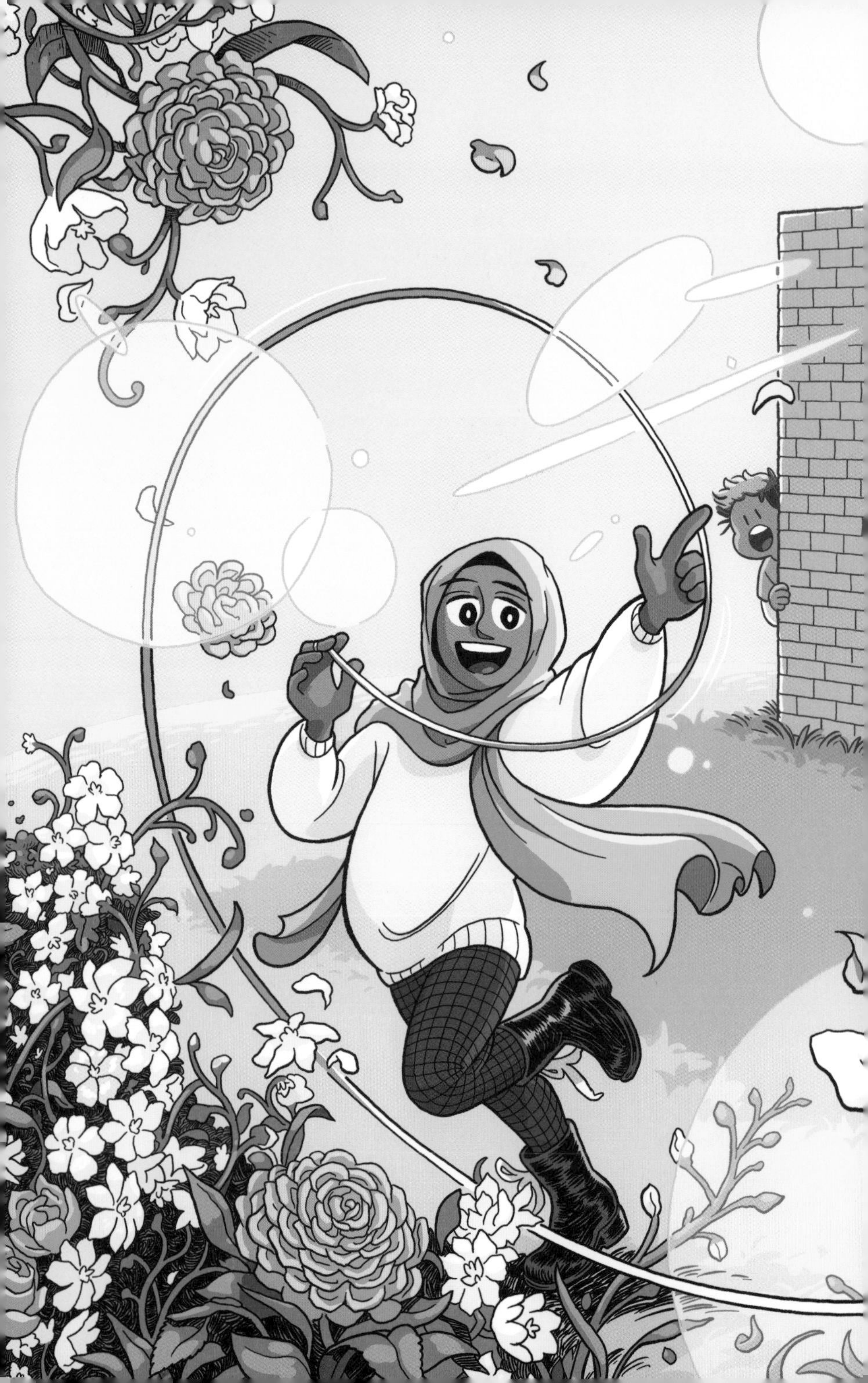

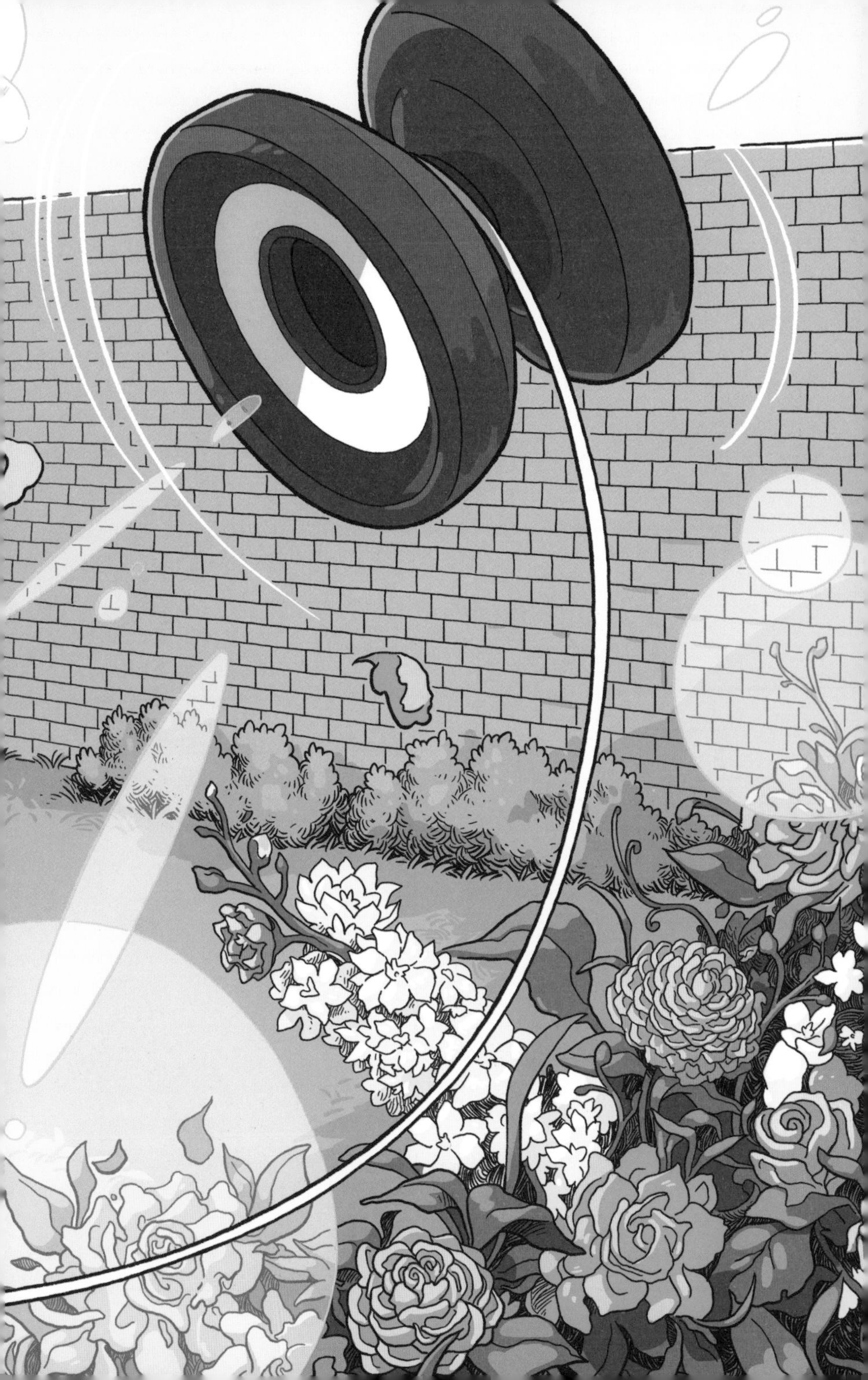

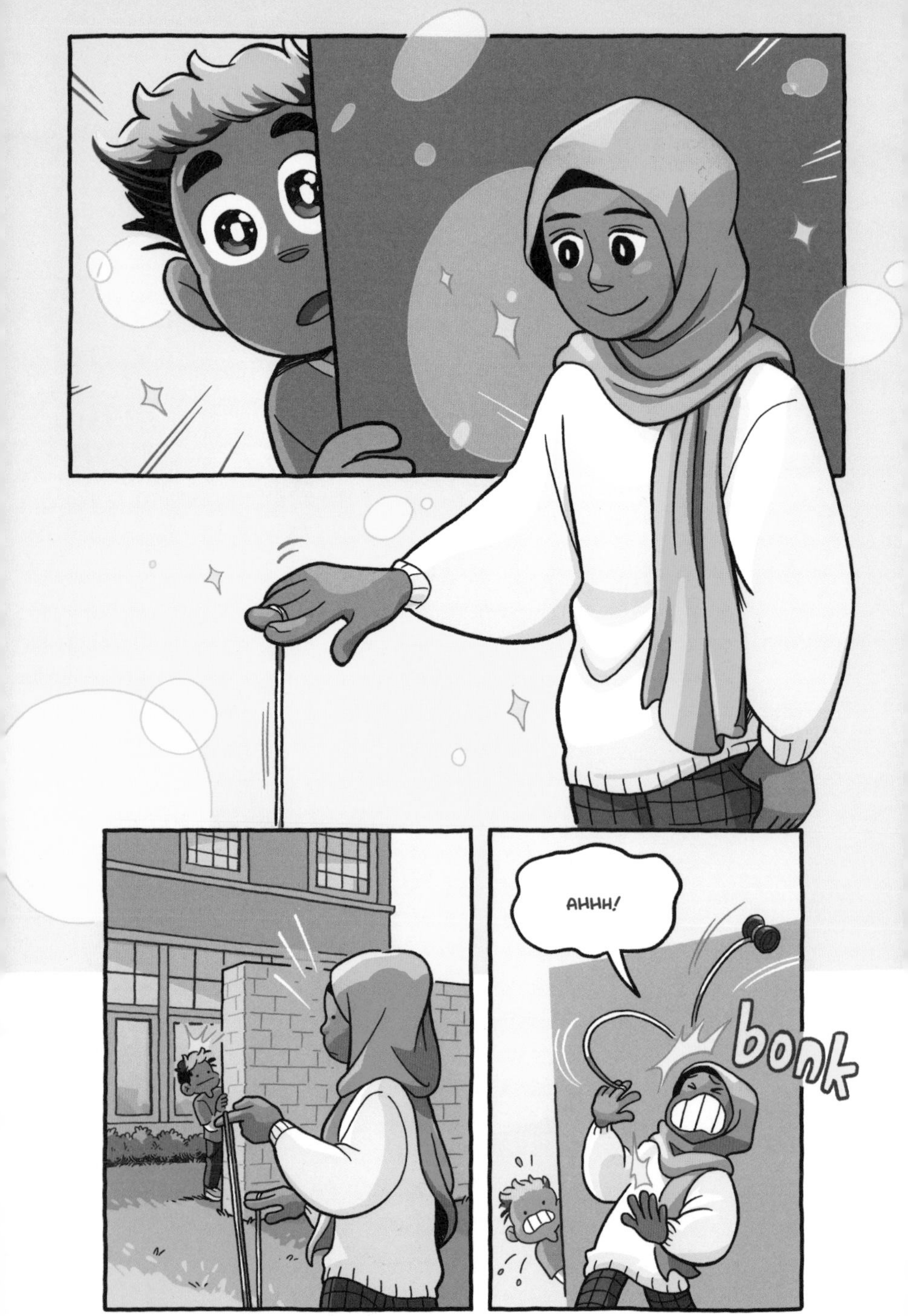
AHHH!
bonk

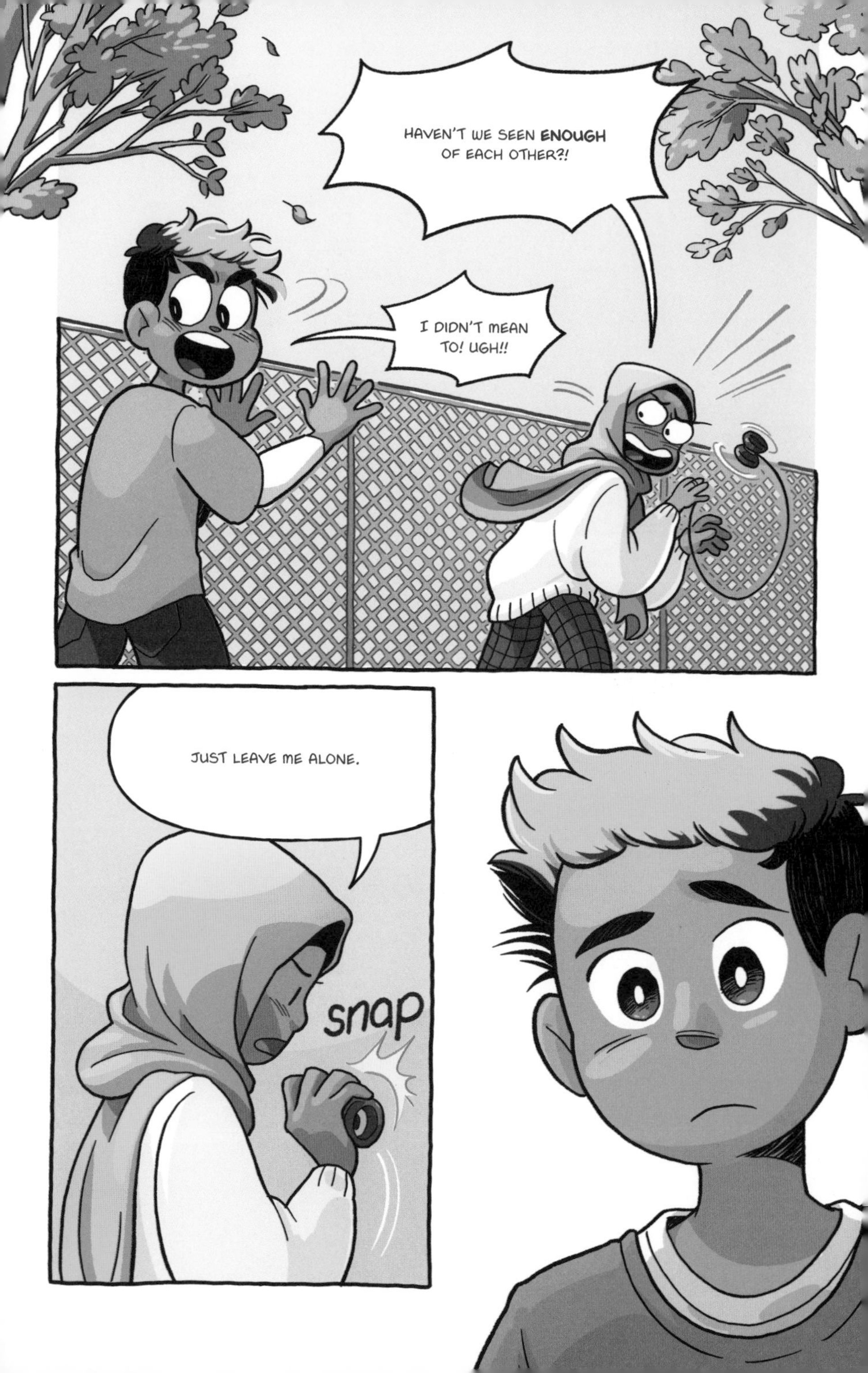
HAVEN'T WE SEEN **ENOUGH** OF EACH OTHER?!
I DIDN'T MEAN TO! UGH!!
JUST LEAVE ME ALONE.
snap

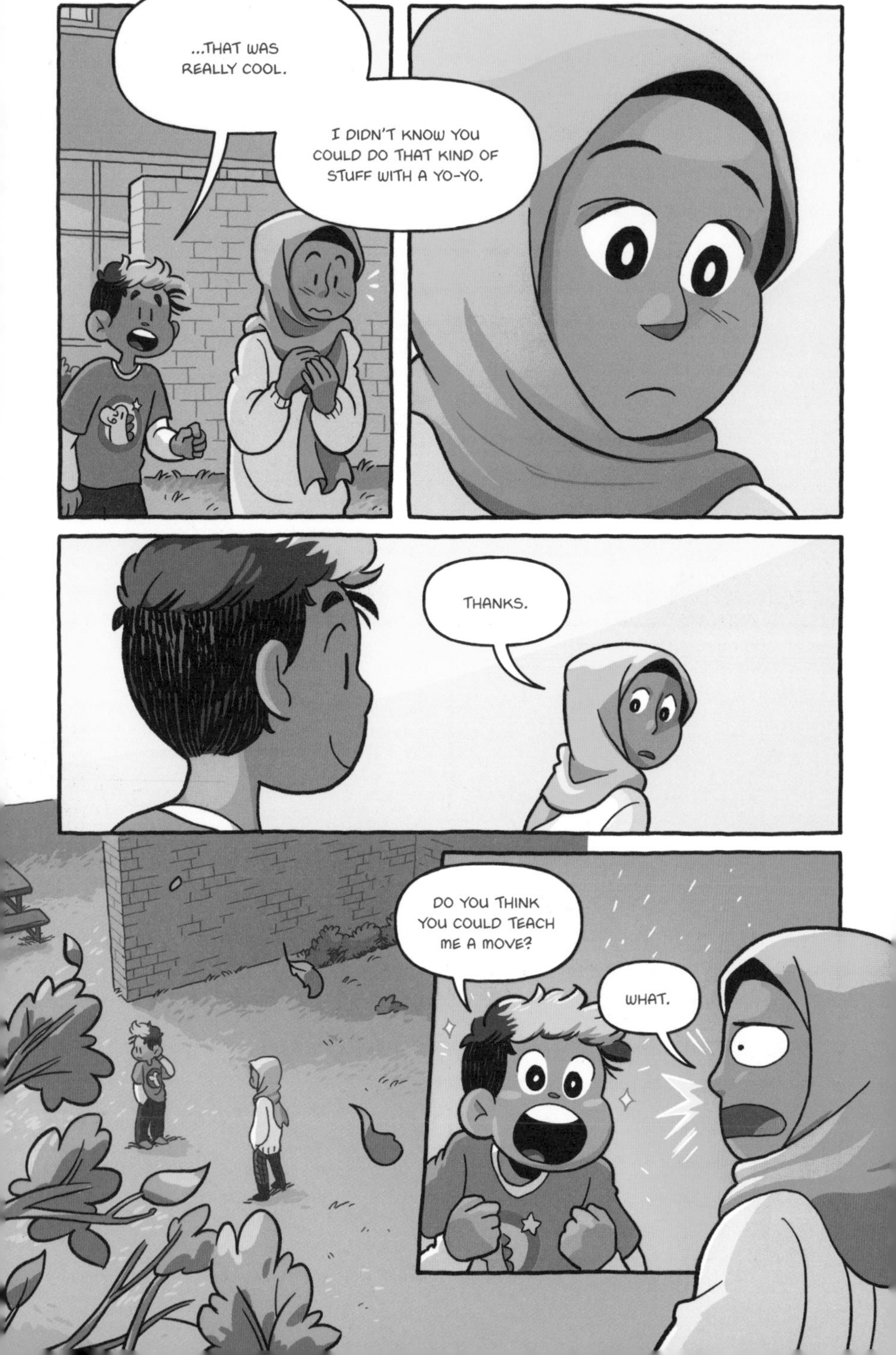
...THAT WAS REALLY COOL.
I DIDN'T KNOW YOU COULD DO THAT KIND OF STUFF WITH A YO-YO.
THANKS.
DO YOU THINK YOU COULD TEACH ME A MOVE?
WHAT.

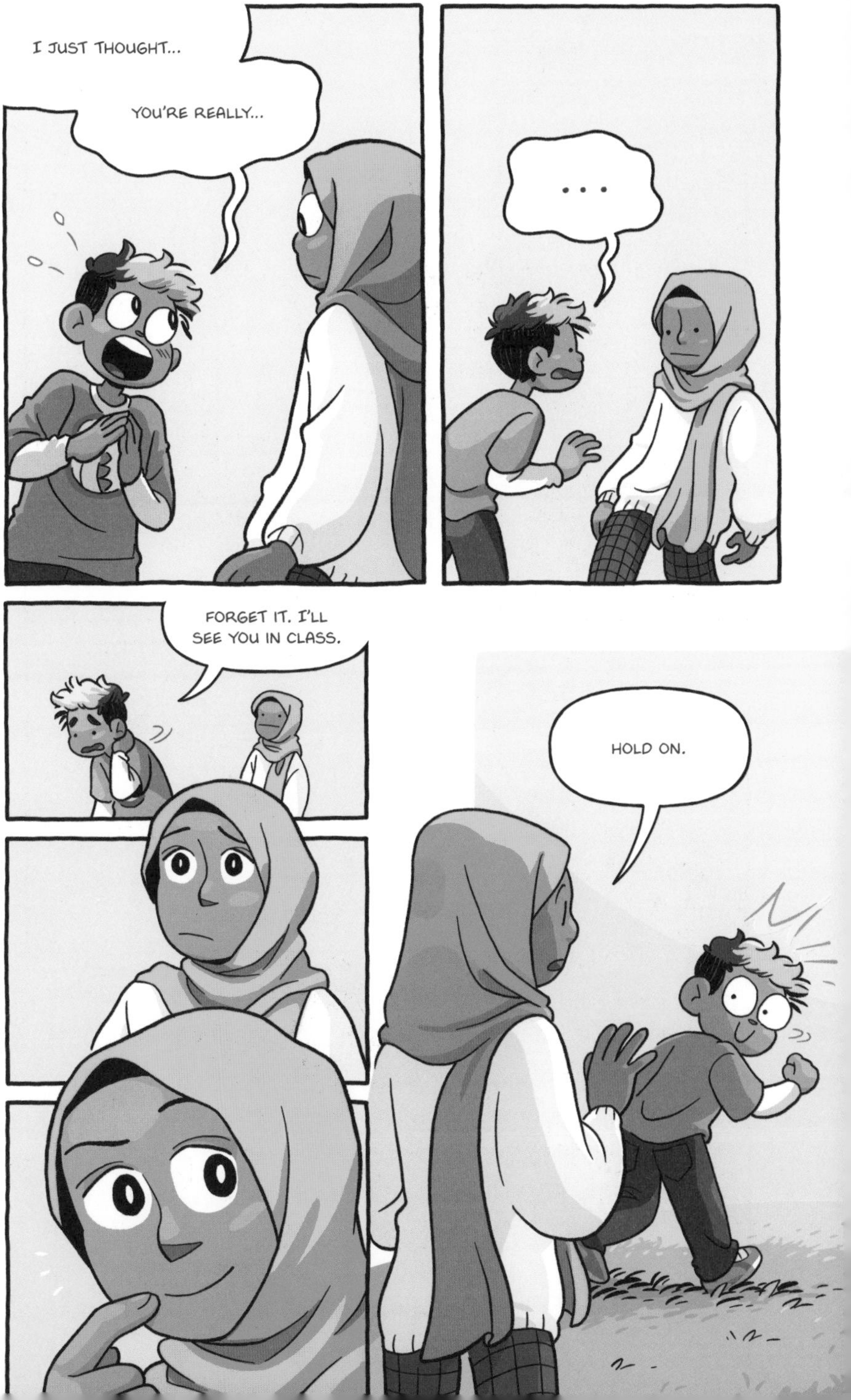
I JUST THOUGHT...
YOU'RE REALLY...
. . .
FORGET IT. I'LL SEE YOU IN CLASS.
HOLD ON.

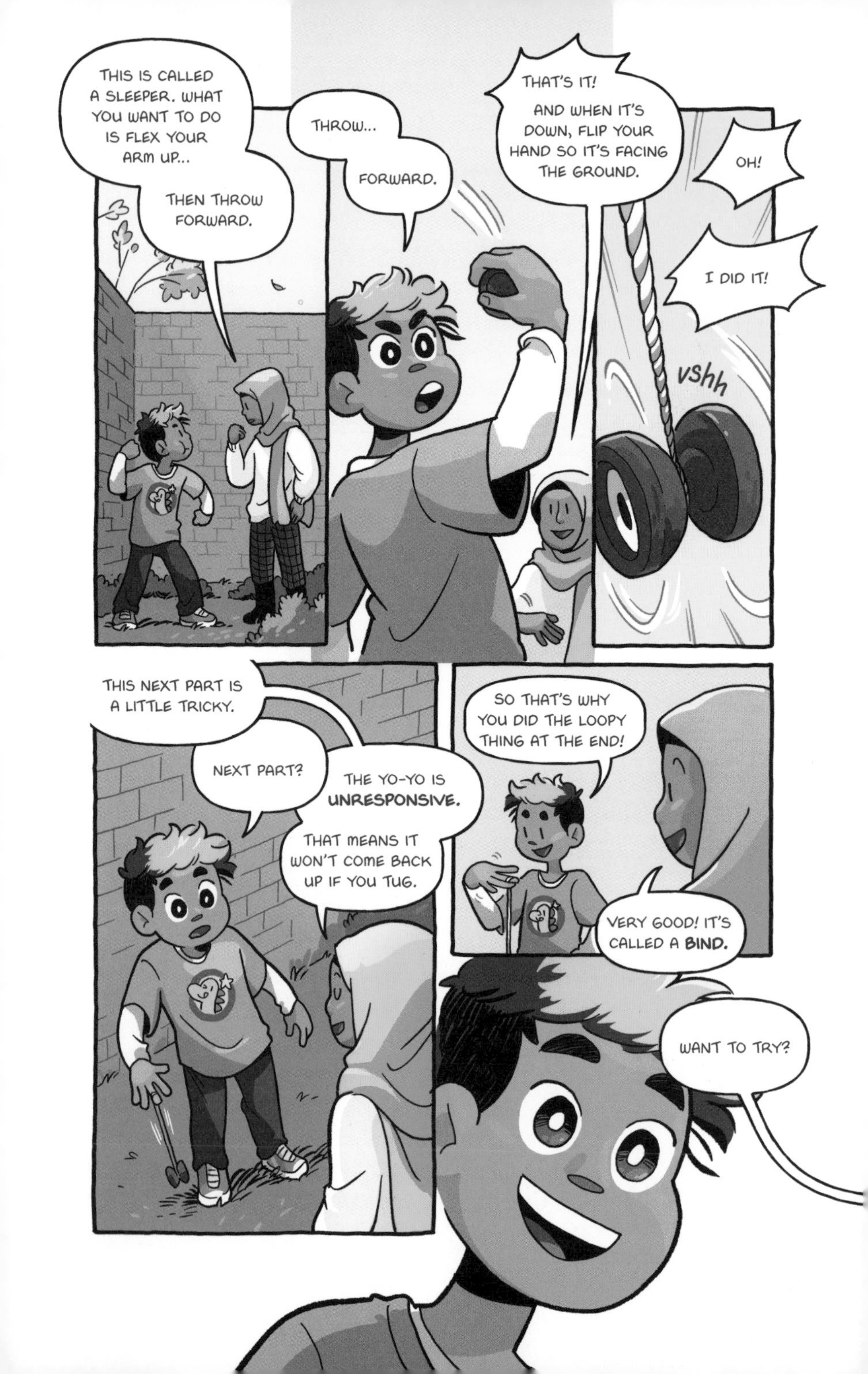

THIS IS CALLED A SLEEPER. WHAT YOU WANT TO DO IS FLEX YOUR ARM UP...
THEN THROW FORWARD.
THROW...
FORWARD.
THAT'S IT!
AND WHEN IT'S DOWN, FLIP YOUR HAND SO IT'S FACING THE GROUND.
OH!
I DID IT!
vshh
THIS NEXT PART IS A LITTLE TRICKY.
NEXT PART?
THE YO-YO IS **UNRESPONSIVE.**
THAT MEANS IT WON'T COME BACK UP IF YOU TUG.
SO THAT'S WHY YOU DID THE LOOPY THING AT THE END!
VERY GOOD! IT'S CALLED A **BIND.**
WANT TO TRY?

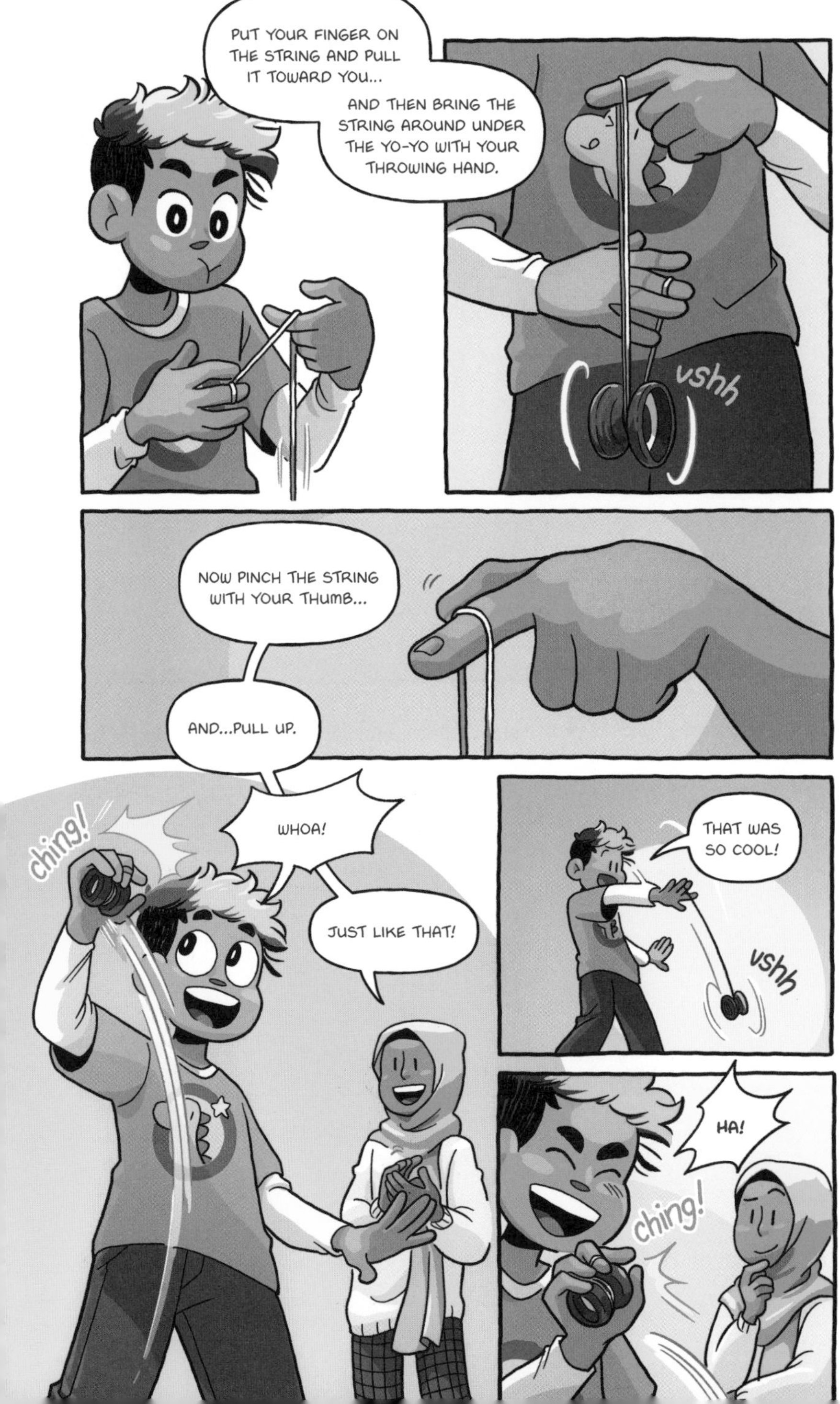
PUT YOUR FINGER ON THE STRING AND PULL IT TOWARD YOU...
AND THEN BRING THE STRING AROUND UNDER THE YO-YO WITH YOUR THROWING HAND.
vshh
NOW PINCH THE STRING WITH YOUR THUMB...
AND...PULL UP.
ching!
WHOA!
JUST LIKE THAT!
THAT WAS SO COOL!
vshh
HA!
ching!

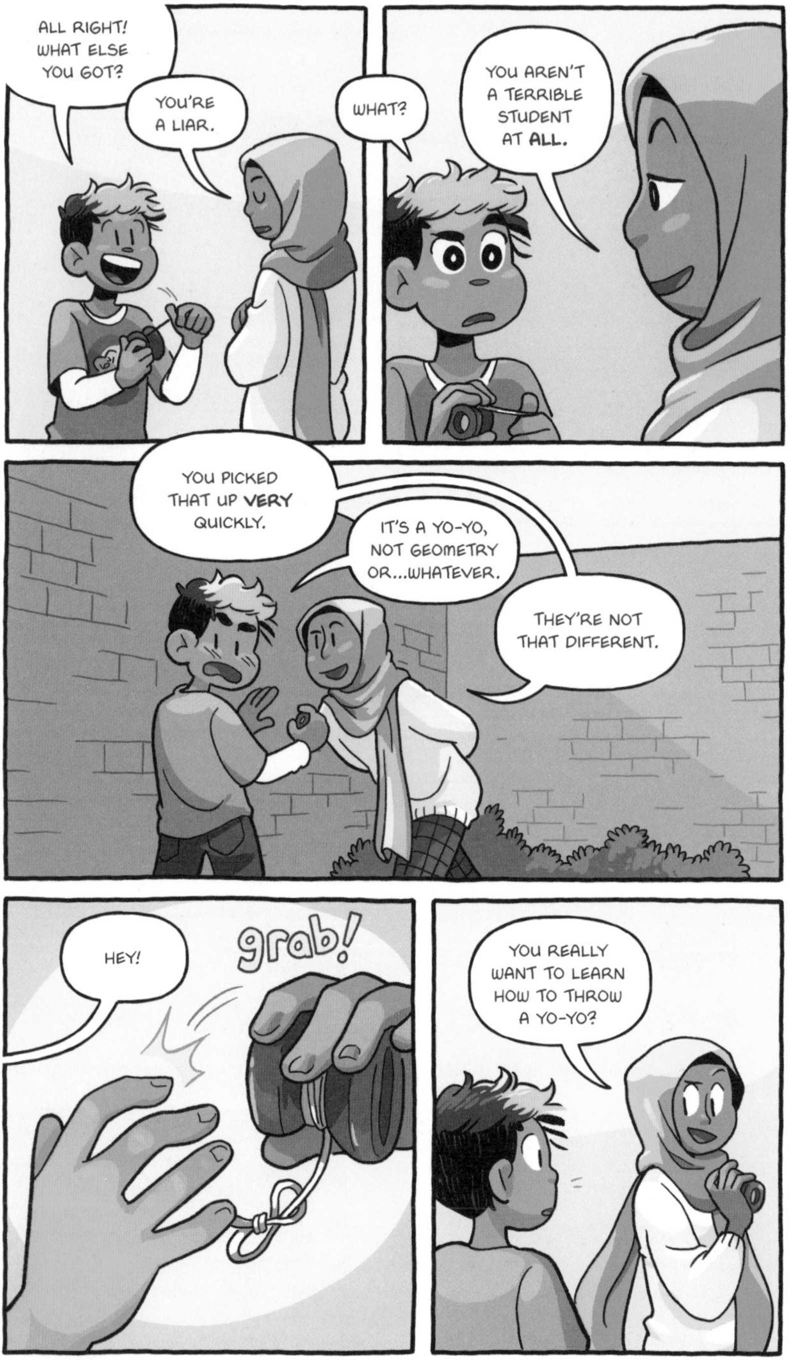
ALL RIGHT! WHAT ELSE YOU GOT?
YOU'RE A LIAR.
WHAT?
YOU AREN'T A TERRIBLE STUDENT AT **ALL.**
YOU PICKED THAT UP **VERY** QUICKLY.
IT'S A YO-YO, NOT GEOMETRY OR...WHATEVER.
THEY'RE NOT THAT DIFFERENT.
HEY!
grab!
YOU REALLY WANT TO LEARN HOW TO THROW A YO-YO?

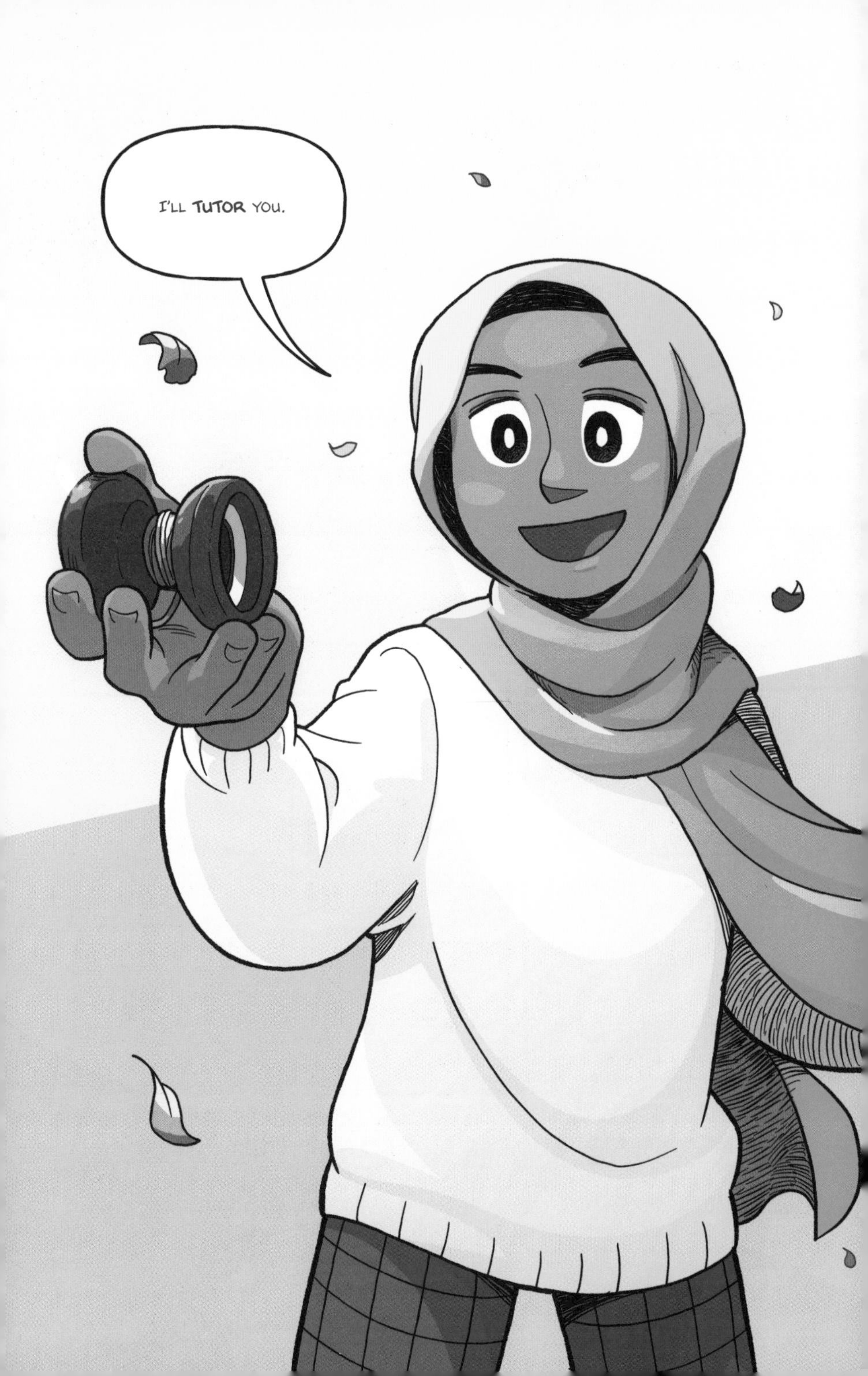
I'LL **TUTOR** YOU.

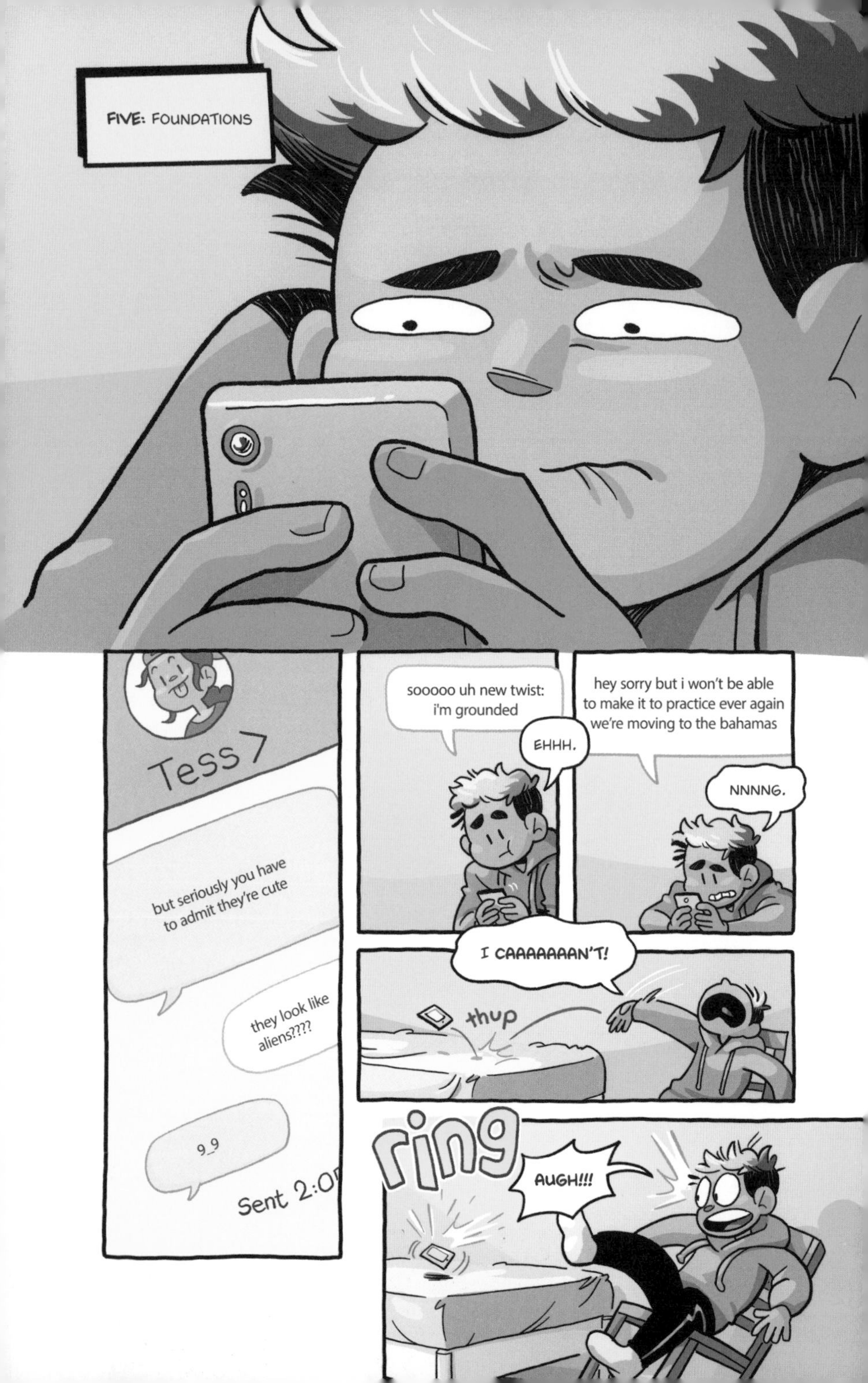
FIVE: FOUNDATIONS
Tess
but seriously you have to admit they're cute
they look like aliens????
9_9
Sent 2:0
sooooo uh new twist: i'm grounded
EHHH.
hey sorry but i won't be able to make it to practice ever again we're moving to the bahamas
NNNNG.
I CAAAAAAAN'T!
thup
ring
AUGH!!!

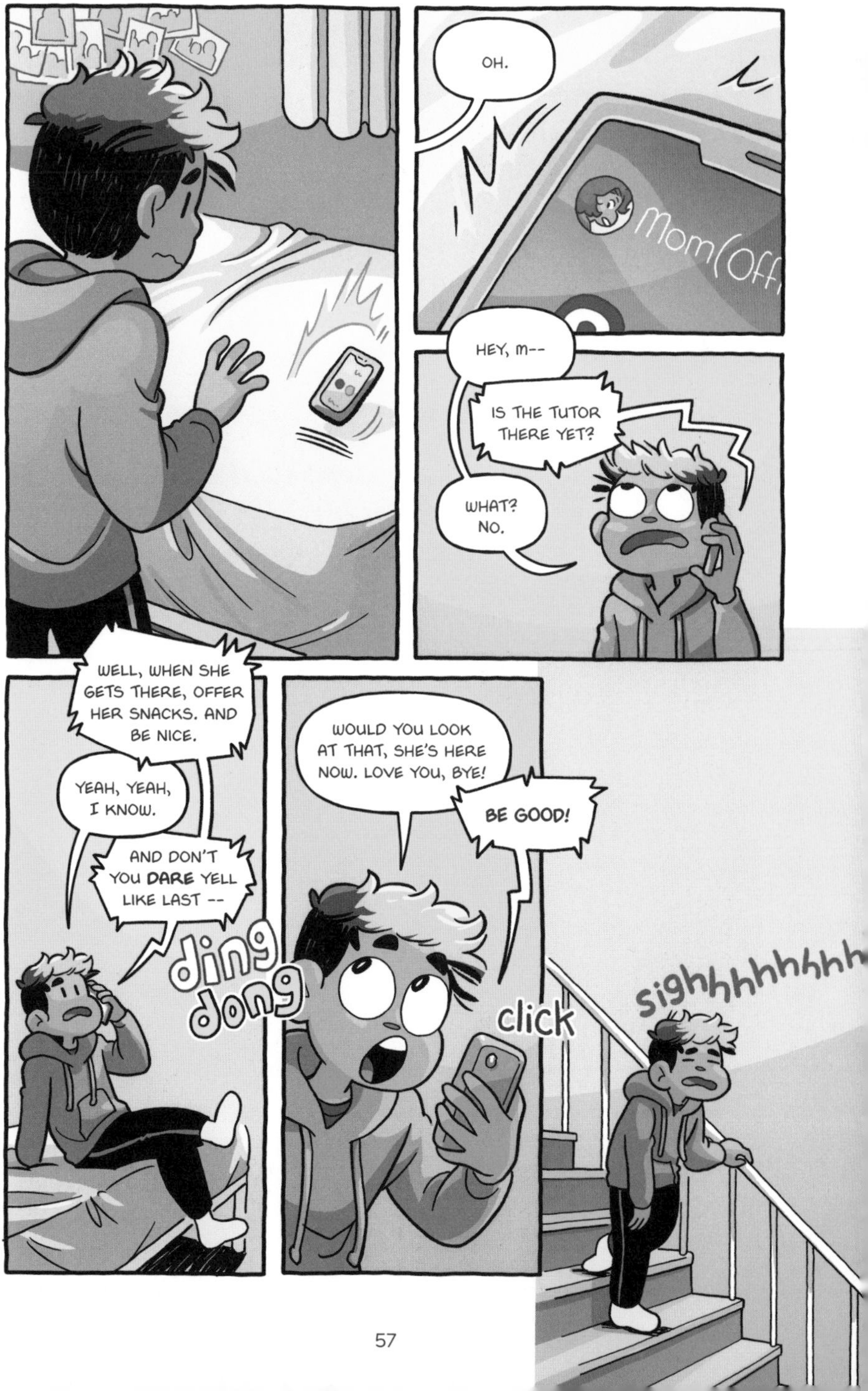
OH.
Mom(Off
HEY, M--
IS THE TUTOR THERE YET?
WHAT? NO.
WELL, WHEN SHE GETS THERE, OFFER HER SNACKS. AND BE NICE.
YEAH, YEAH, I KNOW.
AND DON'T YOU **DARE** YELL LIKE LAST --
ding dong
WOULD YOU LOOK AT THAT, SHE'S HERE NOW. LOVE YOU, BYE!
BE GOOD!
click
sighhhhhhhh

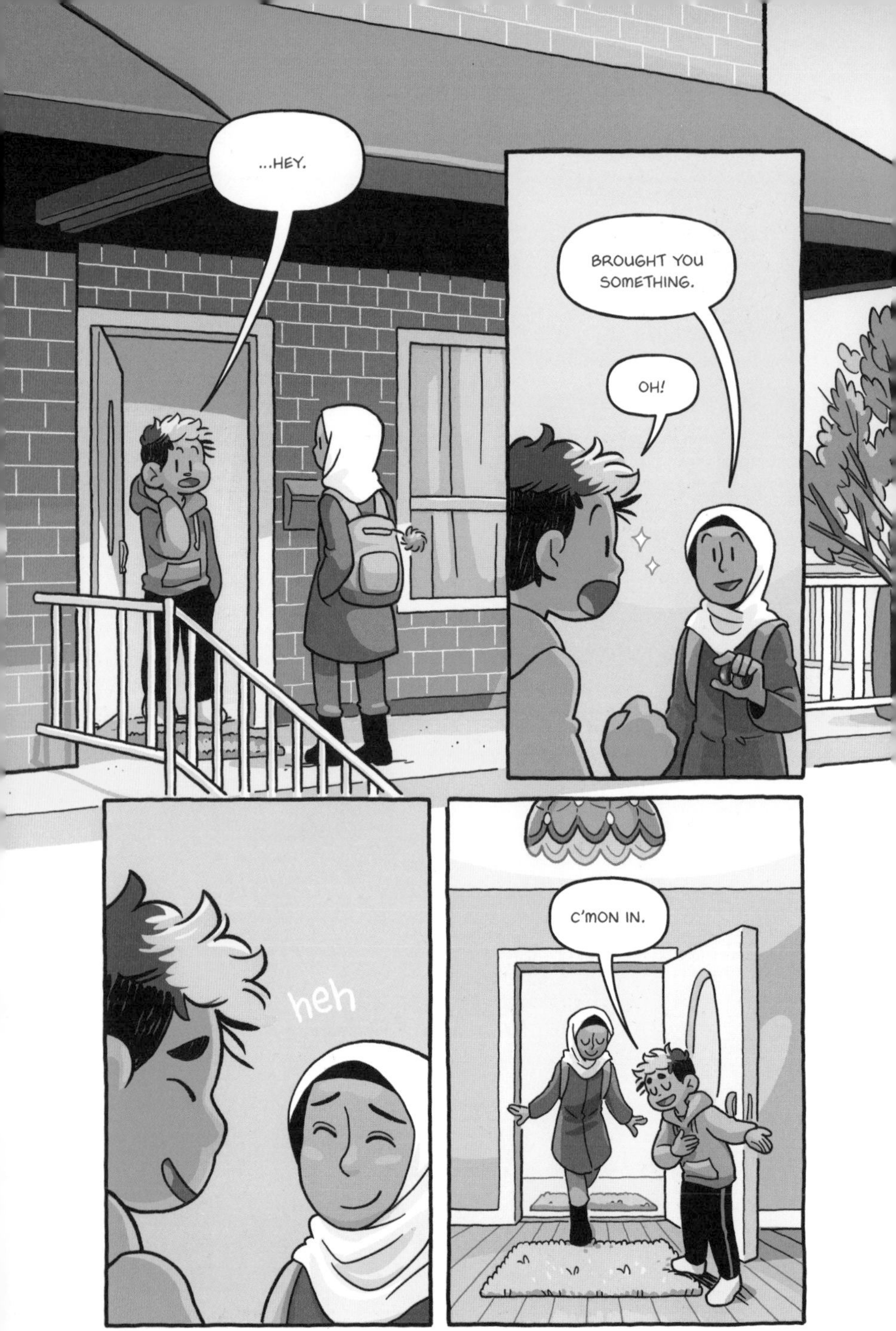
...HEY.
BROUGHT YOU SOMETHING.
OH!
heh
C'MON IN.

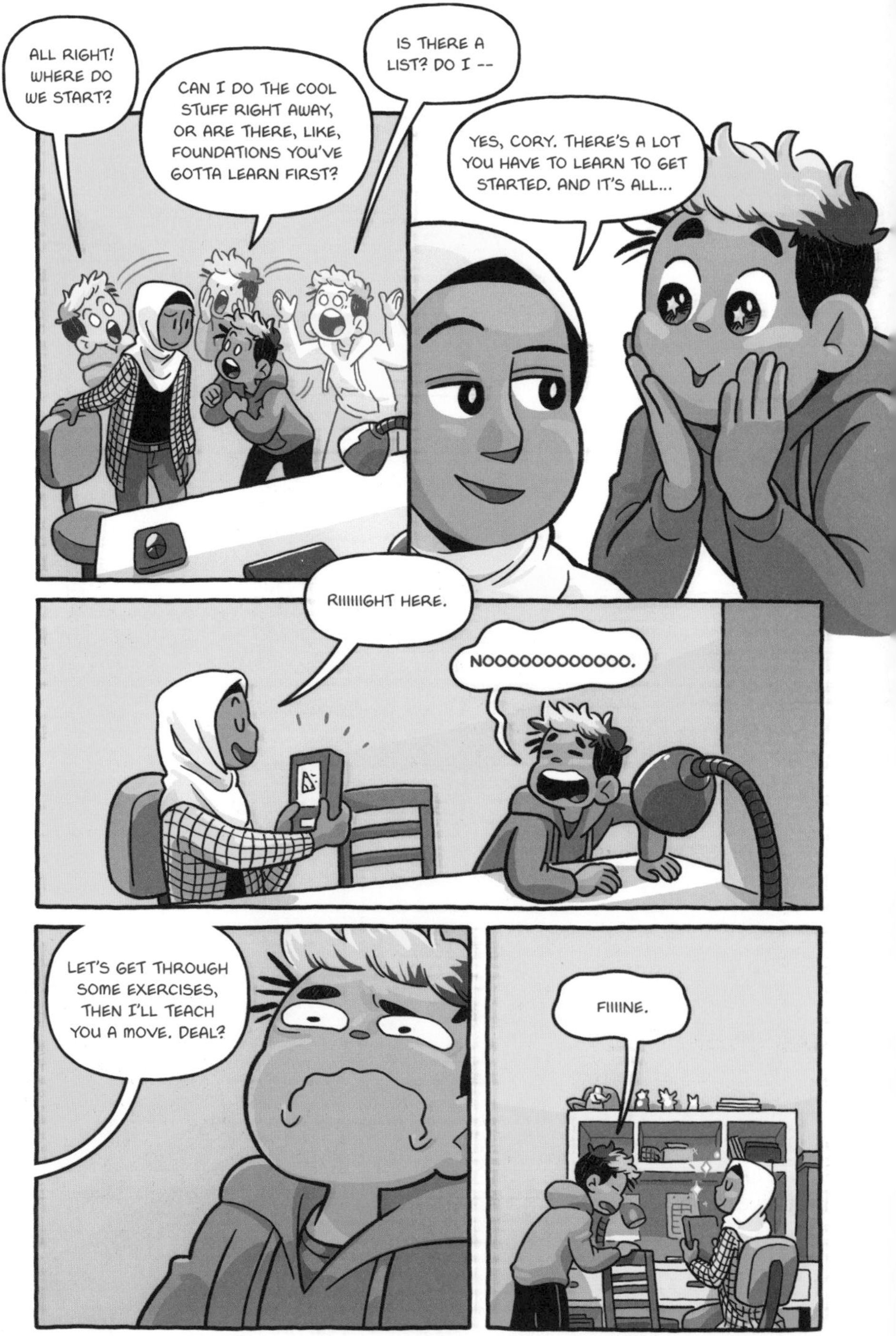
ALL RIGHT! WHERE DO WE START?
CAN I DO THE COOL STUFF RIGHT AWAY, OR ARE THERE, LIKE, FOUNDATIONS YOU'VE GOTTA LEARN FIRST?
IS THERE A LIST? DO I --
YES, CORY. THERE'S A LOT YOU HAVE TO LEARN TO GET STARTED. AND IT'S ALL...
RIIIIIGHT HERE.
NOOOOOOOOOOOO.
LET'S GET THROUGH SOME EXERCISES, THEN I'LL TEACH YOU A MOVE. DEAL?
FIIIINE.

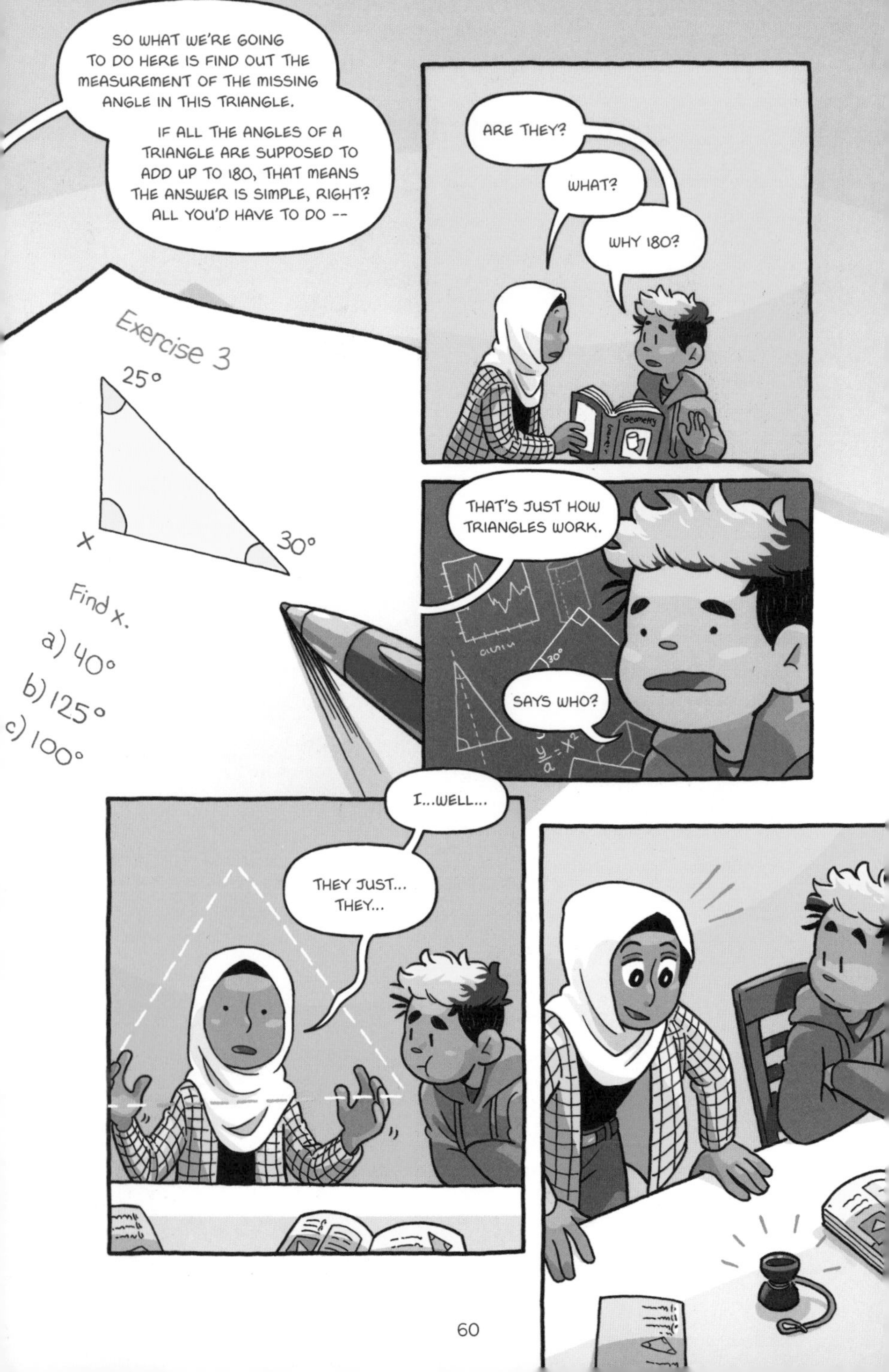
SO WHAT WE'RE GOING TO DO HERE IS FIND OUT THE MEASUREMENT OF THE MISSING ANGLE IN THIS TRIANGLE.
IF ALL THE ANGLES OF A TRIANGLE ARE SUPPOSED TO ADD UP TO 180, THAT MEANS THE ANSWER IS SIMPLE, RIGHT? ALL YOU'D HAVE TO DO --
Exercise 3
25°
X
30°
Find x.
a) 40°
b) 125°
c) 100°
ARE THEY?
WHAT?
WHY 180?
Geometry
THAT'S JUST HOW TRIANGLES WORK.
30°
SAYS WHO?
I...WELL...
THEY JUST... THEY...

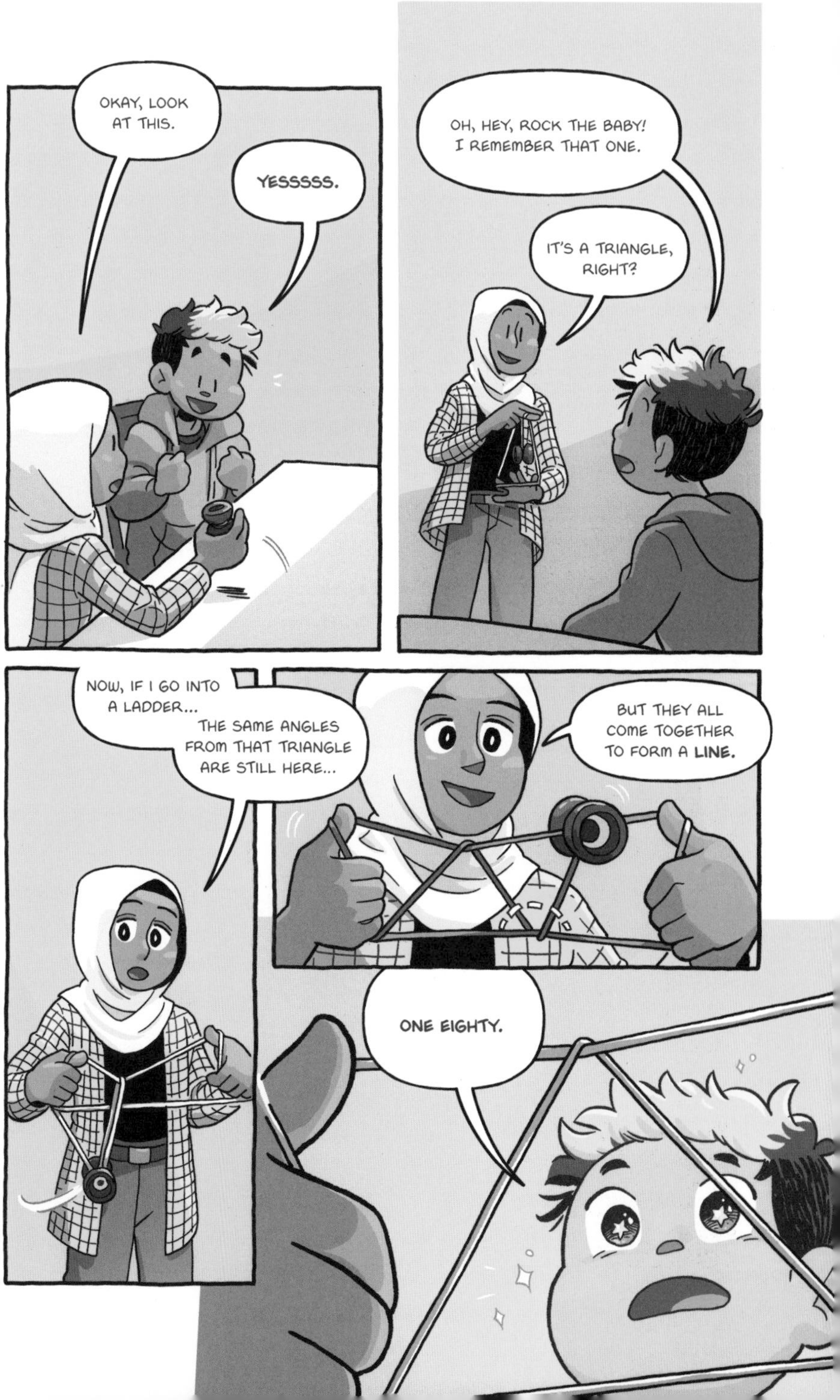
OKAY, LOOK AT THIS.
YESSSSS.
OH, HEY, ROCK THE BABY! I REMEMBER THAT ONE.
IT'S A TRIANGLE, RIGHT?
NOW, IF I GO INTO A LADDER...
THE SAME ANGLES FROM THAT TRIANGLE ARE STILL HERE...
BUT THEY ALL COME TOGETHER TO FORM A **LINE.**
ONE EIGHTY.

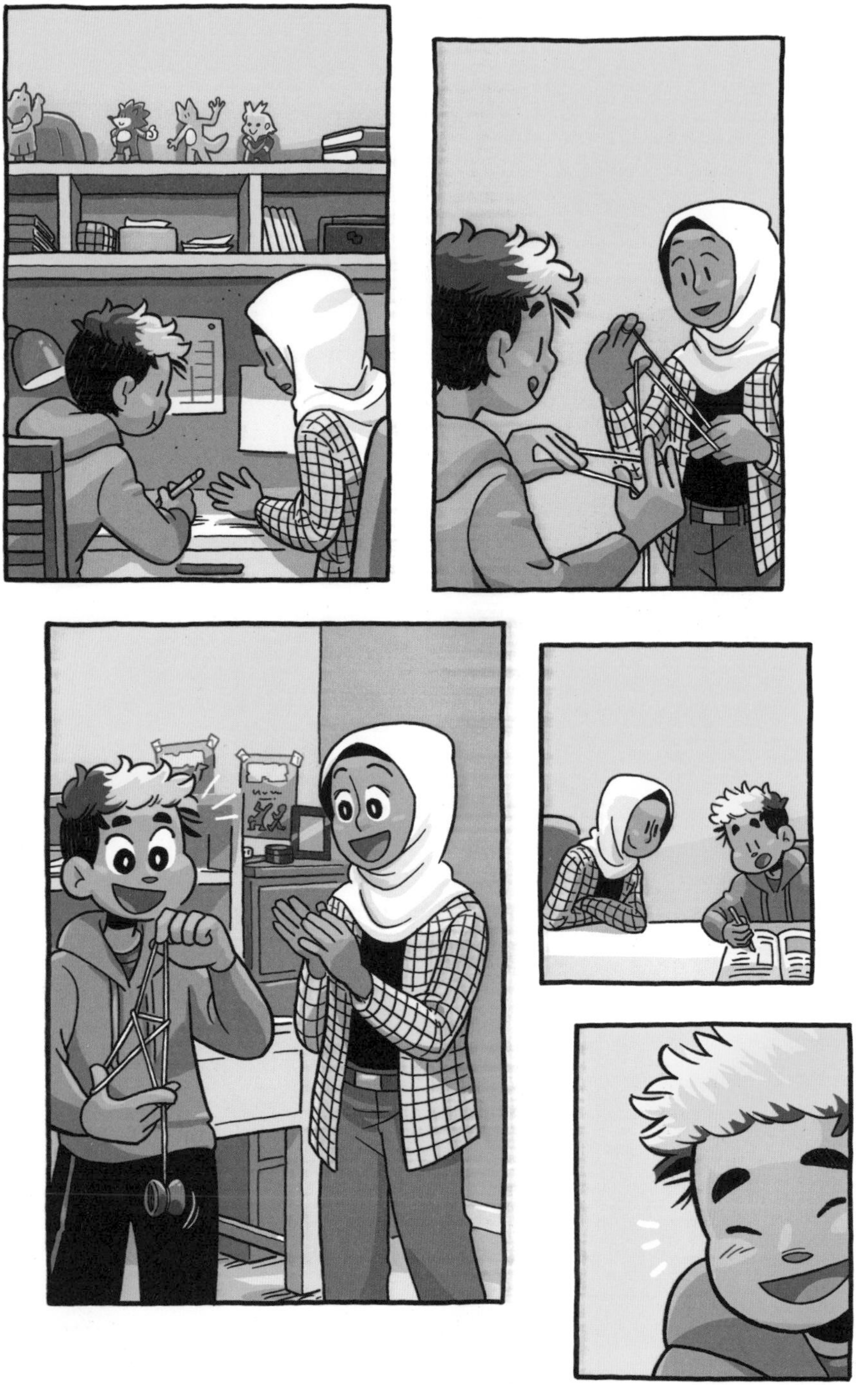

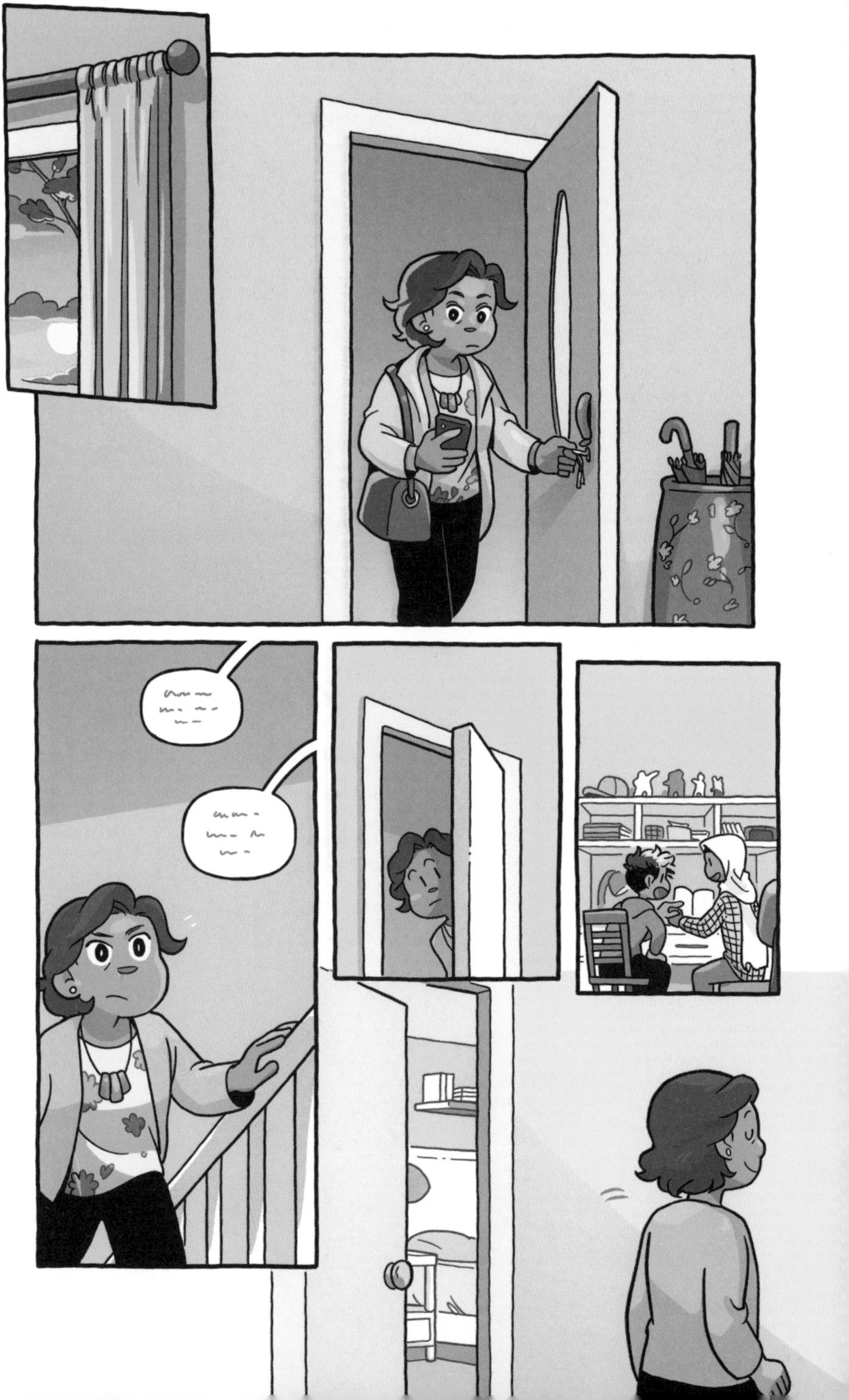

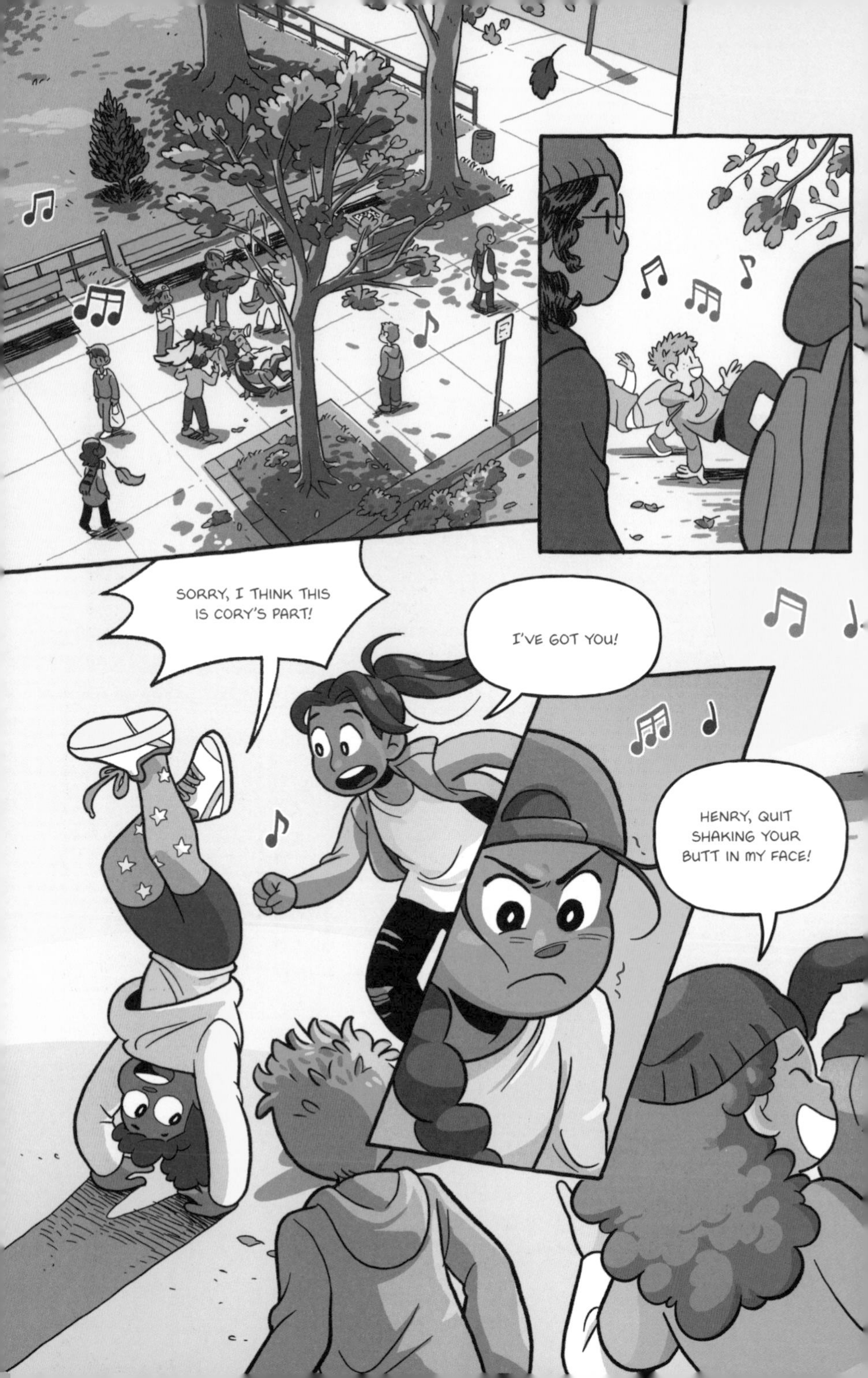
SORRY, I THINK THIS IS CORY'S PART!
I'VE GOT YOU!
HENRY, QUIT SHAKING YOUR BUTT IN MY FACE!

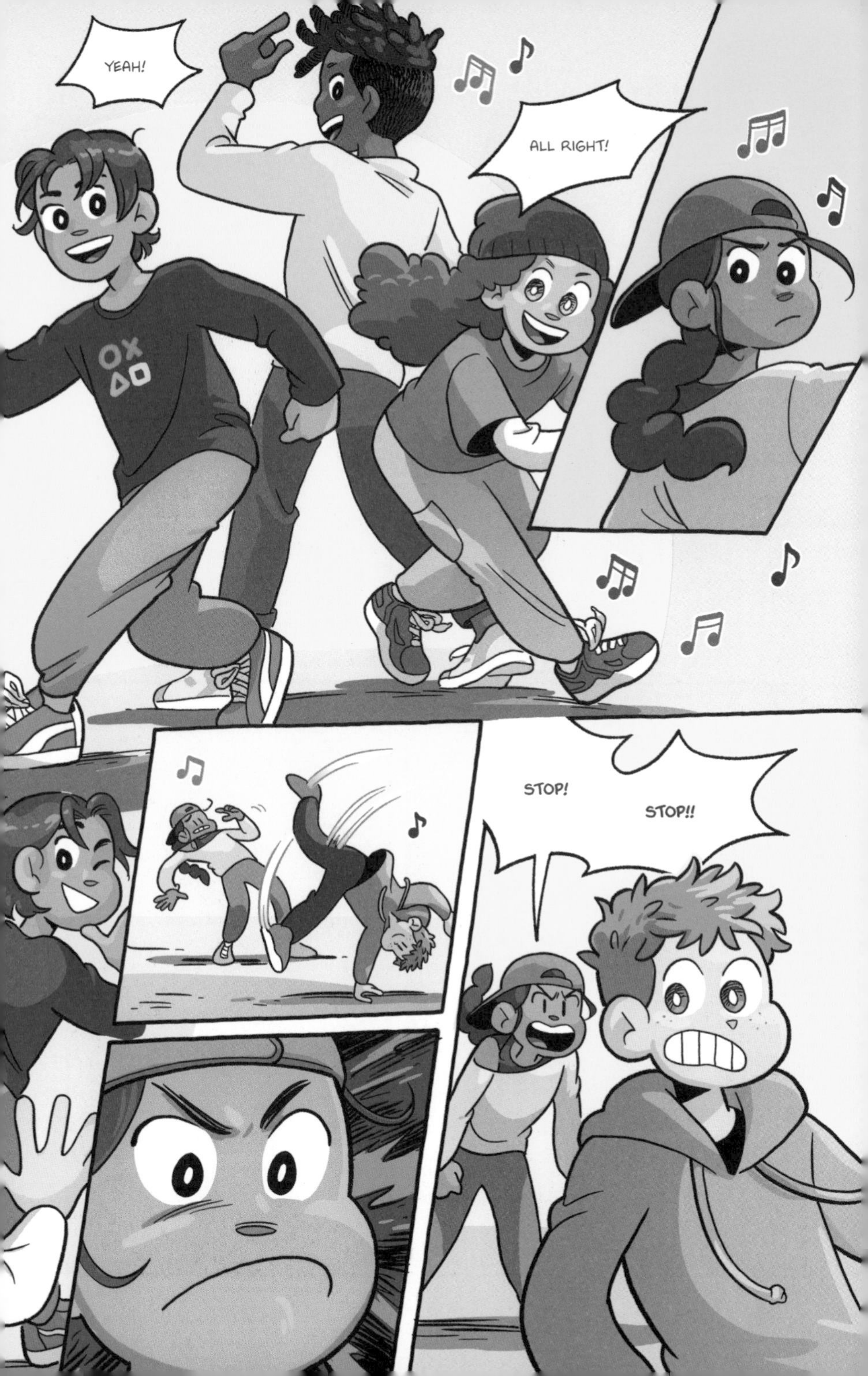
YEAH!
ALL RIGHT!
STOP!
STOP!!

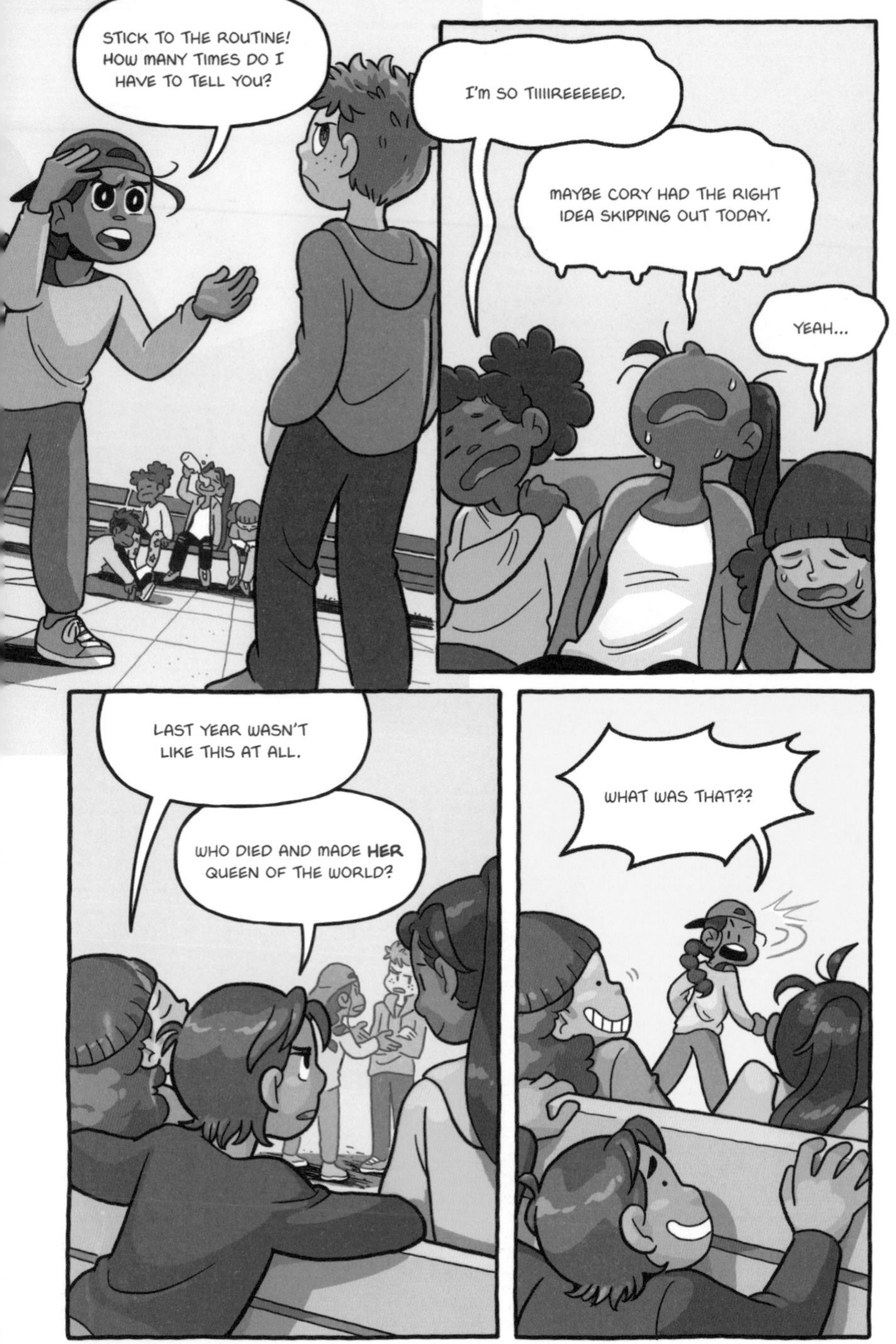
STICK TO THE ROUTINE! HOW MANY TIMES DO I HAVE TO TELL YOU?
I'M SO TIIIIREEEEED.
MAYBE CORY HAD THE RIGHT IDEA SKIPPING OUT TODAY.
YEAH...
LAST YEAR WASN'T LIKE THIS AT ALL.
WHO DIED AND MADE **HER** QUEEN OF THE WORLD?
WHAT WAS THAT??

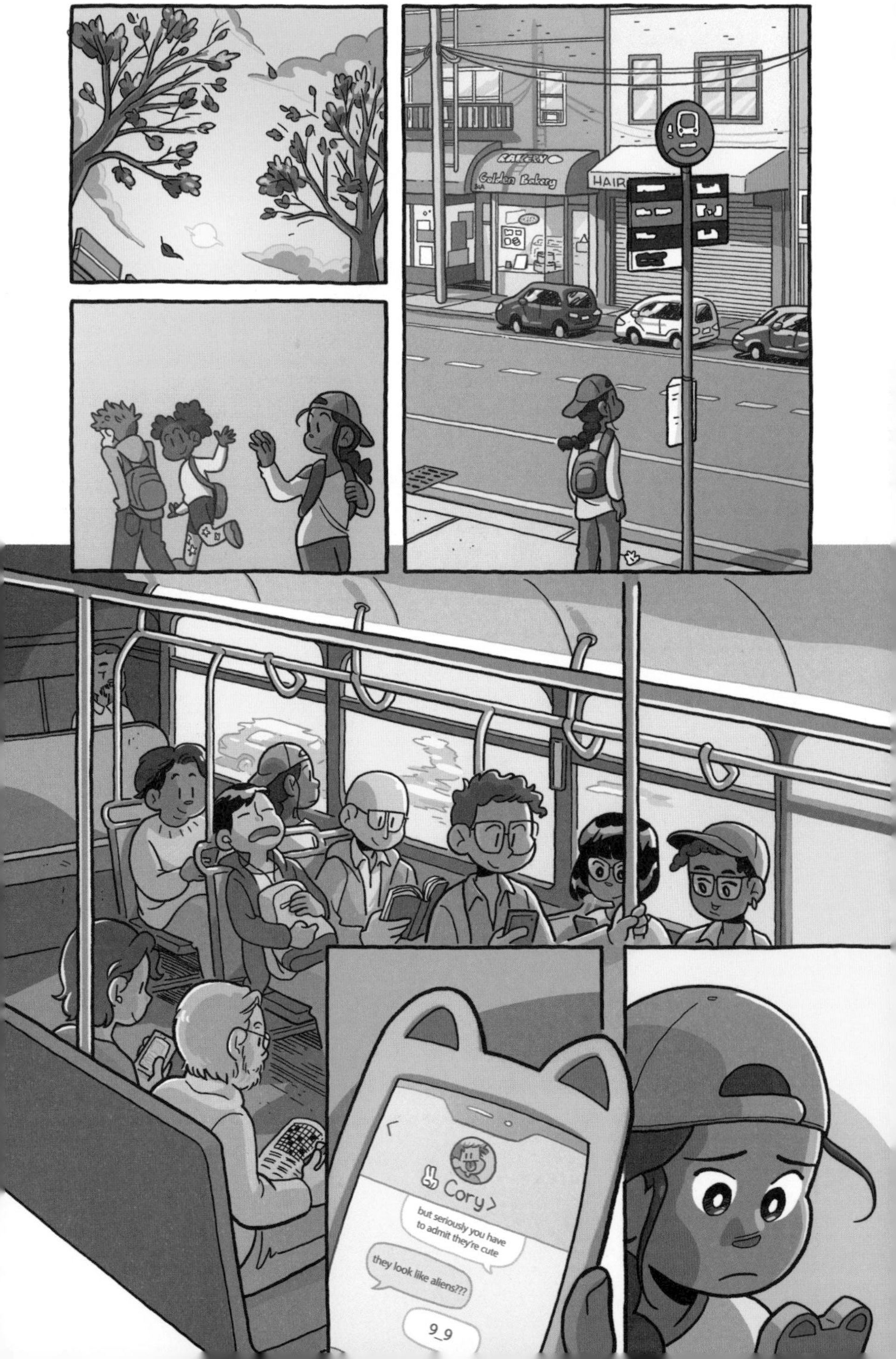
BAKERY
Golden Bakery
HAIR
Cory >
but seriously you have to admit they're cute
they look like aliens???
9_9

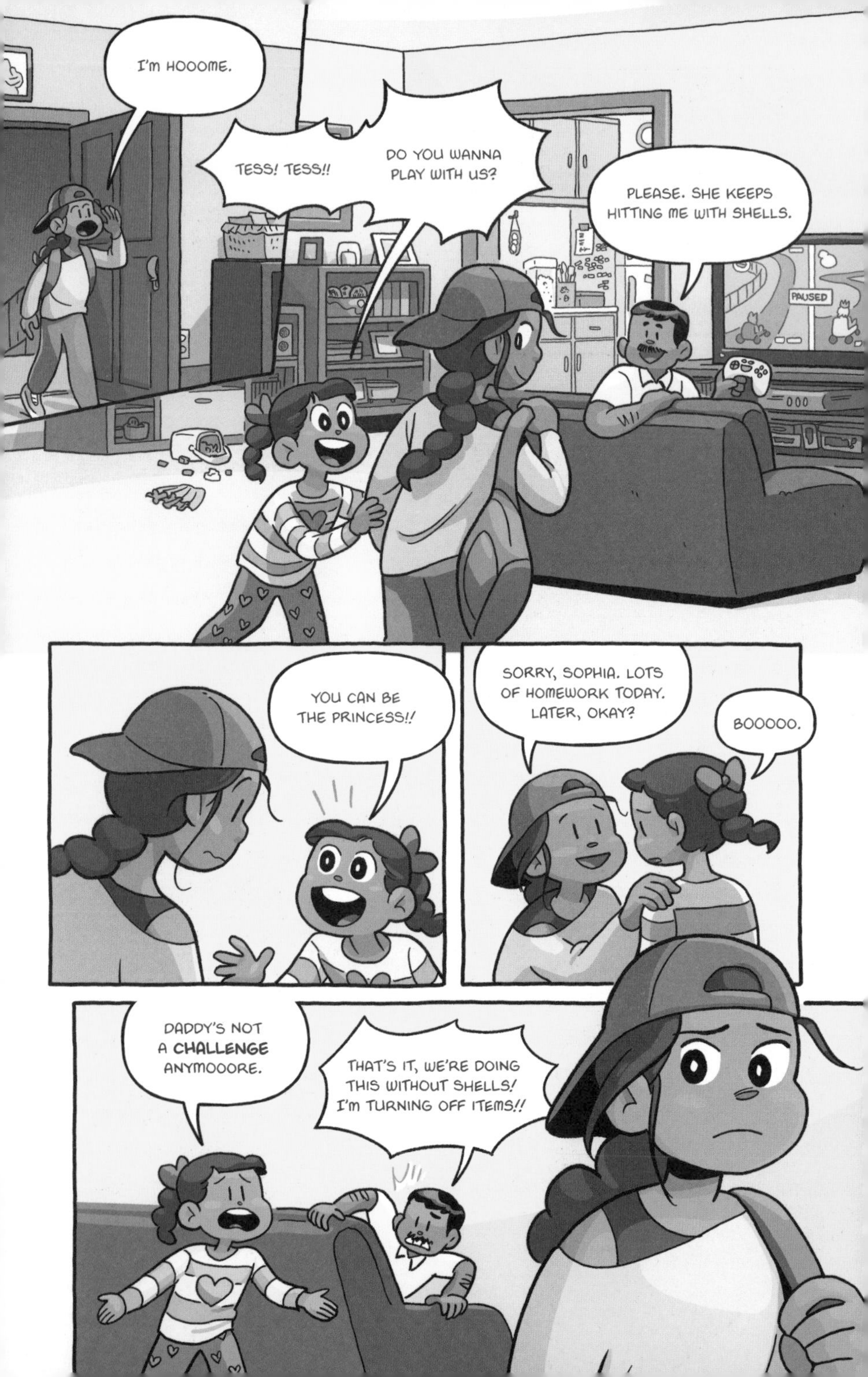
I'M HOOOME.
TESS! TESS!!
DO YOU WANNA PLAY WITH US?
PLEASE. SHE KEEPS HITTING ME WITH SHELLS.
PAUSED
YOU CAN BE THE PRINCESS!!
SORRY, SOPHIA. LOTS OF HOMEWORK TODAY. LATER, OKAY?
BOOOOO.
DADDY'S NOT A **CHALLENGE** ANYMOOORE.
THAT'S IT, WE'RE DOING THIS WITHOUT SHELLS! I'M TURNING OFF ITEMS!!

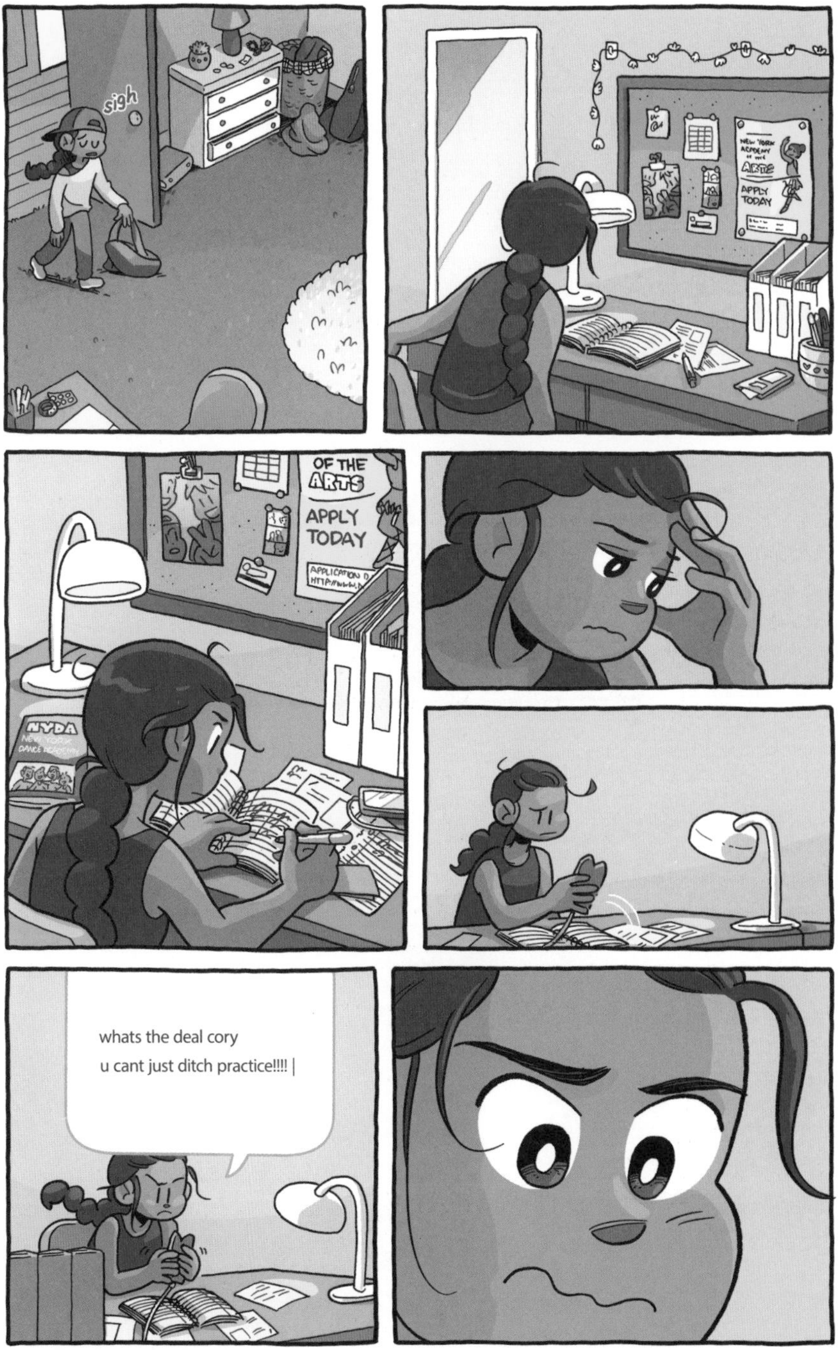
sigh
NEW YORK ACADEMY of the ARTS
APPLY TODAY
OF THE ARTS
APPLY TODAY
NYDA
whats the deal cory
u cant just ditch practice!!!! |

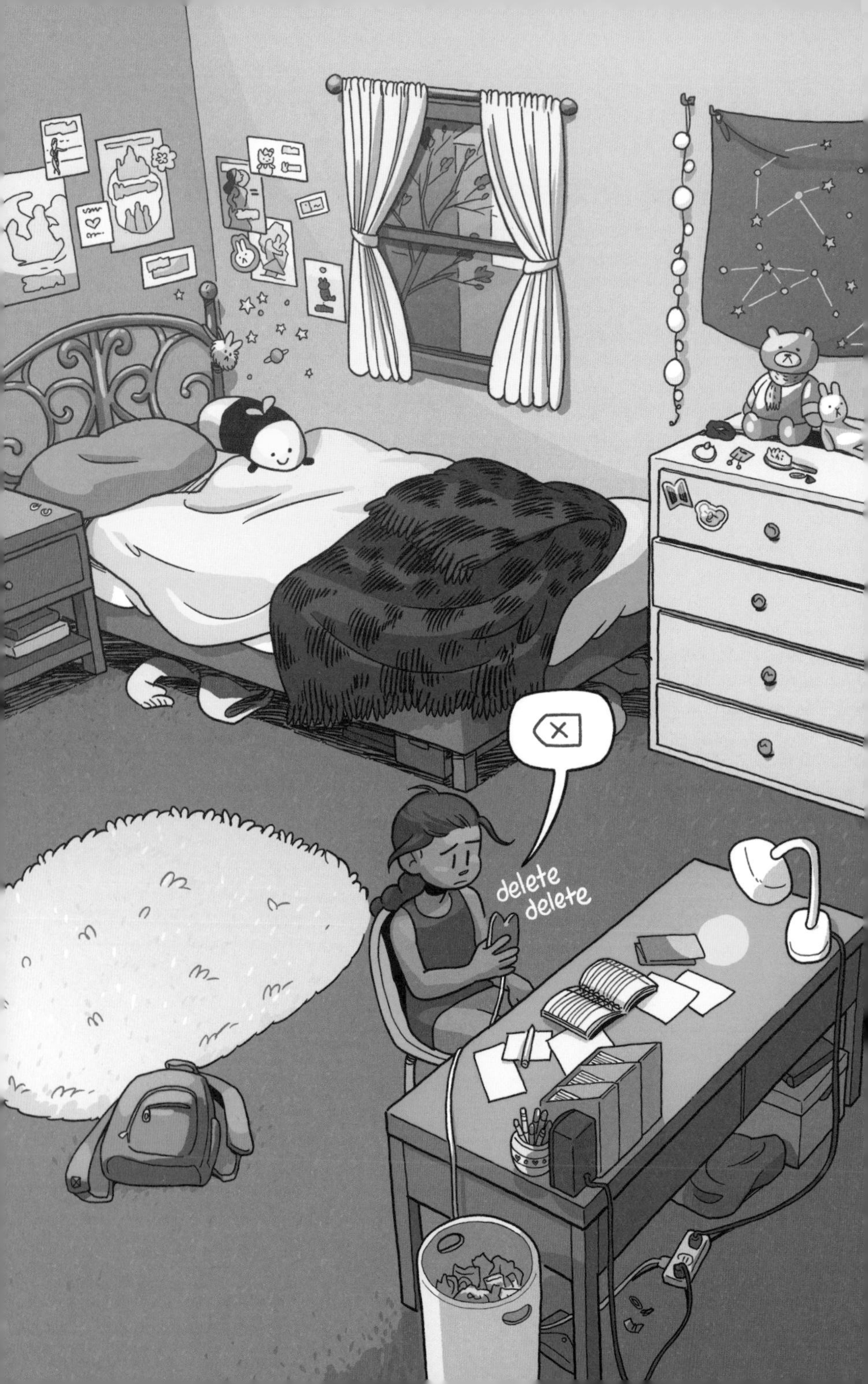
delete
delete

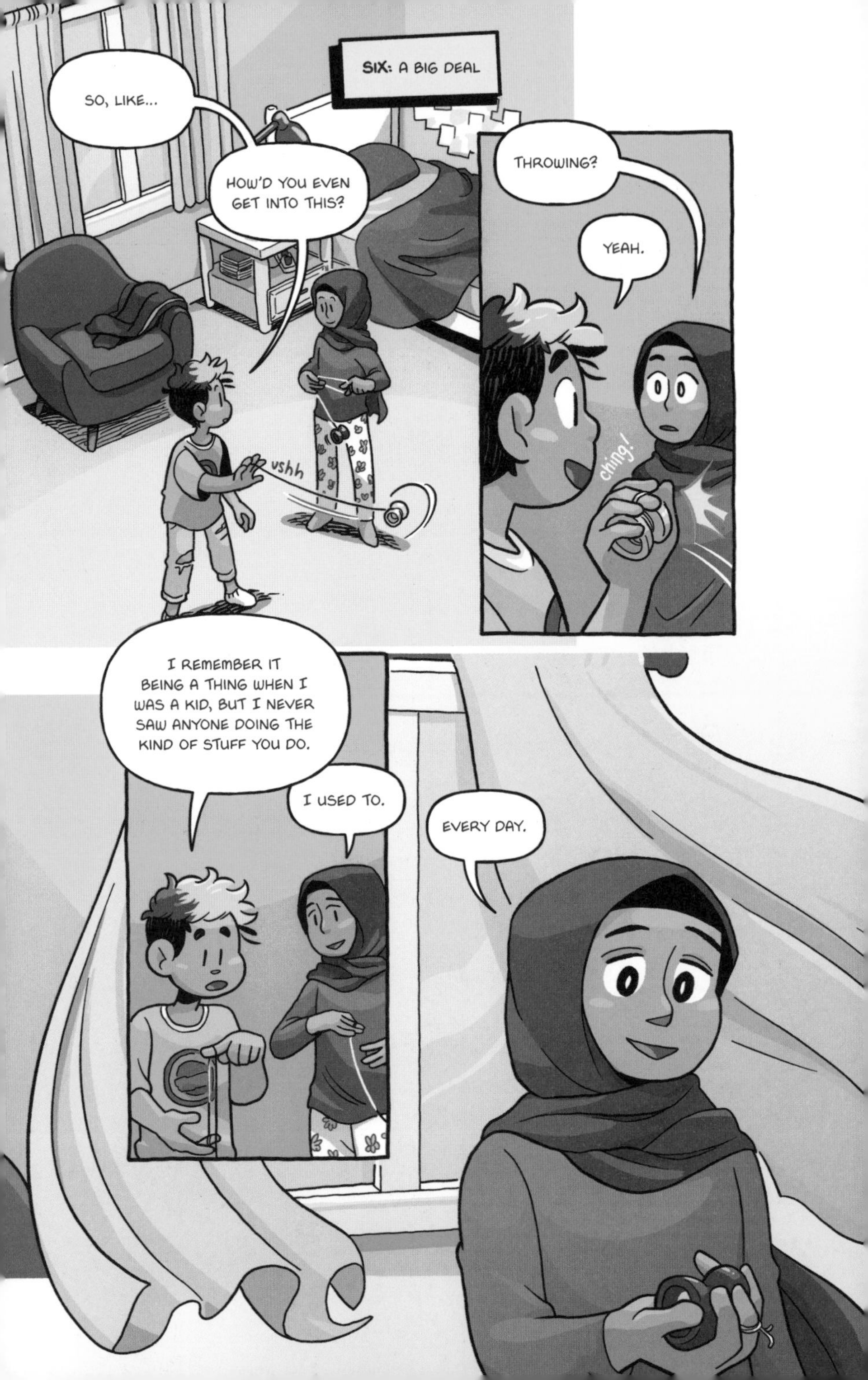
SIX: A BIG DEAL
SO, LIKE...
HOW'D YOU EVEN GET INTO THIS?
vshh
THROWING?
YEAH.
ching!
I REMEMBER IT BEING A THING WHEN I WAS A KID, BUT I NEVER SAW ANYONE DOING THE KIND OF STUFF YOU DO.
I USED TO.
EVERY DAY.

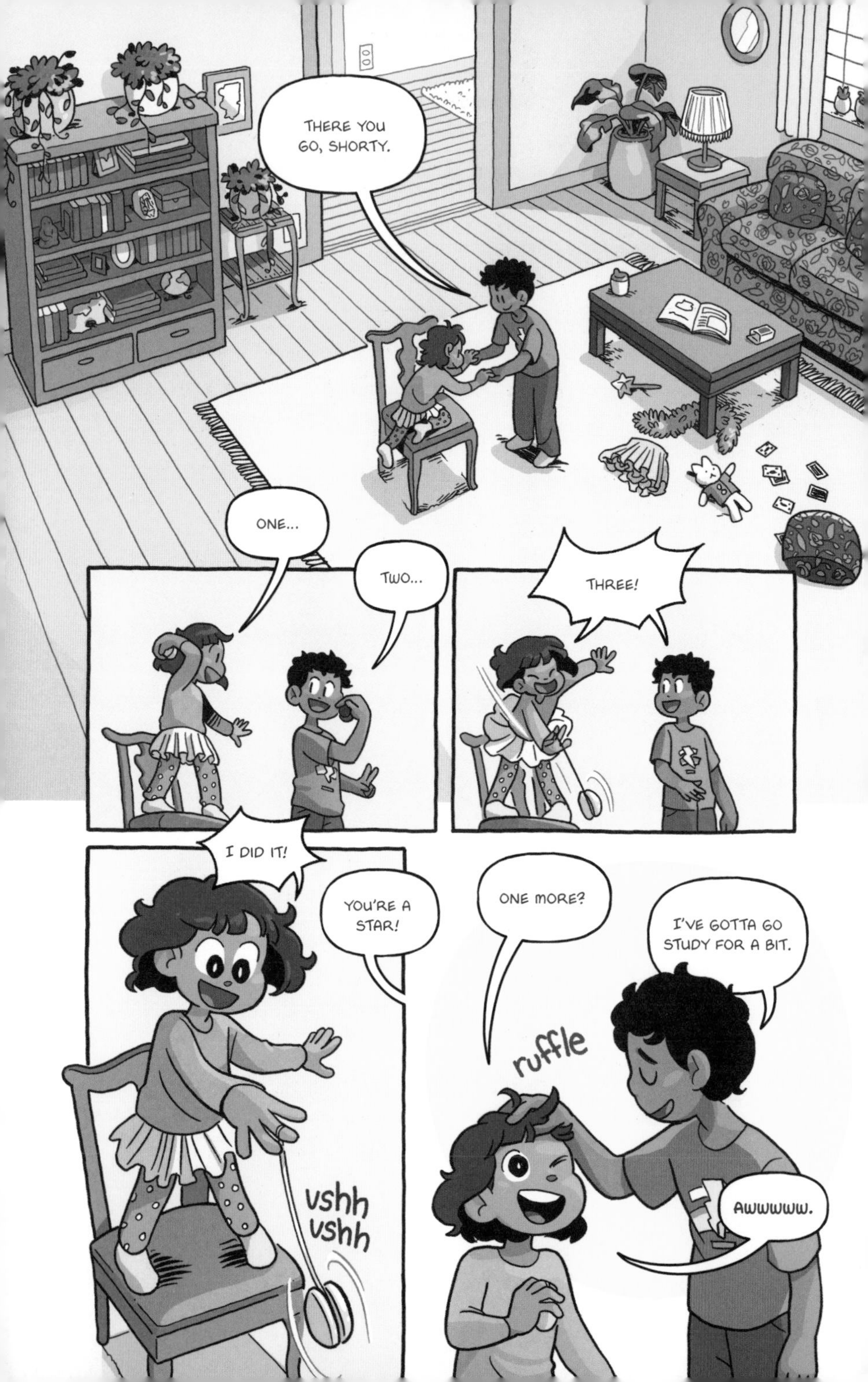
THERE YOU GO, SHORTY.
ONE...
TWO...
THREE!
I DID IT!
YOU'RE A STAR!
vshh vshh
ONE MORE?
I'VE GOTTA GO STUDY FOR A BIT.
ruffle
AWWWWW.

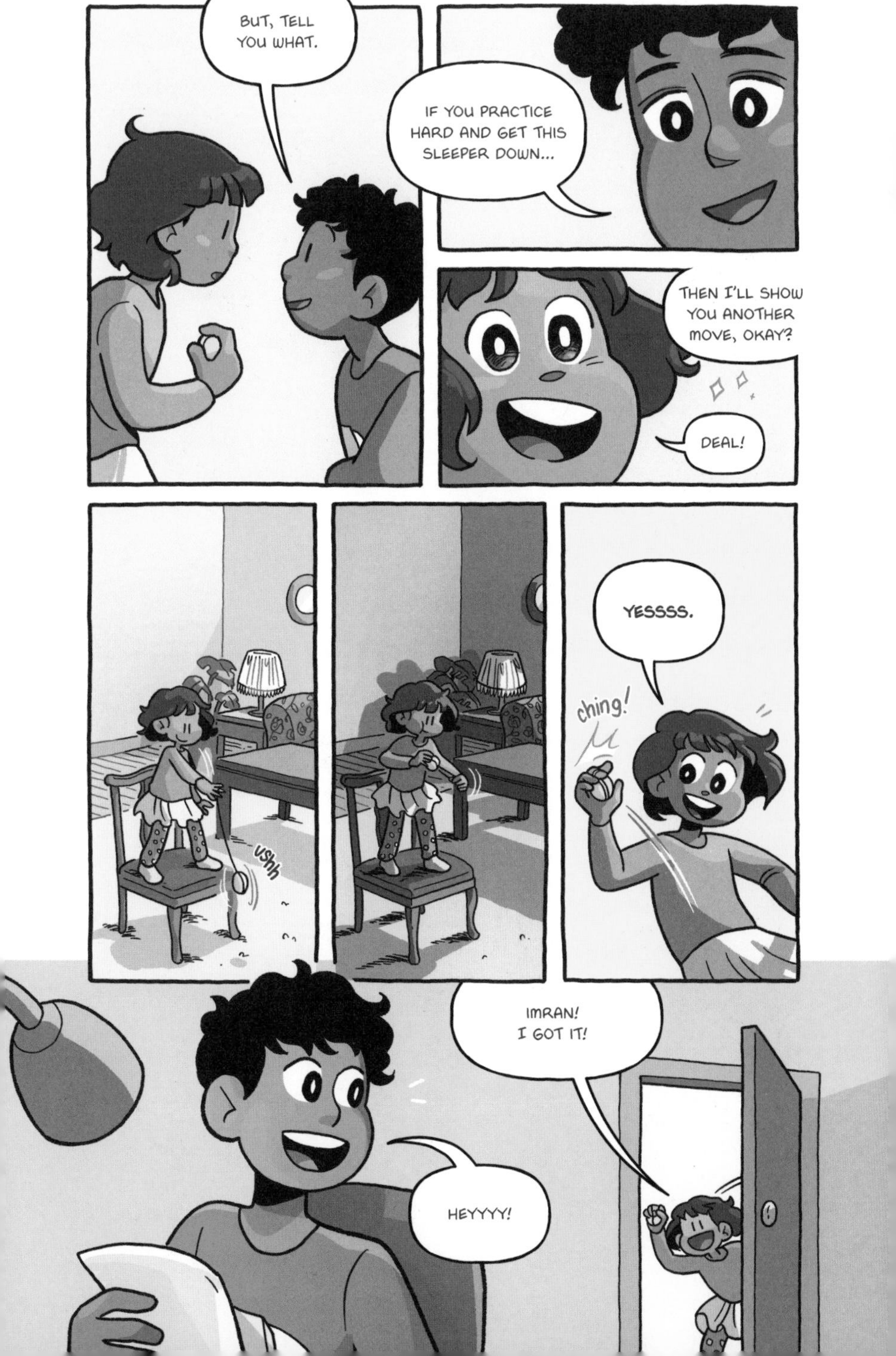

BUT, TELL YOU WHAT.
IF YOU PRACTICE HARD AND GET THIS SLEEPER DOWN...
THEN I'LL SHOW YOU ANOTHER MOVE, OKAY?
DEAL!
USHH
YESSSS.
ching!
IMRAN! I GOT IT!
HEYYYY!

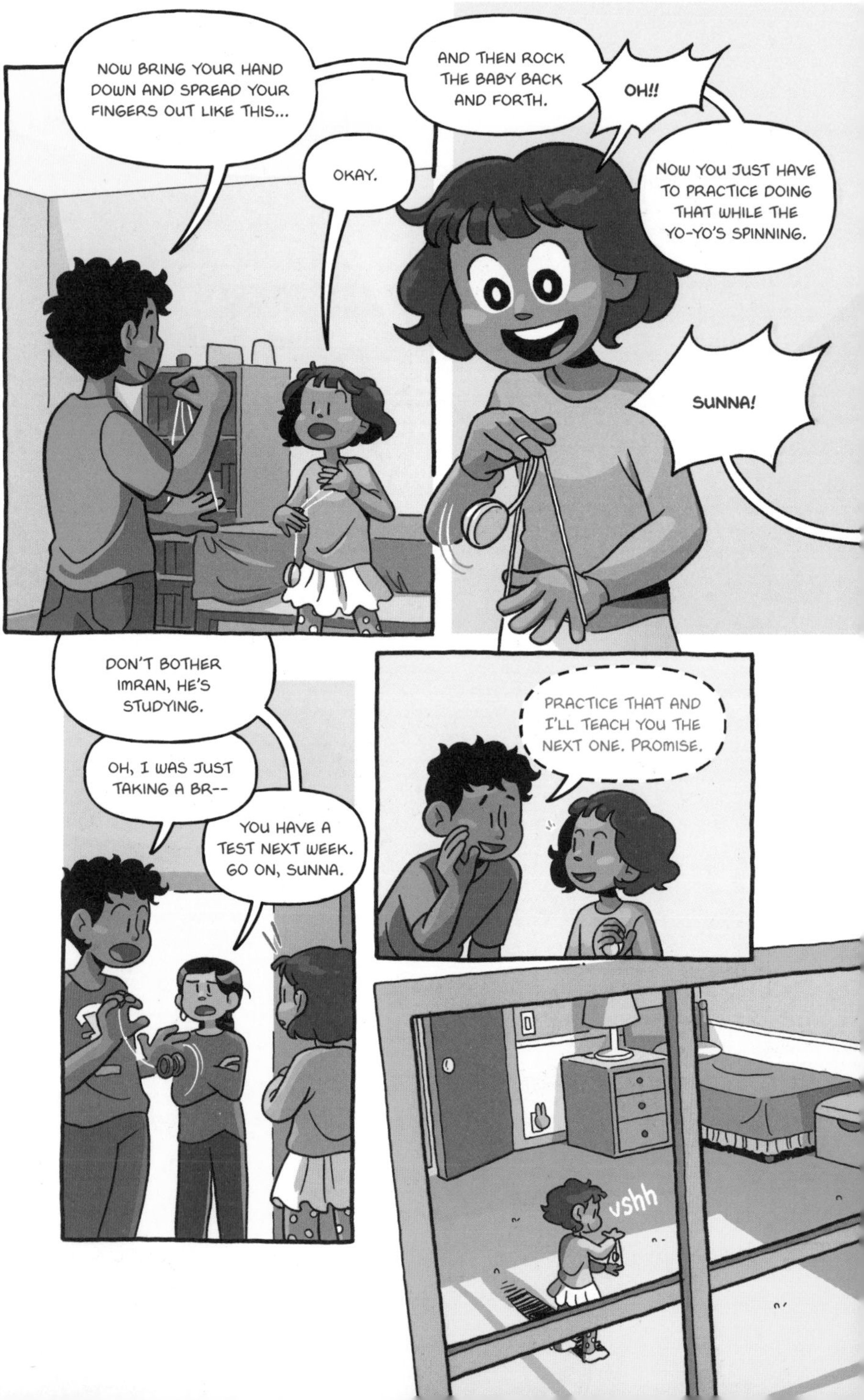
NOW BRING YOUR HAND DOWN AND SPREAD YOUR FINGERS OUT LIKE THIS...
OKAY.
AND THEN ROCK THE BABY BACK AND FORTH.
OH!!
NOW YOU JUST HAVE TO PRACTICE DOING THAT WHILE THE YO-YO'S SPINNING.
SUNNA!
DON'T BOTHER IMRAN, HE'S STUDYING.
OH, I WAS JUST TAKING A BR--
YOU HAVE A TEST NEXT WEEK. GO ON, SUNNA.
PRACTICE THAT AND I'LL TEACH YOU THE NEXT ONE. PROMISE.
vshh

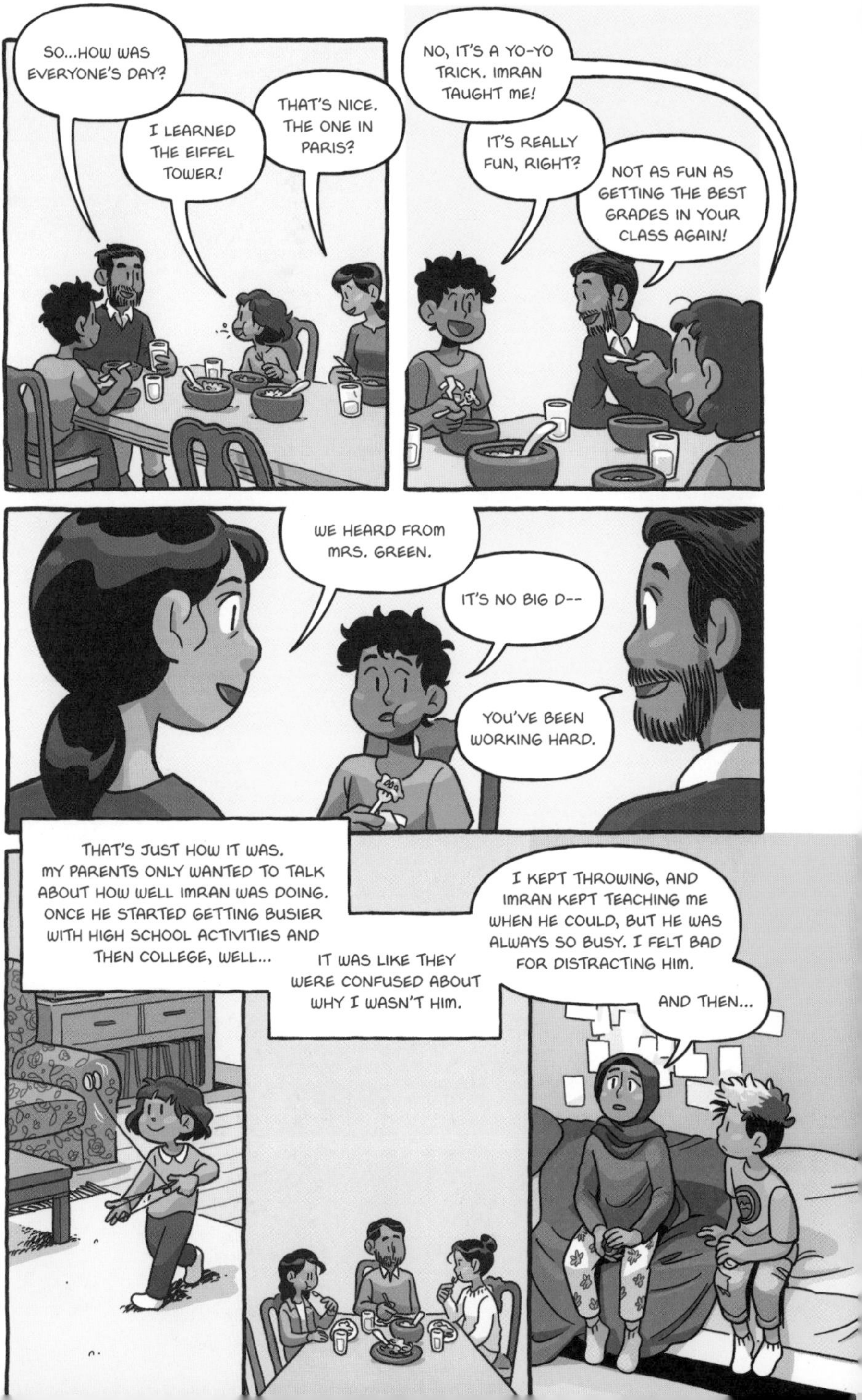
SO...HOW WAS EVERYONE'S DAY?
I LEARNED THE EIFFEL TOWER!
THAT'S NICE. THE ONE IN PARIS?
NO, IT'S A YO-YO TRICK. IMRAN TAUGHT ME!
IT'S REALLY FUN, RIGHT?
NOT AS FUN AS GETTING THE BEST GRADES IN YOUR CLASS AGAIN!
WE HEARD FROM MRS. GREEN.
IT'S NO BIG D--
YOU'VE BEEN WORKING HARD.
THAT'S JUST HOW IT WAS. MY PARENTS ONLY WANTED TO TALK ABOUT HOW WELL IMRAN WAS DOING. ONCE HE STARTED GETTING BUSIER WITH HIGH SCHOOL ACTIVITIES AND THEN COLLEGE, WELL...
IT WAS LIKE THEY WERE CONFUSED ABOUT WHY I WASN'T HIM.
I KEPT THROWING, AND IMRAN KEPT TEACHING ME WHEN HE COULD, BUT HE WAS ALWAYS SO BUSY. I FELT BAD FOR DISTRACTING HIM.
AND THEN...

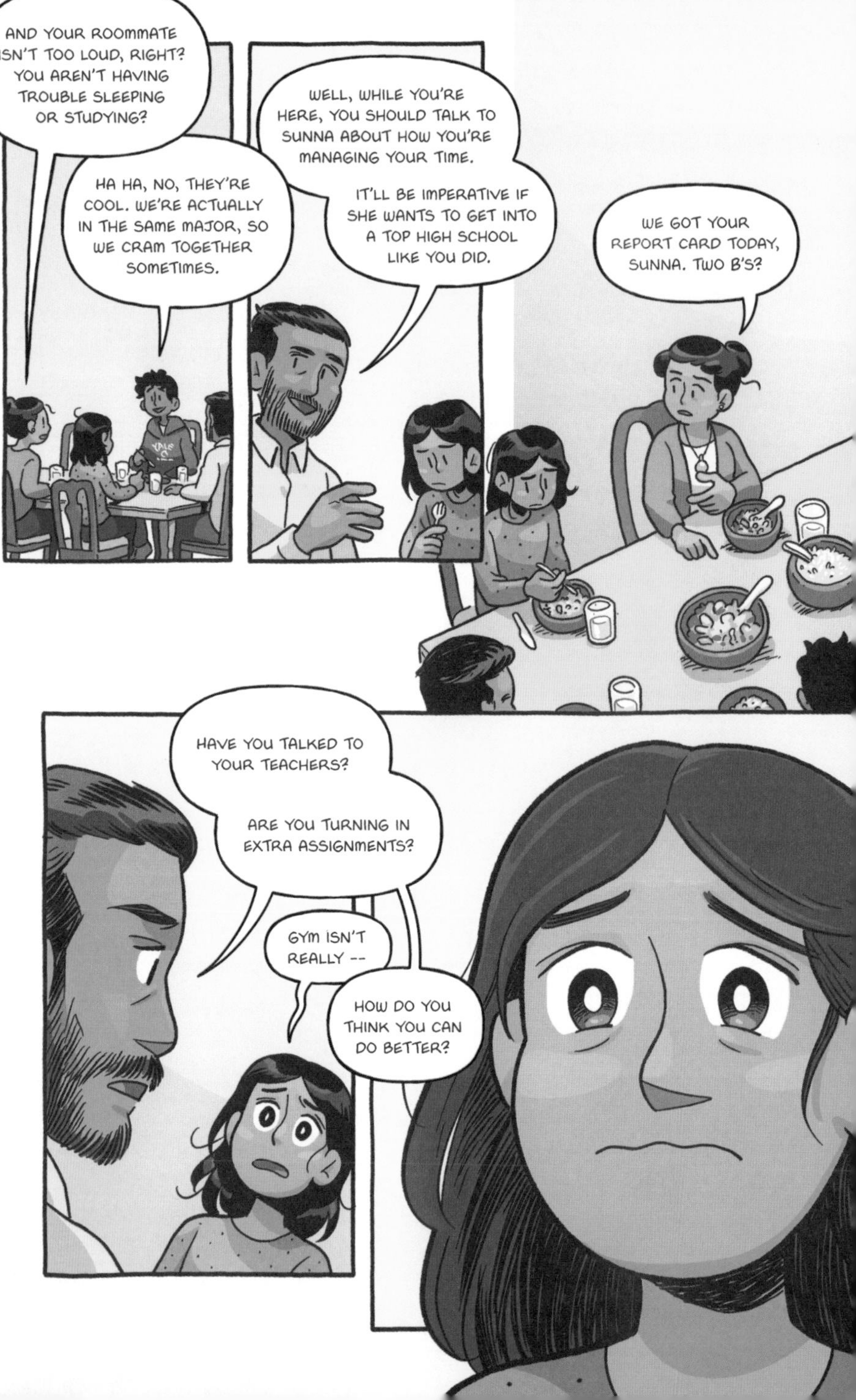
AND YOUR ROOMMATE ISN'T TOO LOUD, RIGHT? YOU AREN'T HAVING TROUBLE SLEEPING OR STUDYING?
HA HA, NO, THEY'RE COOL. WE'RE ACTUALLY IN THE SAME MAJOR, SO WE CRAM TOGETHER SOMETIMES.
WELL, WHILE YOU'RE HERE, YOU SHOULD TALK TO SUNNA ABOUT HOW YOU'RE MANAGING YOUR TIME.
IT'LL BE IMPERATIVE IF SHE WANTS TO GET INTO A TOP HIGH SCHOOL LIKE YOU DID.
WE GOT YOUR REPORT CARD TODAY, SUNNA. TWO B'S?
HAVE YOU TALKED TO YOUR TEACHERS?
ARE YOU TURNING IN EXTRA ASSIGNMENTS?
GYM ISN'T REALLY --
HOW DO YOU THINK YOU CAN DO BETTER?

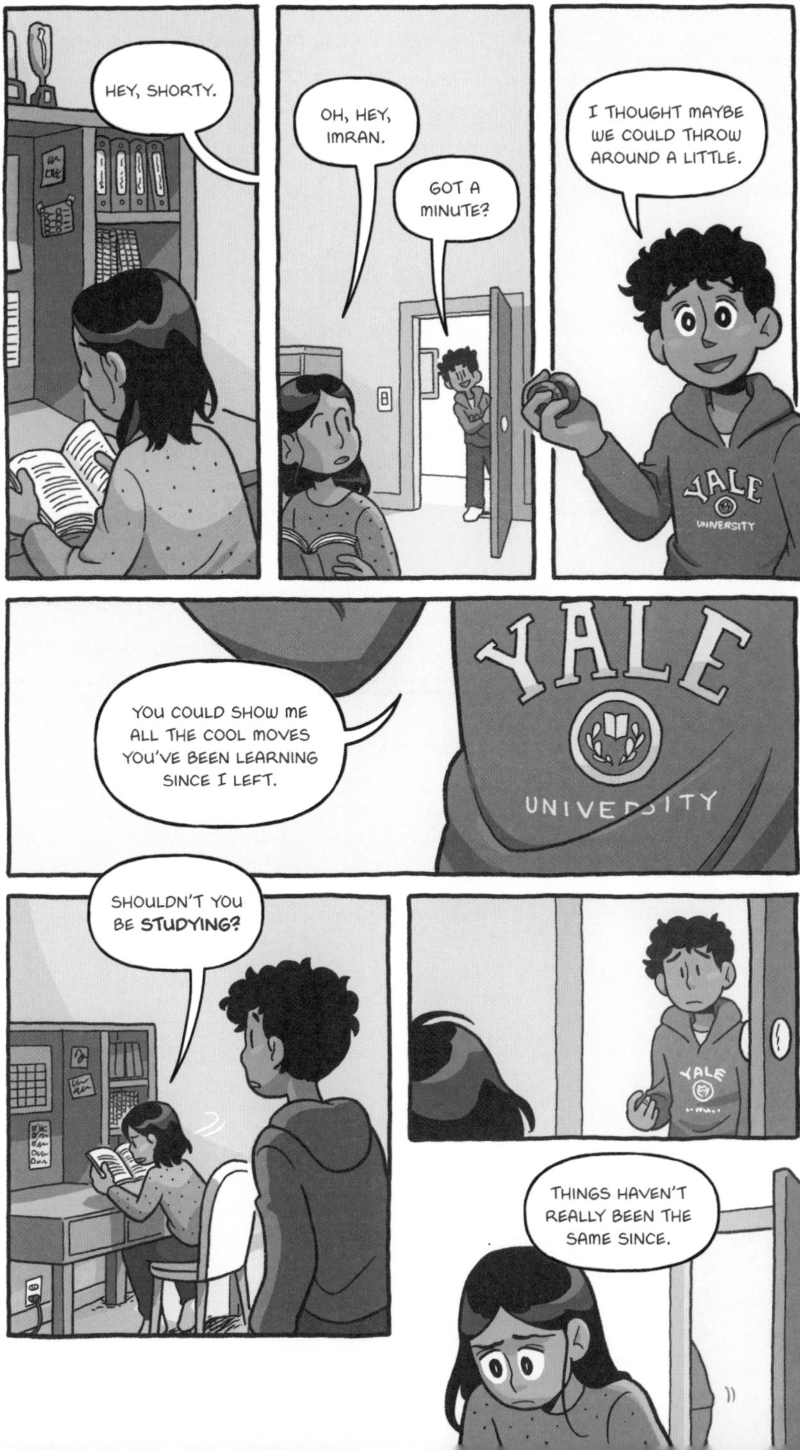
HEY, SHORTY.
OH, HEY, IMRAN.
GOT A MINUTE?
I THOUGHT MAYBE WE COULD THROW AROUND A LITTLE.
YALE UNIVERSITY
YOU COULD SHOW ME ALL THE COOL MOVES YOU'VE BEEN LEARNING SINCE I LEFT.
YALE UNIVERSITY
SHOULDN'T YOU BE **STUDYING?**
YALE
THINGS HAVEN'T REALLY BEEN THE SAME SINCE.

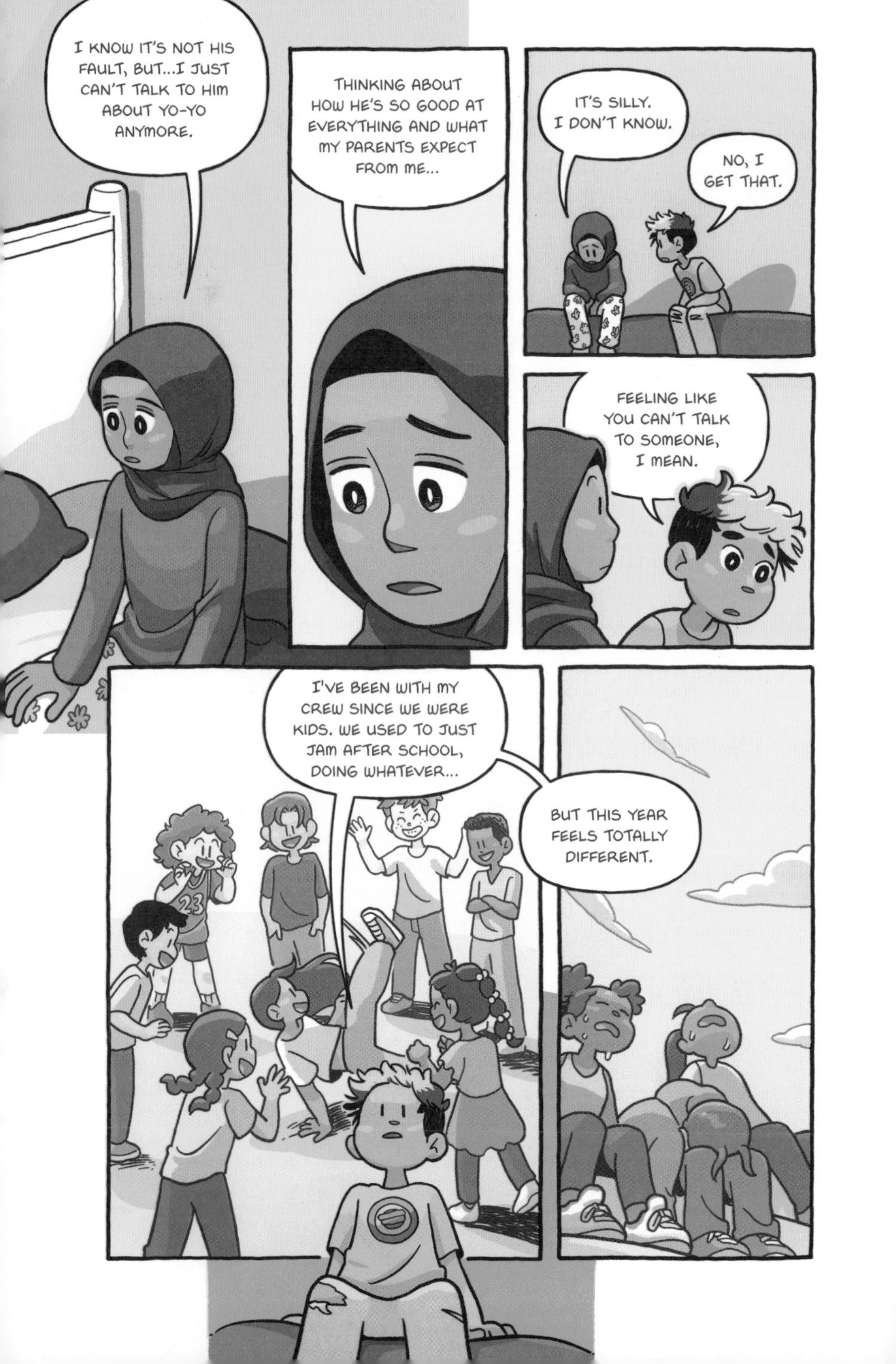
I KNOW IT'S NOT HIS FAULT, BUT...I JUST CAN'T TALK TO HIM ABOUT YO-YO ANYMORE.
THINKING ABOUT HOW HE'S SO GOOD AT EVERYTHING AND WHAT MY PARENTS EXPECT FROM ME...
IT'S SILLY. I DON'T KNOW.
NO, I GET THAT.
FEELING LIKE YOU CAN'T TALK TO SOMEONE, I MEAN.
I'VE BEEN WITH MY CREW SINCE WE WERE KIDS. WE USED TO JUST JAM AFTER SCHOOL, DOING WHATEVER...
BUT THIS YEAR FEELS TOTALLY DIFFERENT.
23

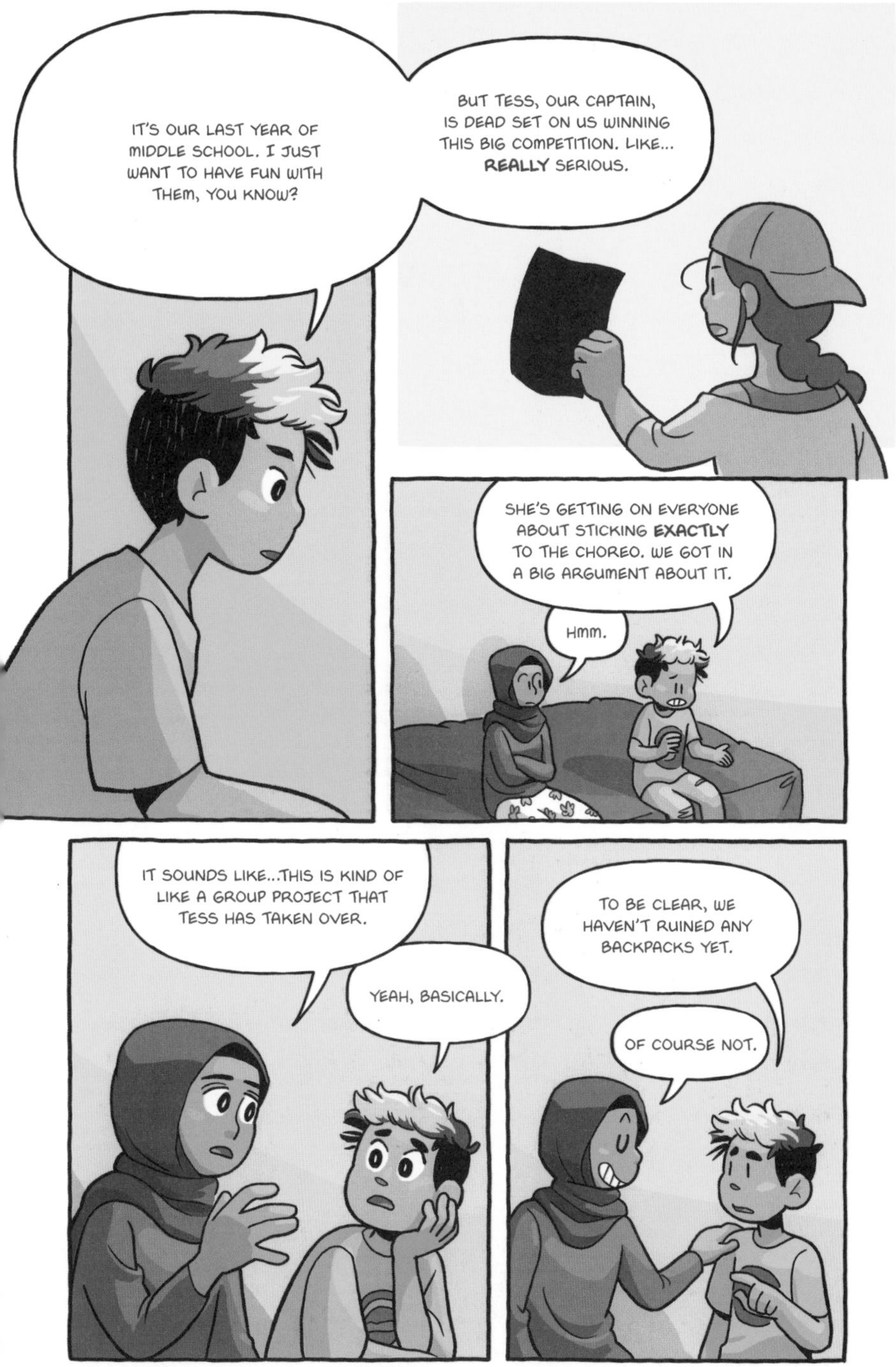
IT'S OUR LAST YEAR OF MIDDLE SCHOOL. I JUST WANT TO HAVE FUN WITH THEM, YOU KNOW?
BUT TESS, OUR CAPTAIN, IS DEAD SET ON US WINNING THIS BIG COMPETITION. LIKE... **REALLY** SERIOUS.
SHE'S GETTING ON EVERYONE ABOUT STICKING **EXACTLY** TO THE CHOREO. WE GOT IN A BIG ARGUMENT ABOUT IT.
HMM.
IT SOUNDS LIKE...THIS IS KIND OF LIKE A GROUP PROJECT THAT TESS HAS TAKEN OVER.
YEAH, BASICALLY.
TO BE CLEAR, WE HAVEN'T RUINED ANY BACKPACKS YET.
OF COURSE NOT.

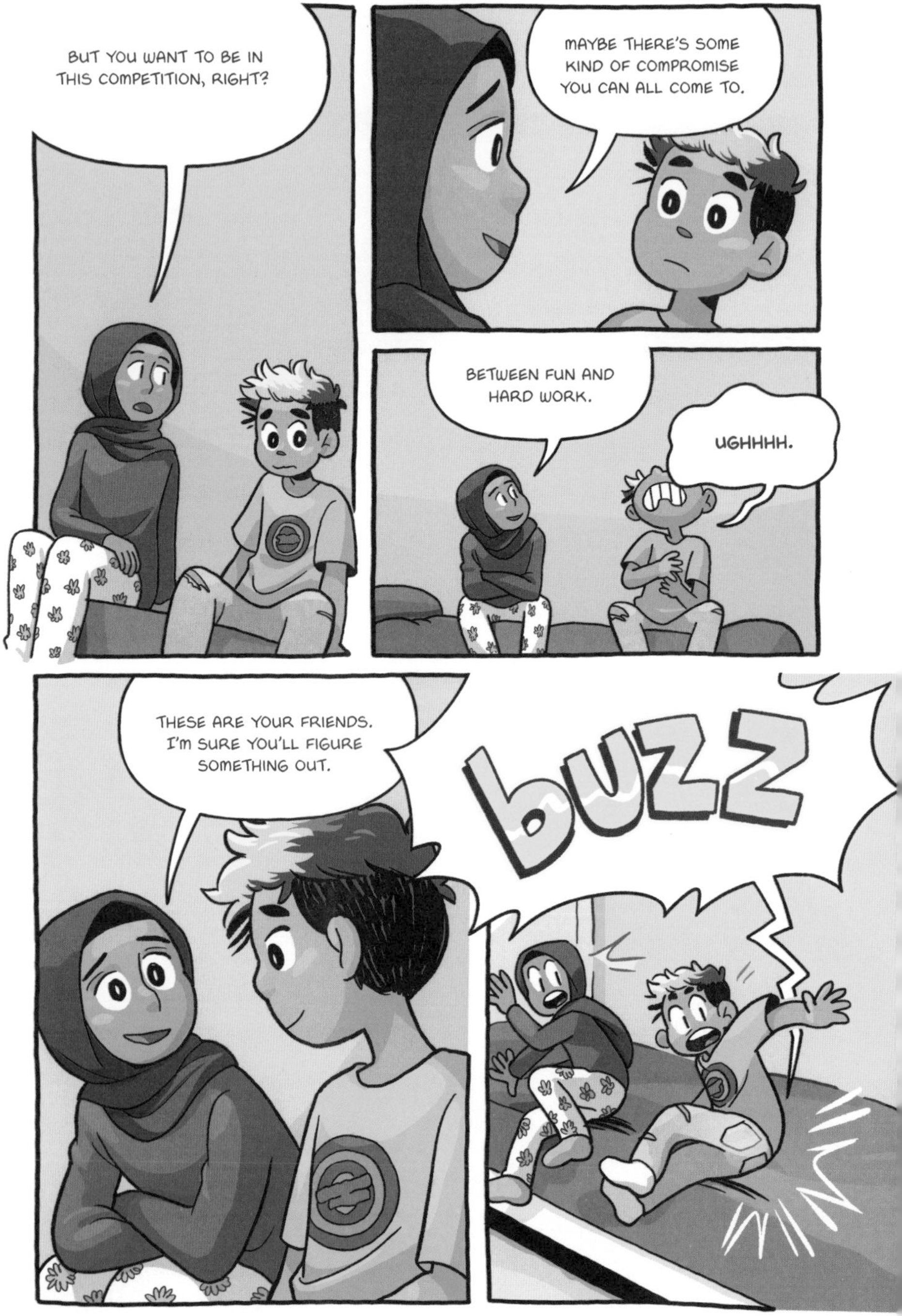

BUT YOU WANT TO BE IN THIS COMPETITION, RIGHT?
MAYBE THERE'S SOME KIND OF COMPROMISE YOU CAN ALL COME TO.
BETWEEN FUN AND HARD WORK.
UGHHHH.
THESE ARE YOUR FRIENDS. I'M SURE YOU'LL FIGURE SOMETHING OUT.
BUZZ

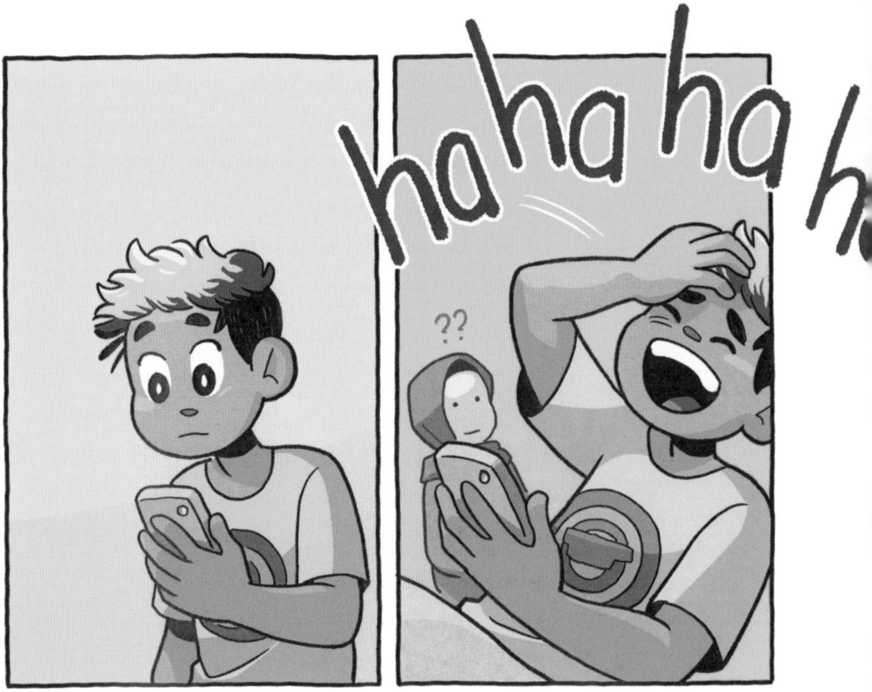
hahahaha h
??

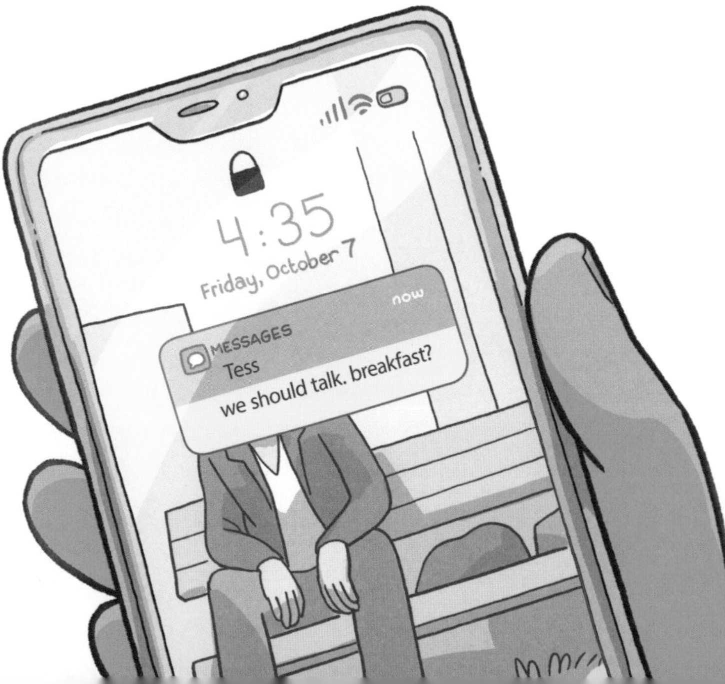
4:35
Friday, October 7
now
MESSAGES
Tess
we should talk. breakfast?

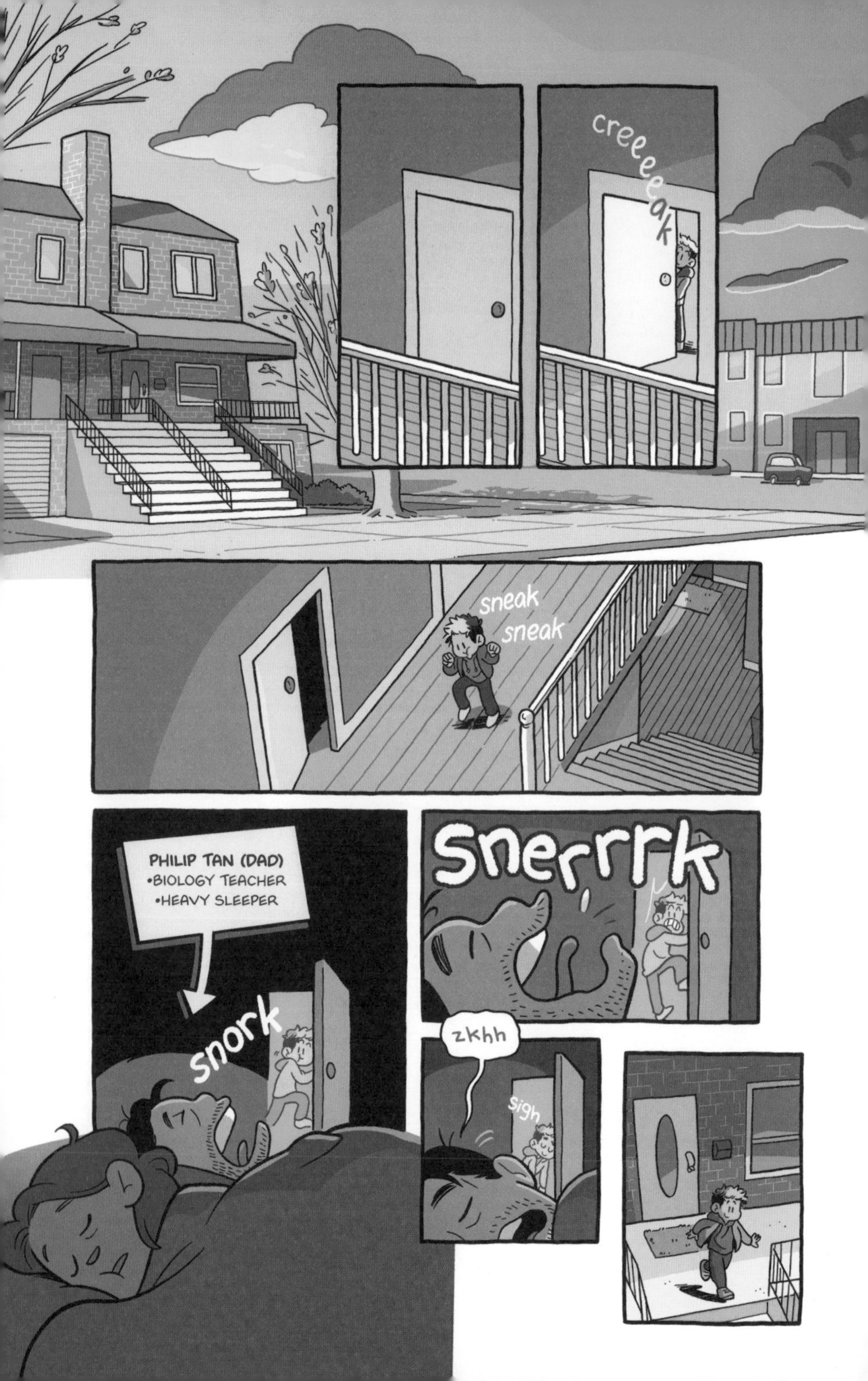
creeeeak
sneak
sneak
PHILIP TAN (DAD)
•BIOLOGY TEACHER
•HEAVY SLEEPER
snork
Snerrrk
zkhh
sigh

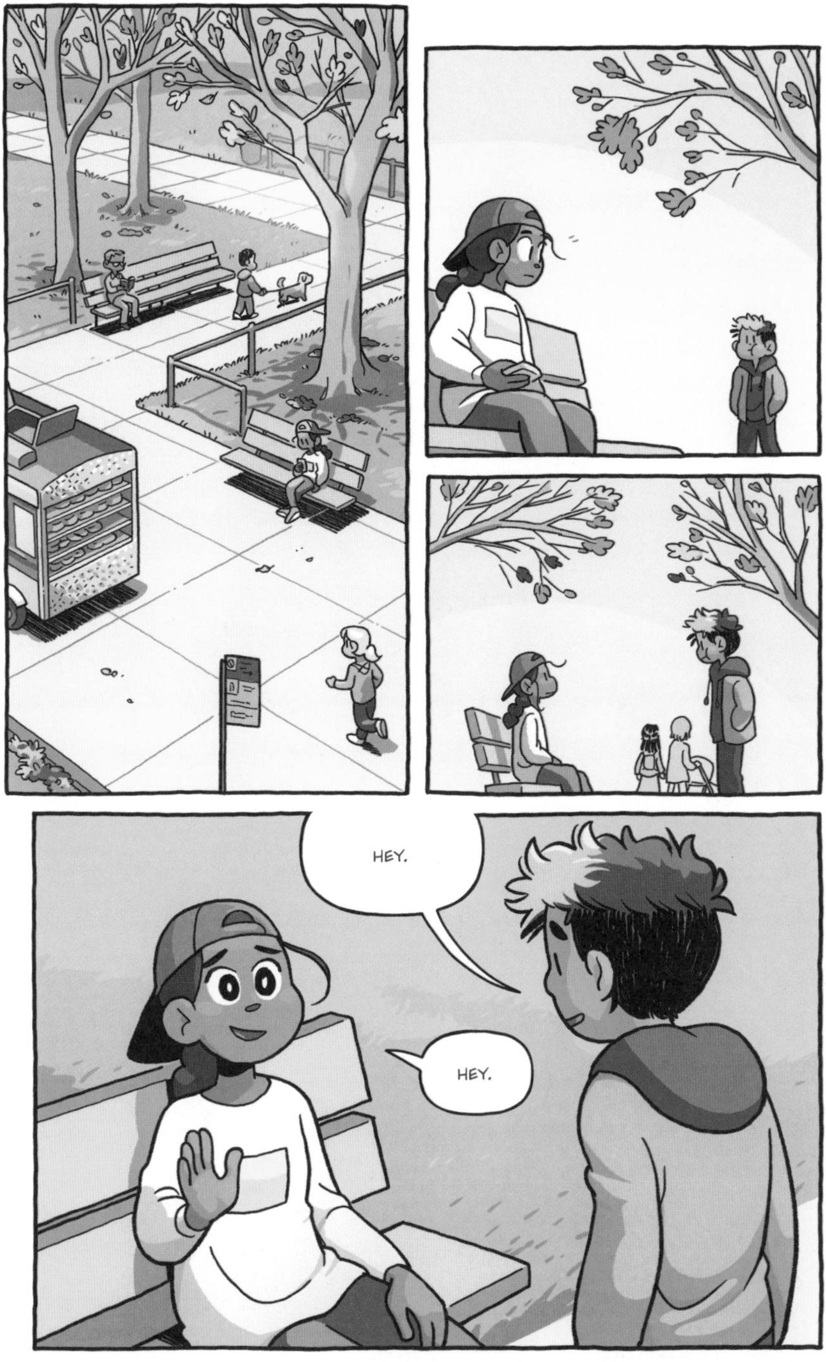
HEY.
HEY.

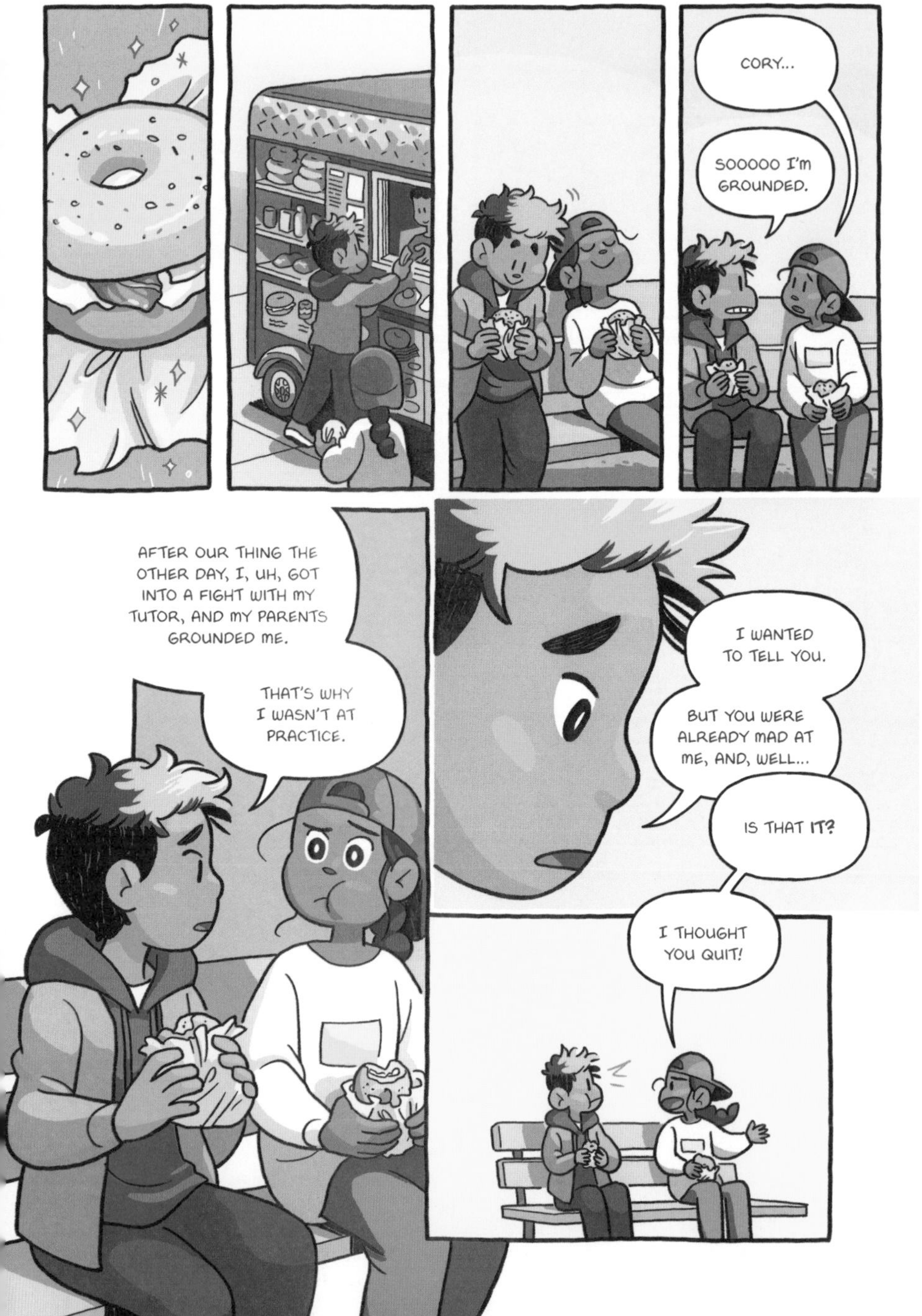
CORY...
SOOOOO I'M GROUNDED.
AFTER OUR THING THE OTHER DAY, I, UH, GOT INTO A FIGHT WITH MY TUTOR, AND MY PARENTS GROUNDED ME.
THAT'S WHY I WASN'T AT PRACTICE.
I WANTED TO TELL YOU.
BUT YOU WERE ALREADY MAD AT ME, AND, WELL...
IS THAT IT?
I THOUGHT YOU QUIT!

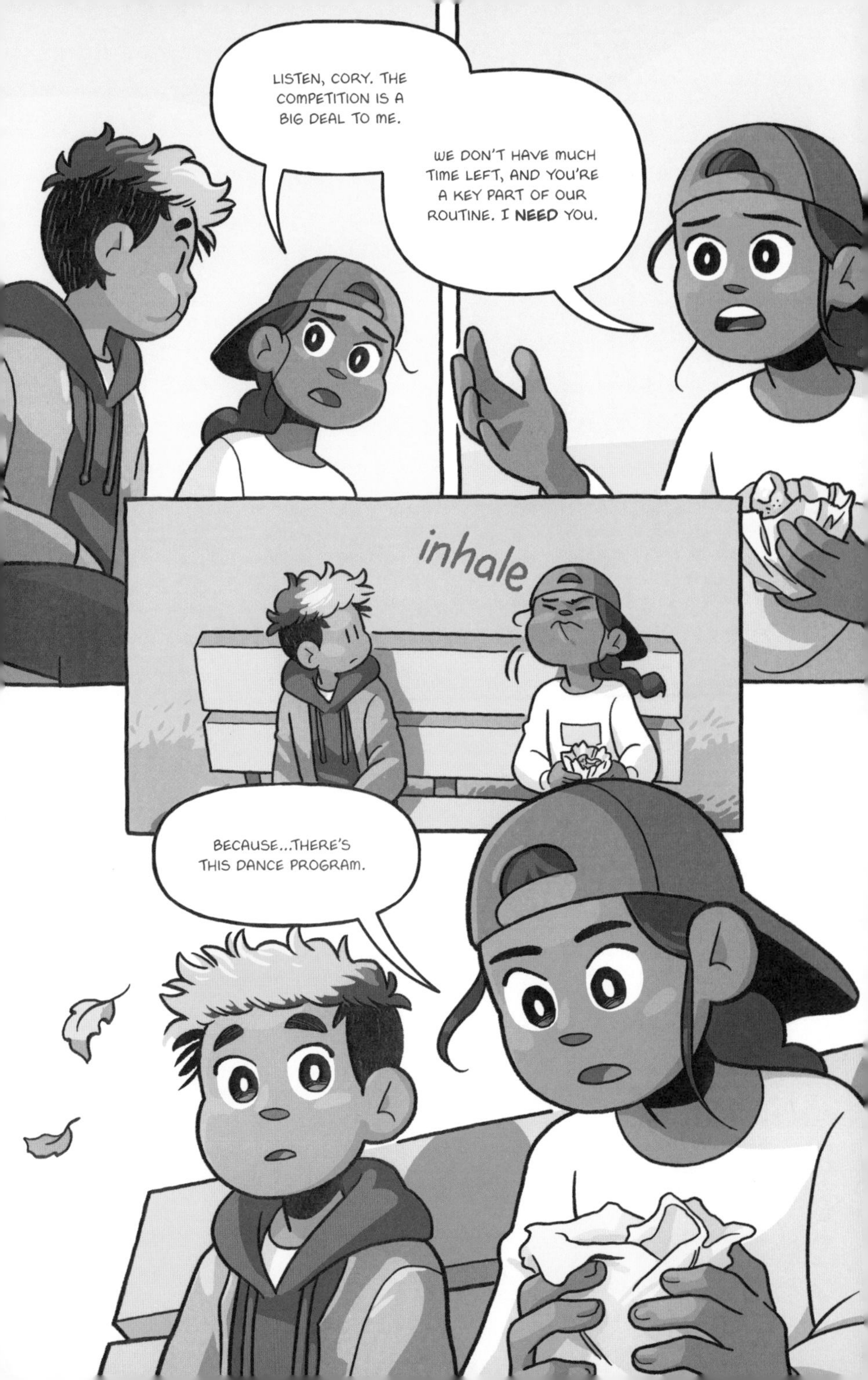
LISTEN, CORY. THE COMPETITION IS A BIG DEAL TO ME.
WE DON'T HAVE MUCH TIME LEFT, AND YOU'RE A KEY PART OF OUR ROUTINE. I **NEED** YOU.
inhale
BECAUSE...THERE'S THIS DANCE PROGRAM.

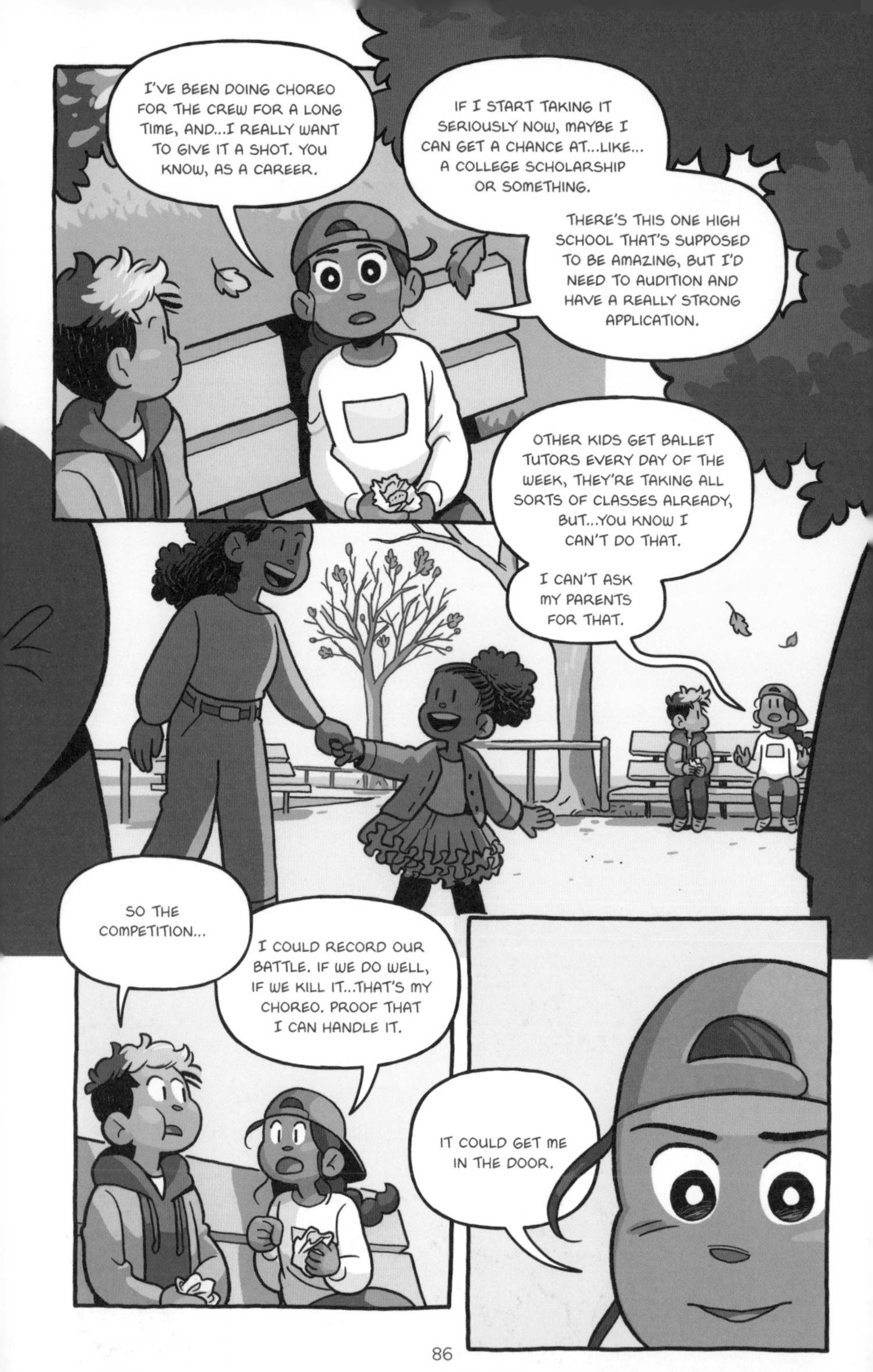
I'VE BEEN DOING CHOREO FOR THE CREW FOR A LONG TIME, AND...I REALLY WANT TO GIVE IT A SHOT. YOU KNOW, AS A CAREER.
IF I START TAKING IT SERIOUSLY NOW, MAYBE I CAN GET A CHANCE AT...LIKE... A COLLEGE SCHOLARSHIP OR SOMETHING.
THERE'S THIS ONE HIGH SCHOOL THAT'S SUPPOSED TO BE AMAZING, BUT I'D NEED TO AUDITION AND HAVE A REALLY STRONG APPLICATION.
OTHER KIDS GET BALLET TUTORS EVERY DAY OF THE WEEK, THEY'RE TAKING ALL SORTS OF CLASSES ALREADY, BUT...YOU KNOW I CAN'T DO THAT.
I CAN'T ASK MY PARENTS FOR THAT.
SO THE COMPETITION...
I COULD RECORD OUR BATTLE. IF WE DO WELL, IF WE KILL IT...THAT'S MY CHOREO. PROOF THAT I CAN HANDLE IT.
IT COULD GET ME IN THE DOOR.

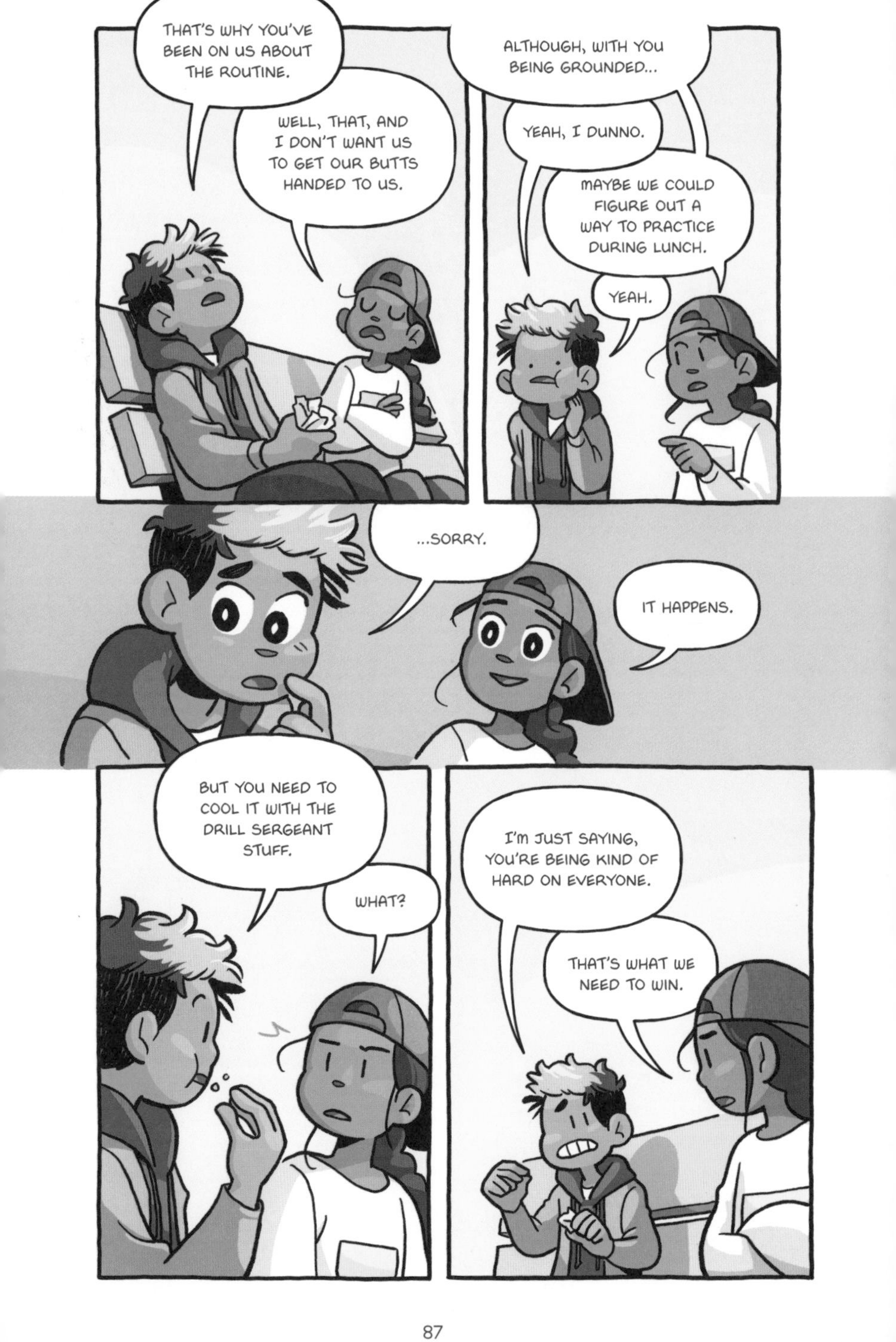
THAT'S WHY YOU'VE BEEN ON US ABOUT THE ROUTINE.
WELL, THAT, AND I DON'T WANT US TO GET OUR BUTTS HANDED TO US.
ALTHOUGH, WITH YOU BEING GROUNDED...
YEAH, I DUNNO.
MAYBE WE COULD FIGURE OUT A WAY TO PRACTICE DURING LUNCH.
YEAH.
...SORRY.
IT HAPPENS.
BUT YOU NEED TO COOL IT WITH THE DRILL SERGEANT STUFF.
WHAT?
I'M JUST SAYING, YOU'RE BEING KIND OF HARD ON EVERYONE.
THAT'S WHAT WE NEED TO WIN.

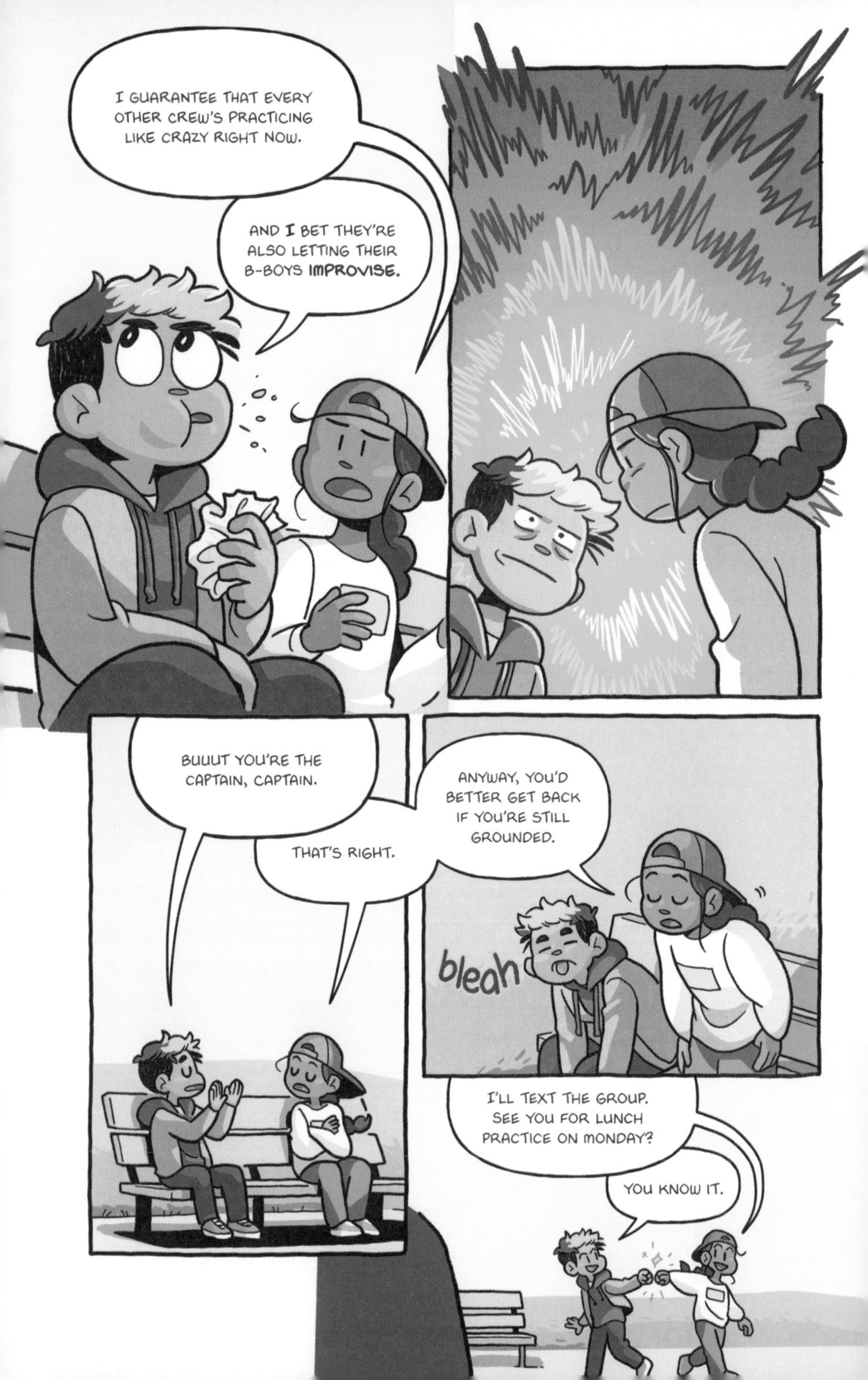
I GUARANTEE THAT EVERY OTHER CREW'S PRACTICING LIKE CRAZY RIGHT NOW.
AND I BET THEY'RE ALSO LETTING THEIR B-BOYS IMPROVISE.
BUUUT YOU'RE THE CAPTAIN, CAPTAIN.
THAT'S RIGHT.
ANYWAY, YOU'D BETTER GET BACK IF YOU'RE STILL GROUNDED.
bleah
I'LL TEXT THE GROUP. SEE YOU FOR LUNCH PRACTICE ON MONDAY?
YOU KNOW IT.

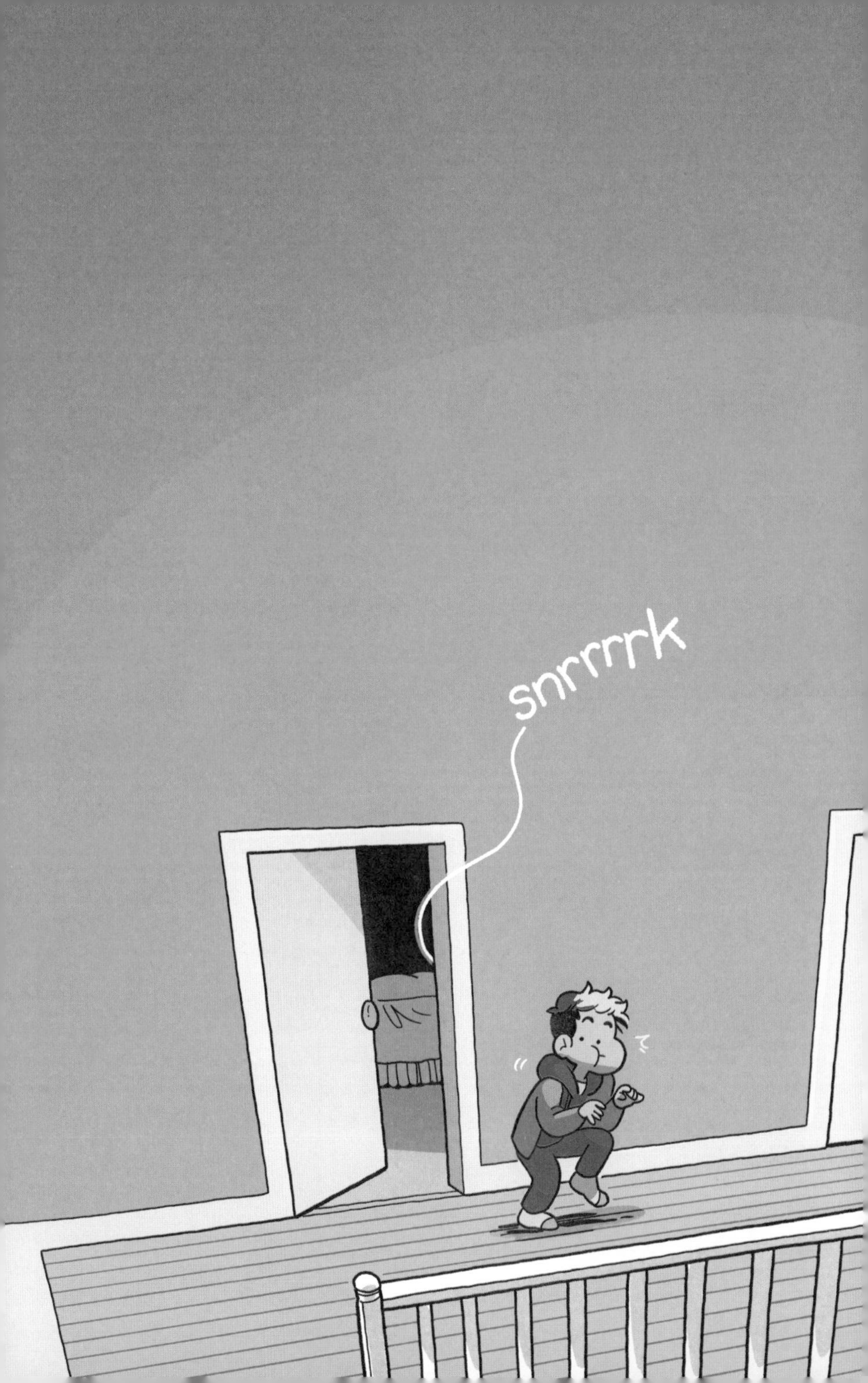
snrrrrk

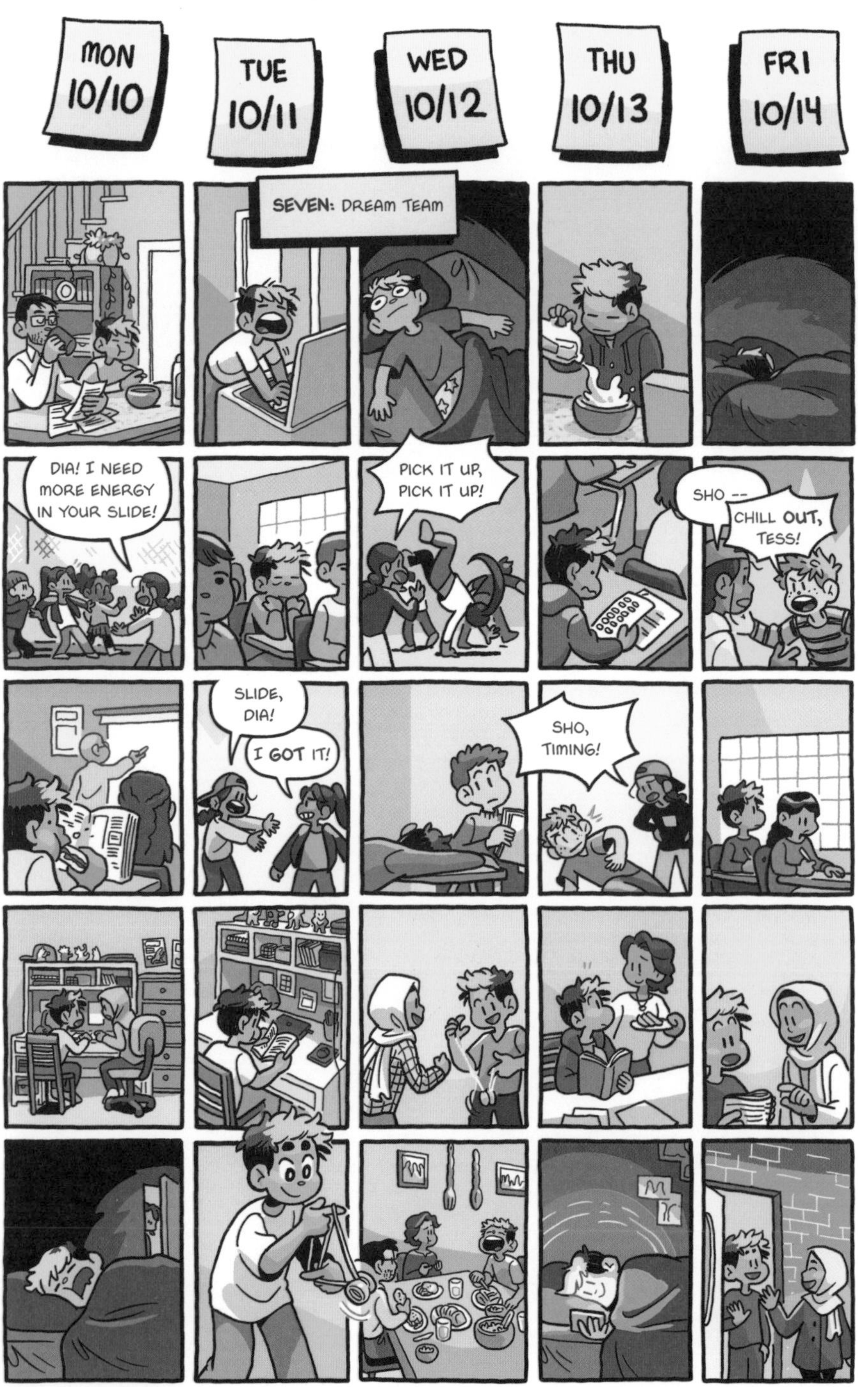
MON 10/10
TUE 10/11
WED 10/12
THU 10/13
FRI 10/14
SEVEN: DREAM TEAM
DIA! I NEED MORE ENERGY IN YOUR SLIDE!
PICK IT UP, PICK IT UP!
SHO --
CHILL OUT, TESS!
SLIDE, DIA!
I GOT IT!
SHO, TIMING!

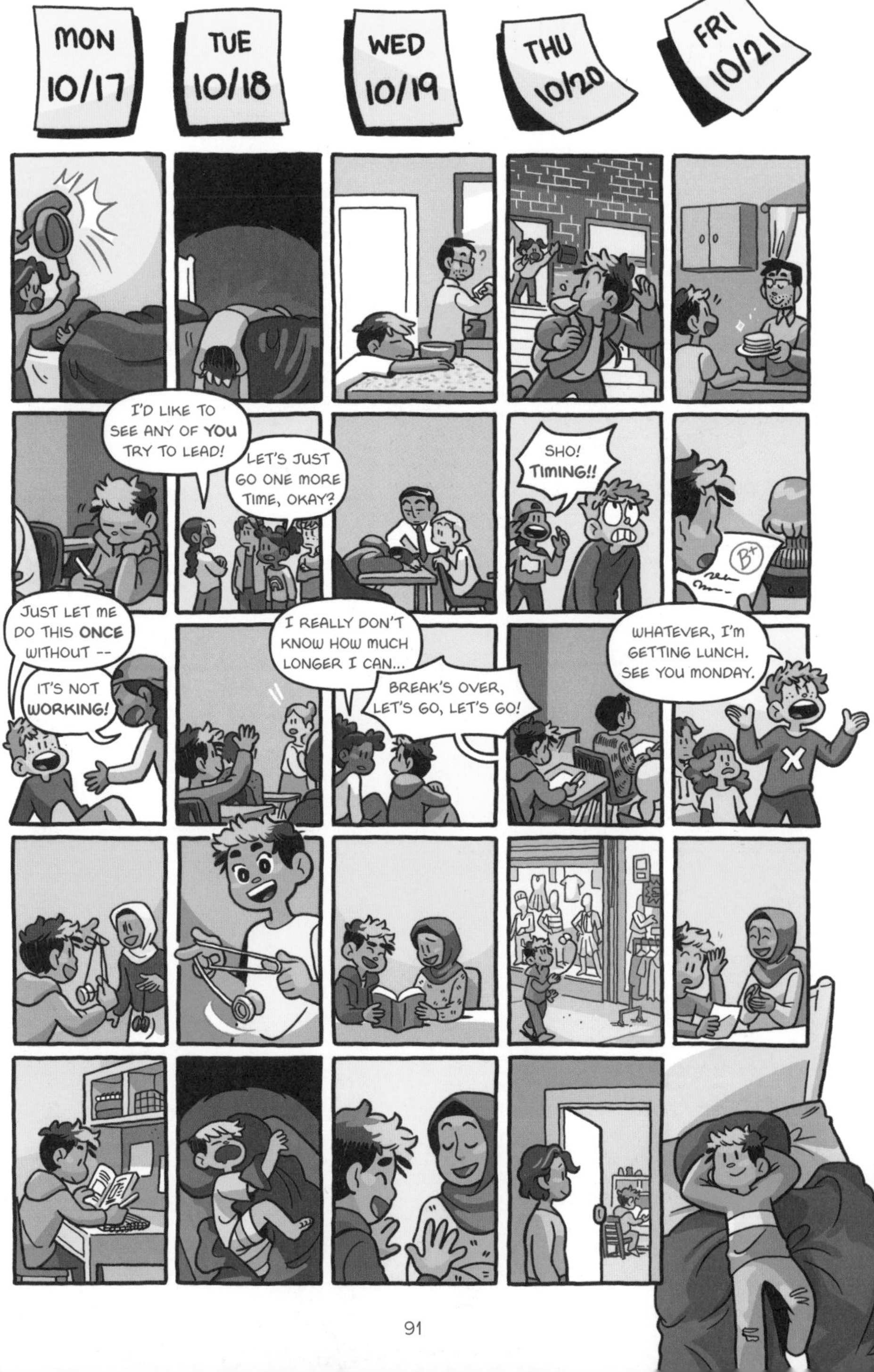

MON 10/17
TUE 10/18
WED 10/19
THU 10/20
FRI 10/21
I'D LIKE TO SEE ANY OF YOU TRY TO LEAD!
LET'S JUST GO ONE MORE TIME, OKAY?
SHO! TIMING!!
JUST LET ME DO THIS ONCE WITHOUT --
IT'S NOT WORKING!
I REALLY DON'T KNOW HOW MUCH LONGER I CAN...
BREAK'S OVER, LET'S GO, LET'S GO!
WHATEVER, I'M GETTING LUNCH. SEE YOU MONDAY.

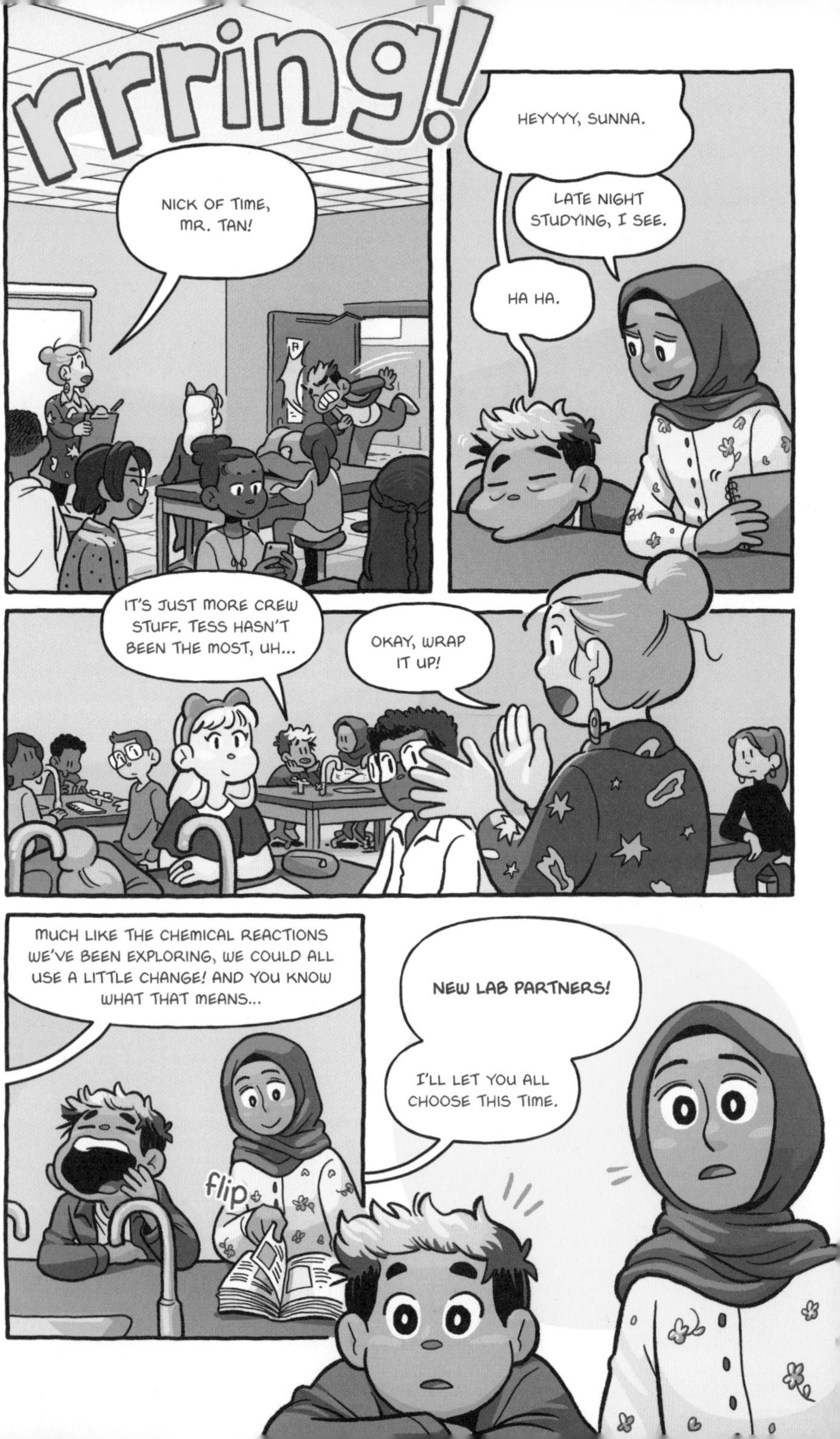
rrring!
NICK OF TIME, MR. TAN!
HEYYYY, SUNNA.
LATE NIGHT STUDYING, I SEE.
HA HA.
IT'S JUST MORE CREW STUFF. TESS HASN'T BEEN THE MOST, UH...
OKAY, WRAP IT UP!
MUCH LIKE THE CHEMICAL REACTIONS WE'VE BEEN EXPLORING, WE COULD ALL USE A LITTLE CHANGE! AND YOU KNOW WHAT THAT MEANS...
NEW LAB PARTNERS!
I'LL LET YOU ALL CHOOSE THIS TIME.
flip

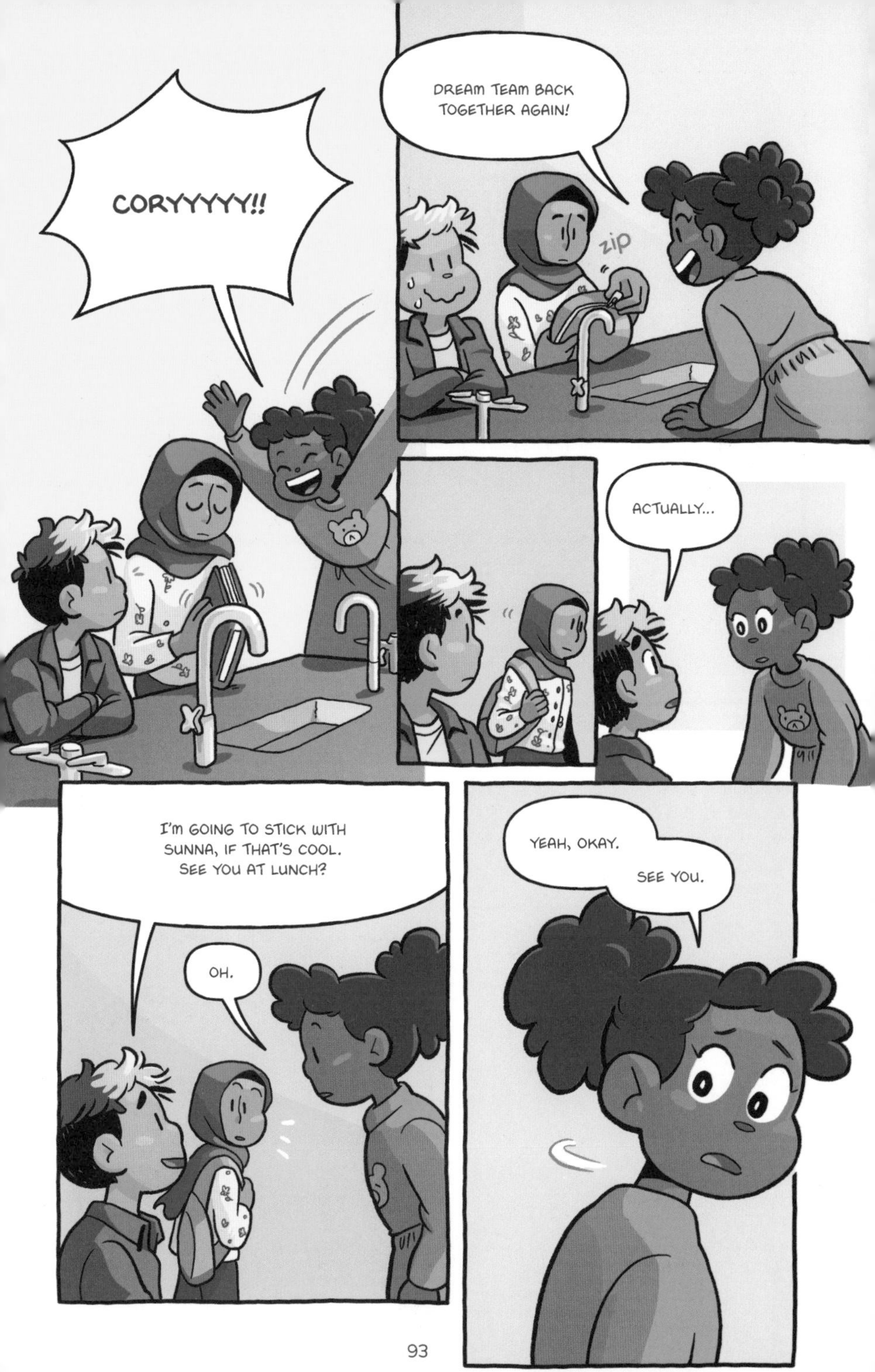
CORYYYYY!!
DREAM TEAM BACK TOGETHER AGAIN!
ZIP
ACTUALLY...
I'M GOING TO STICK WITH SUNNA, IF THAT'S COOL. SEE YOU AT LUNCH?
OH.
YEAH, OKAY.
SEE YOU.

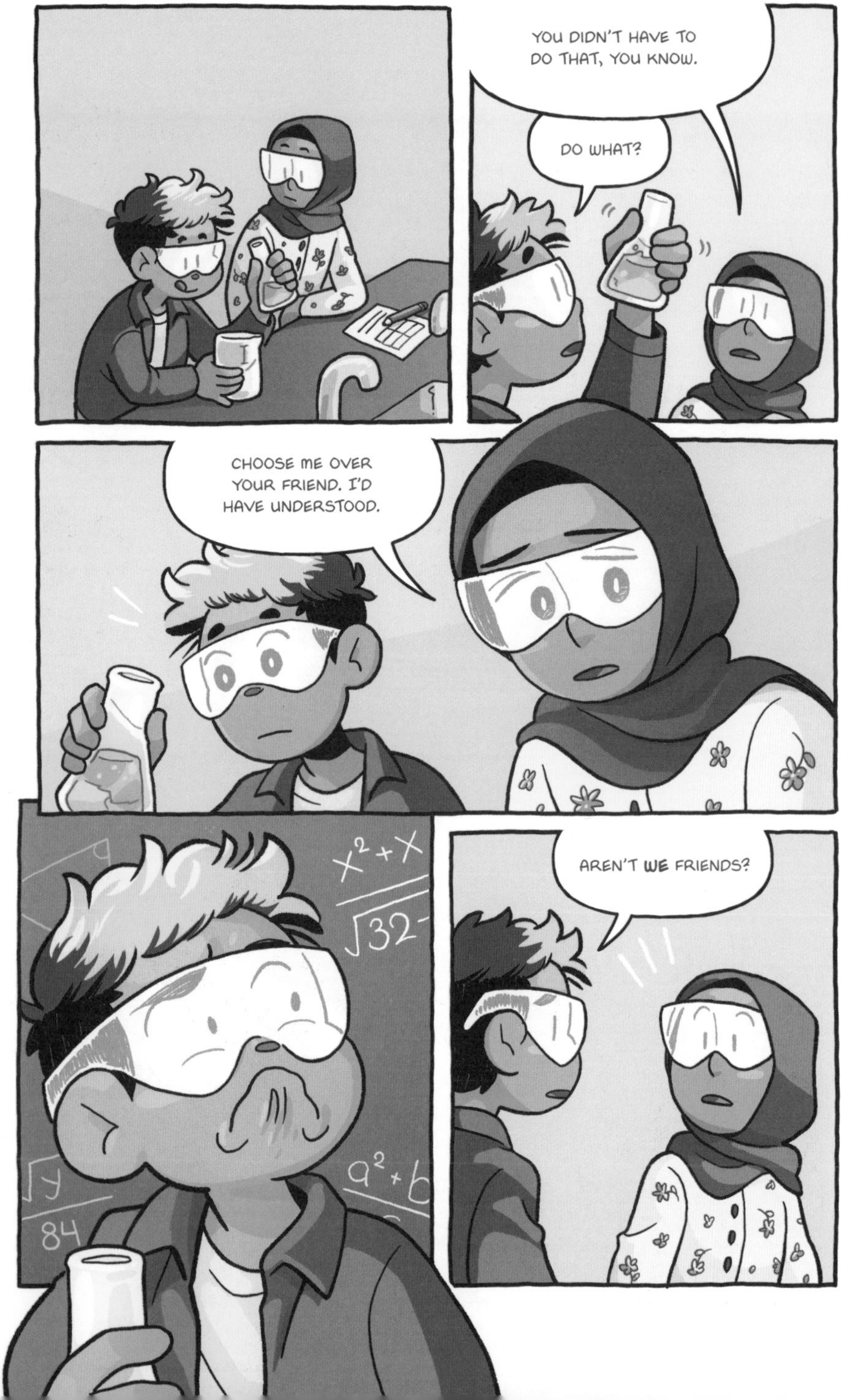
YOU DIDN'T HAVE TO DO THAT, YOU KNOW.
DO WHAT?
CHOOSE ME OVER YOUR FRIEND. I'D HAVE UNDERSTOOD.
x^2+x
$\sqrt{32}$
a^2+b
84
AREN'T **WE** FRIENDS?

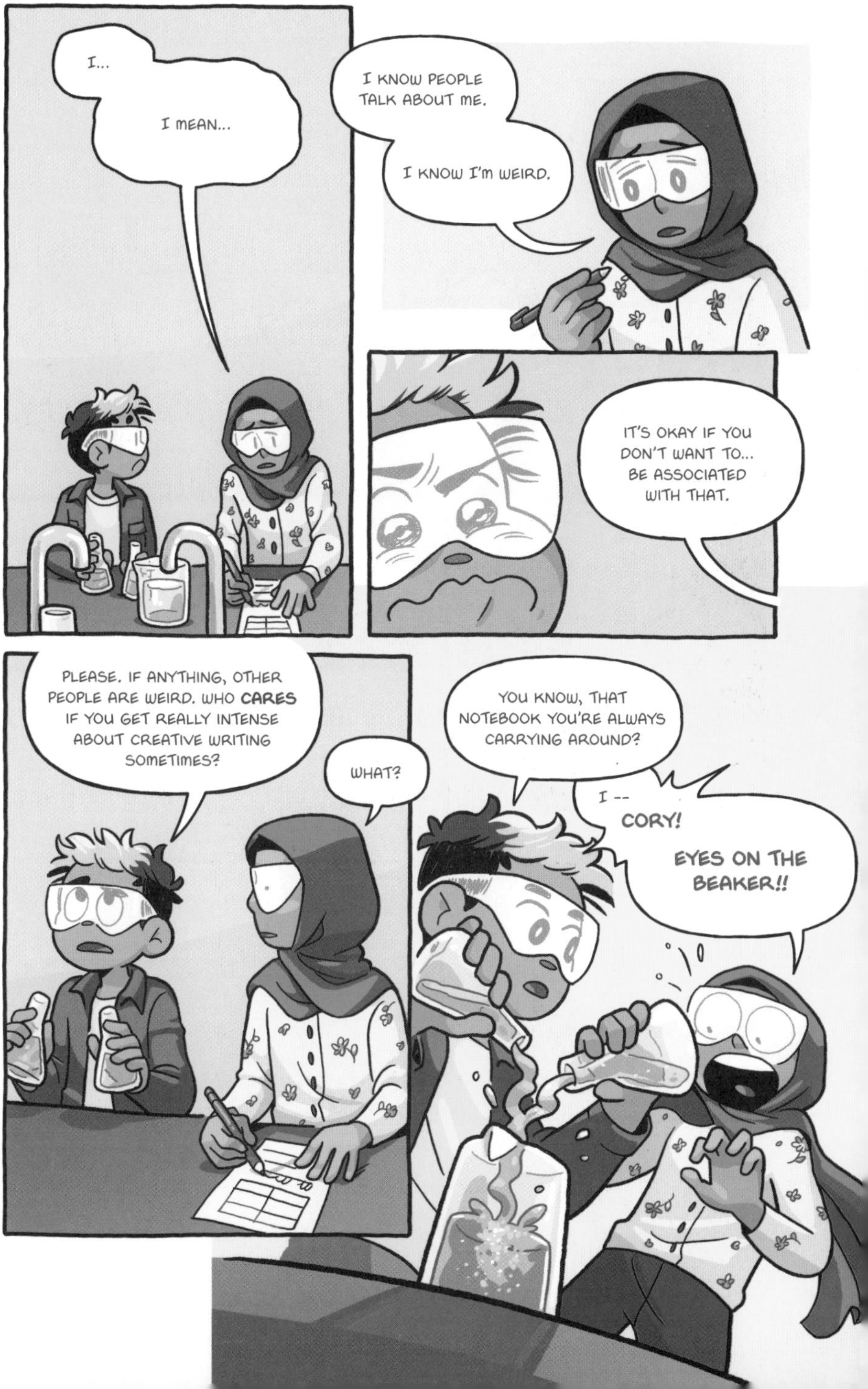
I...
I MEAN...
I KNOW PEOPLE TALK ABOUT ME.
I KNOW I'M WEIRD.
IT'S OKAY IF YOU DON'T WANT TO... BE ASSOCIATED WITH THAT.
PLEASE. IF ANYTHING, OTHER PEOPLE ARE WEIRD. WHO **CARES** IF YOU GET REALLY INTENSE ABOUT CREATIVE WRITING SOMETIMES?
WHAT?
YOU KNOW, THAT NOTEBOOK YOU'RE ALWAYS CARRYING AROUND?
I --
CORY!
EYES ON THE BEAKER!!

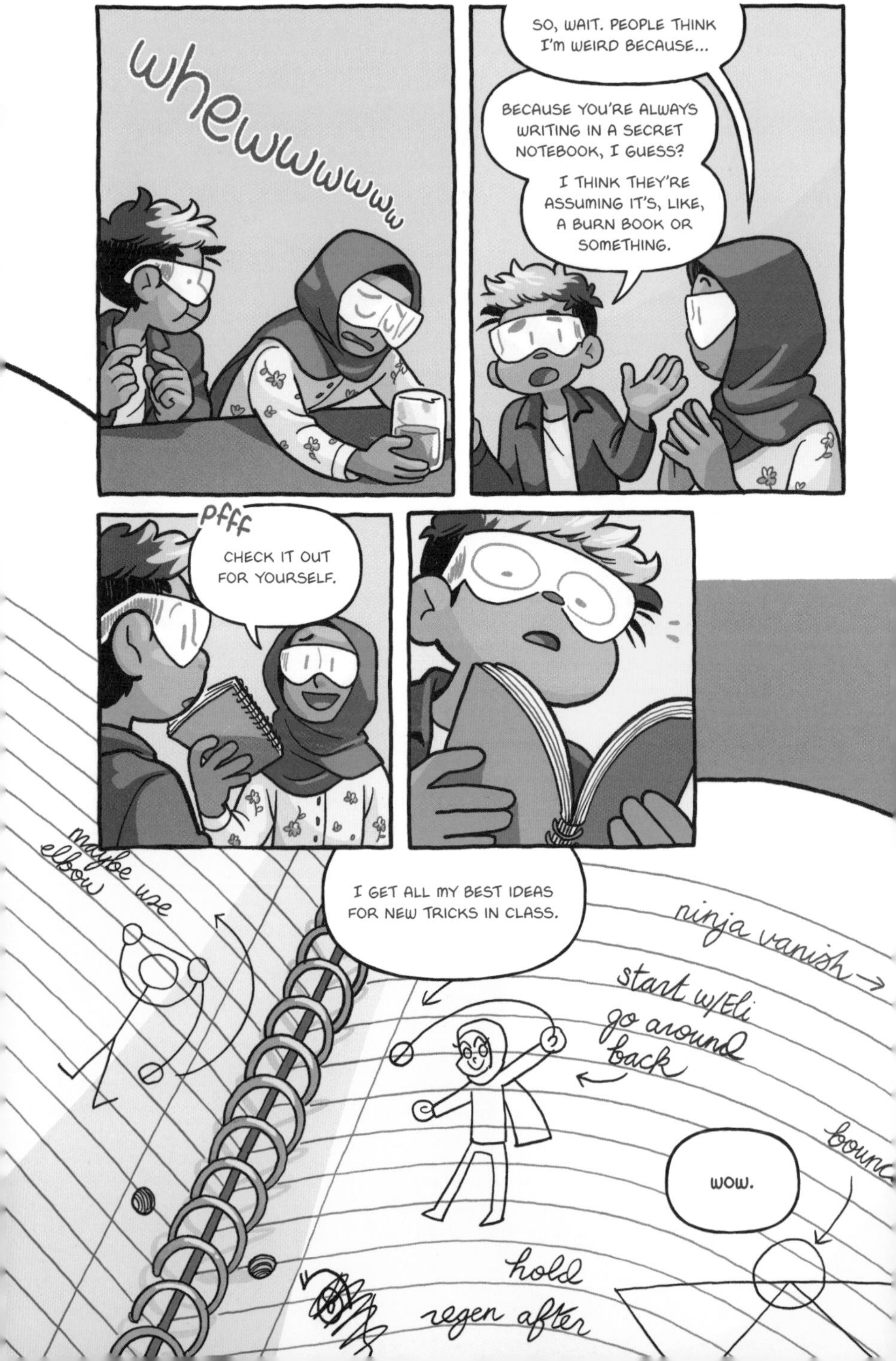
whewwwwwww
SO, WAIT. PEOPLE THINK I'M WEIRD BECAUSE...
BECAUSE YOU'RE ALWAYS WRITING IN A SECRET NOTEBOOK, I GUESS?
I THINK THEY'RE ASSUMING IT'S, LIKE, A BURN BOOK OR SOMETHING.
pfff
CHECK IT OUT FOR YOURSELF.
I GET ALL MY BEST IDEAS FOR NEW TRICKS IN CLASS.
maybe use elbow
ninja vanish
start w/Eli
go around back
WOW.
hold
regen after

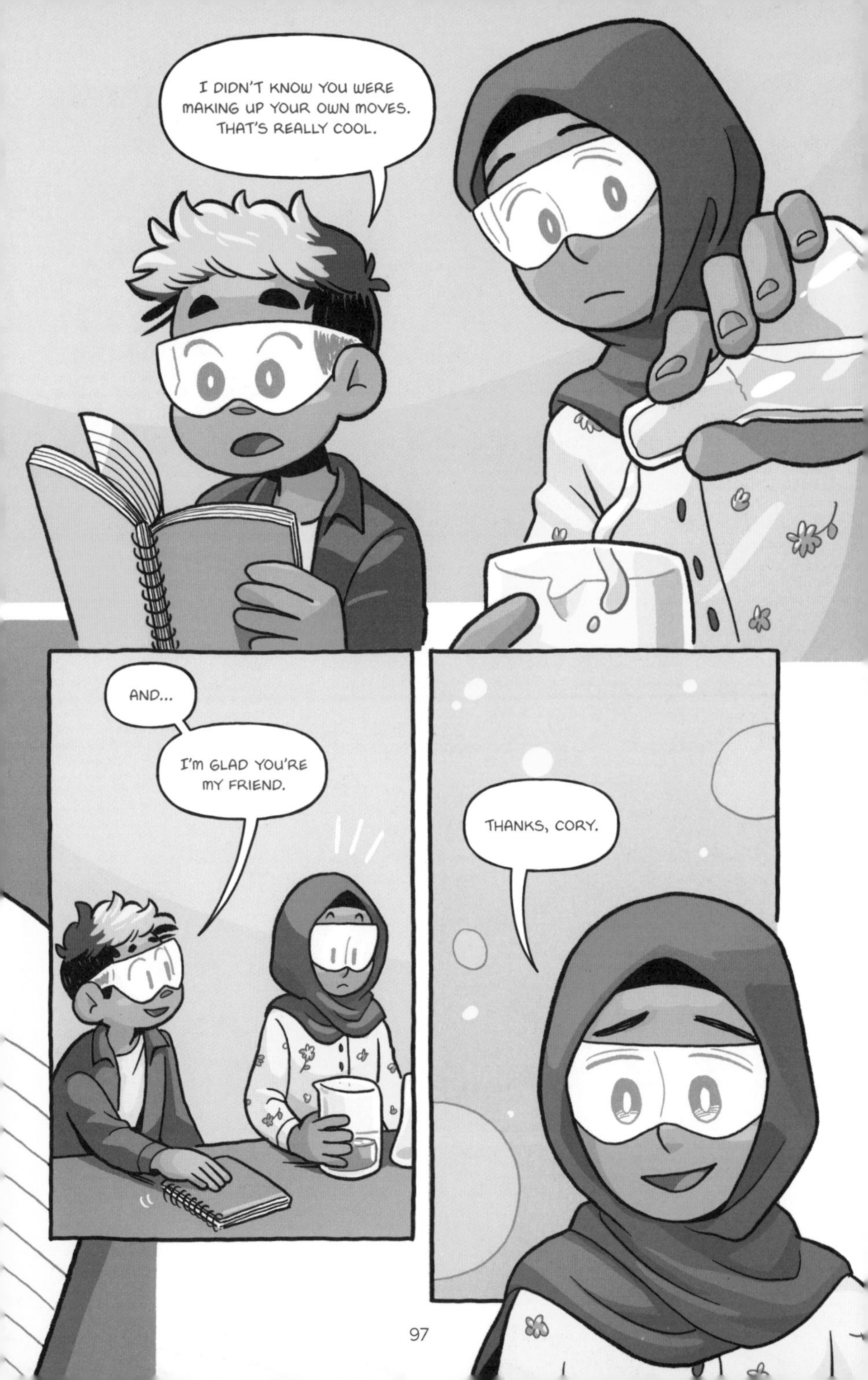
I DIDN'T KNOW YOU WERE MAKING UP YOUR OWN MOVES. THAT'S REALLY COOL.
AND...
I'M GLAD YOU'RE MY FRIEND.
THANKS, CORY.

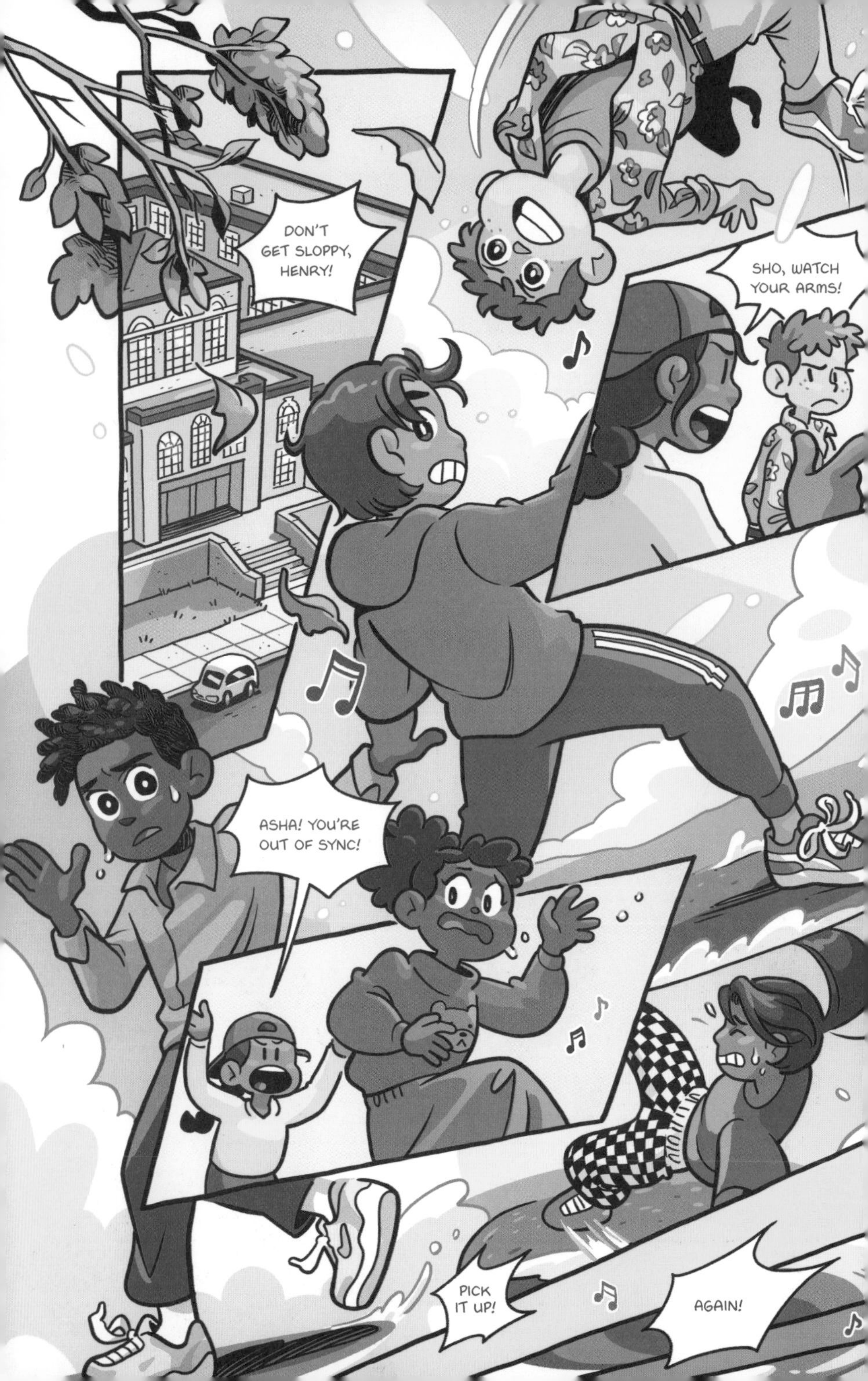

DON'T GET SLOPPY, HENRY!
SHO, WATCH YOUR ARMS!
ASHA! YOU'RE OUT OF SYNC!
PICK IT UP!
AGAIN!

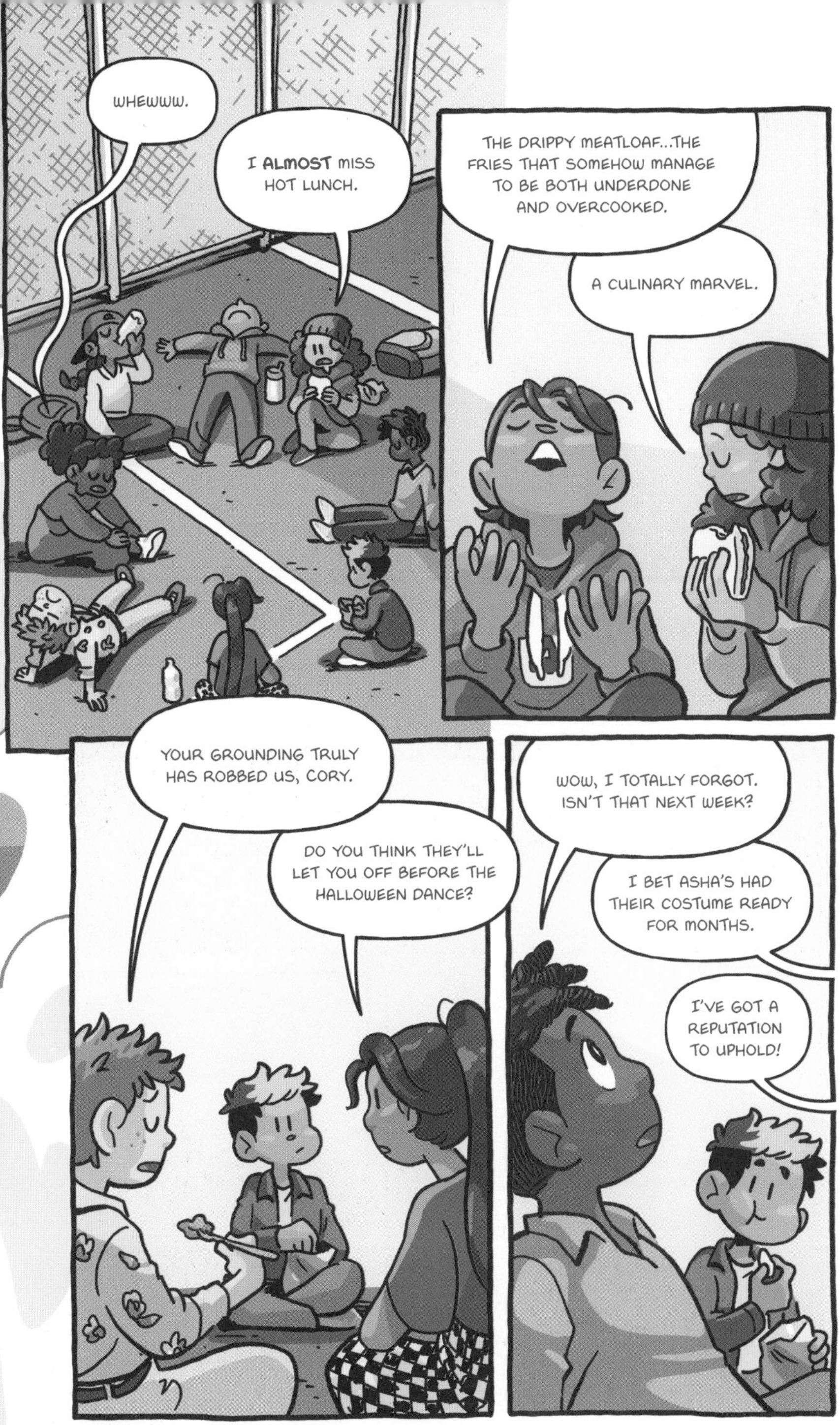
WHEWWW.
I ALMOST MISS HOT LUNCH.
THE DRIPPY MEATLOAF...THE FRIES THAT SOMEHOW MANAGE TO BE BOTH UNDERDONE AND OVERCOOKED.
A CULINARY MARVEL.
YOUR GROUNDING TRULY HAS ROBBED US, CORY.
DO YOU THINK THEY'LL LET YOU OFF BEFORE THE HALLOWEEN DANCE?
WOW, I TOTALLY FORGOT. ISN'T THAT NEXT WEEK?
I BET ASHA'S HAD THEIR COSTUME READY FOR MONTHS.
I'VE GOT A REPUTATION TO UPHOLD!

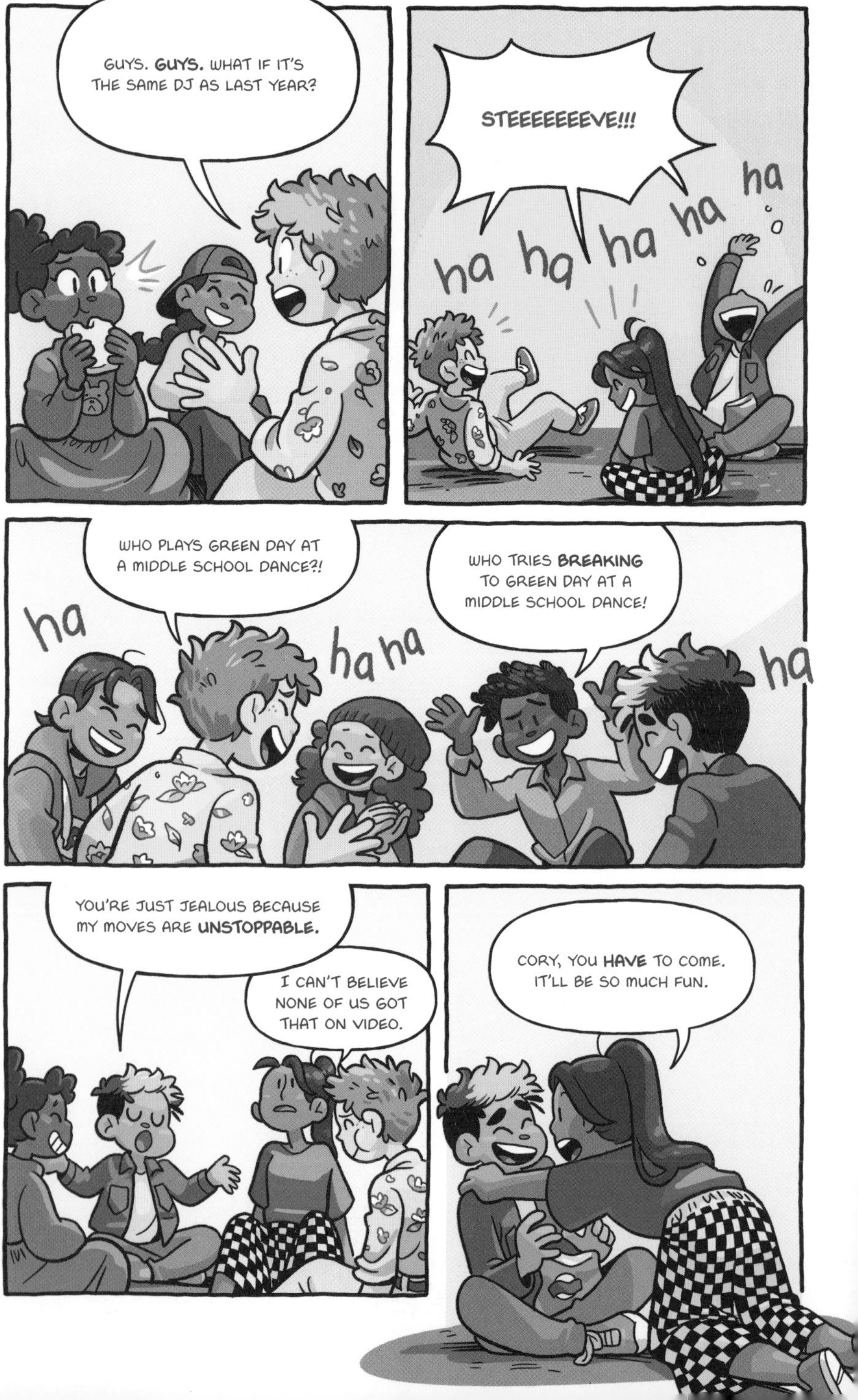
GUYS. **GUYS.** WHAT IF IT'S THE SAME DJ AS LAST YEAR?
STEEEEEEEVE!!!
ha ha ha ha ha
WHO PLAYS GREEN DAY AT A MIDDLE SCHOOL DANCE?!
ha
ha ha
WHO TRIES **BREAKING** TO GREEN DAY AT A MIDDLE SCHOOL DANCE!
ha
YOU'RE JUST JEALOUS BECAUSE MY MOVES ARE **UNSTOPPABLE.**
I CAN'T BELIEVE NONE OF US GOT THAT ON VIDEO.
CORY, YOU **HAVE** TO COME. IT'LL BE SO MUCH FUN.

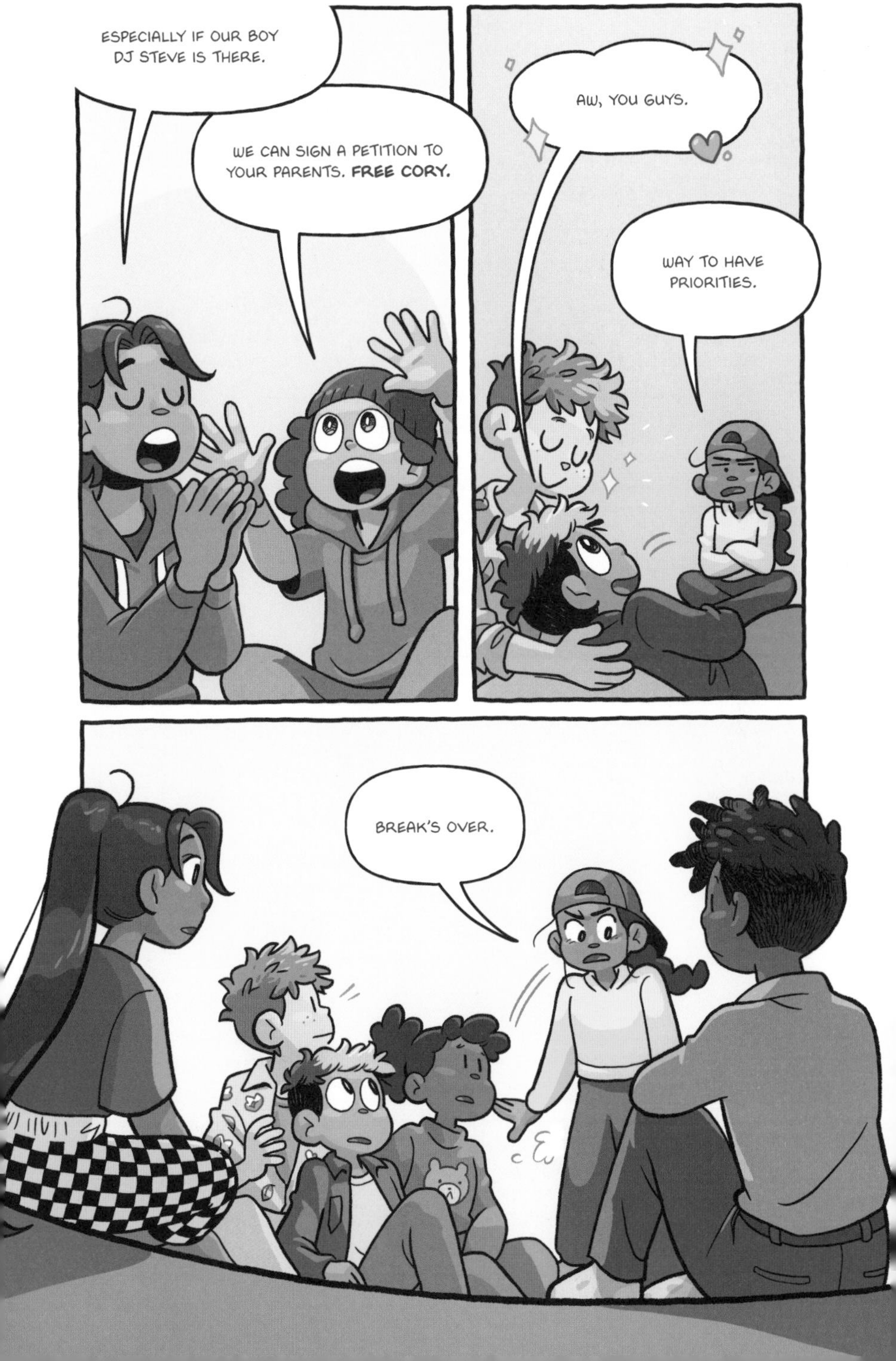
ESPECIALLY IF OUR BOY DJ STEVE IS THERE.
WE CAN SIGN A PETITION TO YOUR PARENTS. **FREE CORY.**
AW, YOU GUYS.
WAY TO HAVE PRIORITIES.
BREAK'S OVER.

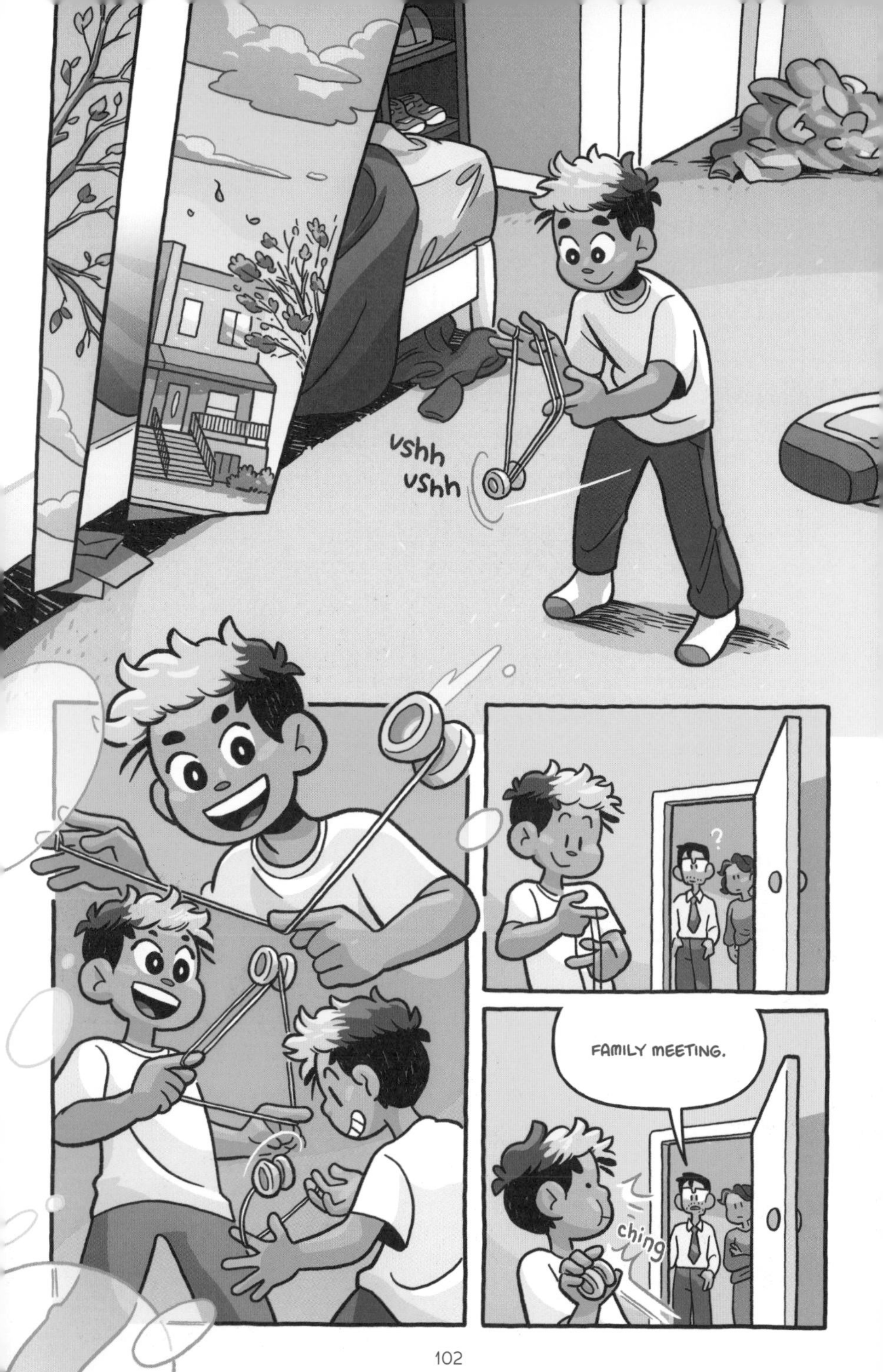

vshh
vshh
?
FAMILY MEETING.
ching

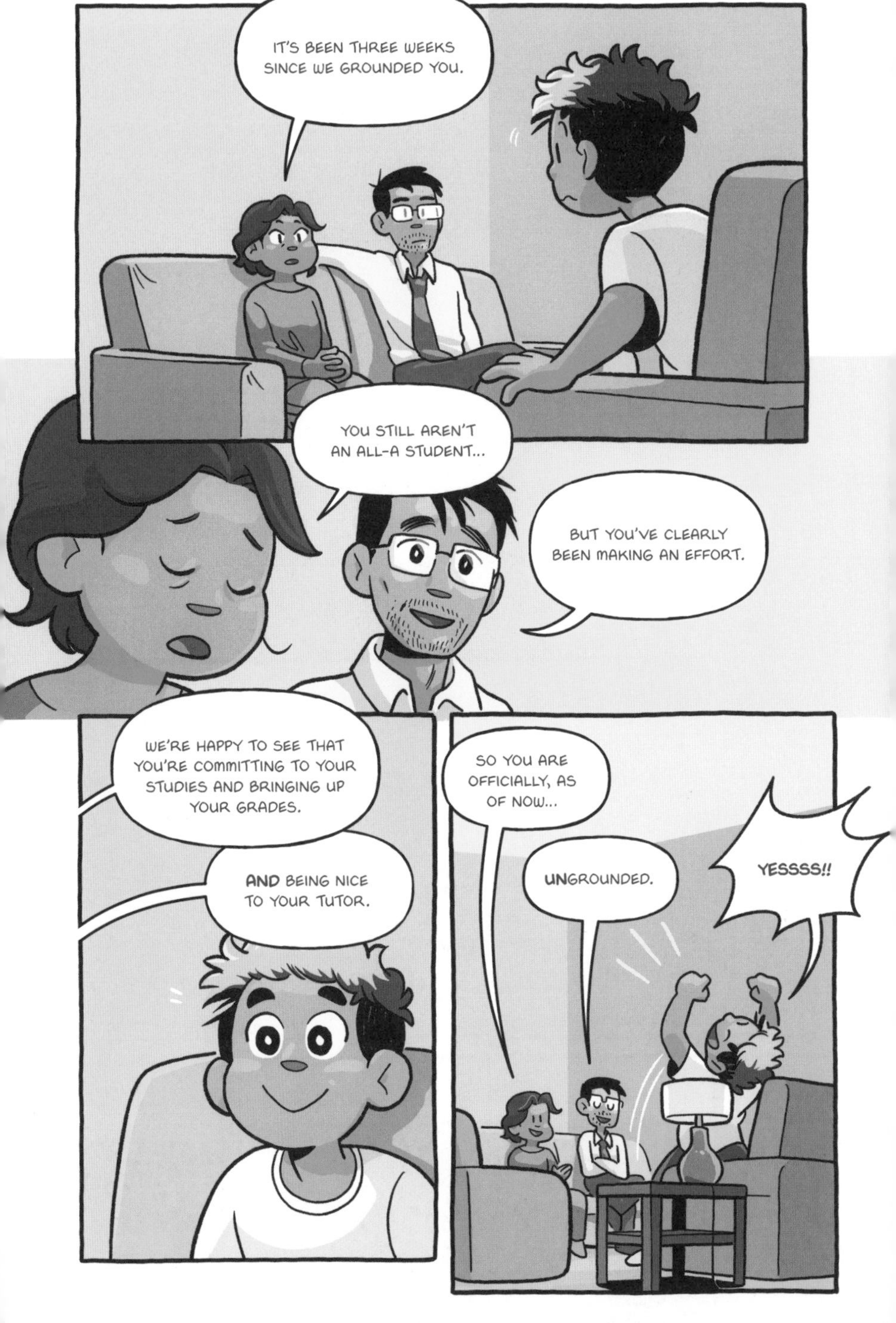
IT'S BEEN THREE WEEKS SINCE WE GROUNDED YOU.
YOU STILL AREN'T AN ALL-A STUDENT...
BUT YOU'VE CLEARLY BEEN MAKING AN EFFORT.
WE'RE HAPPY TO SEE THAT YOU'RE COMMITTING TO YOUR STUDIES AND BRINGING UP YOUR GRADES.
AND BEING NICE TO YOUR TUTOR.
SO YOU ARE OFFICIALLY, AS OF NOW...
UNGROUNDED.
YESSSS!!

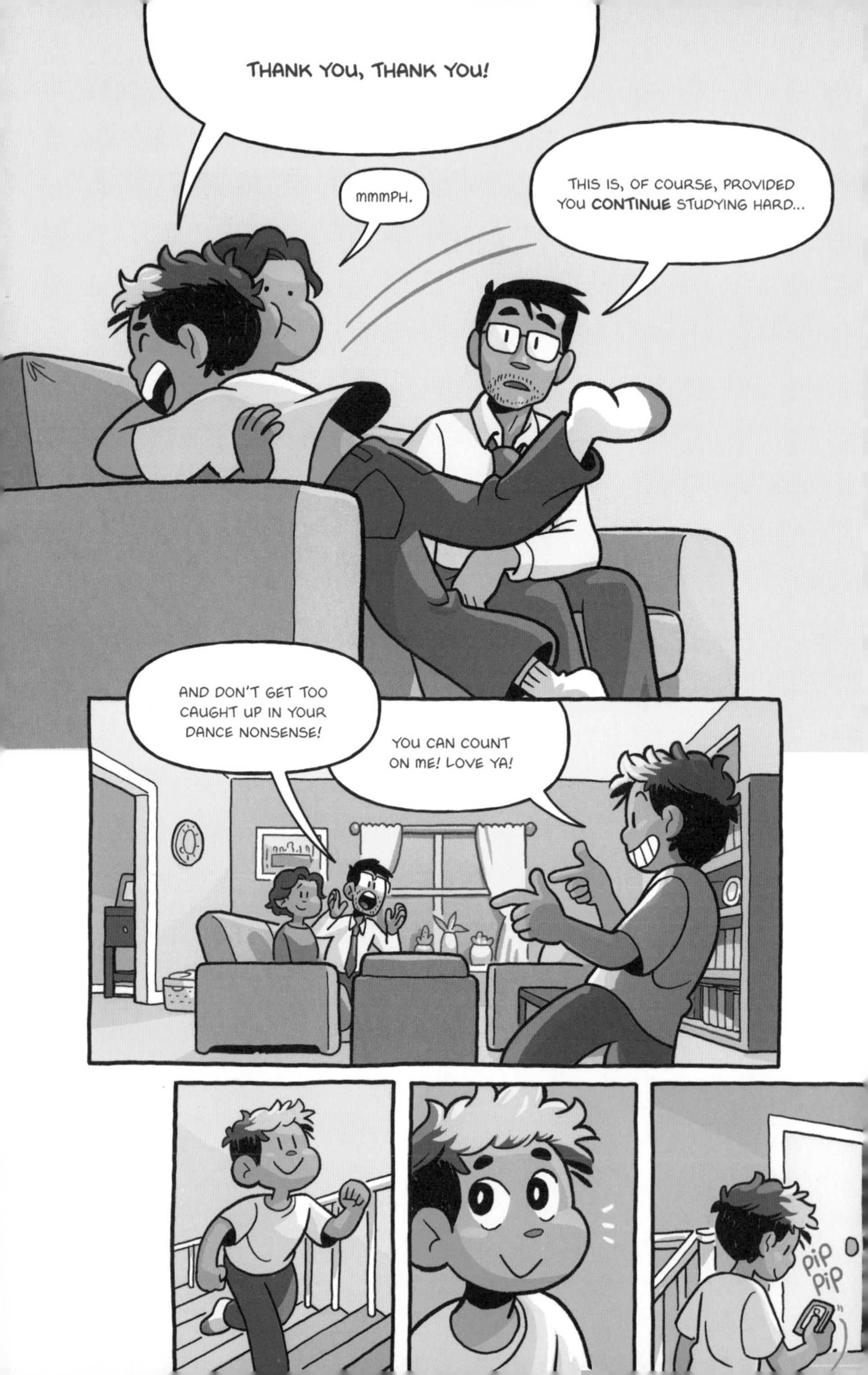
THANK YOU, THANK YOU!
mmmPH.
THIS IS, OF COURSE, PROVIDED YOU CONTINUE STUDYING HARD...
AND DON'T GET TOO CAUGHT UP IN YOUR DANCE NONSENSE!
YOU CAN COUNT ON ME! LOVE YA!
PIP PIP

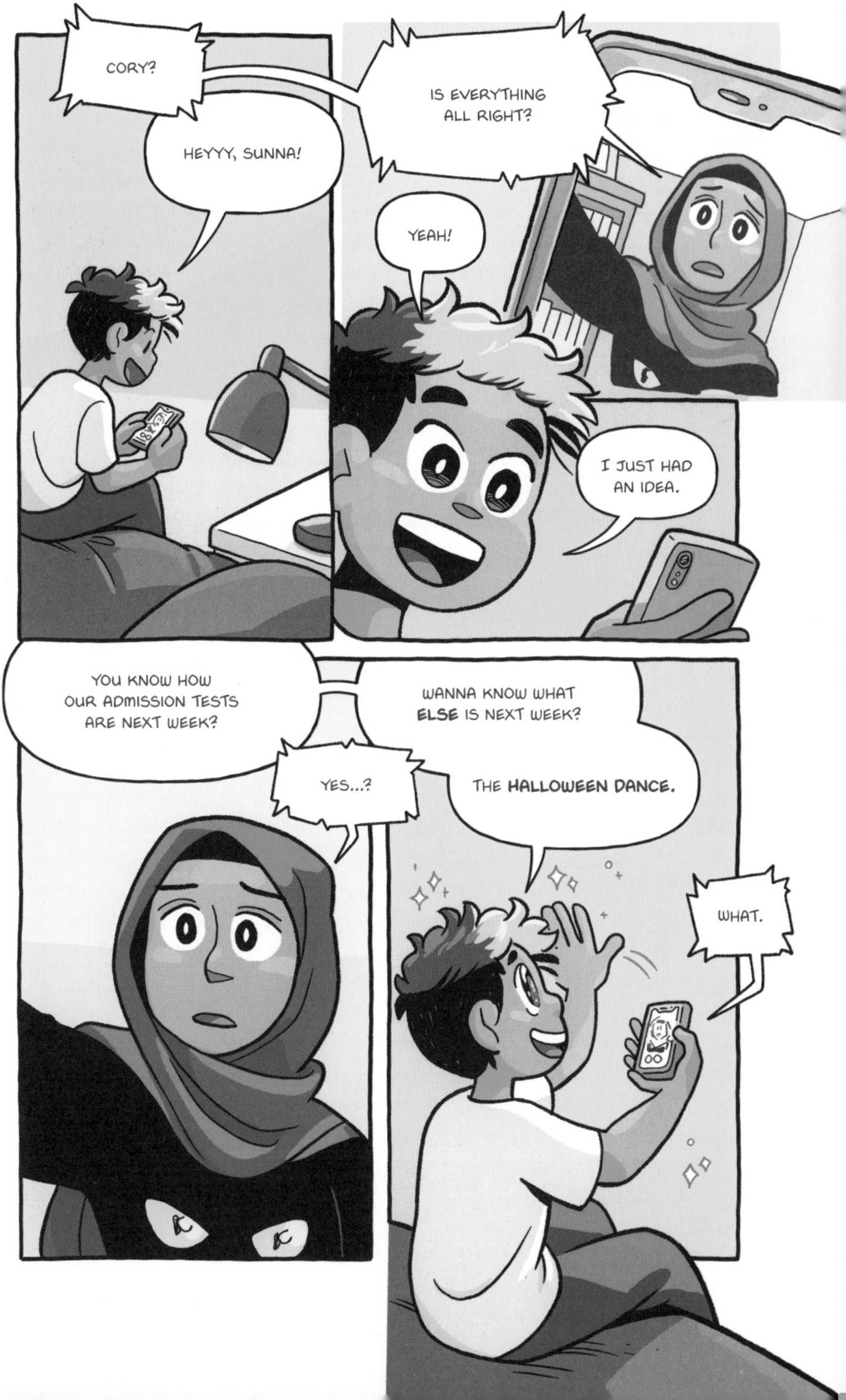
CORY?
HEYYY, SUNNA!
IS EVERYTHING ALL RIGHT?
YEAH!
I JUST HAD AN IDEA.
YOU KNOW HOW OUR ADMISSION TESTS ARE NEXT WEEK?
WANNA KNOW WHAT **ELSE** IS NEXT WEEK?
YES...?
THE **HALLOWEEN DANCE.**
WHAT.

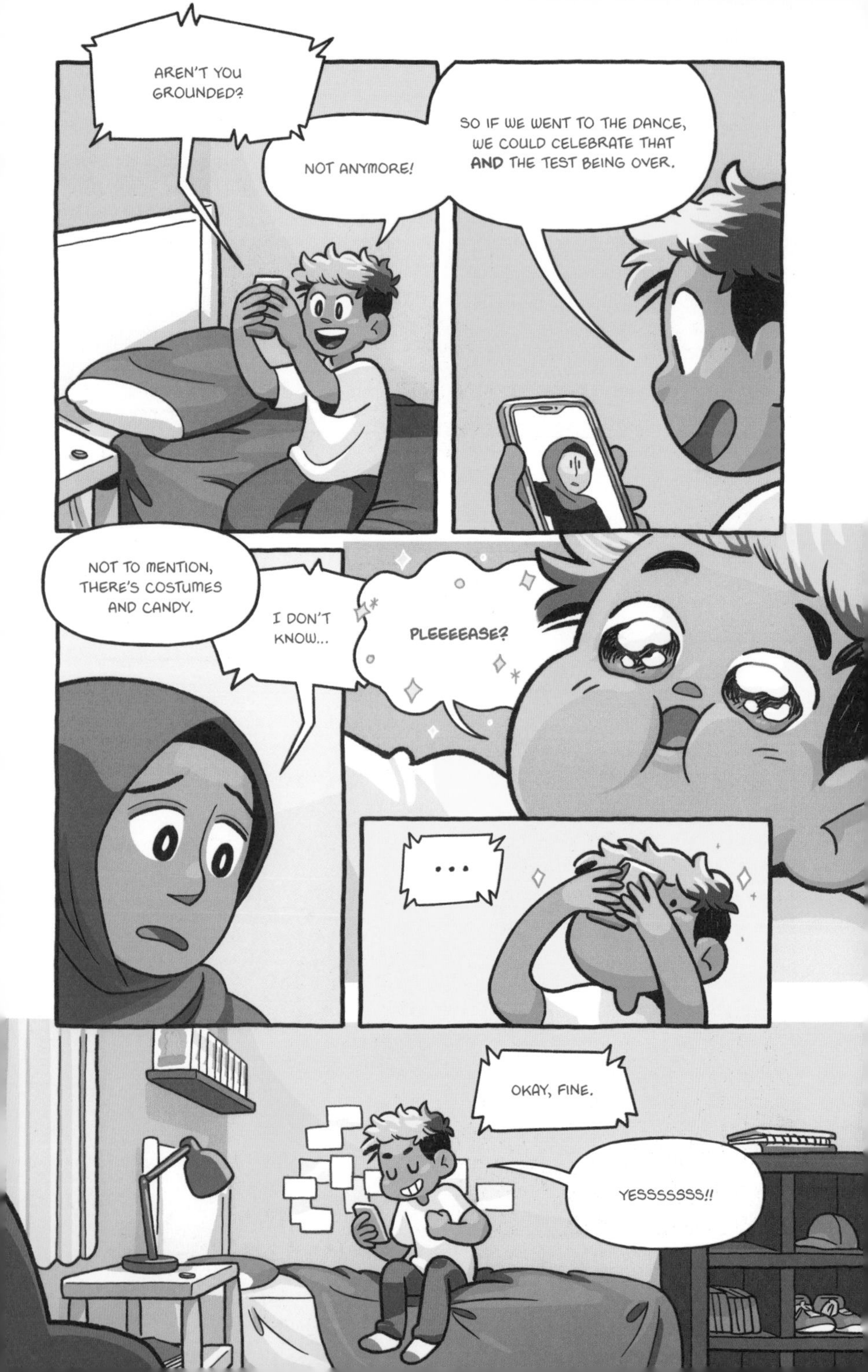
AREN'T YOU GROUNDED?
NOT ANYMORE!
SO IF WE WENT TO THE DANCE, WE COULD CELEBRATE THAT **AND** THE TEST BEING OVER.
NOT TO MENTION, THERE'S COSTUMES AND CANDY.
I DON'T KNOW...
PLEEEEASE?
...
OKAY, FINE.
YESSSSSSS!!

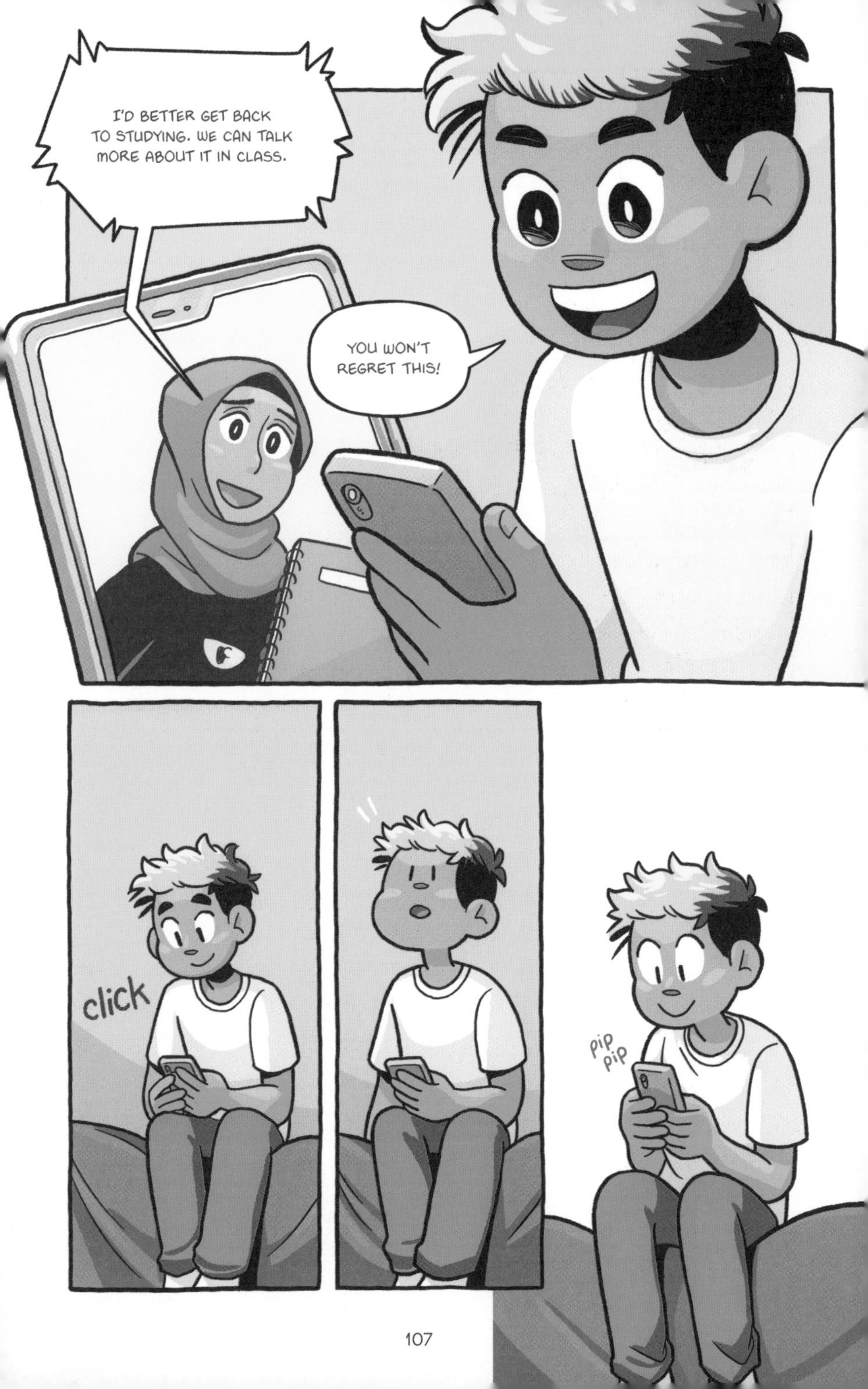
I'D BETTER GET BACK TO STUDYING. WE CAN TALK MORE ABOUT IT IN CLASS.
YOU WON'T REGRET THIS!
click
pip pip

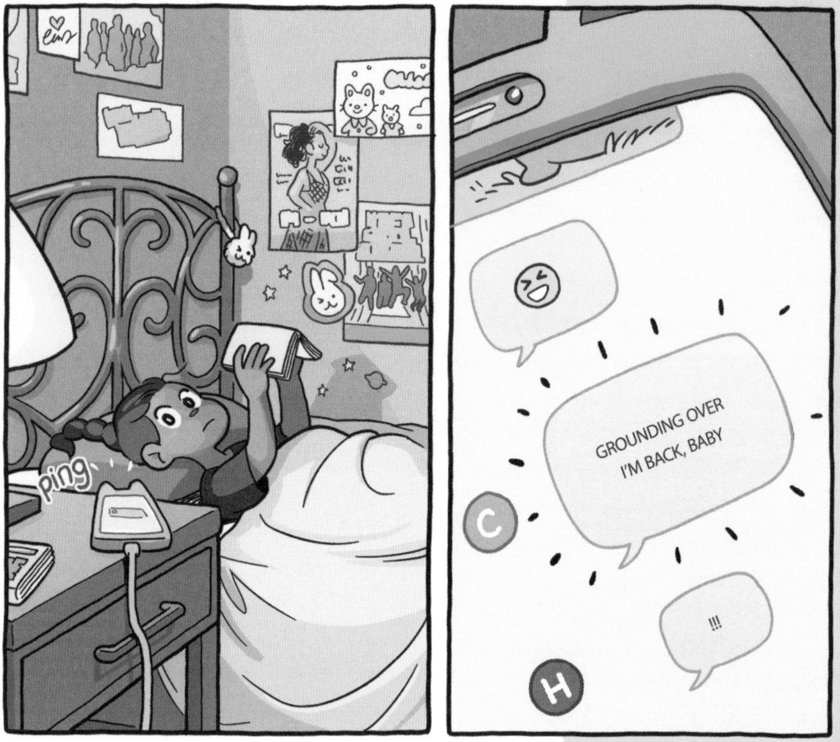
ping
GROUNDING OVER
I'M BACK, BABY
C
!!!
H

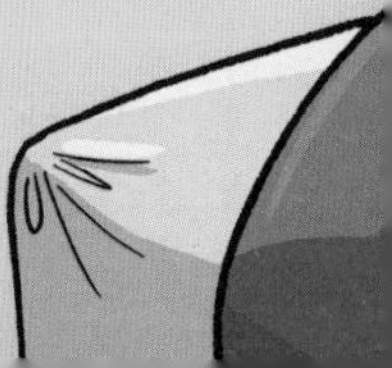

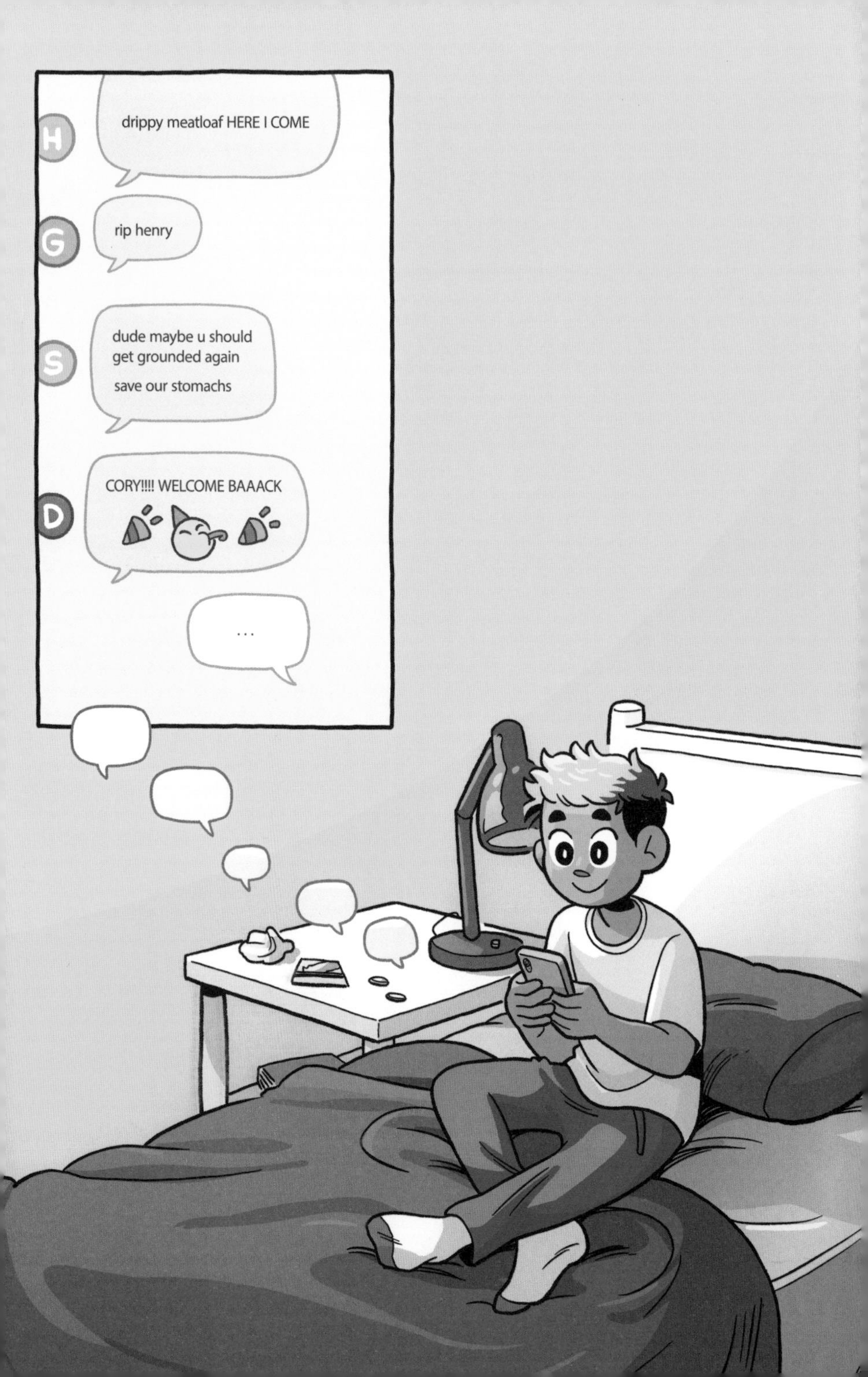
H
drippy meatloaf HERE I COME
G
rip henry
S
dude maybe u should get grounded again
save our stomachs
D
CORY!!!! WELCOME BAAACK
...

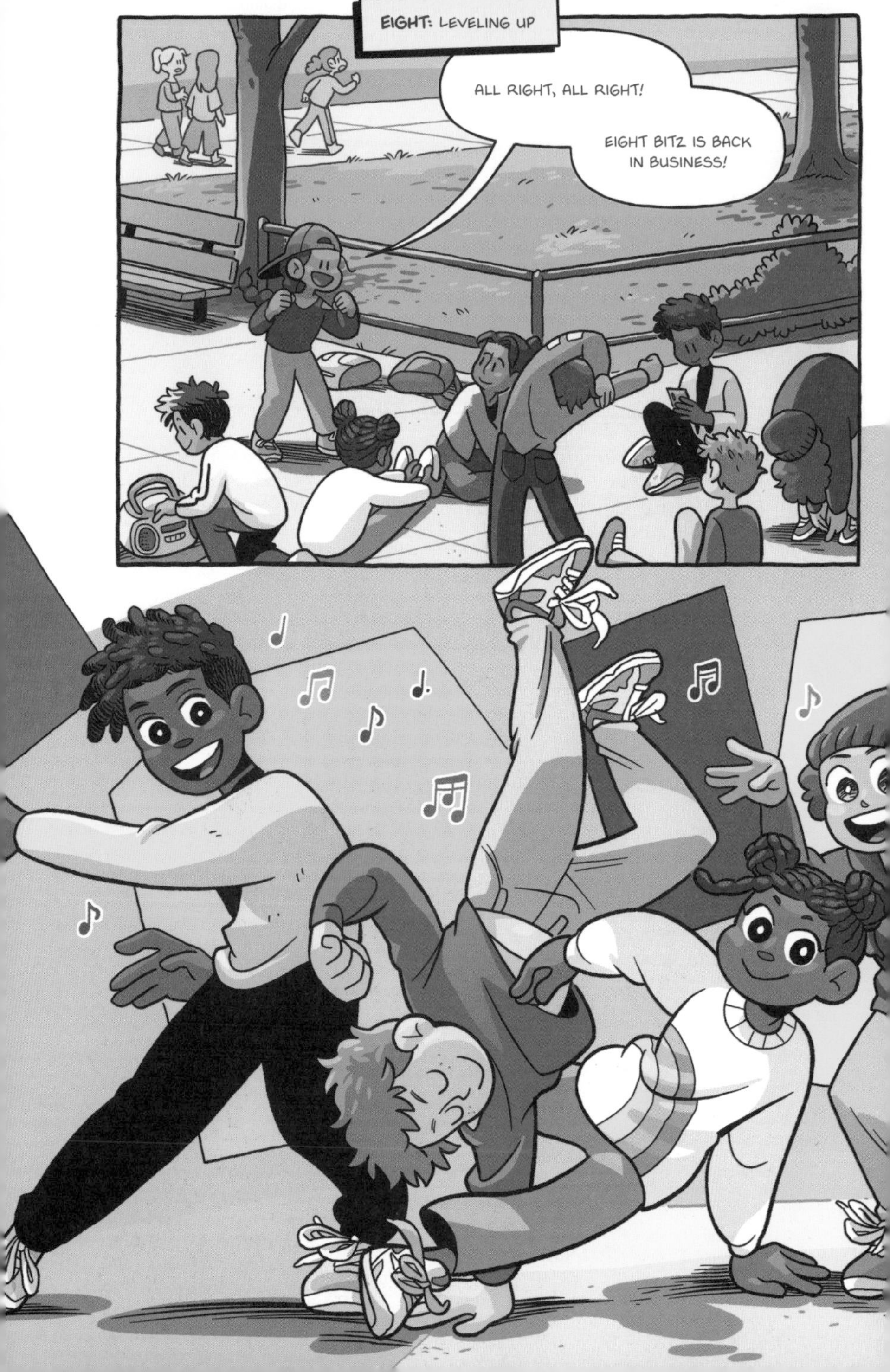
EIGHT: LEVELING UP
ALL RIGHT, ALL RIGHT!
EIGHT BITZ IS BACK IN BUSINESS!

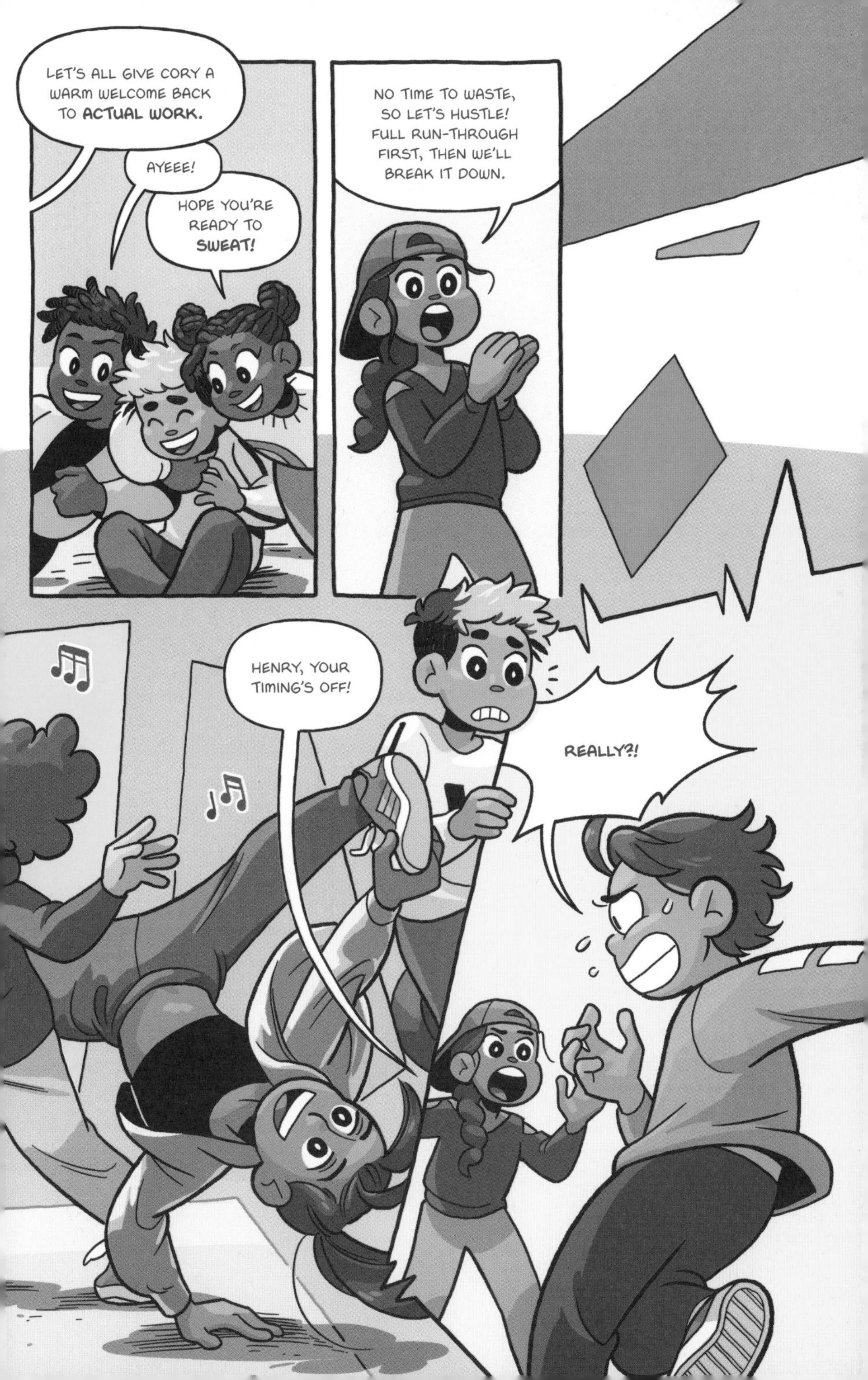

LET'S ALL GIVE CORY A WARM WELCOME BACK TO **ACTUAL WORK.**
AYEEE!
HOPE YOU'RE READY TO **SWEAT!**
NO TIME TO WASTE, SO LET'S HUSTLE! FULL RUN-THROUGH FIRST, THEN WE'LL BREAK IT DOWN.
HENRY, YOUR TIMING'S OFF!
REALLY?!

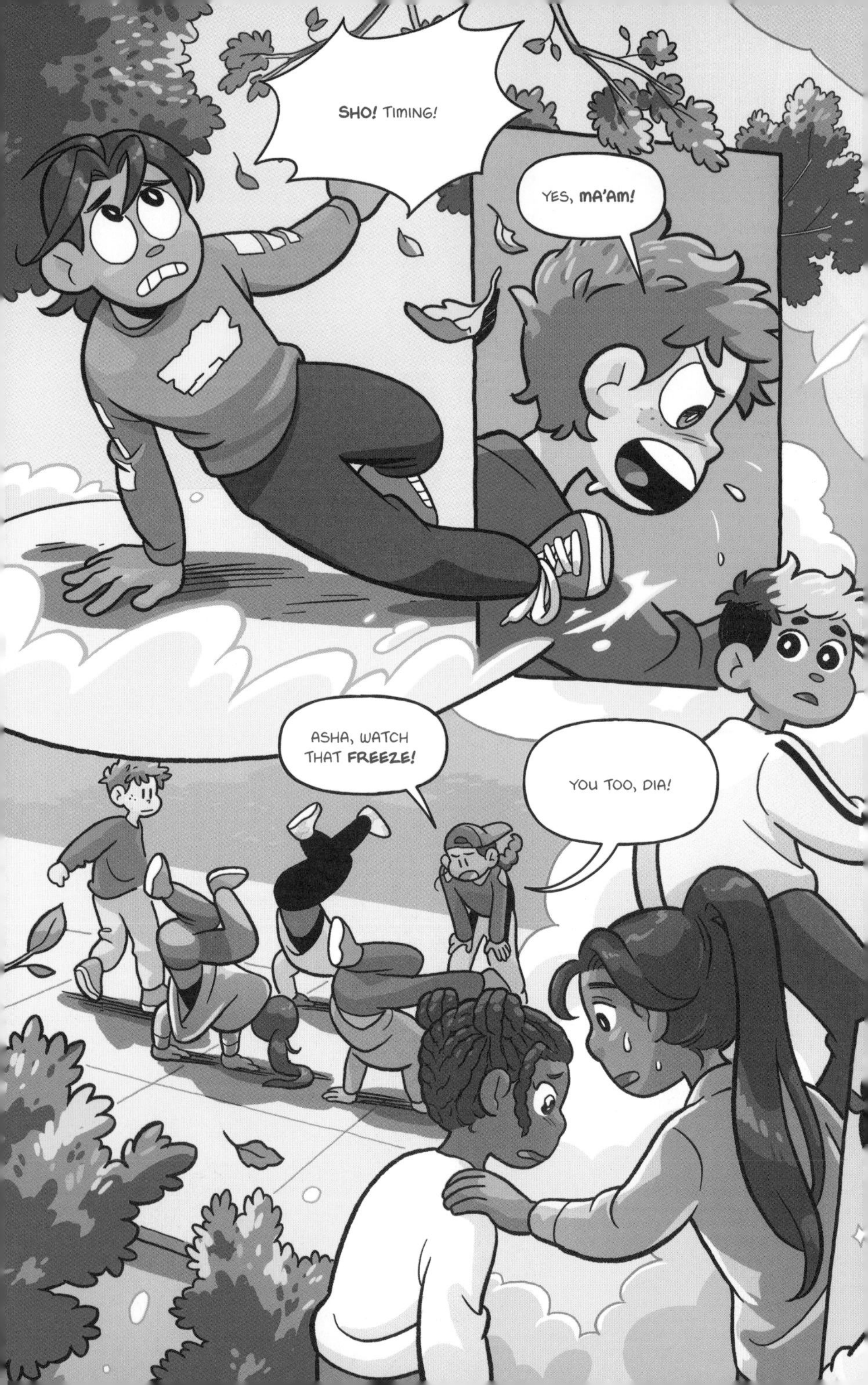
SHO! TIMING!
YES, MA'AM!
ASHA, WATCH THAT FREEZE!
YOU TOO, DIA!

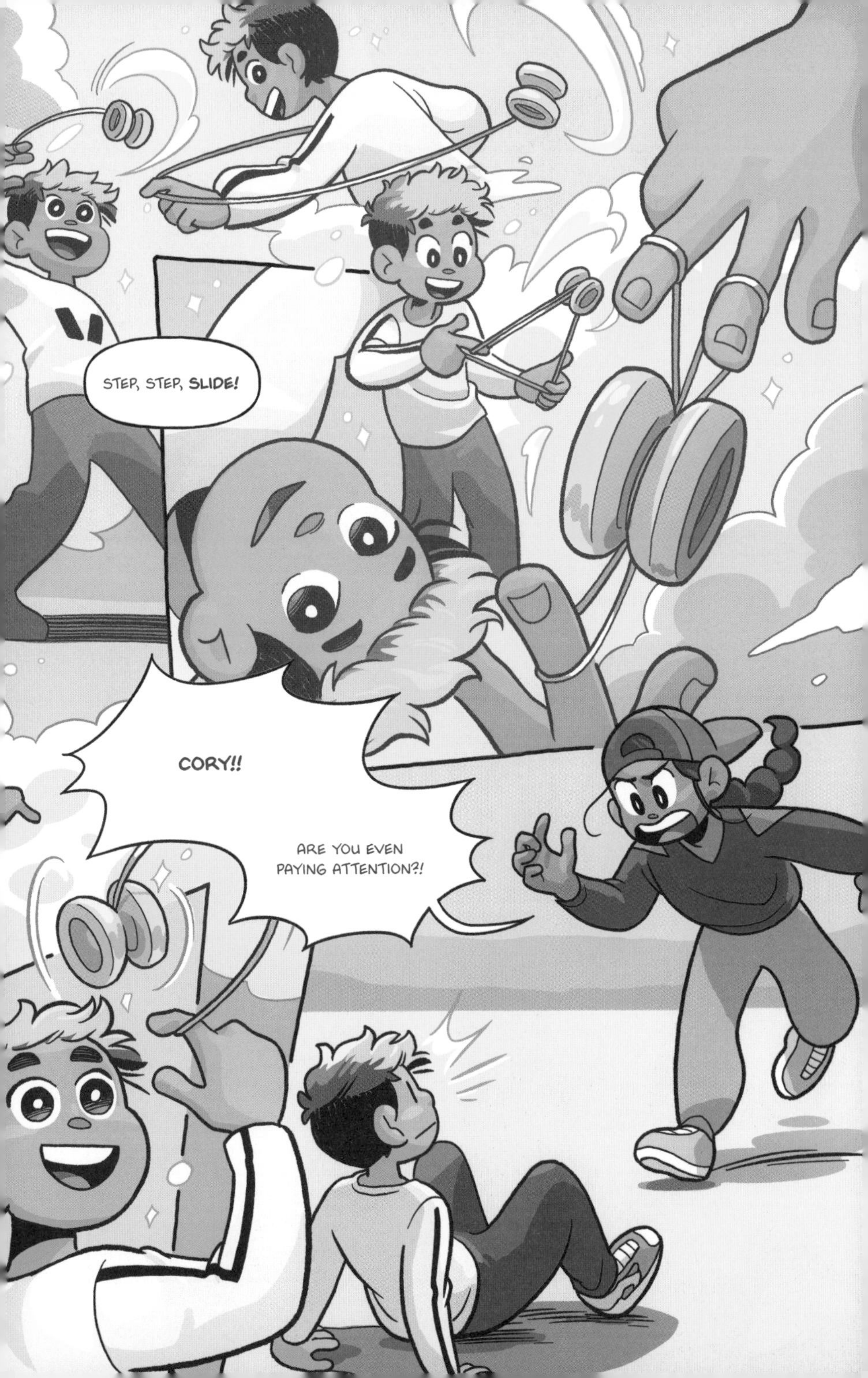
STEP, STEP, **SLIDE!**
CORY!!
ARE YOU EVEN PAYING ATTENTION?!

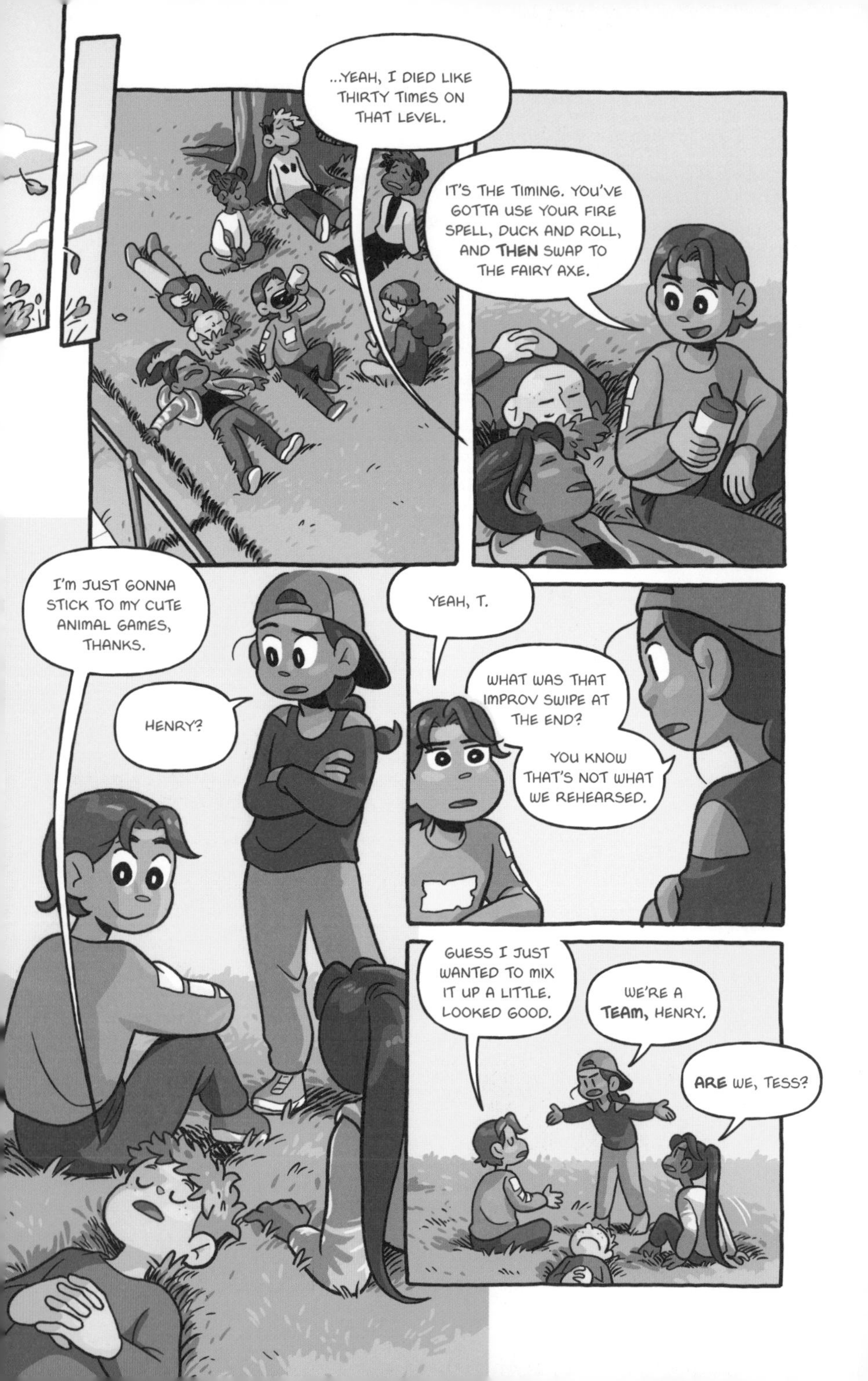
...YEAH, I DIED LIKE THIRTY TIMES ON THAT LEVEL.
IT'S THE TIMING. YOU'VE GOTTA USE YOUR FIRE SPELL, DUCK AND ROLL, AND **THEN** SWAP TO THE FAIRY AXE.
I'M JUST GONNA STICK TO MY CUTE ANIMAL GAMES, THANKS.
HENRY?
YEAH, T.
WHAT WAS THAT IMPROV SWIPE AT THE END?
YOU KNOW THAT'S NOT WHAT WE REHEARSED.
GUESS I JUST WANTED TO MIX IT UP A LITTLE. LOOKED GOOD.
WE'RE A **TEAM,** HENRY.
ARE WE, TESS?

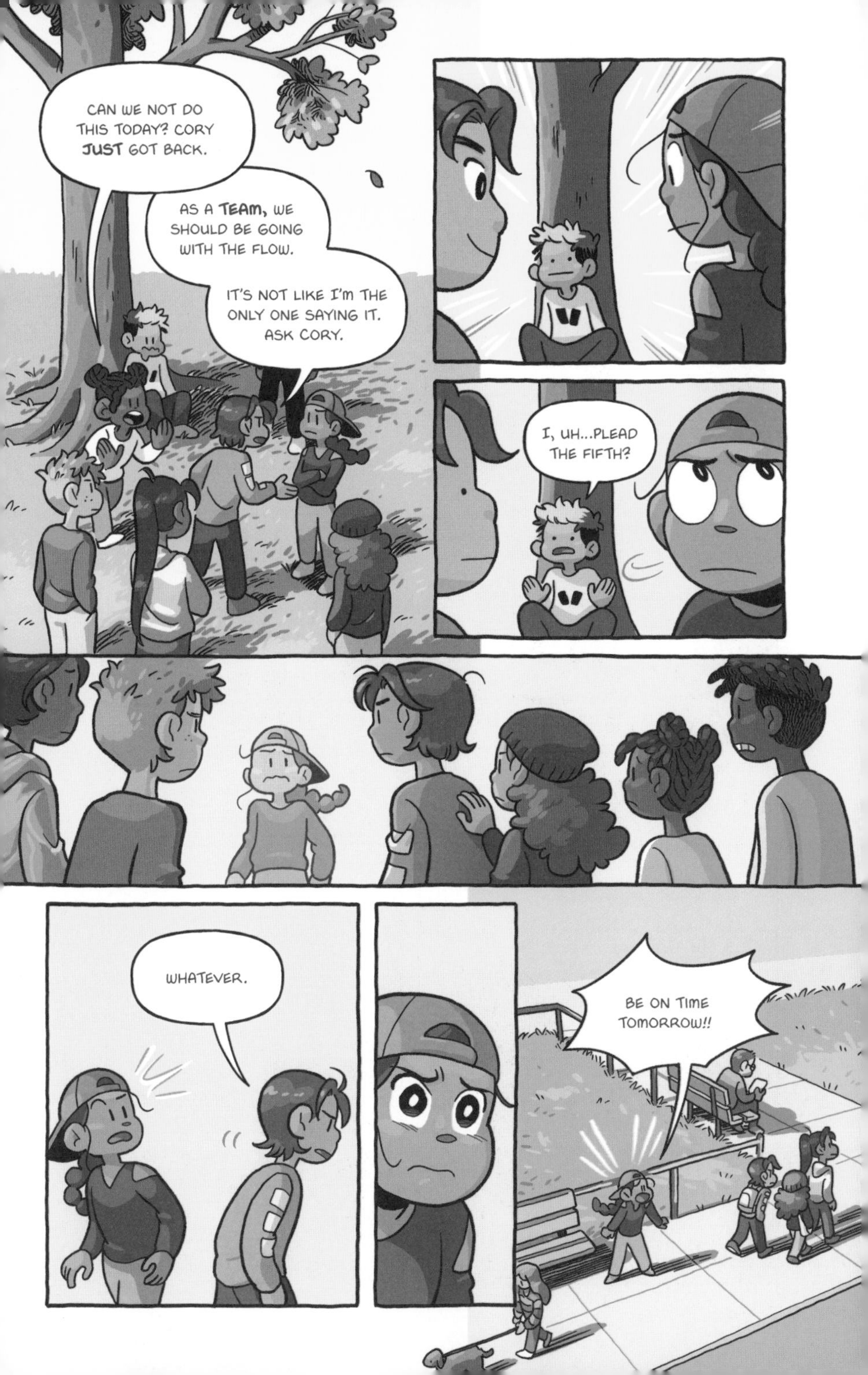
CAN WE NOT DO THIS TODAY? CORY **JUST** GOT BACK.
AS A **TEAM,** WE SHOULD BE GOING WITH THE FLOW.
IT'S NOT LIKE I'M THE ONLY ONE SAYING IT. ASK CORY.
I, UH...PLEAD THE FIFTH?
WHATEVER.
BE ON TIME TOMORROW!!

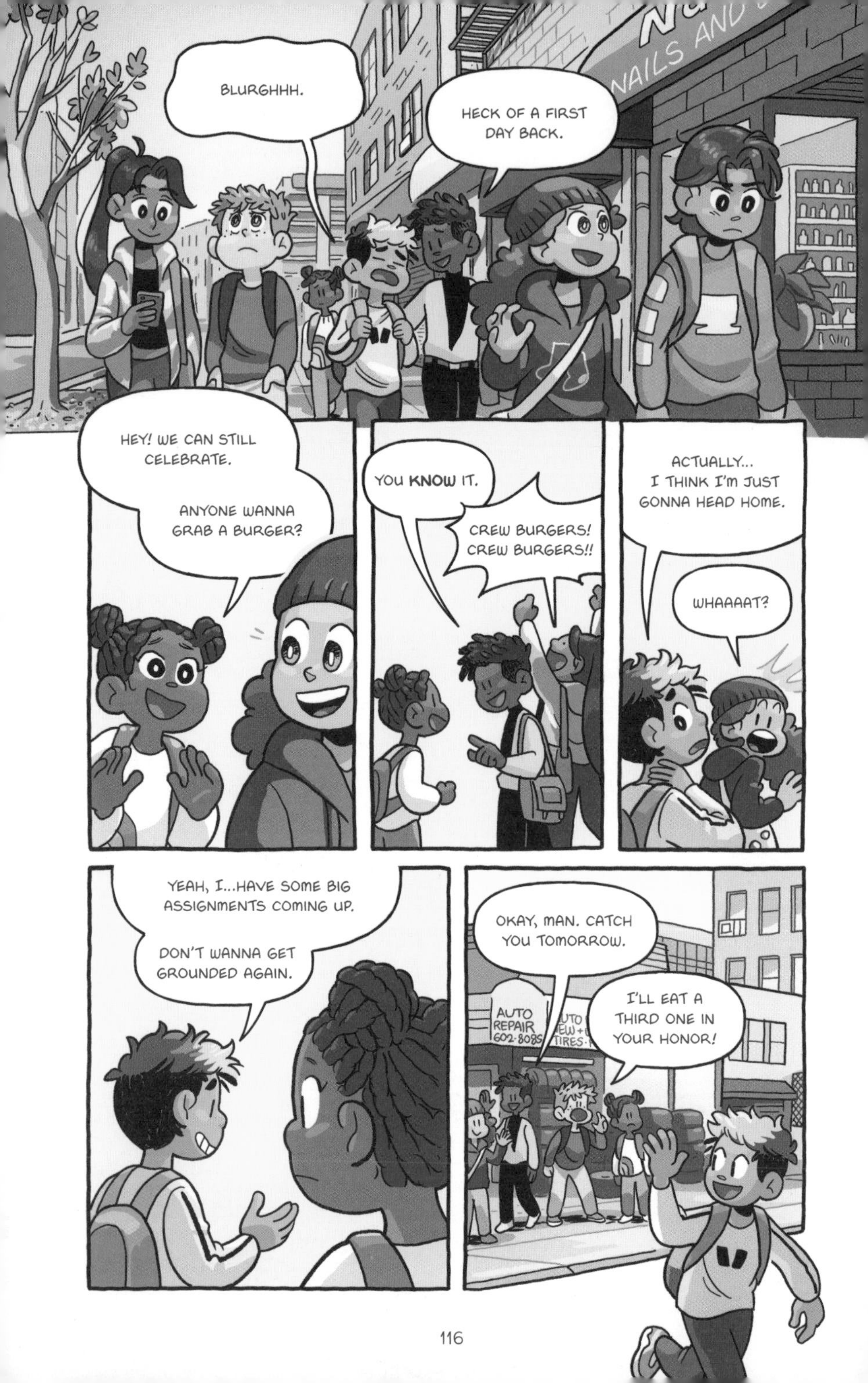
NAILS AND
BLURGHHH.
HECK OF A FIRST DAY BACK.
HEY! WE CAN STILL CELEBRATE.
ANYONE WANNA GRAB A BURGER?
YOU KNOW IT.
CREW BURGERS! CREW BURGERS!!
ACTUALLY... I THINK I'M JUST GONNA HEAD HOME.
WHAAAAT?
YEAH, I...HAVE SOME BIG ASSIGNMENTS COMING UP.
DON'T WANNA GET GROUNDED AGAIN.
OKAY, MAN. CATCH YOU TOMORROW.
I'LL EAT A THIRD ONE IN YOUR HONOR!
AUTO REPAIR 602-8085

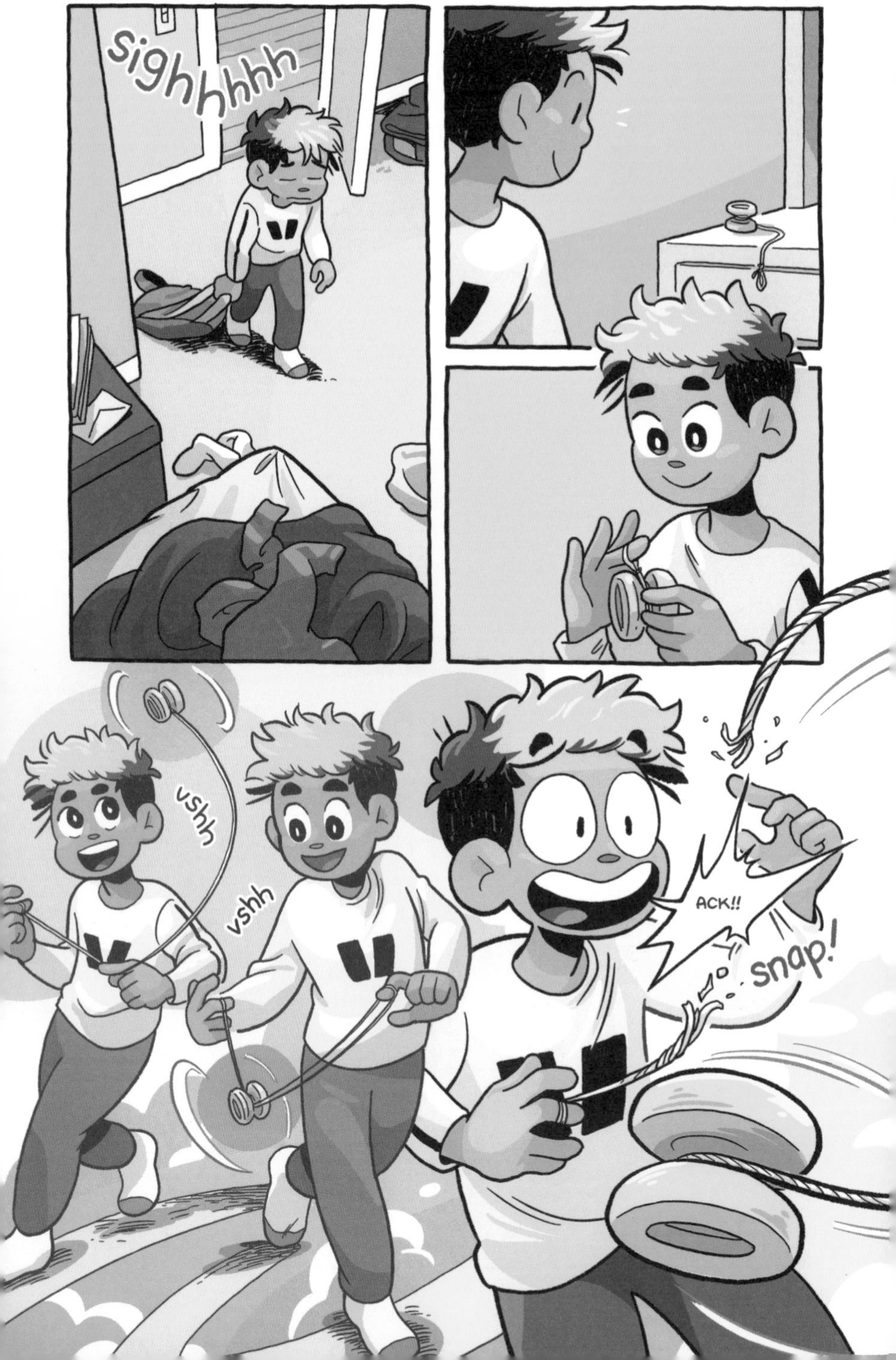

sighhhhh
vshh
vshh
ACK!!
snap!

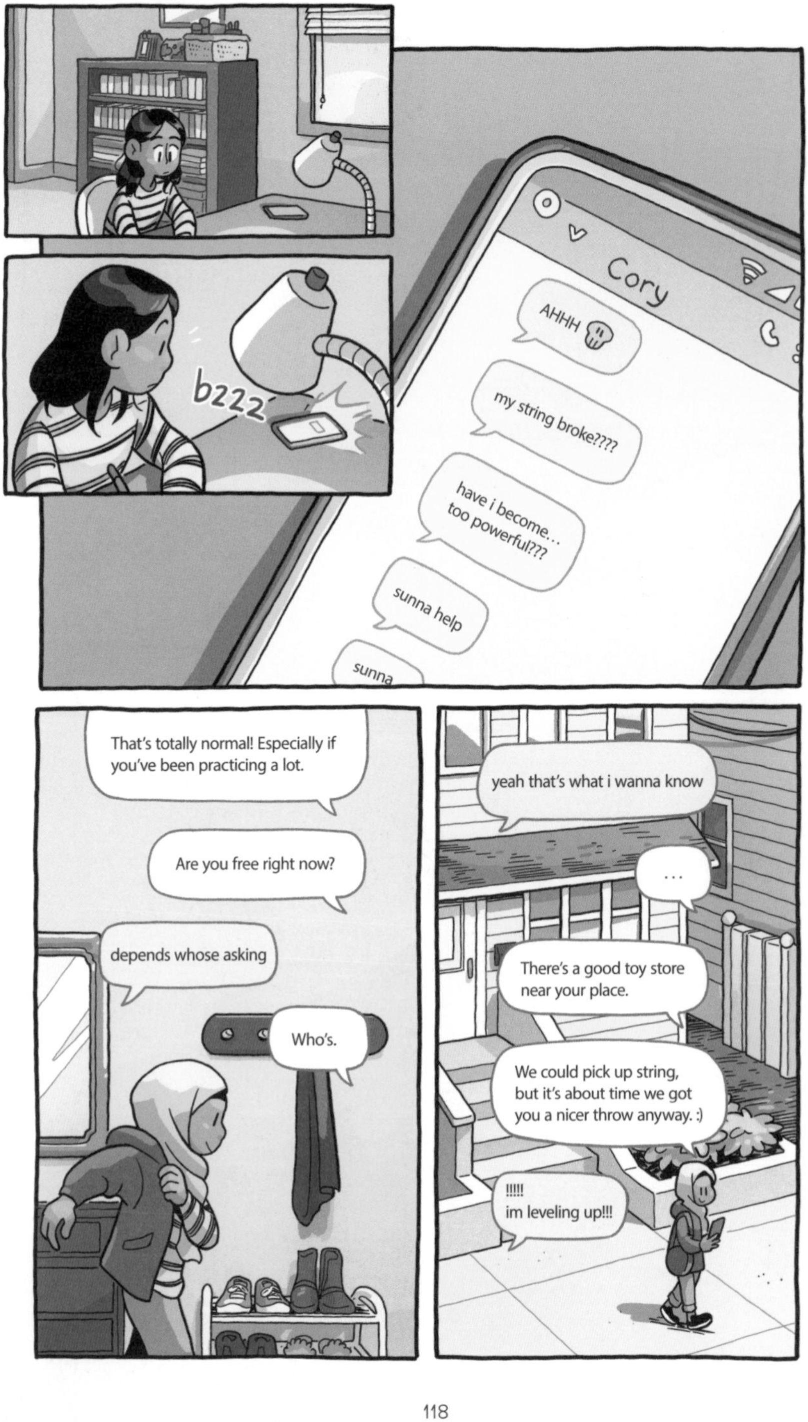
b222
Cory
AHHH
my string broke????
have i become…
too powerful???
sunna help
sunna
That's totally normal! Especially if you've been practicing a lot.
Are you free right now?
depends whose asking
Who's.
yeah that's what i wanna know
…
There's a good toy store near your place.
We could pick up string, but it's about time we got you a nicer throw anyway. :)
!!!!!
im leveling up!!!

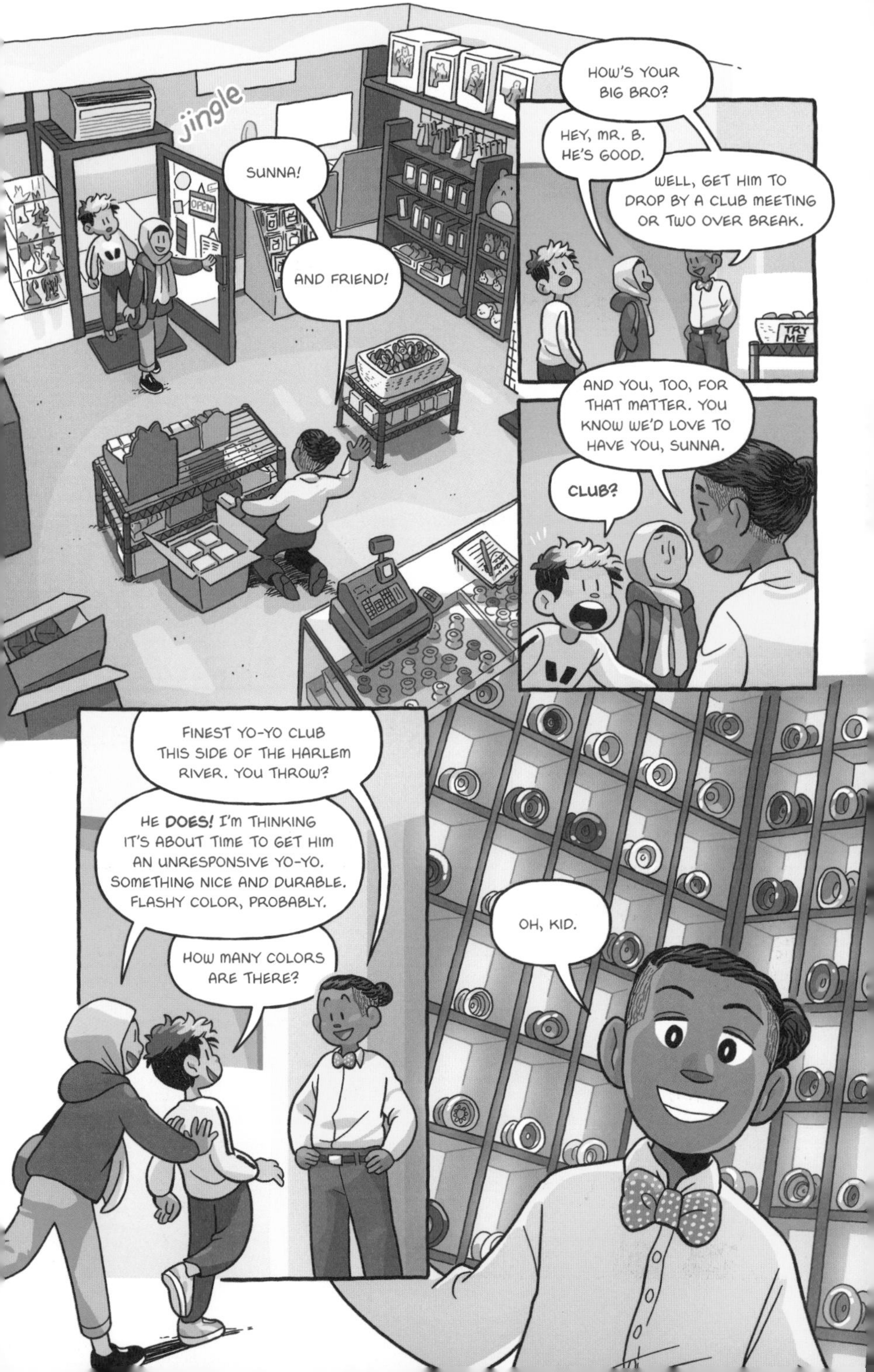
jingle
SUNNA!
AND FRIEND!
HOW'S YOUR BIG BRO?
HEY, MR. B. HE'S GOOD.
WELL, GET HIM TO DROP BY A CLUB MEETING OR TWO OVER BREAK.
TRY ME
AND YOU, TOO, FOR THAT MATTER. YOU KNOW WE'D LOVE TO HAVE YOU, SUNNA.
CLUB?
FINEST YO-YO CLUB THIS SIDE OF THE HARLEM RIVER. YOU THROW?
HE **DOES!** I'M THINKING IT'S ABOUT TIME TO GET HIM AN UNRESPONSIVE YO-YO. SOMETHING NICE AND DURABLE. FLASHY COLOR, PROBABLY.
HOW MANY COLORS ARE THERE?
OH, KID.

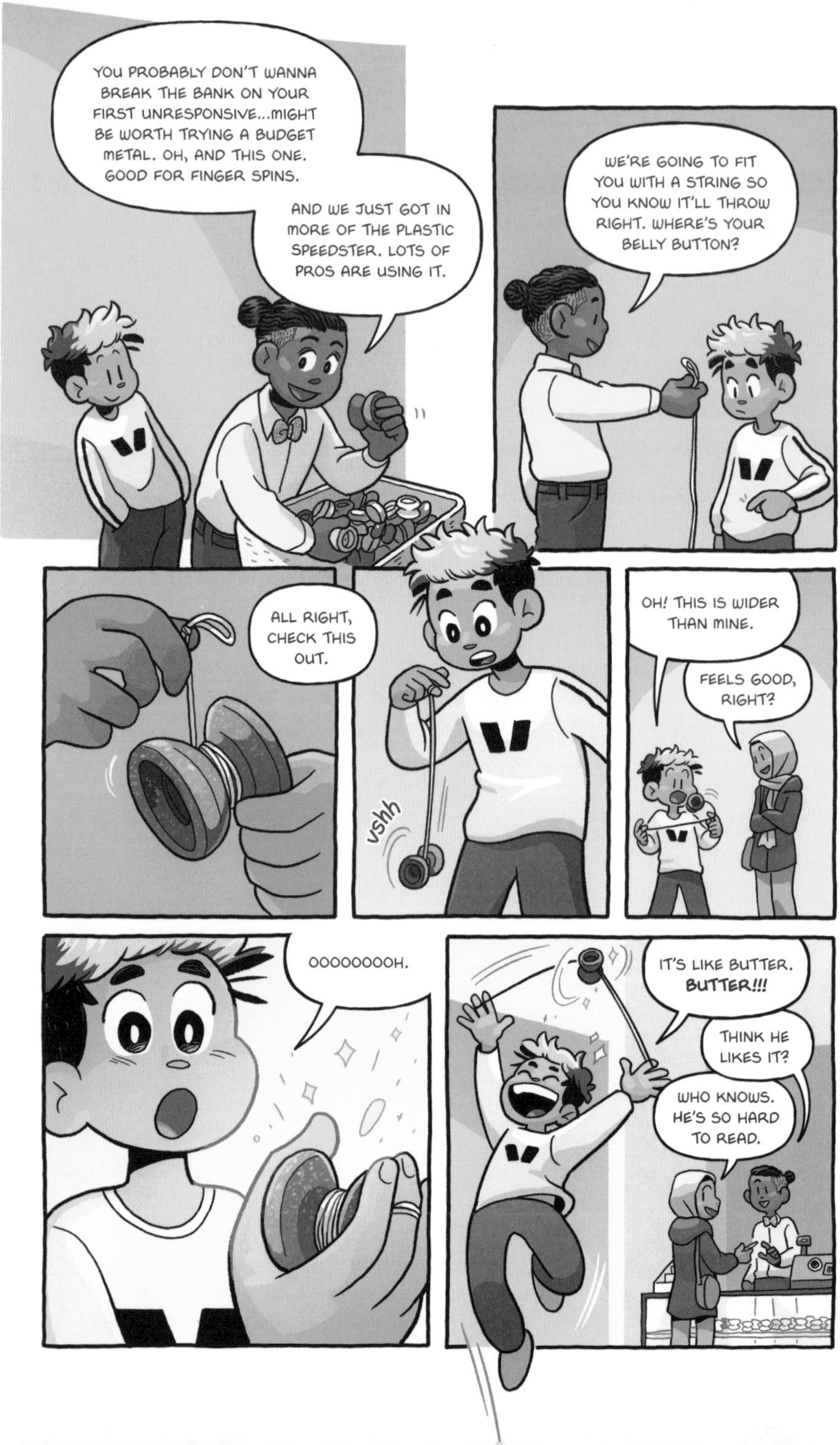
YOU PROBABLY DON'T WANNA BREAK THE BANK ON YOUR FIRST UNRESPONSIVE...MIGHT BE WORTH TRYING A BUDGET METAL. OH, AND THIS ONE. GOOD FOR FINGER SPINS.
AND WE JUST GOT IN MORE OF THE PLASTIC SPEEDSTER. LOTS OF PROS ARE USING IT.
WE'RE GOING TO FIT YOU WITH A STRING SO YOU KNOW IT'LL THROW RIGHT. WHERE'S YOUR BELLY BUTTON?
ALL RIGHT, CHECK THIS OUT.
vshh
OH! THIS IS WIDER THAN MINE.
FEELS GOOD, RIGHT?
OOOOOOOOH.
IT'S LIKE BUTTER. **BUTTER!!!**
THINK HE LIKES IT?
WHO KNOWS. HE'S SO HARD TO READ.

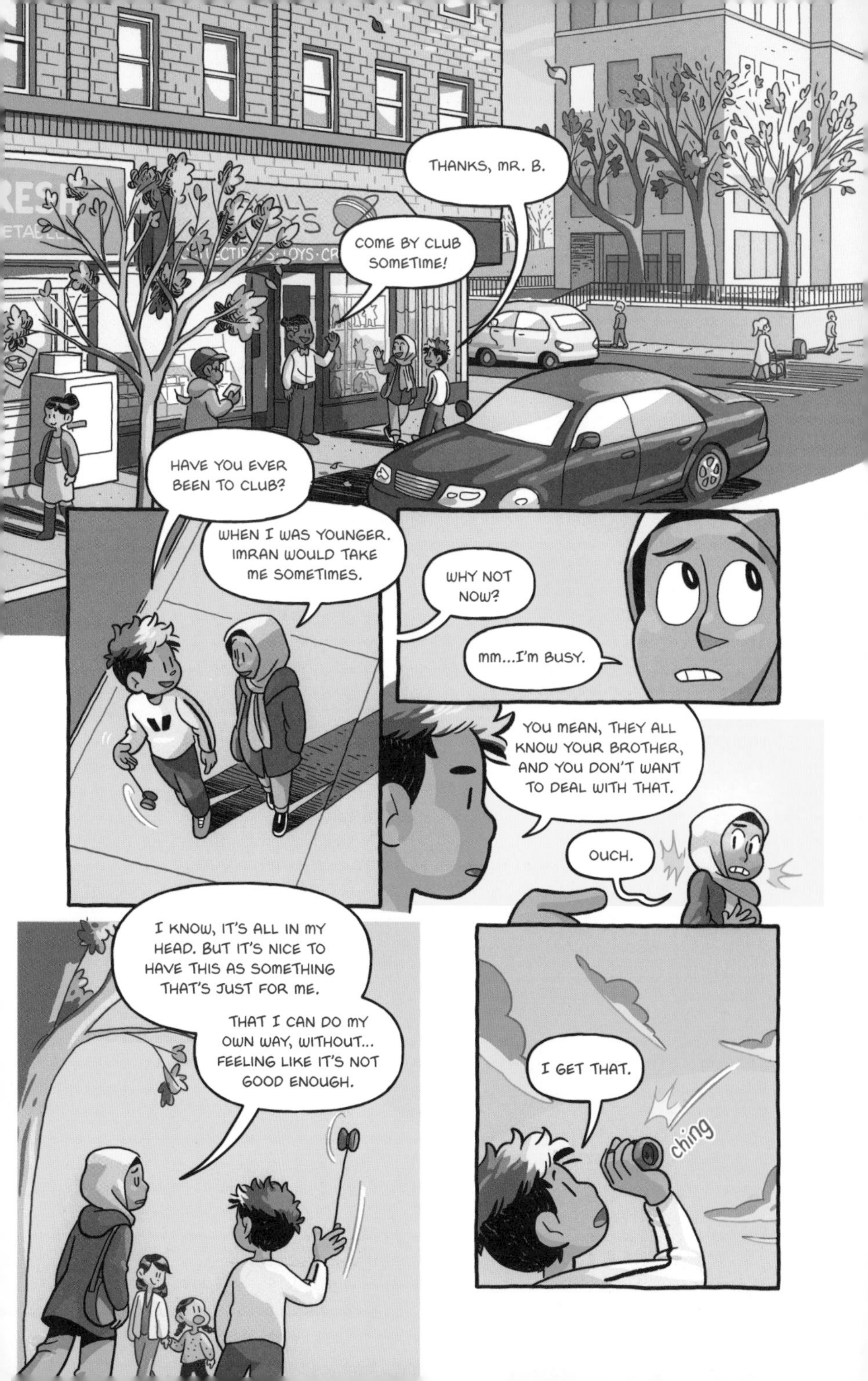
COME BY CLUB SOMETIME!
THANKS, MR. B.
HAVE YOU EVER BEEN TO CLUB?
WHEN I WAS YOUNGER. IMRAN WOULD TAKE ME SOMETIMES.
WHY NOT NOW?
mm...I'm BUSY.
YOU MEAN, THEY ALL KNOW YOUR BROTHER, AND YOU DON'T WANT TO DEAL WITH THAT.
OUCH.
I KNOW, IT'S ALL IN MY HEAD. BUT IT'S NICE TO HAVE THIS AS SOMETHING THAT'S JUST FOR ME.
THAT I CAN DO MY OWN WAY, WITHOUT... FEELING LIKE IT'S NOT GOOD ENOUGH.
I GET THAT.
ching

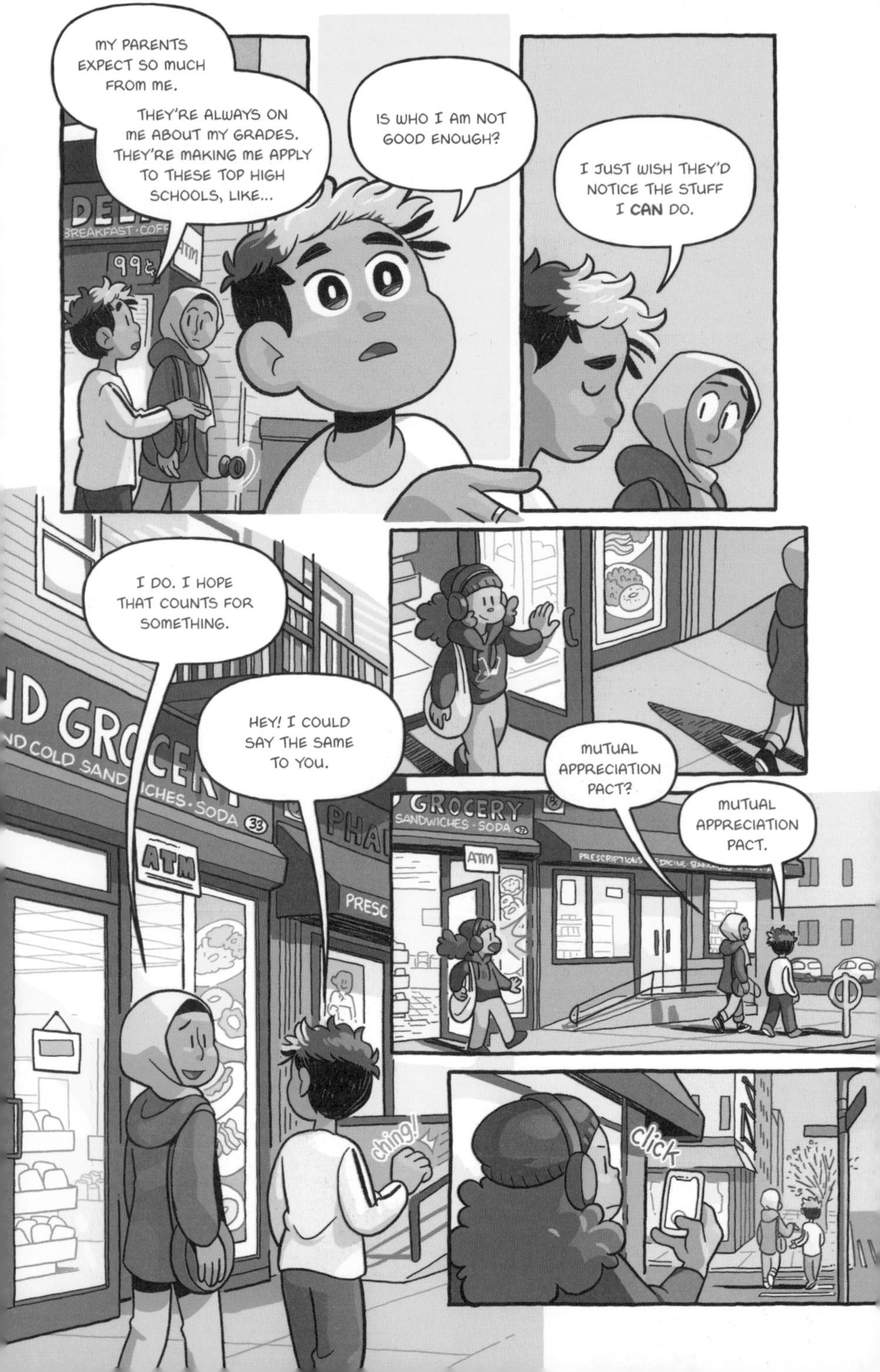
MY PARENTS EXPECT SO MUCH FROM ME.
THEY'RE ALWAYS ON ME ABOUT MY GRADES. THEY'RE MAKING ME APPLY TO THESE TOP HIGH SCHOOLS, LIKE...
DELI
BREAKFAST · COFF
99¢
ATM
IS WHO I AM NOT GOOD ENOUGH?
I JUST WISH THEY'D NOTICE THE STUFF I **CAN** DO.
I DO. I HOPE THAT COUNTS FOR SOMETHING.
D GROCERY
ND COLD SANDWICHES · SODA
ATM
PHA
PRESC
HEY! I COULD SAY THE SAME TO YOU.
ching!
GROCERY
SANDWICHES · SODA
ATM
MUTUAL APPRECIATION PACT?
MUTUAL APPRECIATION PACT.
click

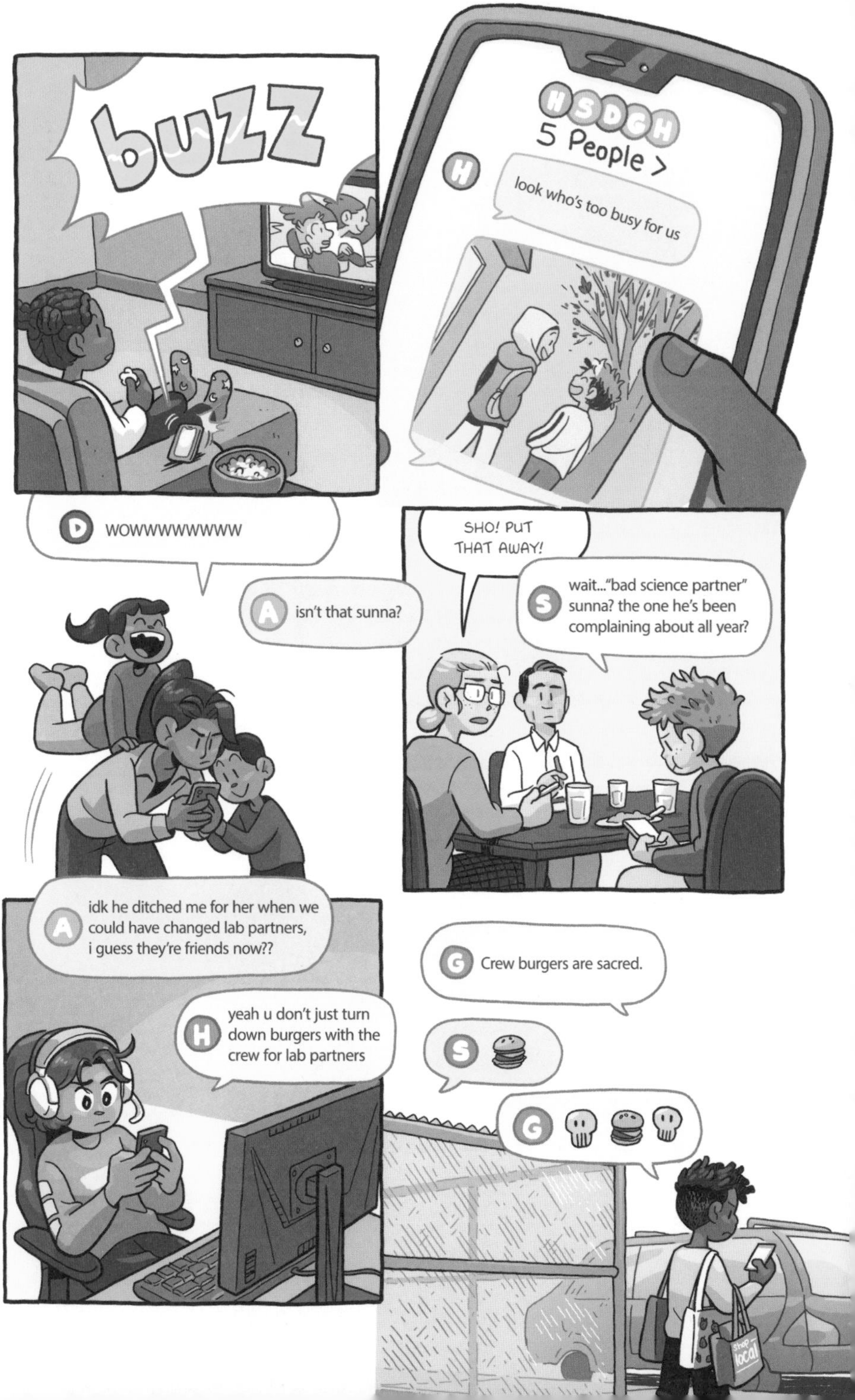

buzz
HSDGH
5 People >
H look who's too busy for us
D WOWWWWWWWWW
A isn't that sunna?
SHO! PUT THAT AWAY!
S wait..."bad science partner" sunna? the one he's been complaining about all year?
A idk he ditched me for her when we could have changed lab partners, i guess they're friends now??
H yeah u don't just turn down burgers with the crew for lab partners
G Crew burgers are sacred.
S
G
shop local

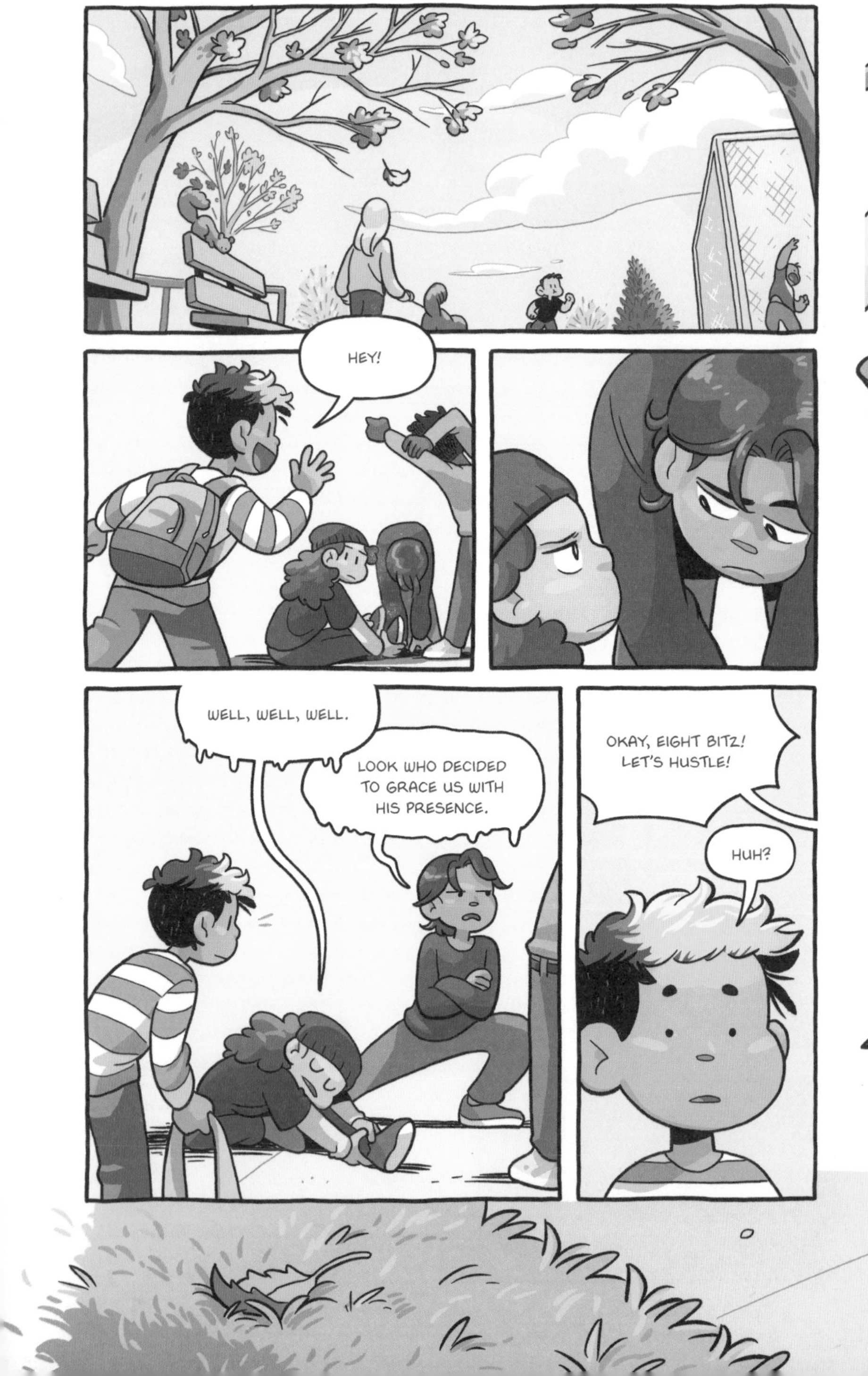
HEY!
WELL, WELL, WELL.
LOOK WHO DECIDED TO GRACE US WITH HIS PRESENCE.
OKAY, EIGHT BITZ! LET'S HUSTLE!
HUH?

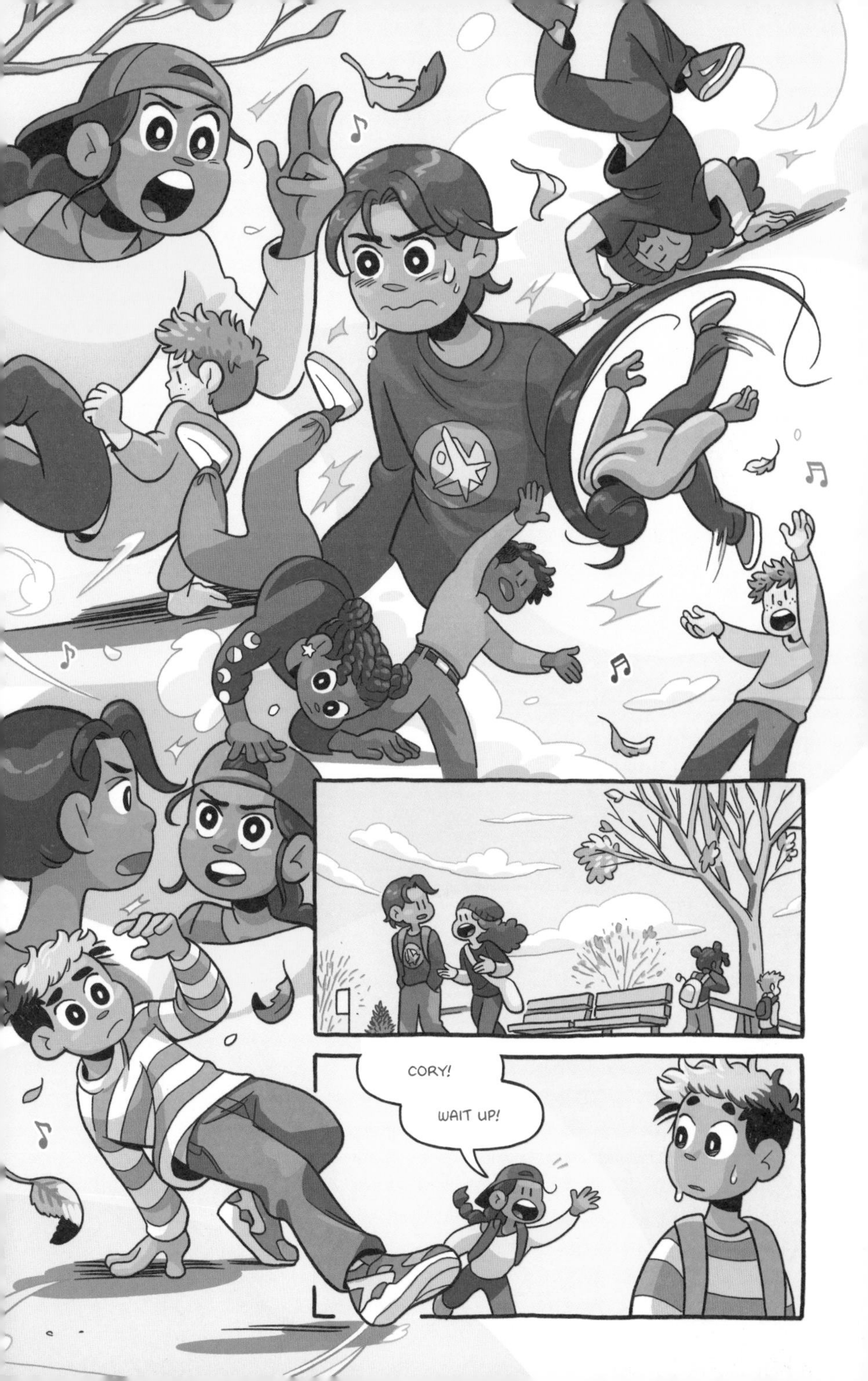
CORY!
WAIT UP!

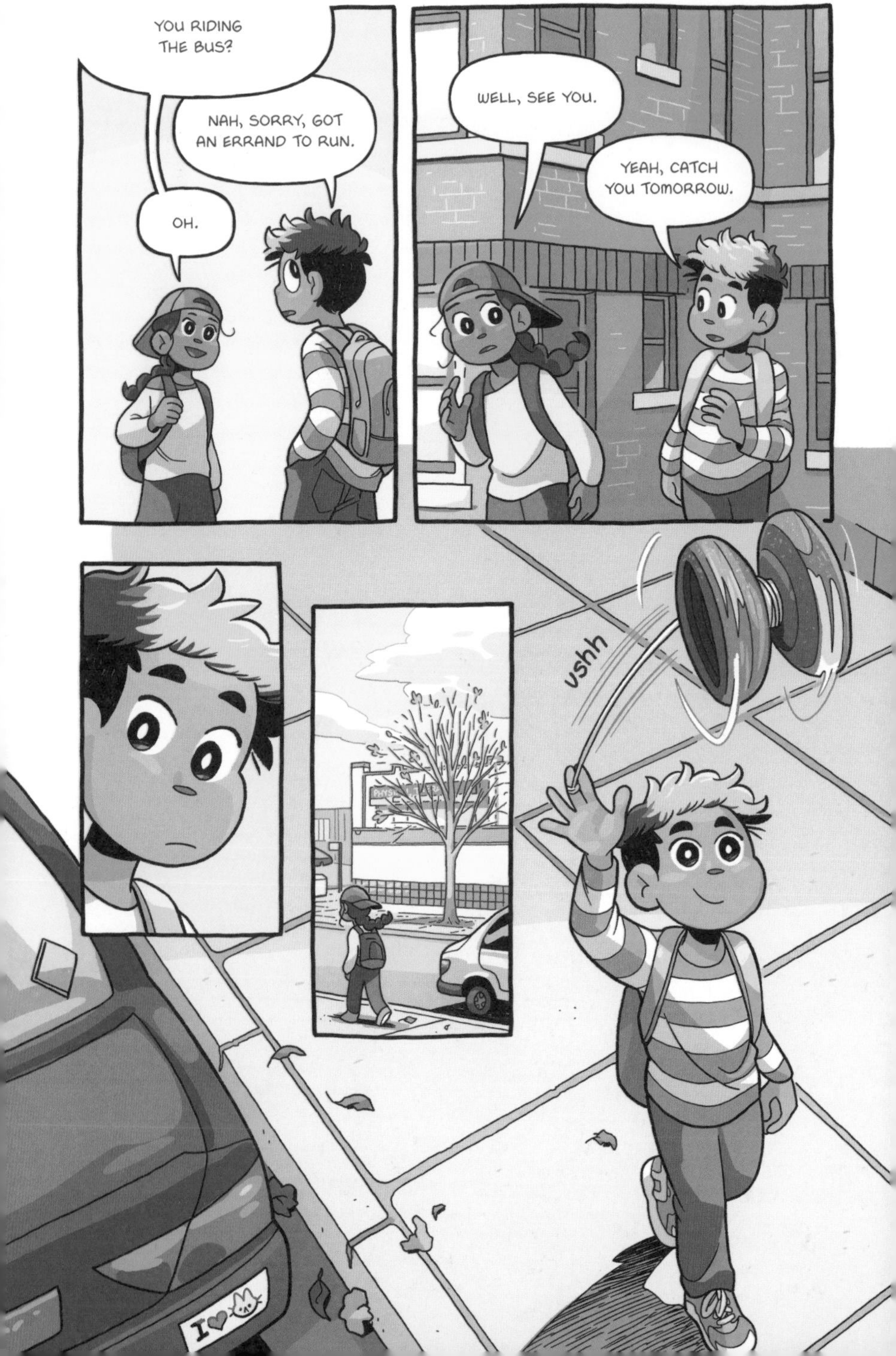
YOU RIDING THE BUS?
NAH, SORRY, GOT AN ERRAND TO RUN.
OH.
WELL, SEE YOU.
YEAH, CATCH YOU TOMORROW.
vshh

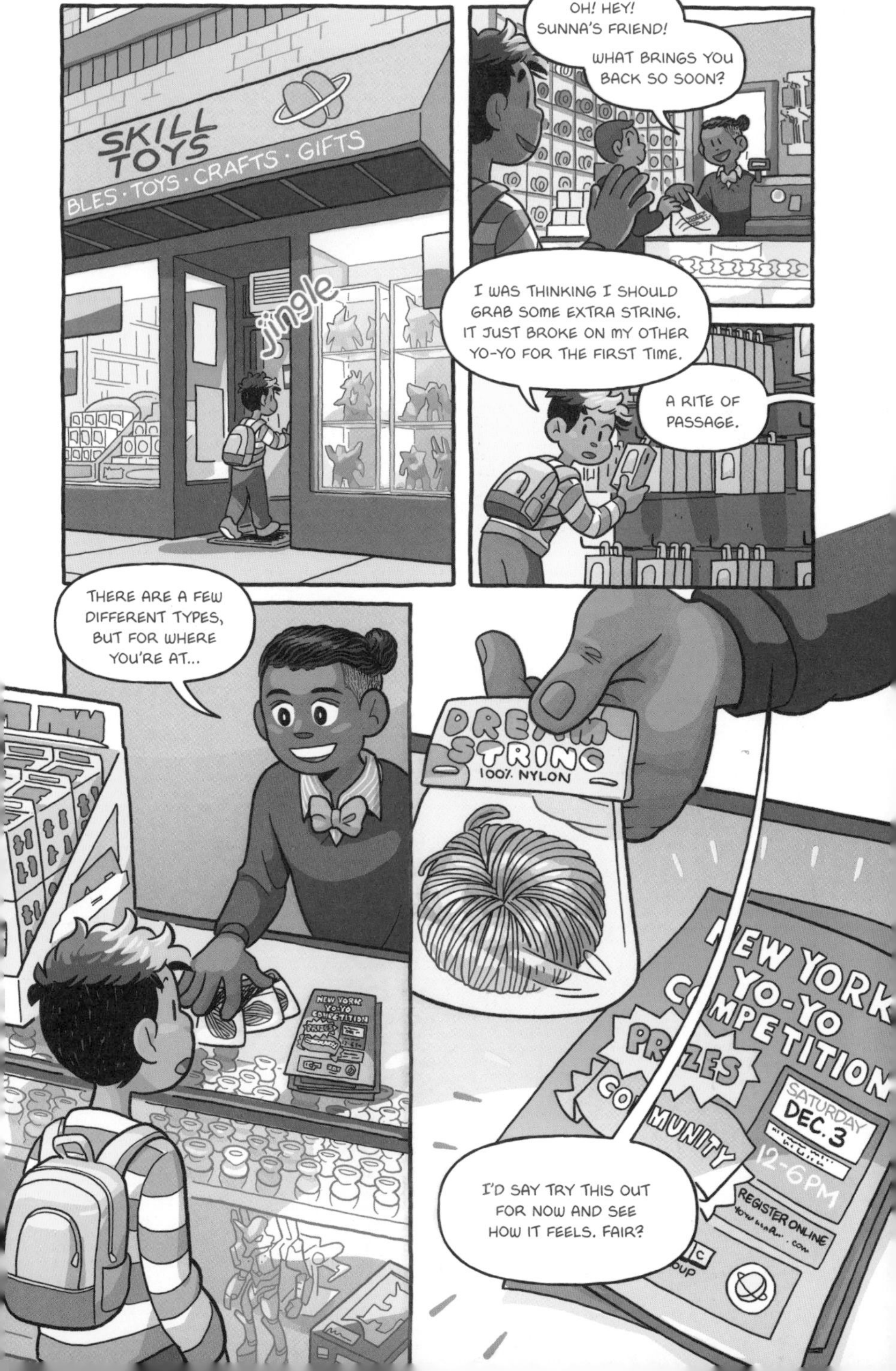

SKILL TOYS
BLES · TOYS · CRAFTS · GIFTS
jingle
OH! HEY! SUNNA'S FRIEND!
WHAT BRINGS YOU BACK SO SOON?
I WAS THINKING I SHOULD GRAB SOME EXTRA STRING. IT JUST BROKE ON MY OTHER YO-YO FOR THE FIRST TIME.
A RITE OF PASSAGE.
THERE ARE A FEW DIFFERENT TYPES, BUT FOR WHERE YOU'RE AT...
DREAM STRING
100% NYLON
NEW YORK YO-YO COMPETITION
PRIZES
COMMUNITY
SATURDAY DEC. 3
12-6PM
REGISTER ONLINE
I'D SAY TRY THIS OUT FOR NOW AND SEE HOW IT FEELS. FAIR?

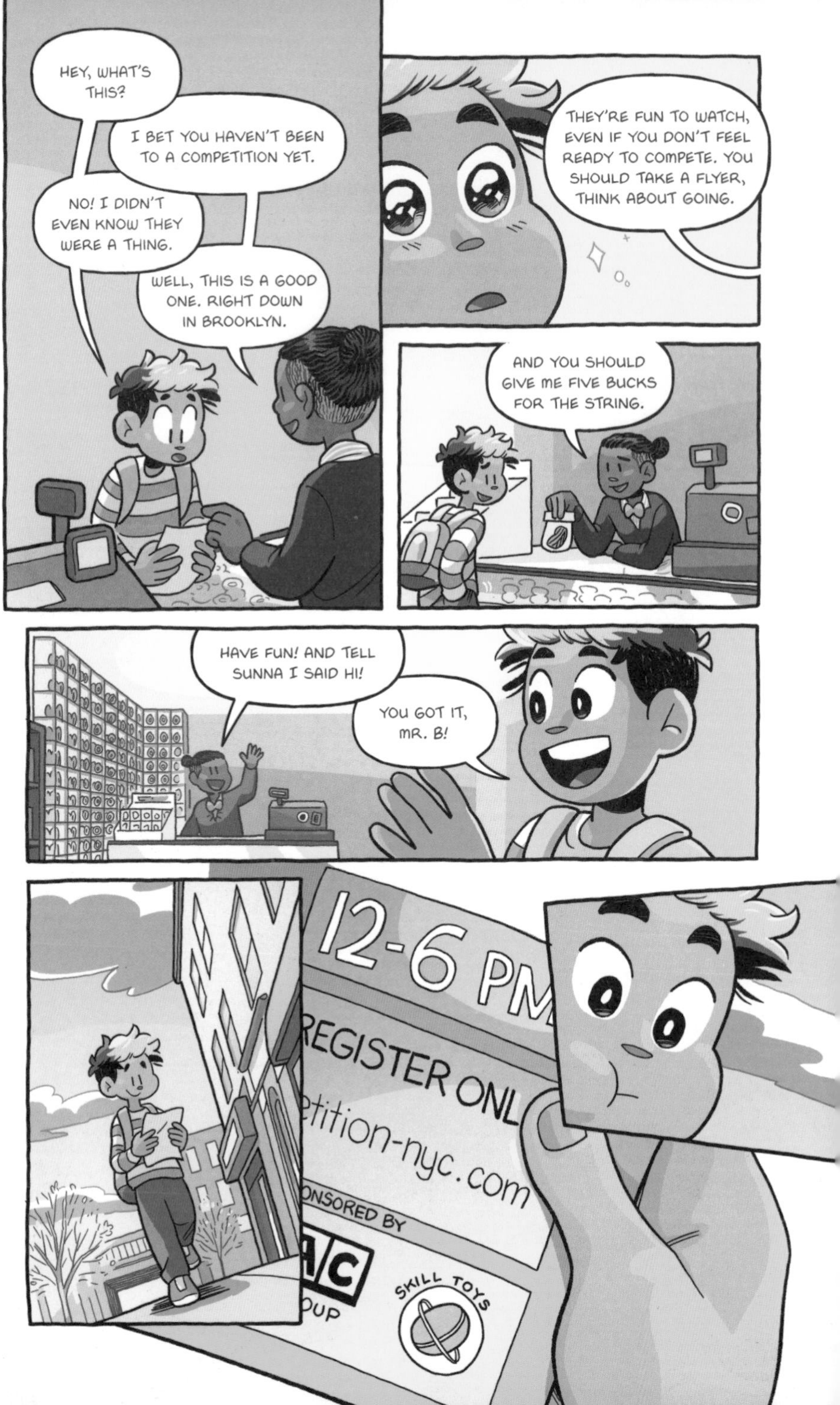
HEY, WHAT'S THIS?
I BET YOU HAVEN'T BEEN TO A COMPETITION YET.
NO! I DIDN'T EVEN KNOW THEY WERE A THING.
WELL, THIS IS A GOOD ONE. RIGHT DOWN IN BROOKLYN.
THEY'RE FUN TO WATCH, EVEN IF YOU DON'T FEEL READY TO COMPETE. YOU SHOULD TAKE A FLYER, THINK ABOUT GOING.
AND YOU SHOULD GIVE ME FIVE BUCKS FOR THE STRING.
HAVE FUN! AND TELL SUNNA I SAID HI!
YOU GOT IT, MR. B!
12-6 PM
REGISTER ONL
etition-nyc.com
ONSORED BY
A/C
OUP
SKILL TOYS

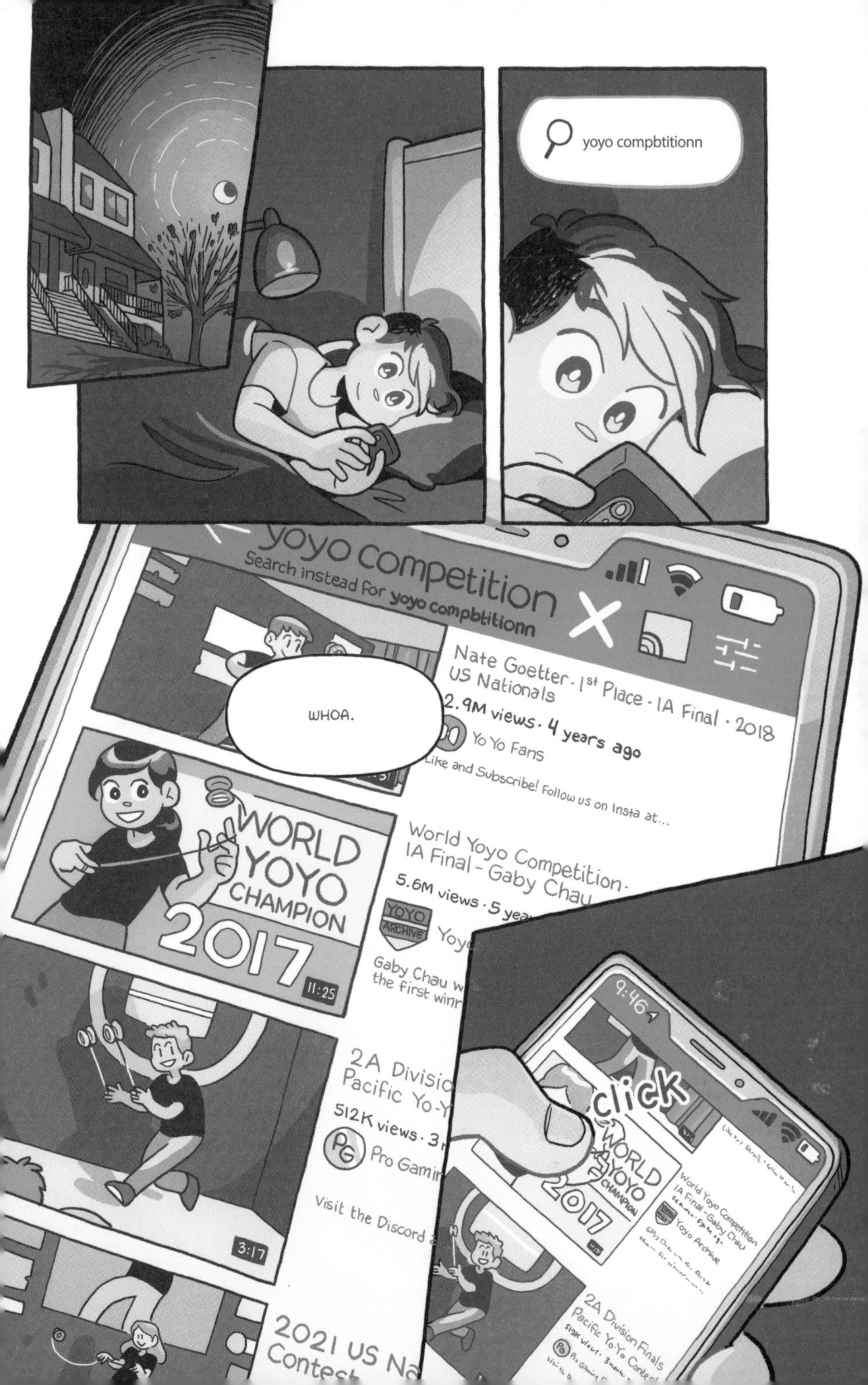
yoyo compbtitionn
yoyo competition
Search instead for yoyo compbtitionn
Nate Goetter - 1st Place - 1A Final - 2018 US Nationals
2.9M views - 4 years ago
Yo Yo Fans
Like and Subscribe! Follow us on Insta at...
WHOA.
WORLD YOYO CHAMPION 2017
11:25
World Yoyo Competition - 1A Final - Gaby Chau
5.6M views - 5 yea
YOYO ARCHIVE
Gaby Chau w
the first winn
2A Divisio
Pacific Yo-Y
512K views - 3
Pro Gamin
Visit the Discord a
3:17
2021 US Na
Contest
9:46
CLICK
World Yoyo Competition 1A Final - Gaby Chau
Yoyo Archive
2A Division Finals
Pacific Yo-Yo Contest

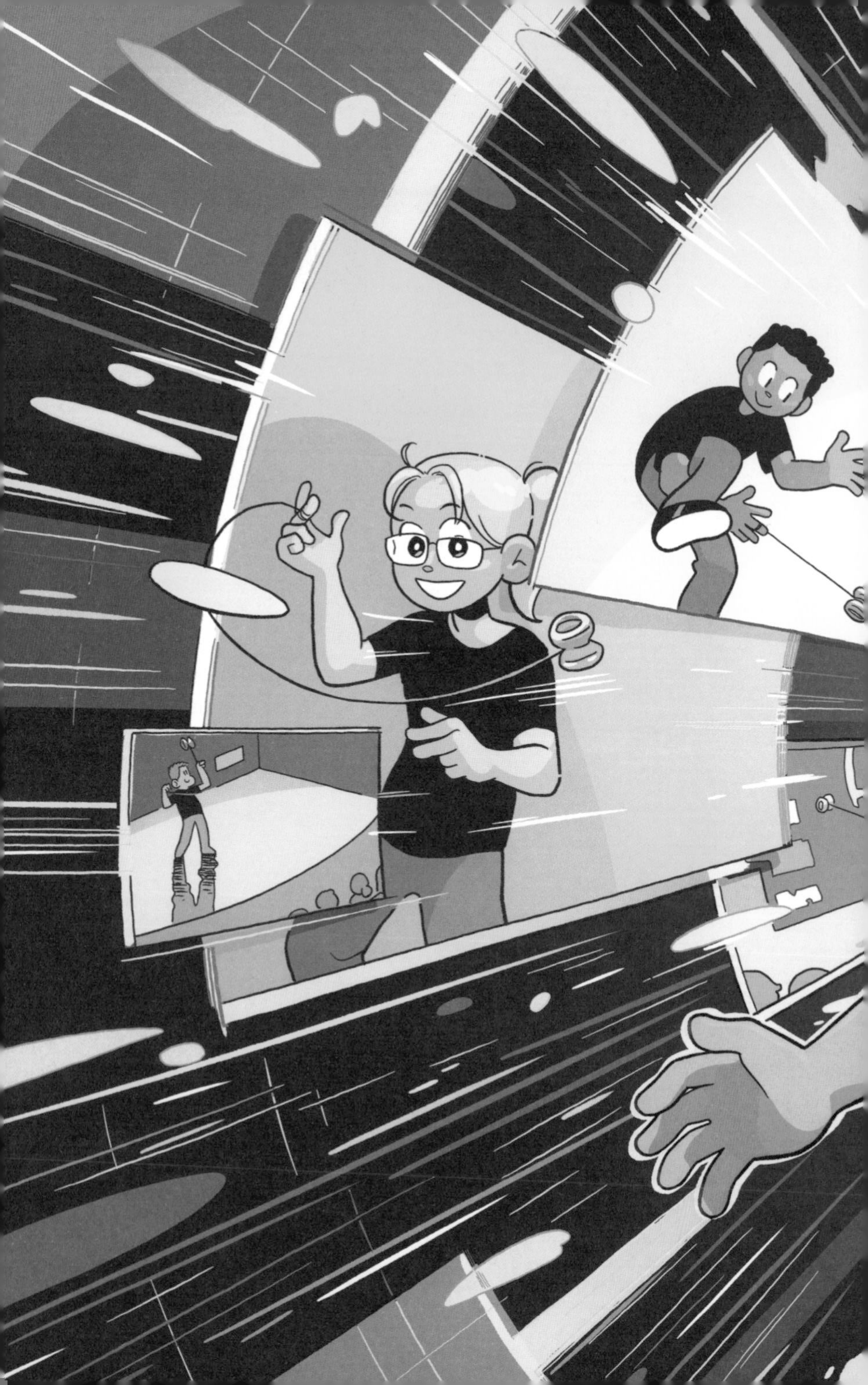

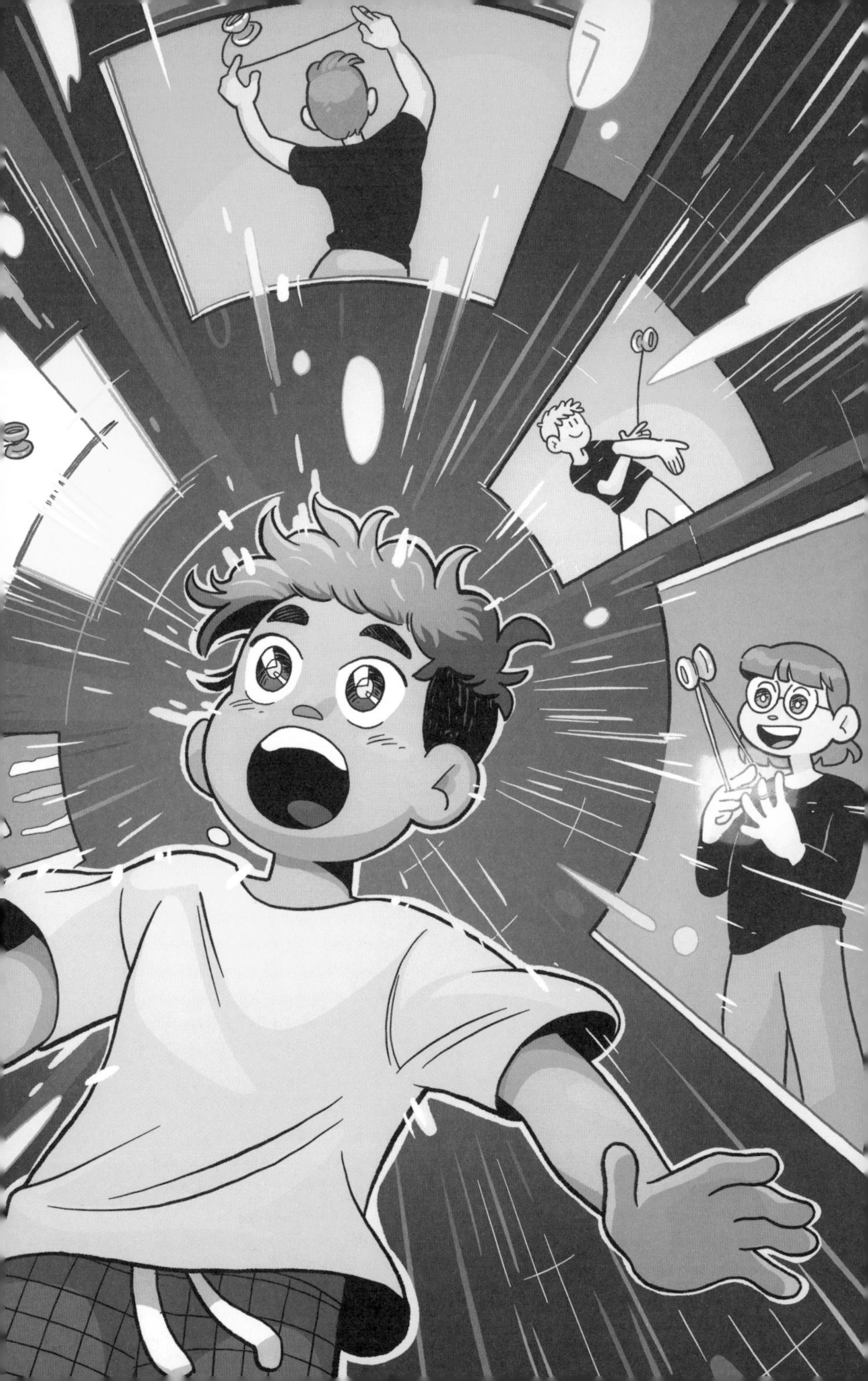

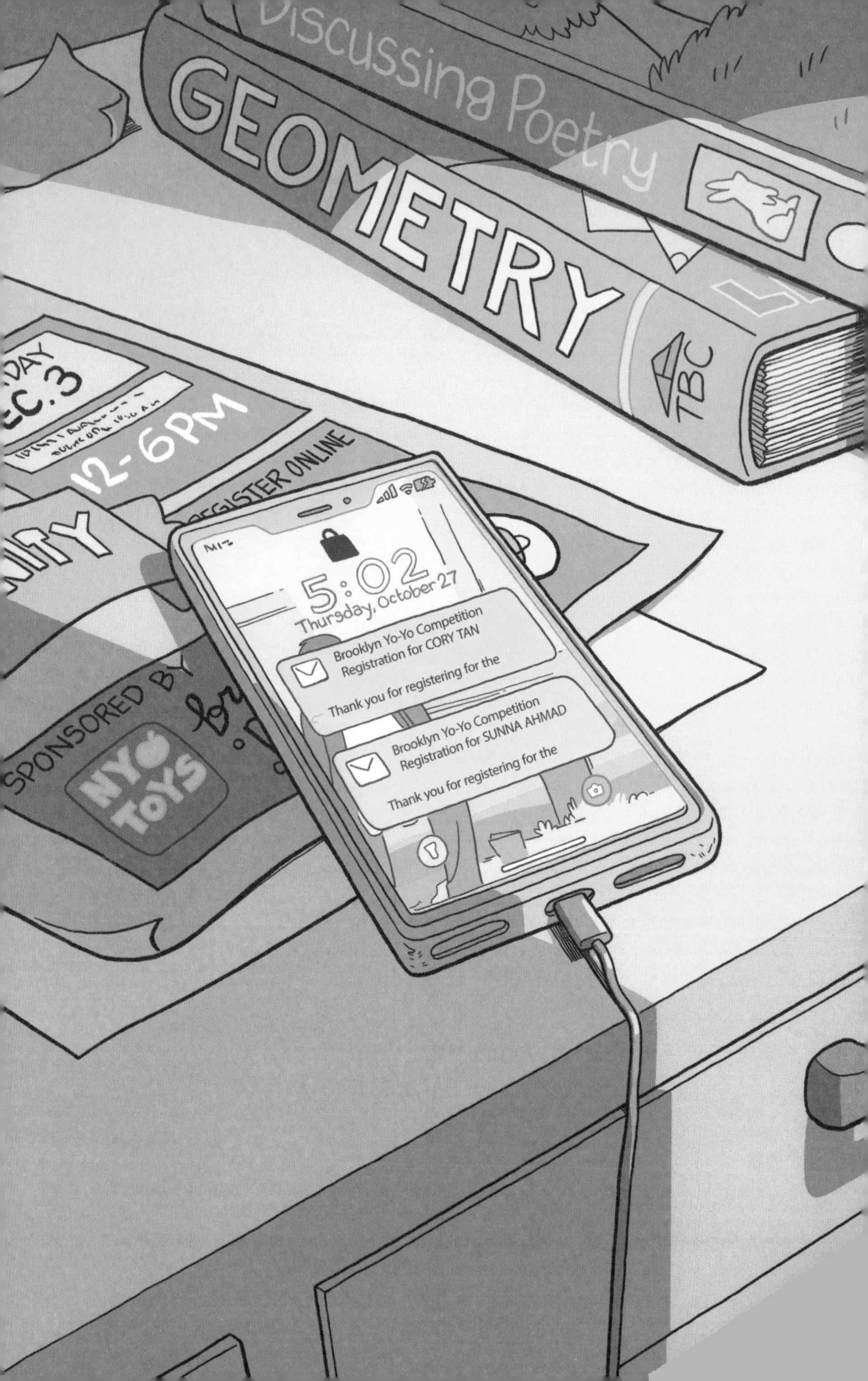

Discussing Poetry
GEOMETRY
TBC
12-6PM
REGISTER ONLINE
SPONSORED BY
NY TOYS
5:02
Thursday, October 27
Brooklyn Yo-Yo Competition
Registration for CORY TAN
Thank you for registering for the
Brooklyn Yo-Yo Competition
Registration for SUNNA AHMAD
Thank you for registering for the

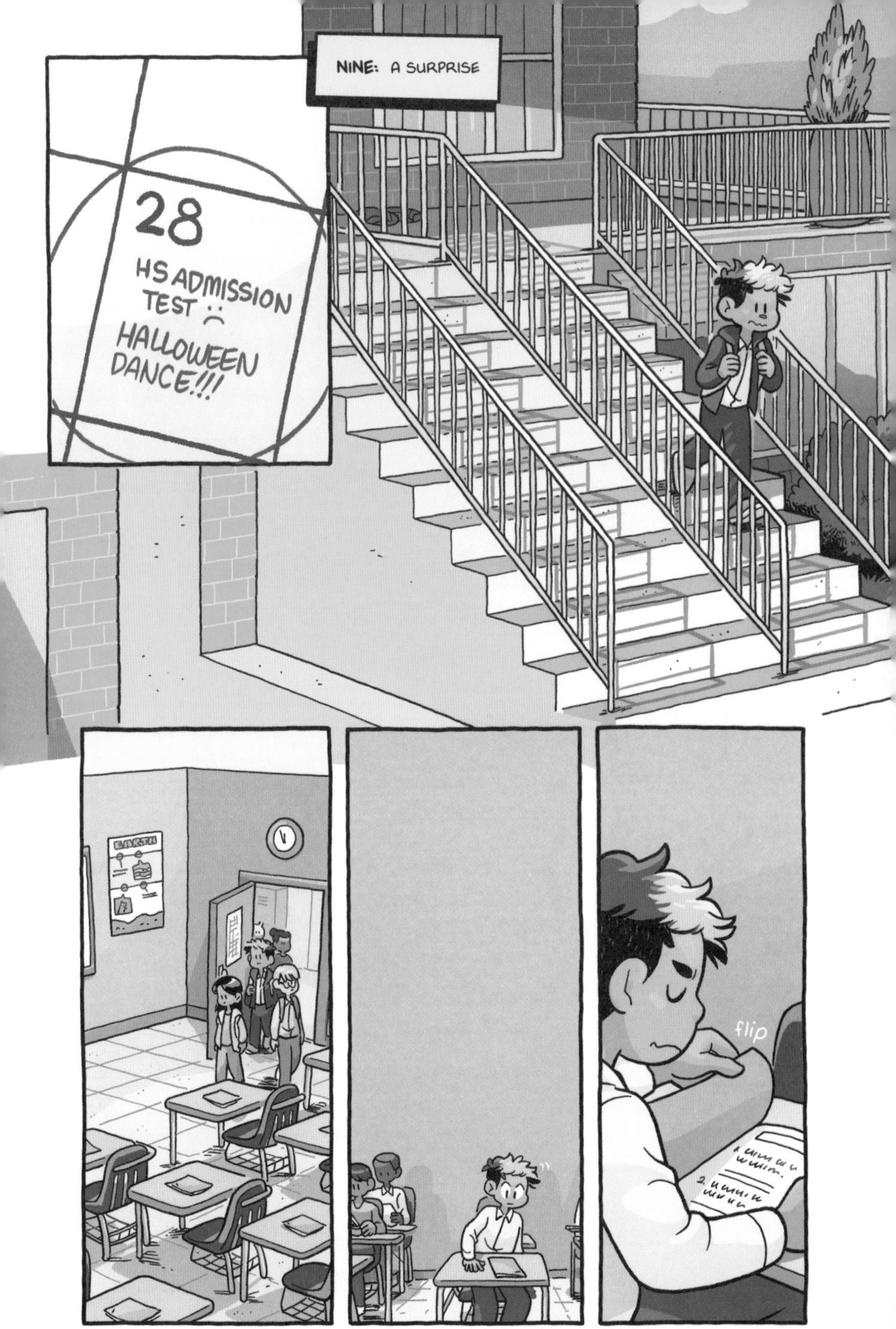

NINE: A SURPRISE
28
HS ADMISSION TEST :(
HALLOWEEN DANCE!!!
EARTH
flip

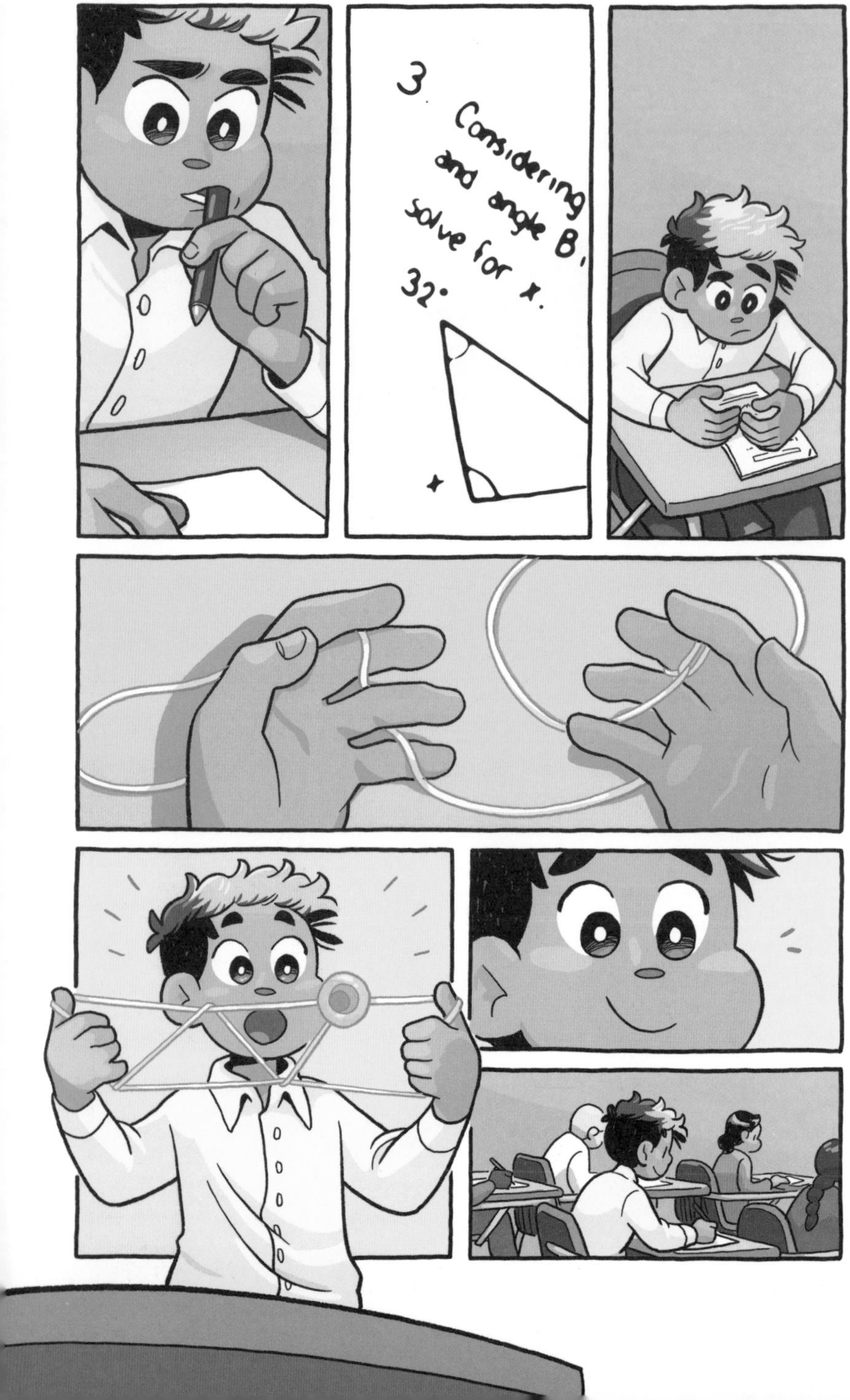
3. Considering angle B, solve for x.
32°
x

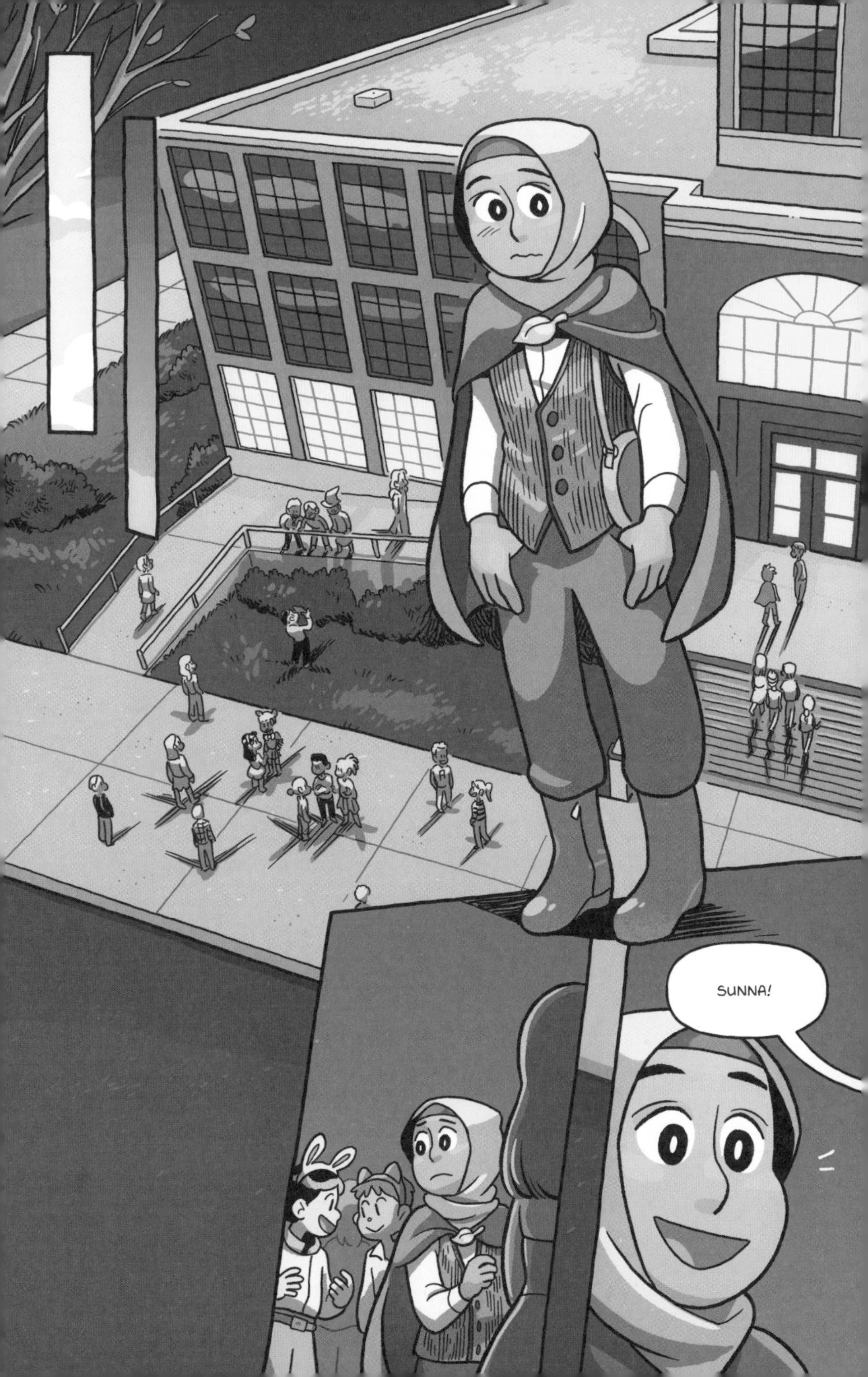
SUNNA!

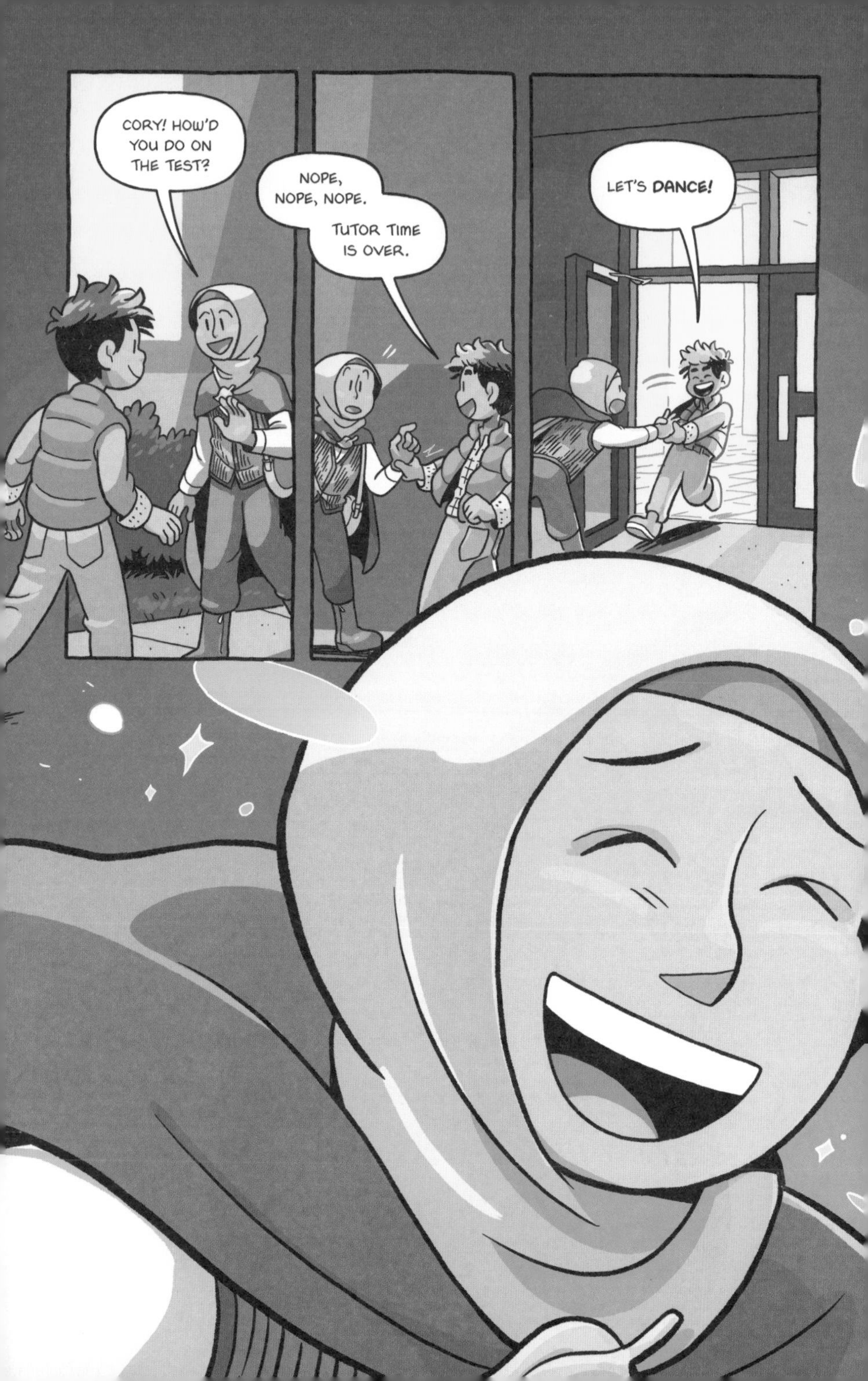
CORY! HOW'D YOU DO ON THE TEST?
NOPE, NOPE, NOPE.
TUTOR TIME IS OVER.
LET'S **DANCE!**

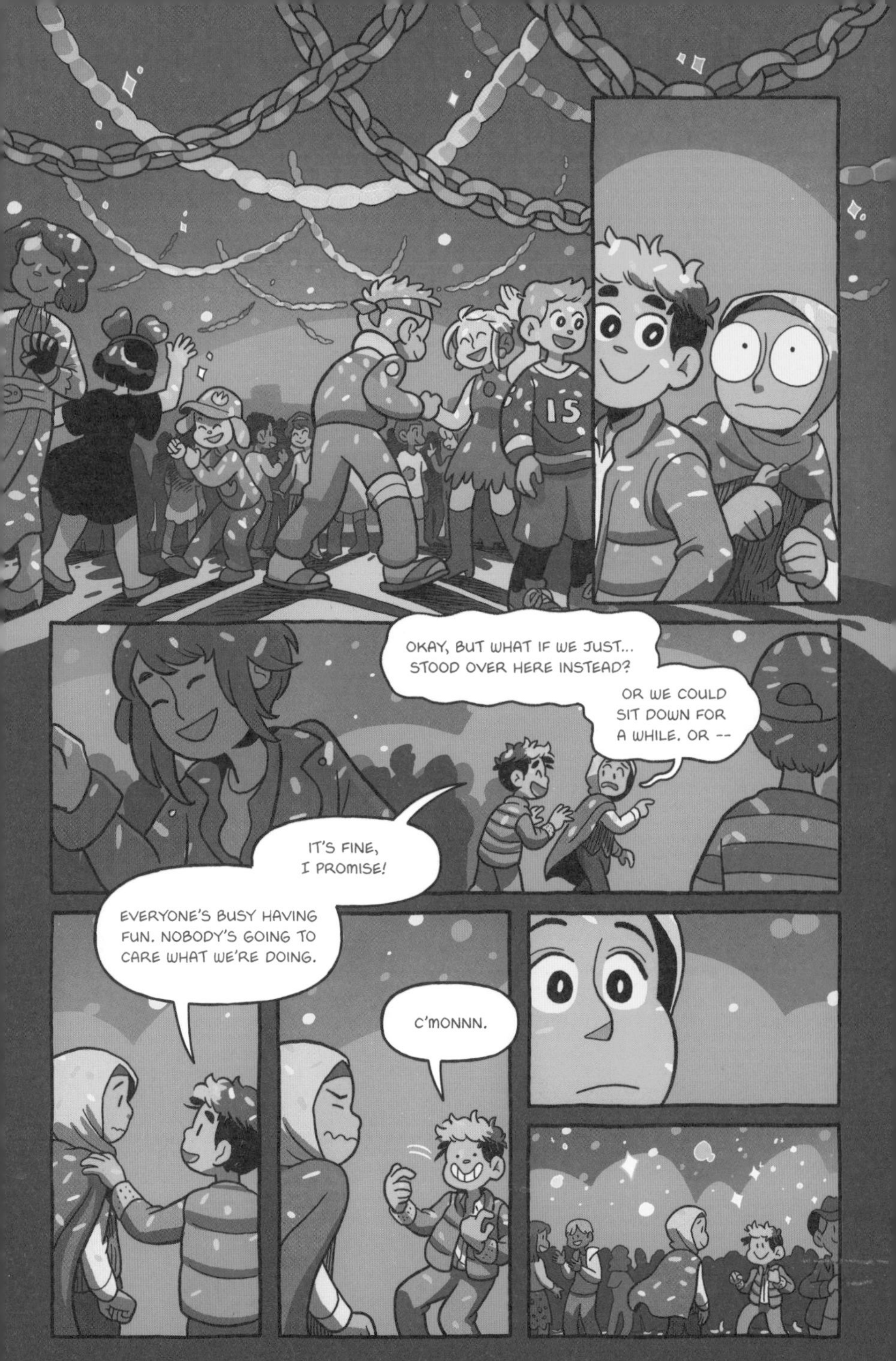
15
OKAY, BUT WHAT IF WE JUST... STOOD OVER HERE INSTEAD?
OR WE COULD SIT DOWN FOR A WHILE. OR --
IT'S FINE, I PROMISE!
EVERYONE'S BUSY HAVING FUN. NOBODY'S GOING TO CARE WHAT WE'RE DOING.
C'MONNN.

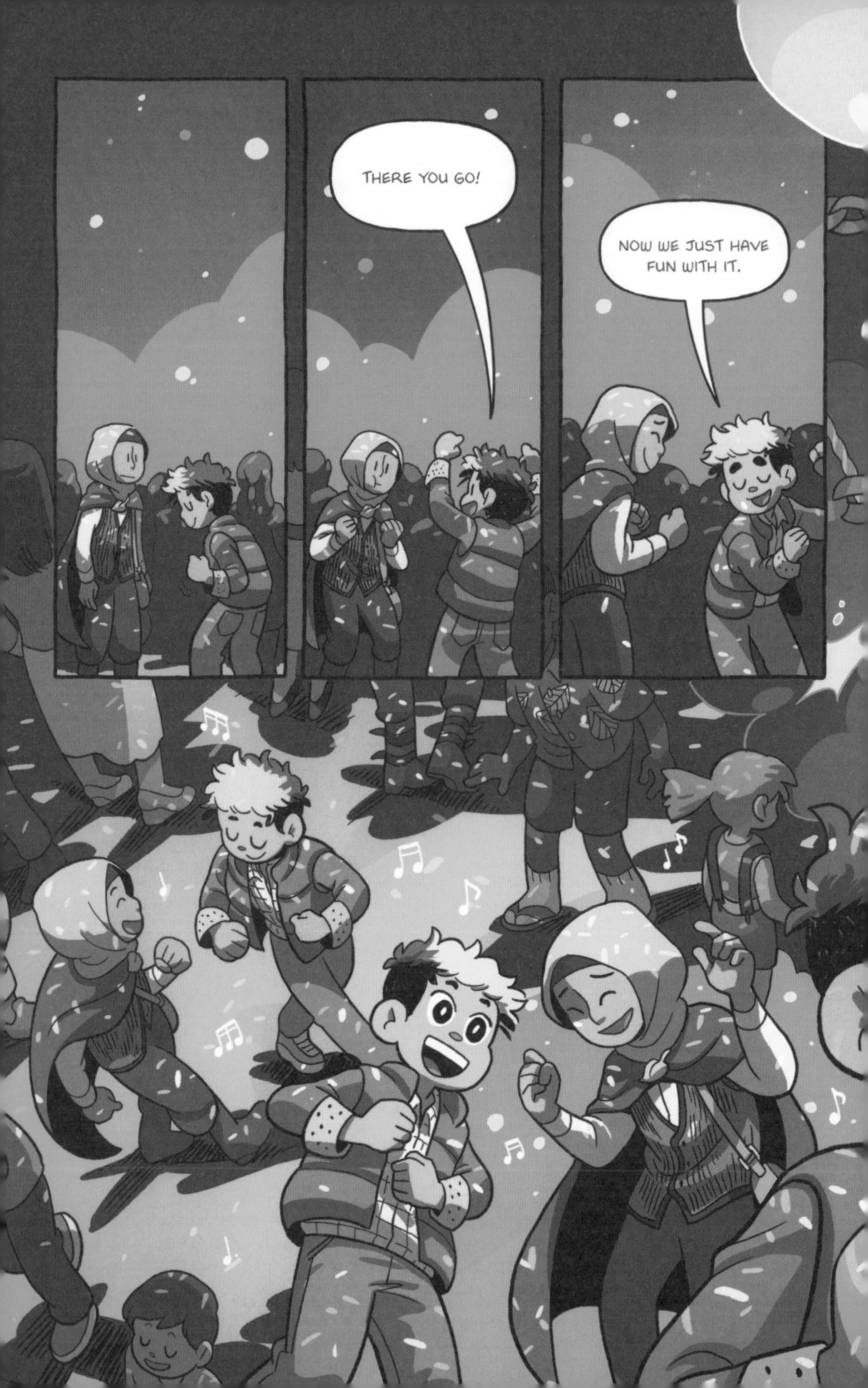
THERE YOU GO!
NOW WE JUST HAVE FUN WITH IT.

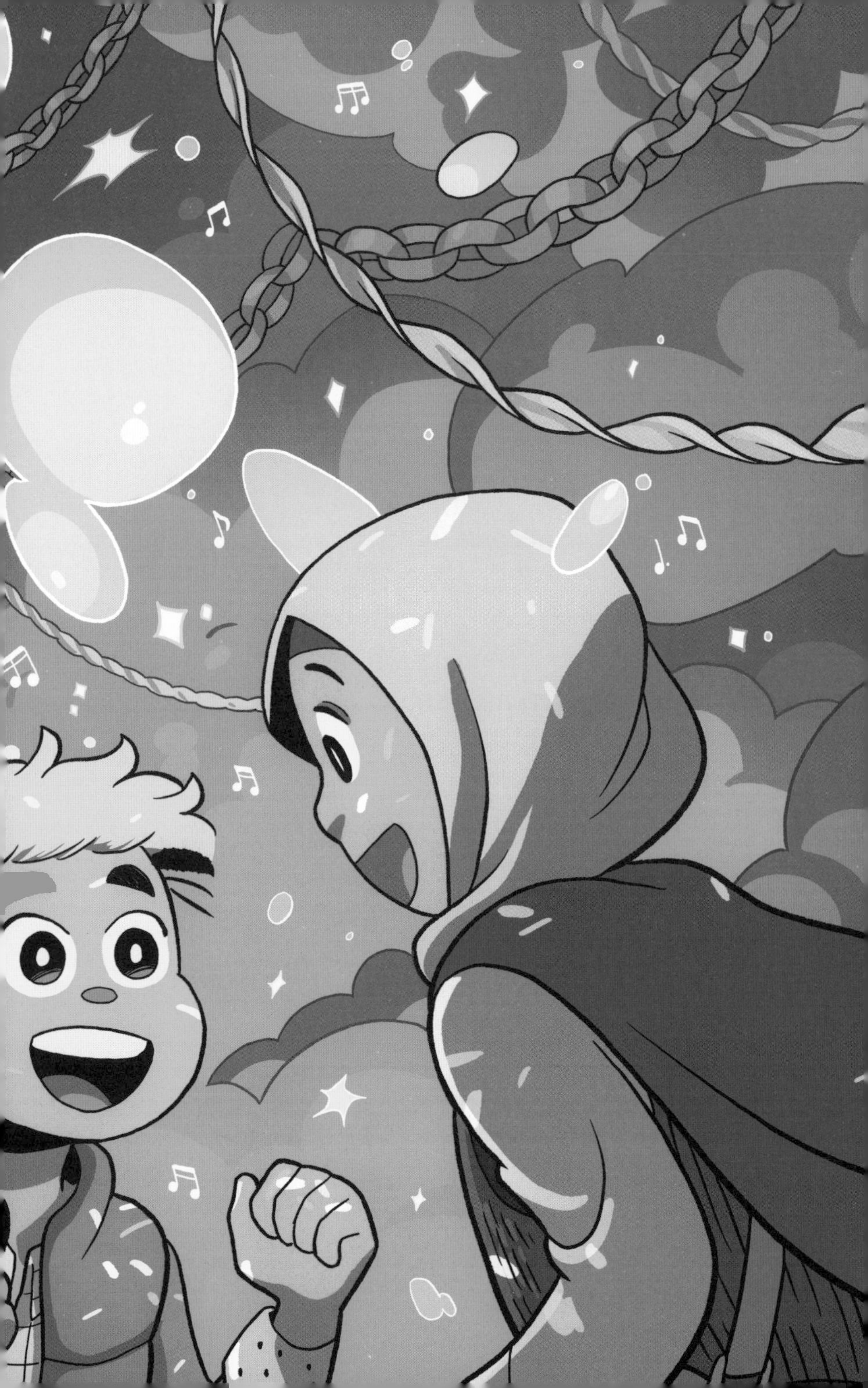

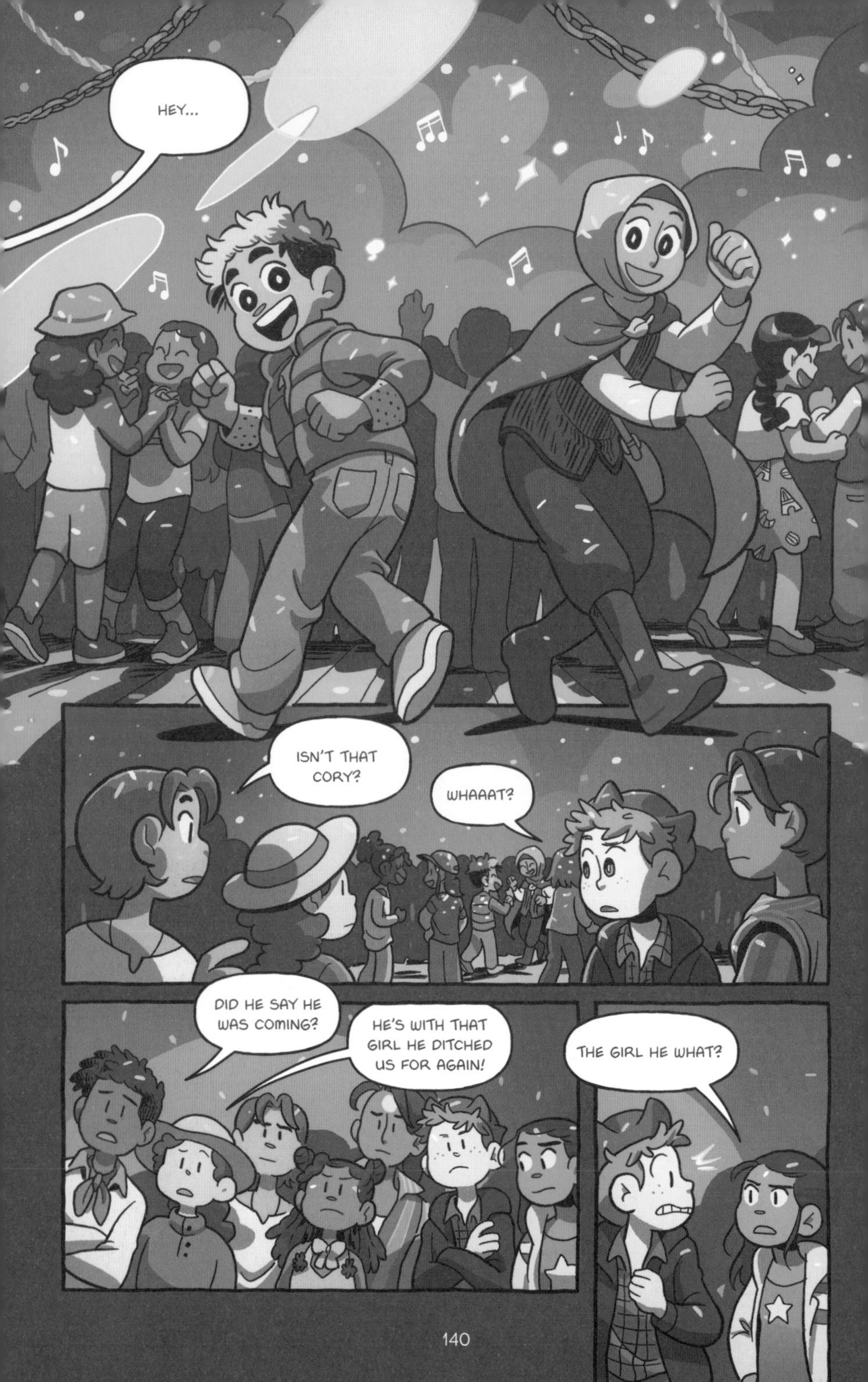
HEY...
ISN'T THAT CORY?
WHAAAT?
DID HE SAY HE WAS COMING?
HE'S WITH THAT GIRL HE DITCHED US FOR AGAIN!
THE GIRL HE WHAT?

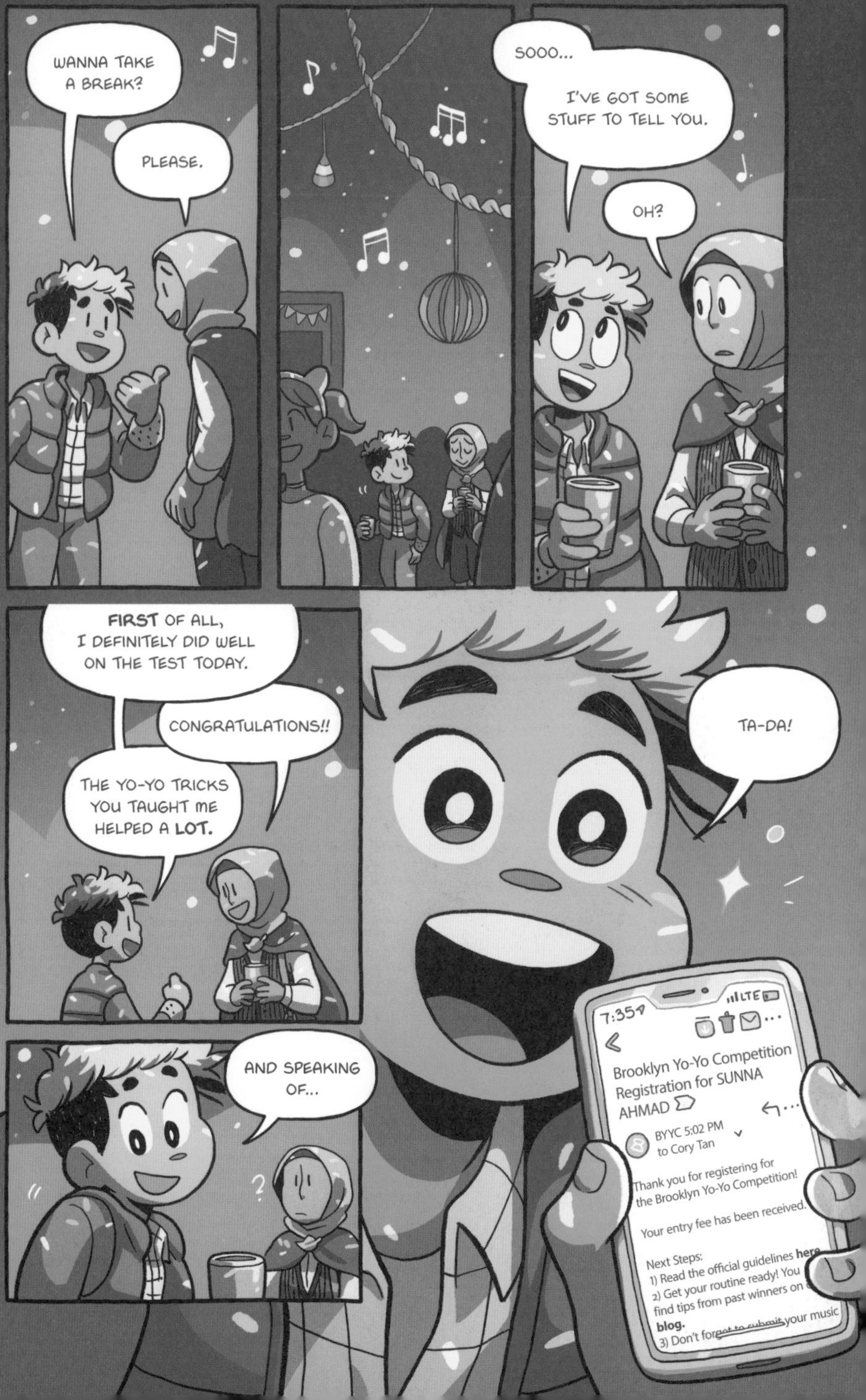
WANNA TAKE A BREAK?
PLEASE.
SOOO...
I'VE GOT SOME STUFF TO TELL YOU.
OH?
FIRST OF ALL, I DEFINITELY DID WELL ON THE TEST TODAY.
CONGRATULATIONS!!
THE YO-YO TRICKS YOU TAUGHT ME HELPED A LOT.
AND SPEAKING OF...
TA-DA!
7:35
LTE
Brooklyn Yo-Yo Competition Registration for SUNNA AHMAD
BYYC 5:02 PM
to Cory Tan
Thank you for registering for the Brooklyn Yo-Yo Competition!
Your entry fee has been received.
Next Steps:
1) Read the official guidelines here
2) Get your routine ready! You
find tips from past winners on
blog.
3) Don't for your music

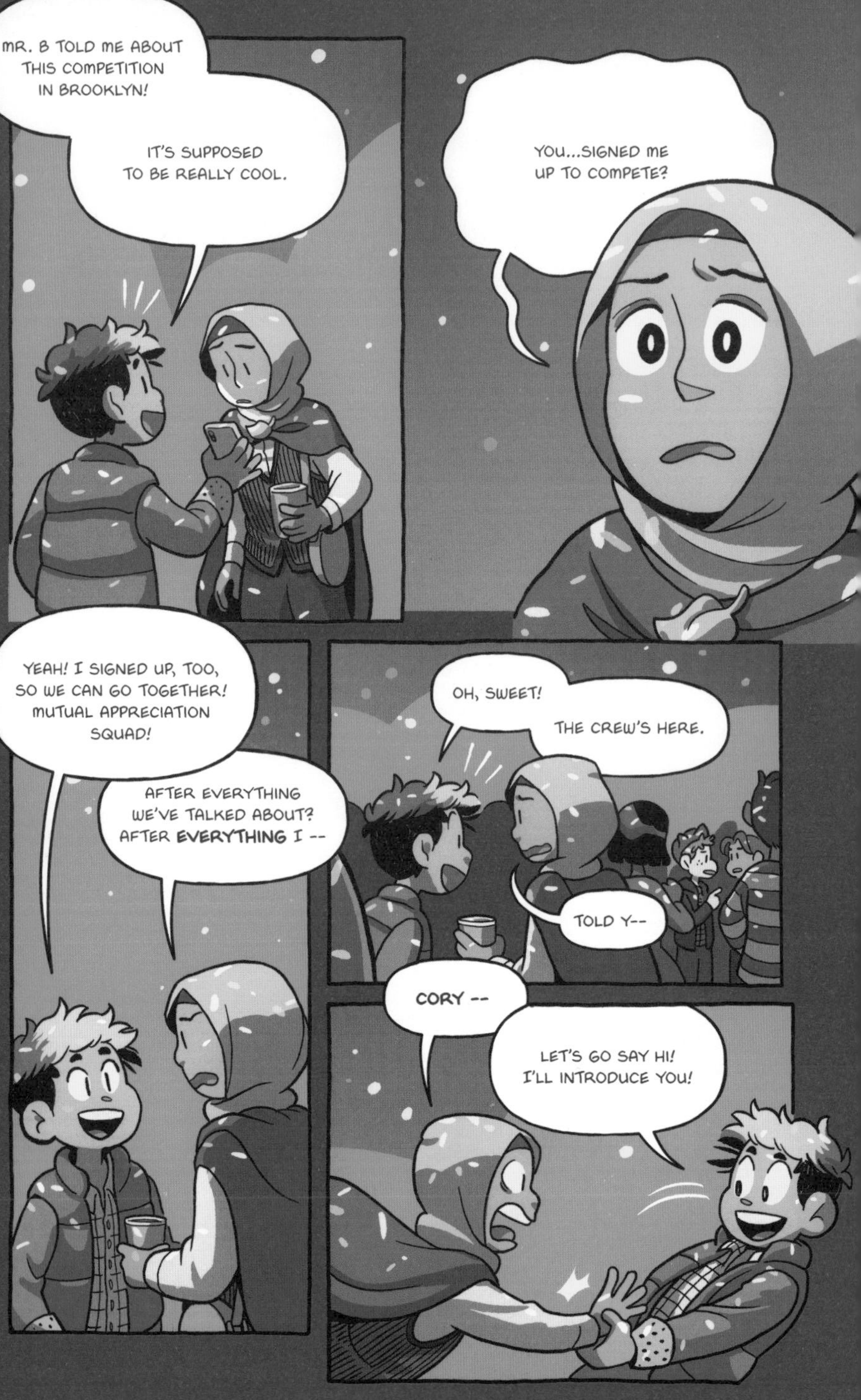
MR. B TOLD ME ABOUT THIS COMPETITION IN BROOKLYN!
IT'S SUPPOSED TO BE REALLY COOL.
YOU...SIGNED ME UP TO COMPETE?
YEAH! I SIGNED UP, TOO, SO WE CAN GO TOGETHER! MUTUAL APPRECIATION SQUAD!
AFTER EVERYTHING WE'VE TALKED ABOUT? AFTER **EVERYTHING** I --
OH, SWEET!
THE CREW'S HERE.
TOLD Y--
CORY --
LET'S GO SAY HI! I'LL INTRODUCE YOU!

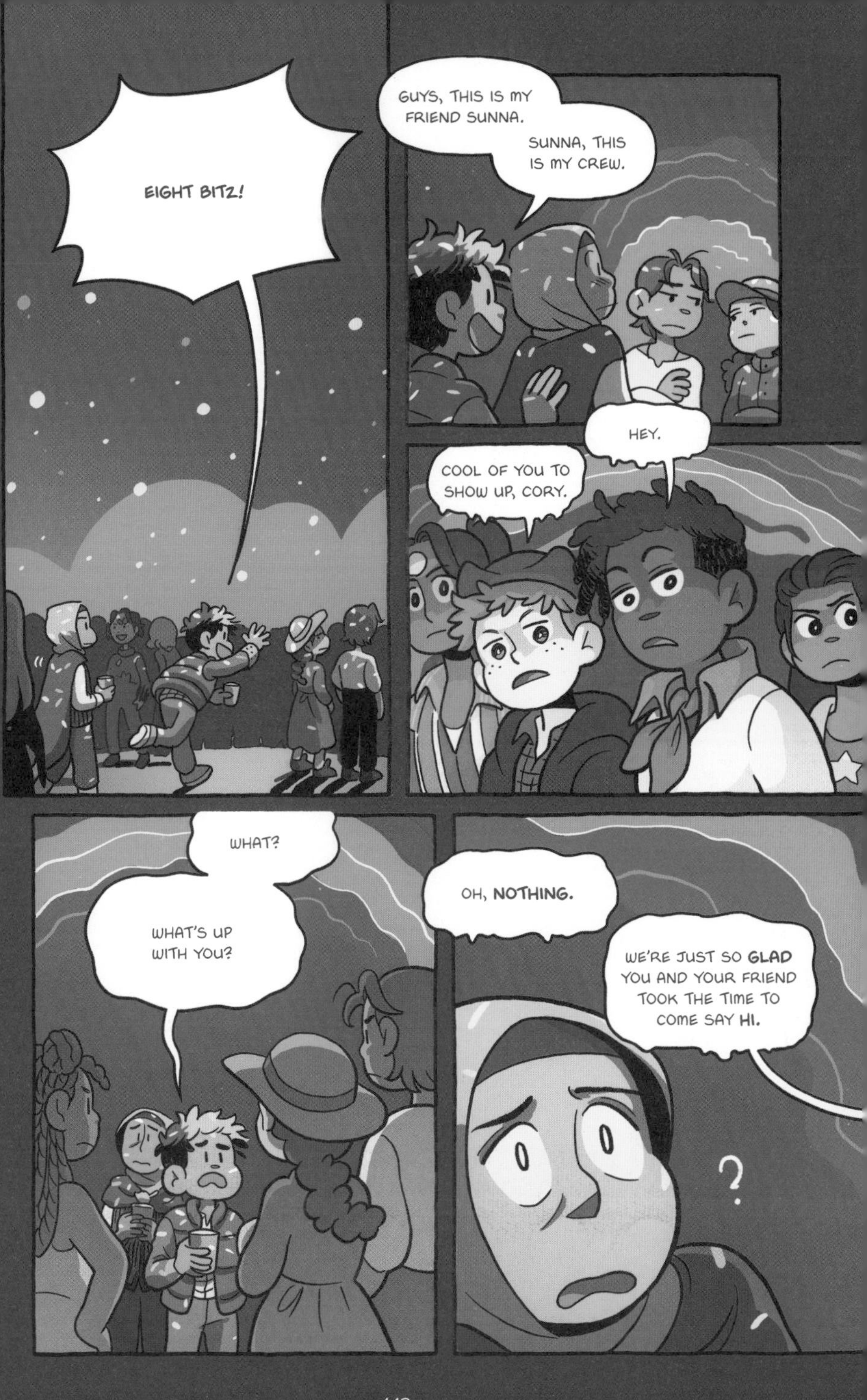
EIGHT BITZ!
GUYS, THIS IS MY FRIEND SUNNA.
SUNNA, THIS IS MY CREW.
COOL OF YOU TO SHOW UP, CORY.
HEY.
WHAT?
WHAT'S UP WITH YOU?
OH, **NOTHING.**
WE'RE JUST SO **GLAD** YOU AND YOUR FRIEND TOOK THE TIME TO COME SAY **HI.**
?

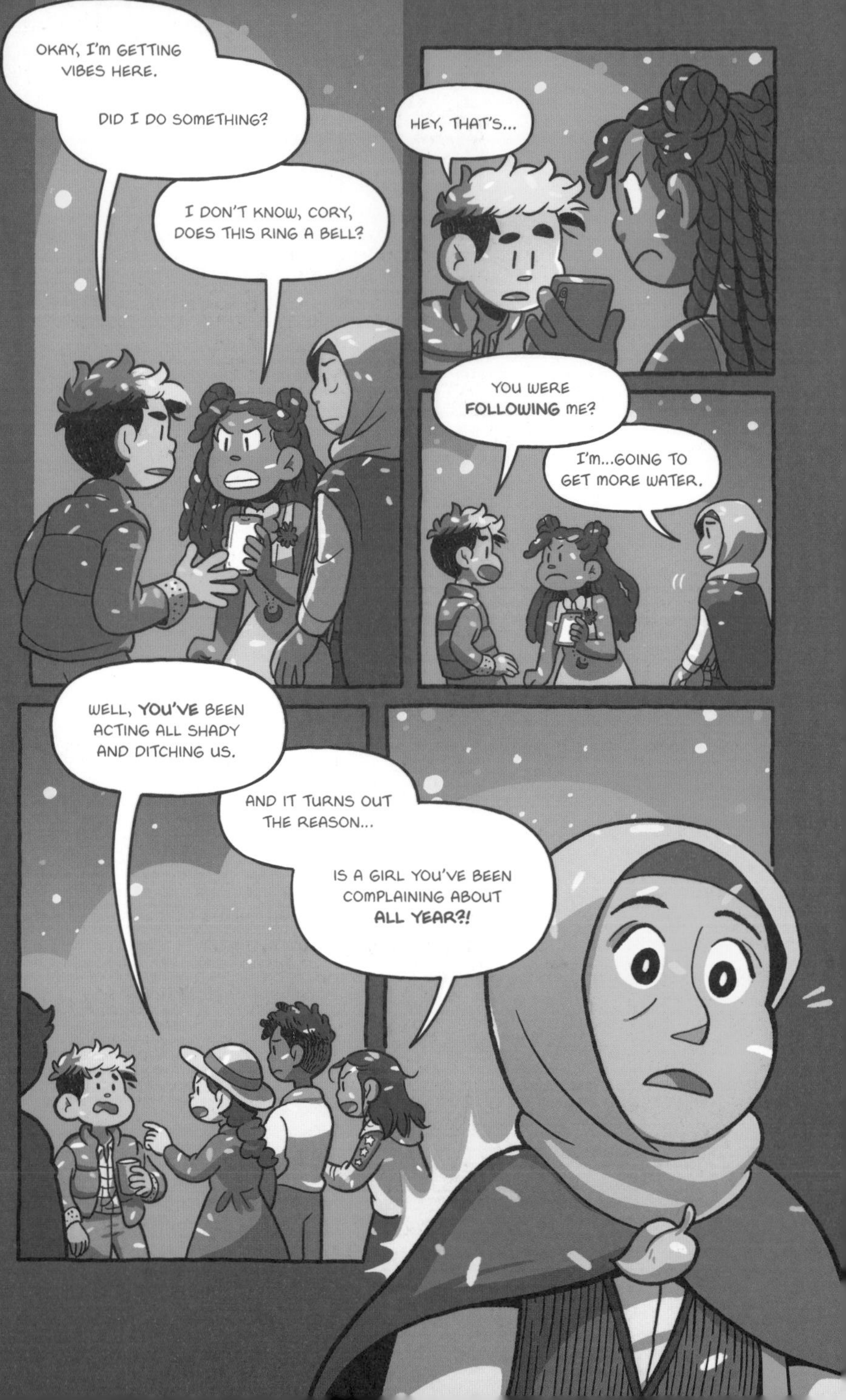
OKAY, I'M GETTING VIBES HERE.
DID I DO SOMETHING?
I DON'T KNOW, CORY, DOES THIS RING A BELL?
HEY, THAT'S...
YOU WERE **FOLLOWING** ME?
I'M...GOING TO GET MORE WATER.
WELL, **YOU'VE** BEEN ACTING ALL SHADY AND DITCHING US.
AND IT TURNS OUT THE REASON...
IS A GIRL YOU'VE BEEN COMPLAINING ABOUT **ALL YEAR?!**

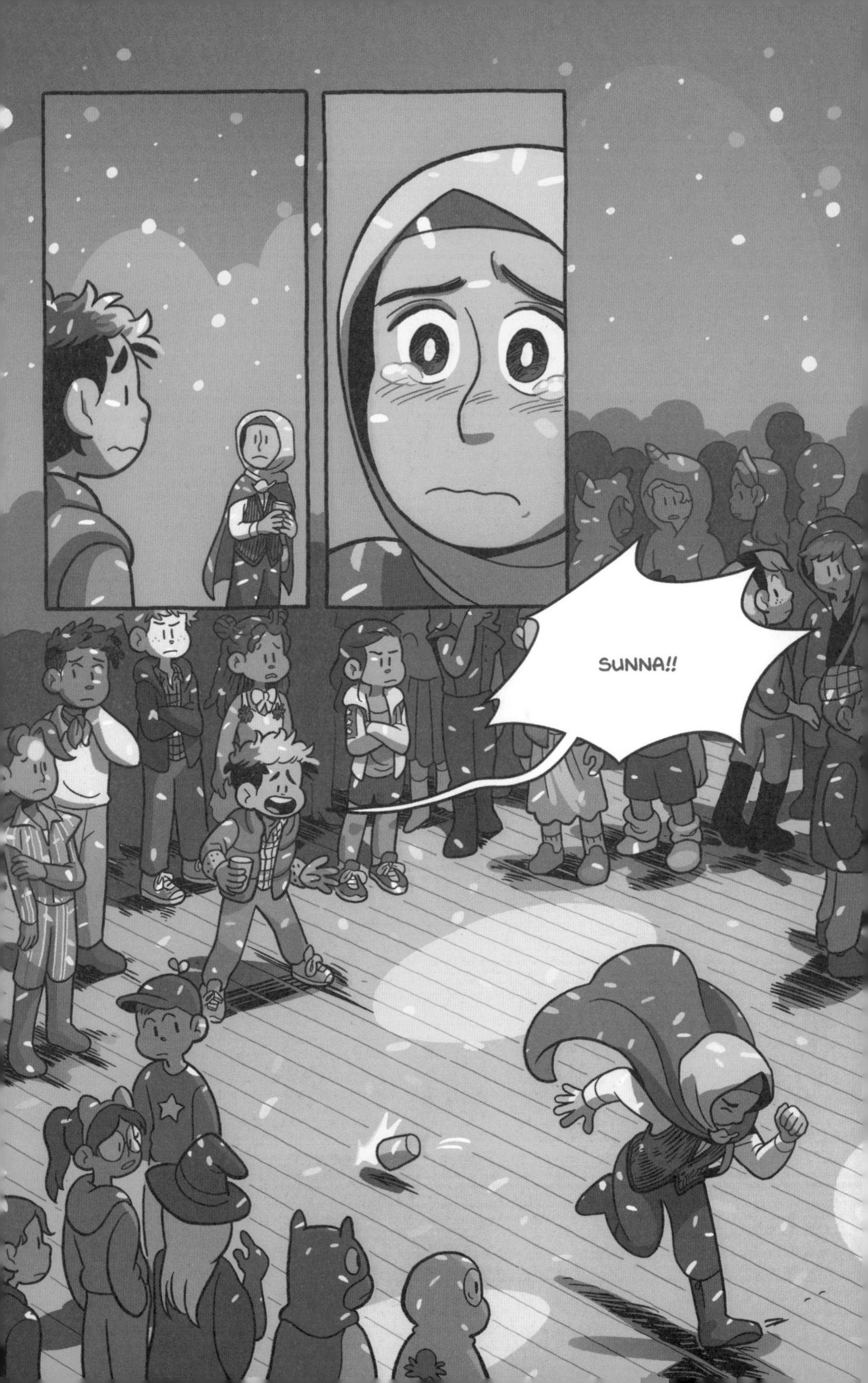
SUNNA!!

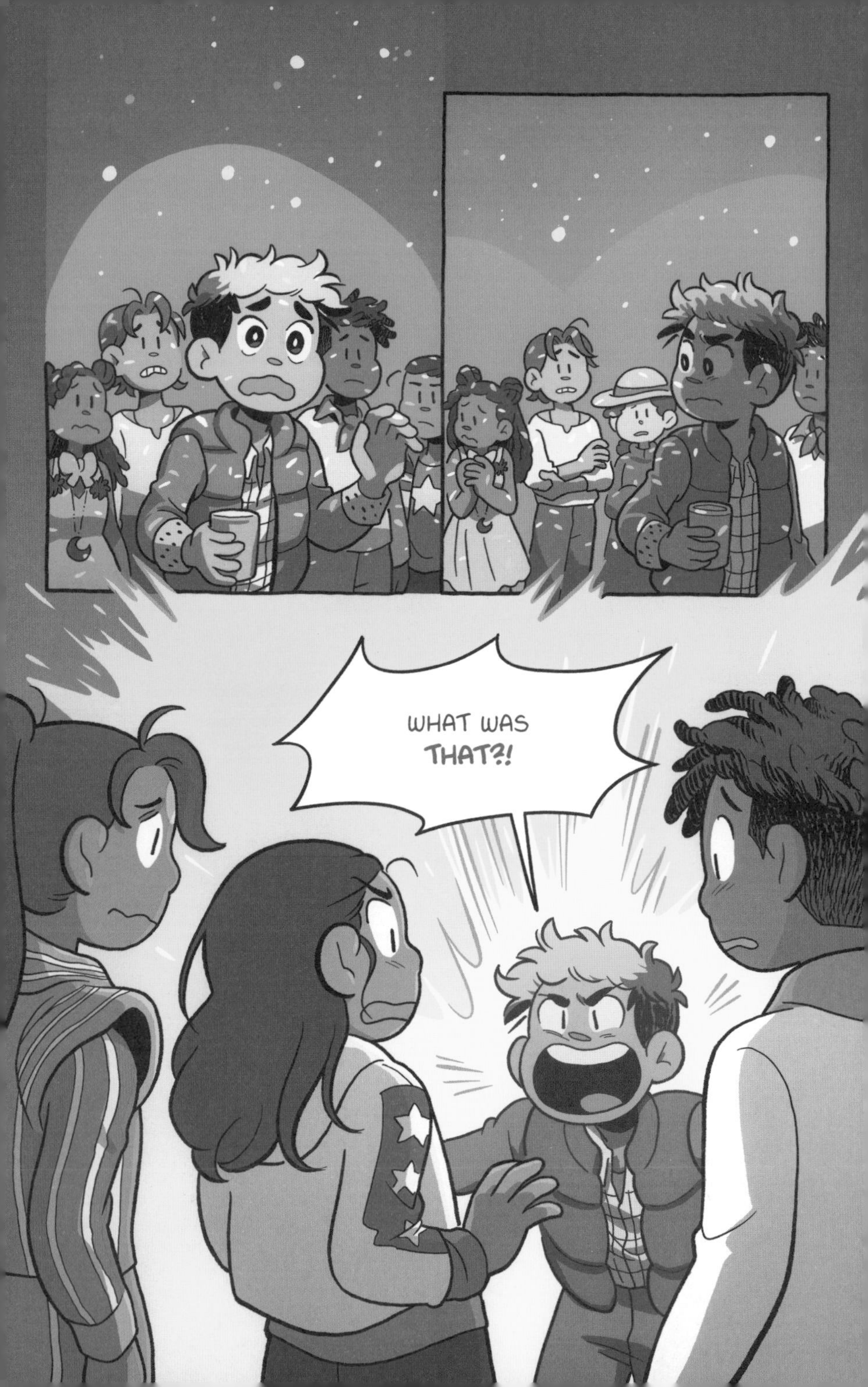
WHAT WAS THAT?!

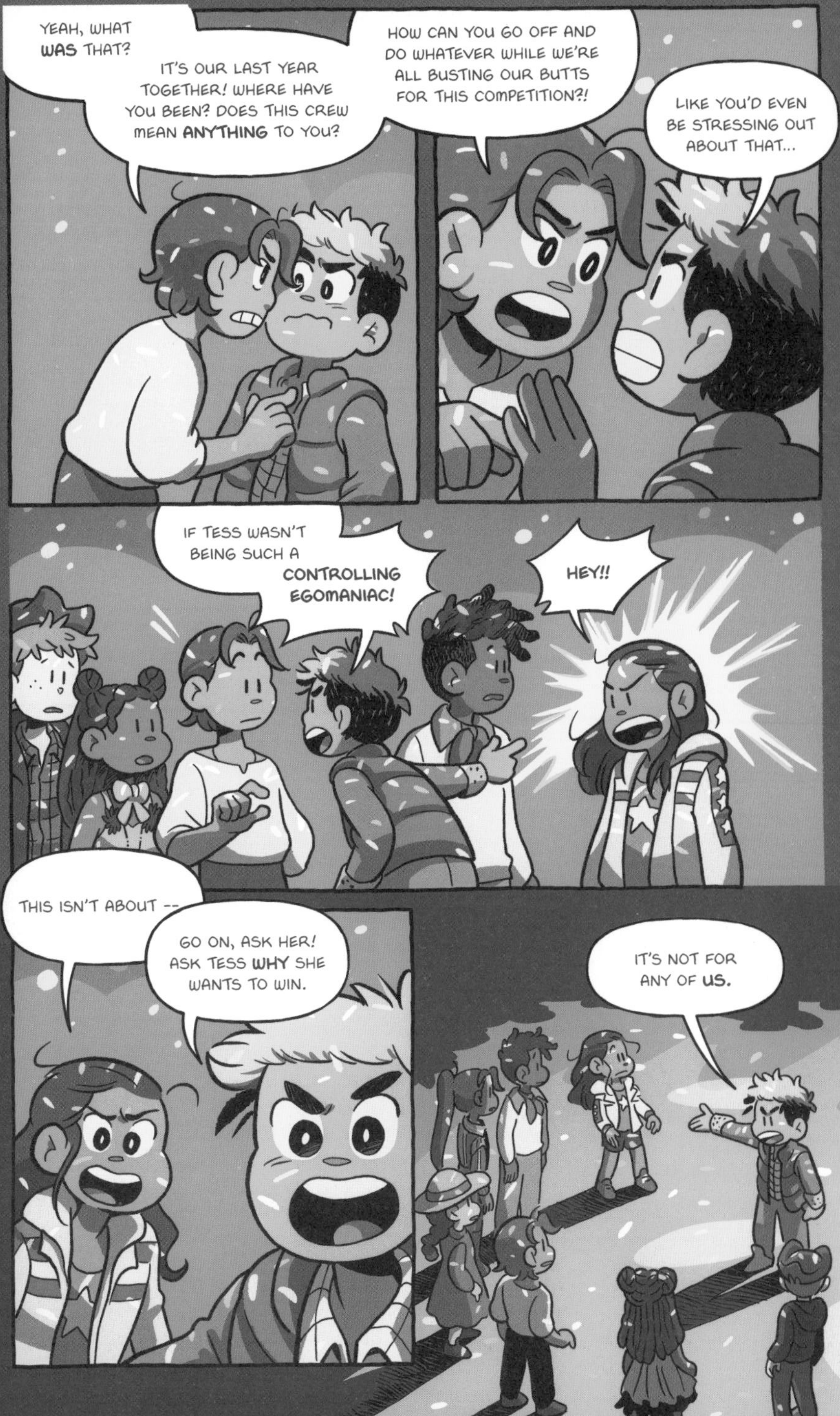
YEAH, WHAT **WAS** THAT?
IT'S OUR LAST YEAR TOGETHER! WHERE HAVE YOU BEEN? DOES THIS CREW MEAN **ANYTHING** TO YOU?
HOW CAN YOU GO OFF AND DO WHATEVER WHILE WE'RE ALL BUSTING OUR BUTTS FOR THIS COMPETITION?!
LIKE YOU'D EVEN BE STRESSING OUT ABOUT THAT...
IF TESS WASN'T BEING SUCH A **CONTROLLING EGOMANIAC!**
HEY!!
THIS ISN'T ABOUT --
GO ON, ASK HER! ASK TESS **WHY** SHE WANTS TO WIN.
IT'S NOT FOR ANY OF **US.**

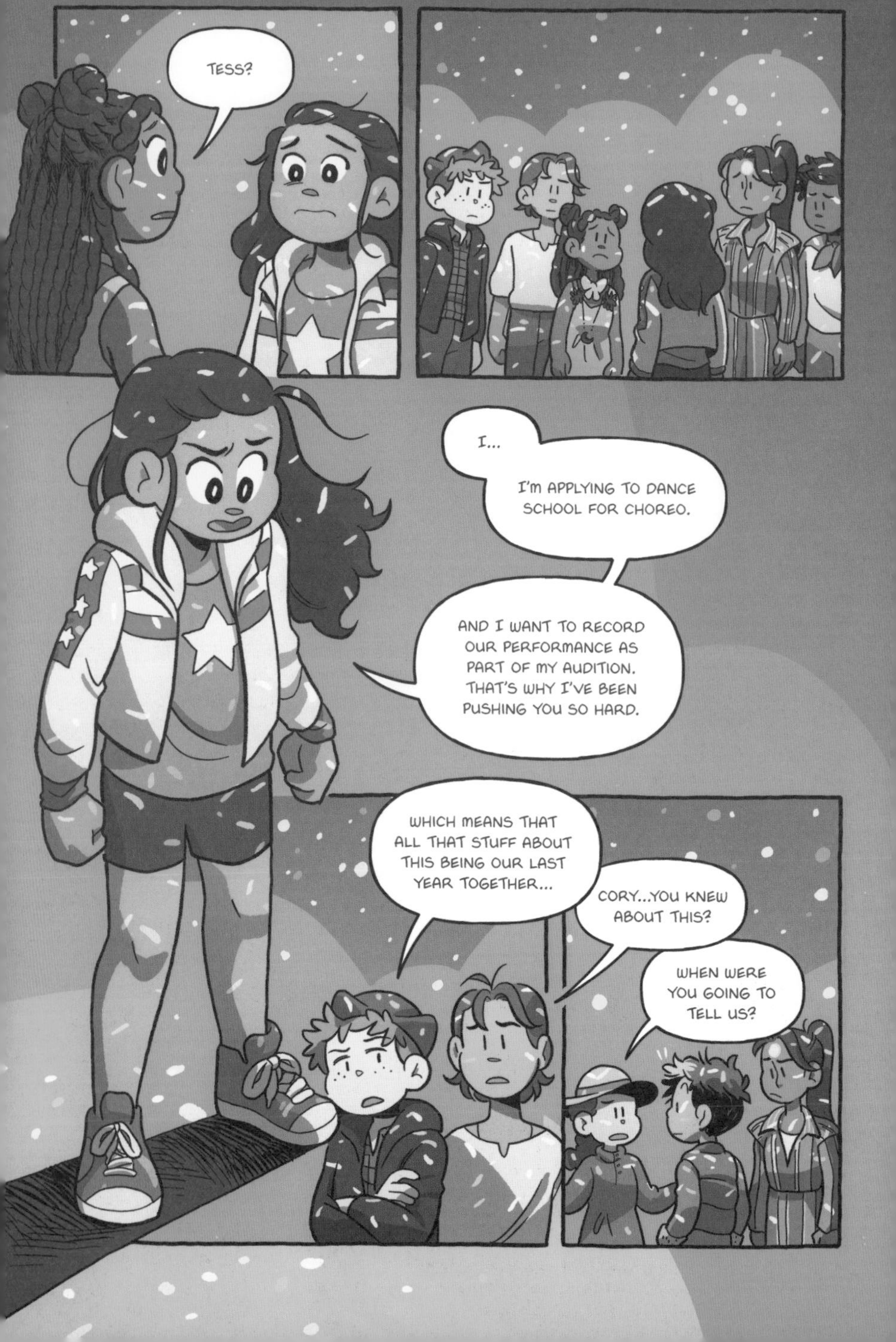
TESS?
I...
I'M APPLYING TO DANCE SCHOOL FOR CHOREO.
AND I WANT TO RECORD OUR PERFORMANCE AS PART OF MY AUDITION. THAT'S WHY I'VE BEEN PUSHING YOU SO HARD.
WHICH MEANS THAT ALL THAT STUFF ABOUT THIS BEING OUR LAST YEAR TOGETHER...
CORY...YOU KNEW ABOUT THIS?
WHEN WERE YOU GOING TO TELL US?

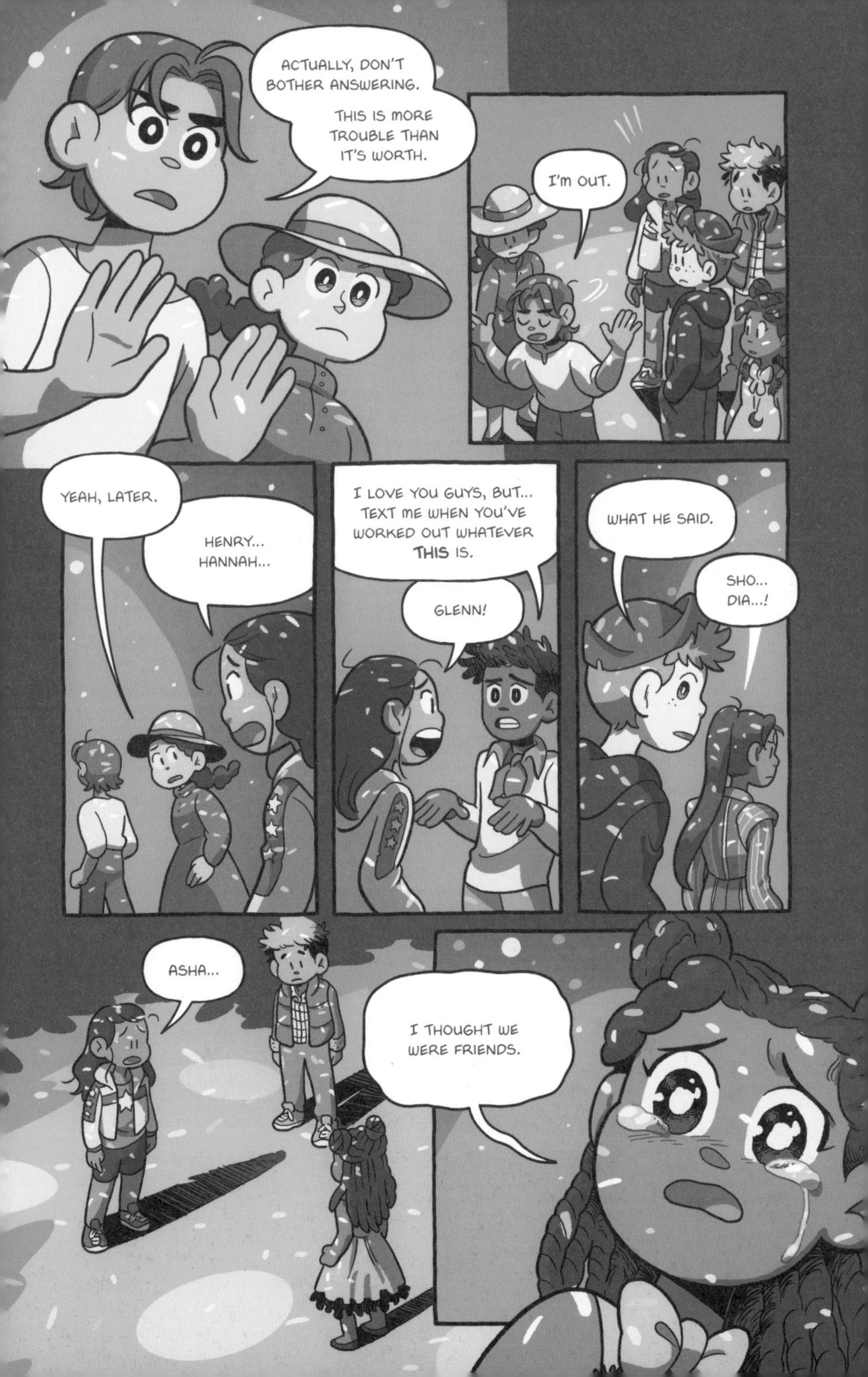

ACTUALLY, DON'T BOTHER ANSWERING.
THIS IS MORE TROUBLE THAN IT'S WORTH.
I'M OUT.
YEAH, LATER.
HENRY... HANNAH...
I LOVE YOU GUYS, BUT... TEXT ME WHEN YOU'VE WORKED OUT WHATEVER THIS IS.
GLENN!
WHAT HE SAID.
SHO... DIA...!
ASHA...
I THOUGHT WE WERE FRIENDS.

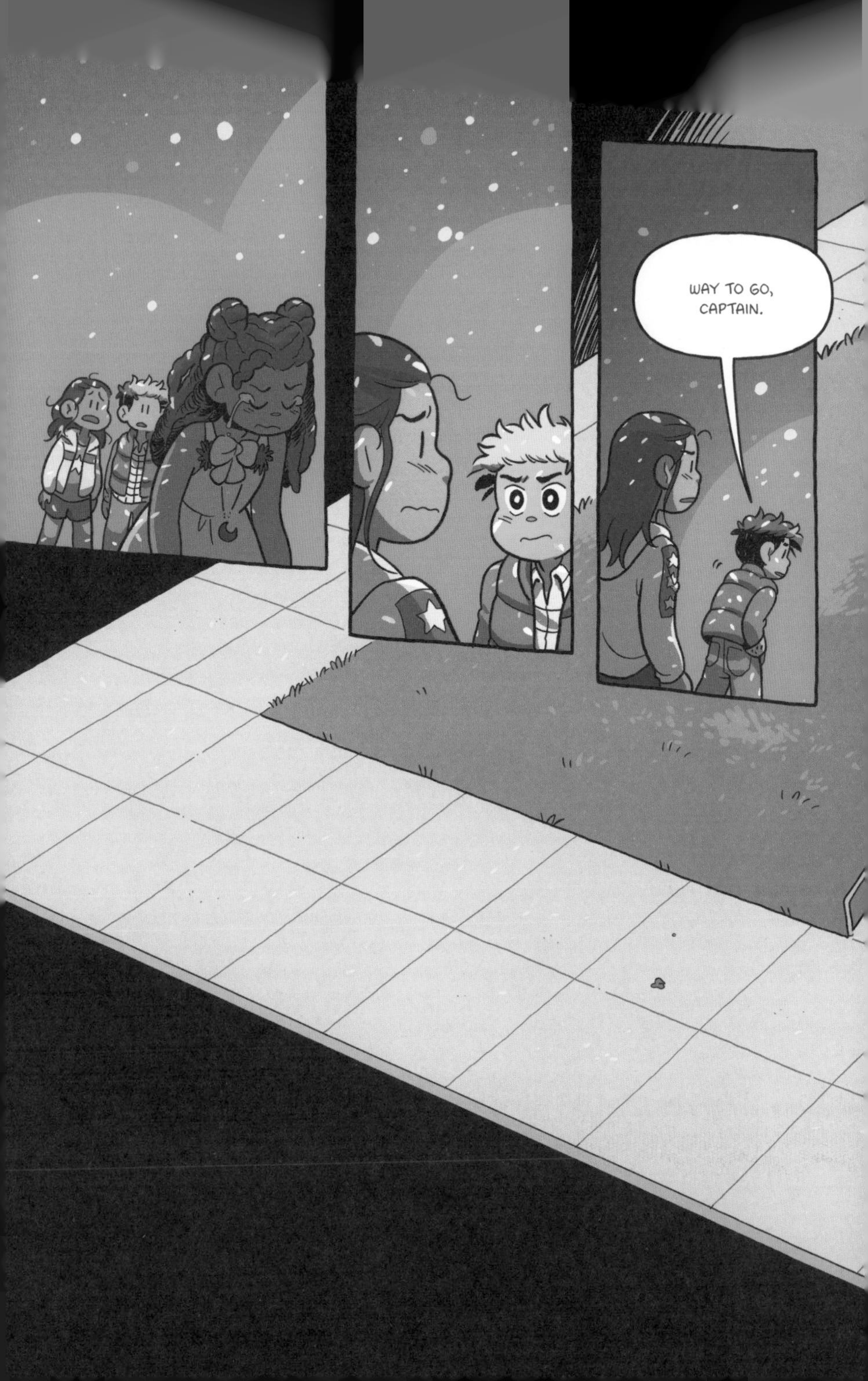
WAY TO GO, CAPTAIN.

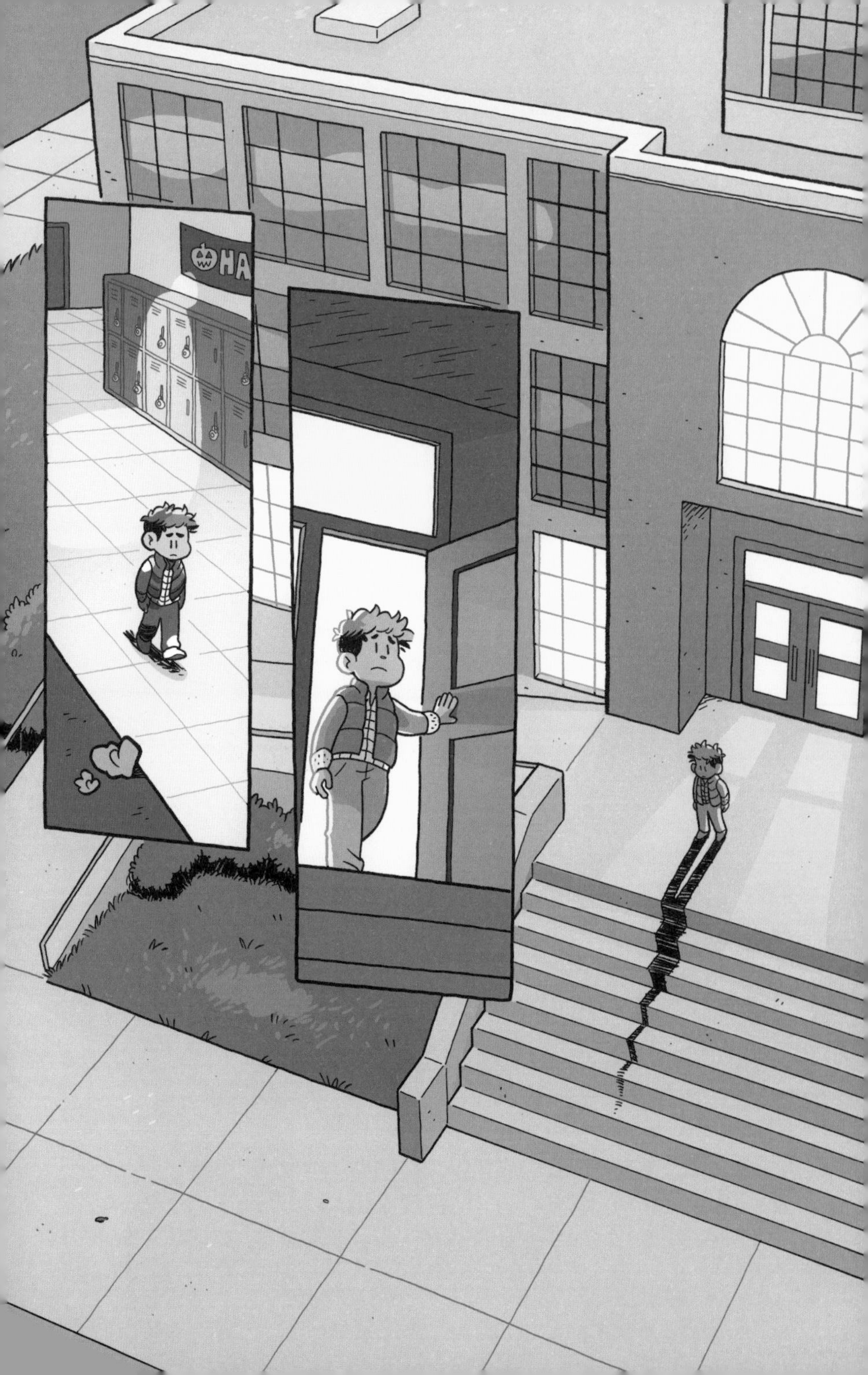

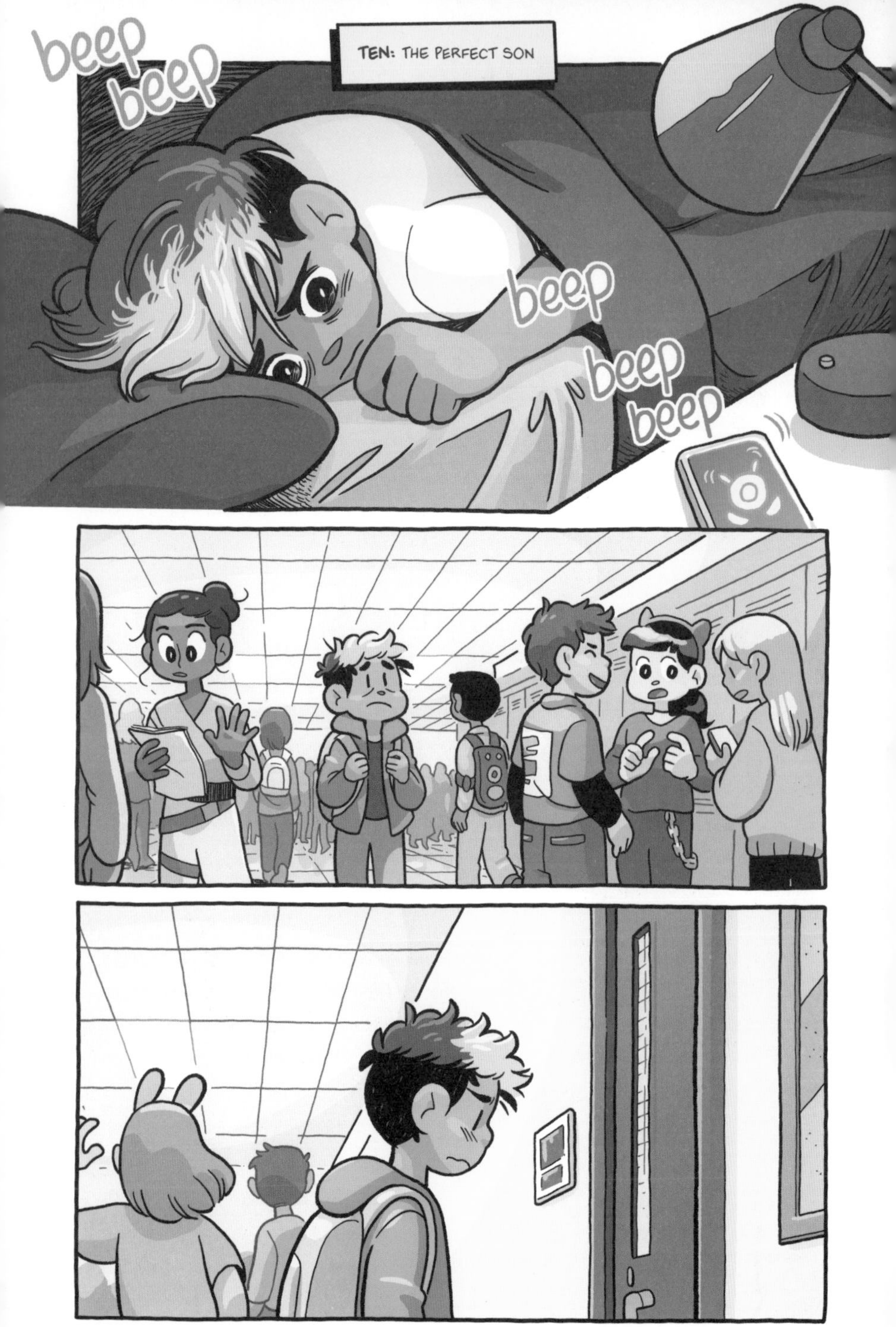
beep
beep
TEN: THE PERFECT SON
beep
beep
beep

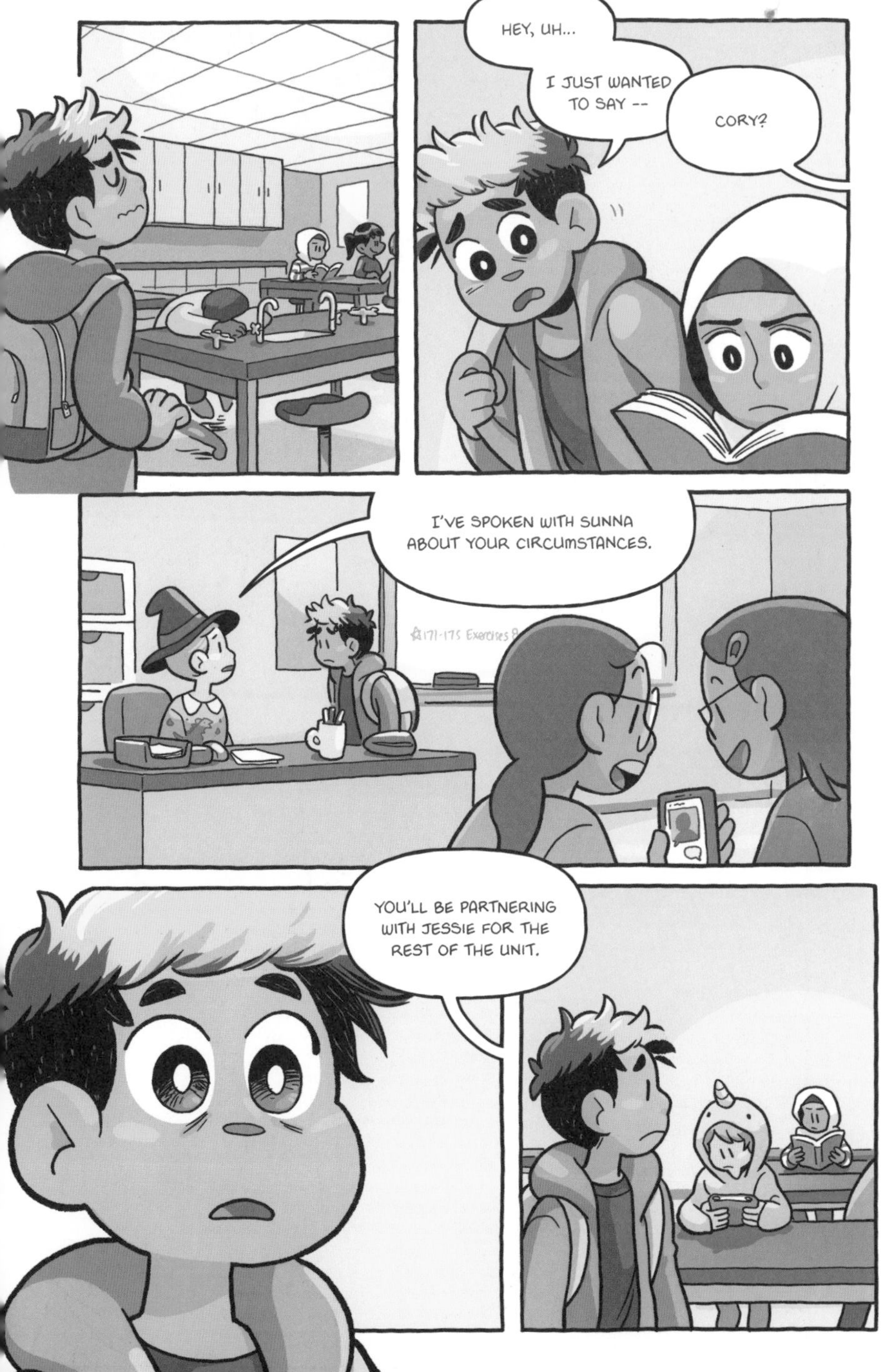
HEY, UH...
I JUST WANTED TO SAY --
CORY?
I'VE SPOKEN WITH SUNNA ABOUT YOUR CIRCUMSTANCES.
171-175 Exercises
YOU'LL BE PARTNERING WITH JESSIE FOR THE REST OF THE UNIT.

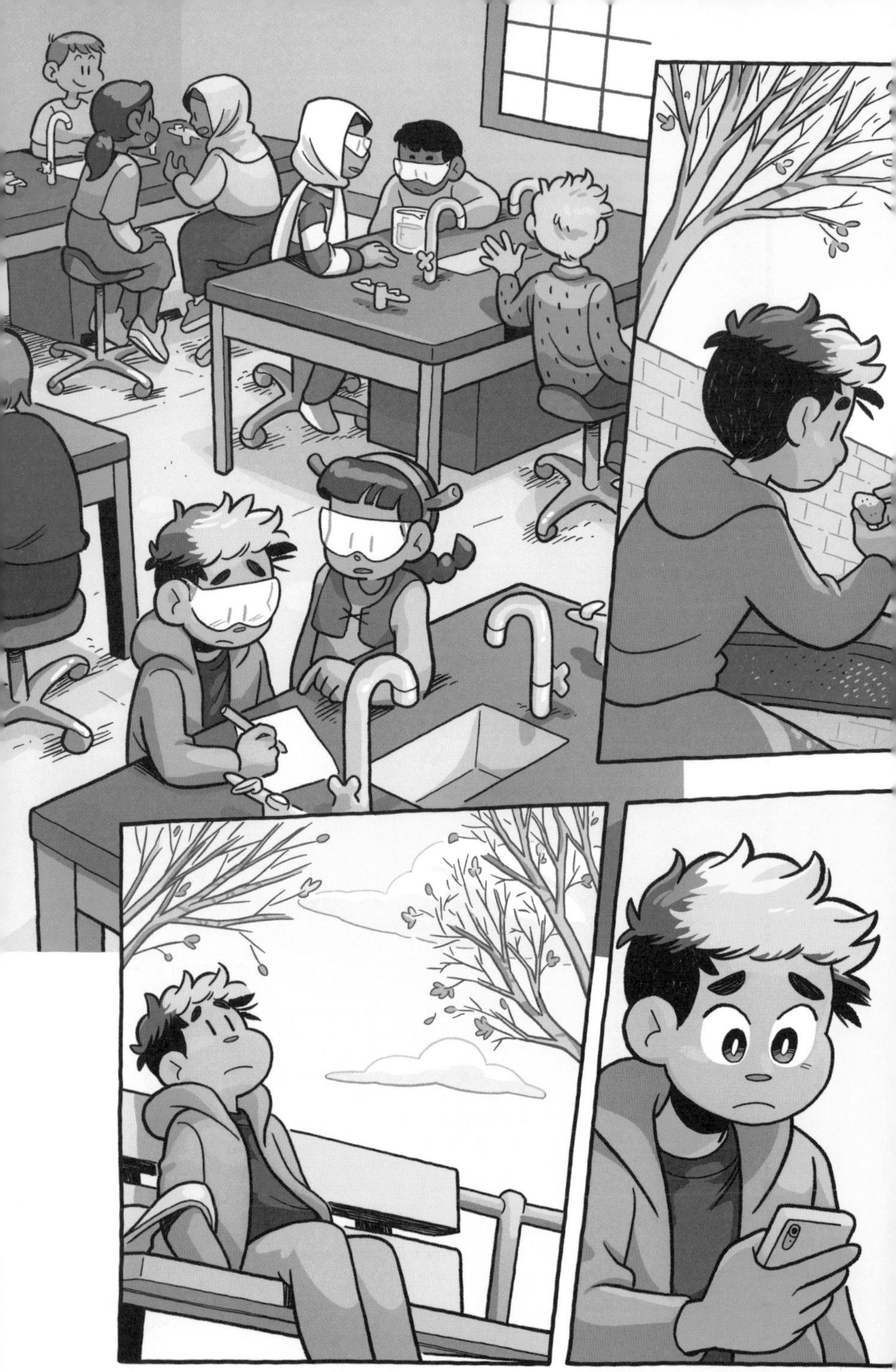

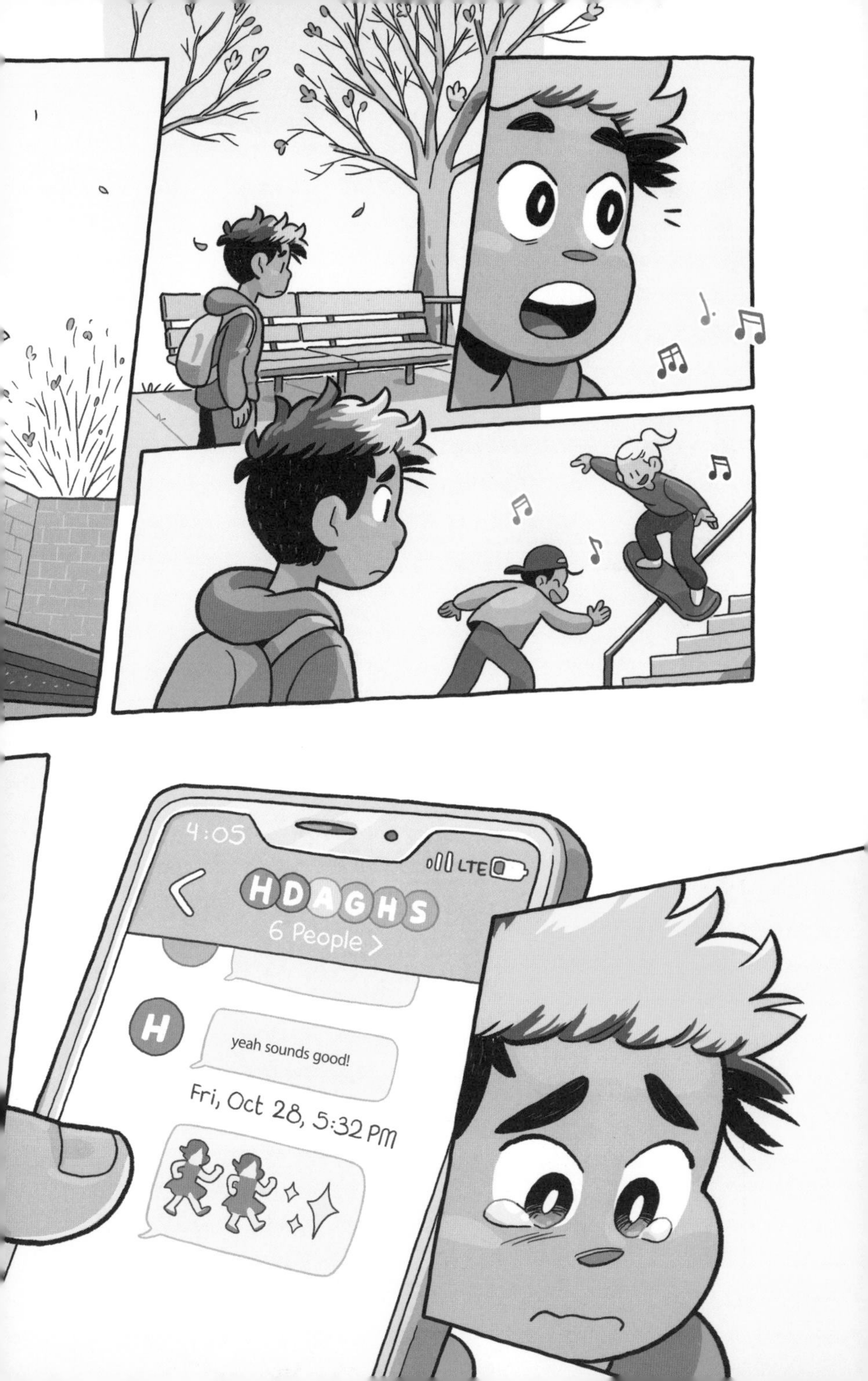

4:05
LTE
HDAGHS
6 People >
yeah sounds good!
Fri, Oct 28, 5:32 PM

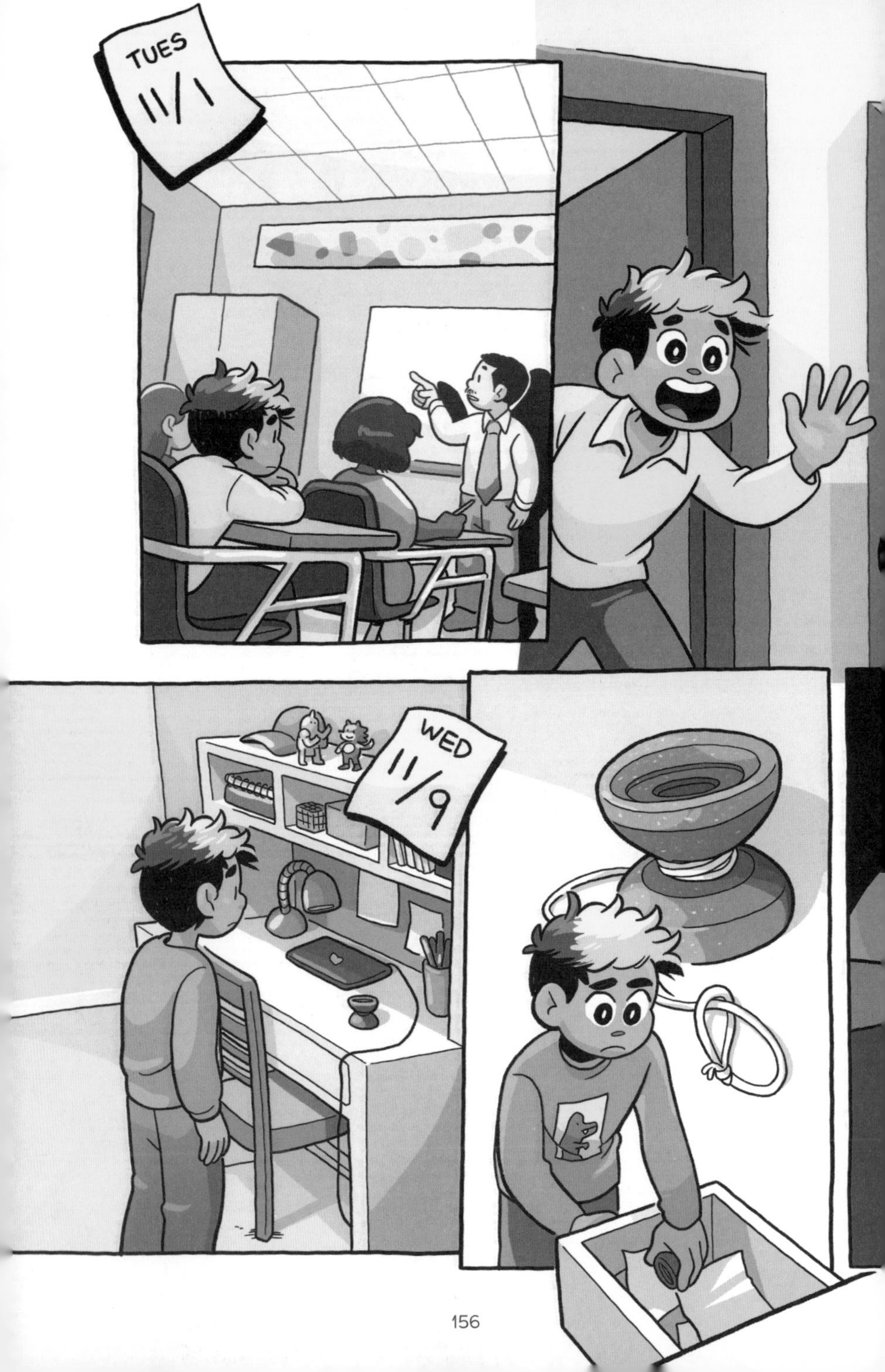
TUES
11/1
WED
11/9

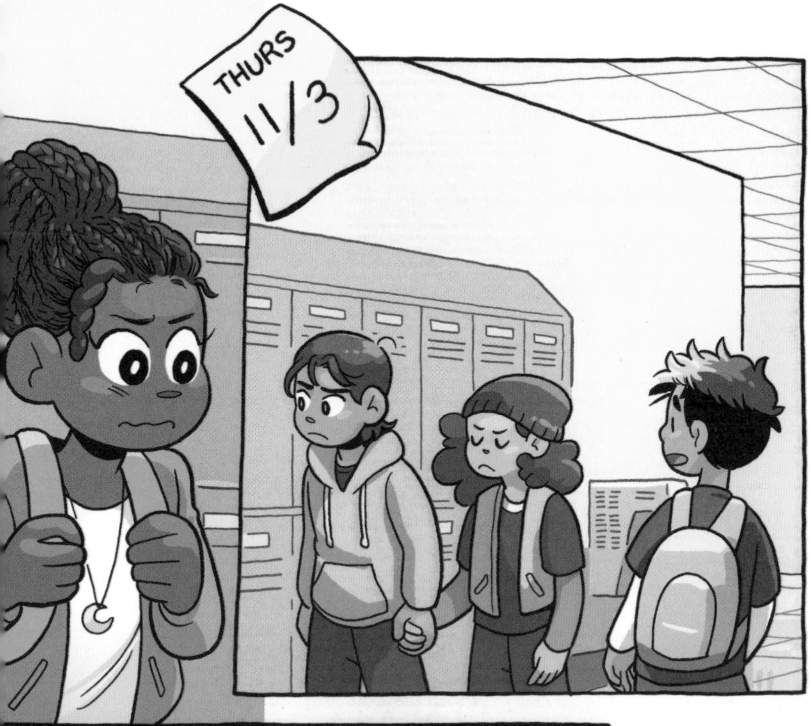
THURS
11/3

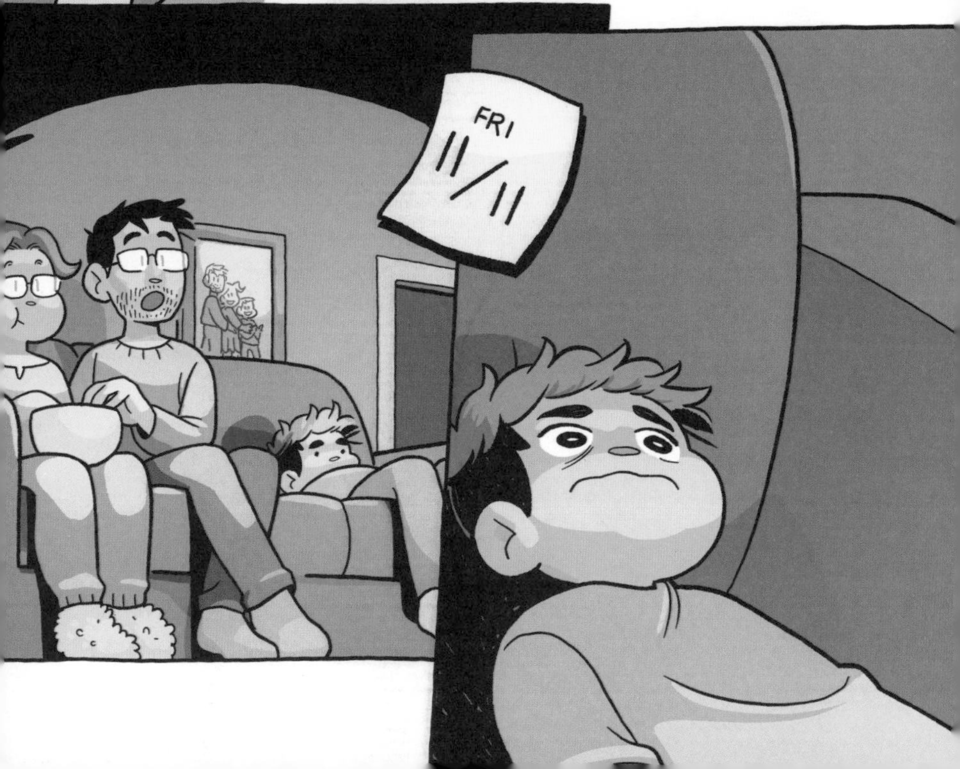
FRI
11/11

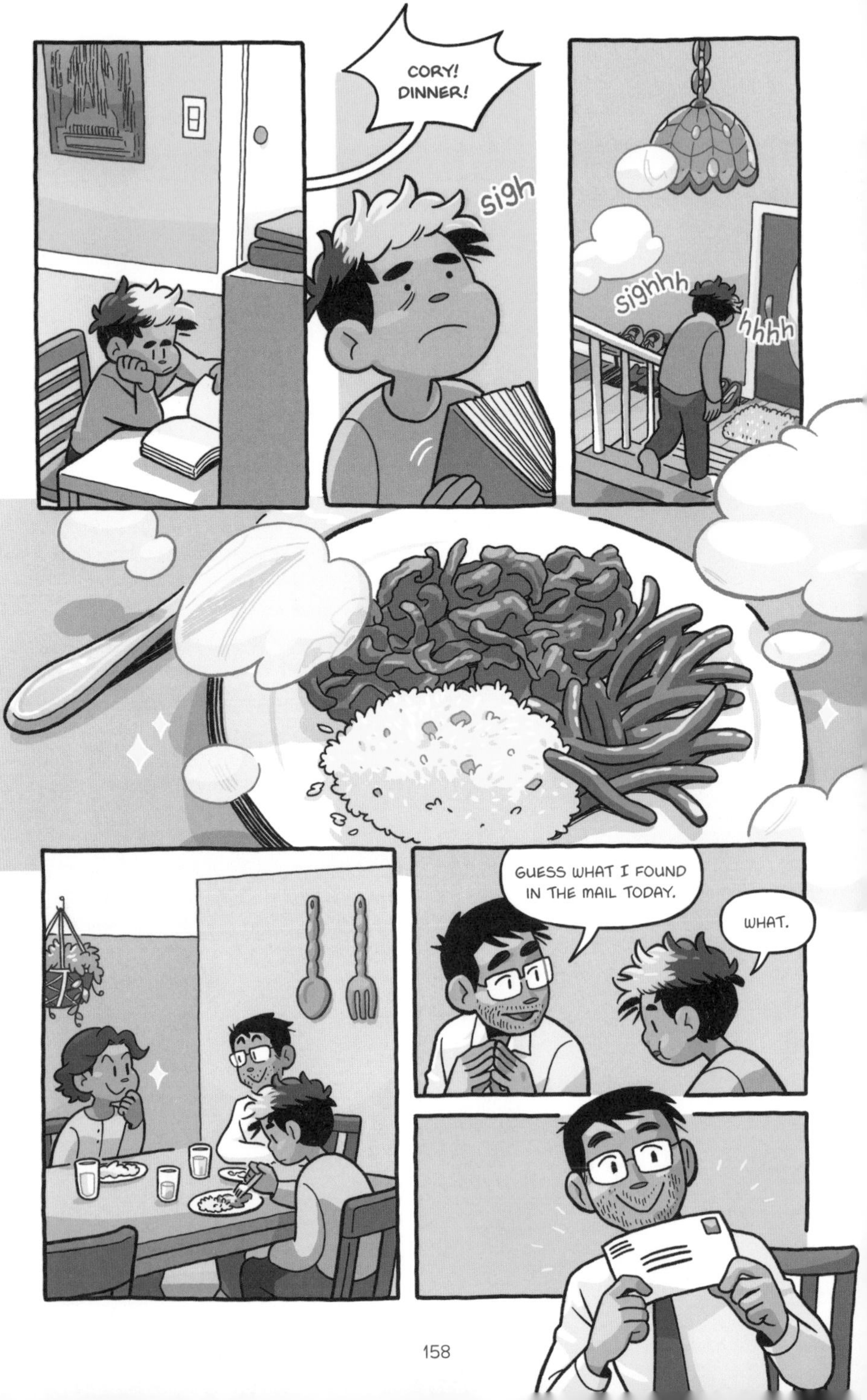

CORY! DINNER!
sigh
sighhh
hhhh
GUESS WHAT I FOUND IN THE MAIL TODAY.
WHAT.

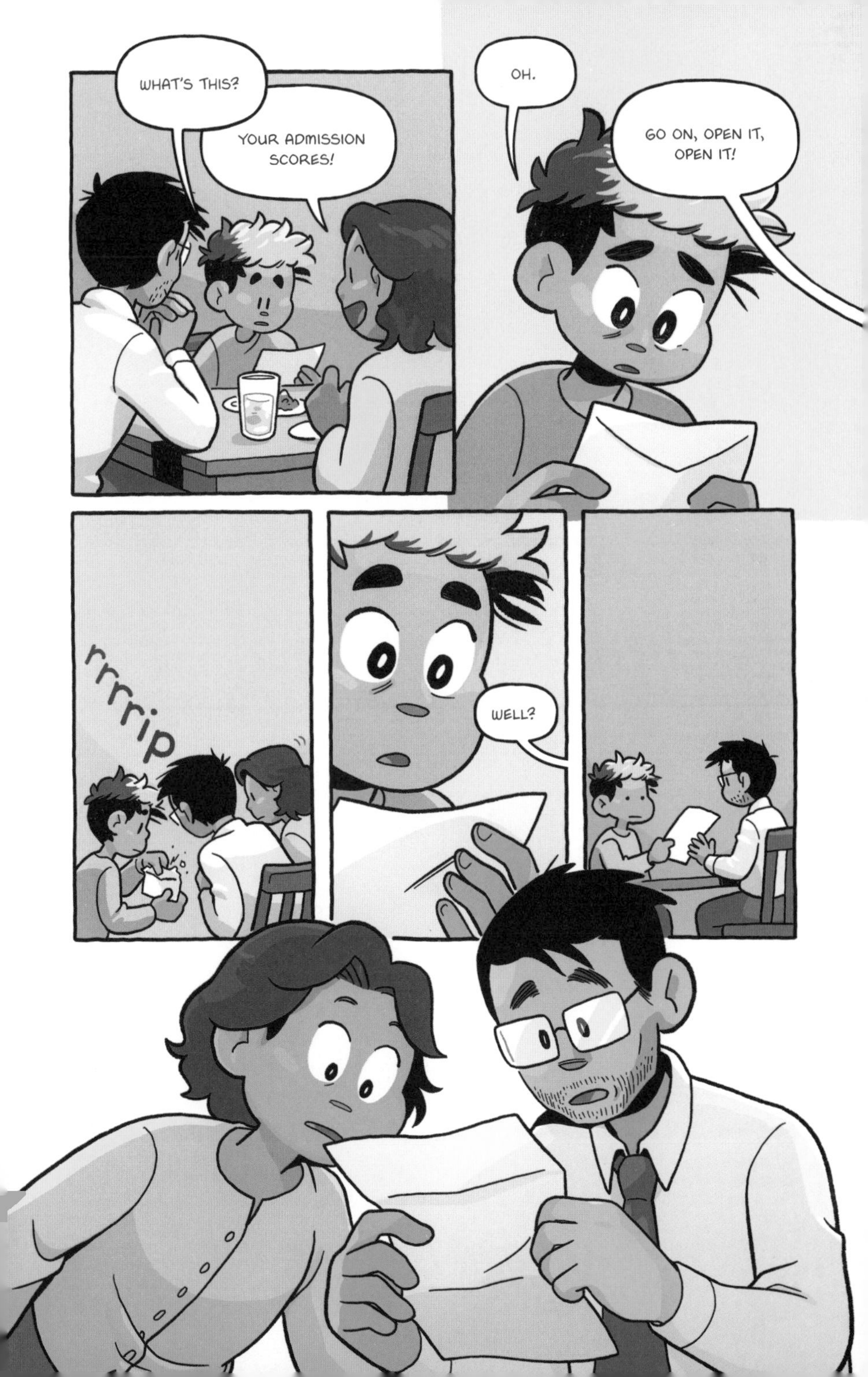
WHAT'S THIS?
YOUR ADMISSION SCORES!
OH.
GO ON, OPEN IT, OPEN IT!
rrrrip
WELL?

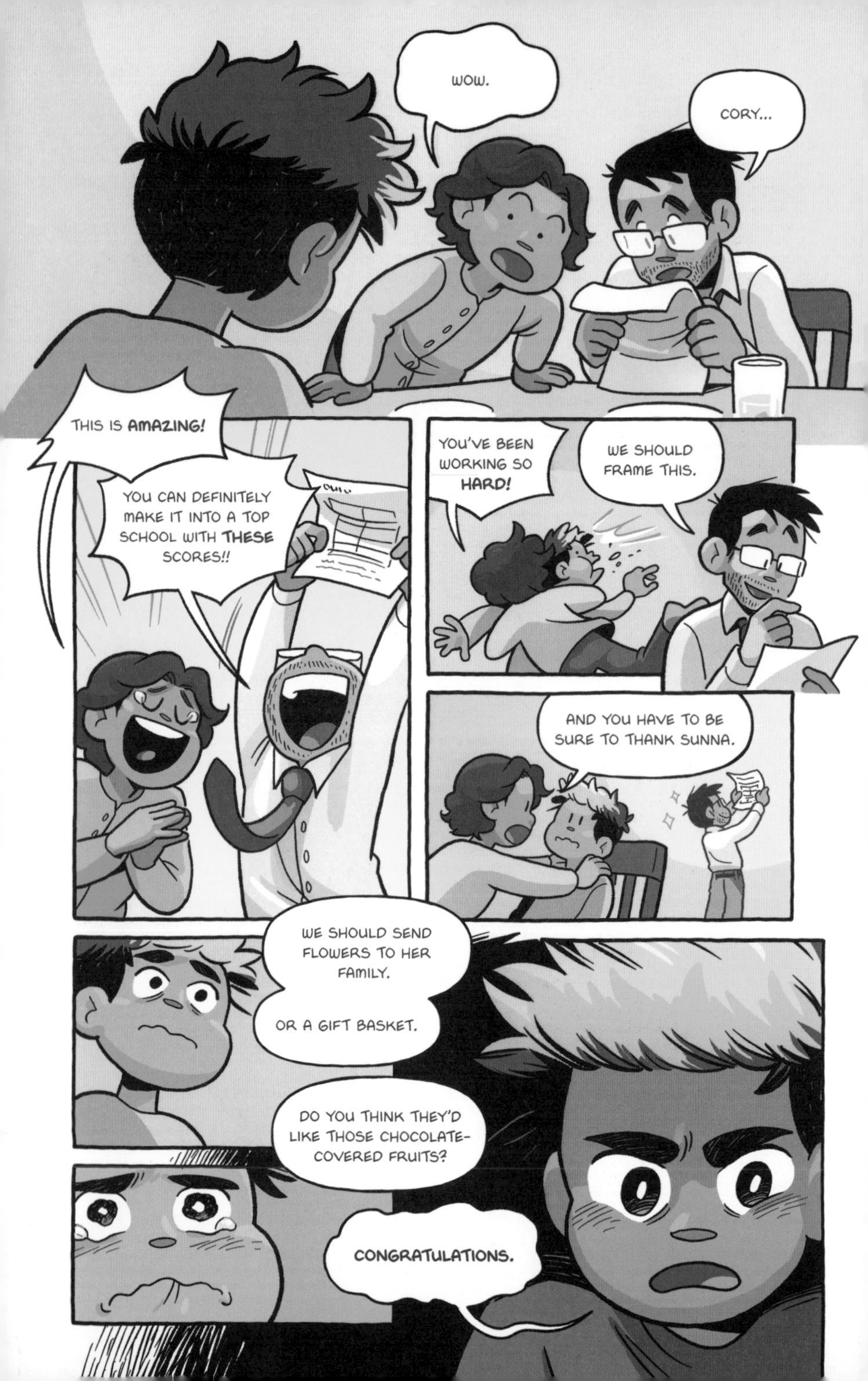
WOW.
CORY...
THIS IS AMAZING!
YOU CAN DEFINITELY MAKE IT INTO A TOP SCHOOL WITH THESE SCORES!!
YOU'VE BEEN WORKING SO HARD!
WE SHOULD FRAME THIS.
AND YOU HAVE TO BE SURE TO THANK SUNNA.
WE SHOULD SEND FLOWERS TO HER FAMILY.
OR A GIFT BASKET.
DO YOU THINK THEY'D LIKE THOSE CHOCOLATE-COVERED FRUITS?
CONGRATULATIONS.

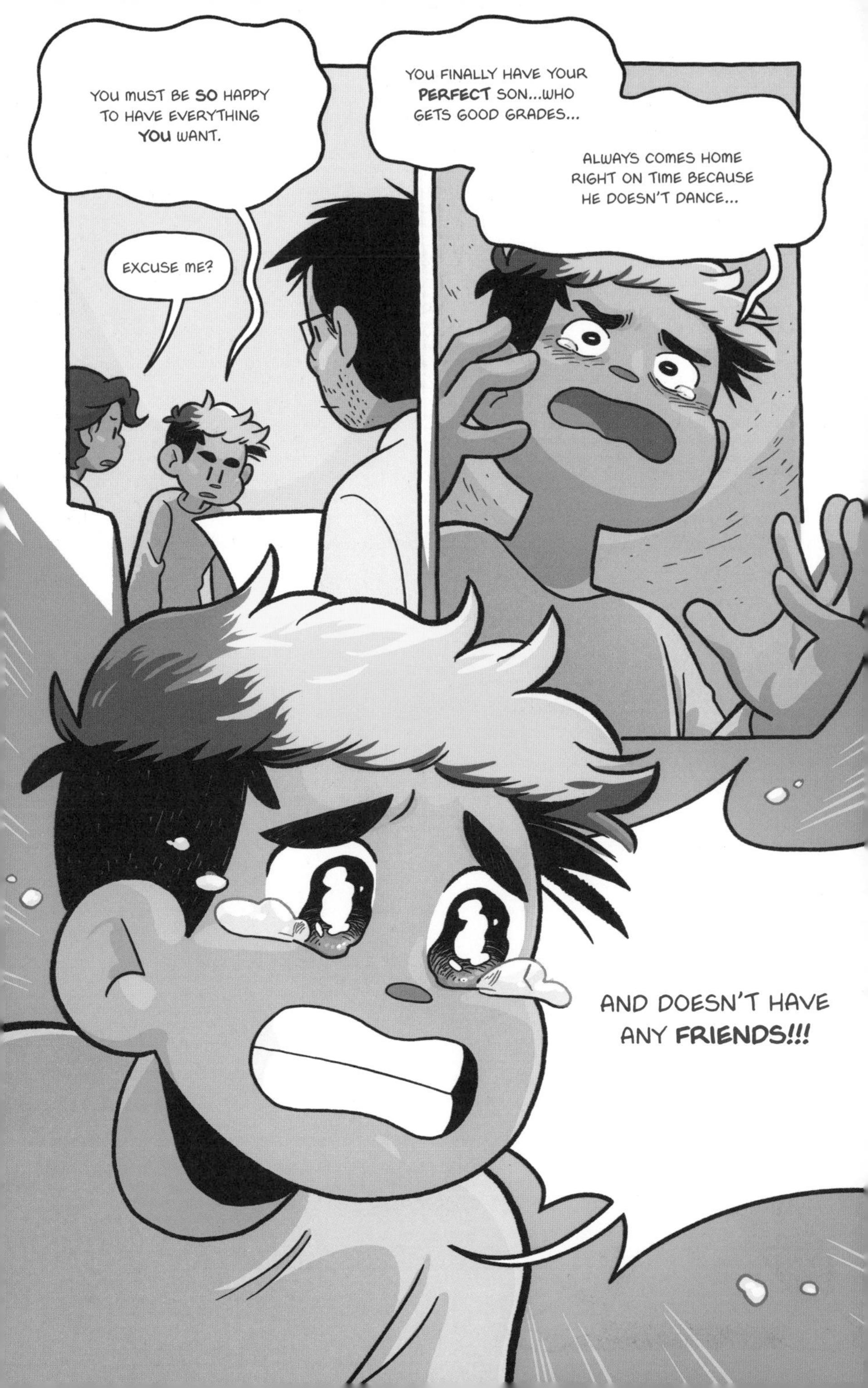
YOU MUST BE SO HAPPY TO HAVE EVERYTHING YOU WANT.
EXCUSE ME?
YOU FINALLY HAVE YOUR PERFECT SON...WHO GETS GOOD GRADES...
ALWAYS COMES HOME RIGHT ON TIME BECAUSE HE DOESN'T DANCE...
AND DOESN'T HAVE ANY FRIENDS!!!

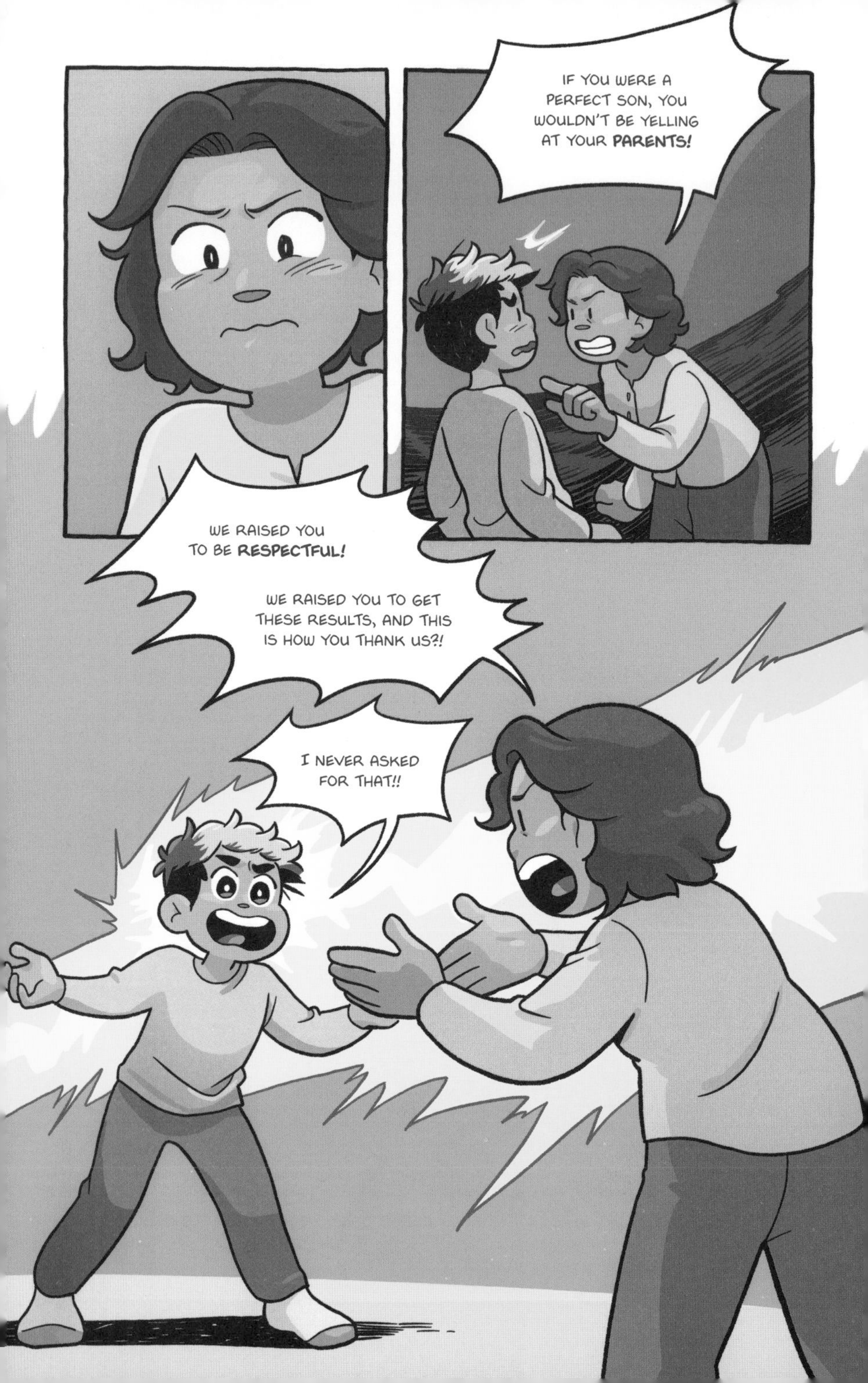
IF YOU WERE A PERFECT SON, YOU WOULDN'T BE YELLING AT YOUR **PARENTS!**
WE RAISED YOU TO BE **RESPECTFUL!**
WE RAISED YOU TO GET THESE RESULTS, AND THIS IS HOW YOU THANK US?!
I NEVER ASKED FOR THAT!!

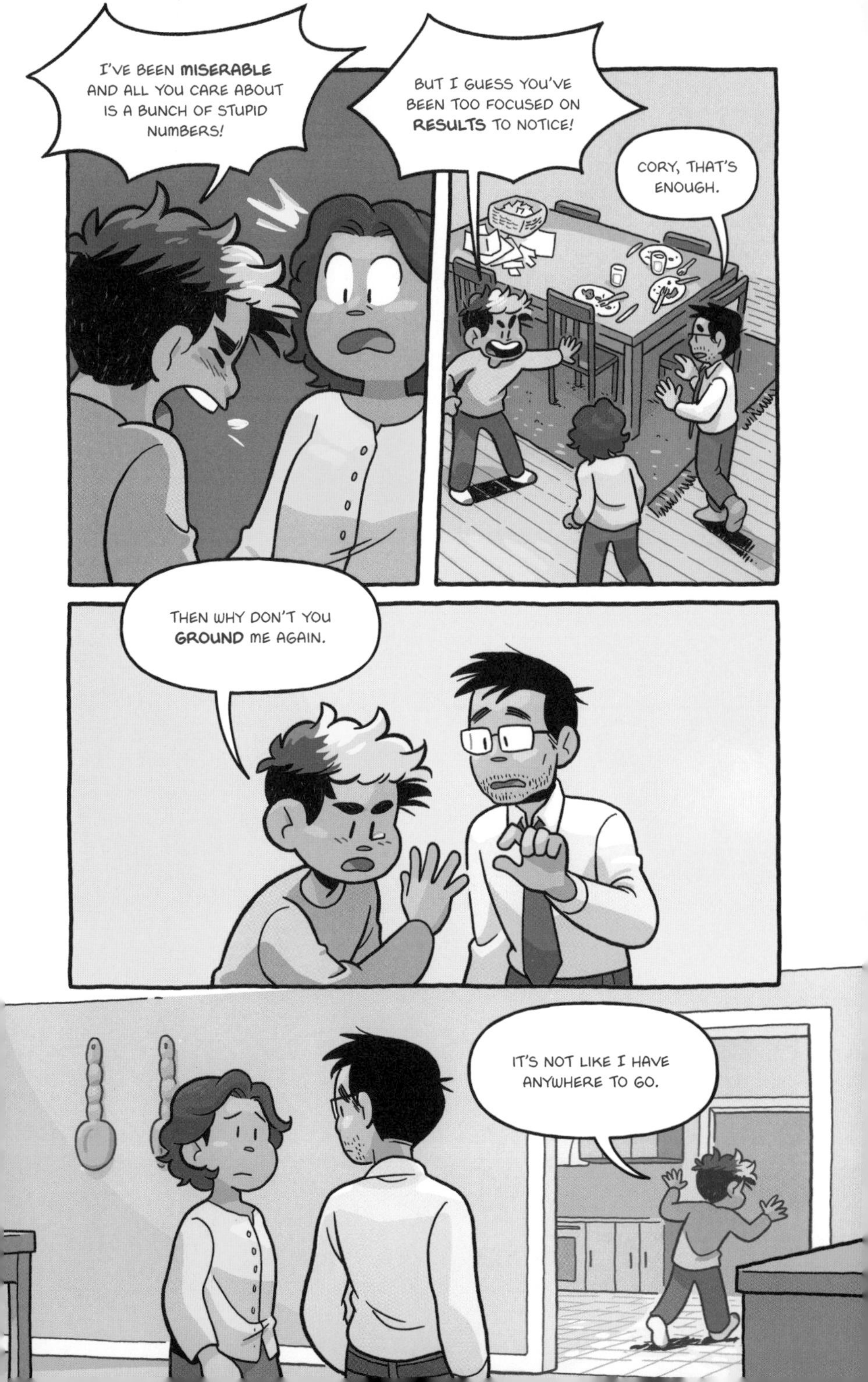
I'VE BEEN **MISERABLE** AND ALL YOU CARE ABOUT IS A BUNCH OF STUPID NUMBERS!
BUT I GUESS YOU'VE BEEN TOO FOCUSED ON **RESULTS** TO NOTICE!
CORY, THAT'S ENOUGH.
THEN WHY DON'T YOU **GROUND** ME AGAIN.
IT'S NOT LIKE I HAVE ANYWHERE TO GO.

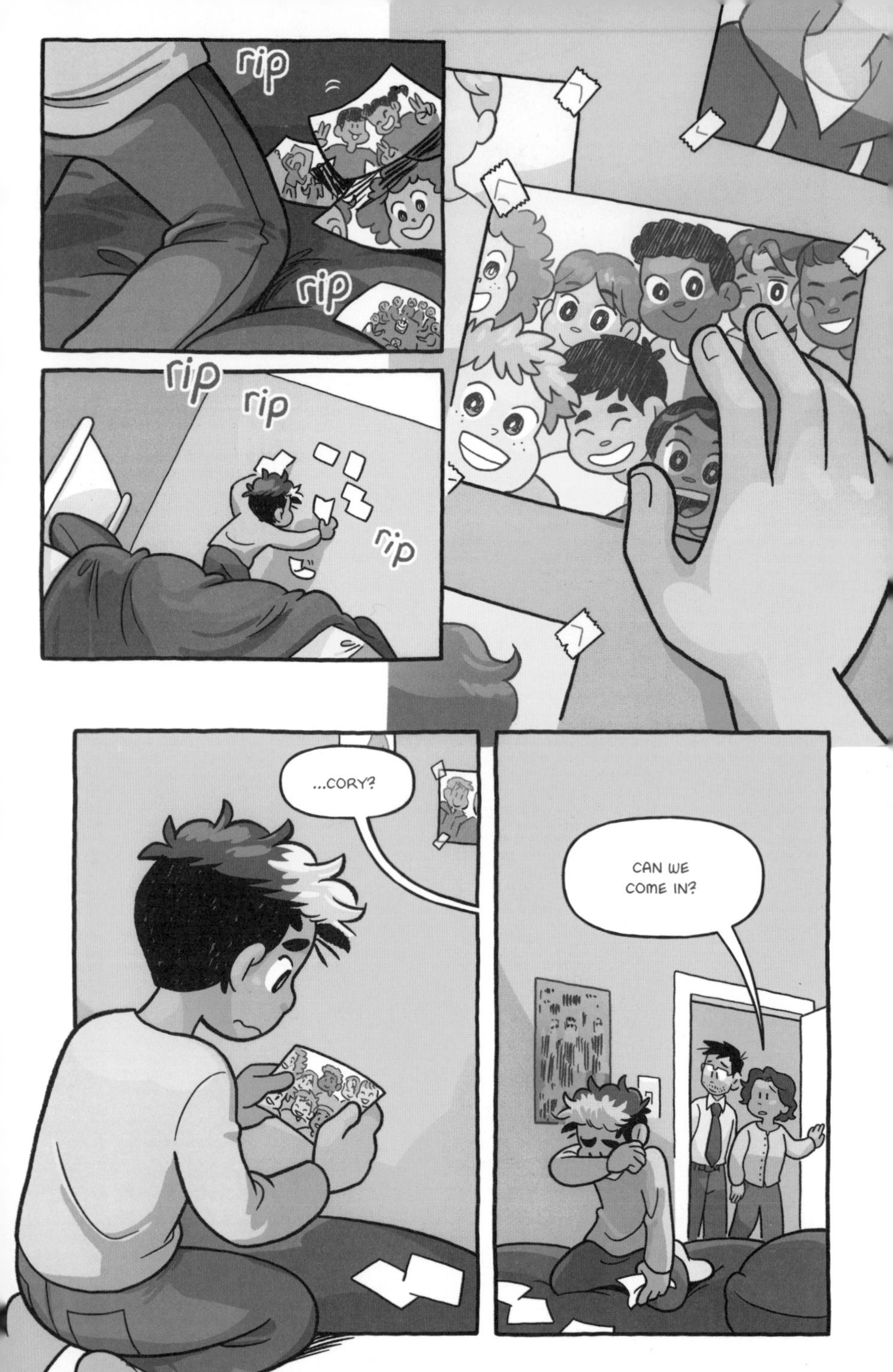
rip
rip
rip
rip
rip
...CORY?
CAN WE COME IN?

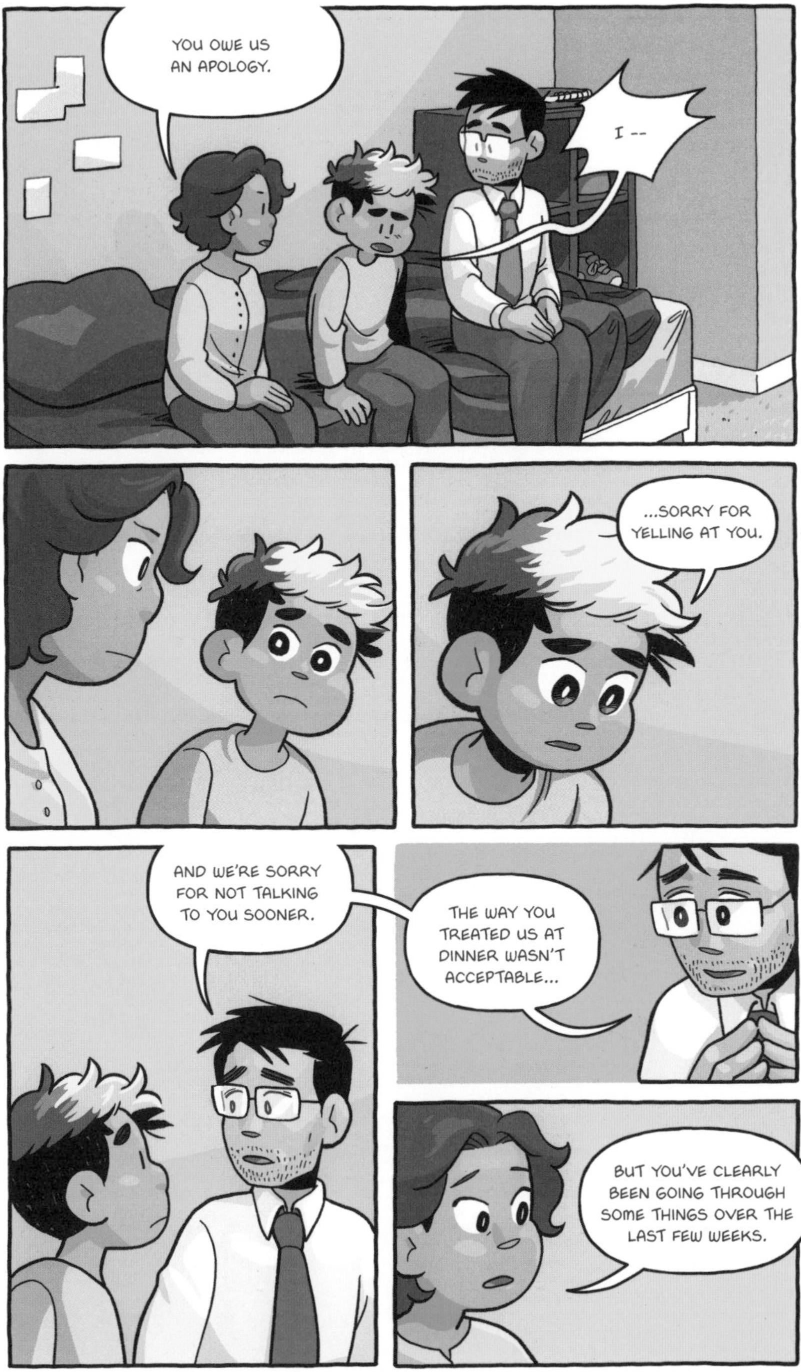
YOU OWE US AN APOLOGY.
I --
...SORRY FOR YELLING AT YOU.
AND WE'RE SORRY FOR NOT TALKING TO YOU SOONER.
THE WAY YOU TREATED US AT DINNER WASN'T ACCEPTABLE...
BUT YOU'VE CLEARLY BEEN GOING THROUGH SOME THINGS OVER THE LAST FEW WEEKS.

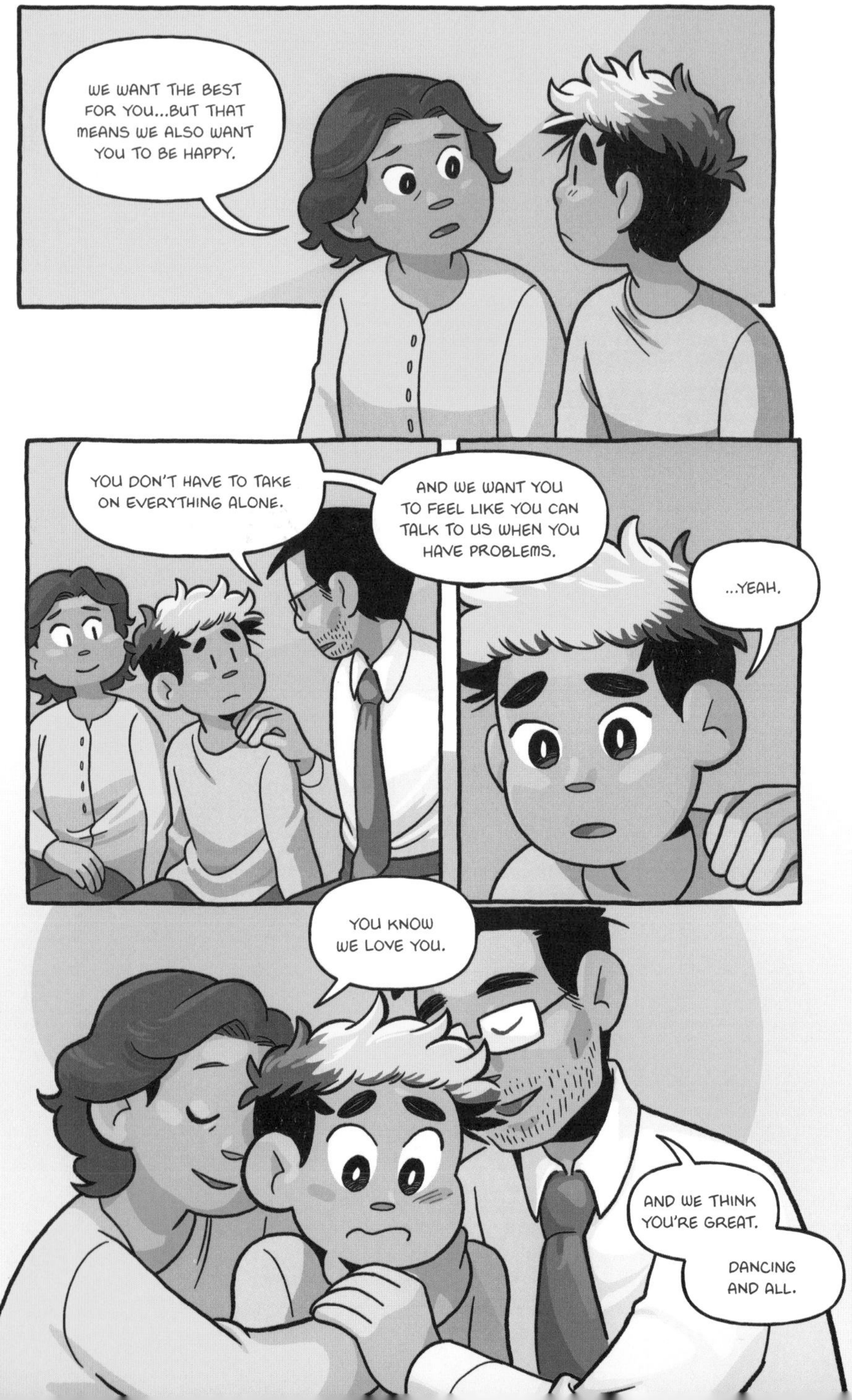
WE WANT THE BEST FOR YOU...BUT THAT MEANS WE ALSO WANT YOU TO BE HAPPY.
YOU DON'T HAVE TO TAKE ON EVERYTHING ALONE.
AND WE WANT YOU TO FEEL LIKE YOU CAN TALK TO US WHEN YOU HAVE PROBLEMS.
...YEAH.
YOU KNOW WE LOVE YOU.
AND WE THINK YOU'RE GREAT.
DANCING AND ALL.

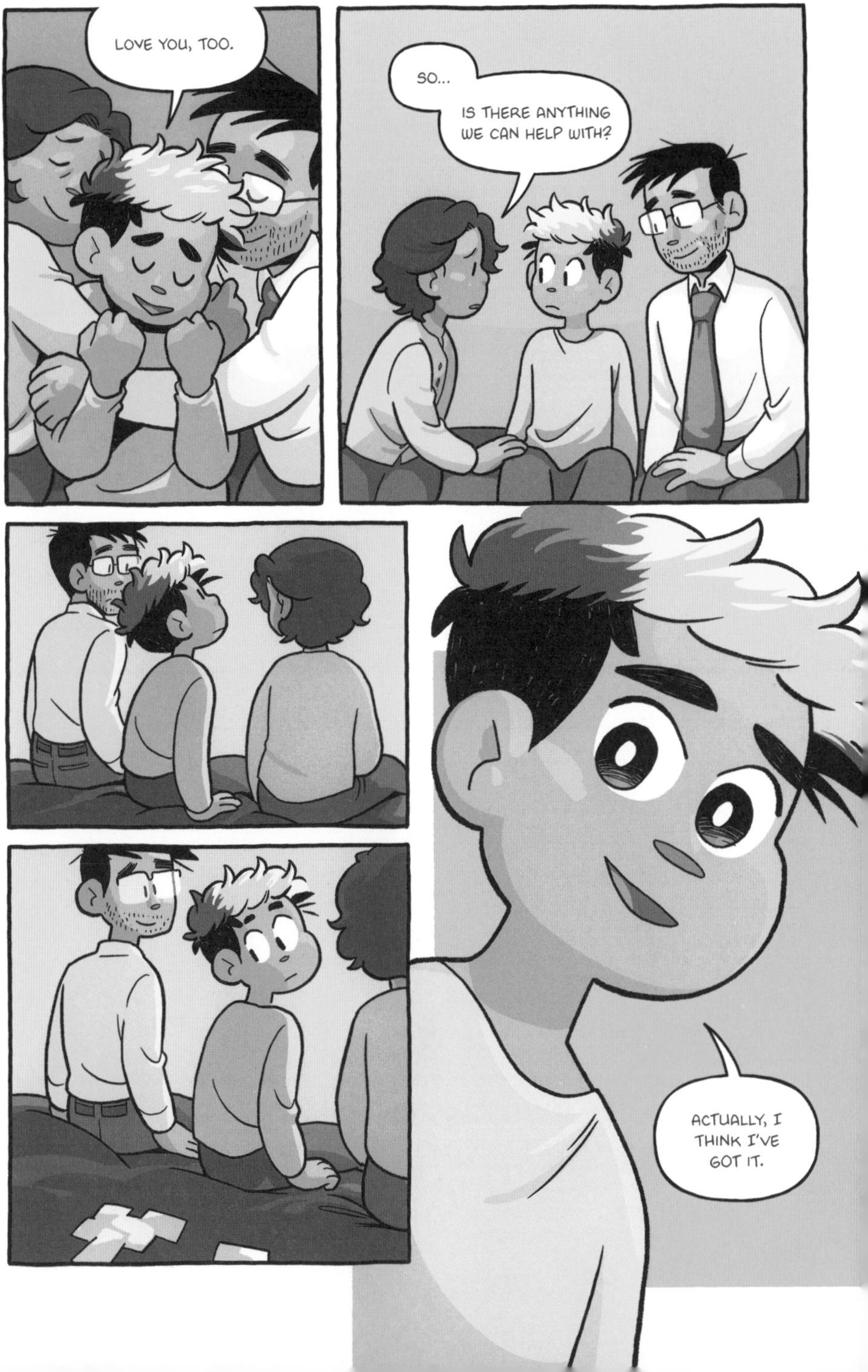
LOVE YOU, TOO.
SO...
IS THERE ANYTHING WE CAN HELP WITH?
ACTUALLY, I THINK I'VE GOT IT.

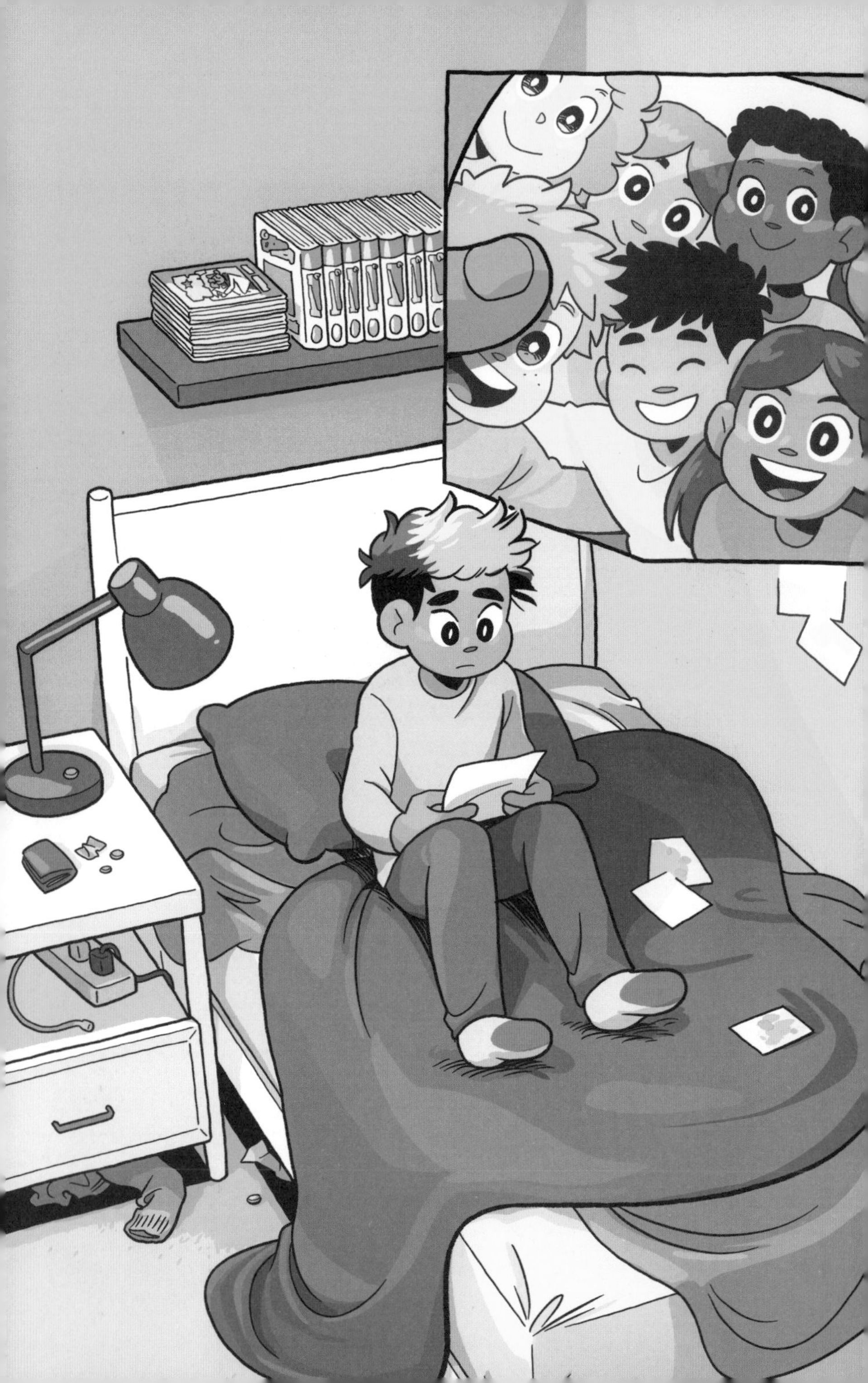

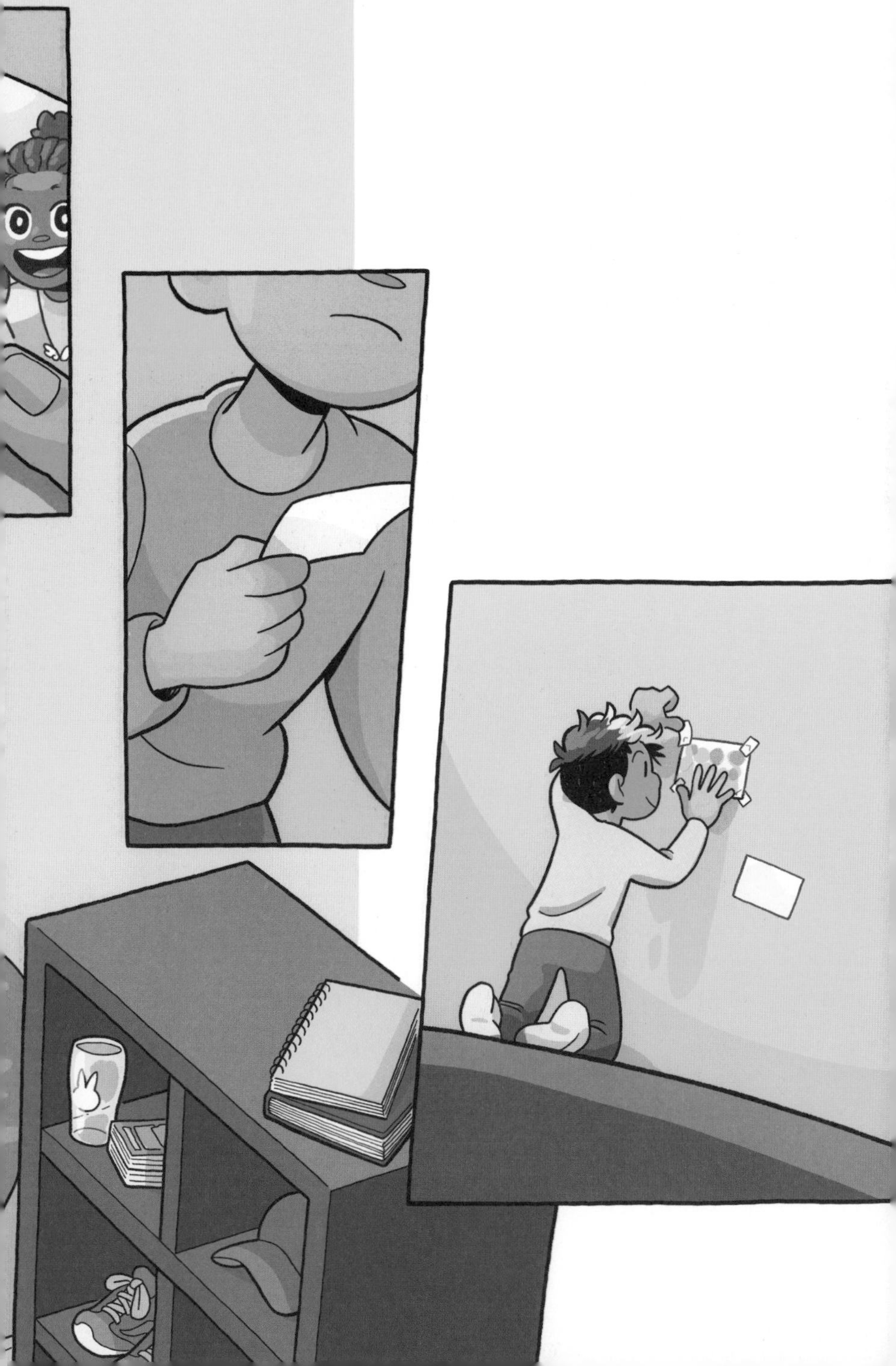

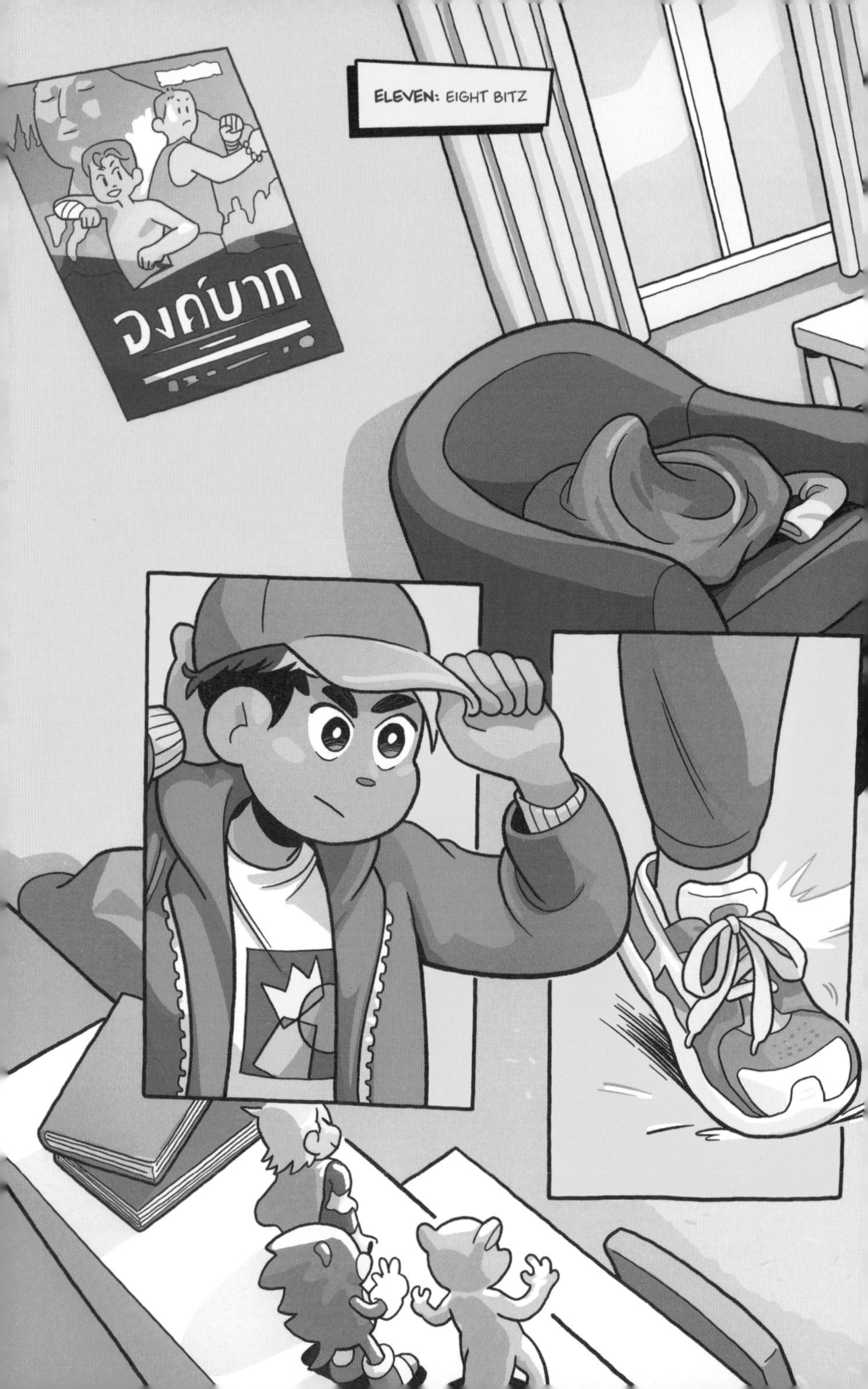
ELEVEN: EIGHT BITZ
องค์บาก

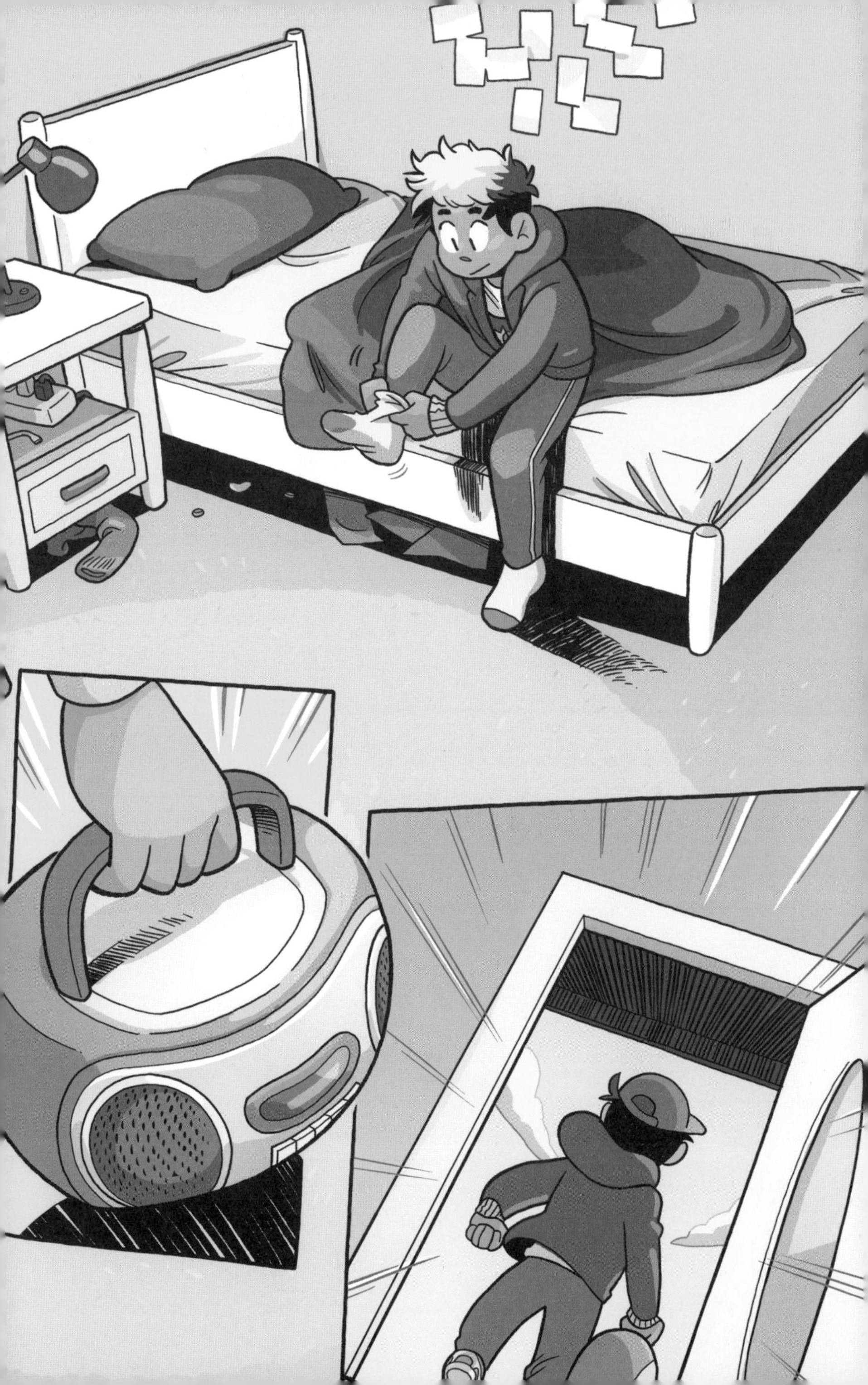

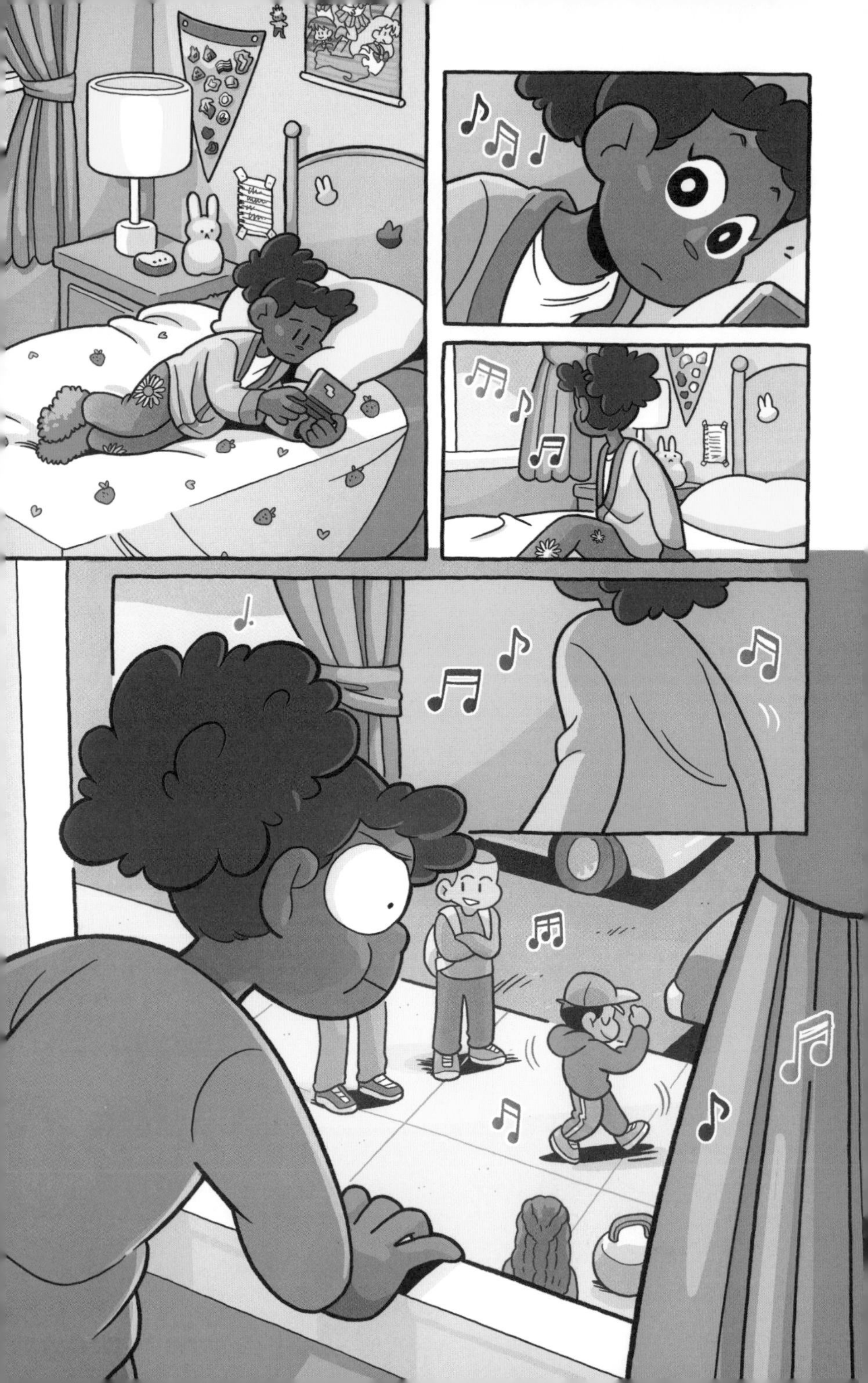

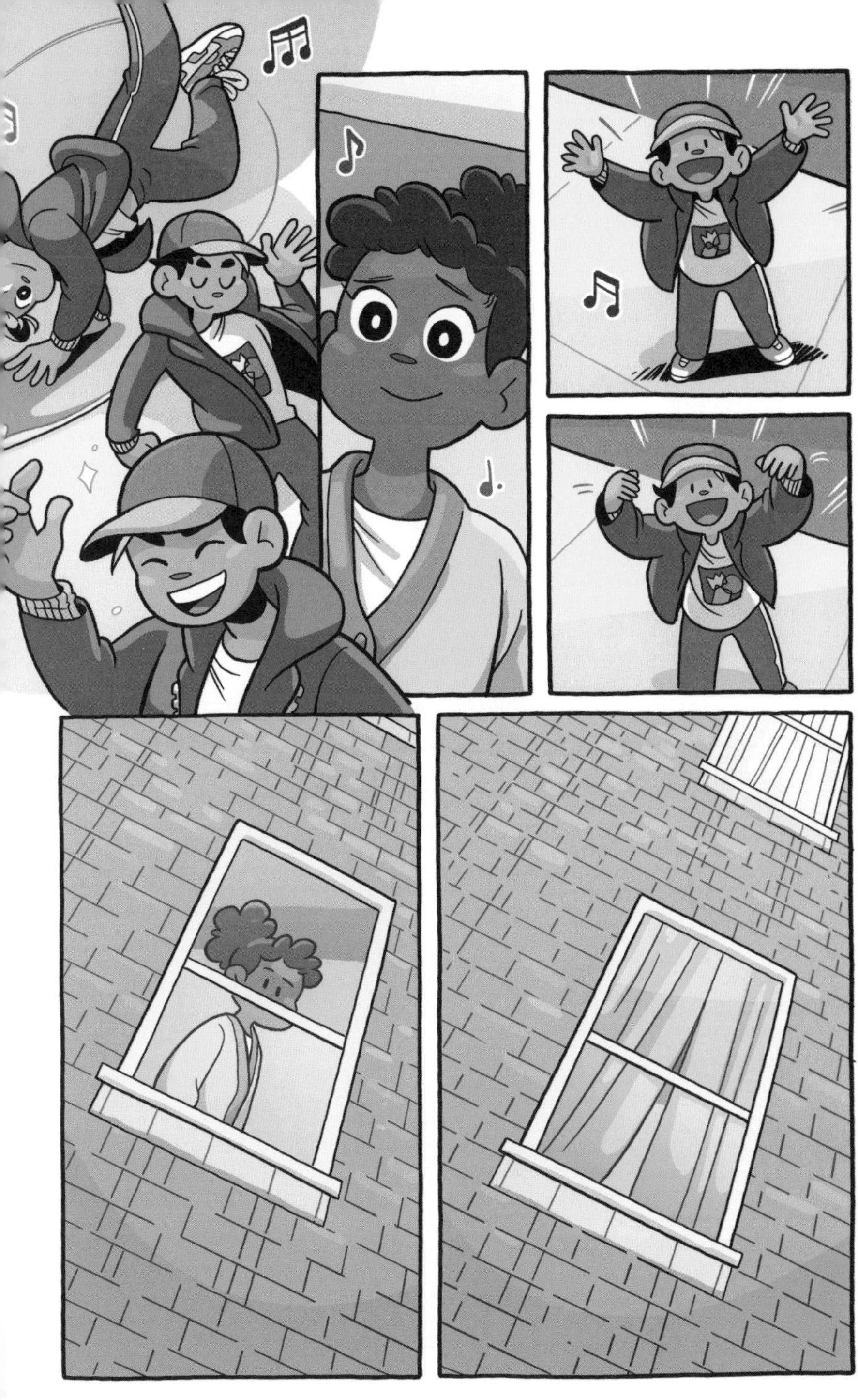

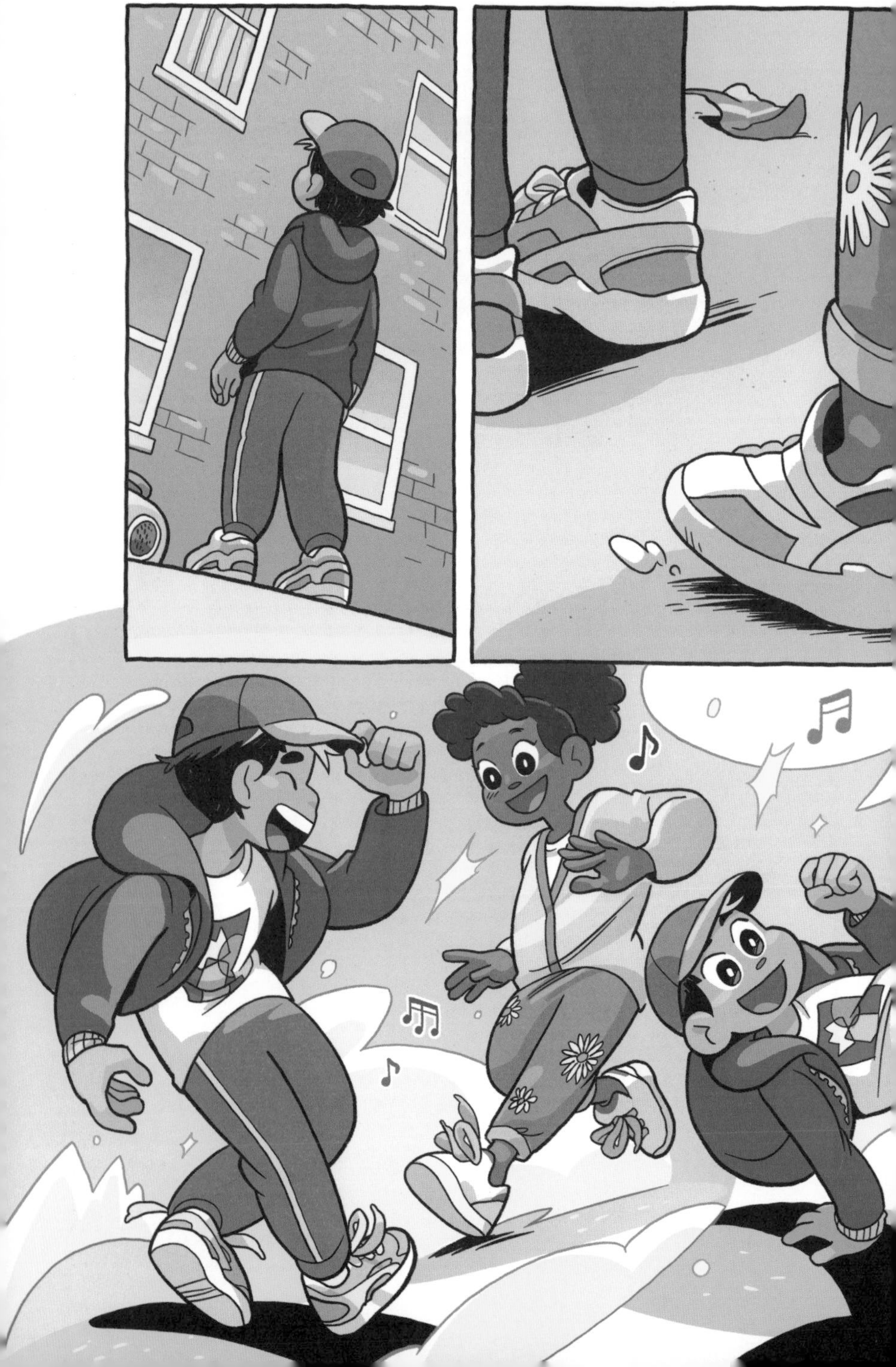

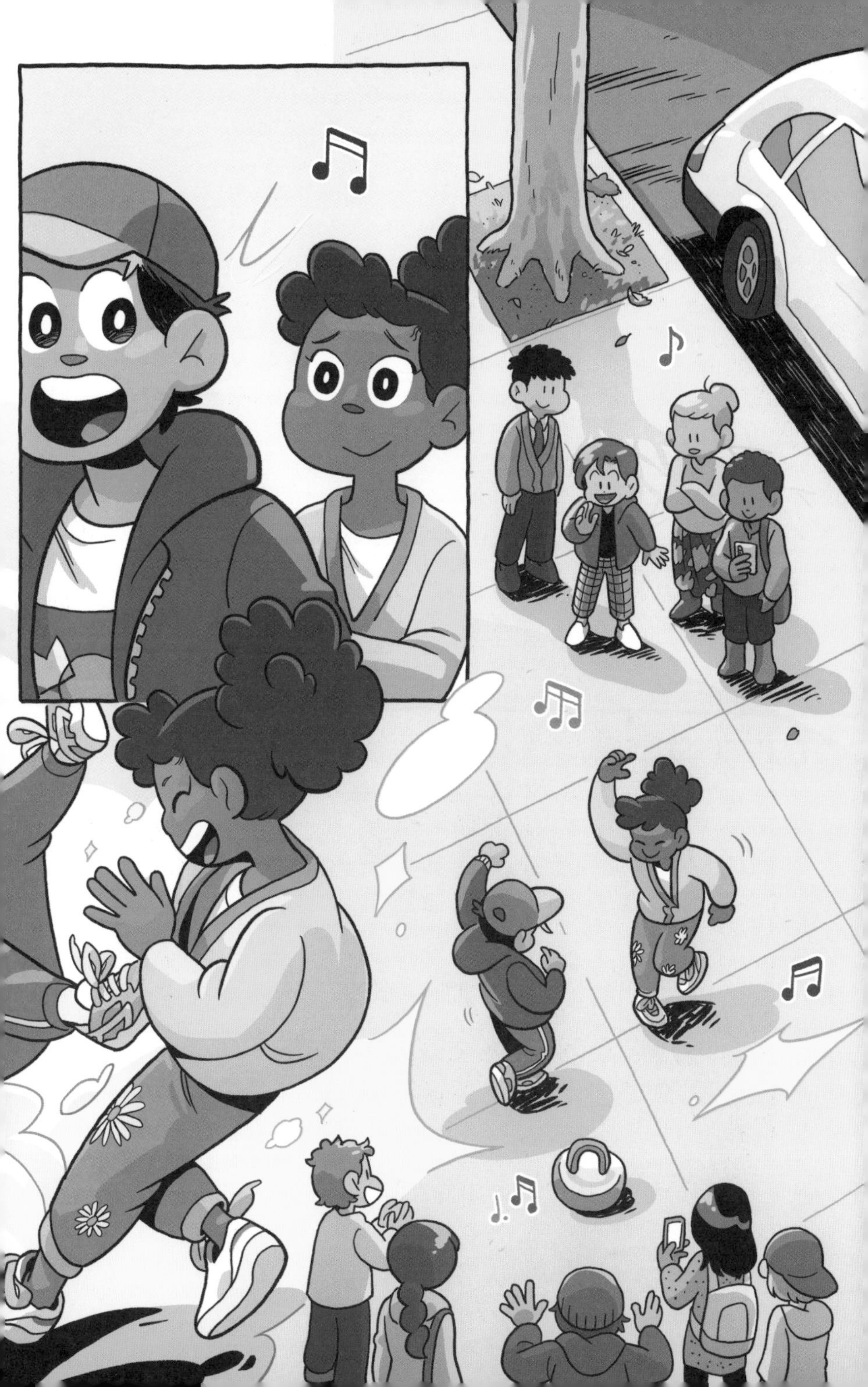

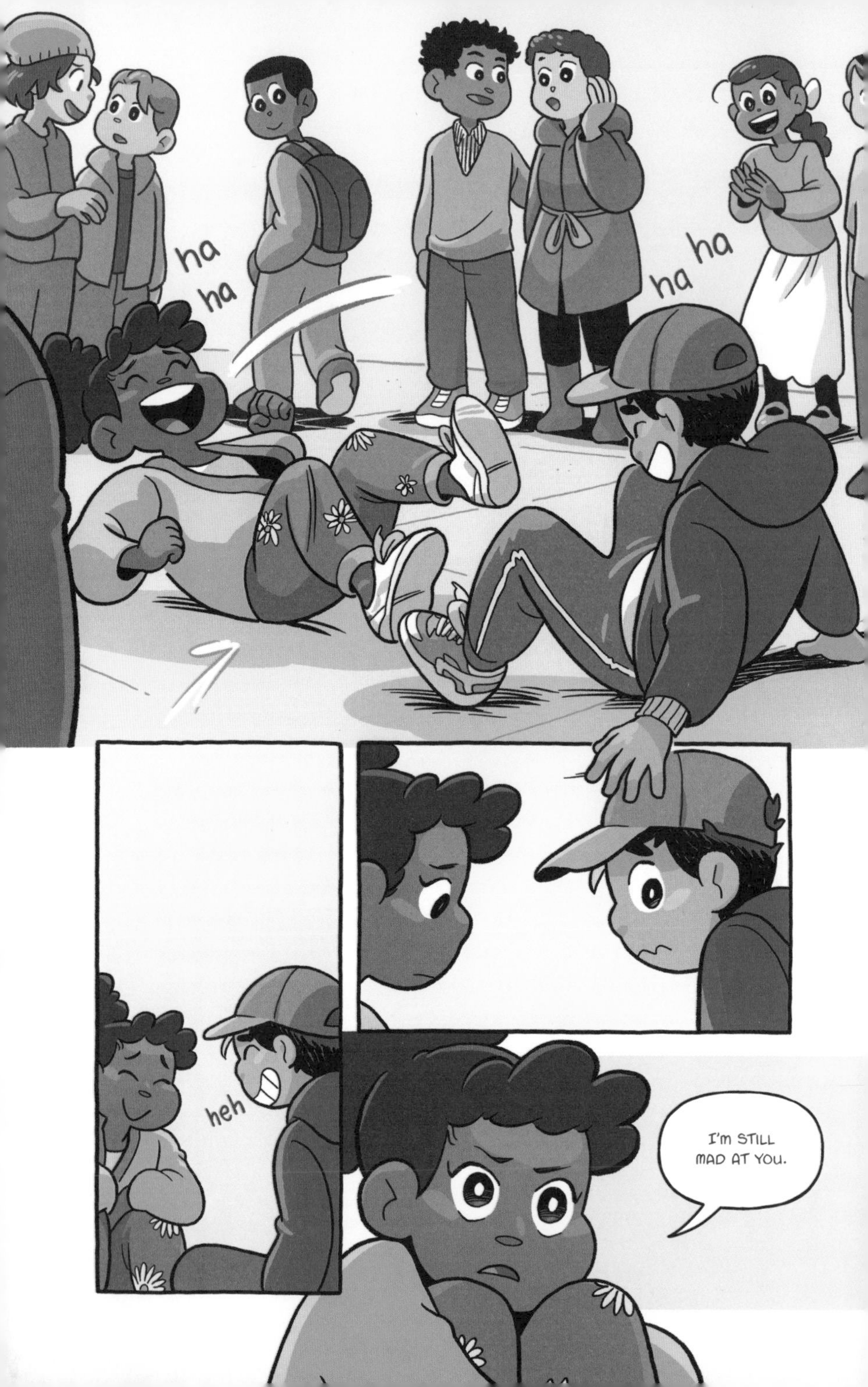
ha
ha
ha
ha
heh
I'M STILL
MAD AT YOU.

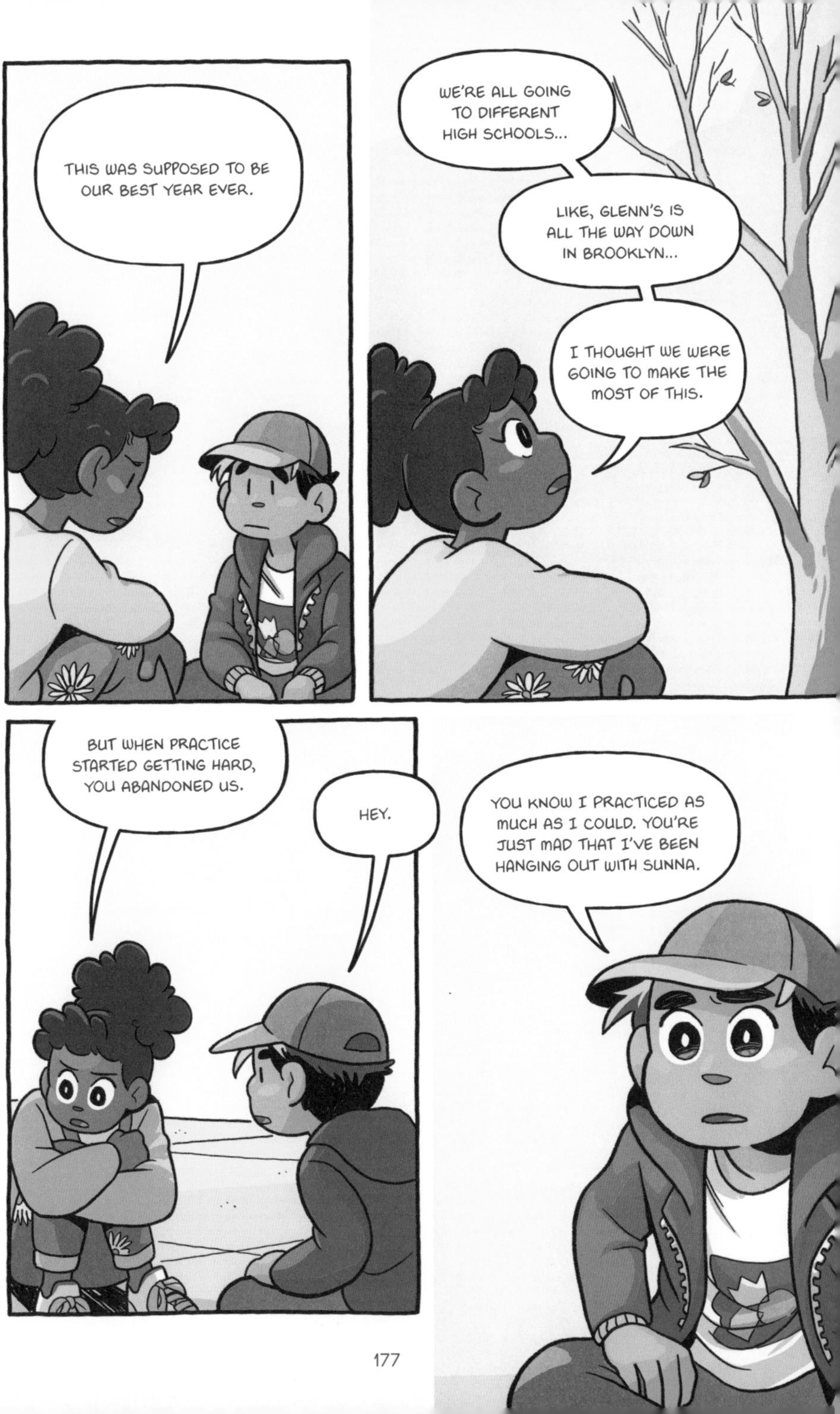
THIS WAS SUPPOSED TO BE OUR BEST YEAR EVER.
WE'RE ALL GOING TO DIFFERENT HIGH SCHOOLS...
LIKE, GLENN'S IS ALL THE WAY DOWN IN BROOKLYN...
I THOUGHT WE WERE GOING TO MAKE THE MOST OF THIS.
BUT WHEN PRACTICE STARTED GETTING HARD, YOU ABANDONED US.
HEY.
YOU KNOW I PRACTICED AS MUCH AS I COULD. YOU'RE JUST MAD THAT I'VE BEEN HANGING OUT WITH SUNNA.

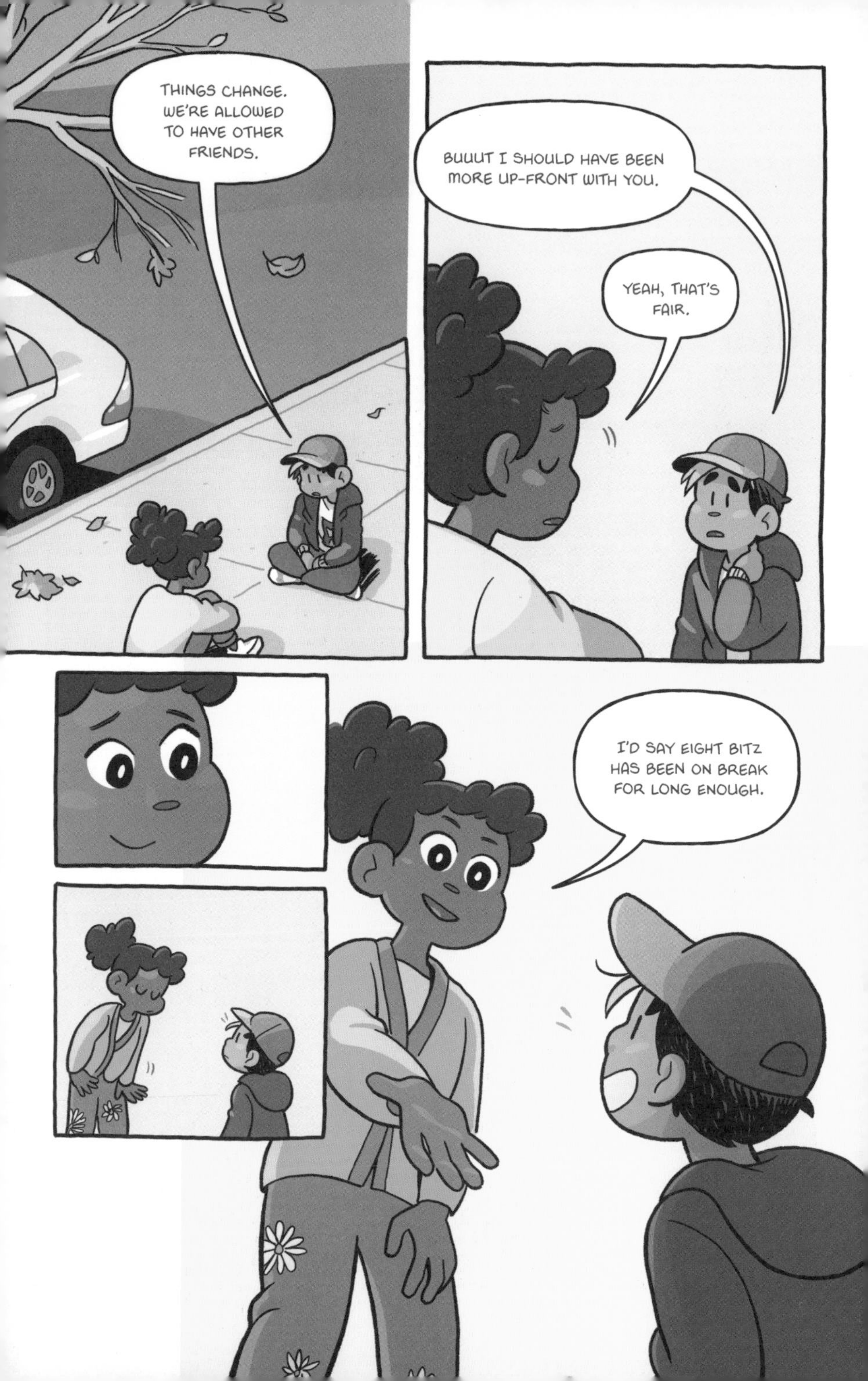
THINGS CHANGE. WE'RE ALLOWED TO HAVE OTHER FRIENDS.
BUUUT I SHOULD HAVE BEEN MORE UP-FRONT WITH YOU.
YEAH, THAT'S FAIR.
I'D SAY EIGHT BITZ HAS BEEN ON BREAK FOR LONG ENOUGH.

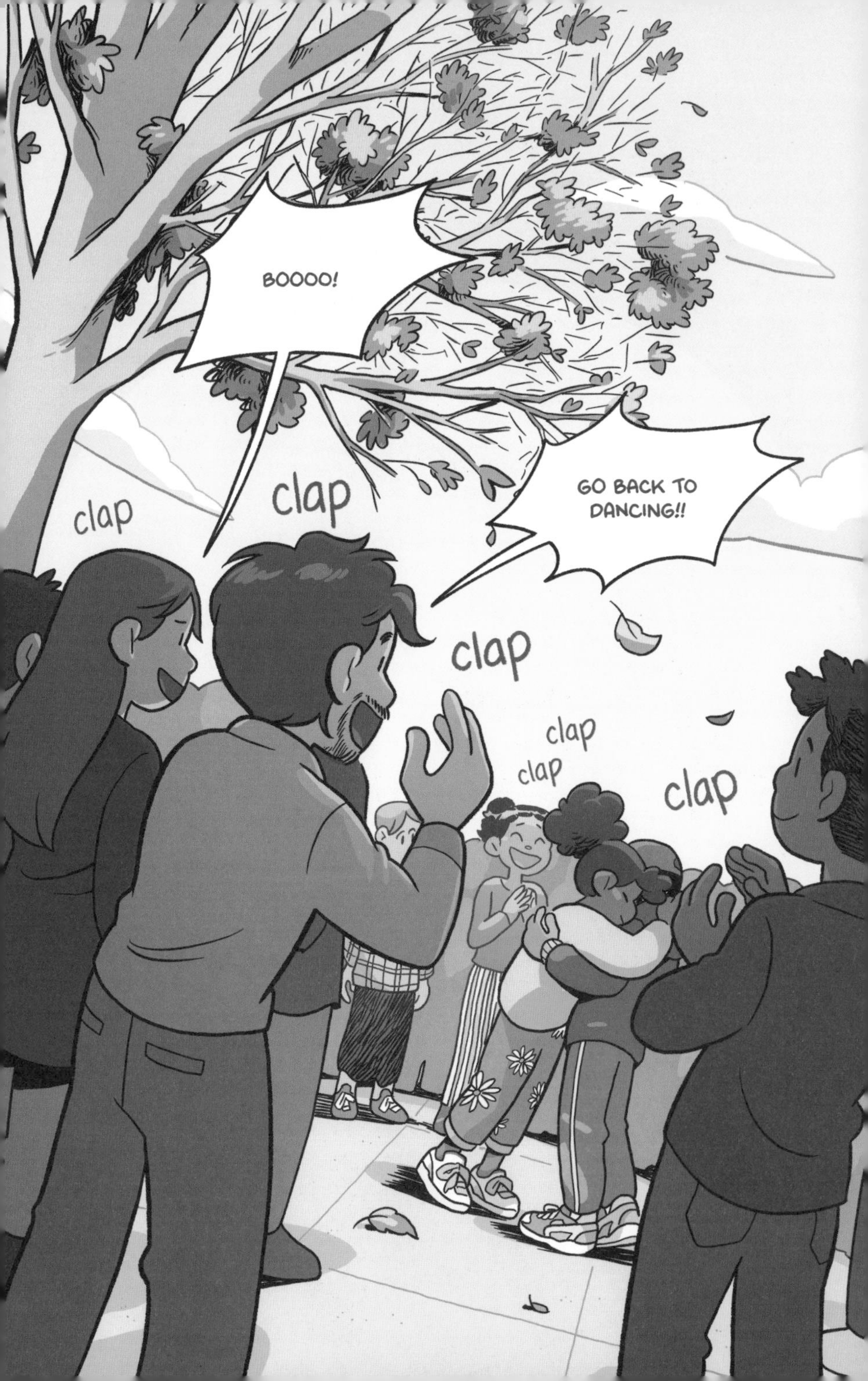
BOOOO!
clap
clap
GO BACK TO DANCING!!
clap
clap
clap
clap

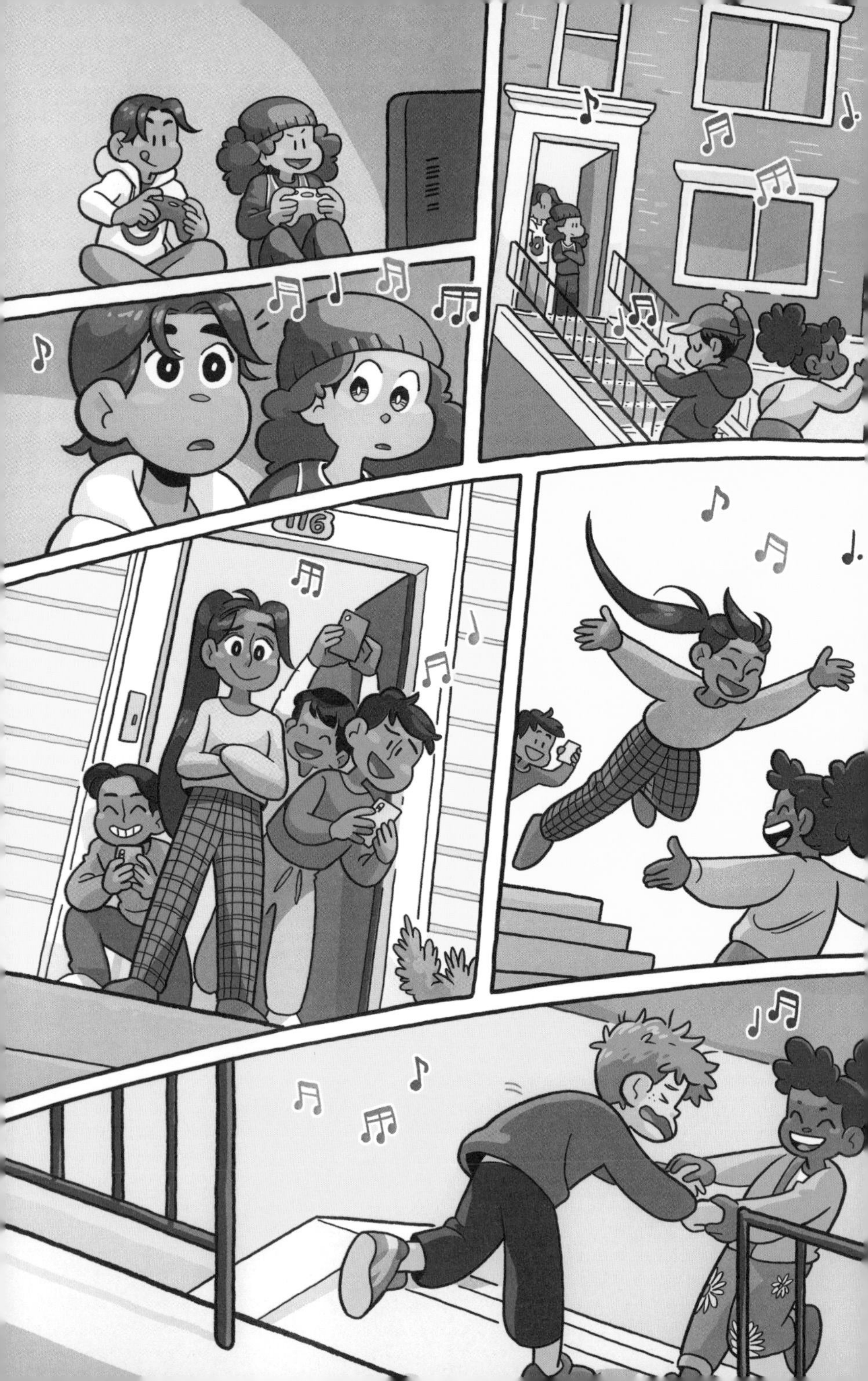
116

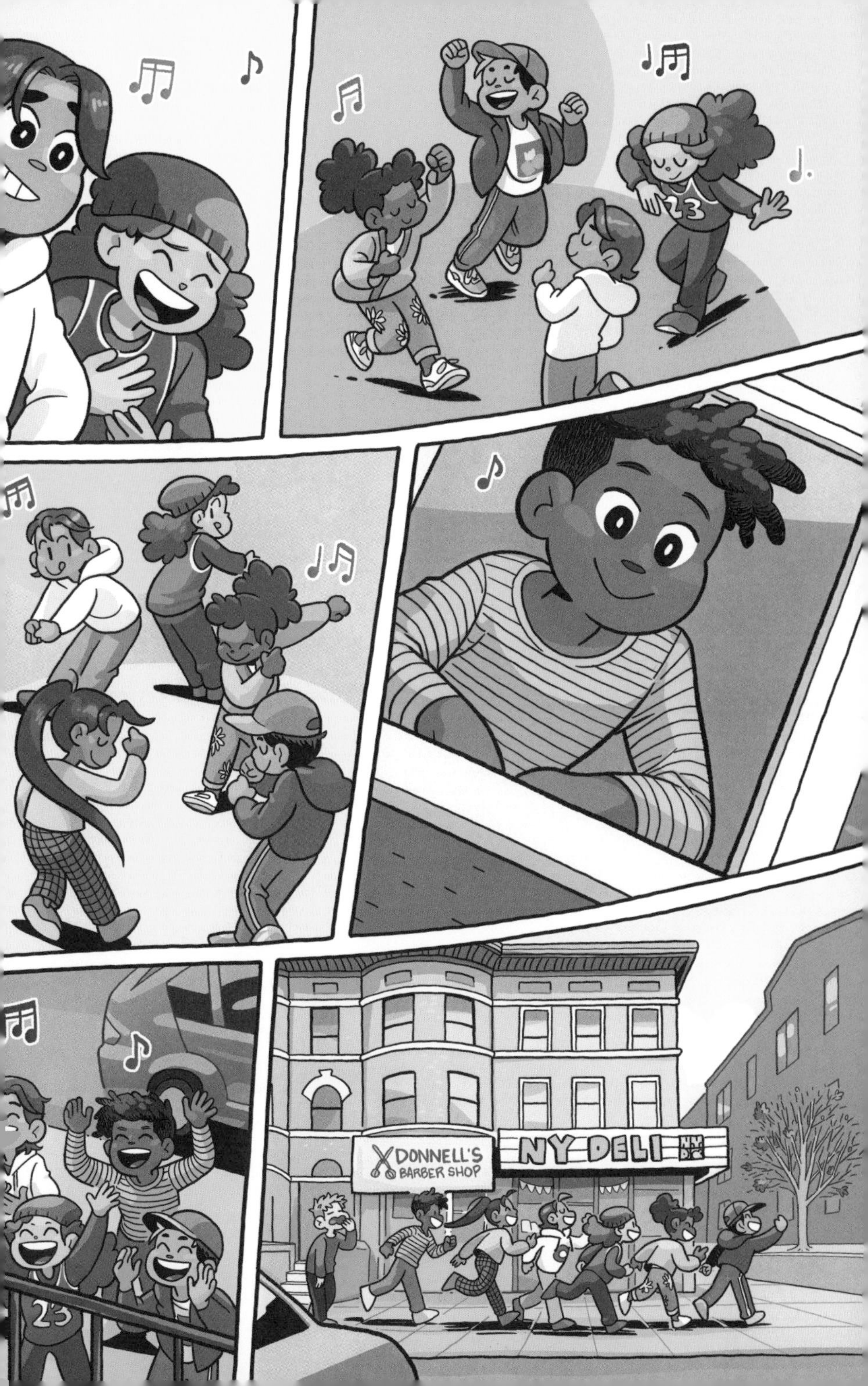
DONNELL'S
BARBER SHOP
NY DELI

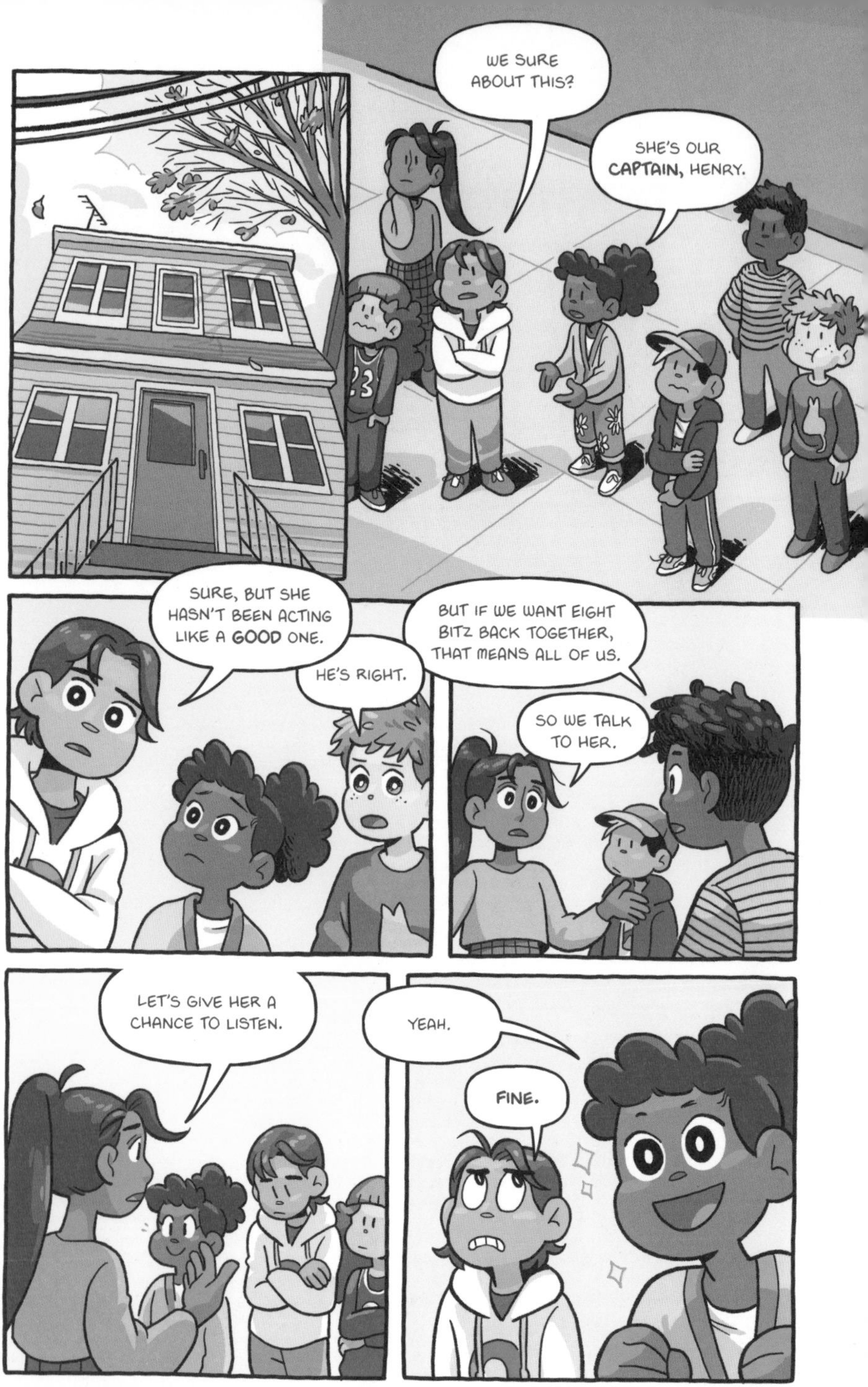
WE SURE ABOUT THIS?
SHE'S OUR CAPTAIN, HENRY.
SURE, BUT SHE HASN'T BEEN ACTING LIKE A GOOD ONE.
HE'S RIGHT.
BUT IF WE WANT EIGHT BITZ BACK TOGETHER, THAT MEANS ALL OF US.
SO WE TALK TO HER.
LET'S GIVE HER A CHANCE TO LISTEN.
YEAH.
FINE.

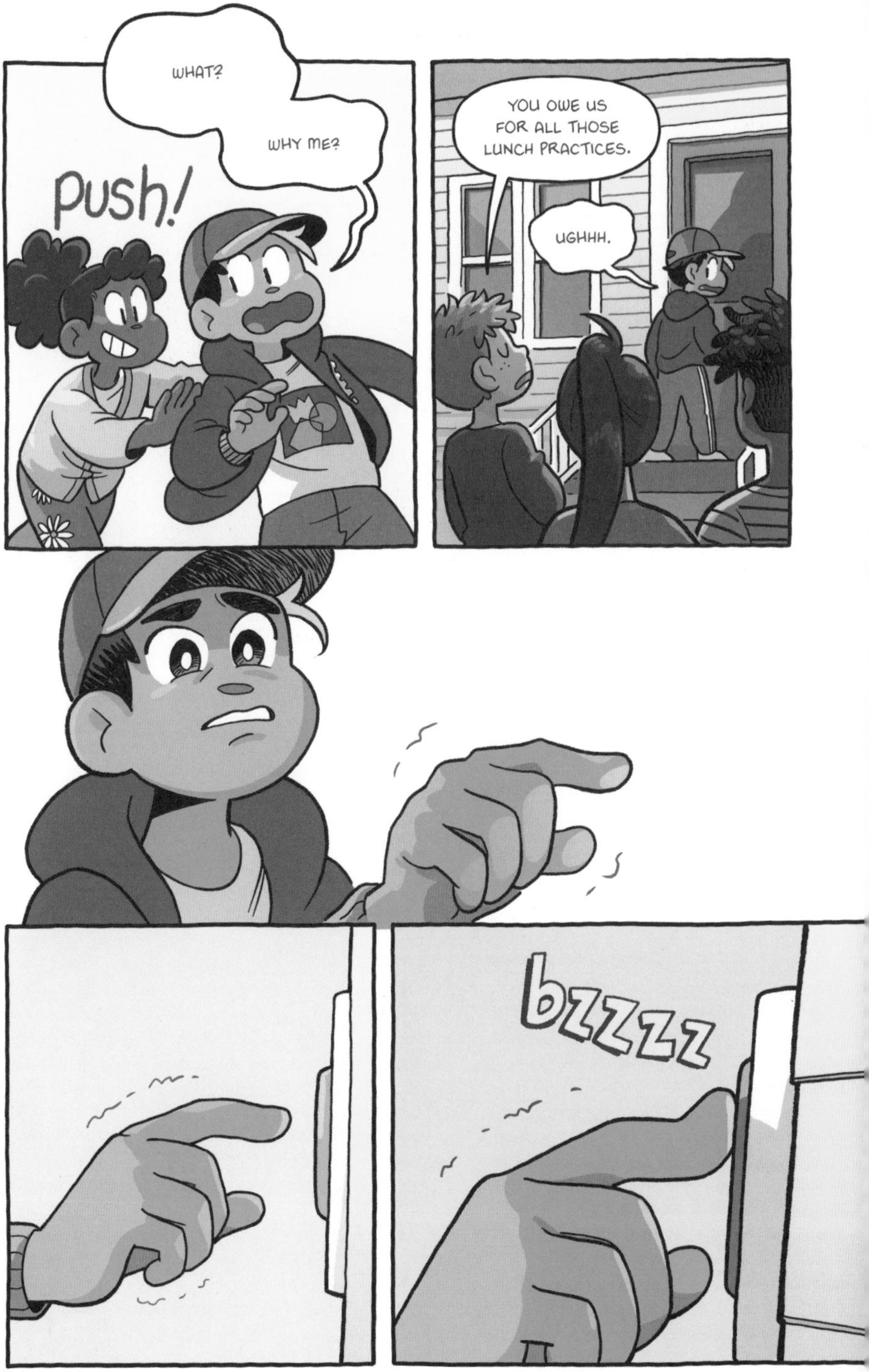

WHAT?
WHY ME?
PUSH!
YOU OWE US FOR ALL THOSE LUNCH PRACTICES.
UGHHH.
BZZZZ

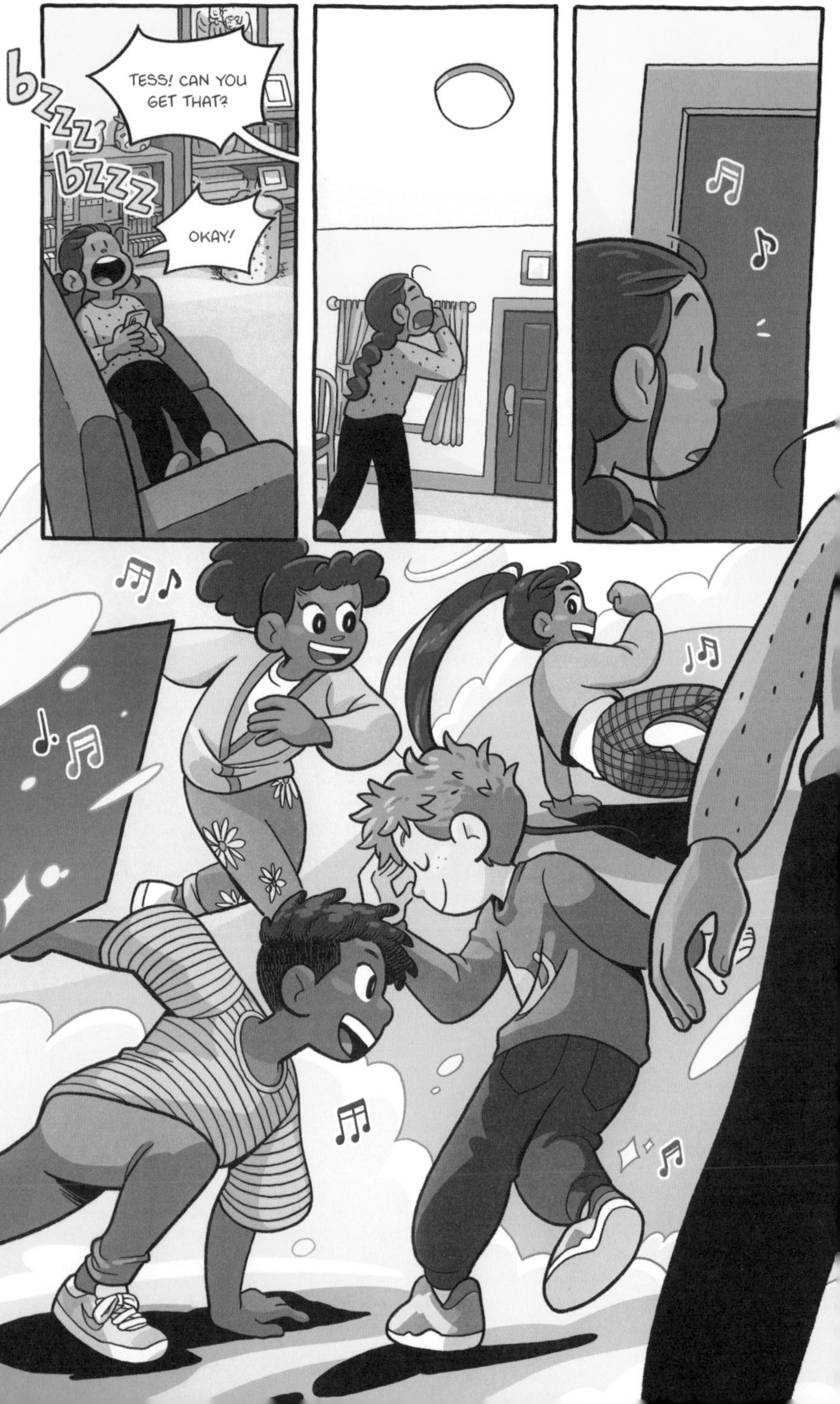
bzzzz
bzzzz
TESS! CAN YOU GET THAT?
OKAY!

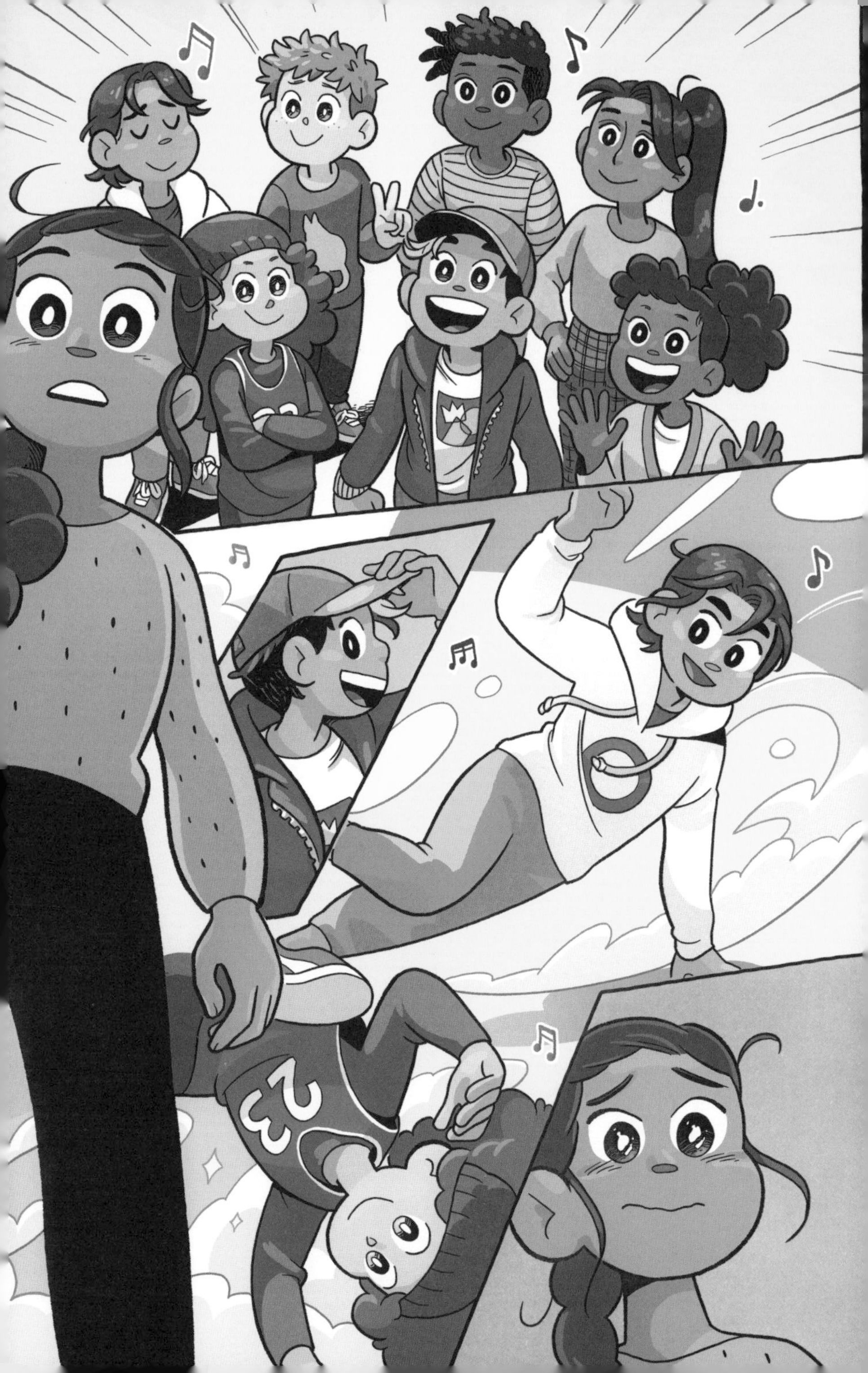

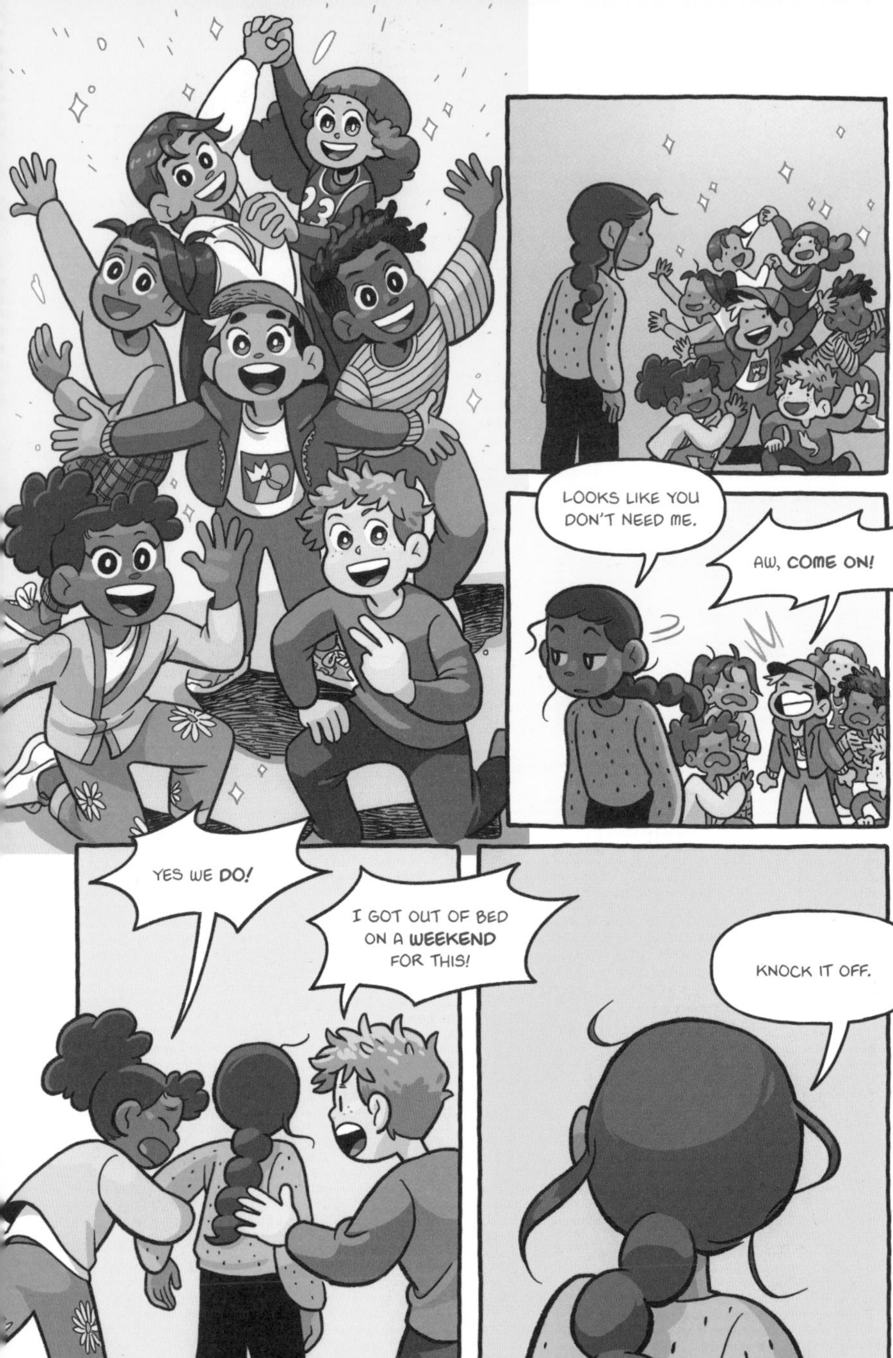
LOOKS LIKE YOU DON'T NEED ME.
AW, **COME ON!**
YES WE **DO!**
I GOT OUT OF BED ON A **WEEKEND** FOR THIS!
KNOCK IT OFF.

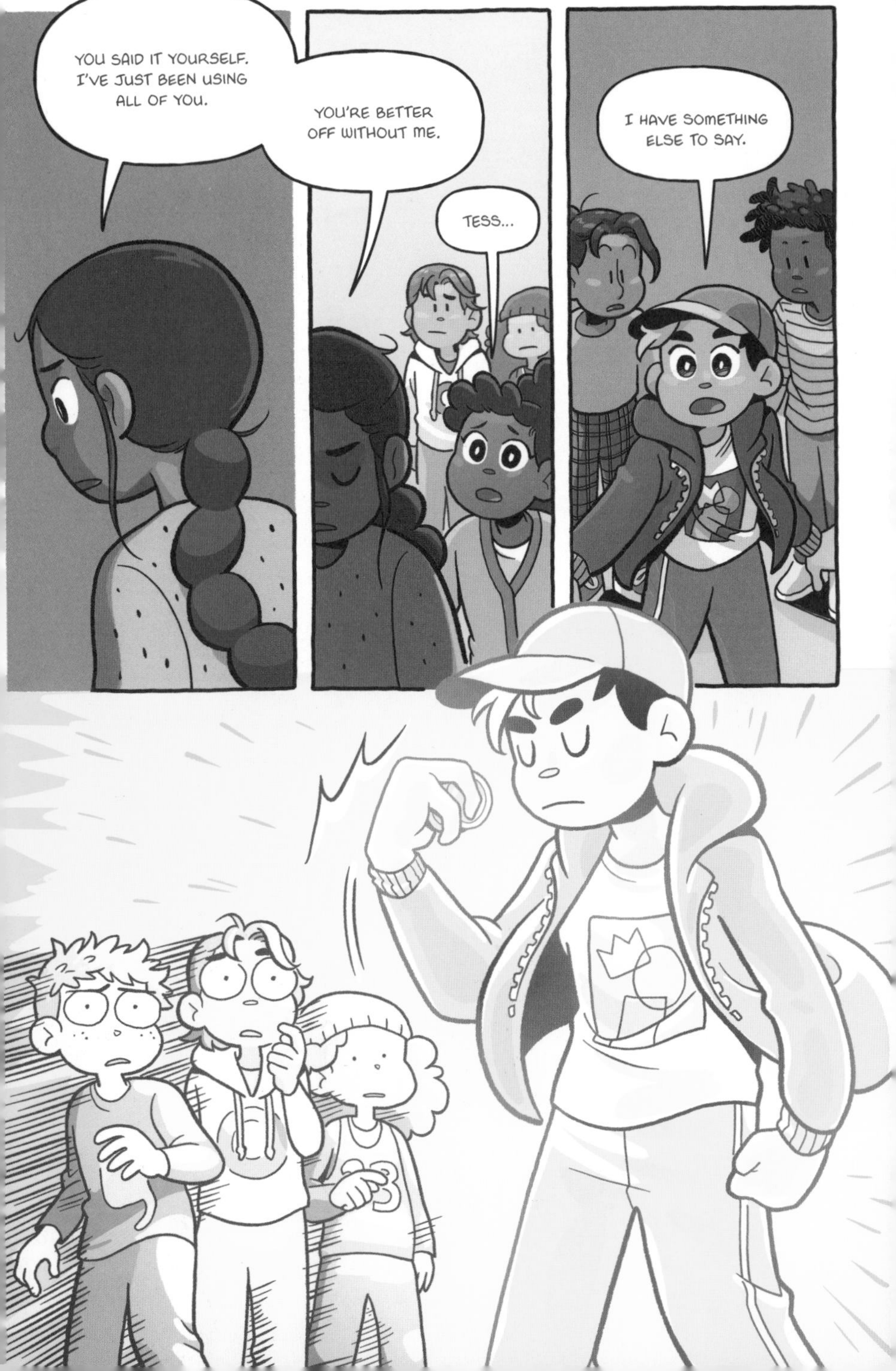
YOU SAID IT YOURSELF. I'VE JUST BEEN USING ALL OF YOU.
YOU'RE BETTER OFF WITHOUT ME.
TESS...
I HAVE SOMETHING ELSE TO SAY.

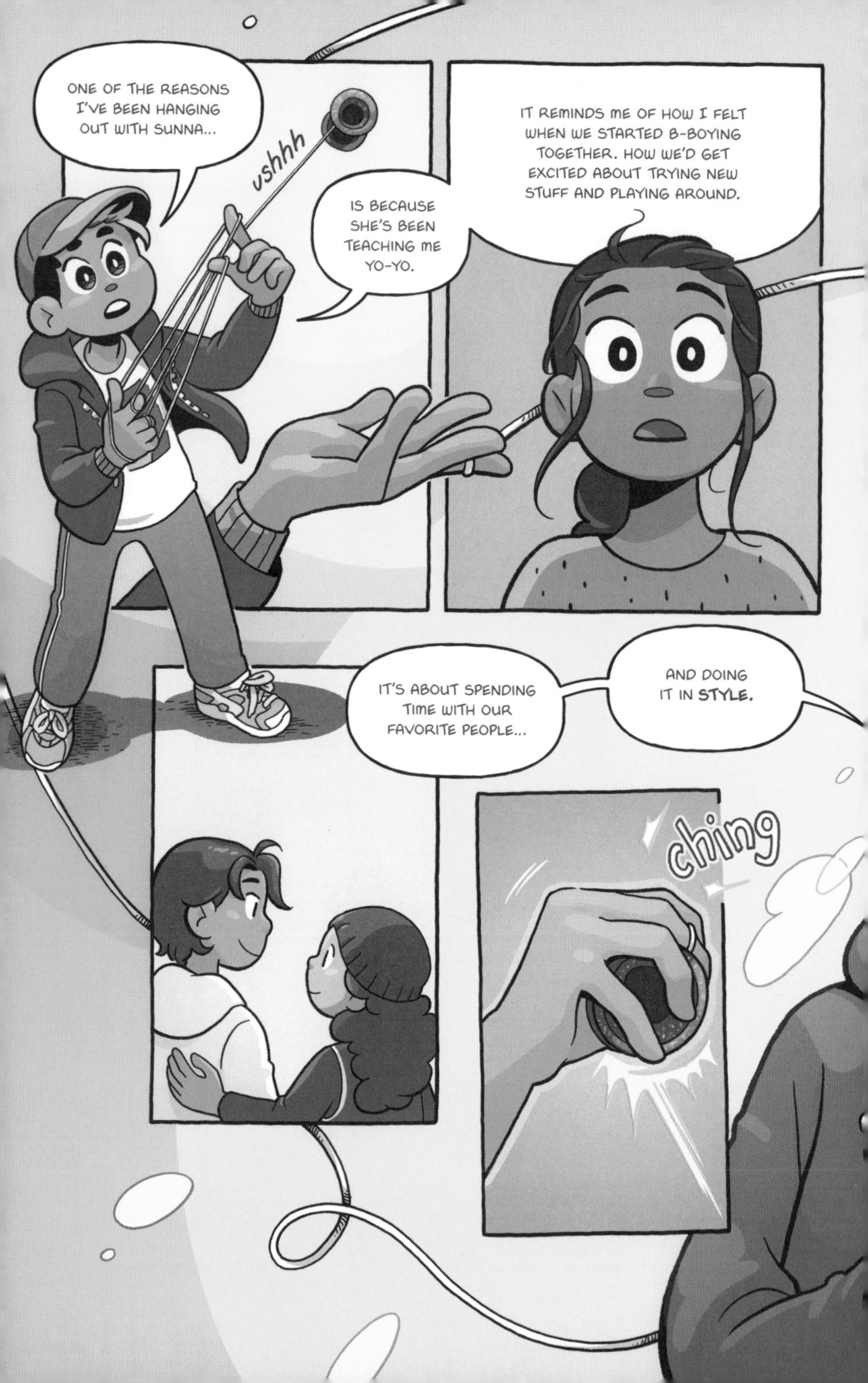
ONE OF THE REASONS I'VE BEEN HANGING OUT WITH SUNNA...
ushhh
IS BECAUSE SHE'S BEEN TEACHING ME YO-YO.
IT REMINDS ME OF HOW I FELT WHEN WE STARTED B-BOYING TOGETHER. HOW WE'D GET EXCITED ABOUT TRYING NEW STUFF AND PLAYING AROUND.
IT'S ABOUT SPENDING TIME WITH OUR FAVORITE PEOPLE...
AND DOING IT IN **STYLE.**
ching

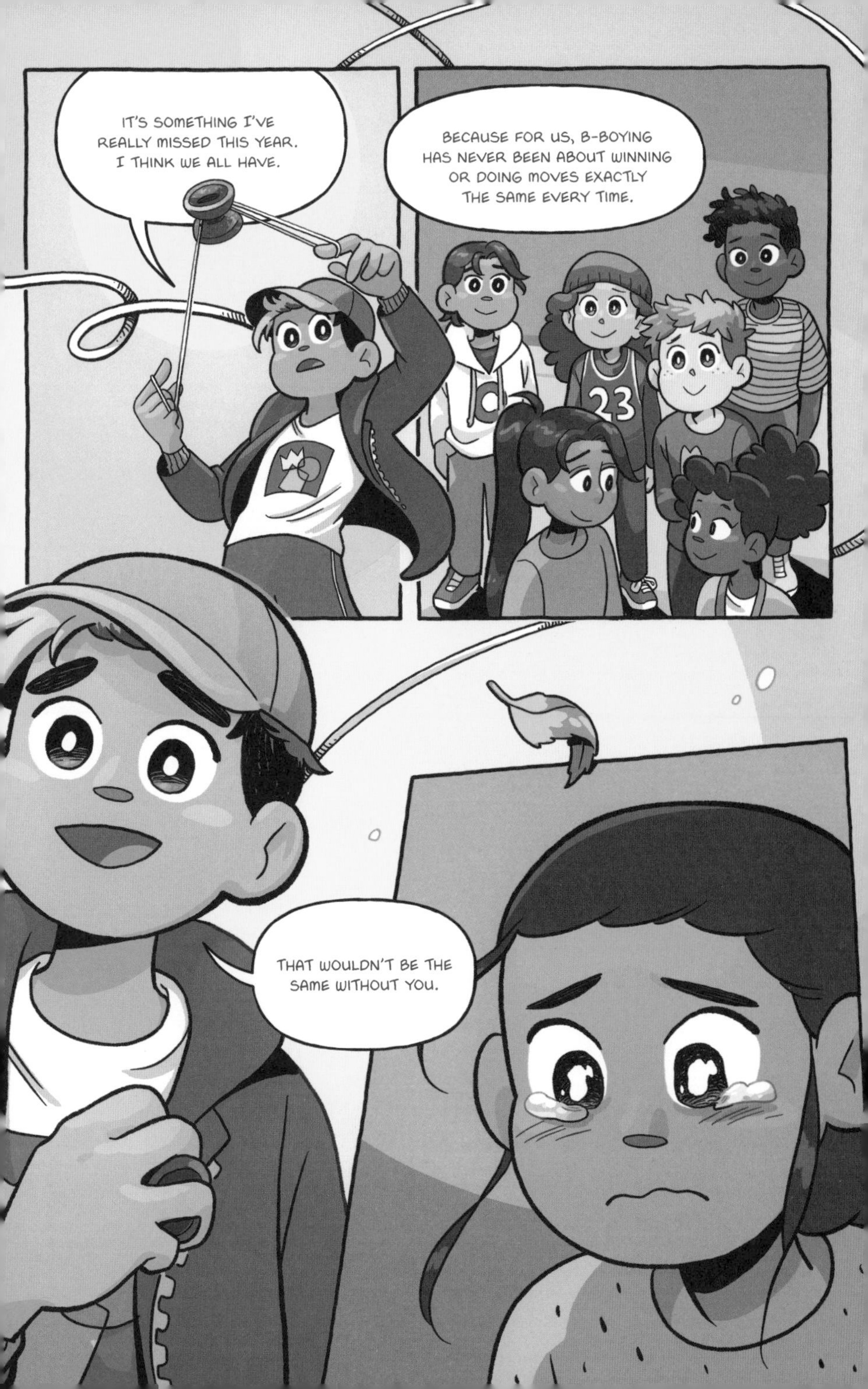
IT'S SOMETHING I'VE REALLY MISSED THIS YEAR. I THINK WE ALL HAVE.
BECAUSE FOR US, B-BOYING HAS NEVER BEEN ABOUT WINNING OR DOING MOVES EXACTLY THE SAME EVERY TIME.
THAT WOULDN'T BE THE SAME WITHOUT YOU.

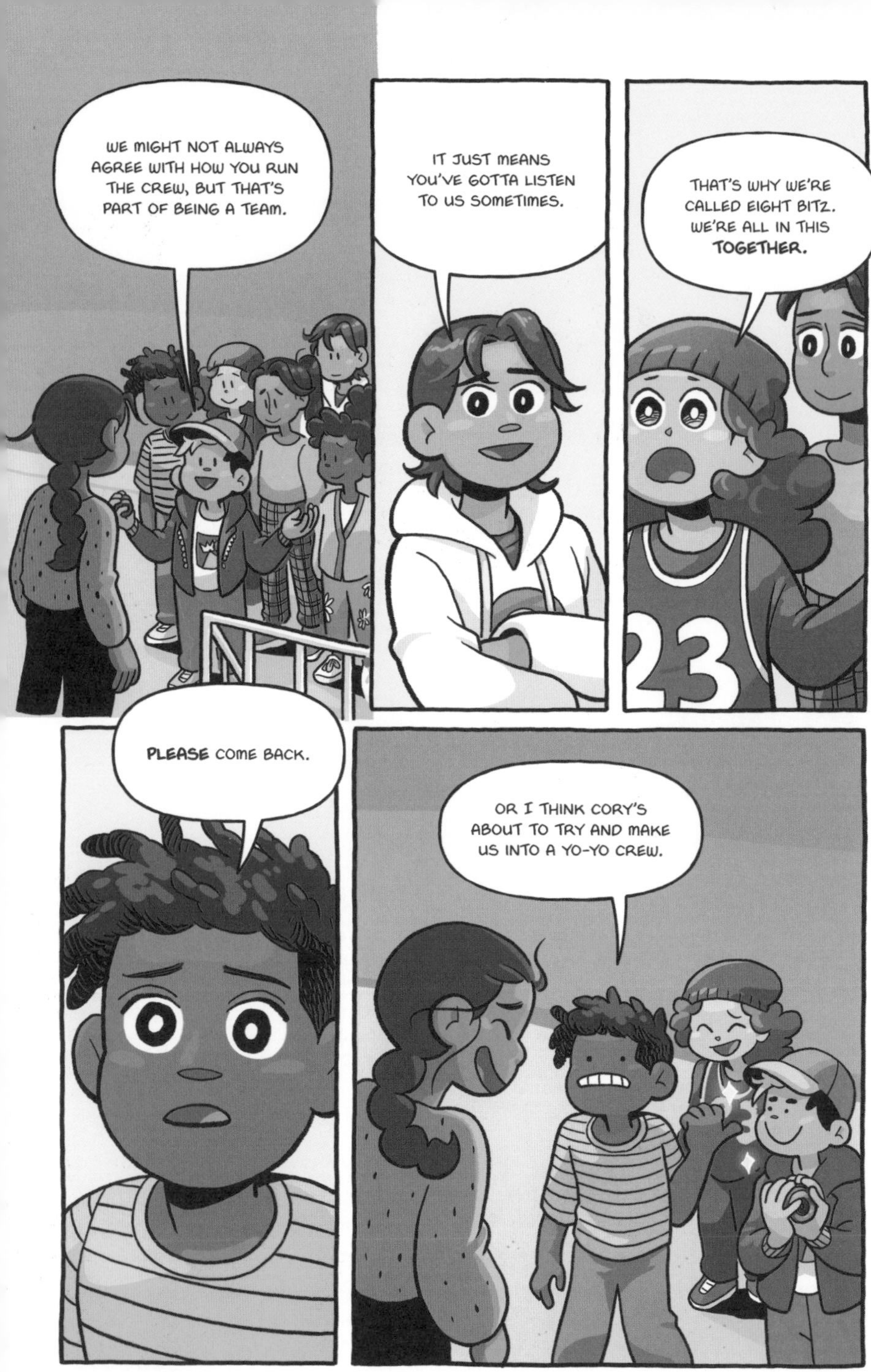
WE MIGHT NOT ALWAYS AGREE WITH HOW YOU RUN THE CREW, BUT THAT'S PART OF BEING A TEAM.
IT JUST MEANS YOU'VE GOTTA LISTEN TO US SOMETIMES.
THAT'S WHY WE'RE CALLED EIGHT BITZ. WE'RE ALL IN THIS **TOGETHER.**
23
PLEASE COME BACK.
OR I THINK CORY'S ABOUT TO TRY AND MAKE US INTO A YO-YO CREW.

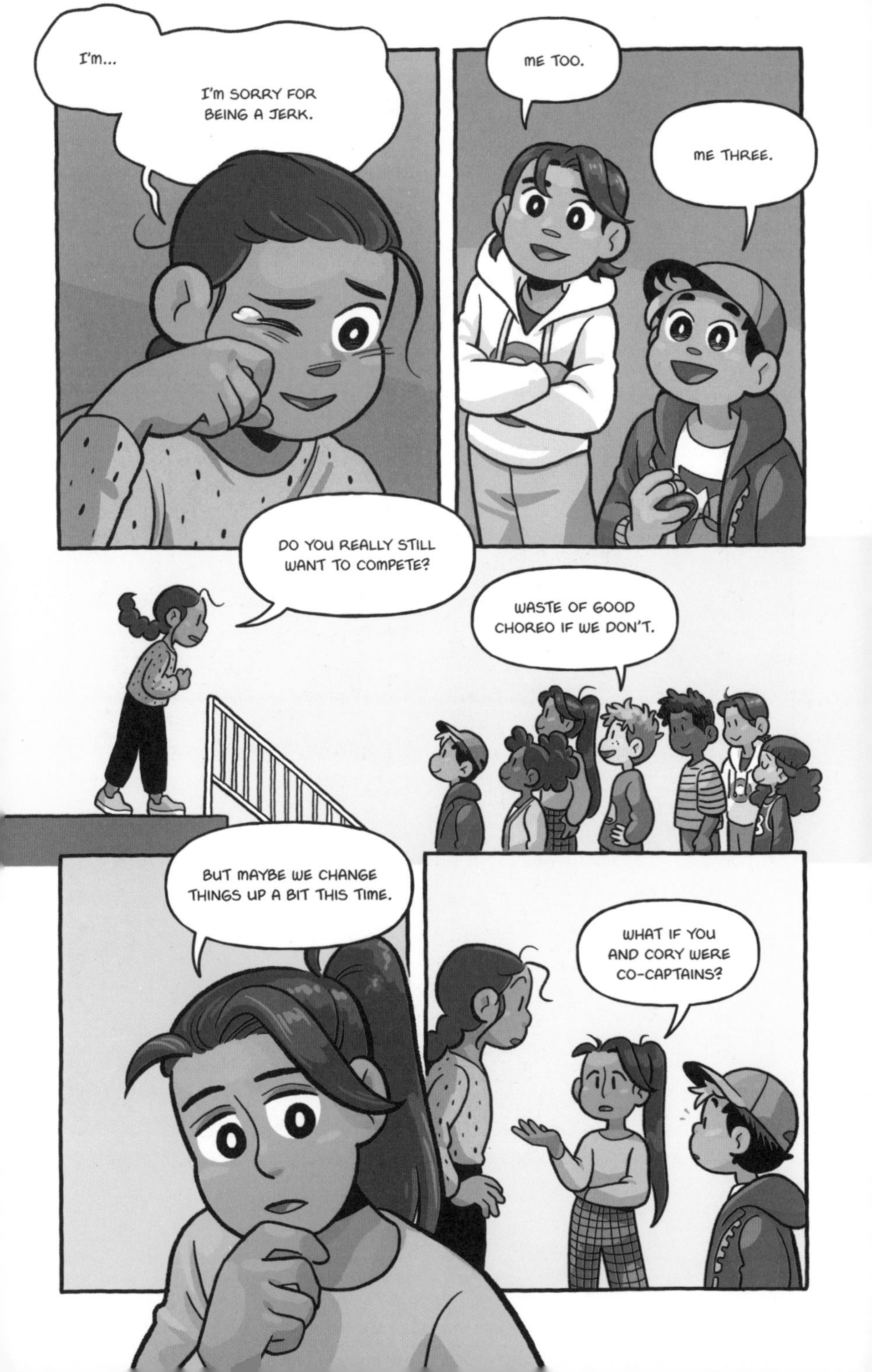
I'm...
I'm SORRY FOR BEING A JERK.
ME TOO.
ME THREE.
DO YOU REALLY STILL WANT TO COMPETE?
WASTE OF GOOD CHOREO IF WE DON'T.
BUT MAYBE WE CHANGE THINGS UP A BIT THIS TIME.
WHAT IF YOU AND CORY WERE CO-CAPTAINS?

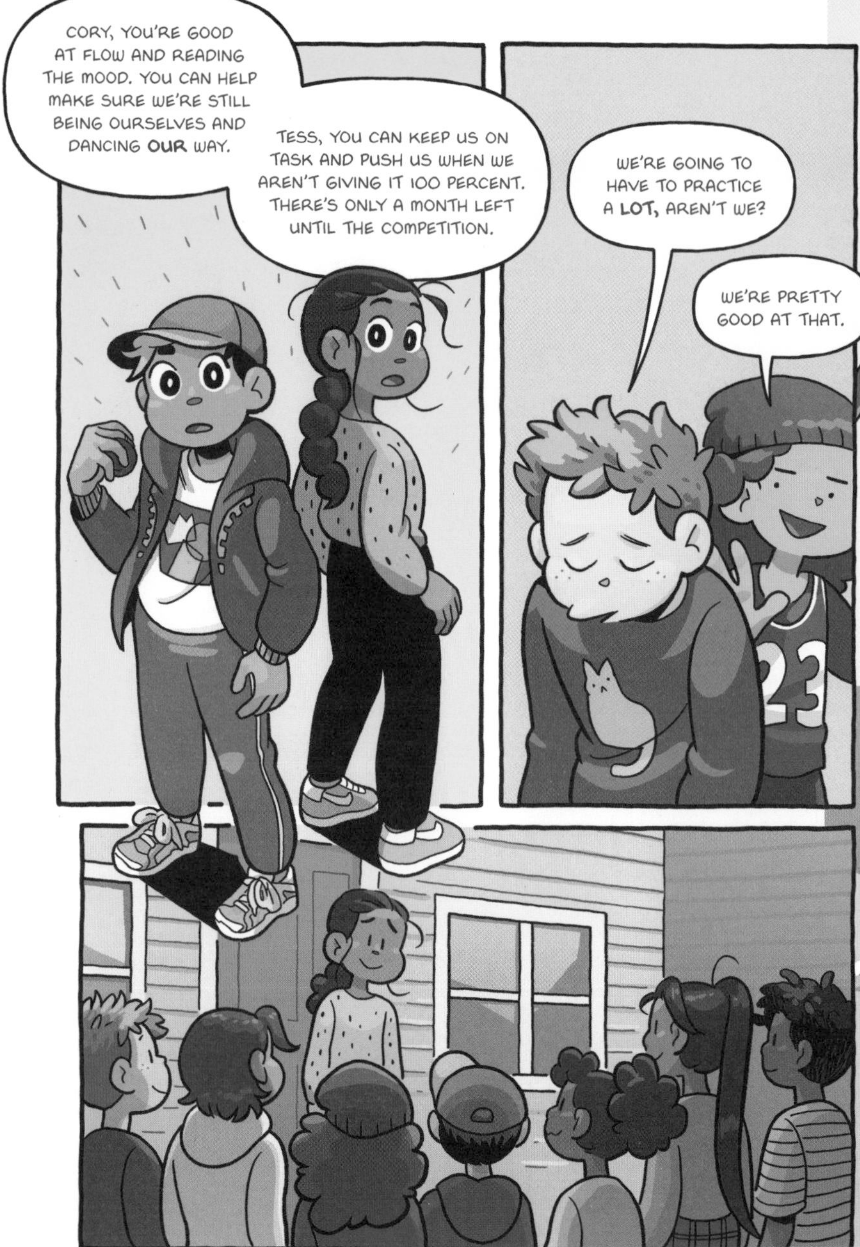
CORY, YOU'RE GOOD AT FLOW AND READING THE MOOD. YOU CAN HELP MAKE SURE WE'RE STILL BEING OURSELVES AND DANCING **OUR** WAY.
TESS, YOU CAN KEEP US ON TASK AND PUSH US WHEN WE AREN'T GIVING IT 100 PERCENT. THERE'S ONLY A MONTH LEFT UNTIL THE COMPETITION.
WE'RE GOING TO HAVE TO PRACTICE A **LOT,** AREN'T WE?
WE'RE PRETTY GOOD AT THAT.
23

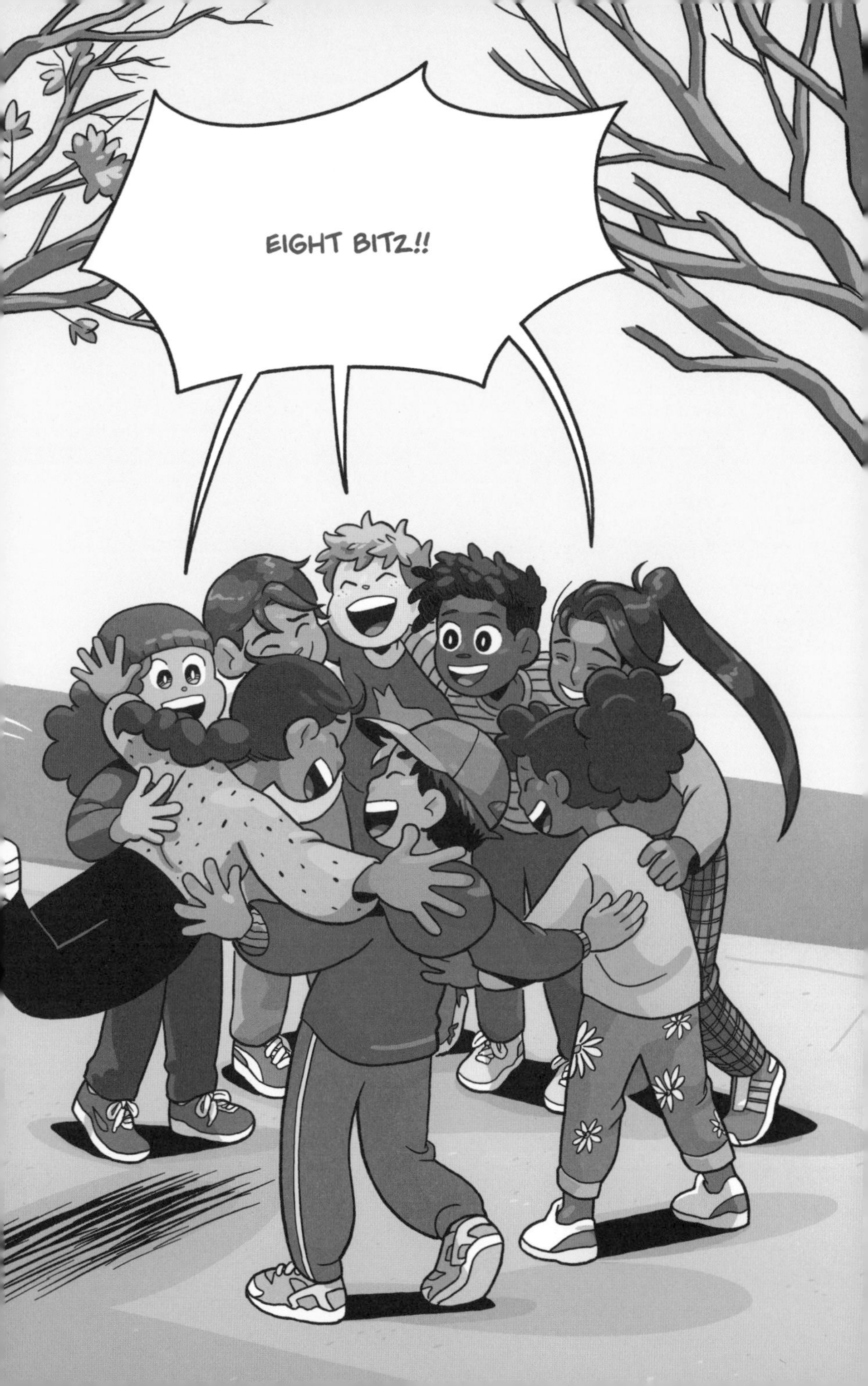
EIGHT BITZ!!

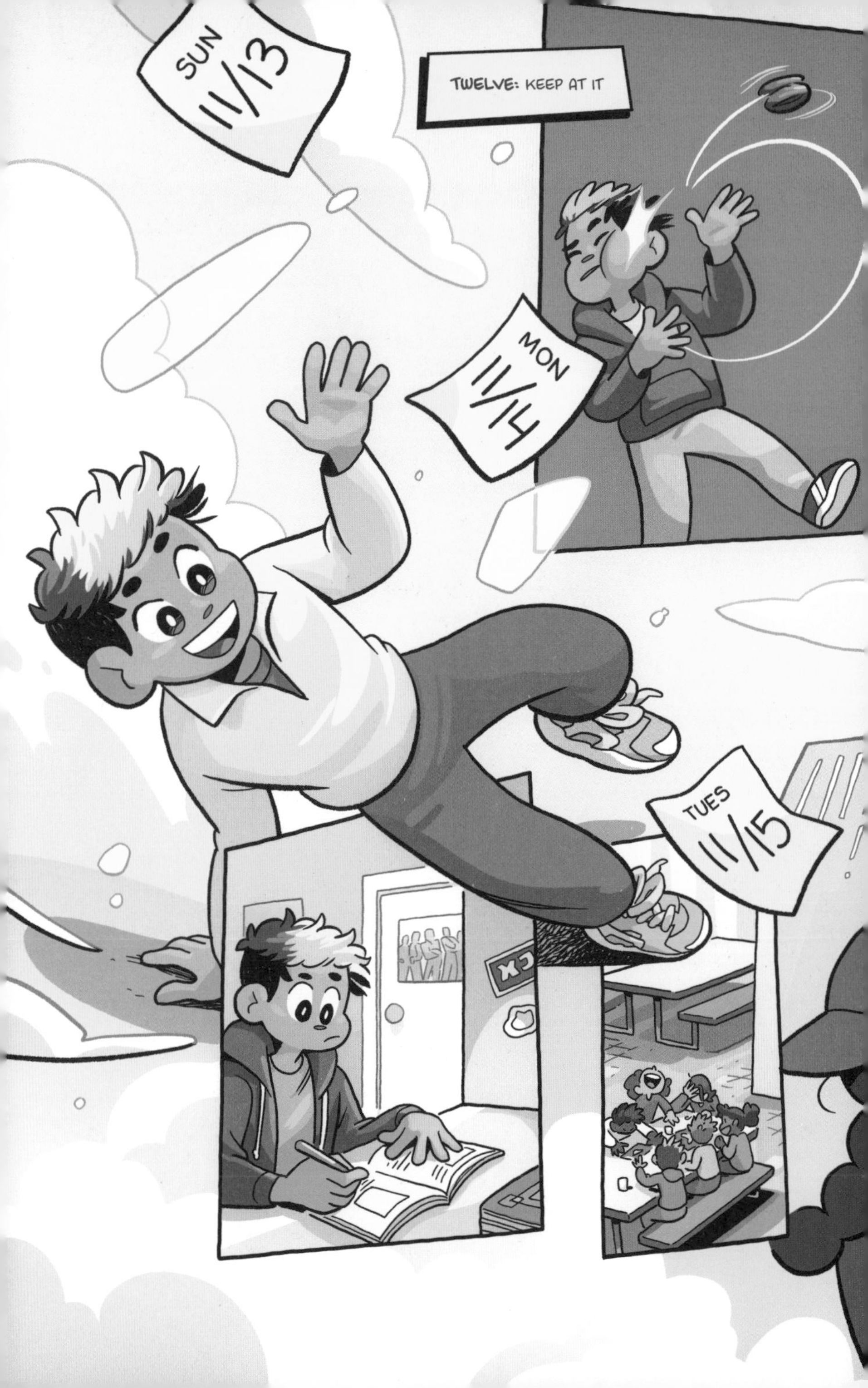
TWELVE: KEEP AT IT
SUN 11/13
MON 11/14
TUES 11/15

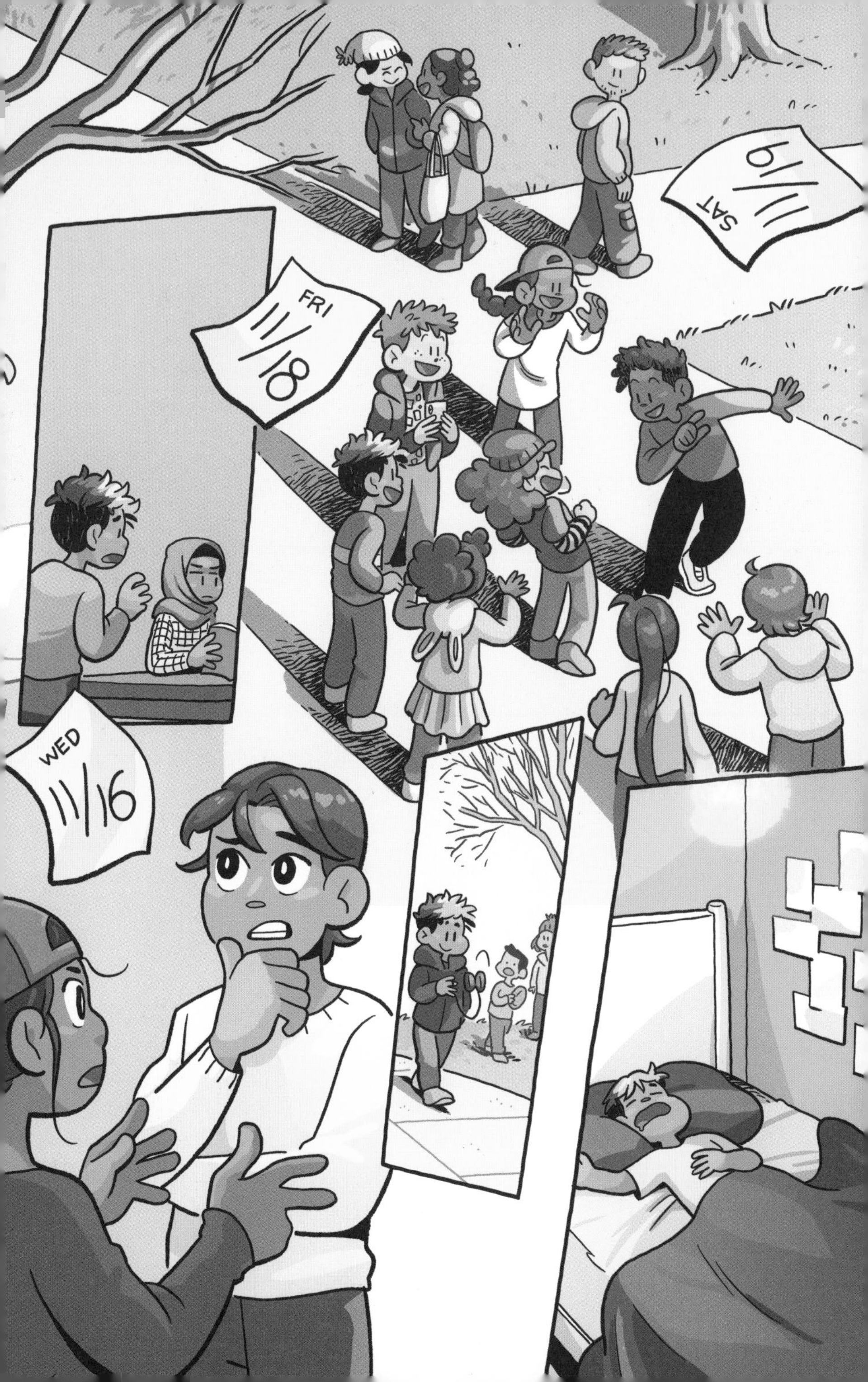
SAT 11/19
FRI 11/18
WED 11/16

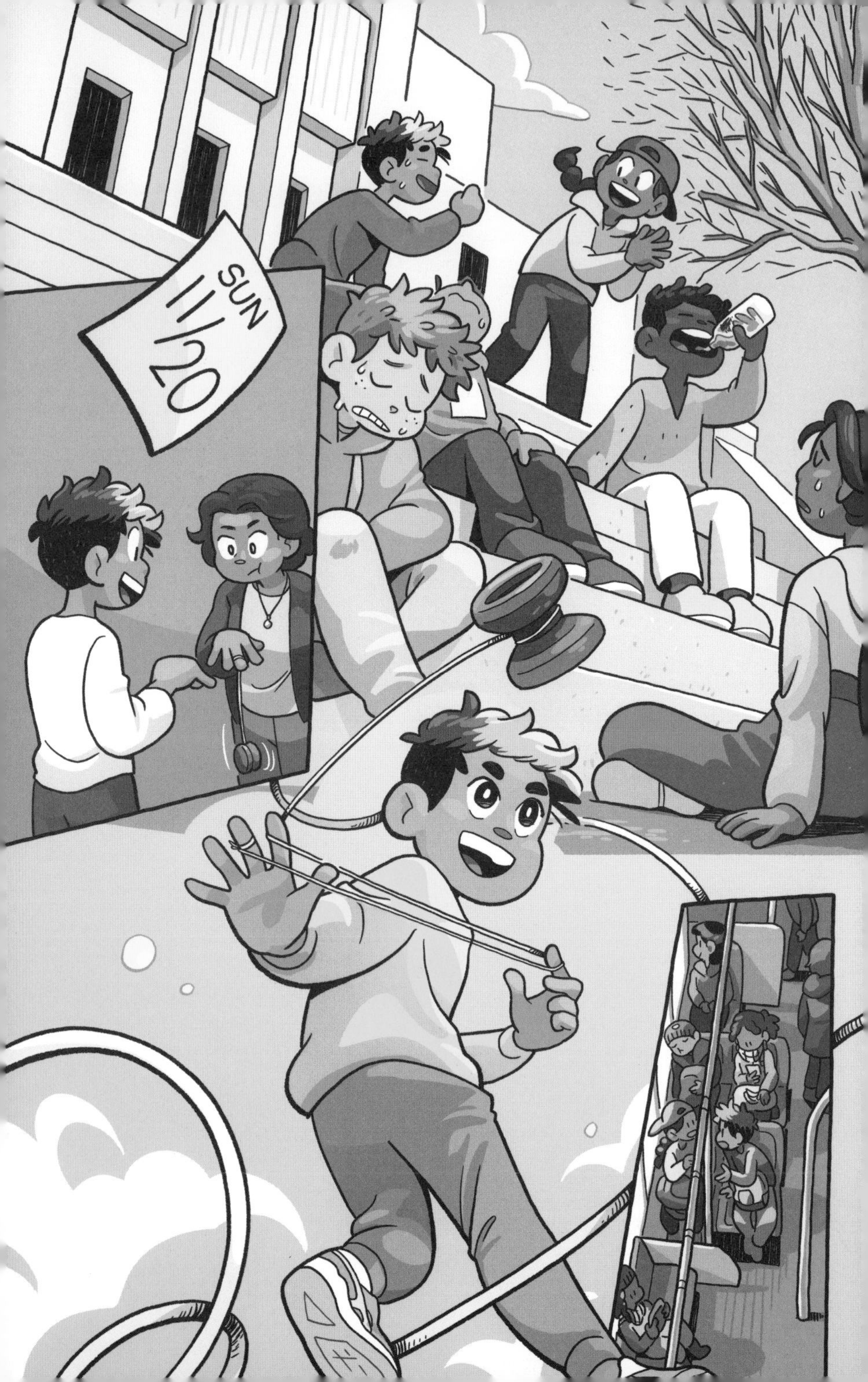
SUN
11/20

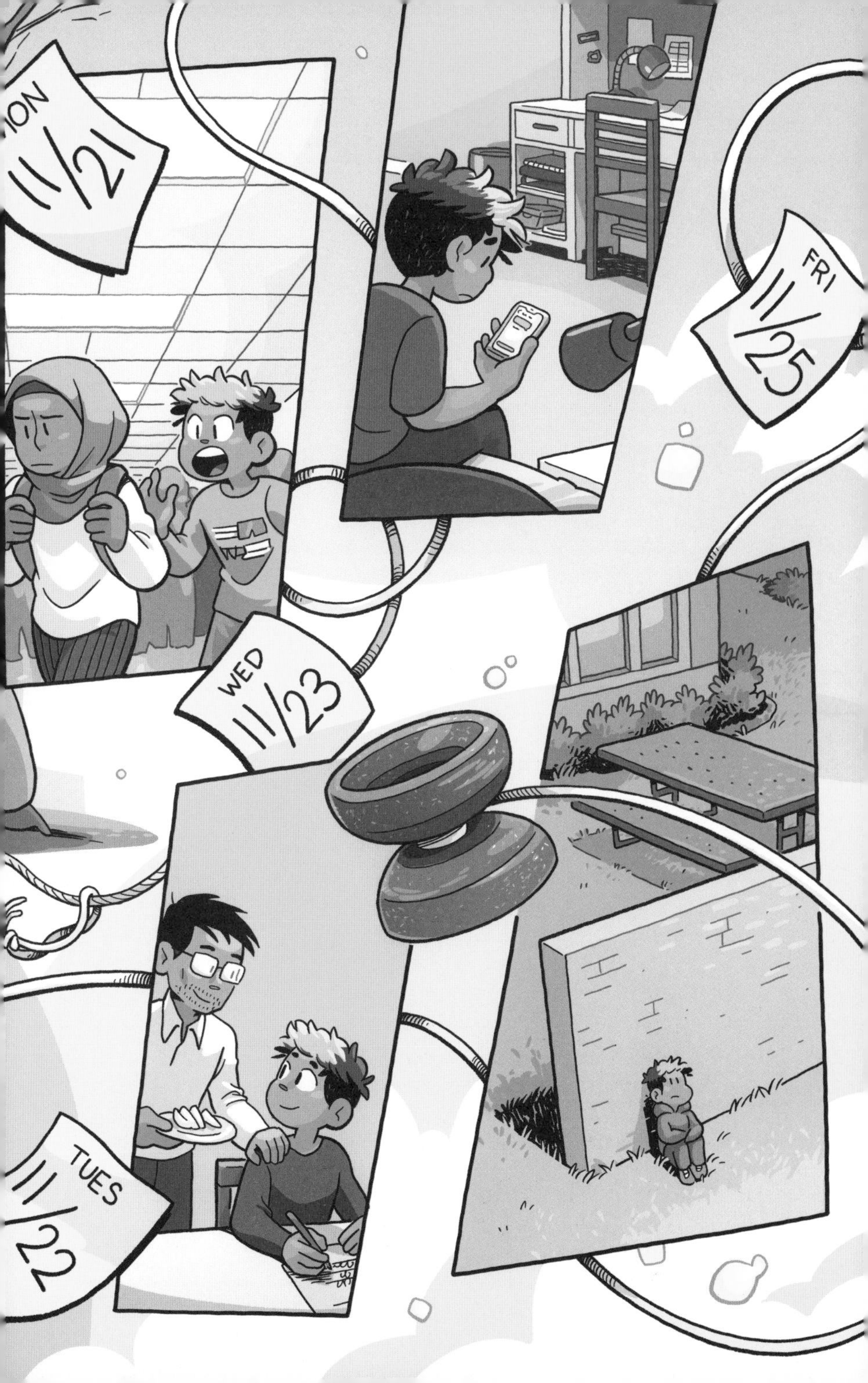

11/21
TUES
11/22
WED
11/23
FRI
11/25

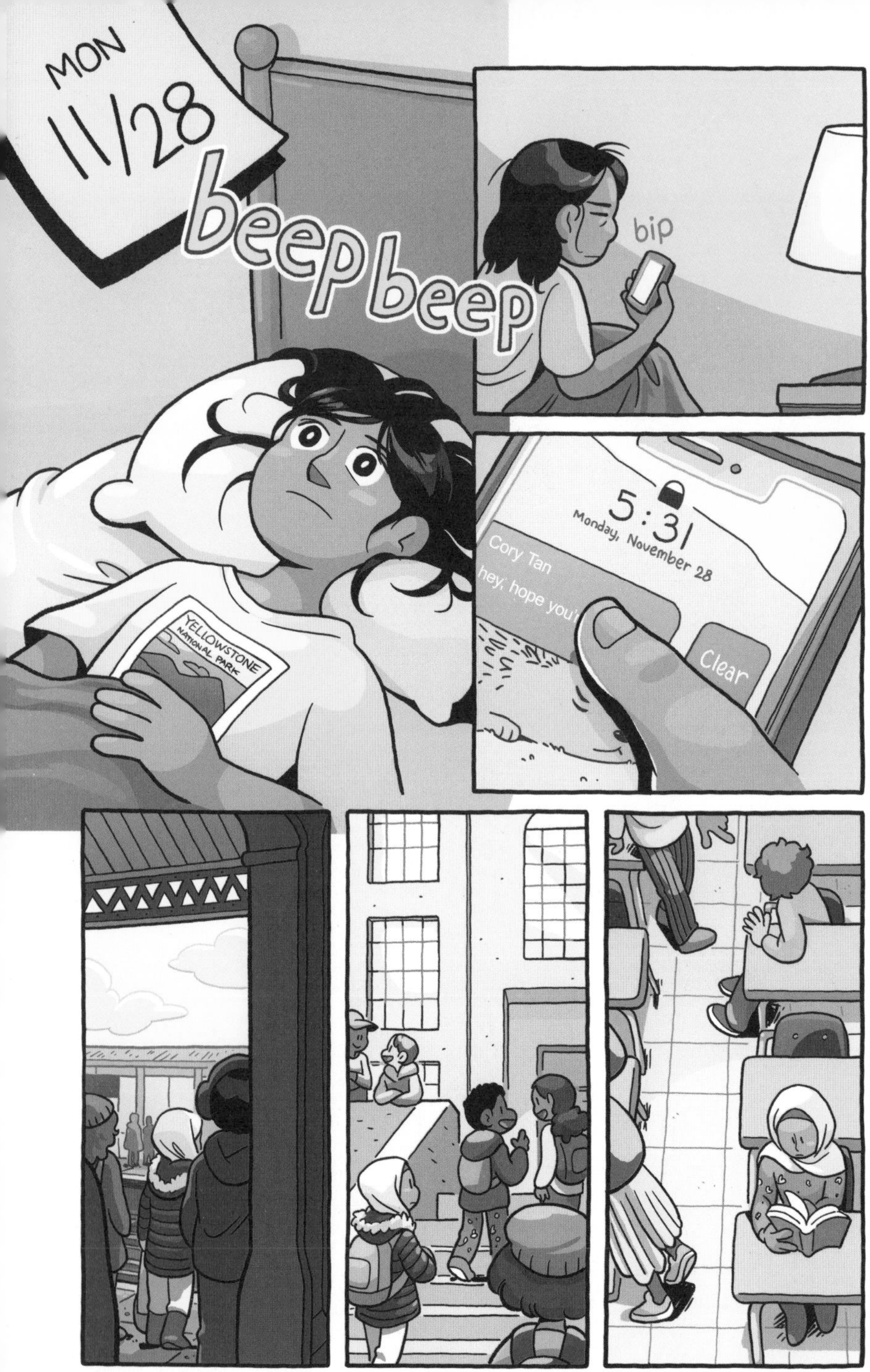
MON
11/28
beep beep
bip
5:31
Monday, November 28
Cory Tan
hey, hope you'
Clear
YELLOWSTONE NATIONAL PARK

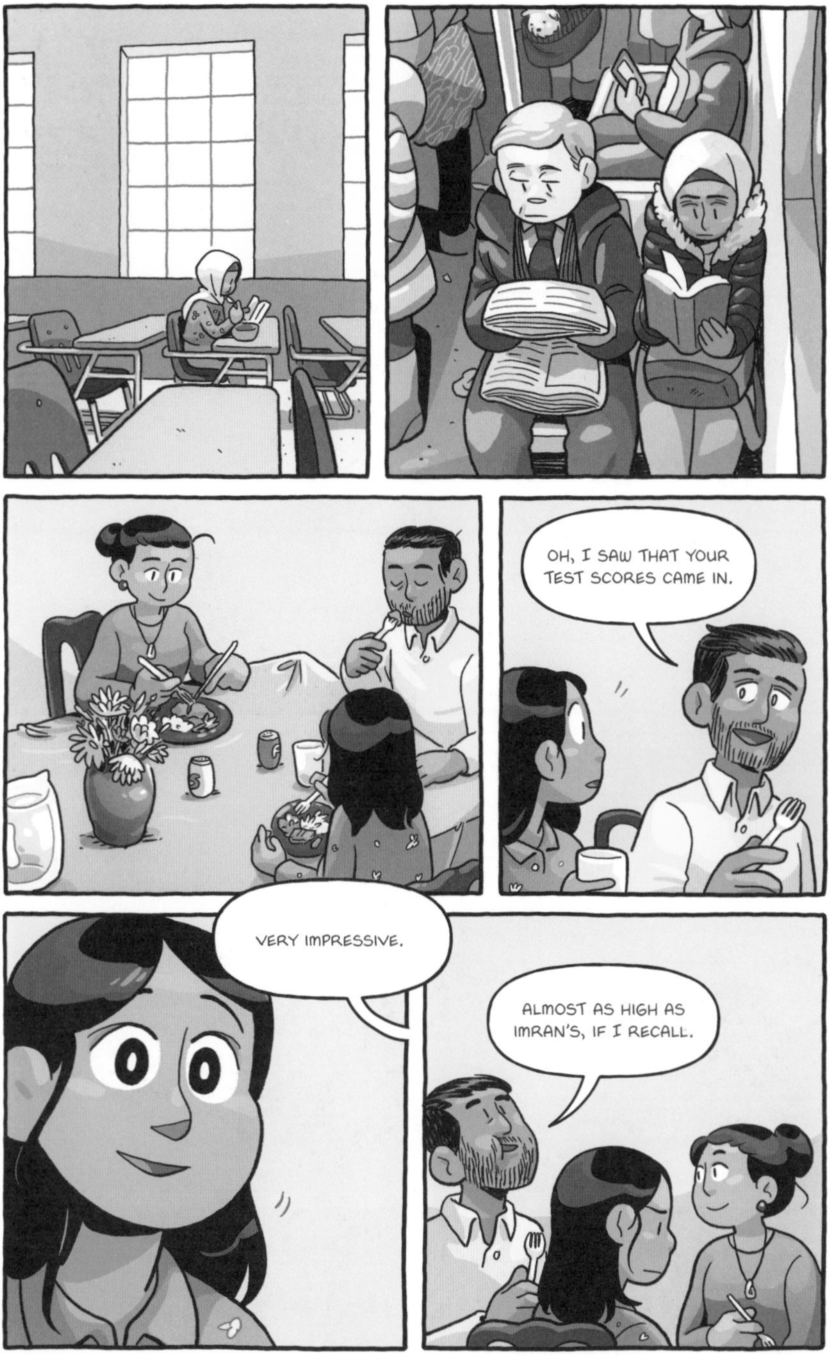
OH, I SAW THAT YOUR TEST SCORES CAME IN.
VERY IMPRESSIVE.
ALMOST AS HIGH AS IMRAN'S, IF I RECALL.

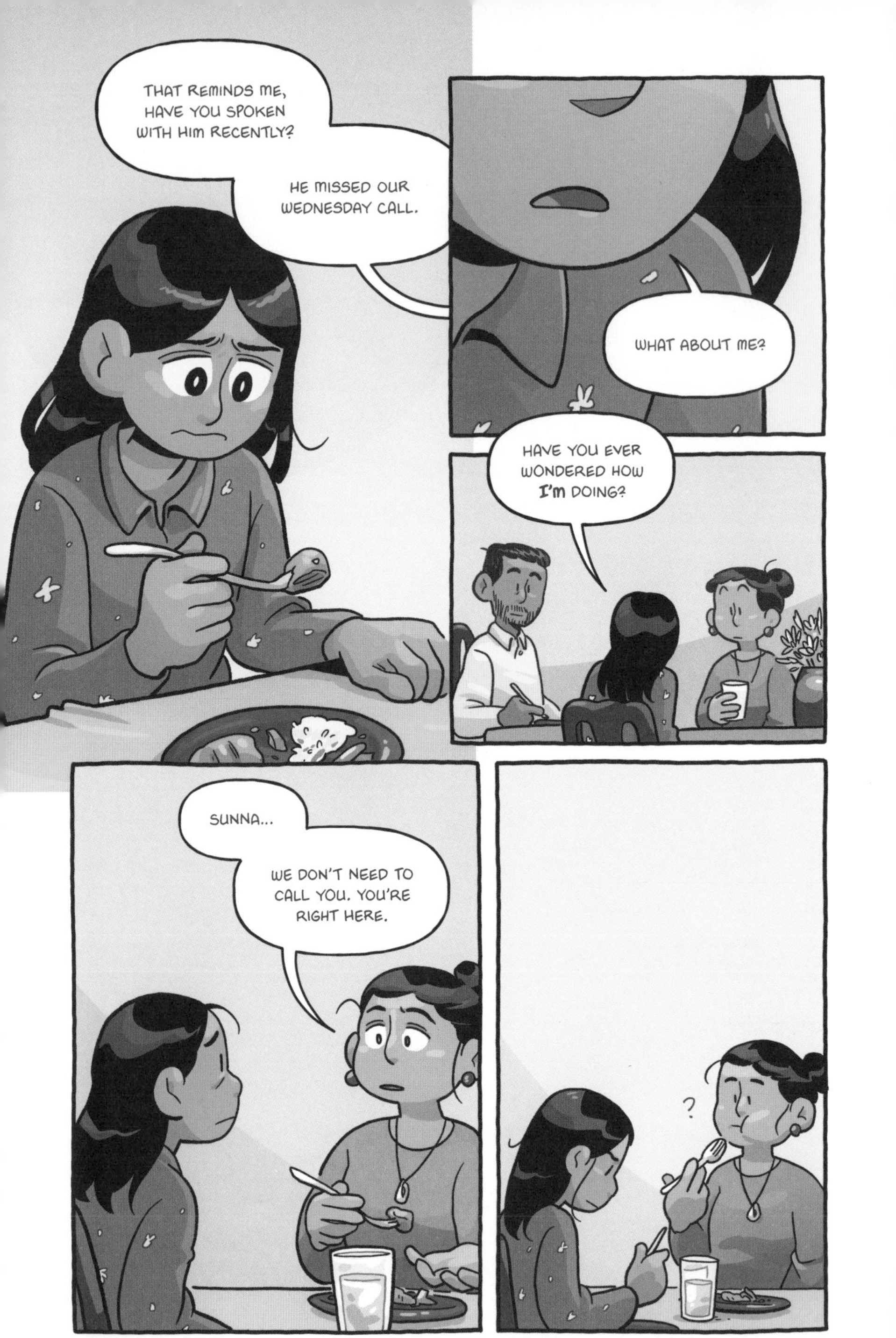
THAT REMINDS ME, HAVE YOU SPOKEN WITH HIM RECENTLY?
HE MISSED OUR WEDNESDAY CALL.
WHAT ABOUT ME?
HAVE YOU EVER WONDERED HOW **I'M** DOING?
SUNNA...
WE DON'T NEED TO CALL YOU. YOU'RE RIGHT HERE.
?

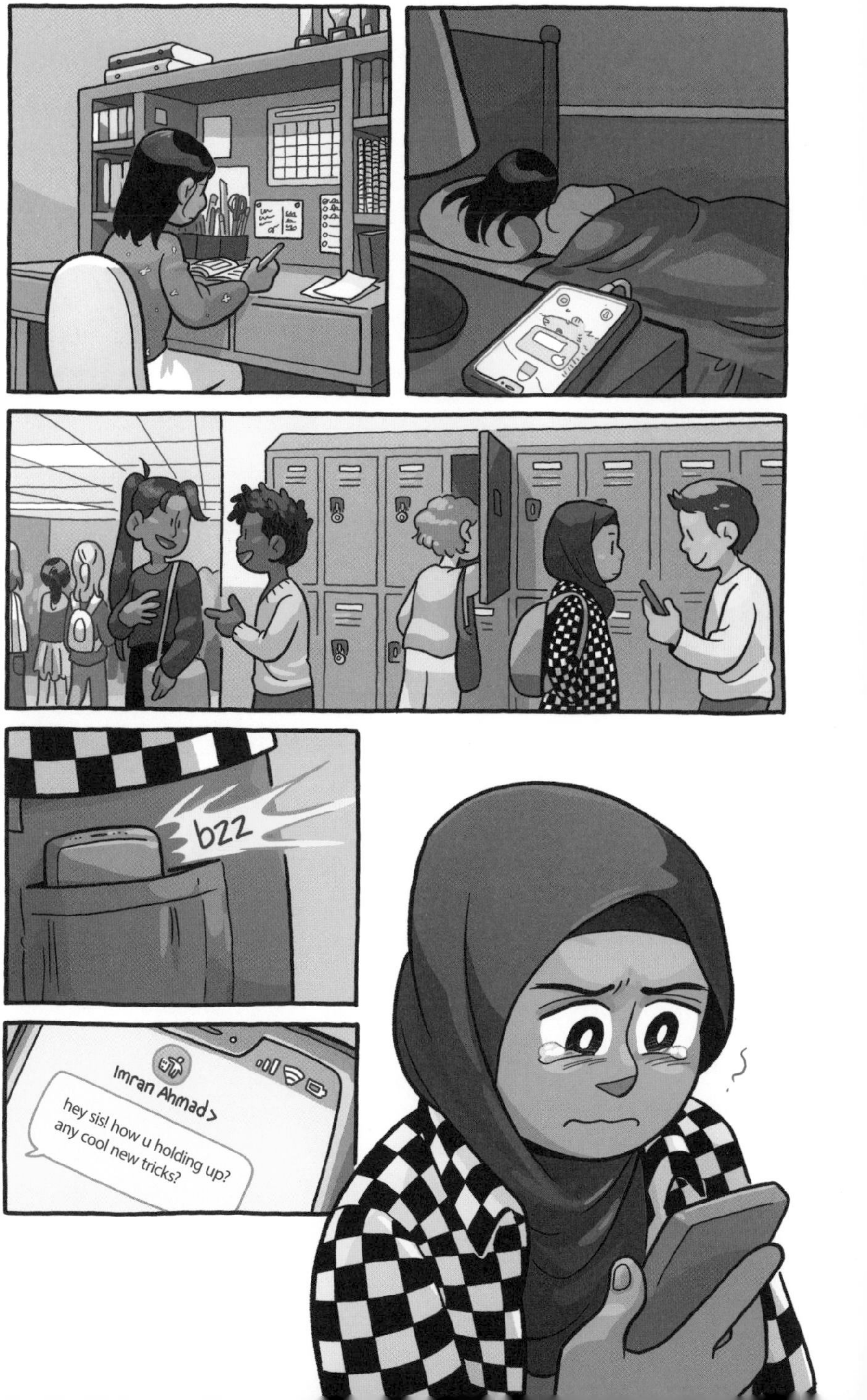
bzz
Imran Ahmad>
hey sis! how u holding up? any cool new tricks?

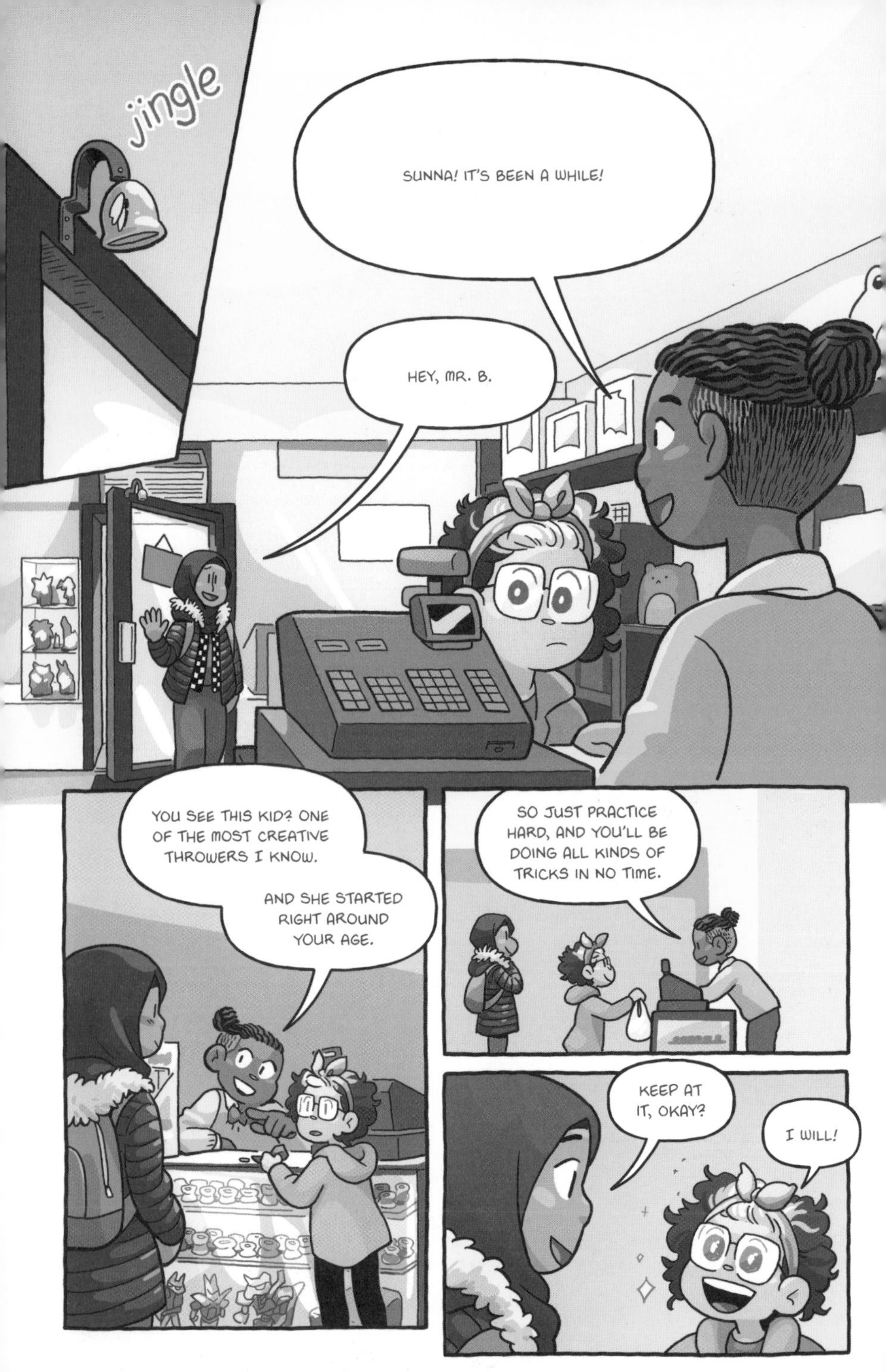
jingle
SUNNA! IT'S BEEN A WHILE!
HEY, MR. B.
YOU SEE THIS KID? ONE OF THE MOST CREATIVE THROWERS I KNOW.
AND SHE STARTED RIGHT AROUND YOUR AGE.
SO JUST PRACTICE HARD, AND YOU'LL BE DOING ALL KINDS OF TRICKS IN NO TIME.
KEEP AT IT, OKAY?
I WILL!

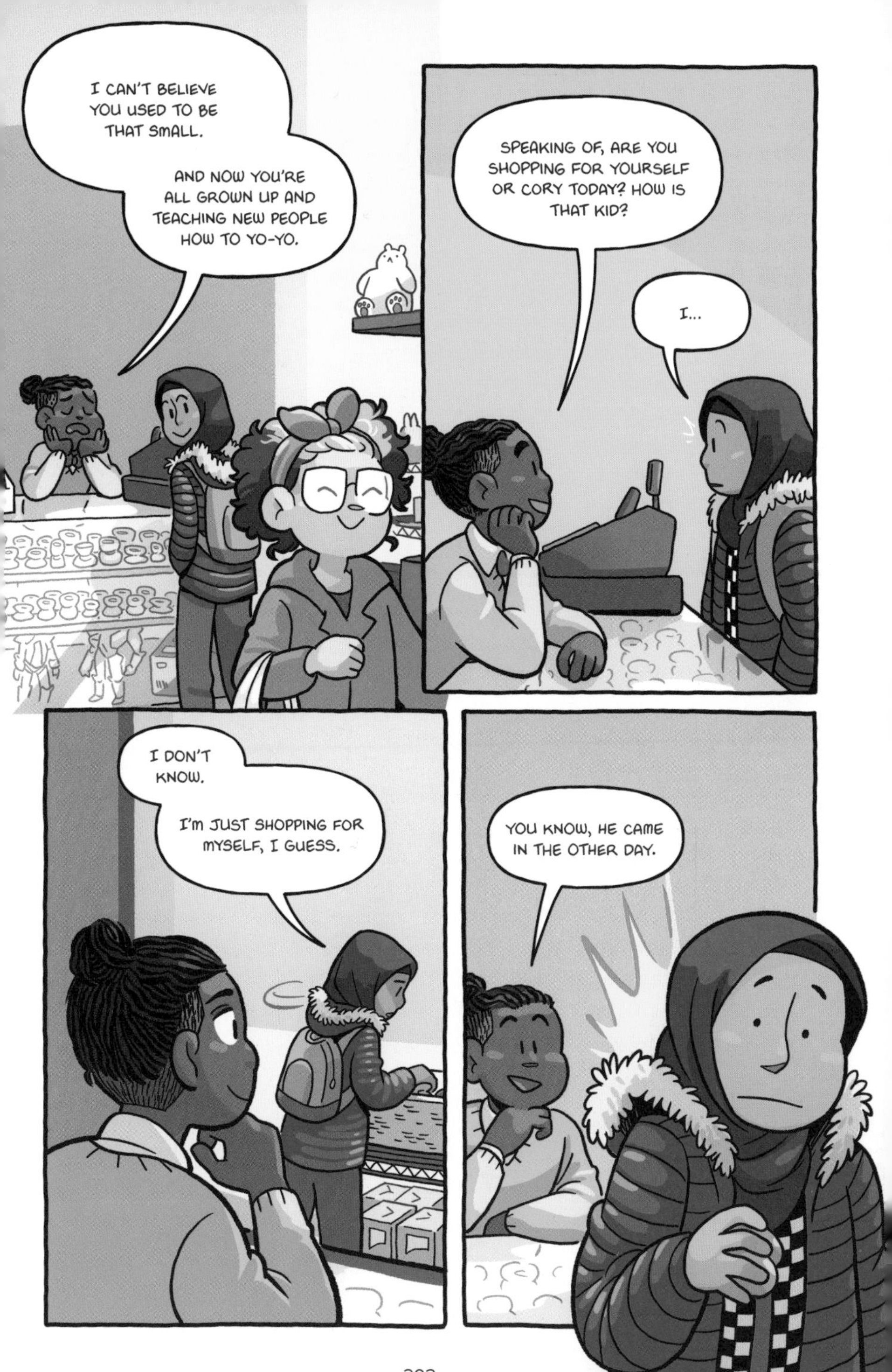
I CAN'T BELIEVE YOU USED TO BE THAT SMALL.
AND NOW YOU'RE ALL GROWN UP AND TEACHING NEW PEOPLE HOW TO YO-YO.
SPEAKING OF, ARE YOU SHOPPING FOR YOURSELF OR CORY TODAY? HOW IS THAT KID?
I...
I DON'T KNOW.
I'M JUST SHOPPING FOR MYSELF, I GUESS.
YOU KNOW, HE CAME IN THE OTHER DAY.

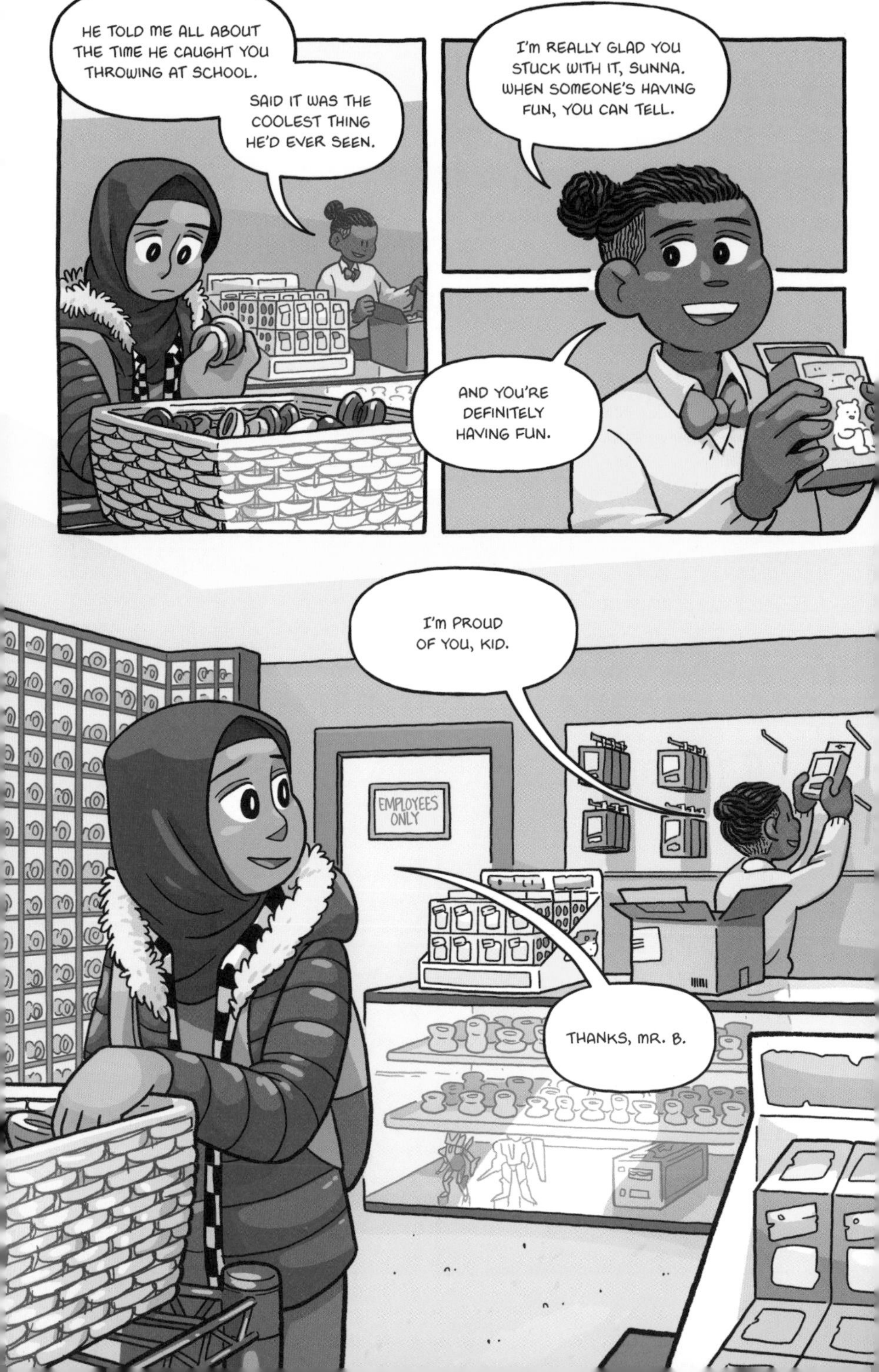
HE TOLD ME ALL ABOUT THE TIME HE CAUGHT YOU THROWING AT SCHOOL.
SAID IT WAS THE COOLEST THING HE'D EVER SEEN.
I'M REALLY GLAD YOU STUCK WITH IT, SUNNA. WHEN SOMEONE'S HAVING FUN, YOU CAN TELL.
AND YOU'RE DEFINITELY HAVING FUN.
I'M PROUD OF YOU, KID.
EMPLOYEES ONLY
THANKS, MR. B.

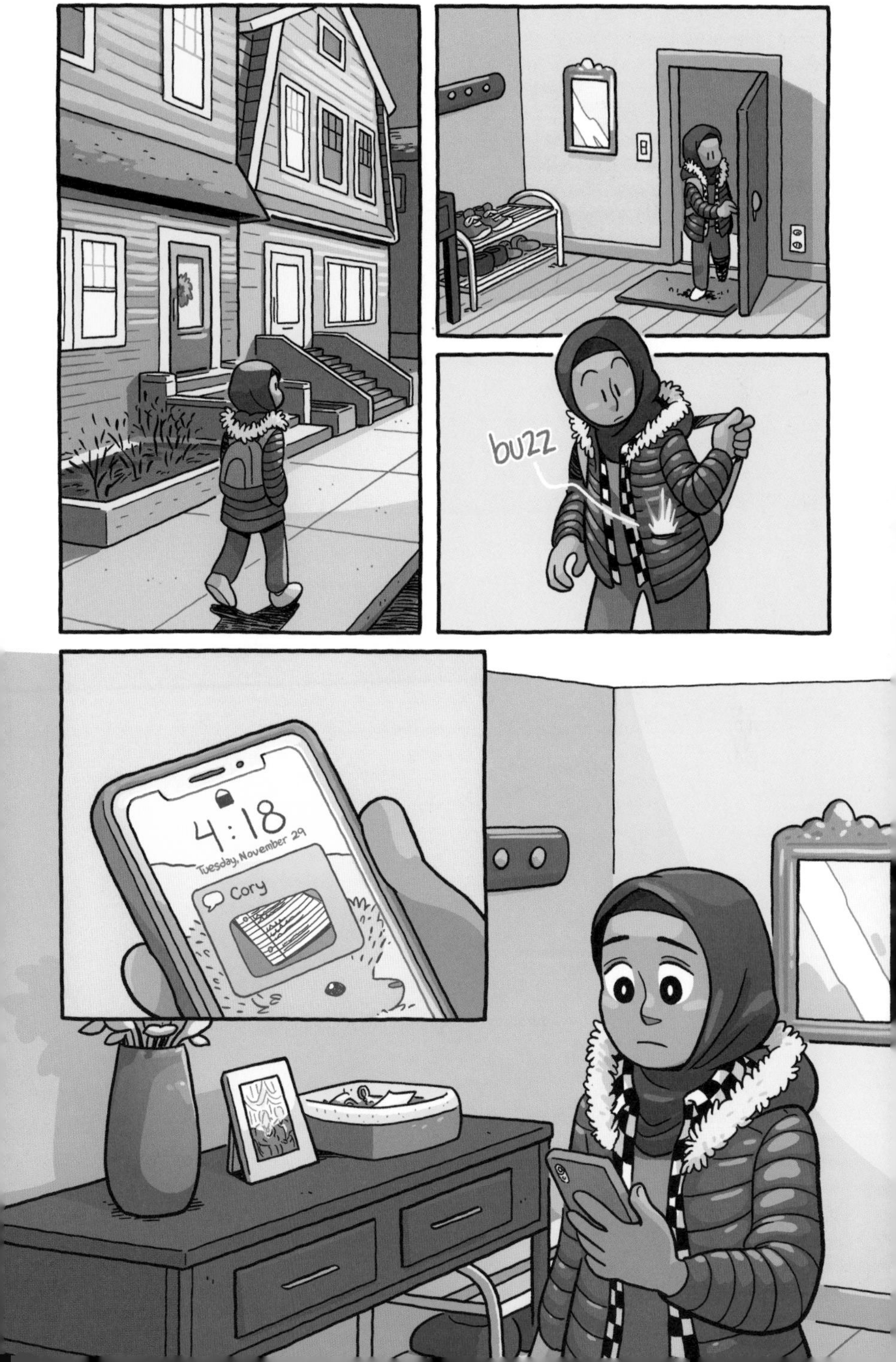
buzz
4:18
Tuesday, November 29
Cory

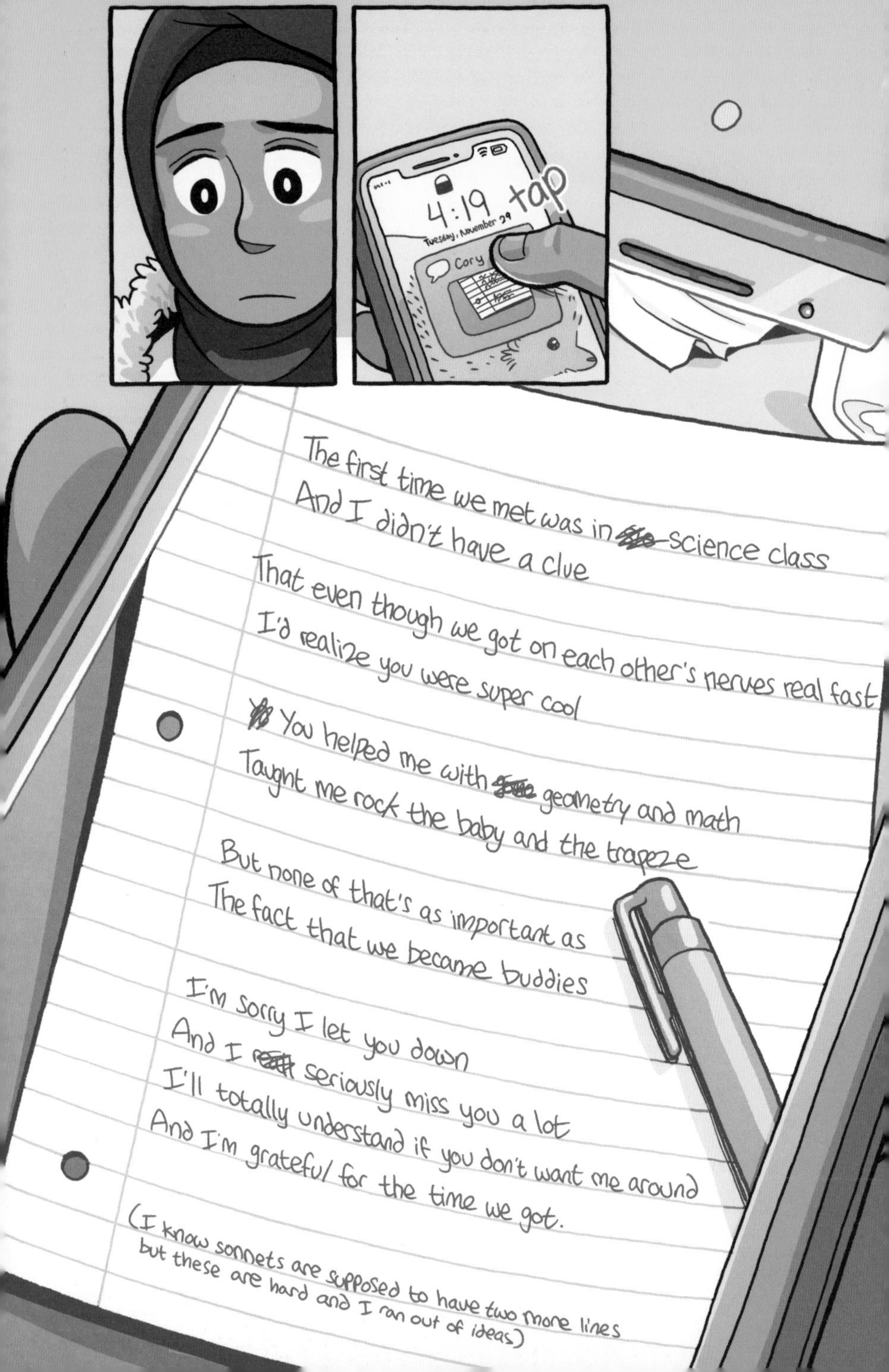

4:19
Tuesday, November 29
Cory
tap
The first time we met was in science class
And I didn't have a clue
That even though we got on each other's nerves real fast
I'd realize you were super cool
You helped me with geometry and math
Taught me rock the baby and the trapeze
But none of that's as important as
The fact that we became buddies
I'm sorry I let you down
And I seriously miss you a lot
I'll totally understand if you don't want me around
And I'm grateful for the time we got.
(I know sonnets are supposed to have two more lines
but these are hard and I ran out of ideas)

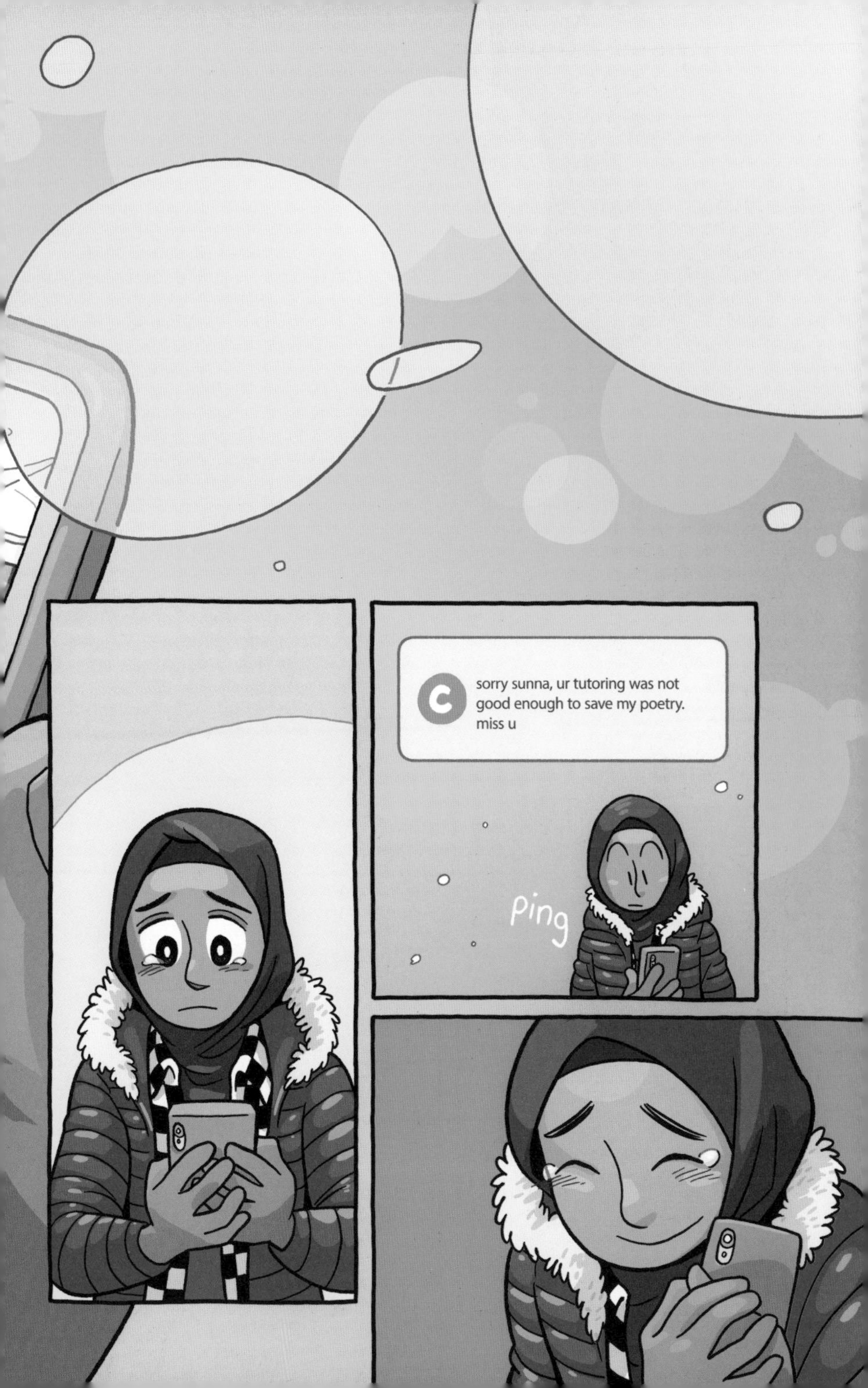
sorry sunna, ur tutoring was not good enough to save my poetry. miss u
ping

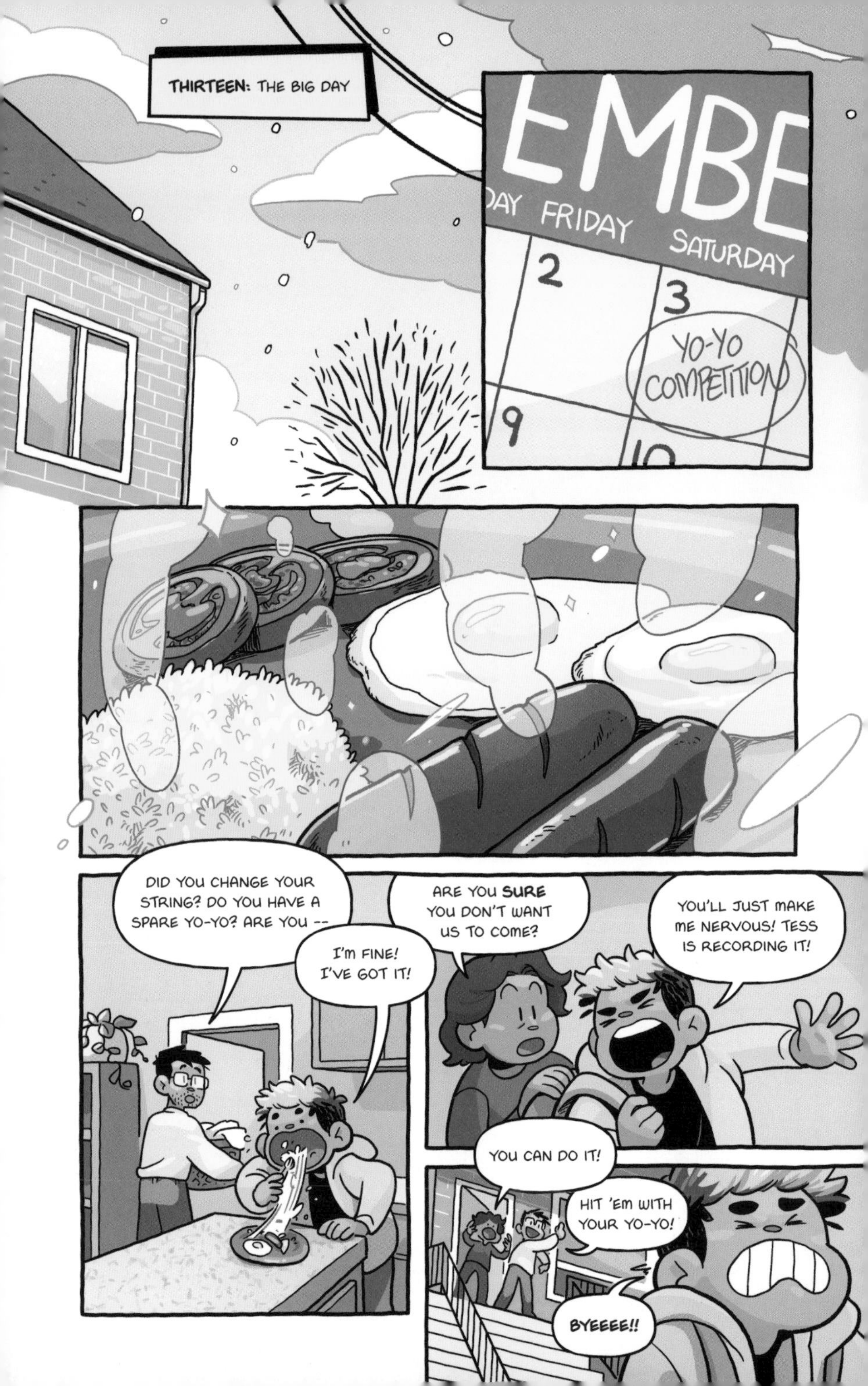
THIRTEEN: THE BIG DAY
EMBE
DAY FRIDAY SATURDAY
2
3
YO-YO COMPETITION
9
10
DID YOU CHANGE YOUR STRING? DO YOU HAVE A SPARE YO-YO? ARE YOU --
I'M FINE! I'VE GOT IT!
ARE YOU SURE YOU DON'T WANT US TO COME?
YOU'LL JUST MAKE ME NERVOUS! TESS IS RECORDING IT!
YOU CAN DO IT!
HIT 'EM WITH YOUR YO-YO!
BYEEEE!!

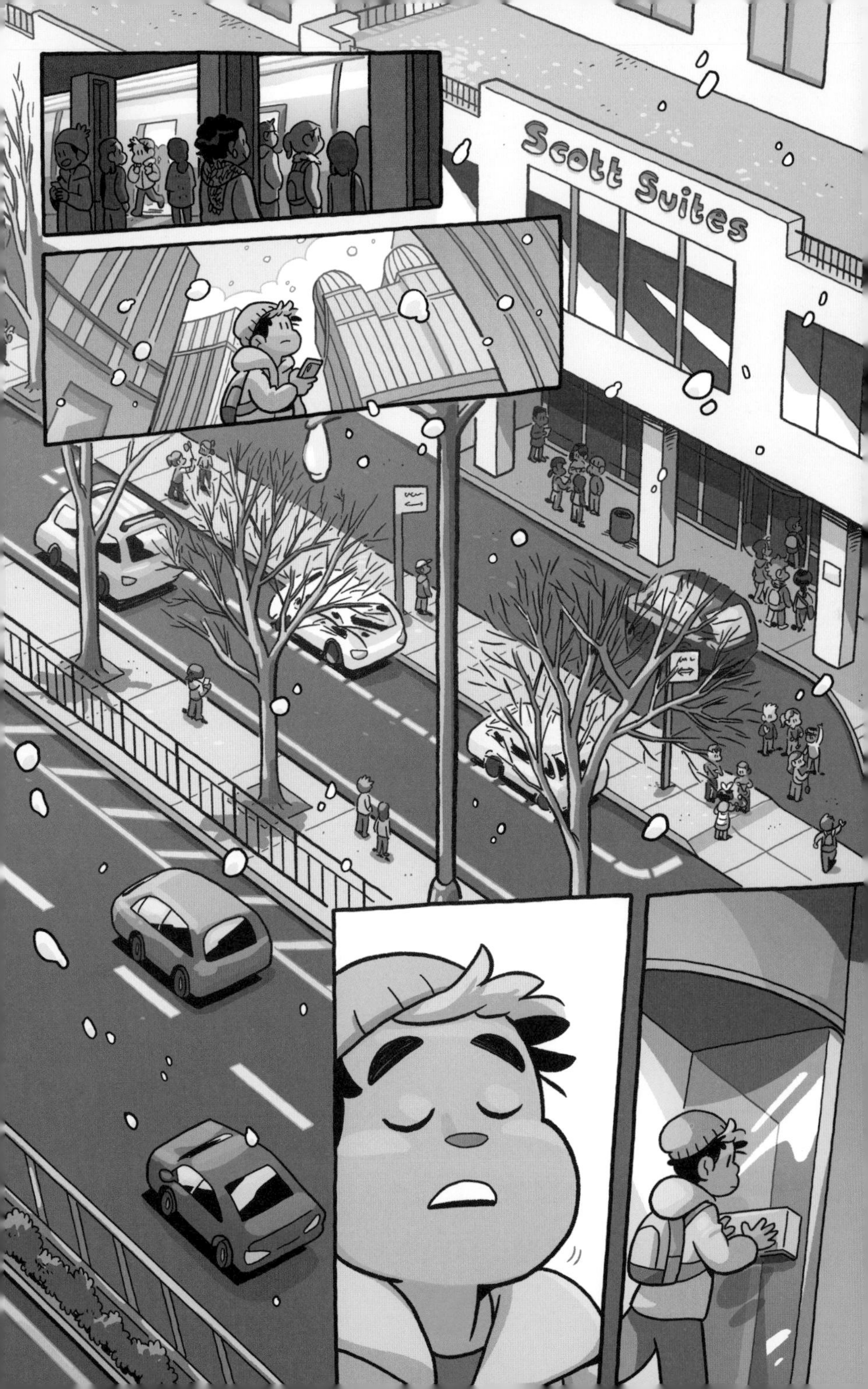
Scott Suites

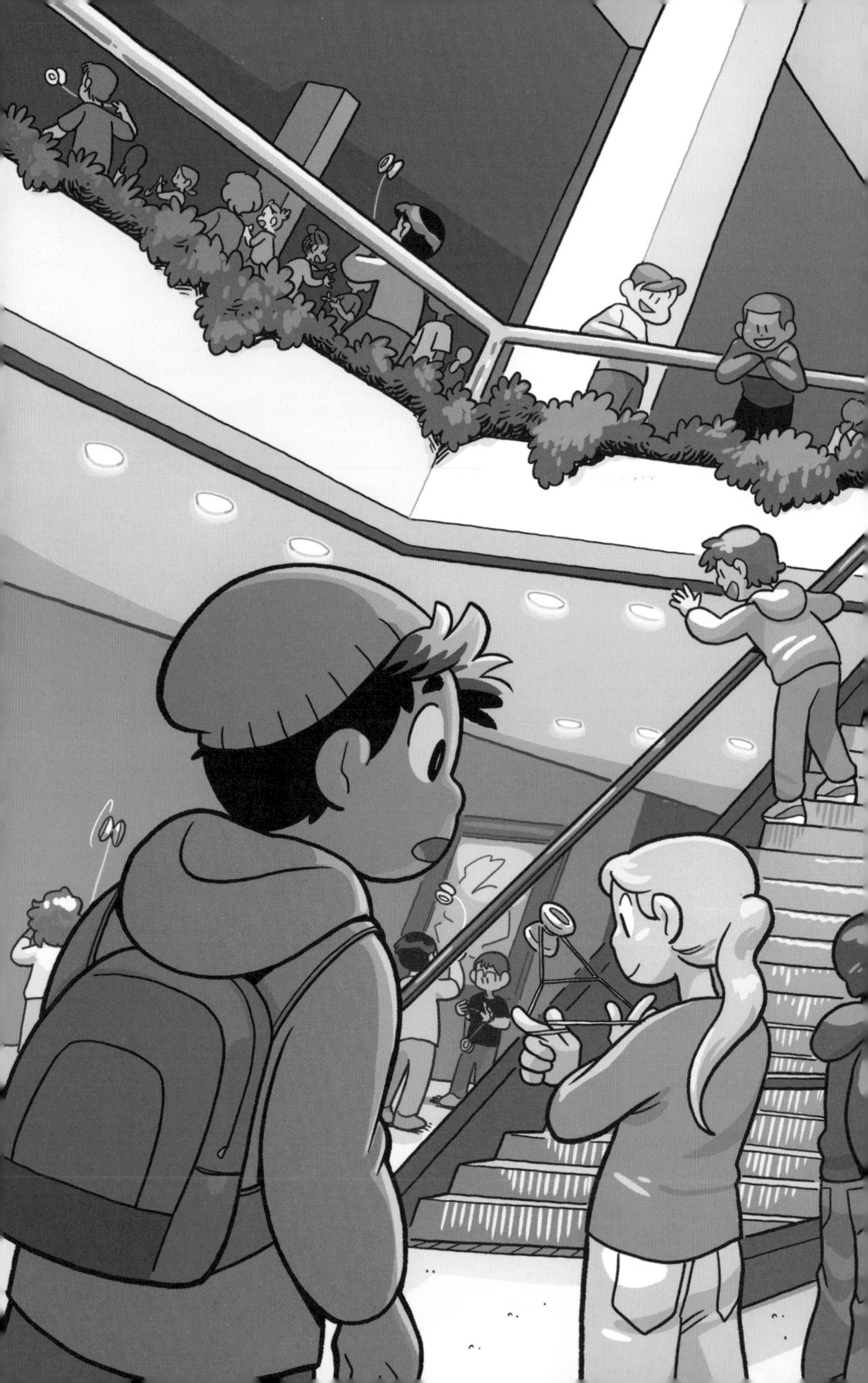

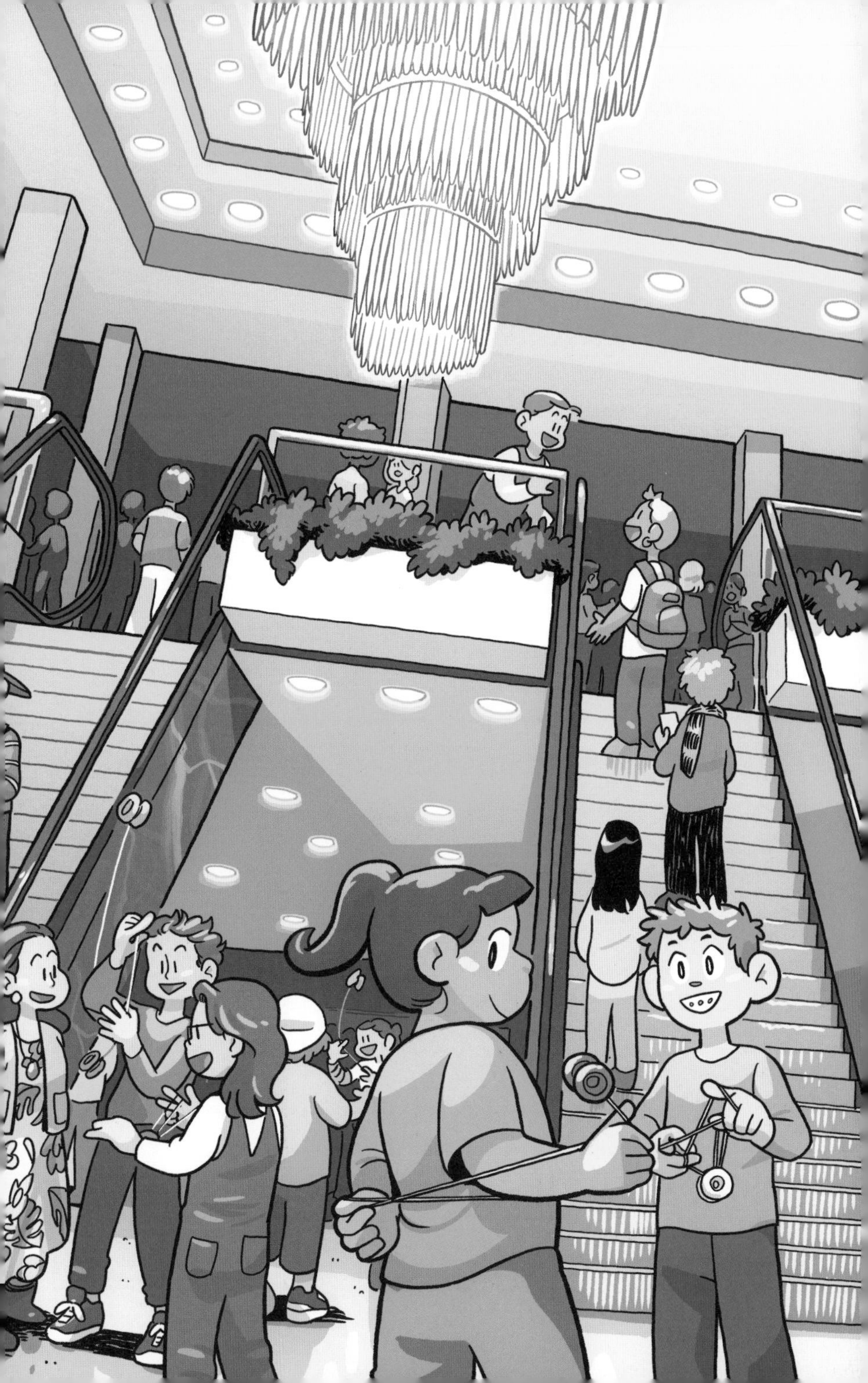

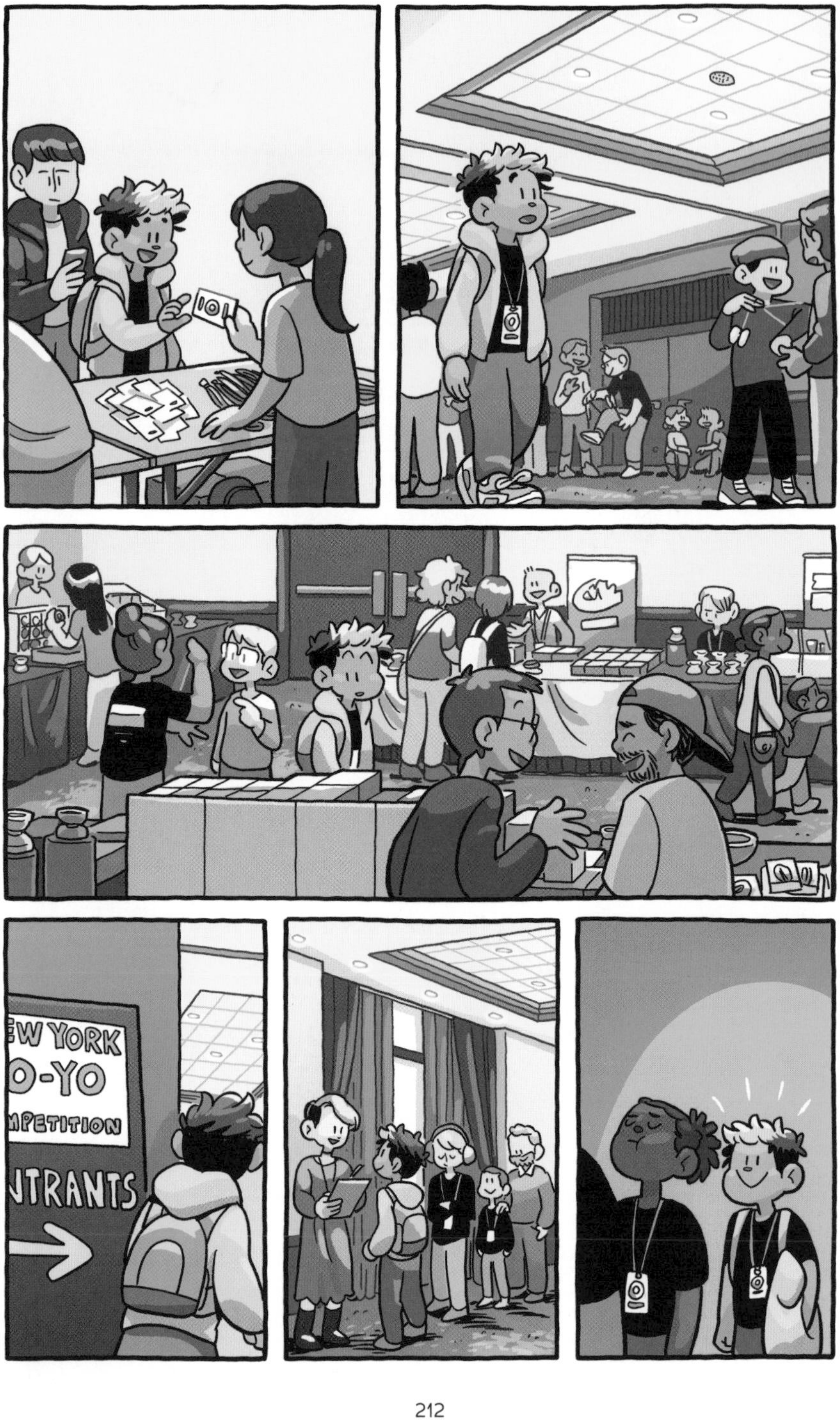
EW YORK
O-YO
MPETITION
NTRANTS

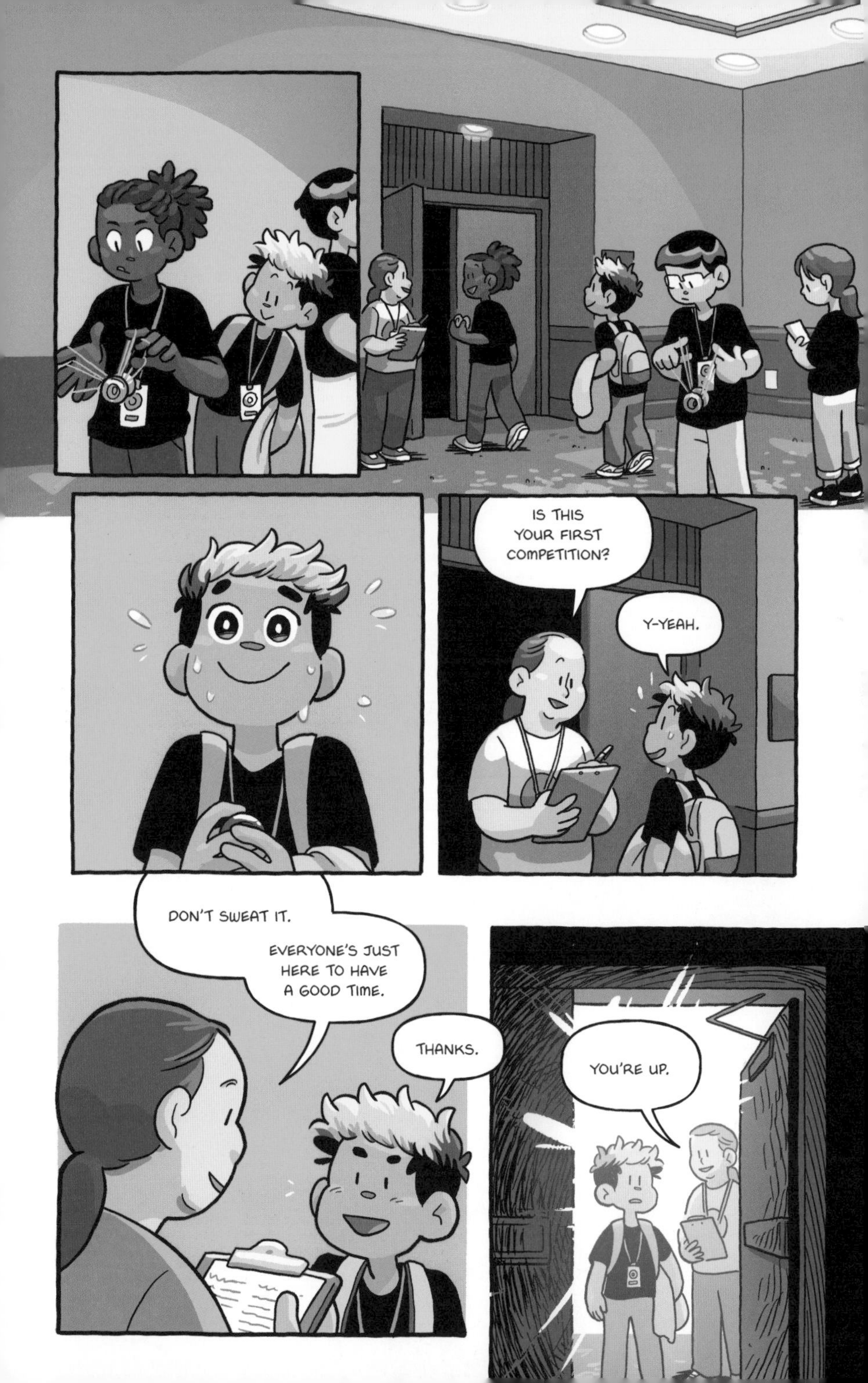
IS THIS YOUR FIRST COMPETITION?
Y-YEAH.
DON'T SWEAT IT.
EVERYONE'S JUST HERE TO HAVE A GOOD TIME.
THANKS.
YOU'RE UP.

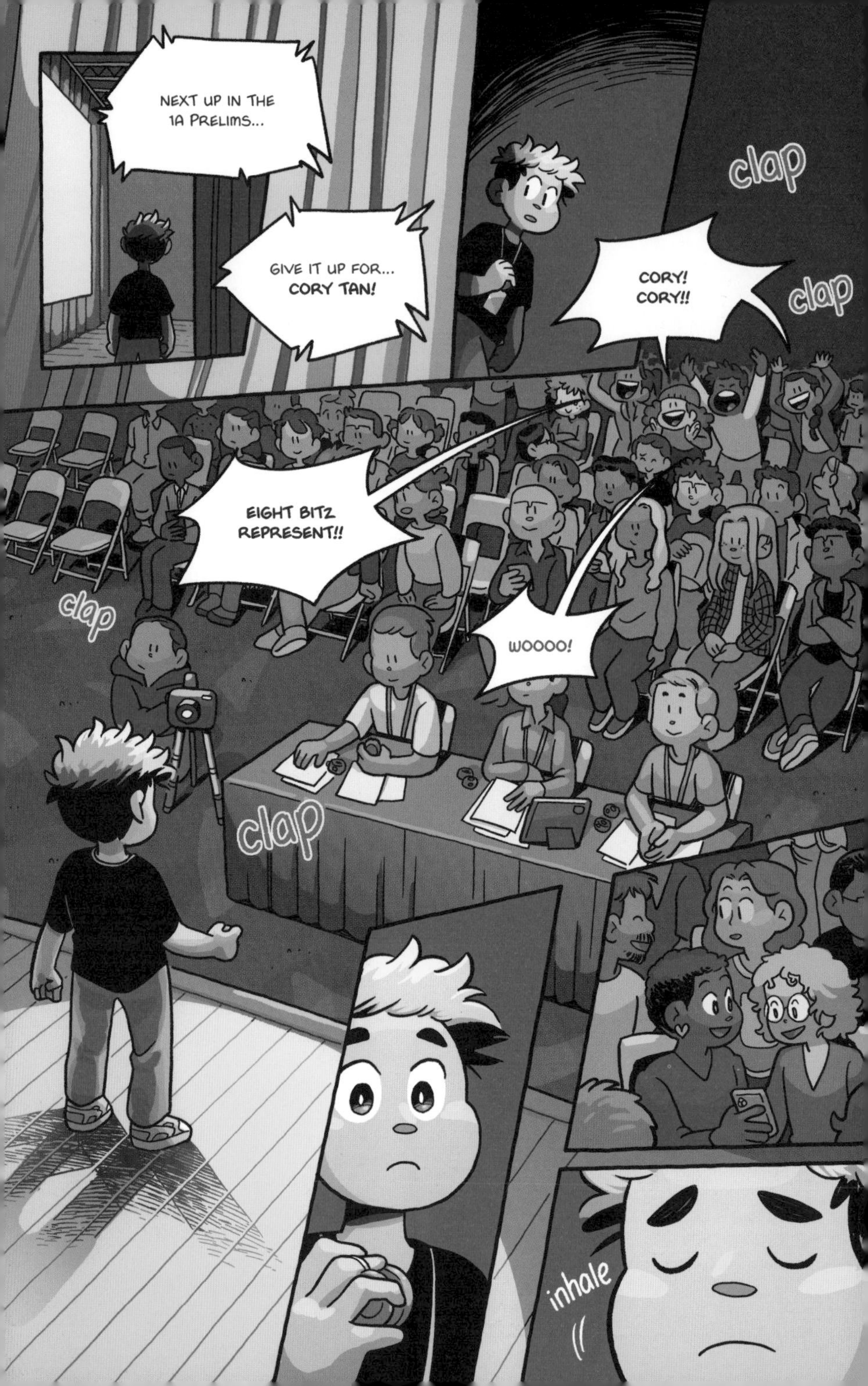
NEXT UP IN THE 1A PRELIMS...
GIVE IT UP FOR... CORY TAN!
clap
CORY! CORY!!
clap
EIGHT BITZ REPRESENT!!
clap
WOOOO!
clap
inhale

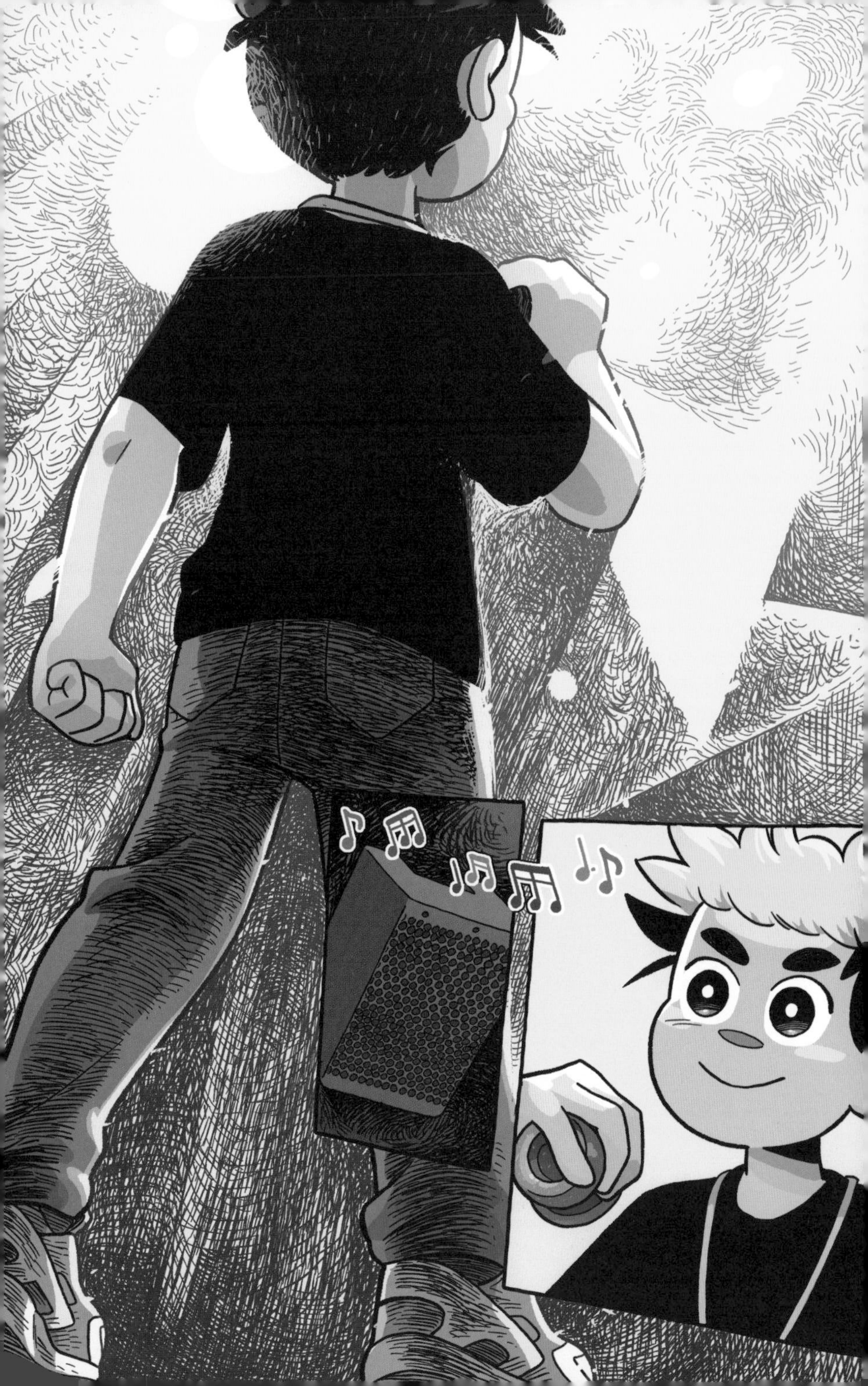

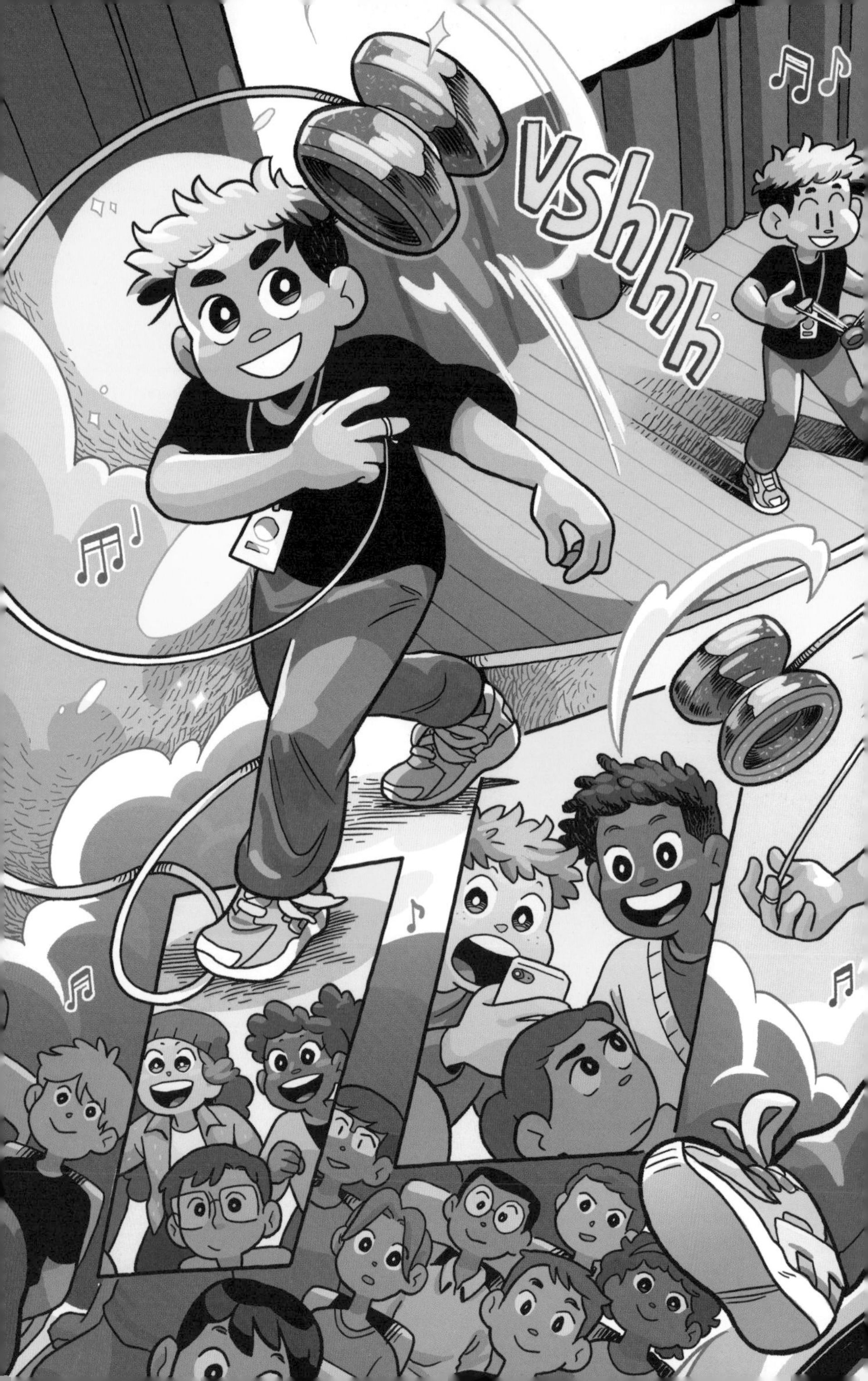
vshhh

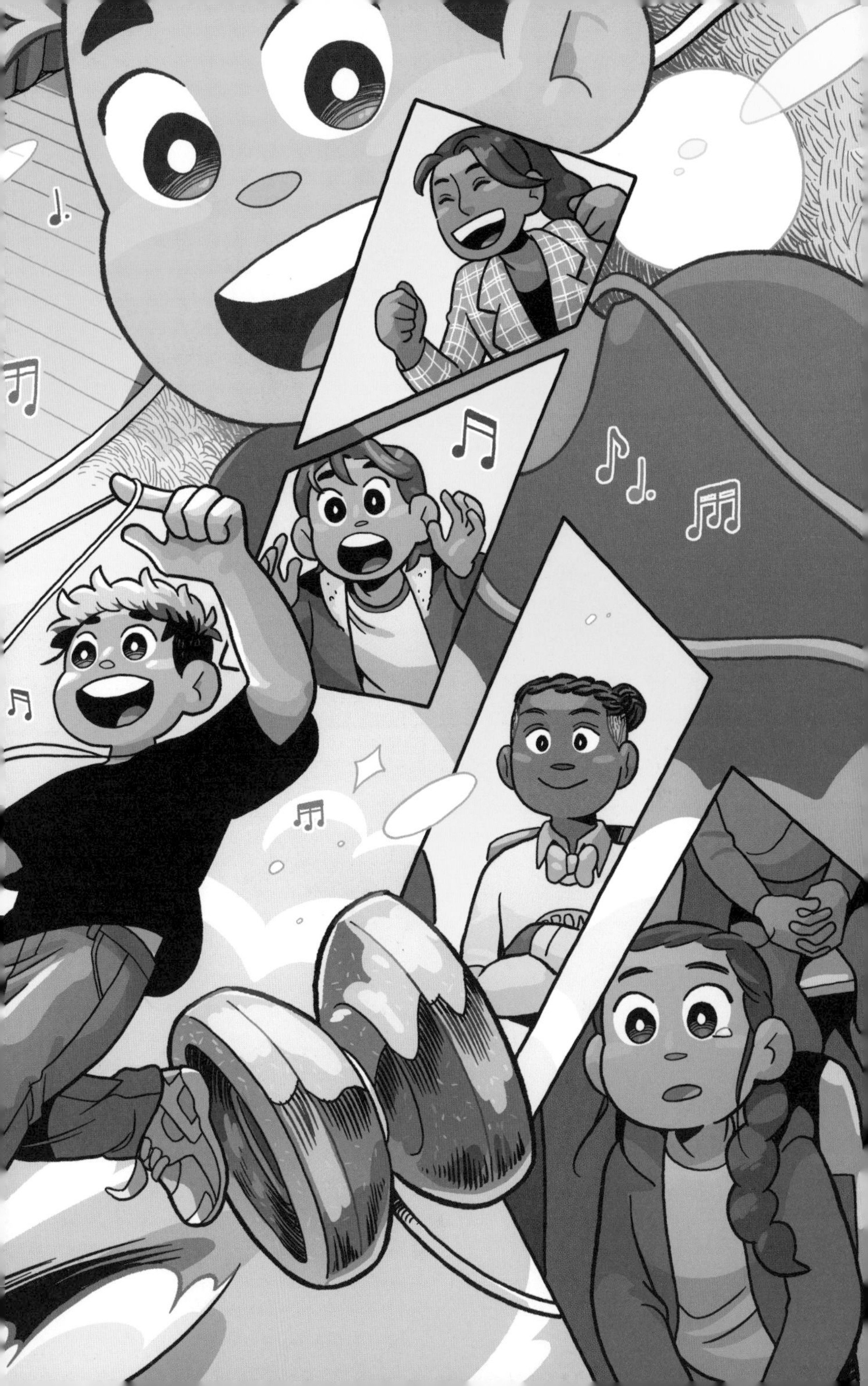

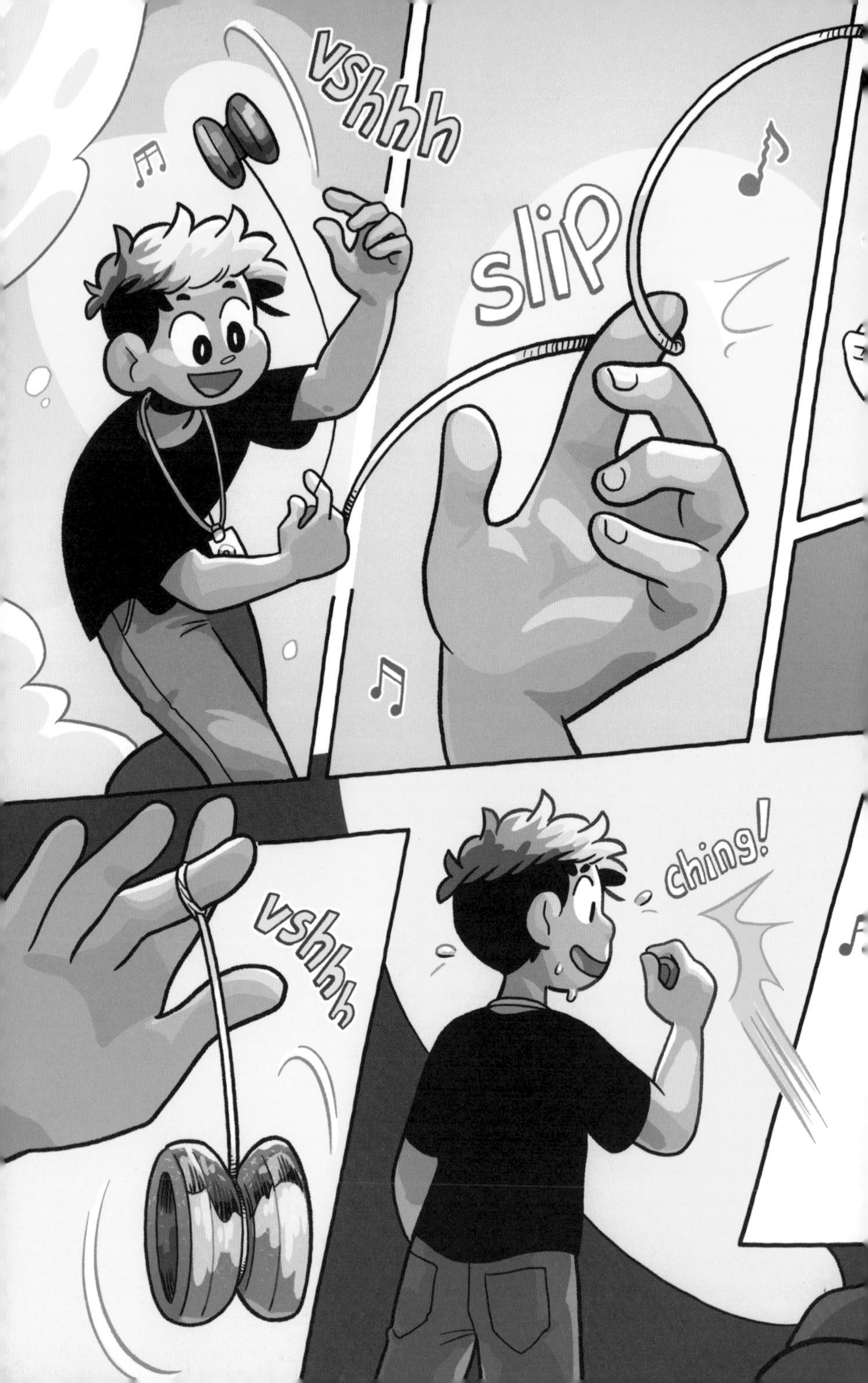
vshhh
slip
vshhh
ching!

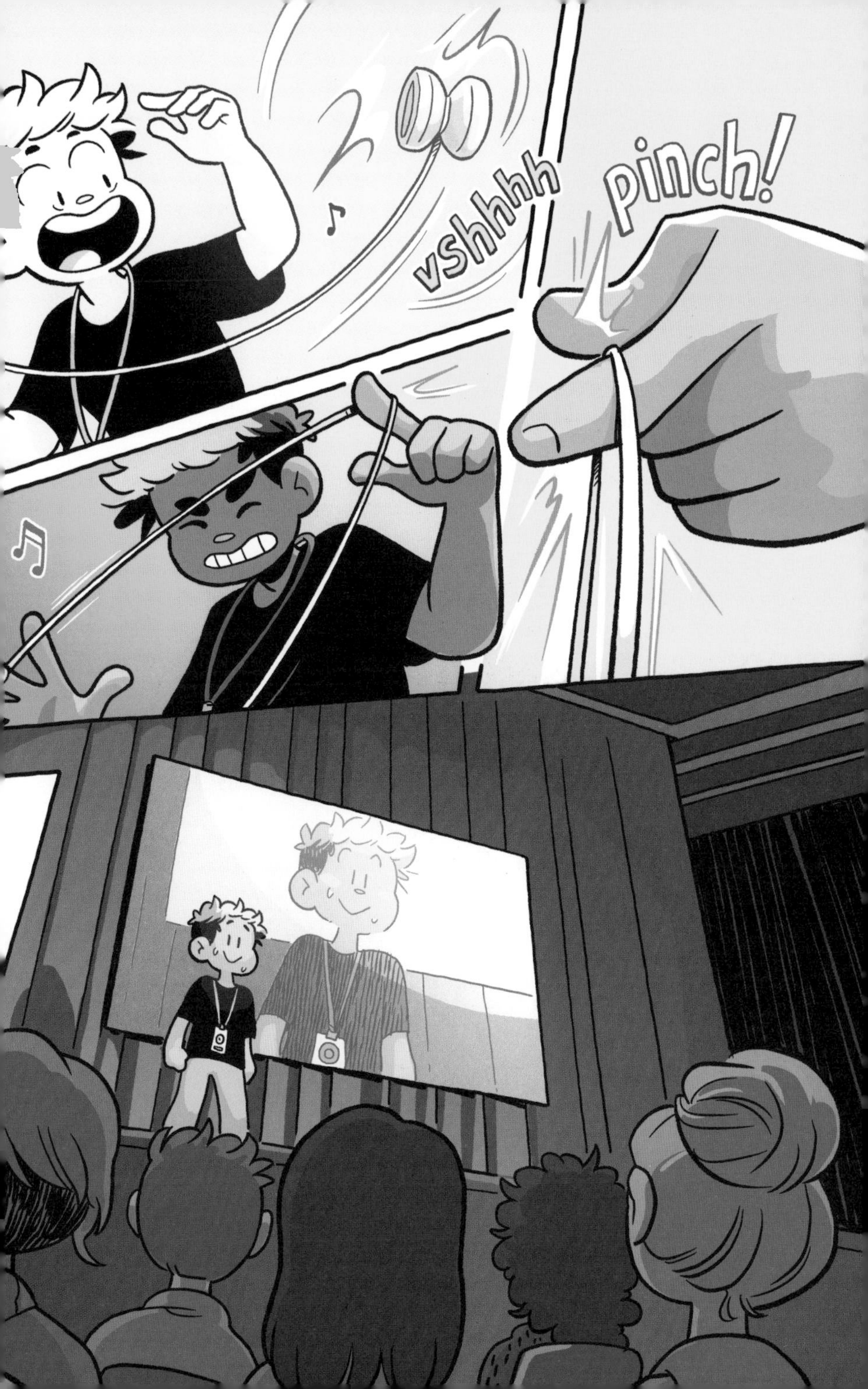
vshhhh
pinch!

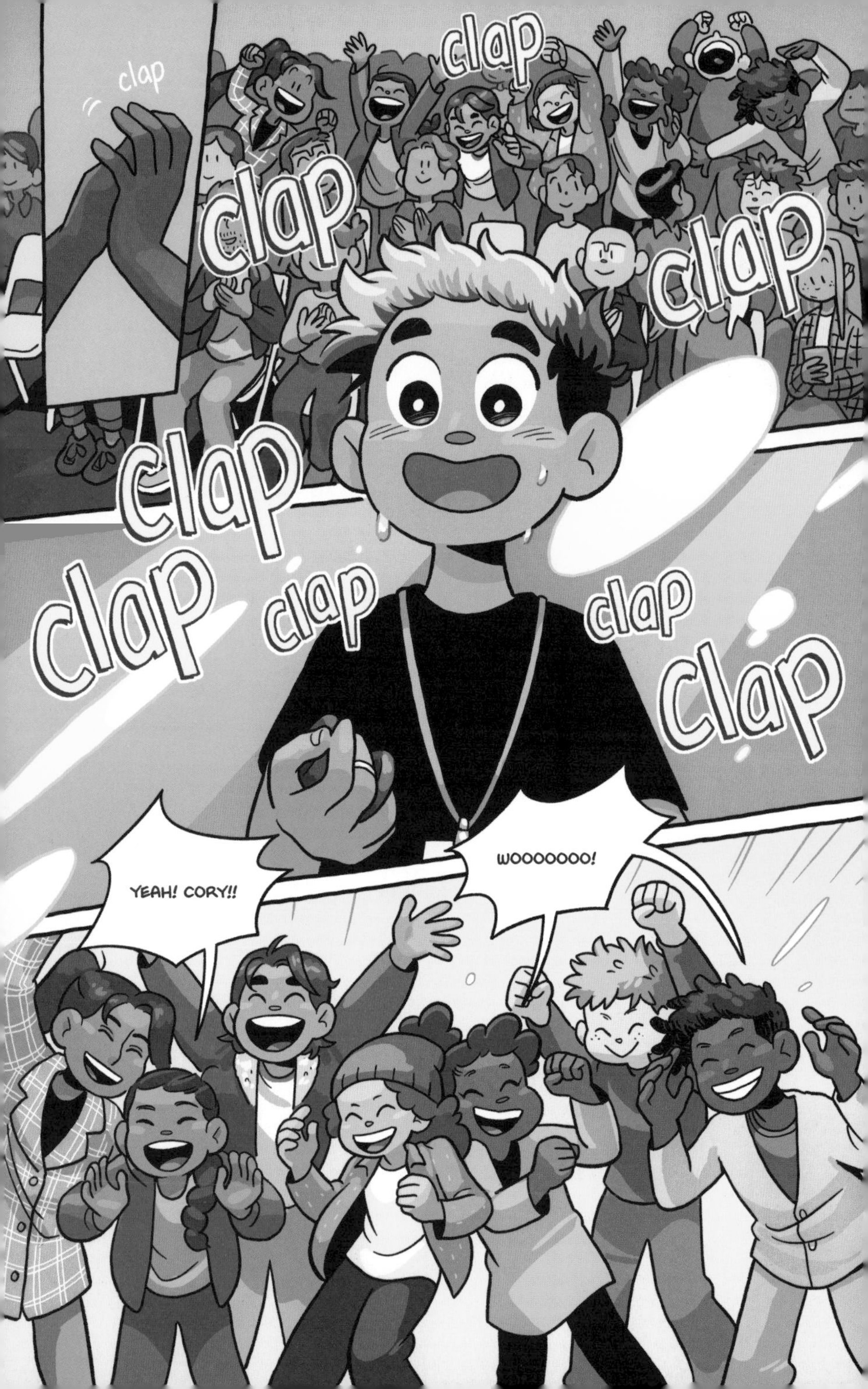
clap
clap
clap
clap
clap
clap
clap
clap
clap
YEAH! CORY!!
WOOOOOOO!

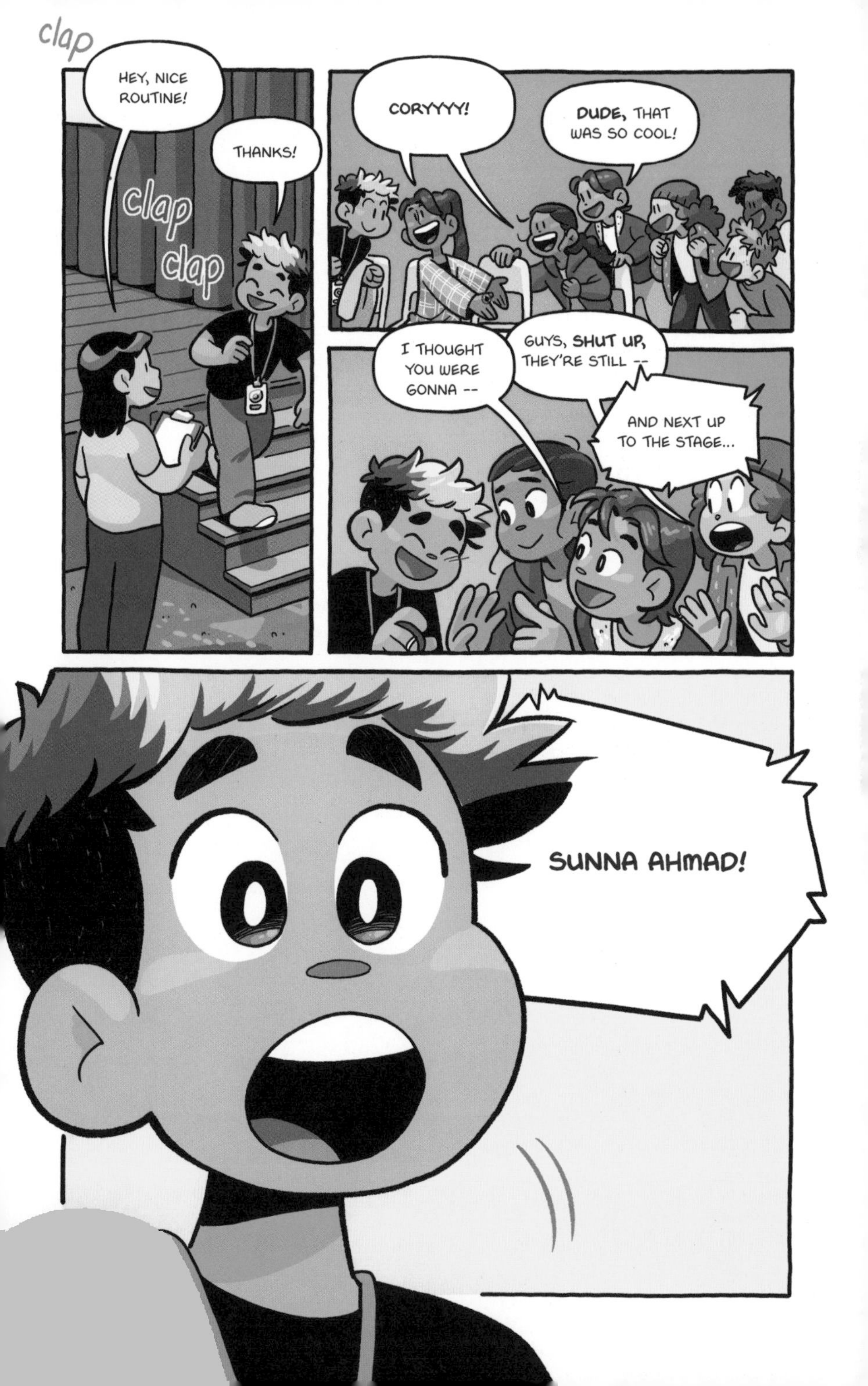
clap
HEY, NICE ROUTINE!
THANKS!
clap
clap
CORYYYY!
DUDE, THAT WAS SO COOL!
I THOUGHT YOU WERE GONNA --
GUYS, SHUT UP, THEY'RE STILL --
AND NEXT UP TO THE STAGE...
SUNNA AHMAD!

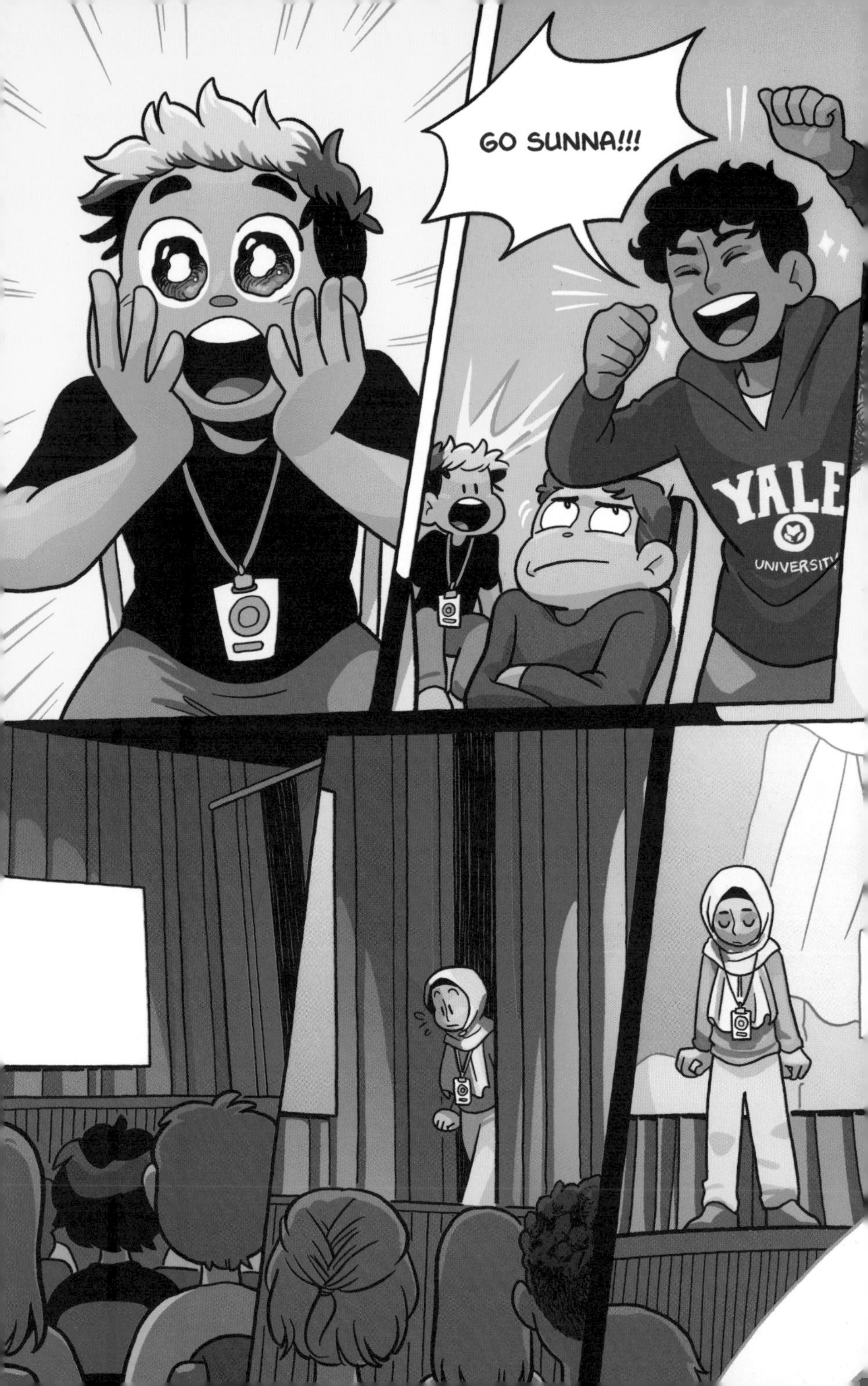
GO SUNNA!!!
YALE
UNIVERSITY

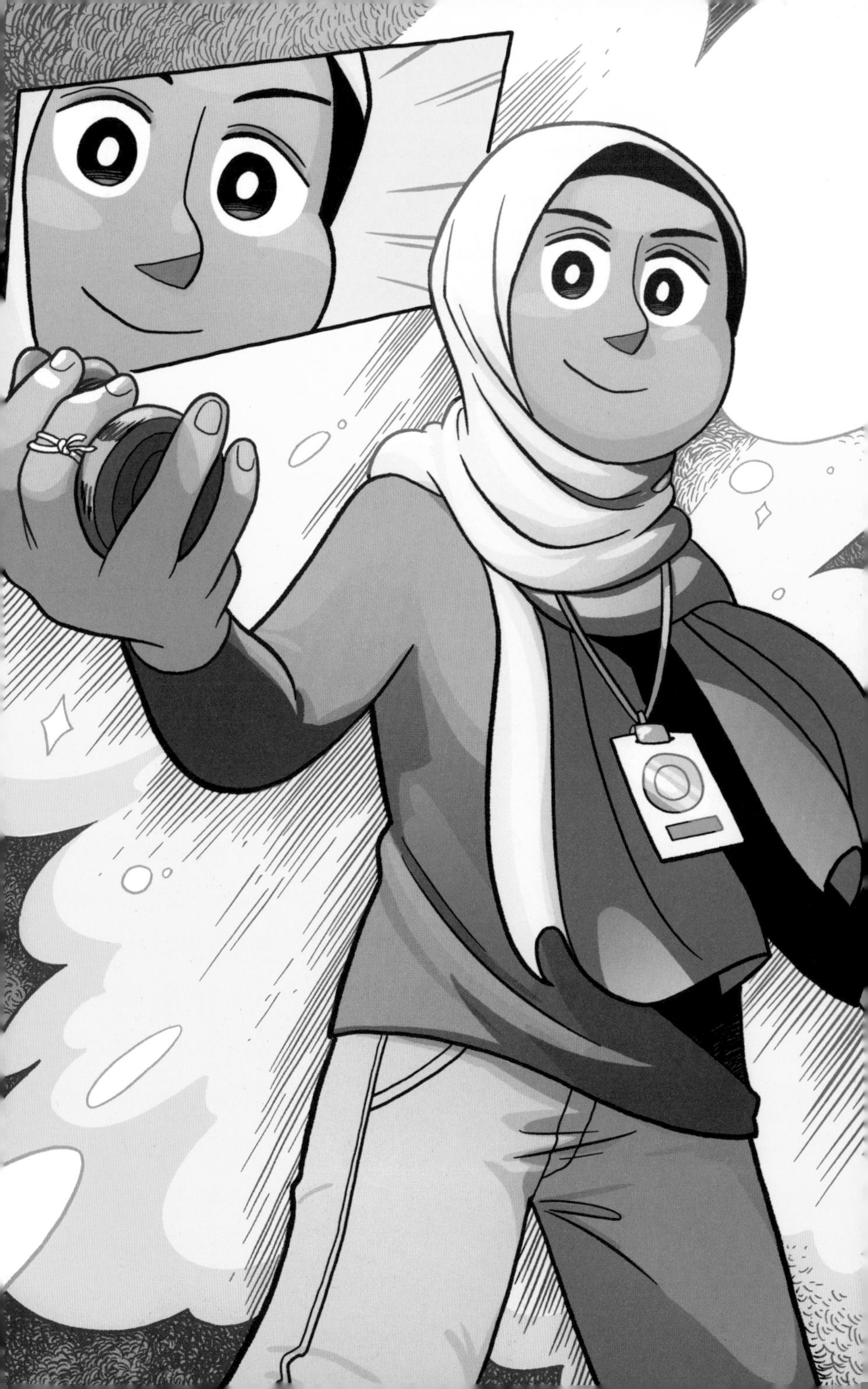

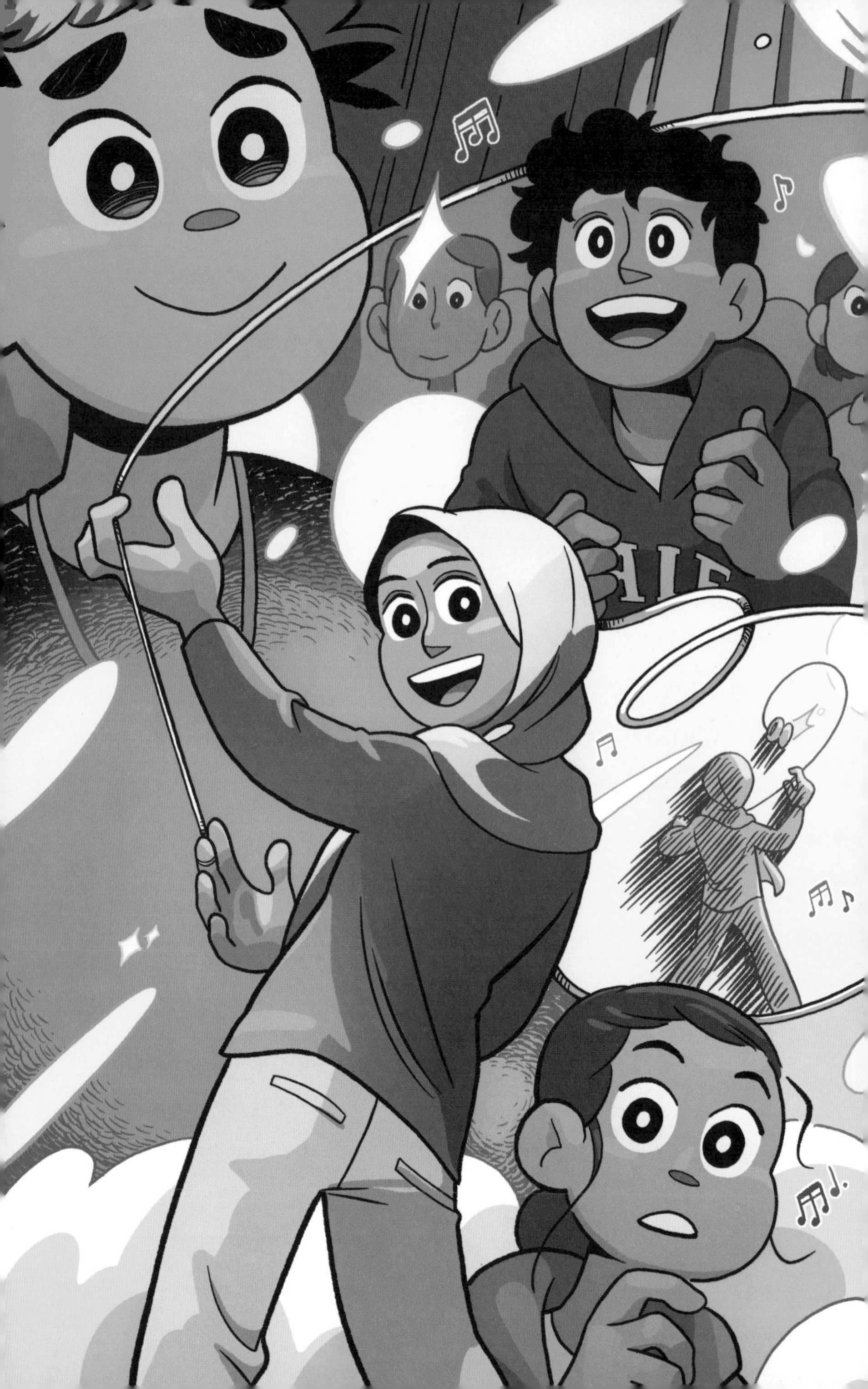

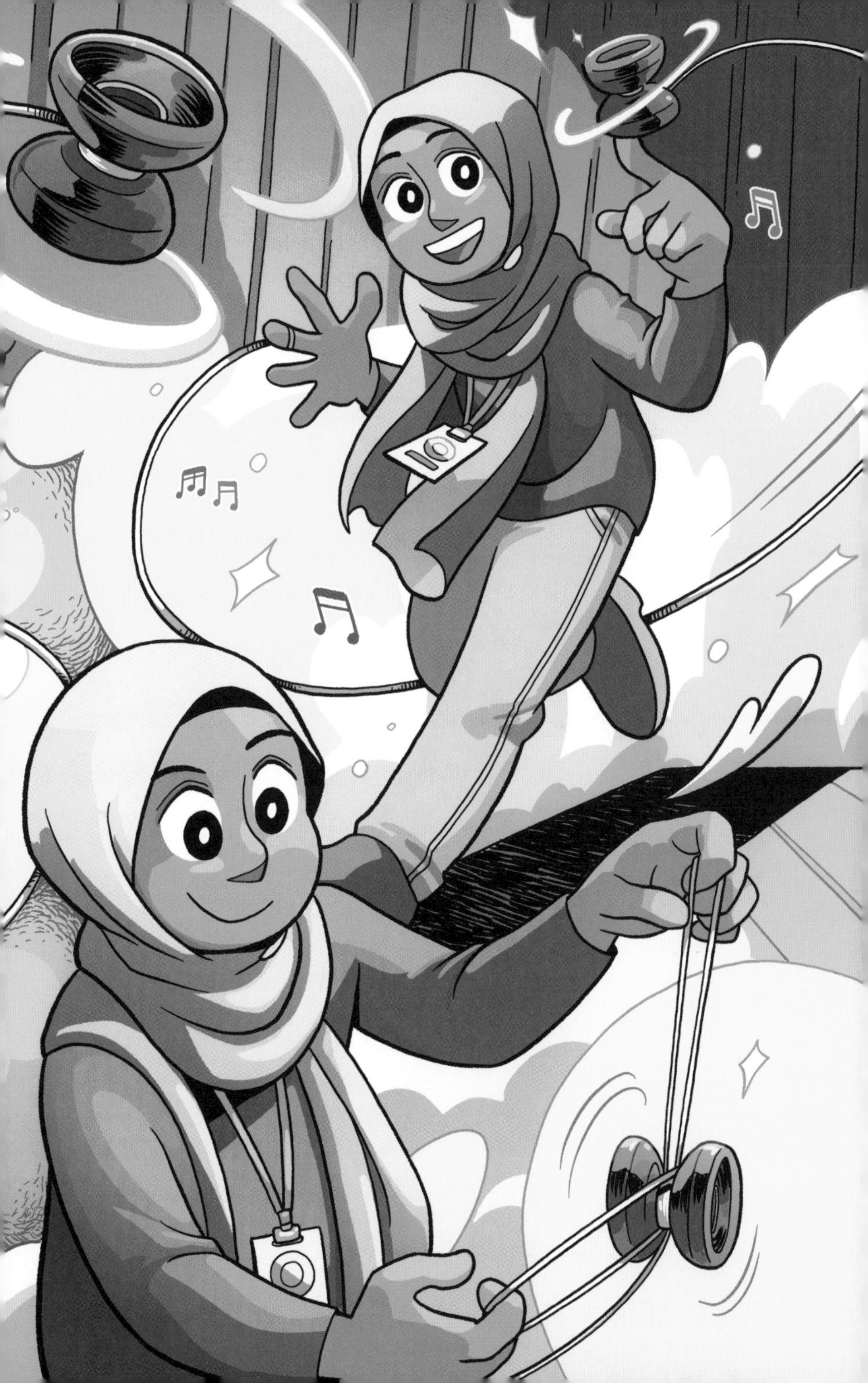

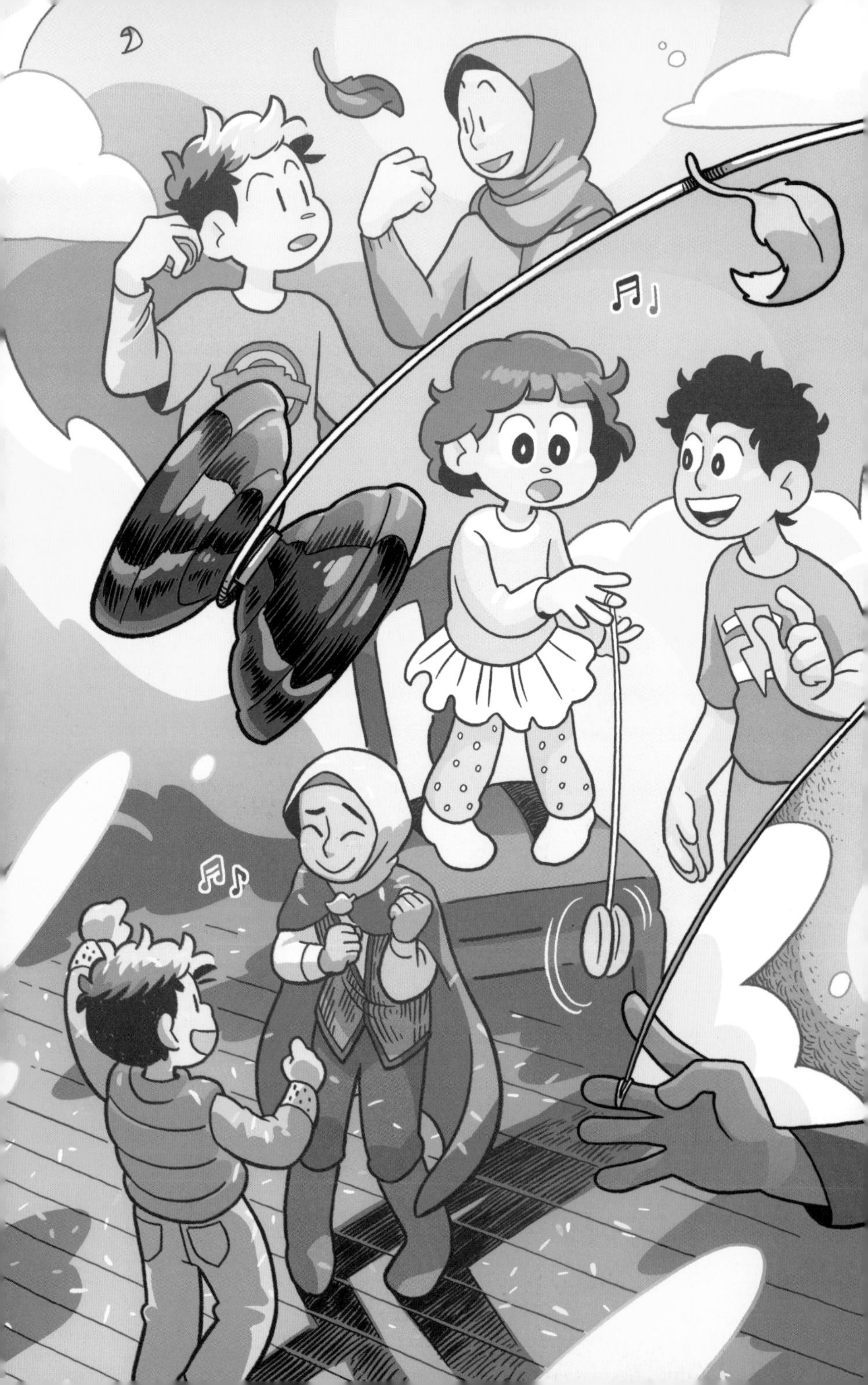

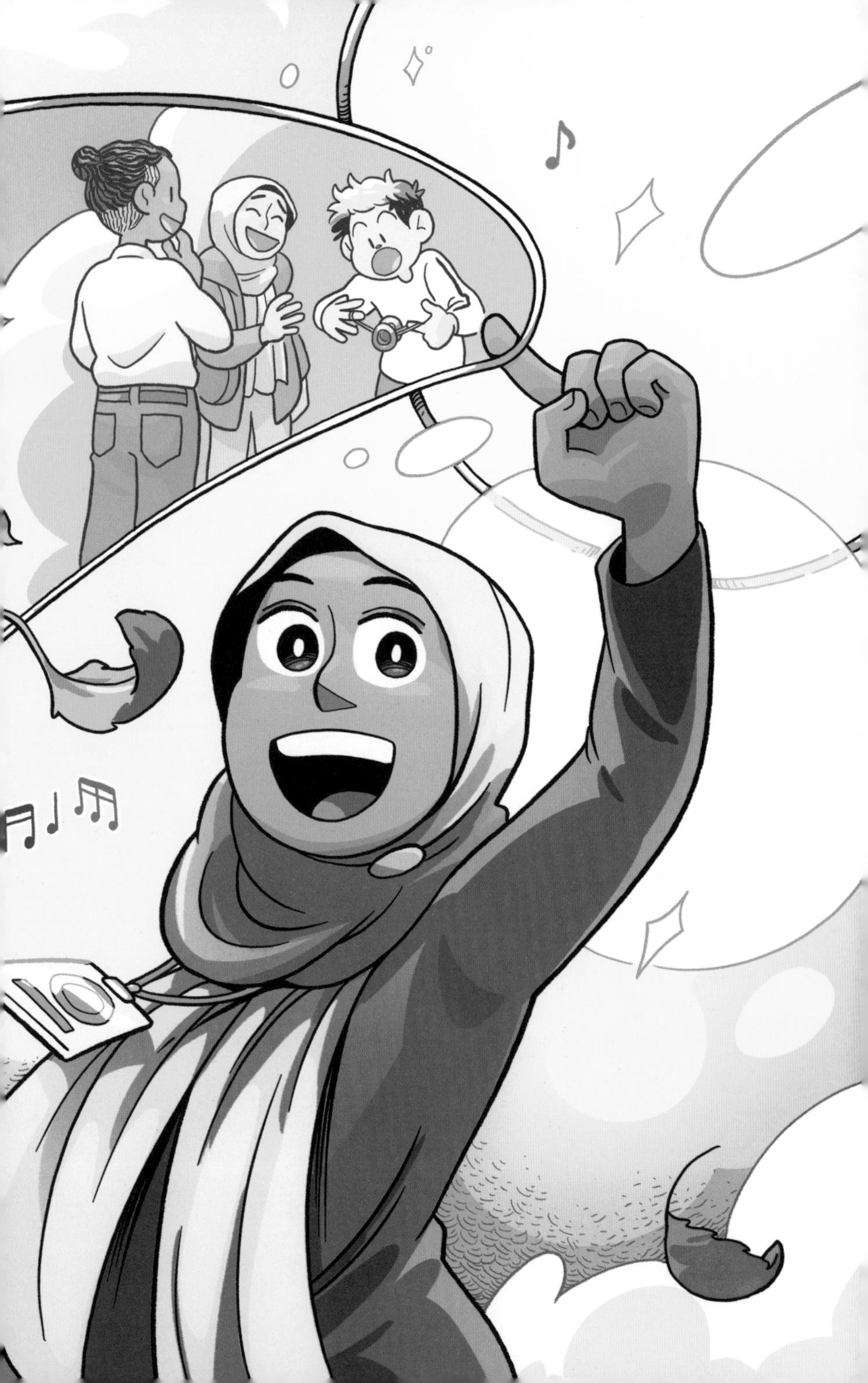

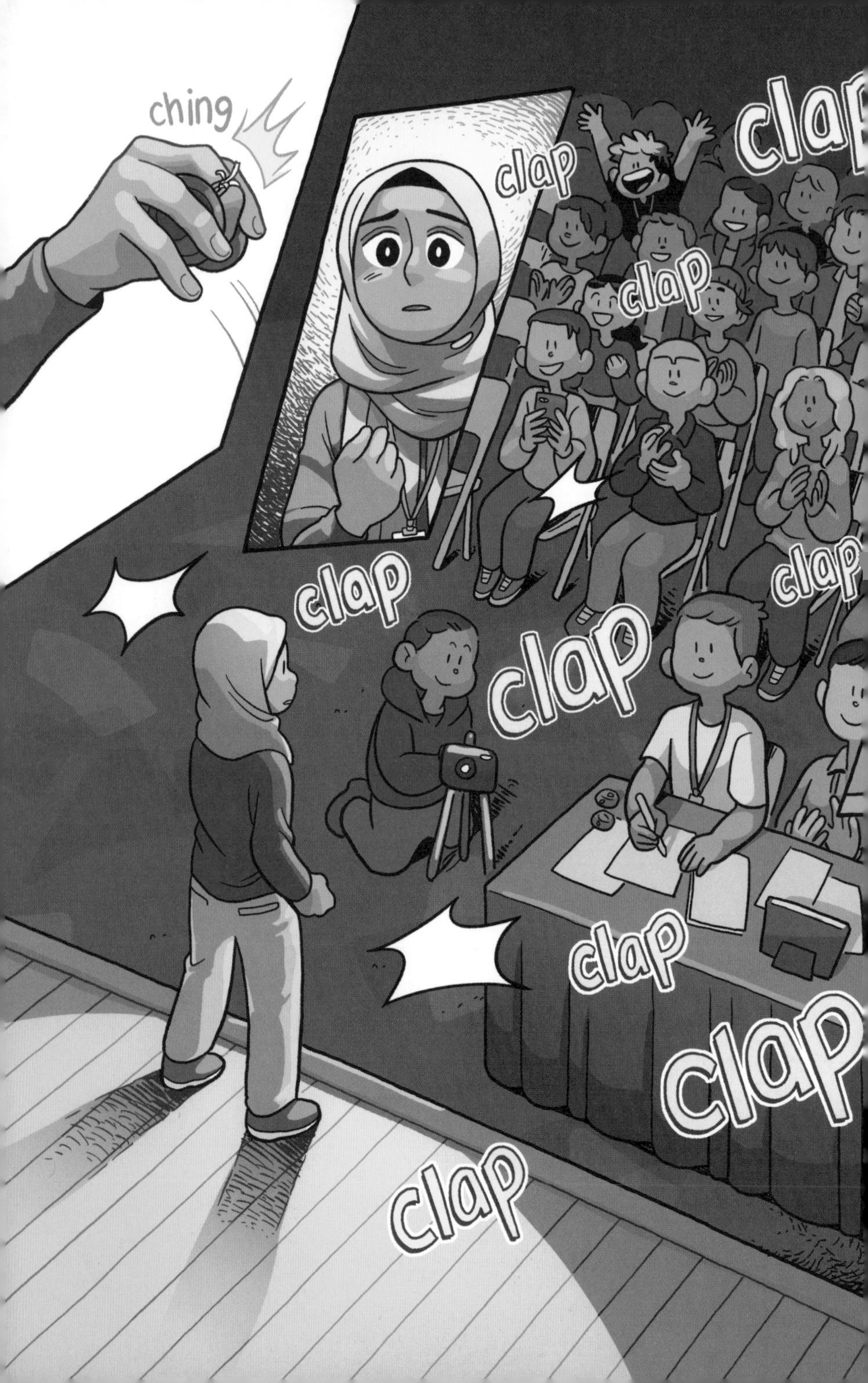
ching
clap
clap
clap
clap
clap
clap
clap
clap
clap

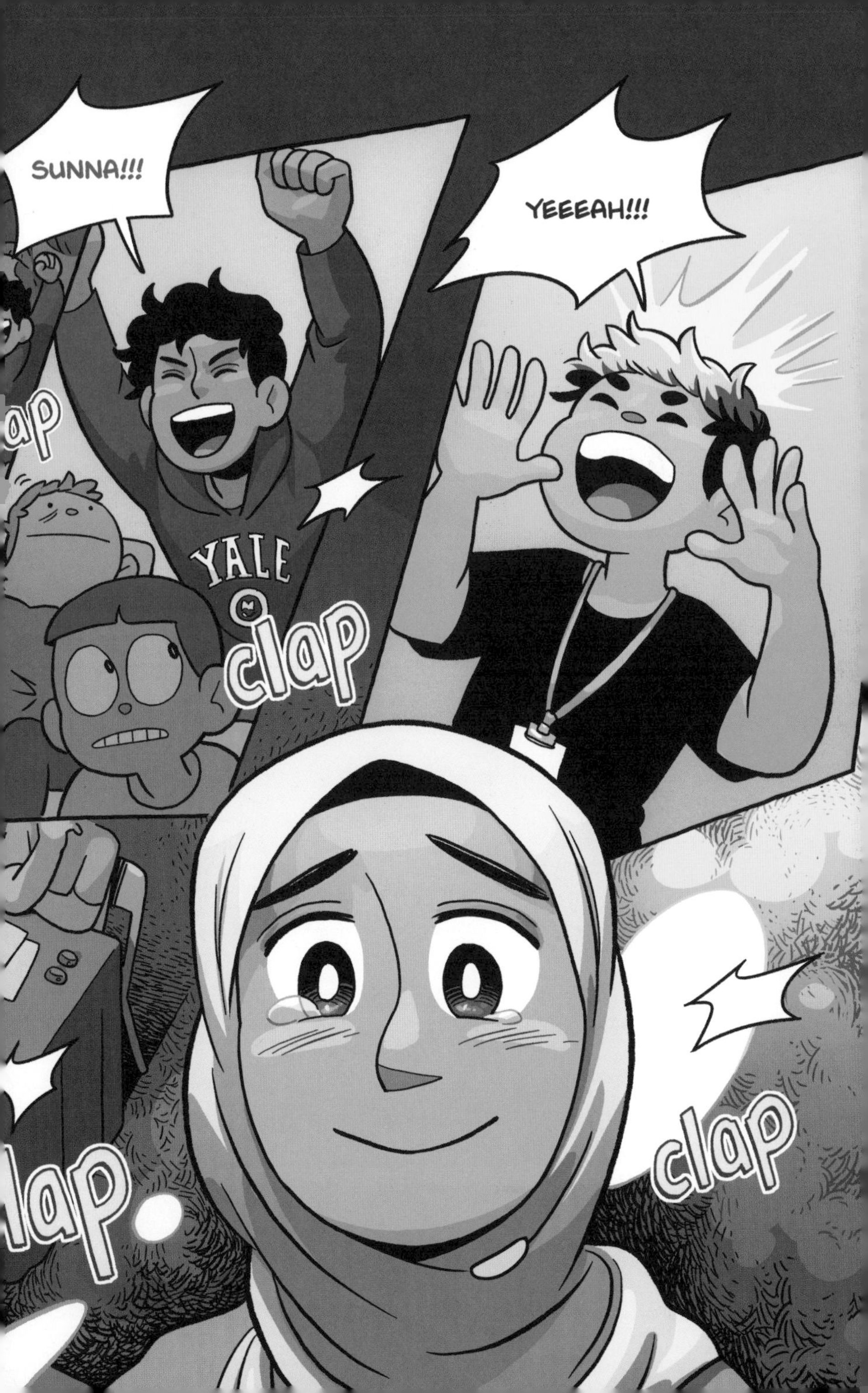
SUNNA!!!
YALE
clap
YEEEAH!!!
clap

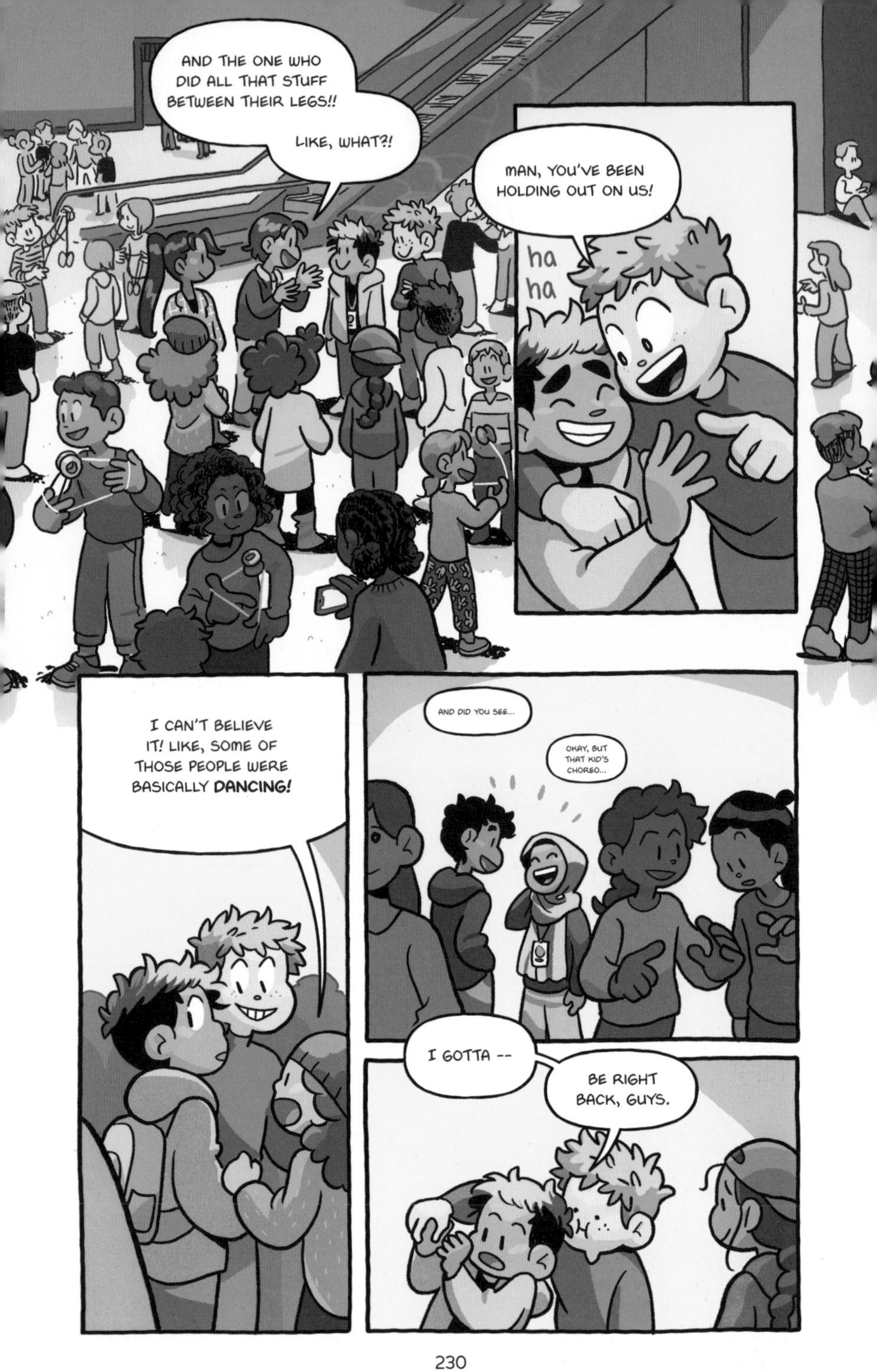

AND THE ONE WHO DID ALL THAT STUFF BETWEEN THEIR LEGS!!
LIKE, WHAT?!
MAN, YOU'VE BEEN HOLDING OUT ON US!
ha ha
I CAN'T BELIEVE IT! LIKE, SOME OF THOSE PEOPLE WERE BASICALLY **DANCING!**
AND DID YOU SEE...
OKAY, BUT THAT KID'S CHOREO...
I GOTTA --
BE RIGHT BACK, GUYS.

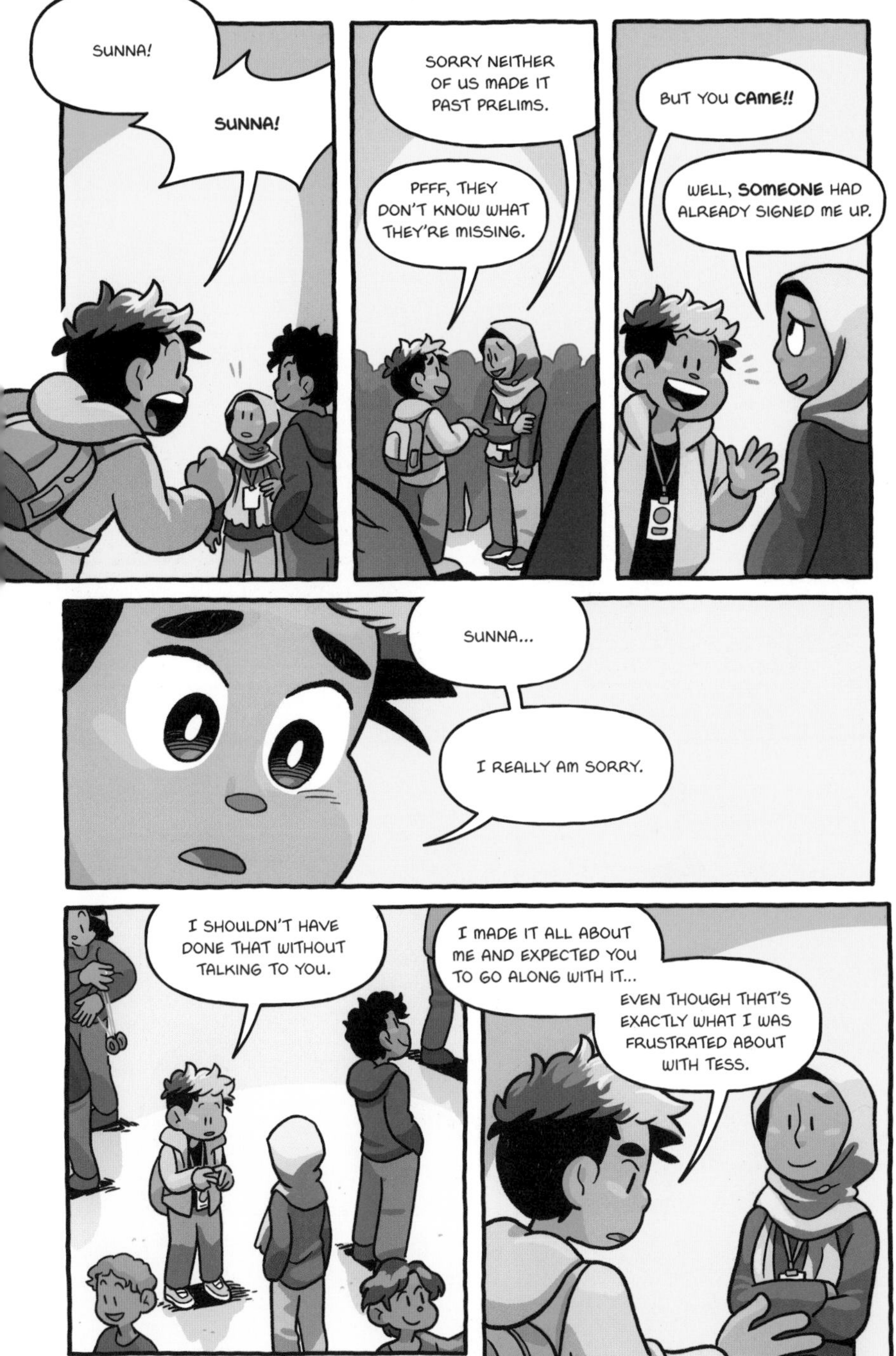
SUNNA!
SUNNA!
SORRY NEITHER OF US MADE IT PAST PRELIMS.
PFFF, THEY DON'T KNOW WHAT THEY'RE MISSING.
BUT YOU CAME!!
WELL, SOMEONE HAD ALREADY SIGNED ME UP.
SUNNA...
I REALLY AM SORRY.
I SHOULDN'T HAVE DONE THAT WITHOUT TALKING TO YOU.
I MADE IT ALL ABOUT ME AND EXPECTED YOU TO GO ALONG WITH IT...
EVEN THOUGH THAT'S EXACTLY WHAT I WAS FRUSTRATED ABOUT WITH TESS.

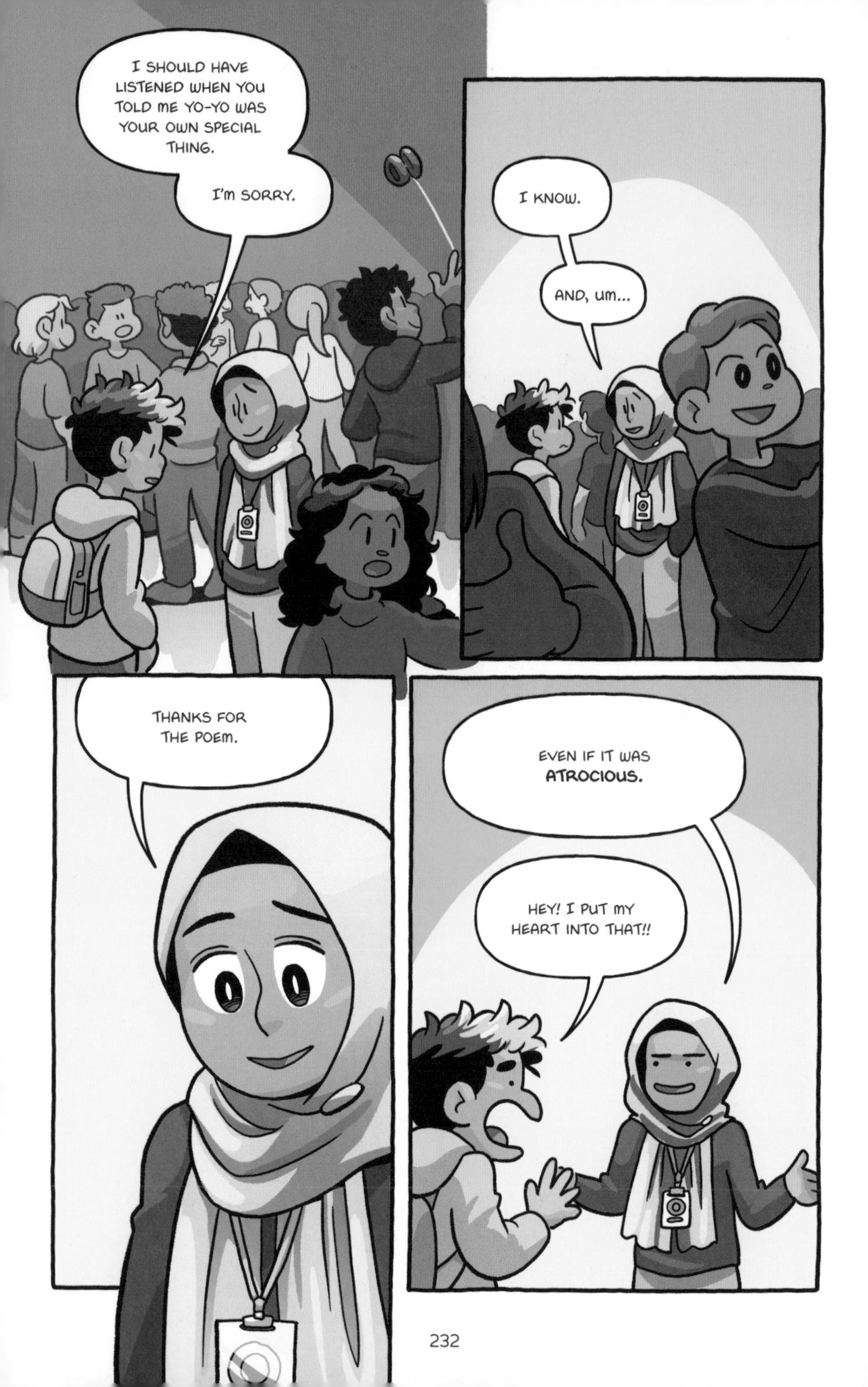
I SHOULD HAVE LISTENED WHEN YOU TOLD ME YO-YO WAS YOUR OWN SPECIAL THING.
I'M SORRY.
I KNOW.
AND, UM...
THANKS FOR THE POEM.
EVEN IF IT WAS **ATROCIOUS.**
HEY! I PUT MY HEART INTO THAT!!

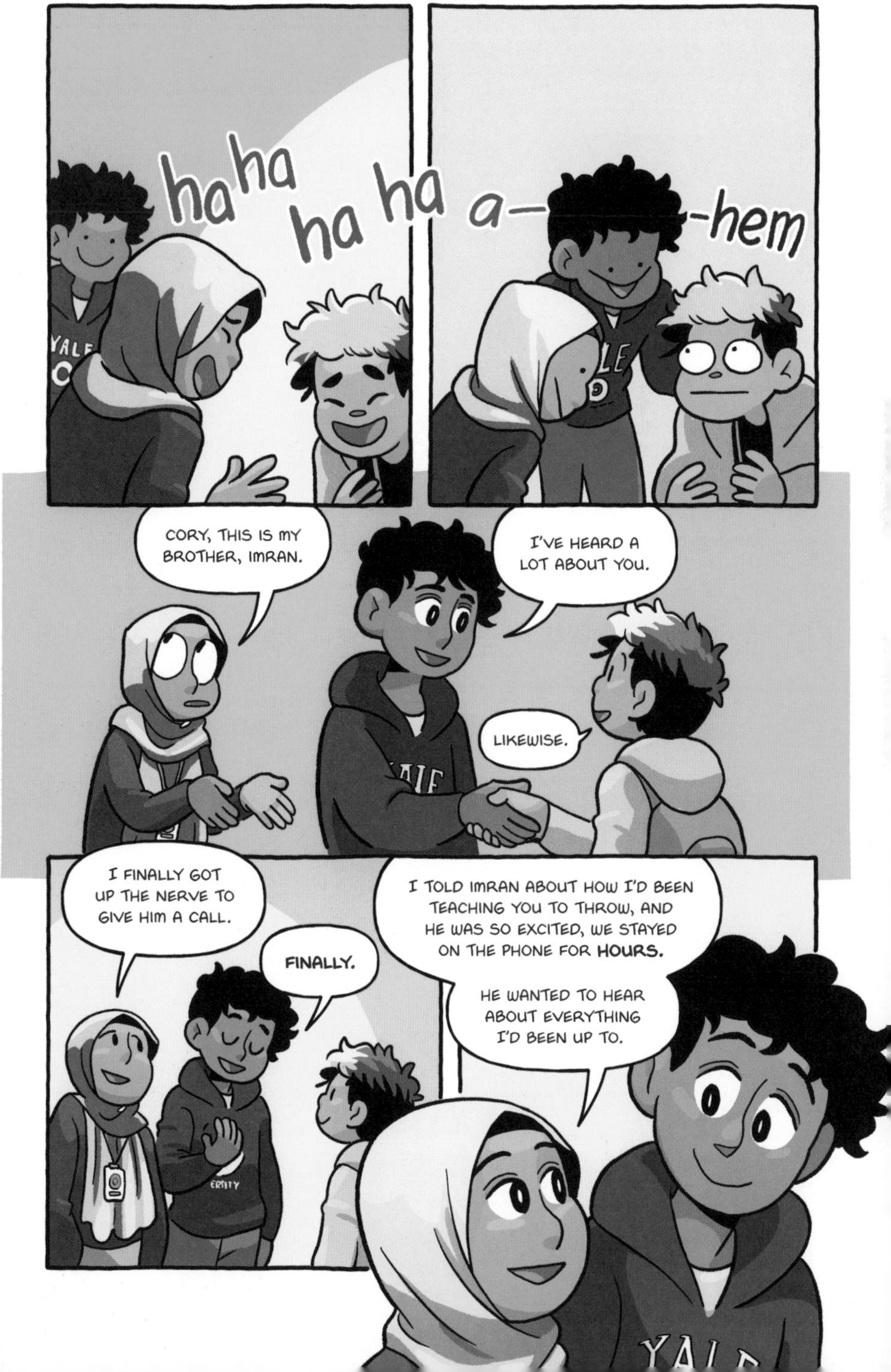

haha
ha ha
a—
-hem
CORY, THIS IS MY BROTHER, IMRAN.
I'VE HEARD A LOT ABOUT YOU.
LIKEWISE.
I FINALLY GOT UP THE NERVE TO GIVE HIM A CALL.
FINALLY.
I TOLD IMRAN ABOUT HOW I'D BEEN TEACHING YOU TO THROW, AND HE WAS SO EXCITED, WE STAYED ON THE PHONE FOR **HOURS.**
HE WANTED TO HEAR ABOUT EVERYTHING I'D BEEN UP TO.

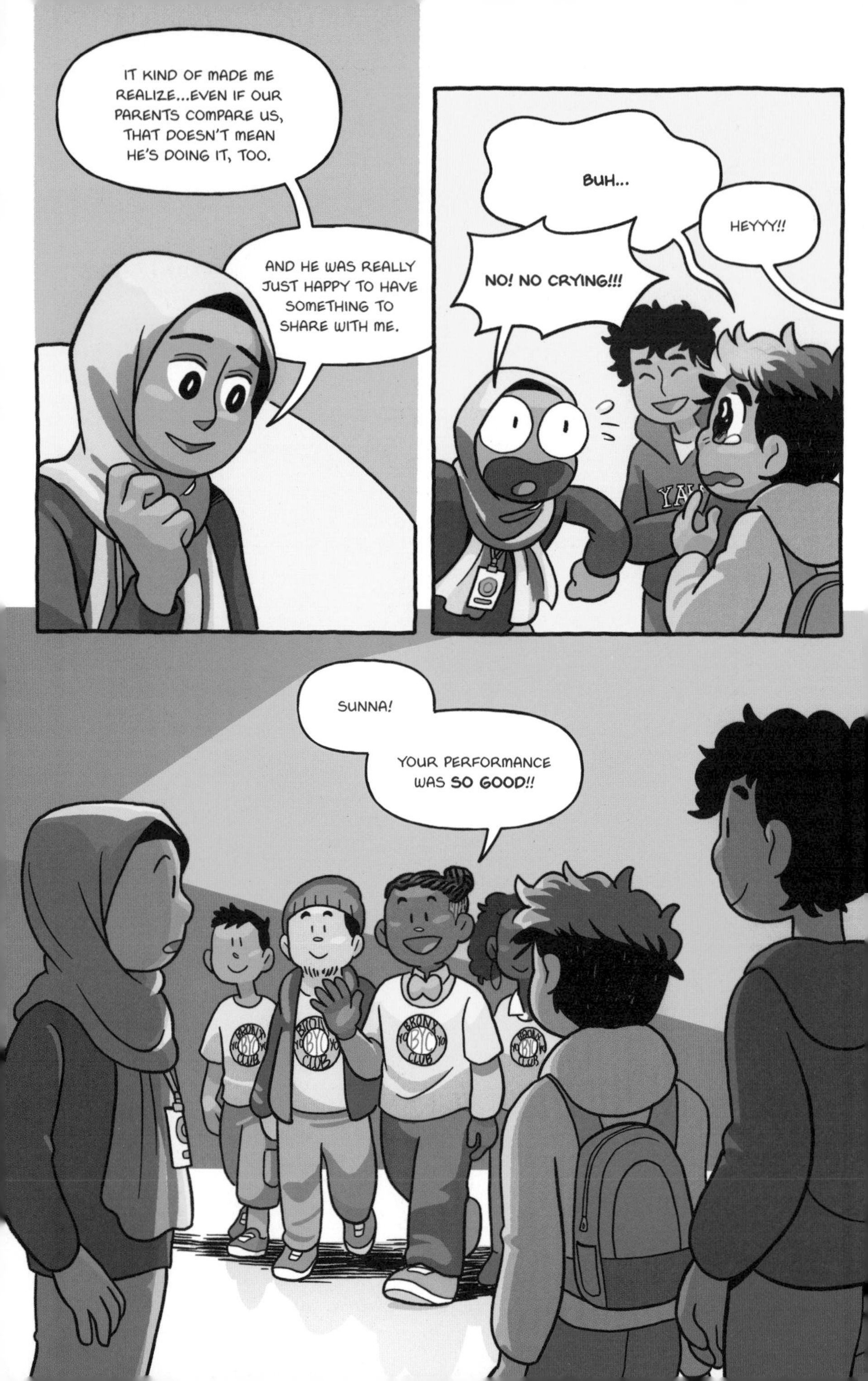
IT KIND OF MADE ME REALIZE...EVEN IF OUR PARENTS COMPARE US, THAT DOESN'T MEAN HE'S DOING IT, TOO.
AND HE WAS REALLY JUST HAPPY TO HAVE SOMETHING TO SHARE WITH ME.
BUH...
HEYYY!!
NO! NO CRYING!!!
SUNNA!
YOUR PERFORMANCE WAS SO GOOD!!

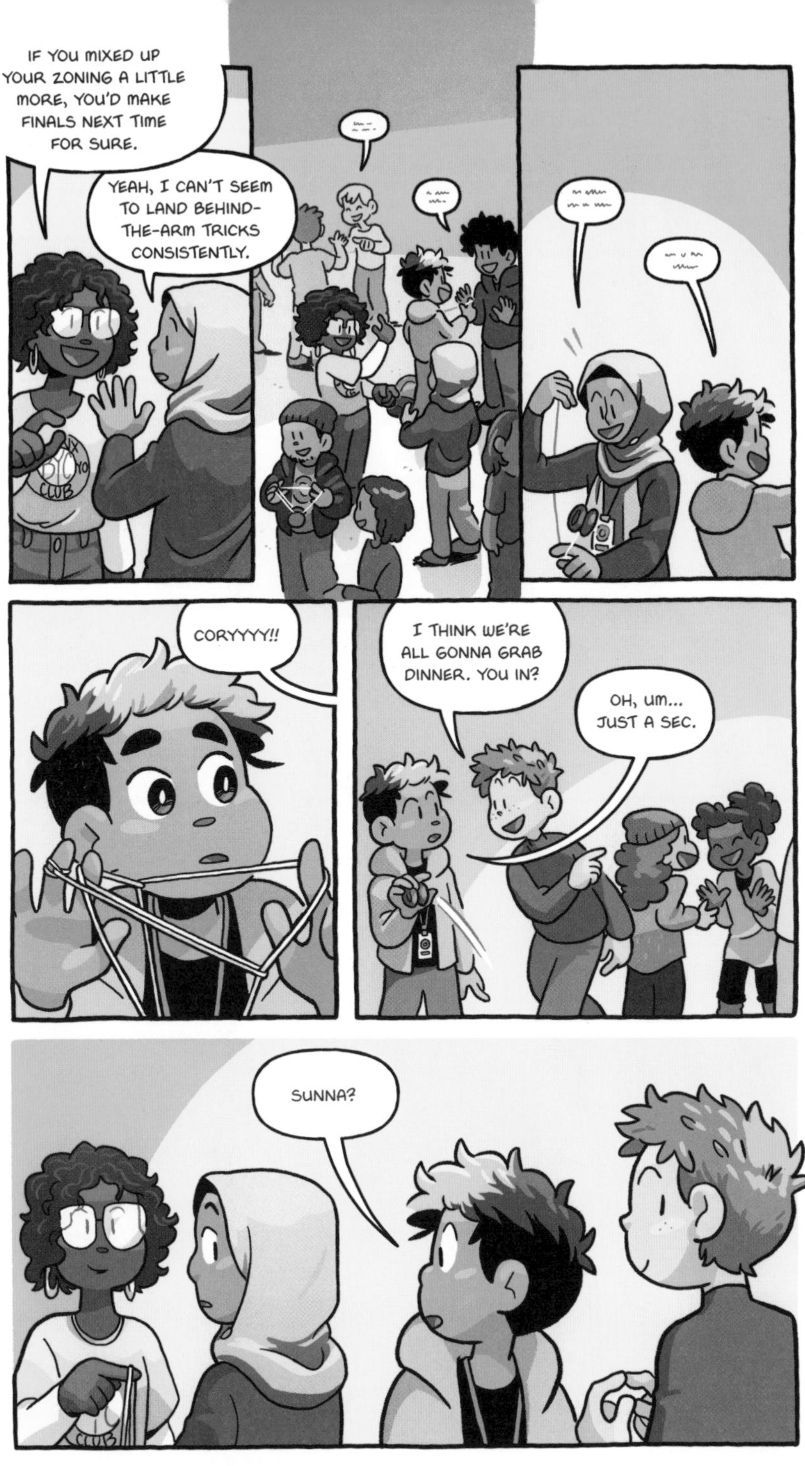
IF YOU MIXED UP YOUR ZONING A LITTLE MORE, YOU'D MAKE FINALS NEXT TIME FOR SURE.
YEAH, I CAN'T SEEM TO LAND BEHIND-THE-ARM TRICKS CONSISTENTLY.
CORYYYY!!
I THINK WE'RE ALL GONNA GRAB DINNER. YOU IN?
OH, UM... JUST A SEC.
SUNNA?

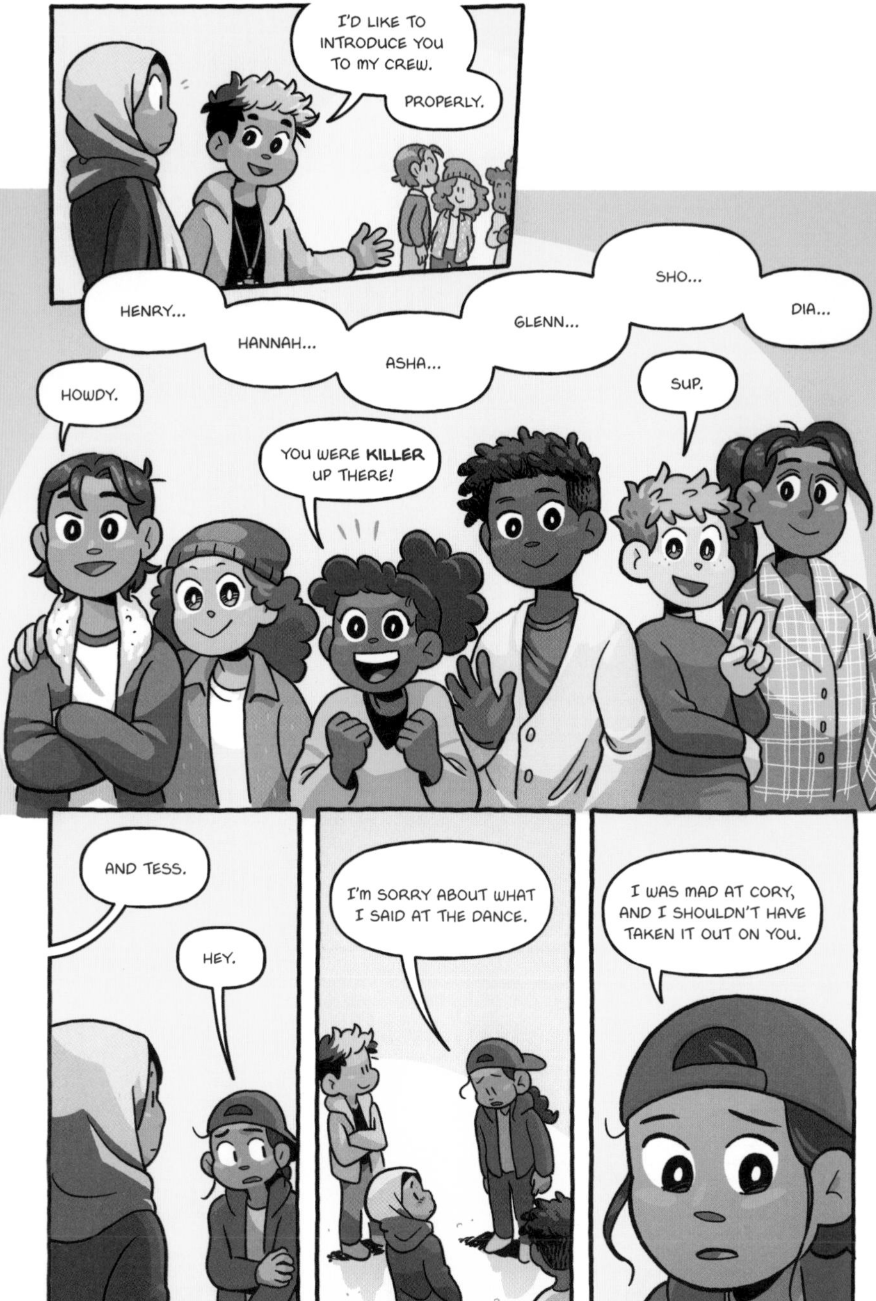
I'D LIKE TO INTRODUCE YOU TO MY CREW.
PROPERLY.
HENRY... HANNAH... ASHA... GLENN... SHO... DIA...
HOWDY.
YOU WERE **KILLER** UP THERE!
SUP.
AND TESS.
HEY.
I'M SORRY ABOUT WHAT I SAID AT THE DANCE.
I WAS MAD AT CORY, AND I SHOULDN'T HAVE TAKEN IT OUT ON YOU.

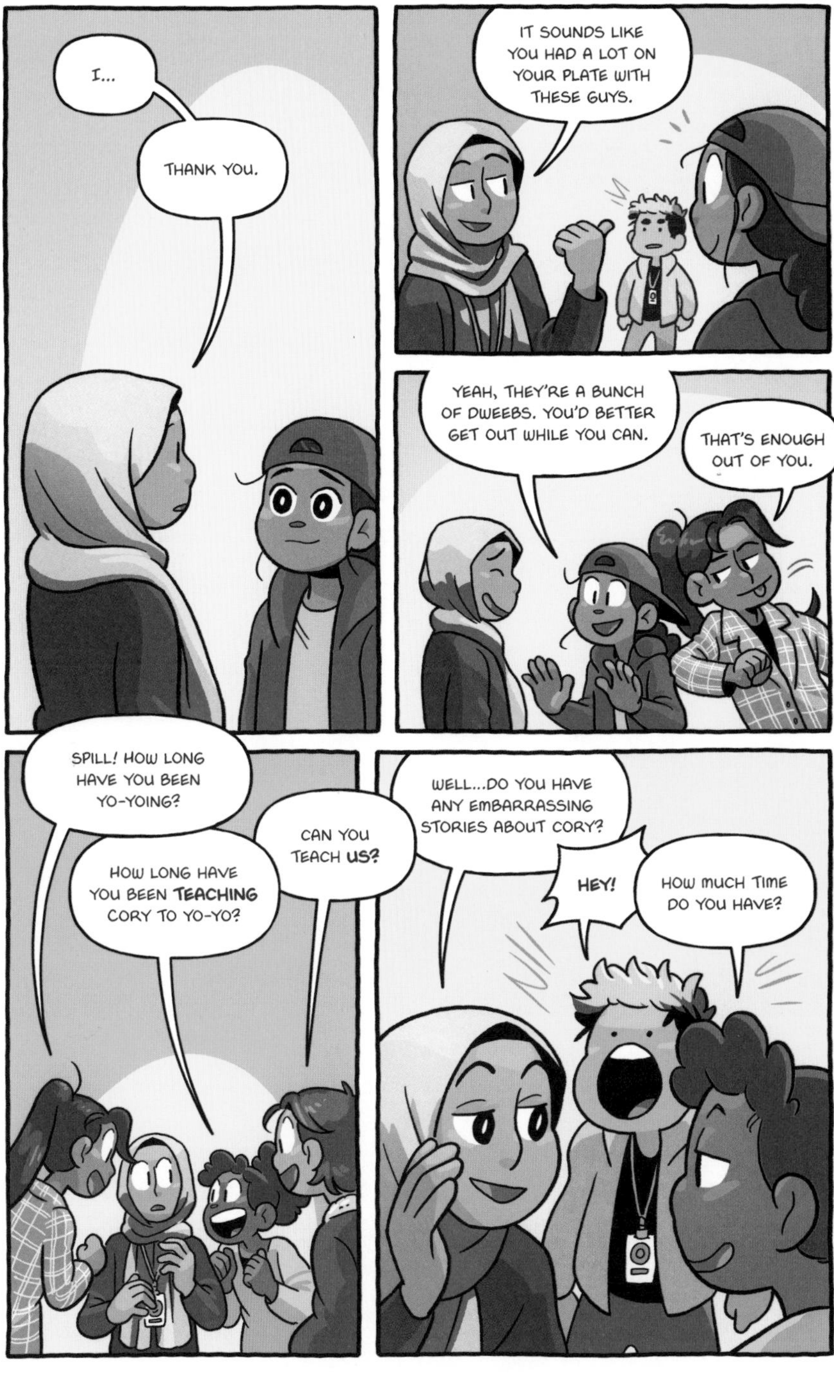
I...
THANK YOU.
IT SOUNDS LIKE YOU HAD A LOT ON YOUR PLATE WITH THESE GUYS.
YEAH, THEY'RE A BUNCH OF DWEEBS. YOU'D BETTER GET OUT WHILE YOU CAN.
THAT'S ENOUGH OUT OF YOU.
SPILL! HOW LONG HAVE YOU BEEN YO-YOING?
HOW LONG HAVE YOU BEEN TEACHING CORY TO YO-YO?
CAN YOU TEACH US?
WELL...DO YOU HAVE ANY EMBARRASSING STORIES ABOUT CORY?
HEY!
HOW MUCH TIME DO YOU HAVE?

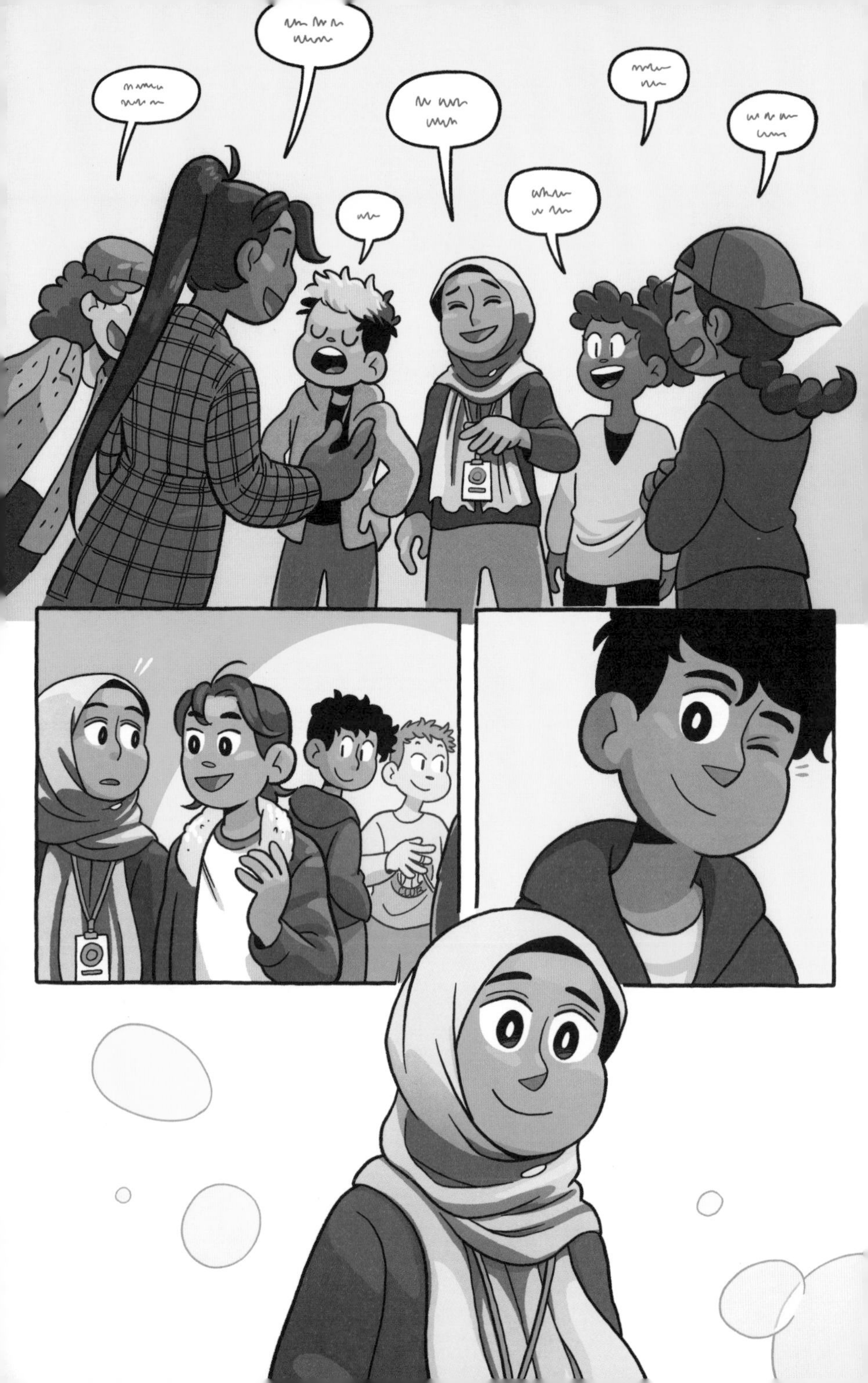

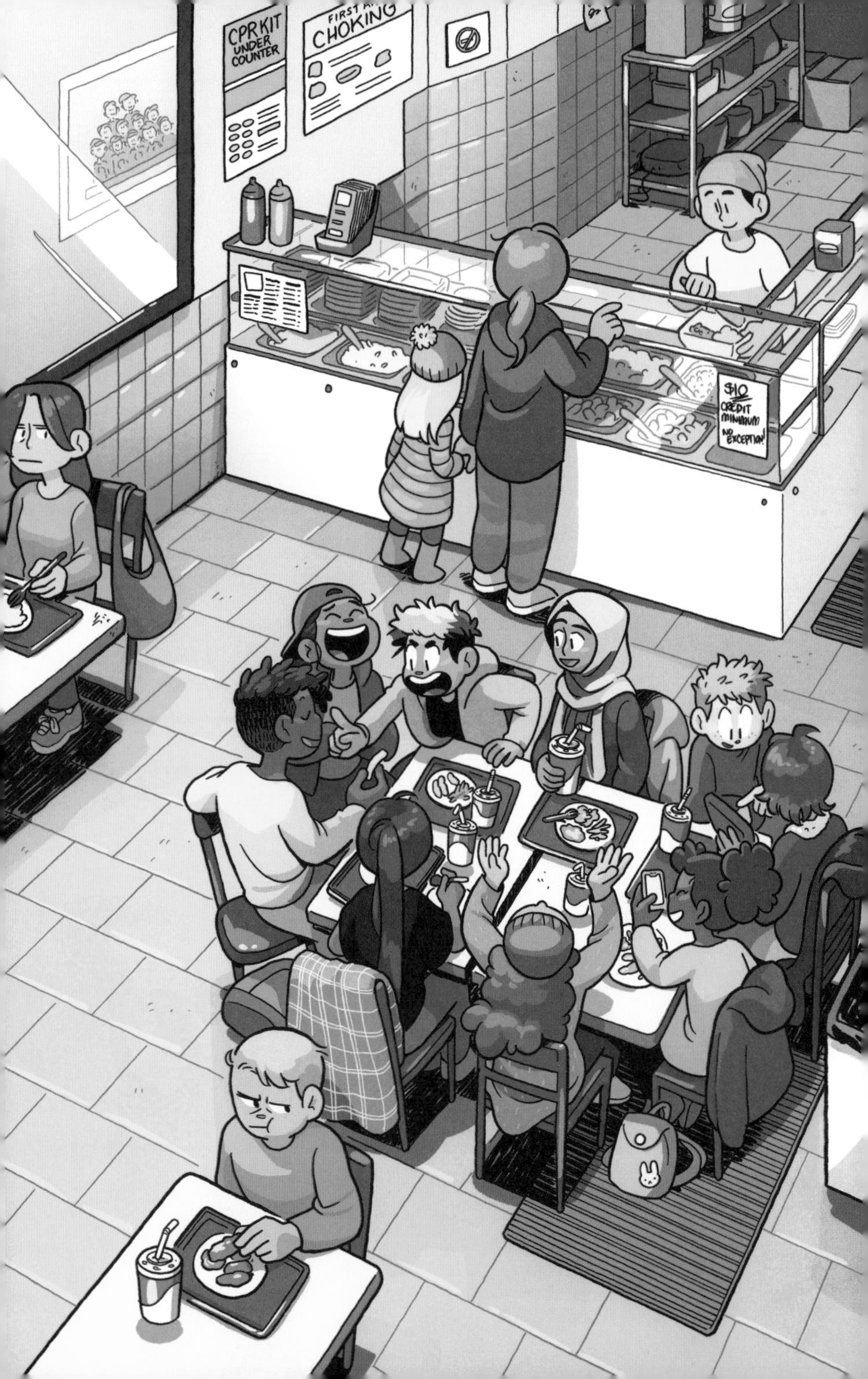
CPR KIT UNDER COUNTER
CHOKING
$10 CREDIT MINIMUM NO EXCEPTION!

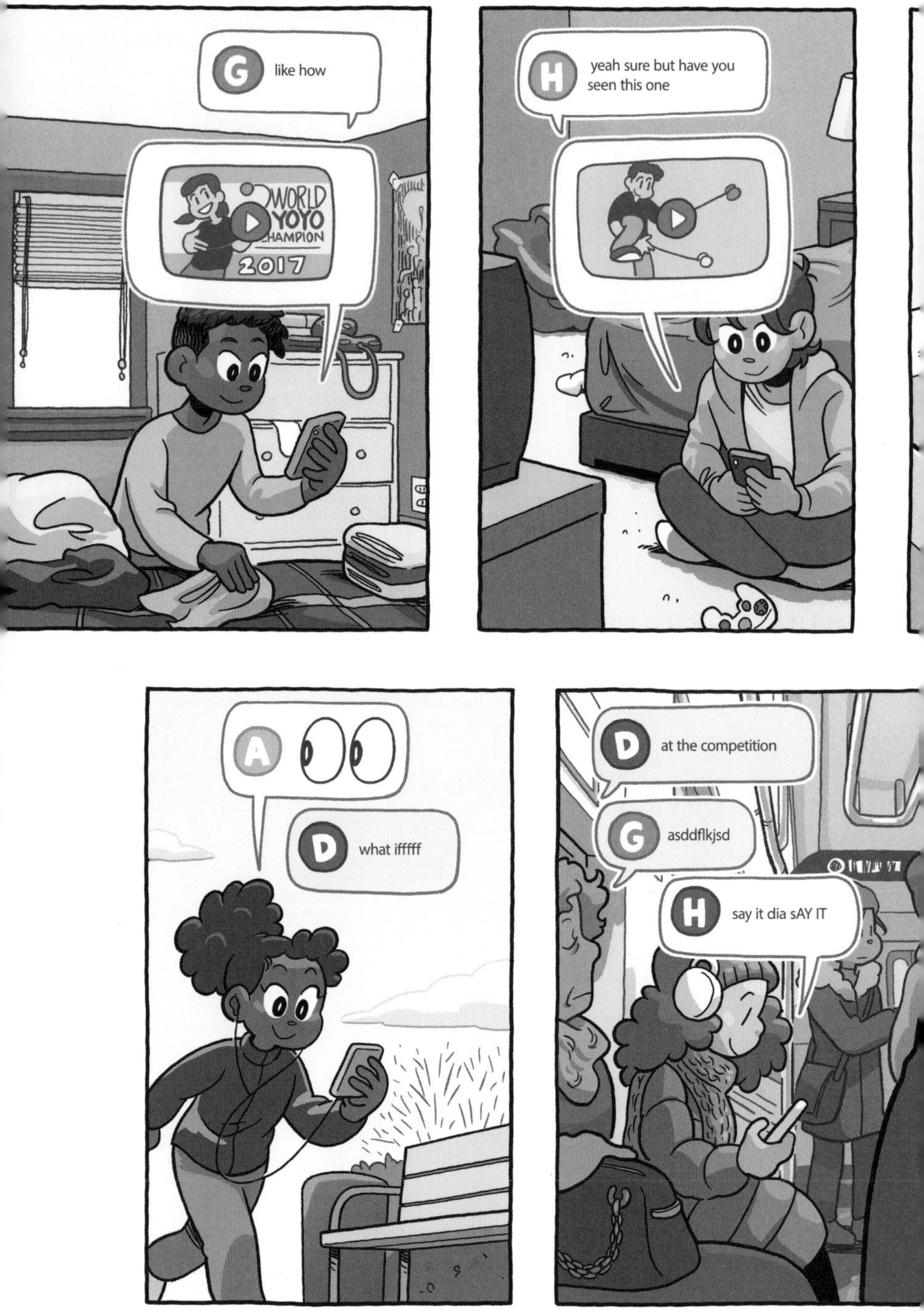
G like how
WORLD YOYO CHAMPION 2017
H yeah sure but have you seen this one
A
D what ifffff
D at the competition
G asddflkjsd
H say it dia sAY IT

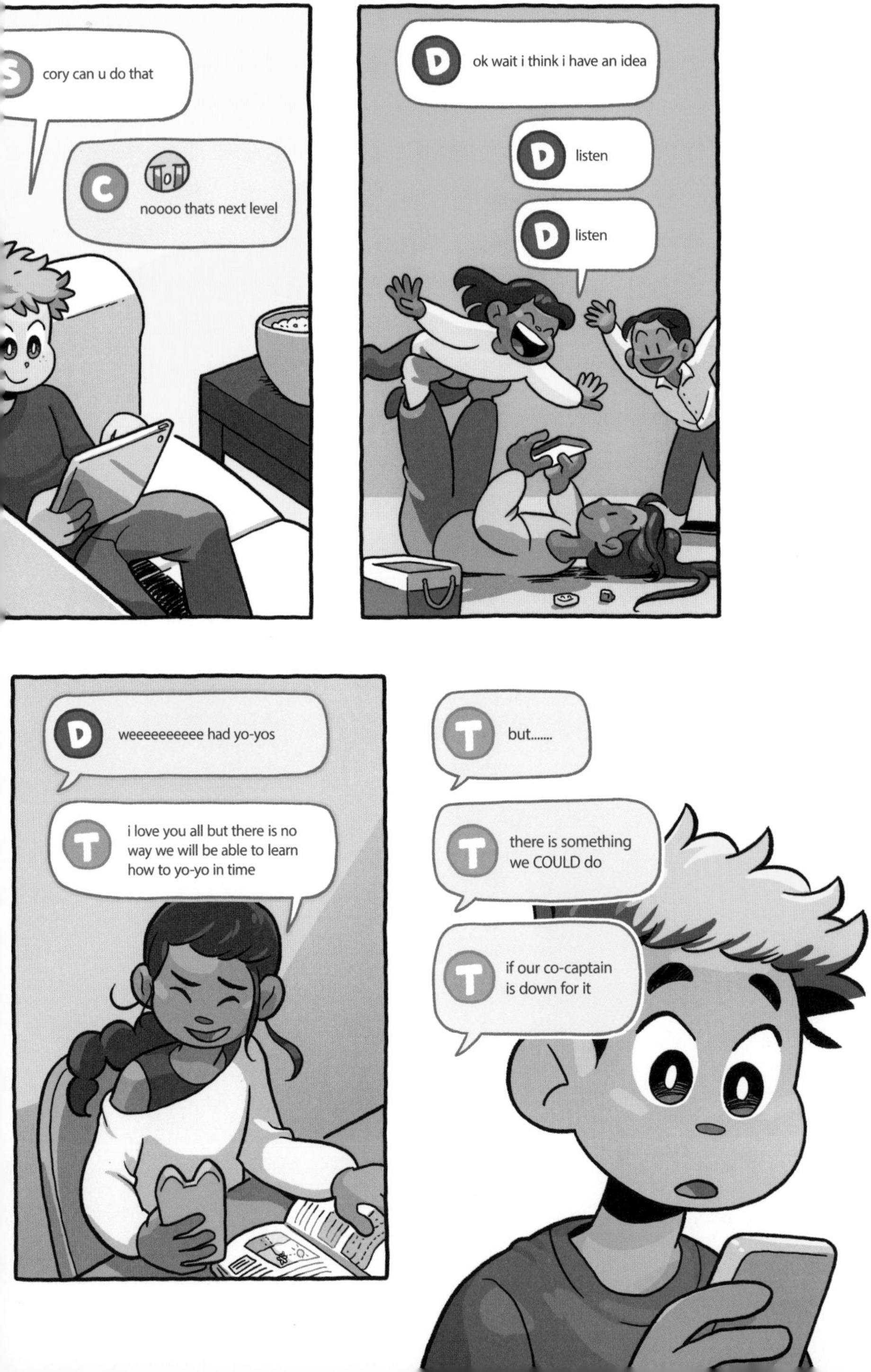
cory can u do that
noooo thats next level
ok wait i think i have an idea
listen
listen
weeeeeeeeee had yo-yos
i love you all but there is no way we will be able to learn how to yo-yo in time
but.......
there is something we COULD do
if our co-captain is down for it

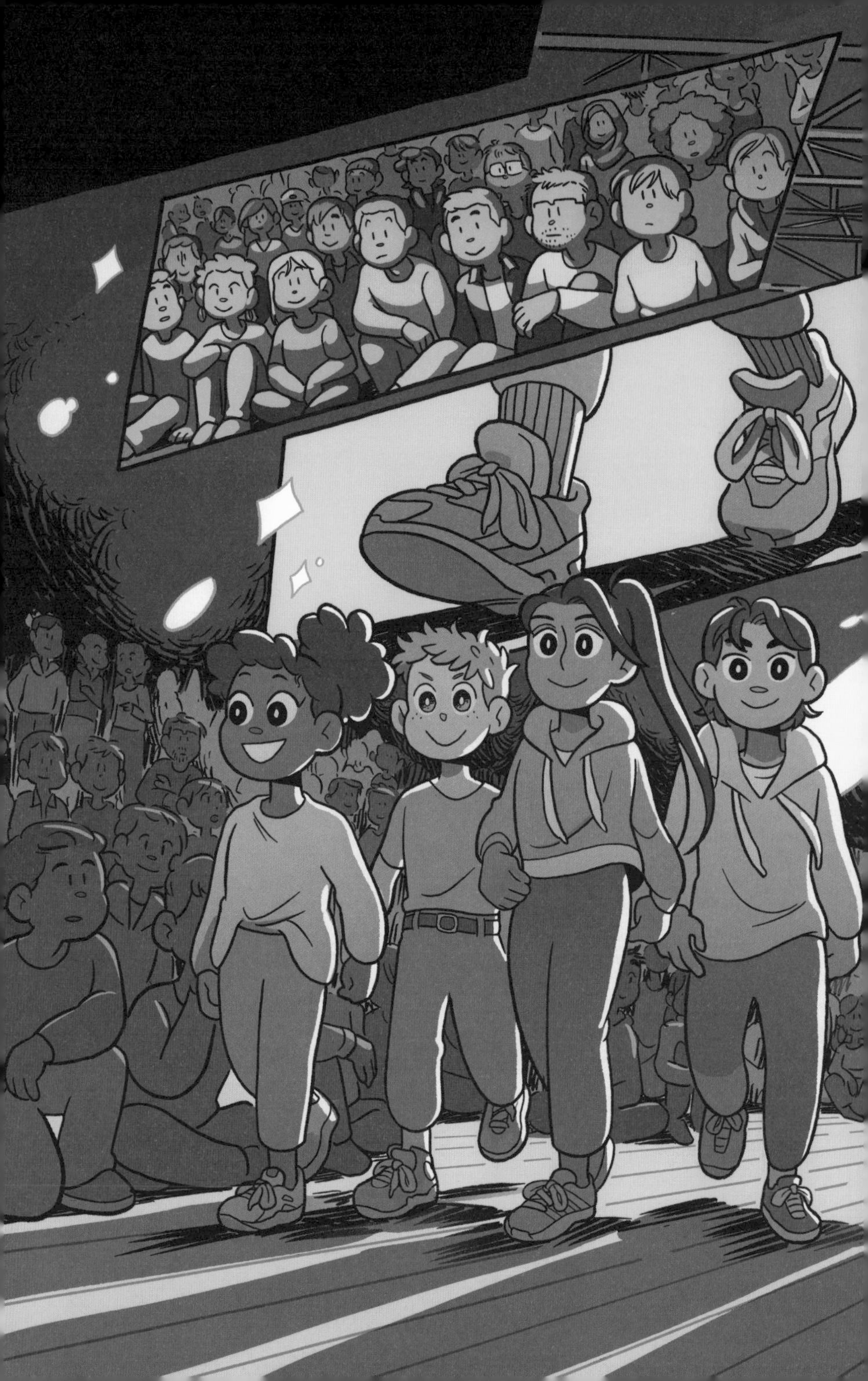

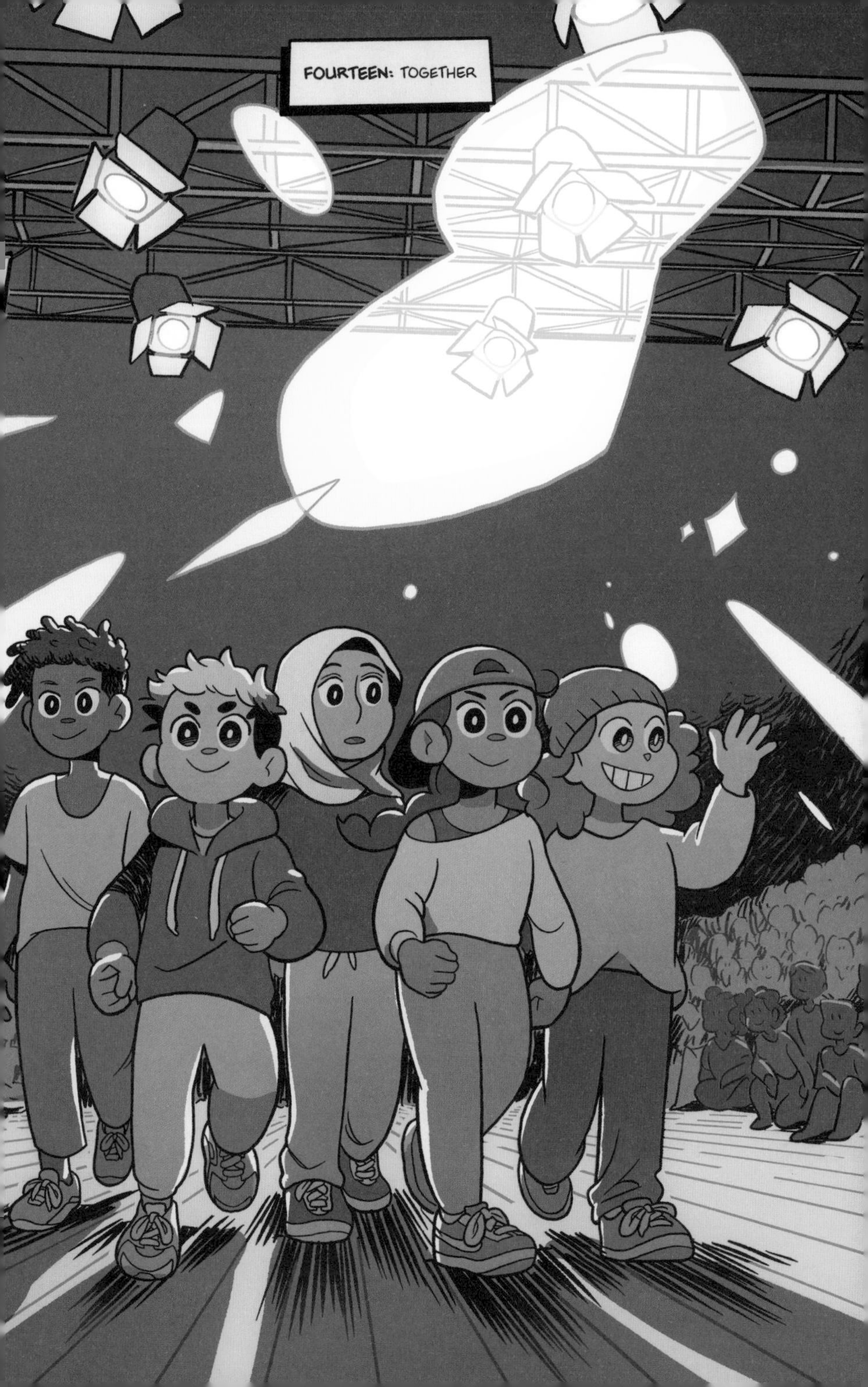
FOURTEEN: TOGETHER

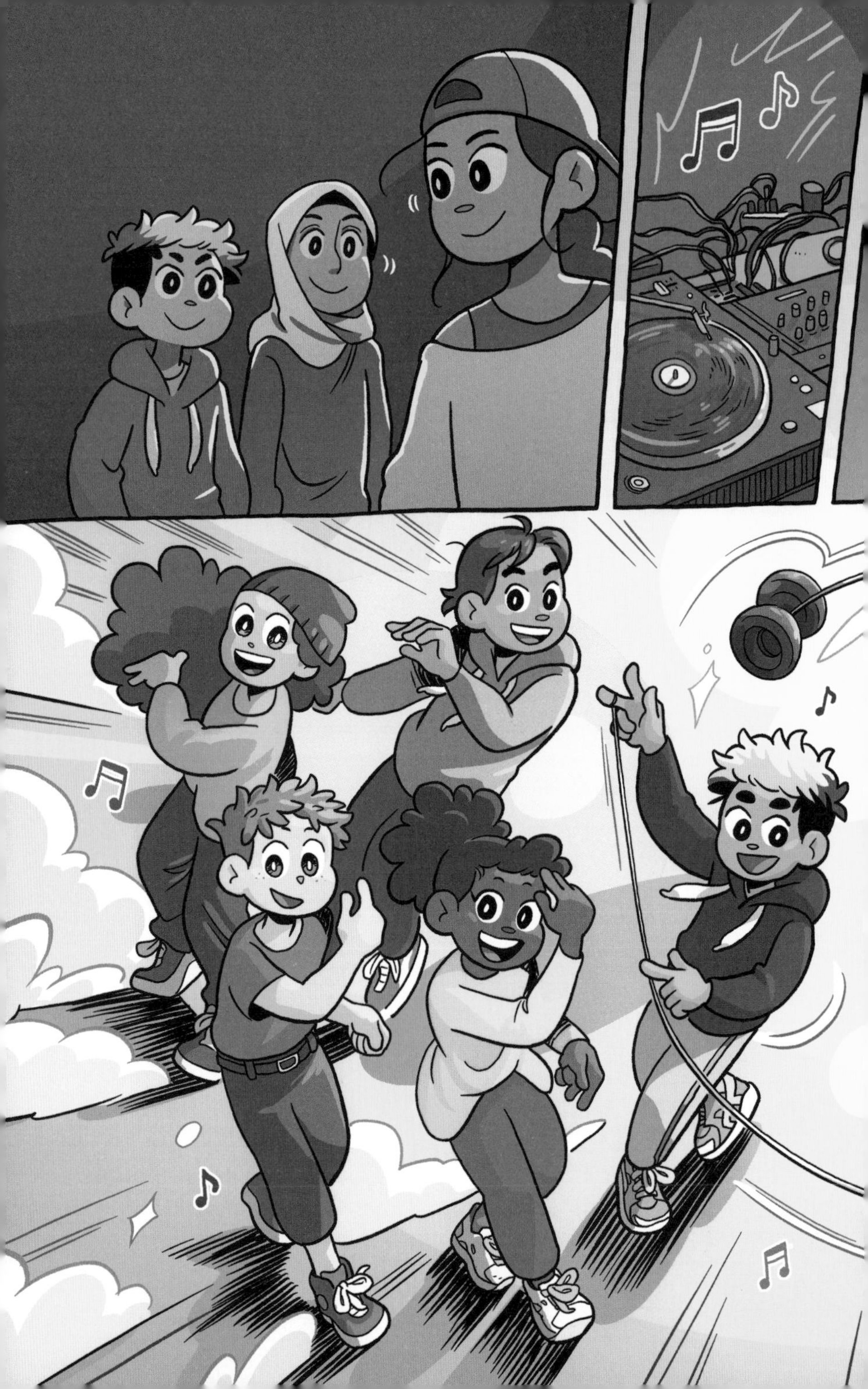

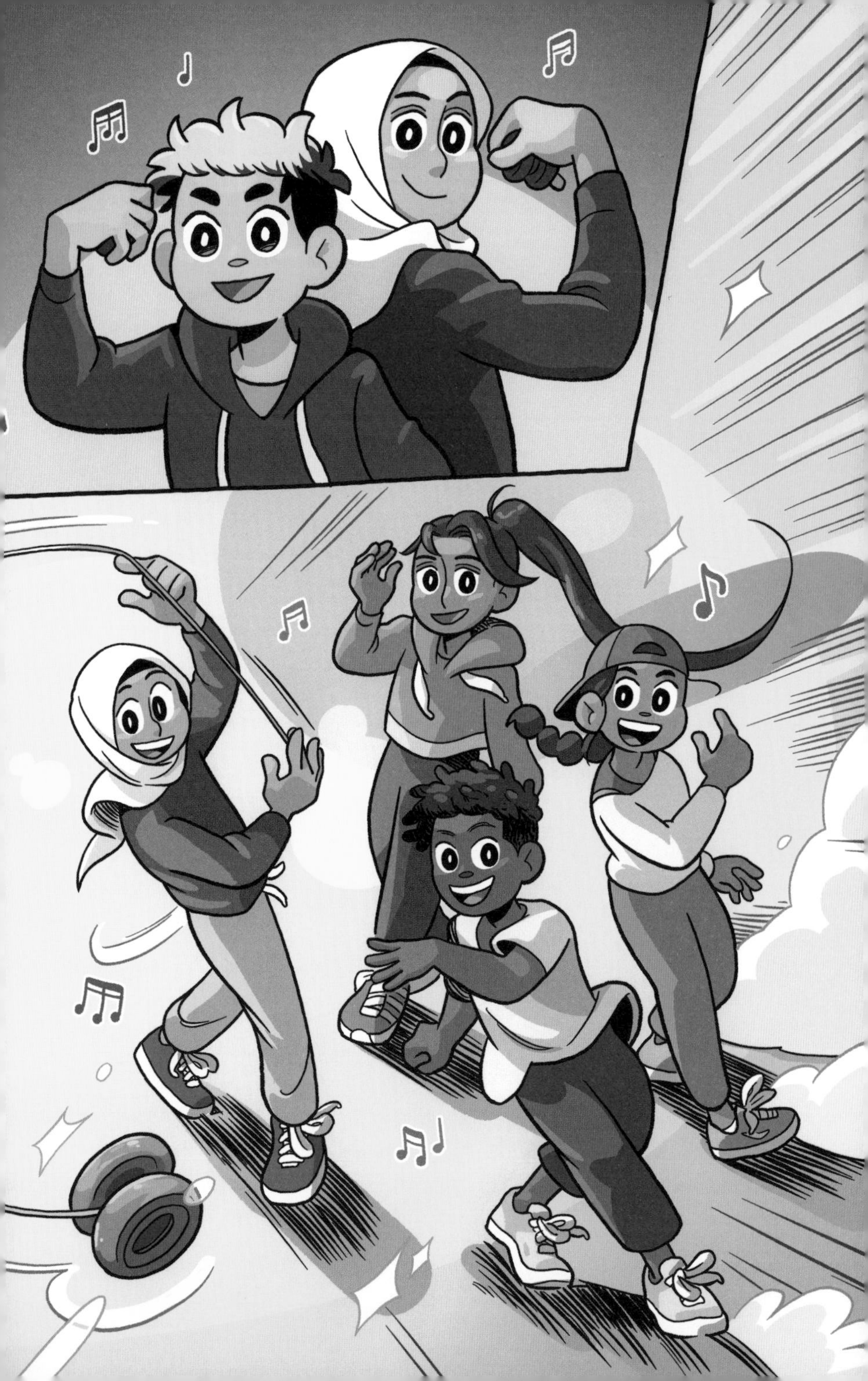

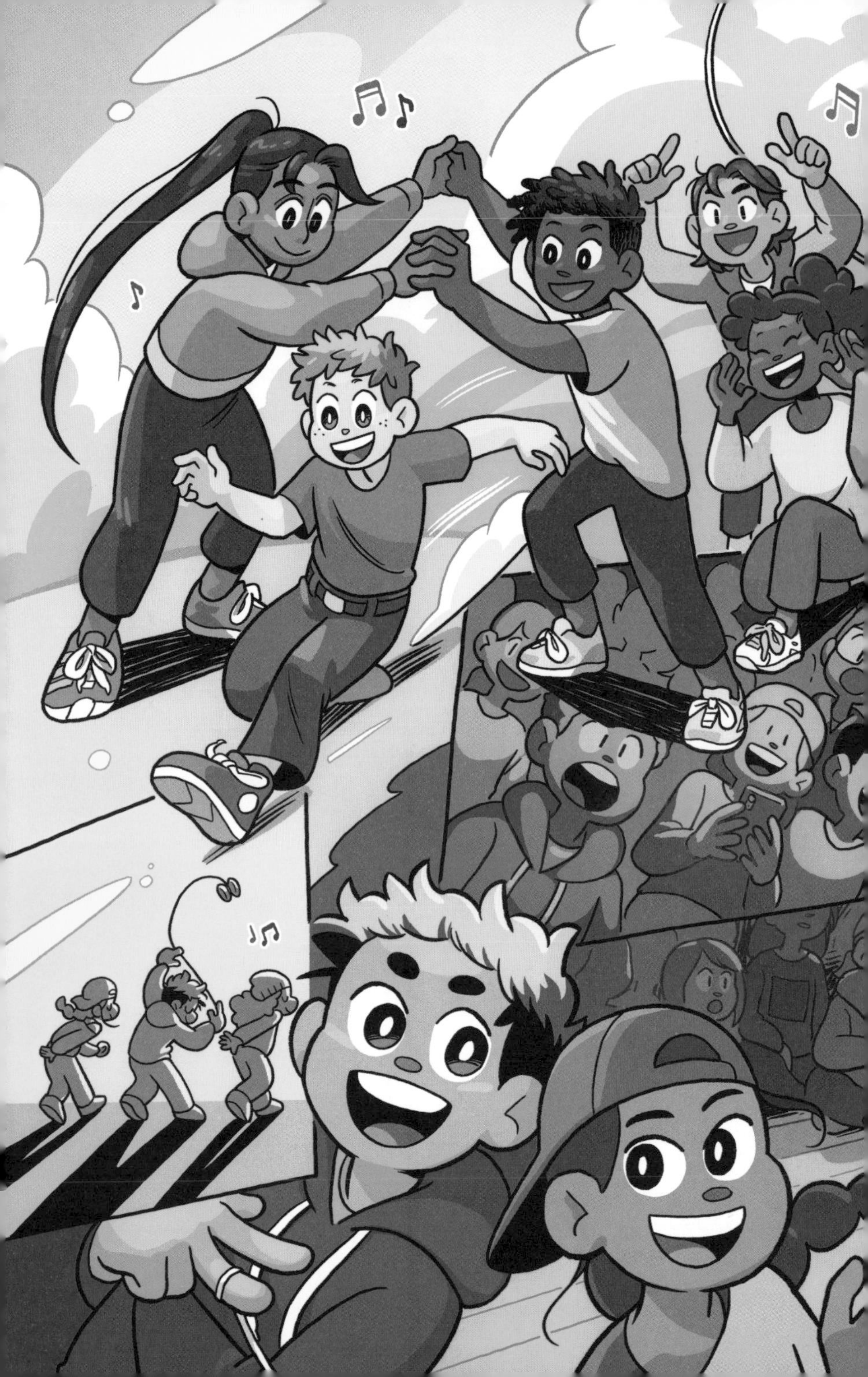

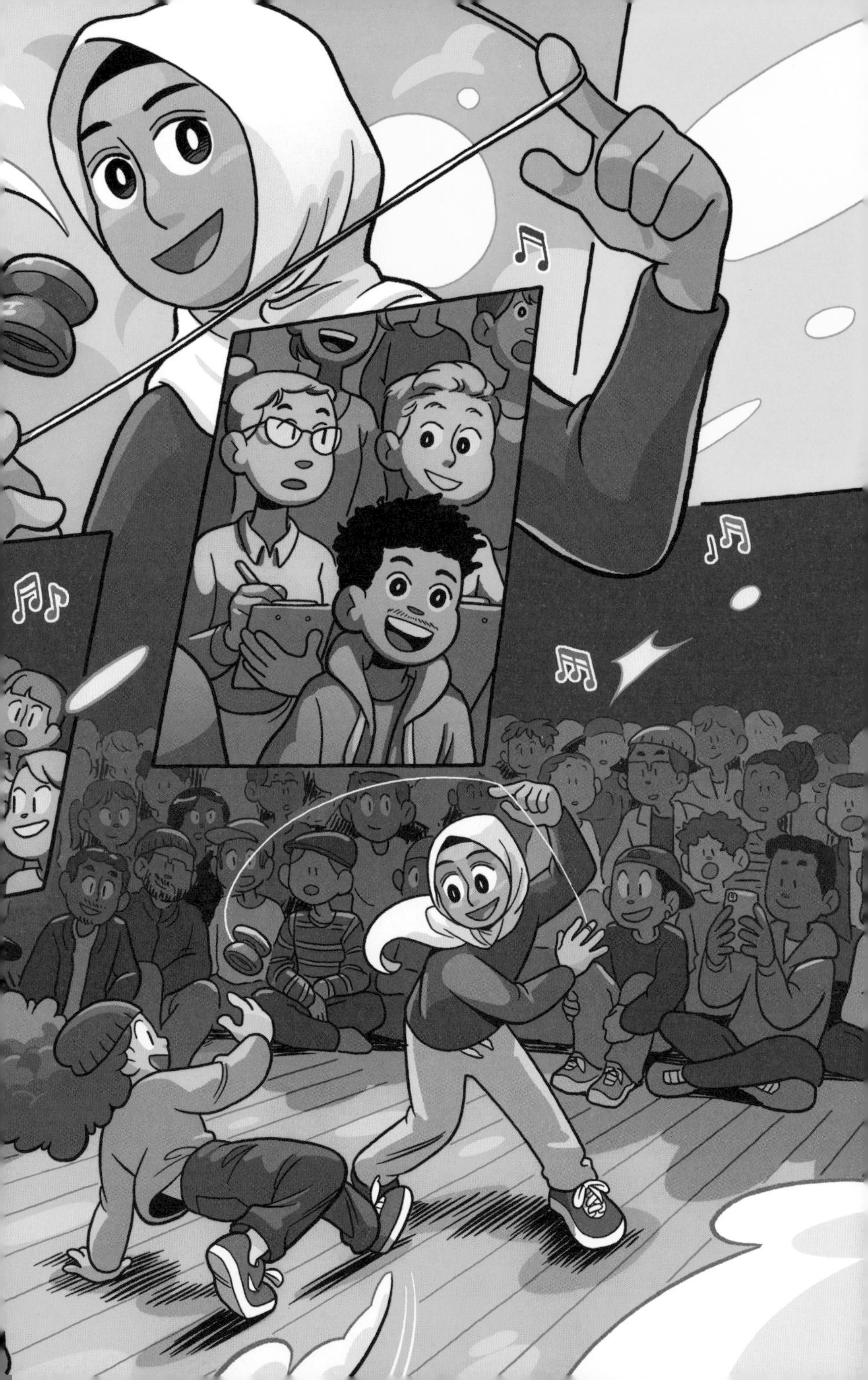

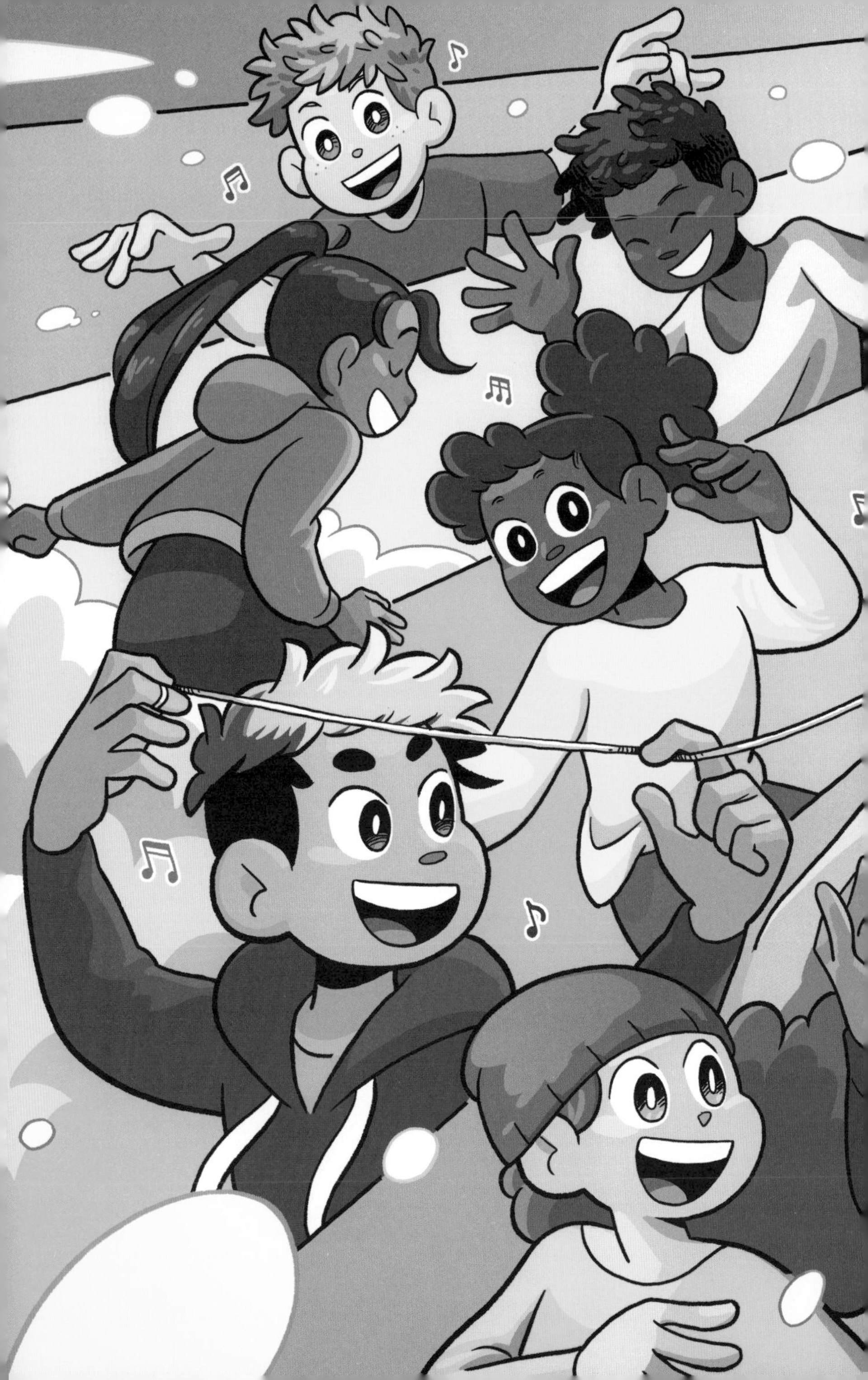

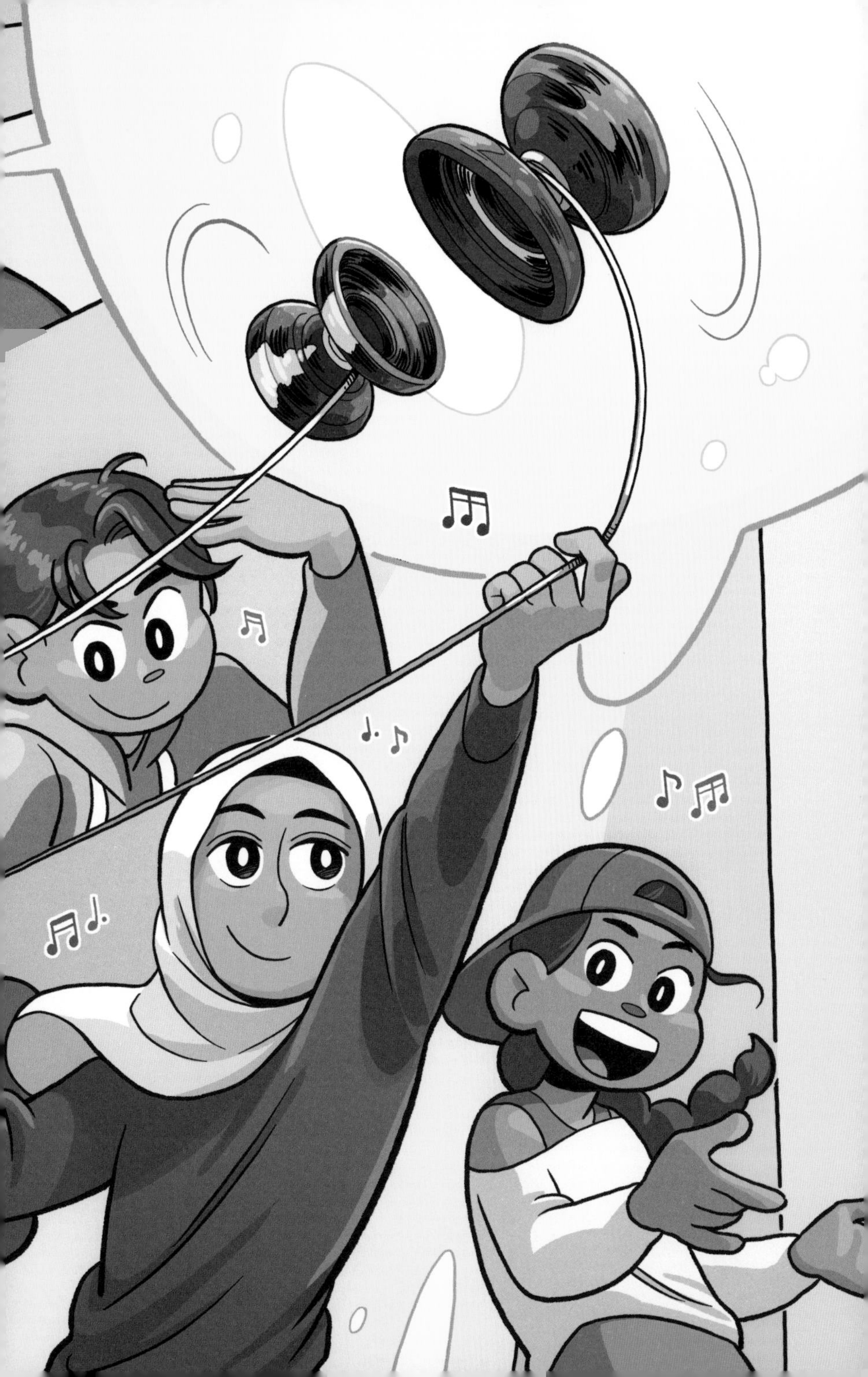

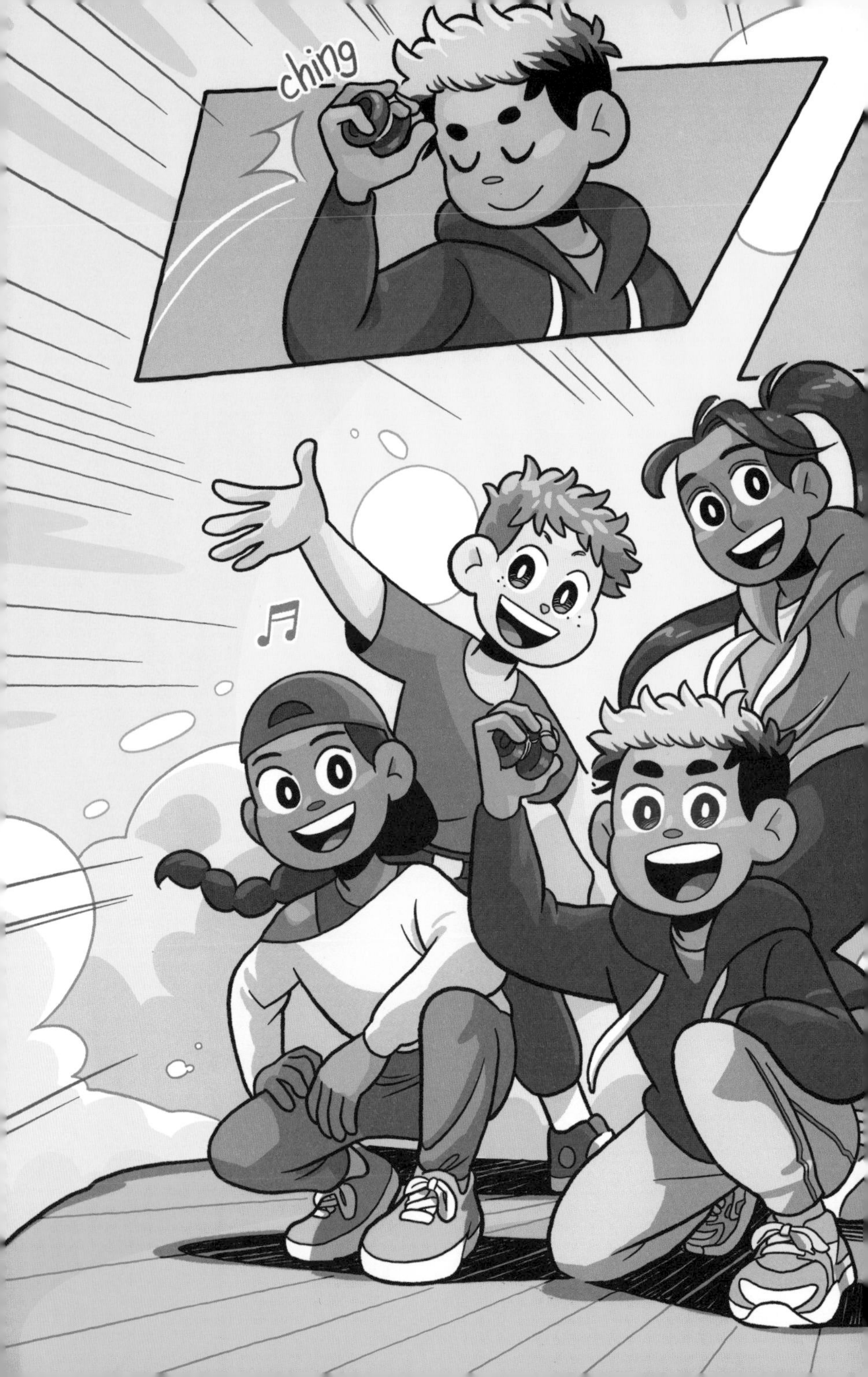
ching

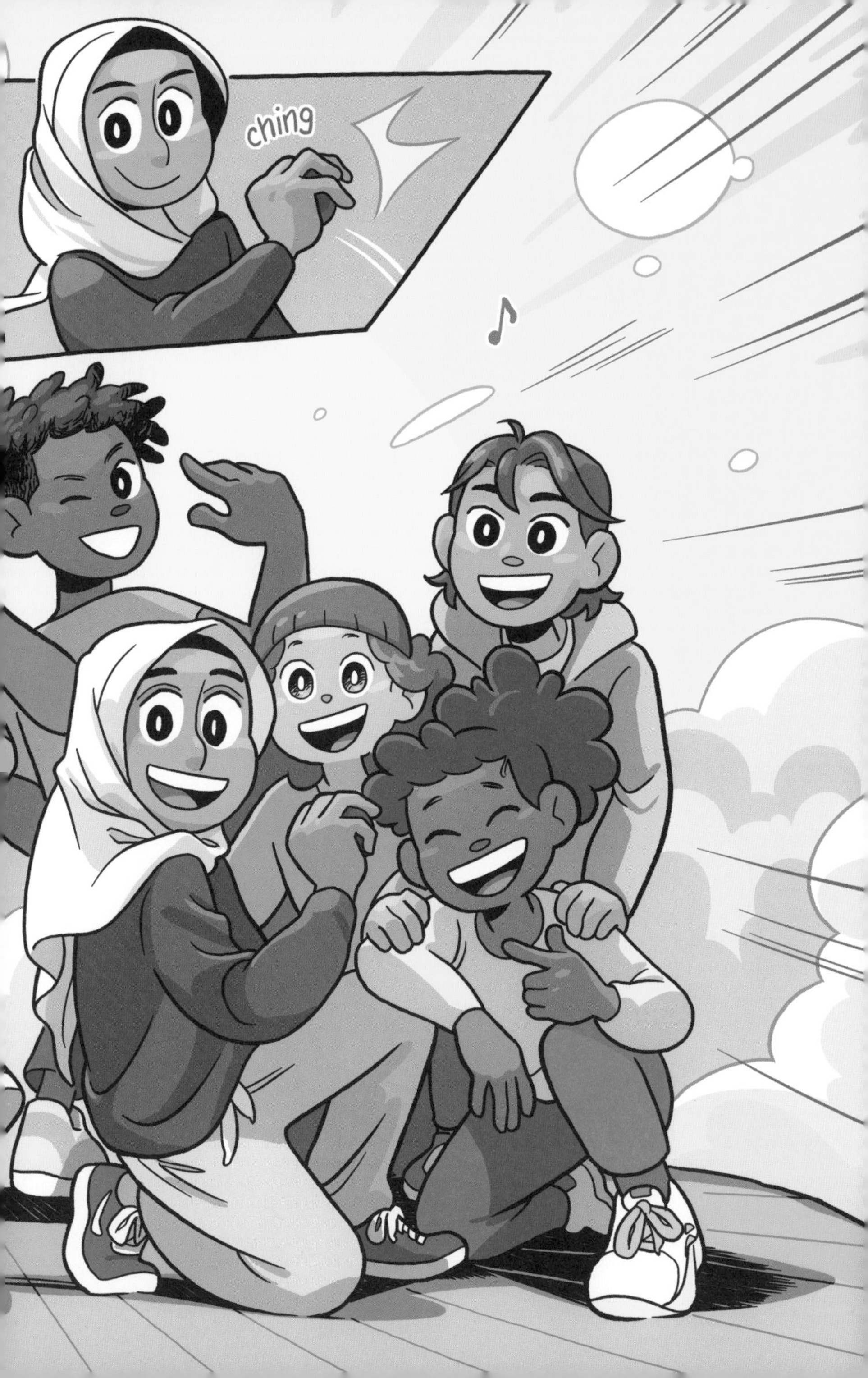
ching

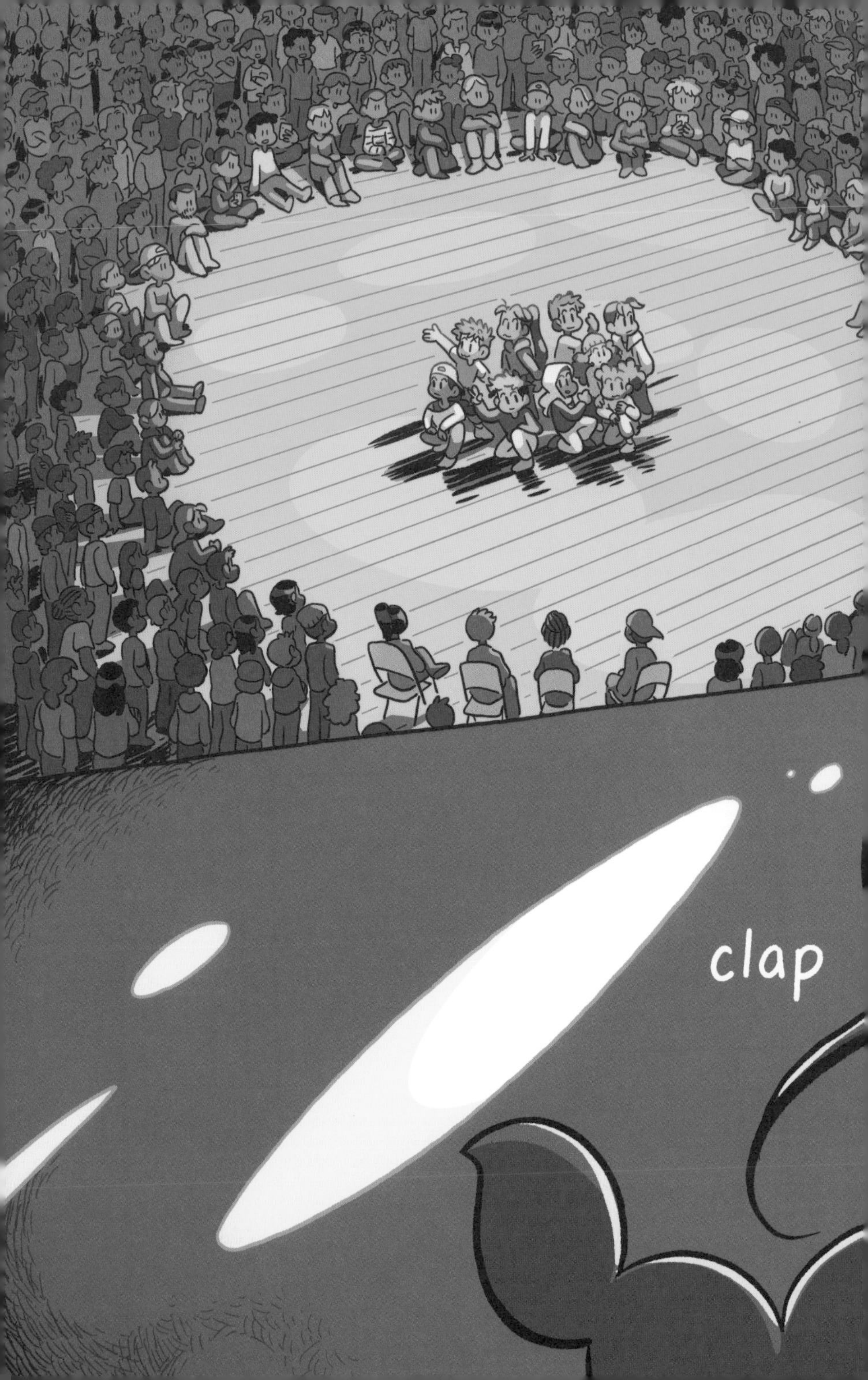
clap

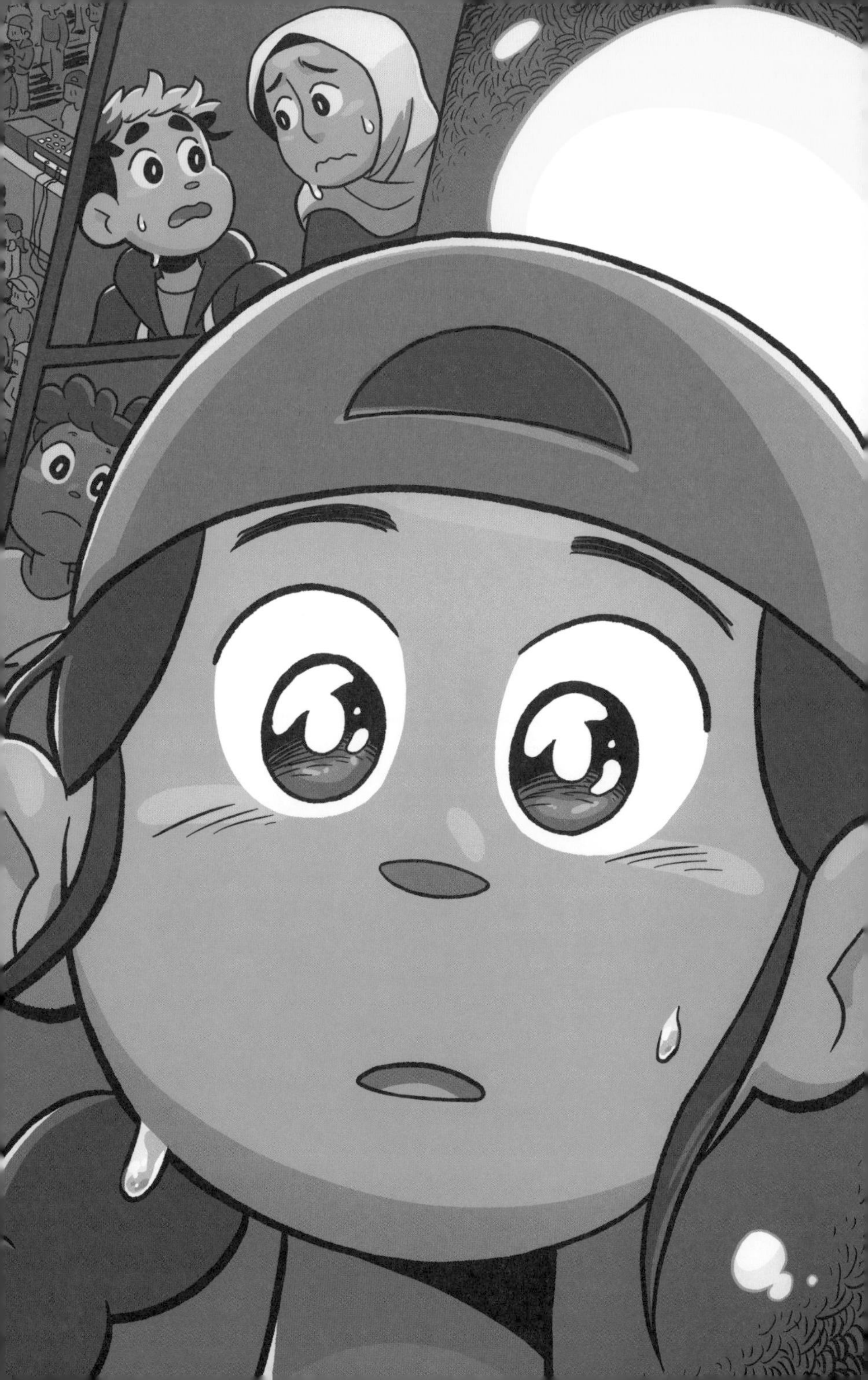

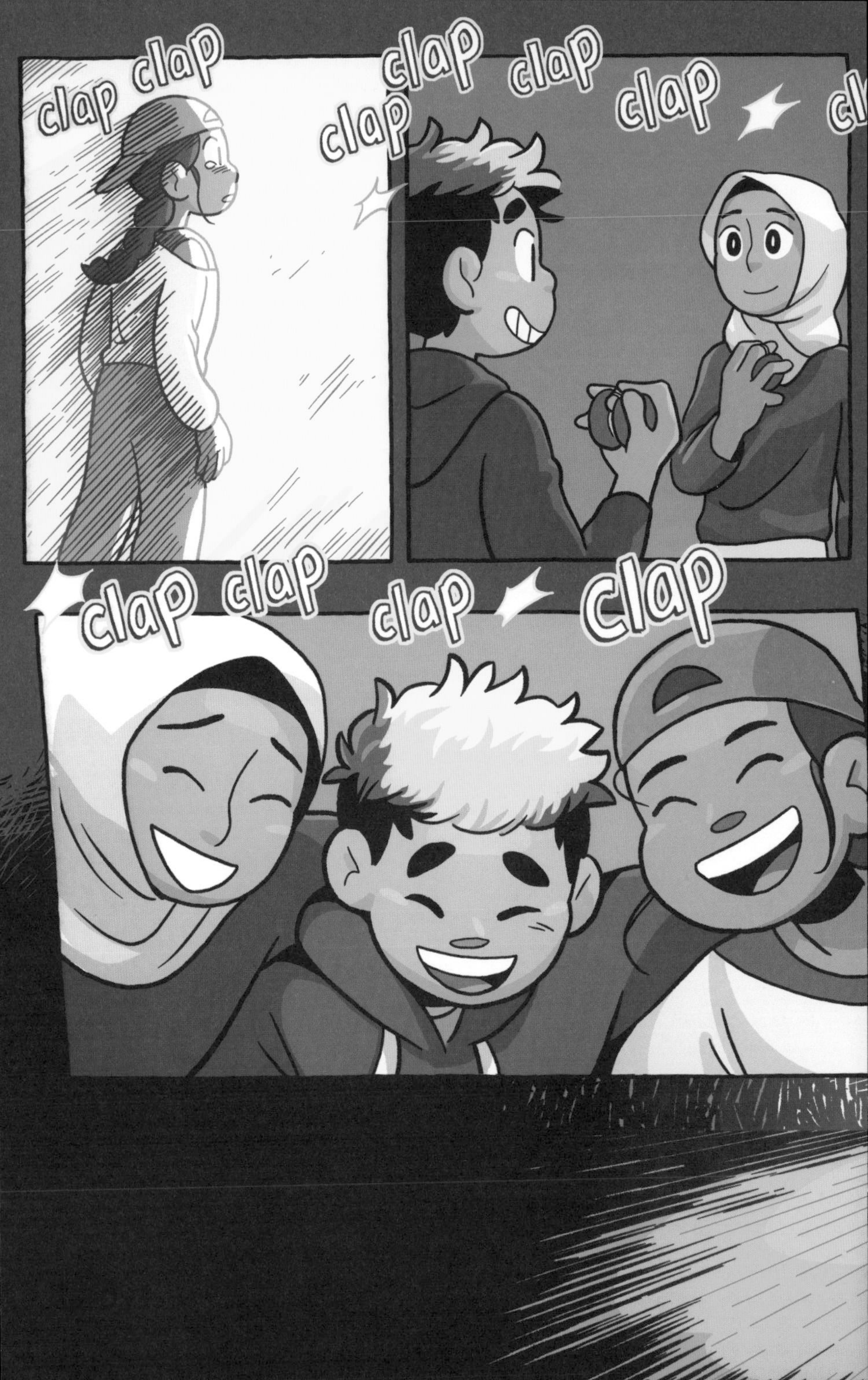
clap clap
clap
clap
clap
clap
clap clap
clap
clap

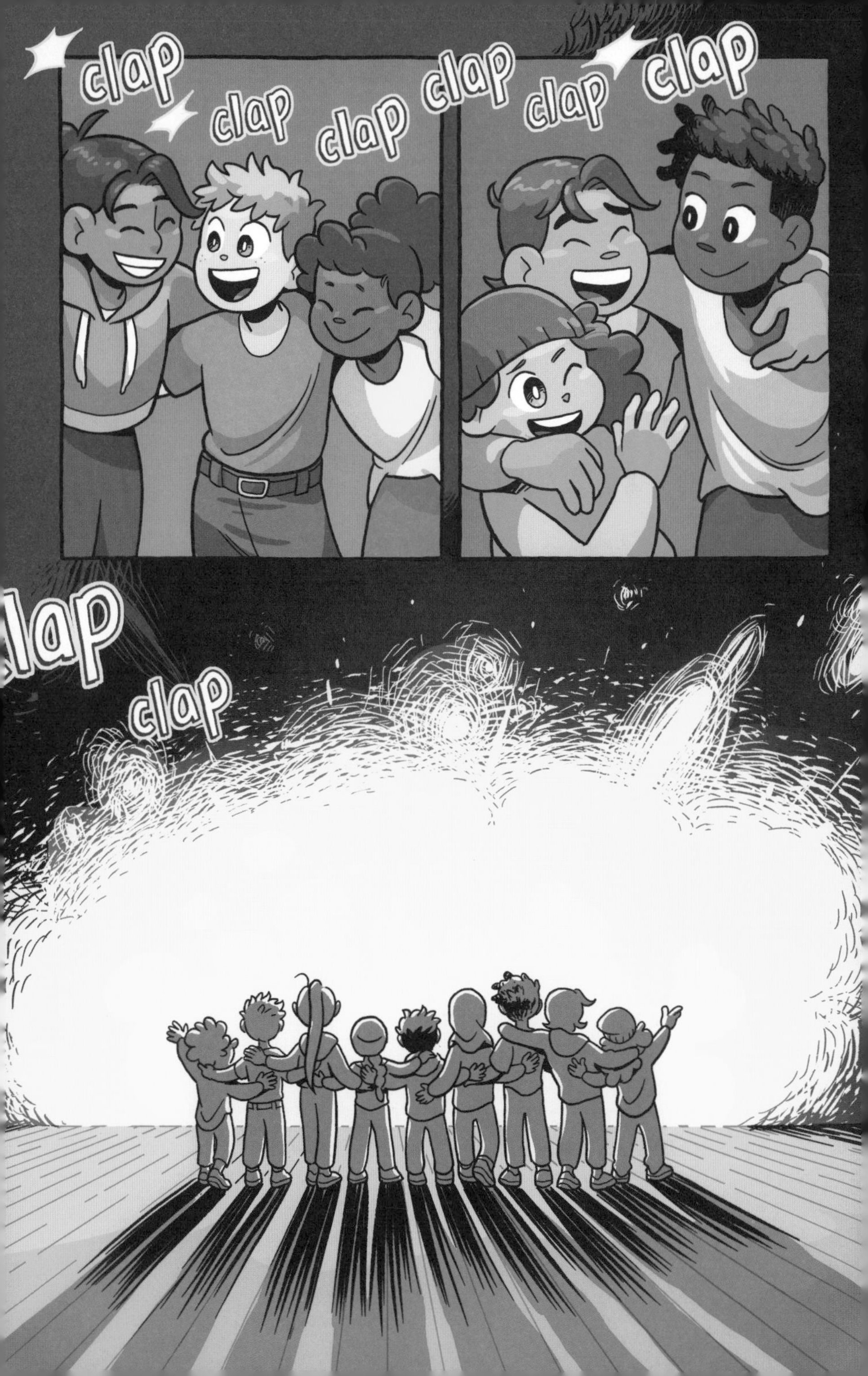
clap
clap
clap
clap
clap
clap
lap
clap

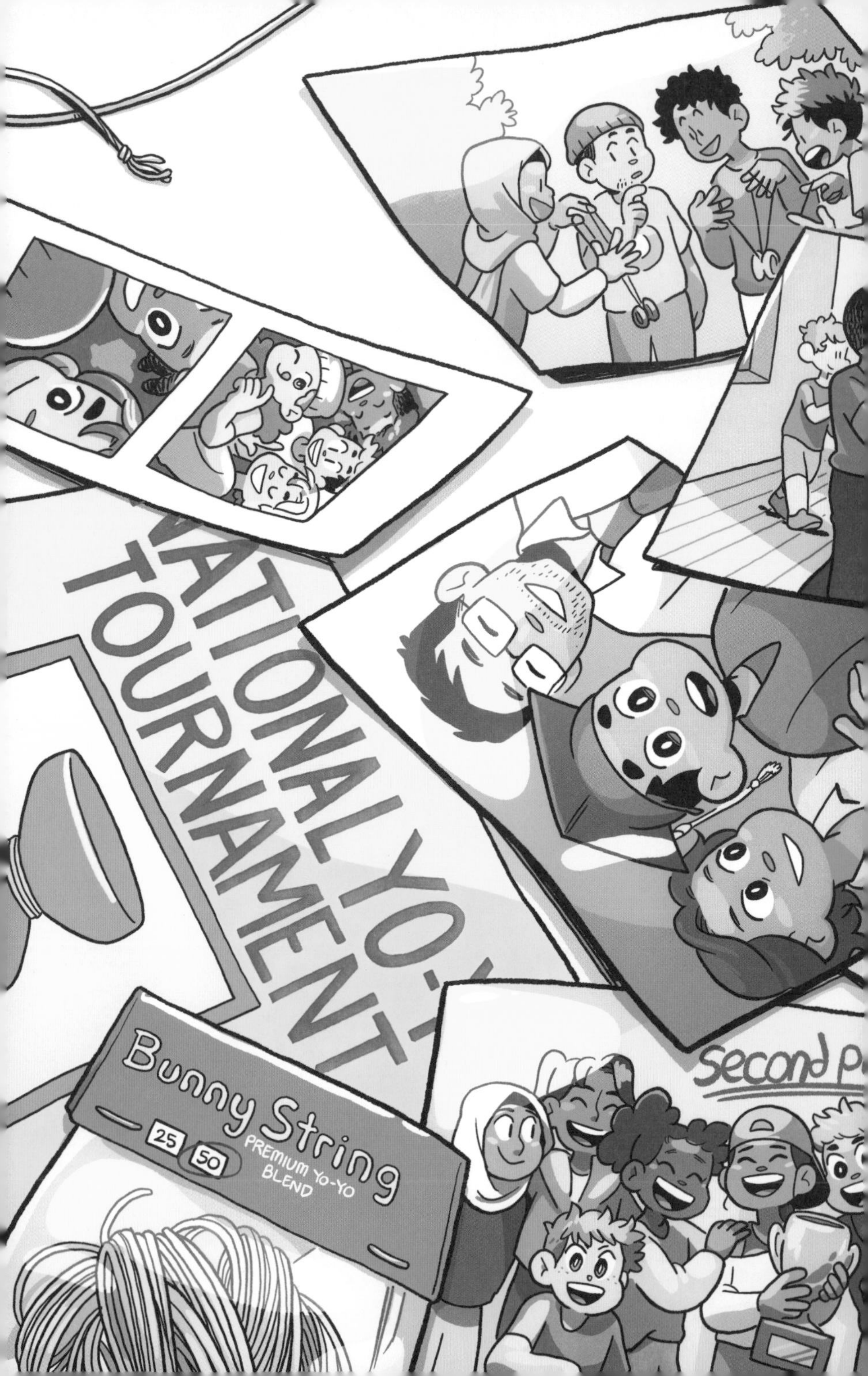
NATIONAL YO-Y
TOURNAMENT
Bunny String
25 50
PREMIUM YO-YO BLEND
Second p

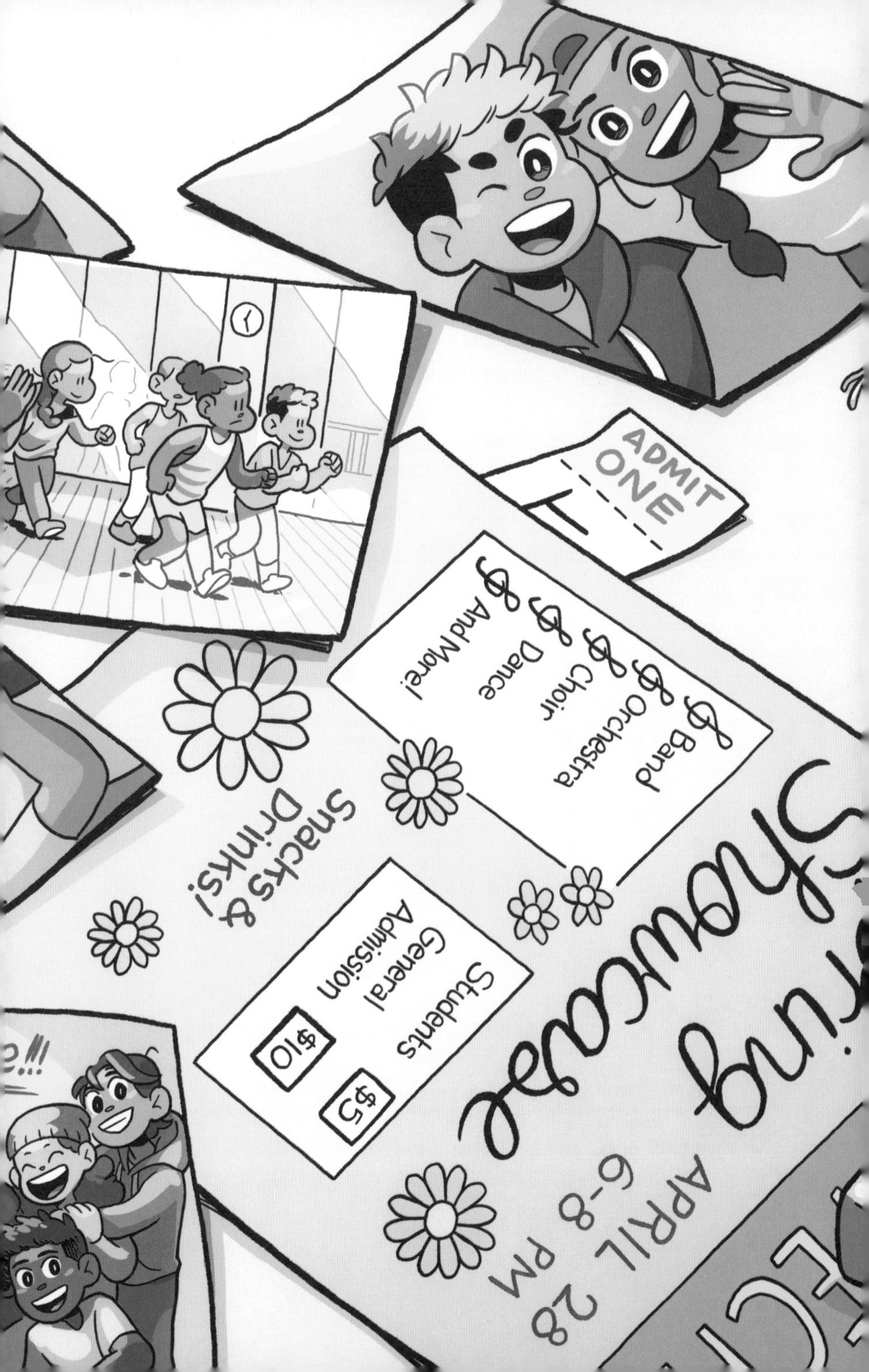

ADMIT ONE
Band
Orchestra
Choir
Dance
And More!
Showcase
APRIL 28
6-8 PM
Students $5
General Admission $10
Snacks & Drinks!

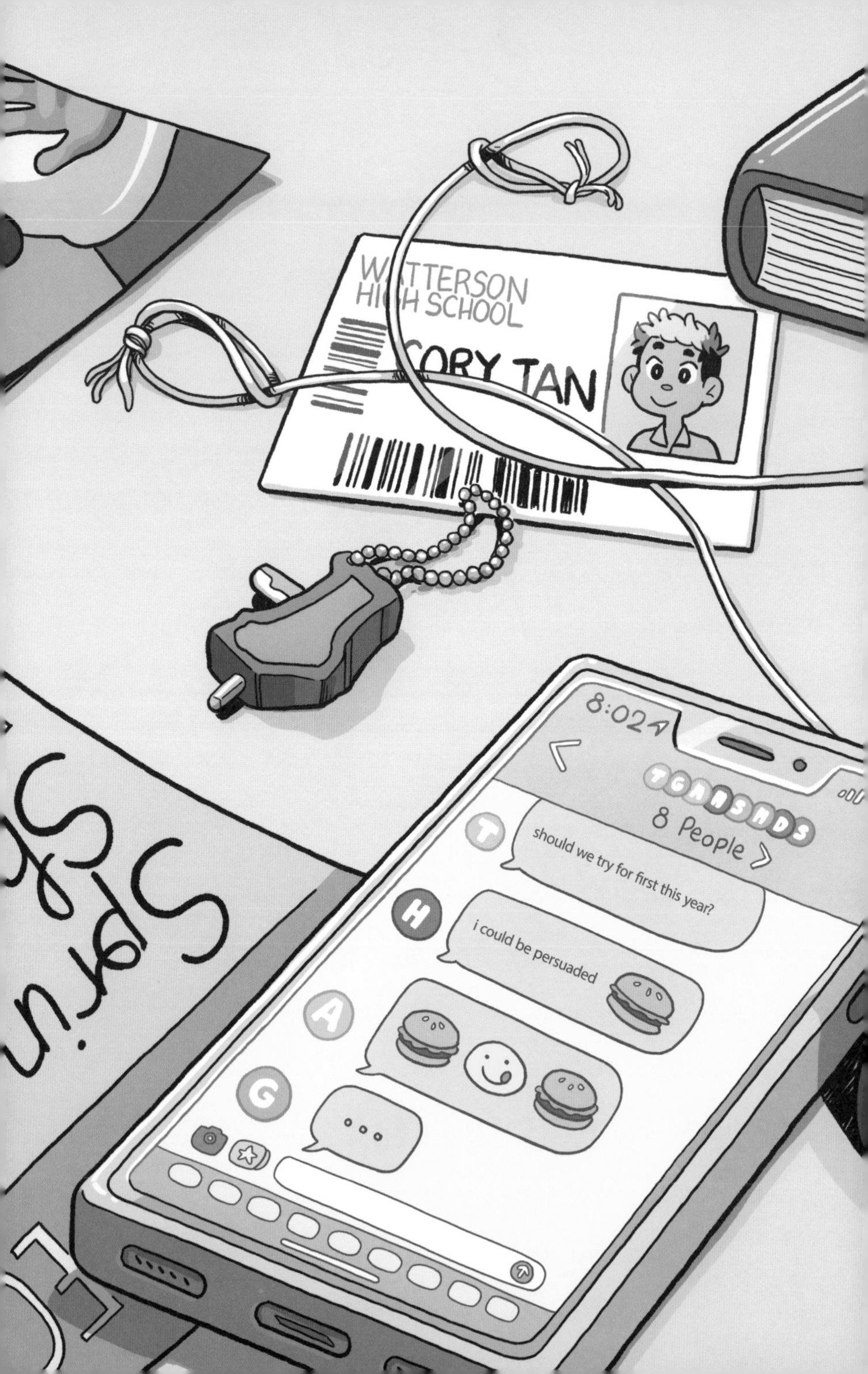

WATTERSON HIGH SCHOOL
CORY TAN
8:02
8 People
should we try for first this year?
i could be persuaded

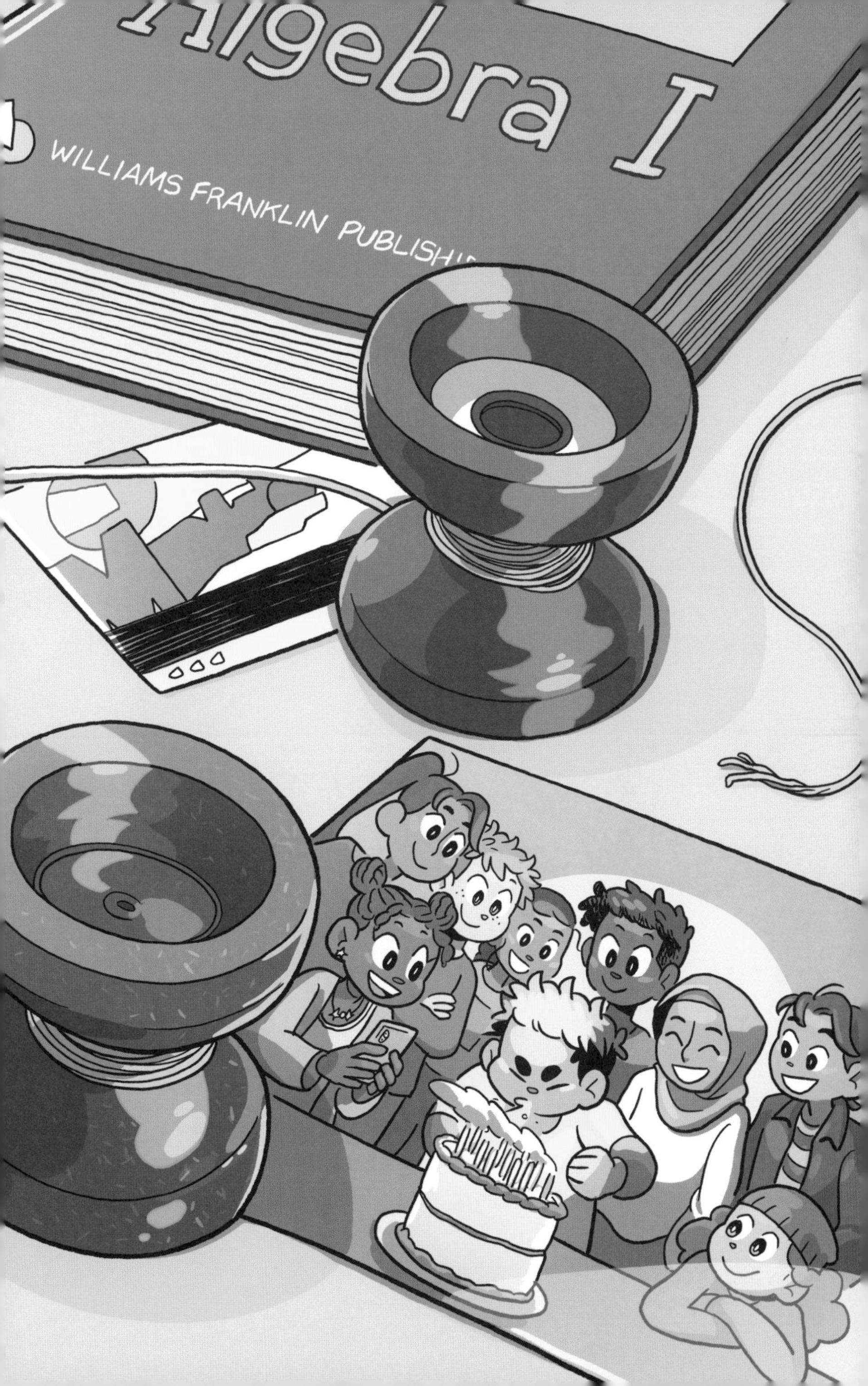
Algebra I
WILLIAMS FRANKLIN PUBLISHI

BONUS COMICS!

Runs in the family.

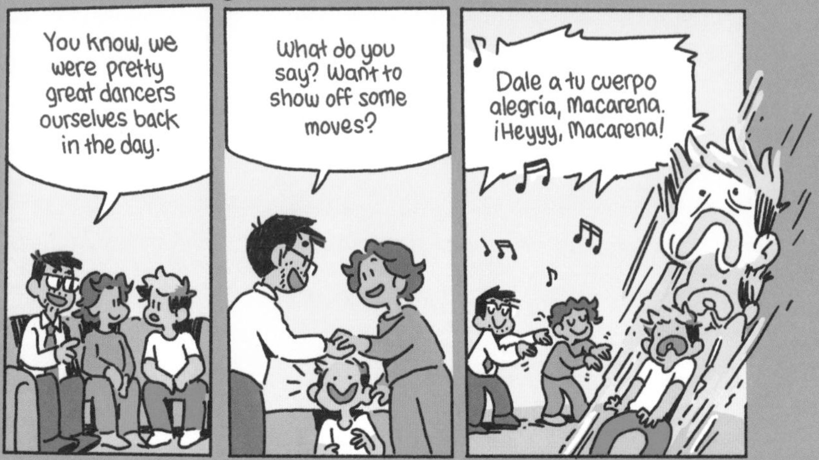
You know, we were pretty great dancers ourselves back in the day.
What do you say? Want to show off some moves?
Dale a tu cuerpo alegría, Macarena. ¡Heyyy, Macarena!

One step at a time.

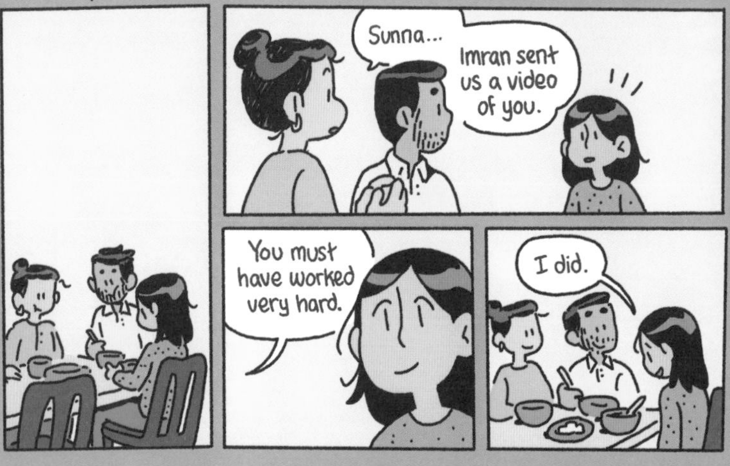
Sunna...
Imran sent us a video of you.
You must have worked very hard.
I did.

ONE STEP AT A TIME.

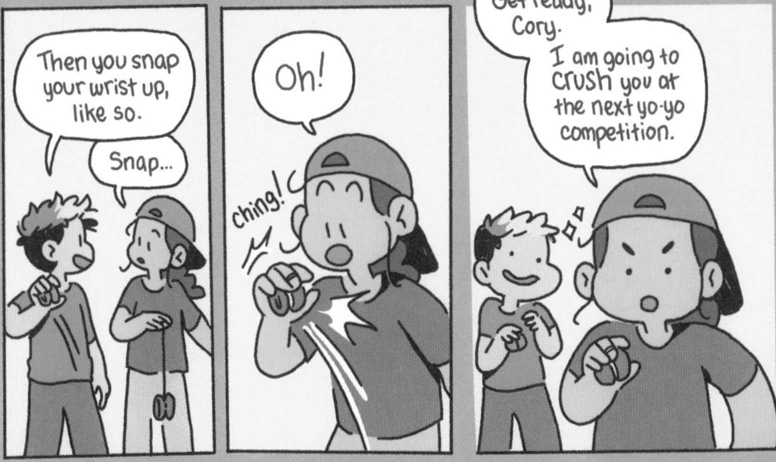
Then you snap your wrist up, like so.
Snap...
Oh!
ching!
Get ready, Cory.
I am going to crush you at the next yo-yo competition.

Discovery.

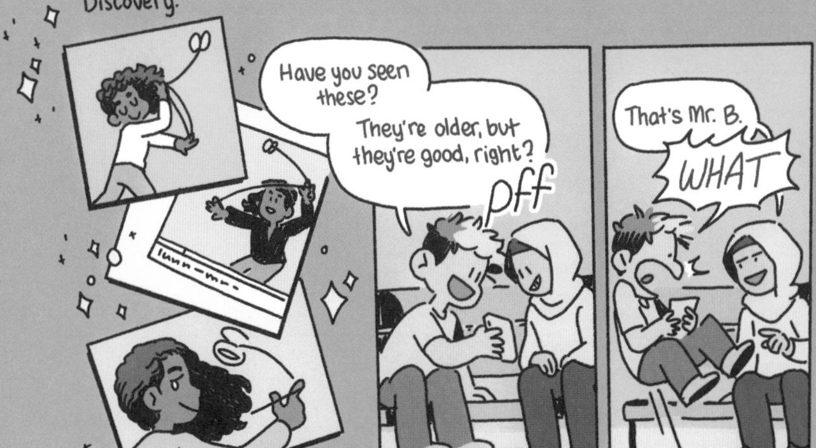
Have you seen these?
They're older, but they're good, right?
pff
That's Mr. B.
WHAT

You know you love me.

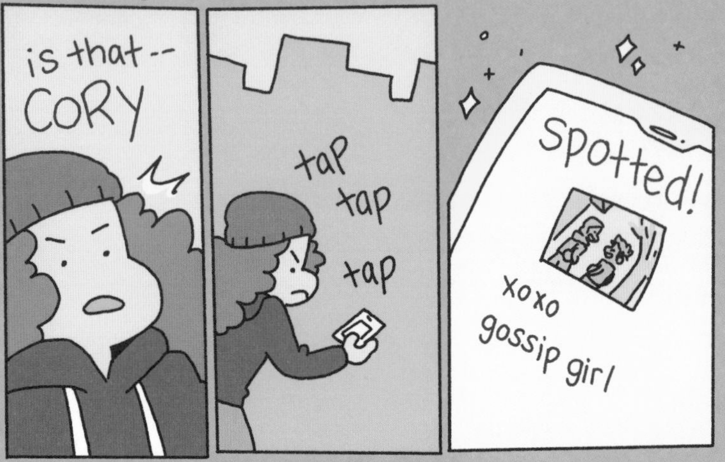
is that--
CORY
tap
tap
tap
Spotted!
xoxo
gossip girl

Getting to the Halloween dance.

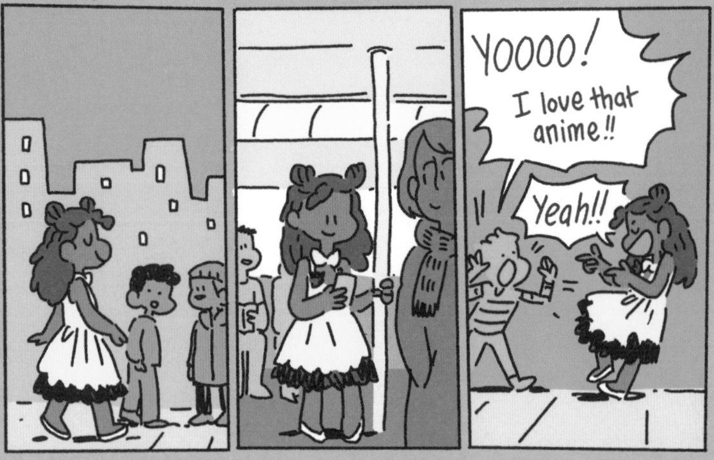
YOOOO!
I love that anime!!
Yeah!!

A very different character journey.

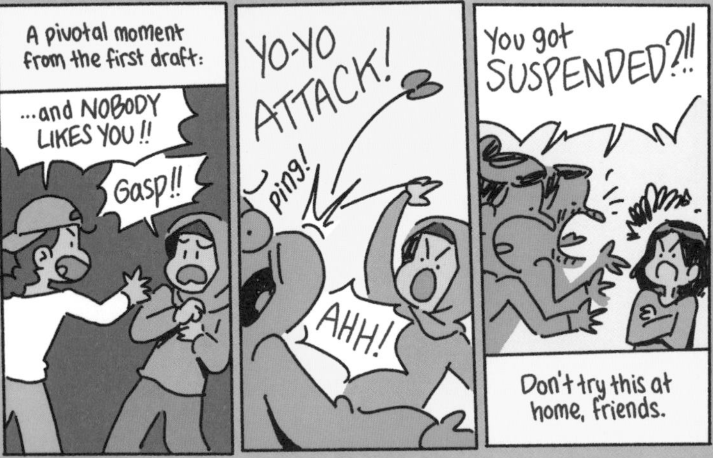

A pivotal moment from the first draft:
...and NOBODY LIKES YOU !!
Gasp!!
YO-YO ATTACK!
ping!
AHH!
You got SUSPENDED?!!
Don't try this at home, friends.

Every day.

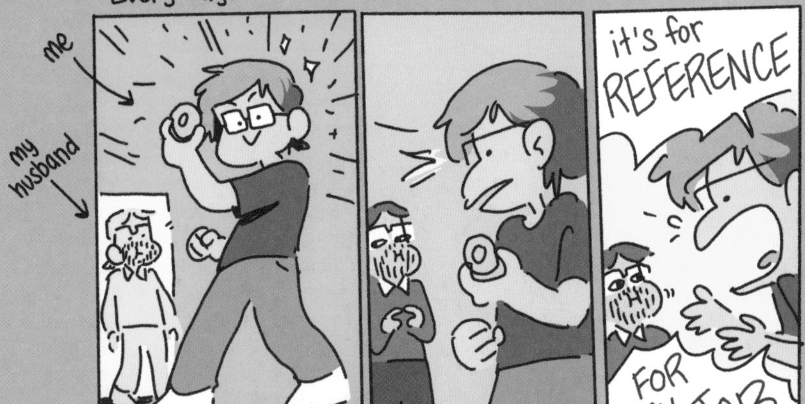

me
my husband
it's for REFERENCE
FOR MY JOB

ACKNOWLEDGMENTS

Freestyle simply would not exist without the efforts, talent, kindness, patience, and care of many, many people. I don't have nearly enough pages to thank them as fervently as they deserve, so please read the following with as much enthusiasm as you can.

Thank you (*fervently!*) to:

Patrick, for your constant encouragement, praise, treats, and the extra child wrangling so I could sneak in a few more minutes of drawing.

Robin, for existing and bringing us all the joy in the world, and also for taking naps sometimes.

Cassandra, for believing in this book from the beginning, and helping me shape it into something I could really be proud of.

Mom, Dad, and Lori, for a lifetime of inspiration.

Greg, Sonja, Durinn, and Astrid, for always being there.

Mary Alice, for helping me make it to the finish line.

Judy Hansen, for being an incomparable agent and lunch companion.

David Saylor, for taking a chance on me.

Phil Falco, Shivana Sookdeo, and Carina Taylor, for making this book actually *look good*.

K Czap, for using your incredible talents to bring this world into such vibrant, gorgeous color, and for continuing to be a cartooning inspiration.

Taylan Salvati and Seale Ballenger, for incredible publicity work in unprecedented times. Thanks especially to Taylan, for displaying heroic restraint upon seeing me spew corn bread all over the table during a very professional book tour lunch.